Charles Towne Belles
TRILOGY

M. L. TYNDALL

ISBN 978-1-61626-215-0

Published by Barbour Publishing, Inc., P.O. Box 719, Uhrichsville, Ohio 44683, www.barbourbooks.com

Our mission is to publish and distribute inspirational products offering exceptional value and biblical encouragement to the masses.

ecpa Member of the
Evangelical Christian
Publishers Association

Printed in the United States of America.

Charles Towne Belles TRILOGY

M. L. TYNDALL

BARBOUR
PUBLISHING

the Red
SIREN

Charles Towne Belles / Book 1

But he who received the seed on stony places,
this is he who hears the word and immediately receives it with joy;
yet he has no root in himself, but endures only for a while.
For when tribulation or persecution arises
because of the word, immediately he stumbles.
MATTHEW 13:20–21 NKJV

CHAPTER 1

*August 17-13, English Channel
off Portsmouth, England*

This was Dajon Waite's last chance. If he didn't sail his father's merchant ship and the cargo she held safely into harbor, his future would be tossed to the wind. With his head held high, he marched across the deck of the *Lady Em* and gazed over the choppy seas of the channel, expecting at any minute to see the lights of Portsmouth pierce the gray shroud of dusk. Another hour and his mission would be completed with success. It had taken two years before his father had trusted him to captain the most prized vessel in his merchant fleet, the *Lady Em*—named after Dajon's mother, Emily—especially on a journey that had taken him past hostile France and Spain and then far into the pirate-infested waters off the African coast.

Fisting his hands on his hips, Dajon puffed out his chest and drew a deep breath of salty air and the scent of musky earth—the smell of home. Returning with a shipload of ivory, gold, and pepper from the Gold Coast, Dajon could almost see the beaming approval on his father's sea-weathered face. Finally, Dajon would prove himself an equal to his older brother, Theodore—obedient, perfect Theodore—who never let his father down. Dajon, however, had been labeled naught but capricious and unruly, the son who possessed neither the courage for command nor the brains for business.

Fog rolled in from the sea, obscuring the sunset into a dull blend of muted colors as it stole the remaining light of what had been a glorious day. Bowing his head, Dajon thanked God for His blessing and protection on the voyage.

"A sail, a sail!" a coarse voice blared from above.

Plucking the spyglass from his belt, Dajon held it to his eye. "Where away, Mules?"

"Directly off our lee, Captain."

Dajon swerved the glass to the port and adjusted it as Cudney, his first mate, halted beside him.

"She seems to be foundering, Captain," Mules shouted.

Through the glass, the dark outline of a ship came into focus, the whites of her sails stark against the encroaching night. Gray smoke spiraled up from her quarterdeck as sailors scrambled across her in a frenzy. The British flag flapped a harried plea from her mainmast.

"Hard to larboard," he yelled aft, lowering the glass. "Head straight for her, Mr. Nelson."

"Straight for her, sir."

"Beggin' your pardon, Captain." Cudney gave him a sideways glance. "But didn't your father give explicit orders never to approach an unknown vessel?"

"My father is not the captain of this ship, and I'll thank you to obey my orders without question." Dajon stiffened his lips, tired of having his decisions challenged. True, he had failed on two of his father's prior ventures—one to the West Indies where a hurricane sank his ship, and the other where he ran aground on the shoals off Portugal. Neither had been his fault. But this time, things would be different. Perhaps his father would even promote Dajon to head overseer of his affairs.

With a nod, Cudney turned. "Mr. Blake, Mr. Gibes, prepare to luff, if you please." His bellowing voice echoed over the decks, sending the men up the shrouds.

"Who is she?" Cudney held out his hand for the glass.

"A merchant ship, perhaps." Dajon handed him the telescope then gripped the railing as the *Lady Em* veered to larboard, sending a spray of seawater over her decks. "But she's British, and she's in trouble."

The ship lumbered over the agitated waves. Dajon watched Cudney as he steadied the glass on his eye and his boots on the sodden deck. A low whistle spilled from his mouth as he twisted the glass for a better look.

"Pray tell, Mr. Cudney, what has caught your eye—one of those new ship's wheels you've been coveting?"

"Nay, Captain. But something nearly as beautiful—a lady."

Dajon snatched the glass back as the *Lady Em* climbed a rising swell and then tromped down the other side. As the vessel's sails snapped in the rising wind, he braced his boots on the deck and focused the glass on the merchant ship. A woman clung to the foremast, panic distorting her features—indistinct through the distant haze. She raised a delicate hand to her forehead as if she were going to faint. Red curls fluttered in the wind behind her. Heat flooded Dajon despite the chill of the channel. Lowering the glass, he tapped it into the palm of his hand, loathing himself for his shameless reaction. Hadn't his weakness for the female gender already caused enough pain?

Yet clearly the vessel was in trouble.

"We shall come alongside her," Dajon ordered.

Cudney glared at the ship. "Something is not right. I can feel it in my gut."

"Nonsense. Where is your chivalry?" Dajon smiled grimly at his friend, ignoring the hair bristling on the back of his own neck.

Cudney's dark eyes shot to Dajon. "But your father—"

"Enough!" Dajon snapped. "My father did not intend for me to allow a lady to drown. Besides, pirates would not dare sail so close to England—especially to Portsmouth, where so many of His Majesty's warships are anchored." Dajon glanced back at the foundering ship, now only half a knot off their bow. Smoke poured from her waist, curling like a snake into the dark sky. Left to burn, the fire would sink her within an hour. "Surely you do not suspect a woman of piracy?"

Cudney cocked one brow. "Begging your pardon, Captain, but I have seen stranger things on these seas."

❧

Faith Louise Westcott flung her red hair behind her and held a quivering hand to her brow, nausea rising in her throat at her idiotic display. How did women feign such weakness without losing the contents of their stomachs?

"They 'ave taken the bait, mistress." A sinister chuckle filled the breeze.

"Oh, thank heavens." Faith released the mast. Planting a hand on her hip, she gave Lucas a mischievous grin. "Well, what are you waiting for? Ready the men."

"Aye, aye." The bulky first mate winked then scuttled across the deck, his bald head gleaming in the light from the lantern hanging on the mainmast.

After checking the pistol that was stuffed in the sash of her gown and the one strapped to her calf, Faith sauntered to the railing to get a better look at her latest victim, a sleek, two-masted brigantine. The orange, white, and blue of the Dutch flag fluttered from her mizzen. A very nice prize, indeed. One that would bring her even closer to winning the private war she waged—a war for the survival of her and her sisters.

The oncoming ship sat low in the water, its hold no doubt packed with valuable cargo. Faith grinned. With this ship and the one she had plundered earlier, loaded with precious spices and silks, she was well on her way to amassing the fortune that would provide for her independence and that of her sisters—at least the two sisters who were left unfettered by unholy matrimony.

She allowed her thoughts to drift for a moment to Charity, the eldest. Last year their father had forced her into a union with Lord Villement, a vile, perverse man who had oppressed and mistreated her beyond what anyone should endure. Faith feared for her sister's safety and prayed for God to deliver Charity, but to no avail.

Then, of course, there was the incident with Hope, their younger sister.

That was when Faith had stopped praying, had stopped hoping, had stopped believing in a God who claimed to love and care for His children.

She would rather die than see her two younger sisters chained to abusive men, and the only way to avoid that fate was to shield them with their own fortune—a fortune she must provide since British law prohibited women from inheriting their father's wealth. Cringing, she stifled the fury bubbling in her stomach. She mustn't think of it now. She had a ship to plunder, and this was as much for Charity as it was for any of them.

The bowsprit of the brigantine bowed in obedience to her as it plunged over the white-capped swells. Gazing into the hazy mist, Faith longed to get a peek at the ninnies who had been so easily duped by her ruse, but she dared not raise the spyglass to her eye.

Putting on her most flirtatious smile, she waved at her prey, beckoning the fools onward, then she scanned the deck as her crew rushed to their stations. Aboard her ship, she was in control; she was master of her life, her future—here and nowhere else. And oh, how she loved it!

Lucas's large frame appeared beside her. "The rest of the men be waitin' yer command below hatches, mistress." He smacked his oversized lips together in a hungry sound Faith had become accustomed to before a battle. Nodding, she scanned her ship. Wilson manned the helm; Grayson and Lambert hovered over the fire, pretending to put it out; and Kane and Mac clambered up the ratlines in a pretense of fear. She spotted Morgan pacing the special perch Faith had nailed into the mainmast just for him. She whistled, and the red macaw halted, bobbed his head up and down, and squawked, "Man the guns, man the guns!"

Faith smiled. She had purchased the bird from a trader off Morocco and named him after Captain Henry Morgan, the greatest pirate of all time. The feisty parrot had been a fine addition to her crew.

Bates, her master gunner, hobbled to her side, wringing his thick hands together in anticipation. "Can I just fire one shot at 'em, Cap'n? The guns grow cold from lack of use." His expression twisted into a pout that reminded her of Hope, her younger sister. "I won't hurt 'em none; ye have me word."

"I cannot take that chance, Bates. You know the rules," Faith said as the gunner's soot-blackened face fell in disappointment. "No one gets hurt, or we abandon the prize. But I promise we shall test the guns soon enough."

With a grunt, Bates hobbled away and disappeared below.

Returning her gaze to her unsuspecting prey, Faith inhaled a breath of the crisp air. Smoke bit her throat and nose, but she stifled a cough as the thrill of her impending victory charged through her, setting every nerve aflame. The merchant ship was nigh upon them. She could already make out the worried expressions upon the crew's faces as they charged to her rescue.

This is for you, Charity, and for you, Mother.

Heavy fog blanketed the two ships in gray that darkened with each passing minute. Faith tugged her shawl tighter against her body, both to ward off the chill and to hide the pistol in her sash. A vision of her mother's pale face formed in the fog before her, blood marring the sheets on the birthing bed where she lay.

"Take care of your sisters, Faith."

A gust of wind chilled Faith's moist cheeks. A tear splattered onto the deck by her shoes before she brushed the rest from her face. "I will, Mother. I promise."

"Ahoy there!" A booming voice shattered her memories.

She raised her hand in greeting toward the brigantine as it heaved ten yards off their starboard beam. "Ahoy, kind sir. Thank God you have arrived in time," she yelled back, sending the sailors scurrying across the deck. Soon they lowered a cockboat, filled it with men, and shoved off.

A twinge of guilt poked at Faith's resolve. These men had come to her aid with kind intentions. She swallowed hard, trying to drown her nagging conscience. They were naught but rich merchants, she told herself, and she, merely a Robin Hood of the seas, taking from the rich to feed the poor. Well, perhaps not the poor, but certainly the needy. Besides, she had exhausted all legal means of acquiring the money she needed, and present society offered her no other choice.

The boat thumped against her hull, and she nodded at Kane and Mac, who had jumped down from the shrouds and tossed the rope ladder over the side.

"Permission to come aboard?" The man who appeared to be the captain shouted toward Lucas as he swung his legs over the bulwarks, but his eyes were upon Faith.

By all means. Faith shoved a floppy fisherman's hat atop her head, obscuring her features from his view, and smiled sweetly.

❧

"Aye, I beg ye, be quick about it afore our ship burns to a cinder," the massive bald man beckoned to Dajon.

Dajon hesitated. He knew he should obey his father's instructions, he knew he shouldn't risk the hoard of goods in his hold, he knew he should pay heed to the foreboding of dread that now sank like an anchor in his stomach, but all he could see was the lady's admiring smile beneath the shadow of her hat, and he led his men over the bulwarks.

After directing them to assist in putting out the fire, he marched toward the dark bald man and bowed.

"Captain Dajon Waite at your service."

When his gaze drifted to the lady, she slunk into the shadows by the foremast, her features lost in the dim light. Odd. Somehow he had envisioned a much warmer reception. At the very least, some display of feminine appreciation.

"Give 'em no quarter! Give 'em no quarter!" a shrill voice shrieked, drawing Dajon's attention behind him to a large red parrot perched on a peg jutting from the mainmast.

A sharp blade of fear stabbed him.

"Captain," one of his crew called from the quarterdeck. "The ship ain't on fire. It's just a barrel with flaming rubbish inside it!"

The anchor that had sunk in Dajon's stomach dropped into his boots with an ominous clunk.

He spun back around, hoping for an explanation, but all he received was a sinister grin on the bald man's mouth.

Alarm seized Dajon, sucking away his confidence, his reason, his pride. Surely he could not have been this daft. He glanced back at the *Lady Em*, bobbing in the sea beside them—the pride of his father's fleet.

"To battle, men!" the woman roared in a commanding voice belying her gender—a voice that pummeled Dajon's heart to dust.

Dozens of pirates spat from the hatches onto the deck. Brandishing weapons, they rushed toward his startled crew. One by one, his men dropped their buckets to the wooden planks with hollow thuds and slowly raised their hands. Their anxious gazes shot to Dajon, seeking his command. The pirates chortled as Dajon's fear exploded into a searing rage. They were surrounded.

The woman drew a pistol from her sash. Dajon could barely make out the tilted lift of her lips. He wiped the sweat from his brow and prayed to God that he would wake up from this nightmare.

"I thank you, Captain, for your chivalrous rescue." The woman pointed her pistol at him and cocked it with a snap. "But I believe I'll be taking over your ship."

CHAPTER 2

August 1718, Charles Towne, Carolina

With a light kick to his gelding's sides, Dajon prodded his horse into a trot as he made his way down Bay Street. To his right, over the wall that surrounded Charles Towne, the Cooper River swept past the city in smooth ripples that, joined by the Ashley River to the west, poured fresh water into Charles Towne Bay. A muggy breeze eased over him, stealing away the icy chill that had seeped into his bones from a winter spent patrolling the English Channel. Though he had heard tales of the brutal summer heat in the British province of Carolina, he looked forward to the warm sunshine boasted about by the settlers. He had never been fond of the continual dome of fog and clouds draped over England.

He nodded at the women strolling in front of the town's shops and warehouses, shrugging off their admiring gazes, telling himself the women's interest stemmed purely from the Royal Navy uniform he wore. Had it really been four years since he had rejoined His Majesty's Navy—and five years since that accursed woman pirate had stolen his father's ship and forced Dajon to return home in humiliation? Somehow it seemed only yesterday.

Passing one of the town's many taverns, he grimaced at the swarm of men already visible through the windows and pouring out the door into the street so early in the evening. Bawdy music accompanied by the raised voices of men playing billiards and the laughter of women oozed over Dajon like the slimy bilge from his ship, reminding him of a time when he, too, had wallowed in the filth with the worst of them.

Shaking off the bad memories, he urged his mount forward past a brick Presbyterian church, framed with dogwood and oak trees, that rose like a beacon of hope. Dajon scratched his head at the dichotomy of a place where debauchery and holiness coexisted without contention. In fact, more than ten churches graced this tiny port of nearly four thousand citizens, branding it the "Holy City," a title that warmed Dajon to his soul.

Thunder rumbled as he turned his mount onto Hasell Street, where moss-draped trees stood like sentinels dressed in royal robes on each side of the dirt path. Dajon examined the houses lining the avenue for the one that matched the description given him by his old friend Rear Admiral Westcott. Though quite pleased to have unexpectedly run into the admiral at the Powder Magazine the night before, Dajon couldn't halt the pang of trepidation he felt for what the admiral wished to discuss with him.

Rain drizzled from the darkening sky, and Dajon tugged his dark blue bicorn farther down upon his head just as the only cherry red house on the street came into view. Guiding the horse through the open iron gate and down the gravel path, he lightly drew back the reins at the front entrance and slid from the saddle. A brawny man with wiry, long black hair and skin the color of copper sped around the corner of the house much faster than his bulk seemed to allow and took the reins. When the man's dark eyes met his, a spike of familiarity halted Dajon.

"I'll take care of yer horse, sir." He snapped his gaze to the ground and shuffled his feet in the mud before turning away.

"Hold up there. Have we met before?"

The man let out a nervous chuckle. "No, sir." And kept his eyes leveled at the dirt. "They's awaitin' ye inside, sir," he said then led the horse around the corner.

A strong breeze blew in from the bay, sending the palmettos dancing in the front yard and immersing Dajon in the spicy incense of moist earth as he took the stairs in one leap and ducked under the porch's covering. Doffing his hat, he slapped the rain from it on his knee and rapped the brass door knocker. It was only after the clang tolled through the humid air that he noticed it was shaped like a three-masted frigate. He smiled.

The thick oak door opened to reveal a middle-aged man of small stature and rounded belly.

"Mr. Waite, I presume?" He pursed his thin lips and stepped back, allowing Dajon entrance. "Please follow me. The admiral is expecting you." Closing the door, he adjusted his silk waistcoat and led the way through a spacious entrance hall. A marble staircase with shiny brass posts rose to a second story. Candlelight and feminine giggles floated down from above and danced around Dajon, sparking his interest and bristling his nerves.

"May I?" The steward turned and proffered his hand when he reached an open door to his right. Dajon shrugged off his frock and handed it to him, along with his bicorn, and entered the parlor. The admiral sat by a fireplace, intently perusing a document.

"Mr. Waite, sir," the steward announced, and the admiral stood.

"Commander." Rear Admiral Westcott dropped the papers onto a table. "Good to see you again." He shook Dajon's hand and directed him to a sofa.

"Thank you for your invitation, Admiral." Seating himself, Dajon scanned the room. Mahogany bookcases and cabinets lined the walls, an oak desk and chair perched beside open french doors that led to a wide porch, and imported rugs warmed the hardwood floor.

The admiral resumed his seat by the brick fireplace, where smoldering embers added unnecessary warmth to the stifling summer heat. Or maybe it was only Dajon's jittery nerves that caused the beads of sweat to form on his forehead. Could this be the promotion to post captain he had been waiting for? Certainly during the past two years as commander, he had more than proven himself capable during skirmishes with the Spanish and the French. He had heard that promotions came more quickly in the colonies because of a shortage of good officers. It was one of the reasons he had requested a transfer to Carolina.

Wiping the moisture from the back of his neck, he smiled at the admiral, noticing the man wore his gold-trimmed blue coat even when at home. Although the British Navy required no uniform, Dajon took pride in wearing his as well.

An uncomfortable silence permeated the room. "What brings you to Charles Towne, sir?" Dajon began. "I must admit my shock when I came across you in town."

The admiral stared out the window, suddenly looking older than his fifty years. "I fear I needed a change of scenery. Portsmouth holds far too many memories for me."

Dajon swallowed, chiding himself for bringing up the subject and only now remembering that the admiral's wife had died some years ago. "You have my deepest condolences."

The admiral shifted in his seat. "It was a long time ago," he huffed, the sorrow on his face tightening into firm lines. "But I thought it would be wise for the girls and me to start afresh. And what better place than the American colonies?"

"The girls?"

The admiral sighed. "I have been *blessed* with four daughters. Would you believe it? Three have traveled to Charles Towne with me. The fourth remains in Portsmouth with her husband."

Dajon smiled, finding it difficult indeed to fathom the admiral as a father. He was a gruff old man whose booming voice and piercing gaze frightened the most stalwart of sailors. He could not imagine their effect on a genteel woman.

The admiral stuffed a pipe into his mouth and took a puff, folding his hands over his stomach and examining Dajon as if he were a cadet taking his first lieutenant's exam. "I'm a direct man, Mr. Waite, so I'll get to the point of your visit." The pipe wobbled in his mouth as he spoke. "In your time serving under my command, I found you to be an honorable, trustworthy man."

"Thank you, sir." Anticipation rang within Dajon. He moved to the edge of his seat.

"I have rarely encountered a man so naturally skilled and suited for command in His Majesty's Navy."

Dajon broadened his shoulders. "Due to your excellent tutelage, sir. I was fortunate to learn from one of the best officers in the navy." In fact, Dajon owed his quick rise to commander to Admiral Westcott's hearty recommendation. He clamped his sweaty hands together, his heart skipping a beat.

"Yes, yes." The admiral waved a hand in the air. He scratched his gray hair and flashed his auburn eyes to Dajon—that imperious gaze that could wither the staunchest of hearts.

"But I fear you did not bring me here to recount my success in the navy," Dajon said.

"No, quite right." The admiral stood and began to pace in front of the fireplace, the tails of his coat flapping on the back of his white breeches.

The muted sound of a bird squawking reached Dajon's ears, and he glanced above him curiously.

"Ah yes, my daughter's infernal parrot." The admiral shook his head, drawing Dajon's attention back to him. "She refused to leave the blasted beast behind. Noisy creature and quite messy, to be sure." He puffed on his pipe. "But back to business. I am afraid I have been called away suddenly."

"Sir?" Dajon feigned ignorance at the admiral's reasons for disclosing his plans. But why else would he mention his sudden departure unless he wanted Dajon to assume command of a higher-rated ship in his absence?

"As you have no doubt heard, the Spanish are causing problems in Italy. They have landed a fleet on Sardinia."

"Yes, I have read the dispatches." Dajon blinked, wishing the man would get to the point.

"I am to report overseas in a month in preparation for the possibility of war."

"Nothing to fear, sir. I am sure it will not come to that."

"Egad, man, I am not afraid! 'Tis my daughters that concern me." The admiral's eyes flared with the same sternness Dajon had grown accustomed to when he had sailed under the admiral's command. "This barbarous town is no place for young ladies. When I heard you were stationed here indefinitely, I knew you were the man for the job."

Dajon slowly rose and lengthened his stance. Indeed, he was the man for the job, but what did that have to do with the admiral's daughters? A slight disturbance ruffled his anticipation, like the beginnings of a quarrel in the dark corner of a tavern, but he shrugged it off. "You can count on me, sir."

"I knew I could." The admiral smiled. " 'Tis a big responsibility to force on you so suddenly."

Responsibility? Not to Dajon. Being post captain gave him more power, and more power meant he could protect more people—could play a bigger part in guarding his country, her colonies, and her citizens—and perhaps make some amends for past wrongs. "I am up to the task, sir."

"Very well, then. I shall make arrangements to have your things moved as soon as possible. That way, my daughters can get used to having you around before I set sail."

Dajon's exuberance sank to the floor. "Your daughters?" his voice squeaked.

"Why yes. There is no better man than you to be their guardian in my absence. With the Spanish and Indian attacks of late, not to mention the savage nature of some of the settlers, they need a naval officer to protect them."

No promotion? Dajon's breath halted in his throat. He wiped the sweat from his brow. A guardian? Of women? Every encounter he'd ever had with females had ended in disaster.

And drastically changed the course of his life.

For the worse.

'Twas one of the reasons he had joined the navy. No women.

Dajon stared at the admiral and knew he could never trust himself to protect a woman again. "Sir, I fear you have the wrong man. I could not possibly—"

"Of course you will not be staying here in the house." The admiral snorted, ignoring him. "That would not be proper, but I will have Edwin prepare a bed for you in the guesthouse out back. I have no doubt you will find it quite comfortable. No need for you to stay on your ship while you are at anchor."

Dajon felt as though he were tumbling headlong into a dark void. "I appreciate your trust in me, Admiral, but 'tis a most untoward request, sir, and I must refuse it."

"I know. You fear your duties will keep you away overmuch?" The admiral slapped him on the back. "Of course your responsibilities in the Royal Navy come first. I only ask that you check on my girls daily and be aware of their comings and goings."

Dajon took a forceful step toward the admiral, trying to formulate his words. How could he deny this man's request—this man who had done so much for him?

The admiral stomped a boot atop the brick hearth and stared into the dying embers, puffing on his pipe. "I daresay any man who can successfully command my three daughters and run my home like a tight ship during my absence"—he chuckled, a disbelieving kind of laughter that said

19

the feat had yet to be accomplished—"now that man would have more than proven his ability to command." He tapped his pipe into a tray on the mantel. "In fact, I might be inclined to promote such a man to post captain." He slowly turned around and gave Dajon a sly look.

Dajon swallowed. So that was the way of it. Admiral Westcott continued to hold Dajon's future solely in his hands. Making post captain was no easy feat. A commander or lieutenant had to have political influence—of which Dajon had none—win some daring battle at sea—hard to do when one's country was currently not at war—or wait until someone above him died—a rather morbid way to be promoted. The only other hope was by the recommendation of an admiral. And it was clear now to Dajon that he would not receive such an honor unless he did as the admiral requested.

But how could he?

Either way, doom cast an ominous cloud over his naval career like the endless black fog over London. Nevertheless, if he were to remain a commander forever, the position would be more easily borne without the added tarnish of having caused harm to innocent young ladies. And yet he could not agree, no matter the cost to his career. He opened his mouth to speak when a shuffle sounded at the door.

"Ah, there they are." The admiral smiled.

Dajon swerved about to see three women enter the room: One was a petite girl with hair the color of the sun pinned up in a bounty of curls; another had dark hair pulled tight in a bun, a book cradled in her arms. But it was the third woman who drew Dajon's attention and sent his blood racing. She sashayed into the room, flinging her brazen red curls behind her and wearing a saucy smirk on her plump lips.

Dajon's heart crashed into his ribs.

CHAPTER 3

Faith forced the shock from her face at seeing the man whose ship she had once pirated—the man whose ship she still sailed. Perhaps he did not recognize her. Nearly five years had passed, and it had been foggy and dismal that night. If she were still a praying woman, she would pray for no remembrance of her to form in his mind, for if he disclosed her secret, she would face not only her father's wrath but quite possibly the gallows, as well. Alarm stiffened every nerve as she slunk deeper into the shadows behind the door.

"Ladies, may I present Mr. Dajon Waite, commander of the HMS *Enforcer*." The admiral approached his daughters, gestured toward Faith, and then frowned. "Faith, how oft must I impress upon you to put up your hair as befitting a proper young lady? And quit cowering against the wall and come hither to meet Mr. Waite."

Faith took a tentative step forward, keeping her gaze on the floor.

Her father huffed. "Miss Westcott." Then he gestured toward her sisters. "Miss Hope and Miss Grace."

Faith risked a peek at Mr. Waite as he bowed toward all three of them. Then the man opened his mouth as if attempting to say something. Yet not a word proceeded out of it.

"Does he speak, Father?" Faith asked, eliciting giggles from her sisters.

Mr. Waite turned a wary gaze upon her, his blue eyes like ice. A barb of unfamiliar fear scraped down her back. Perhaps he was trying to find a way to break the news to the admiral that his daughter was a pirate.

She looked away as her stomach coiled in a knot.

The admiral gave Mr. Waite a puzzled look. "He was doing quite nicely before you entered."

Mr. Waite's harsh expression melted, and he puffed a breath as if a giant ball in his throat had instantly dissolved. His face reddened. "My apologies, ladies. 'Tis a great pleasure to meet you."

Hope rushed to him and raised her hand.

"Oh, Hope, must you throw yourself at every man who enters the house?" Grace shook her head and turned to replace her book in one of the bookcases.

Ignoring her sister, Hope gave Mr. Waite an alluring smile and fluttered her lashes as he placed a kiss upon her hand. Her low neckline drew his attention, as it did all men's. Faith winced at her sister's blatant coquetry. Why was she always seeking the wrong sort of attention? Yet the commander surprised Faith when he quickly averted his eyes and turned to address her. No recognition tinged his features, just a curious admiration.

He does not know me.

Relief blanketed her tight nerves.

"Father." Hope's voice sounded strained. "I hope Mr. Waite's presence here does not mean you'll be leaving us again?" She glanced at Mr. Waite. "No disrespect to you, Mr. Waite."

Mr. Waite nodded but shifted his stance uncomfortably.

Jutting out his chin, the admiral stared at the bookcases behind Hope. "I have not received my final orders yet, my dear, but you know my job is upon the sea."

"But we have just moved here, Father." Grace clasped her hands together and took a step toward him. "We hardly know a soul, and the customs are so different than in England."

" 'Tis a savage place," Hope added with a snort. "Too frightening for us to be left all alone." She twirled a lock of hair at her neck, her features scrunched with worry. "And you must introduce us into society, or we shall be terribly bored."

Faith studied her father. Muscles of annoyance twitched in his jaw. Yet behind his staunch expression, she detected a glimmer of excitement in his eyes. And she knew. She knew he planned to sail away soon. She knew because she felt the same thrill every time she was about to head out upon the sea. If she and her father were so much alike, then why did he constantly disappoint her?

He straightened his blue coat and put on the indomitable expression of his position. "There are worse things than boredom, Hope. Besides, you have your sisters to keep you company."

Hope lowered her gaze. "With Mother. . .with Mother. . ." She gulped. "And you always at sea, I feel like I am an orphan."

"Egad, an orphan who lives in luxury! Have you ever heard of such a thing?" The admiral gave an angry laugh, his face reddening; then he glanced at Mr. Waite, but the commander had turned aside, pretending to examine a brass figurine on the table.

Grace placed her arm around Hope's shoulders. " 'Tis all right, Hope. Clearly, Father cannot abandon his duty to Britain. And we must always remember that we have a Father in heaven who loves us very much."

Hope flattened her lips and stared at the floor.

Faith touched her father's arm and met his gaze. "Father, can you not stay a little while longer, just until Hope feels more at ease?" But she already knew his answer. She had long ago learned to live without her father's presence, as her mother had before her.

The admiral frowned. A hard sheen covered his brown eyes. He opened his mouth to speak what Faith knew would be an angry retort when Edwin's dull voice interrupted them from the doorway. "Sir Wilhelm Carteret has arrived, Admiral, and Molly informs me that dinner is served."

"Ah yes. Shall we, then?" The admiral blew out a heavy sigh and gestured toward the foyer.

Mr. Waite turned and hastened toward the door as if he couldn't wait to escape. Deciding to face her enemy head-on, Faith slid her arm through his as he passed. "Mr. Waite, please do forgive us for forcing you to endure our family squabbles."

Although he smiled, the muscles in his arm remained as tight as a full sail under a strong wind.

Hope tossed her nose in the air at Faith before exiting the parlor in a swish of satin—no doubt she'd intended to grab the commander herself. Grace and the admiral followed behind.

"Sir Wilhelm," the admiral bellowed. "How good of you to come."

At the sight of Sir Wilhelm, a chill seeped through Faith. He straightened his white periwig and allowed his eyes to slink over her before they landed on Mr. Waite and narrowed. A smile returned when he faced the admiral and bowed. "My pleasure, as always."

"Sir Wilhelm Carteret," the admiral said. "May I present Mr. Dajon Waite."

"An honor, sir." The commander bowed.

Sir Wilhelm grunted and gave him a cursory glance.

"Sir Wilhelm is an acquaintance of the family and dines with us often," the admiral explained as Edwin led the party down the hall to the dining room.

White linen and china glistened in the candlelight on the oblong table that filled the small room. The admiral took his seat at the head, his back to a window overlooking the gardens; rain puddled across the glass, distorting the trees, bushes, stables, and servants' quarters that filled the back gardens.

Once everyone was seated, kitchen maids placed platters of meat, fresh flounder, rice, corn, and biscuits onto the table, in addition to pitchers of wine and water. The savory aroma of beef and creamy butter spiraled over Faith but soured in her churning stomach. She cast a wary eye upon the two men responsible for her lack of appetite: Sir Wilhelm, who flapped his coattails behind him as he lowered to his chair, and Mr. Waite, who took his seat directly across from her.

"A grand feast." Her father rubbed his hands together before saying grace over the food.

"Sir Wilhelm." Mr. Waite passed a plate of mutton to the man who sat beside him. "Your name is familiar to me. Where have I heard it?"

Sir Wilhelm took the plate and served himself a huge pile of meat, thrusting his chin out before him. "My grandfather, George Carteret, was one of the original eight proprietors of the realm."

"Indeed?" Mr. Waite tucked a strand of wayward hair behind his ear. "Not the same George Carteret who was treasurer of the navy?"

"The same." Sir Wilhelm sniffed and directed his pointed nose at Faith. His epicurean smile sent a shudder through her, and she looked away and grabbed the bowl of rice in front of her.

"Not only that"—the admiral poured wine into his goblet—"but Wilhelm's grandfather was also a vice admiral and comptroller of the navy. A brilliant, powerful man."

Faith watched Sir Wilhelm's scrawny shoulders rise with each praise. She used to think him a large man, but sitting next to the commander, he shriveled in stature. Her gaze shifted to Mr. Waite. His broad chest pressed against his blue navy coat. One rebellious strand of dark brown hair—the color of the rich soil she'd once seen on the coast of Ireland—sprang from his queue, and when his bright blue eyes met hers, glimmering in the candlelight, an unusual warmth spread throughout her.

"So you can imagine," Sir Wilhelm said, leaning forward and drawing all attention his way, "how thrilled I was to discover that an admiral had been stationed here in Charles Towne. I arranged to make his acquaintance as soon as I could. But I never imagined Admiral Westcott would have such lovely daughters." His brash gaze landed on Faith, and she shifted in her chair, wondering why she had the misfortune of being the center of this man's attentions.

"Then do you share your grandfather's love of the sea?" Mr. Waite asked Sir Wilhelm.

Wilhelm poured wine into his glass, clanking the decanter against his goblet so loudly Faith thought it would break. "No, I am afraid my many obligations keep me ashore."

"Indeed?" Faith gave him a crooked smile. "The rumor about town is that you suffer from seasickness."

Hope giggled.

"Faith!" Her father's gruff voice boomed across the room like a cannon blast. "You know better than to put any credence to the foolhardy prattle of the town's biddies. You will apologize to Sir Wilhelm at once."

Sir Wilhelm sniffed and wiggled his nose. "No need. There are many who are jealous of my power and enjoy nothing more than to spread ugly tales about me." He withdrew a handkerchief from his embroidered satin waistcoat and held it to his nose. "I trust, Miss Westcott, you are too clever to fall for such fabrications."

"Forgive my impertinence." She took a bite of beef and eyed him. The ghostly pallor of his face matched the powder in his wig. A dark mole peeked out from behind a cusp of white hair near his right ear, like a bat from a cave.

"Faith is far too wise for such nonsense," Hope added. "She is by far the most intelligent woman I know."

"That she surpasses your own intelligence is no accomplishment." The admiral chortled, plunging his fork into a mound of corn. "My dear Hope was never proficient in her studies."

Hope lowered her eyes, and Faith longed to kick her father beneath the table. Why did he insist on showering Hope with his constant disapproval? Could he not see how it crushed the poor girl, especially now that their mother was gone?

Grace squeezed Hope's arm and cast a matronly look around the table. "It is the condition of the heart that matters most."

"Well said, Miss Grace." Mr. Waite nodded then raised his gaze to Faith. "Forgive me, but I cannot shake the feeling that we have met somewhere before."

Her heart froze. She gulped and willed the screeching voice within her to calm before she dared utter a word. "I fear you are mistaken, Mr. Waite. Unless, perhaps"—she stabbed a piece of meat with her fork, hoping the trembling of her hands was not evident—"you frequented Portsmouth? We may have passed on the streets." She placed the beef into her mouth, but the savory flavor became bitter before it reached her throat.

"Perhaps. But 'tis the strangest thing. Your groomsman seemed quite familiar to me, as well." A hint of suspicion tainted his voice.

"Lucas?" Faith coughed. "He has a common face." She bent over, trying to dislodge the food stuck in her throat. The commander was toying with her, after all. *He knows. He has to know.* Dread stung every nerve as she pounded on her chest, finally loosening the clump of meat. It wasn't that she feared the gallows. It wasn't that she feared death.

What she feared most of all was leaving her sisters all alone in the world.

"Are you ill, daughter?" The admiral leaned from his seat beside her and laid a hand on her shoulder.

Sir Wilhelm took a sip of wine and gazed at Faith. Something sinister crept behind his grin. " 'Tis probably the climate. Every new settler suffers local infections as they grow accustomed to this humid environment. They call it the seasoning."

"I am quite well, I assure you." Faith glared at Wilhelm. "We have been here over two months and have yet to fall ill."

"Then you have been fortunate, indeed," Sir Wilhelm commented. "In the past twenty years, Charles Towne has been struck by both smallpox and the Barbados fever. Horrid diseases." He shuddered in disgust. "Hundreds died." He gave them a superior look. "Only those of strong constitution survived."

Faith snarled. Strong, indeed. Or too weak and despicable for the disease to waste its energy upon.

The admiral cleared his throat. "Hardly appropriate dinner conversation in front of the ladies."

"We have nothing to fear," Grace interjected. "God will protect us."

"If we live, dear sister, God will have naught to do with it," Faith snapped.

"You cannot mean that."

"Come now, ladies." The admiral shook his head and gestured for more wine, his face flushed with embarrassment. "Faith, you must repent for such a statement."

Faith flattened her lips and flung her hair behind her.

Grace smiled at Mr. Waite. "Are you a godly man?"

"For heaven's sake, Grace, is that all that concerns you?" Hope sighed, poking at her food.

Mr. Waite swallowed and smiled, grabbing his cup. "Yes, I am, miss."

"To what church do you belong?"

He took a sip of water and set down his cup. "I aspire to the doctrine that the Bible is the divine Word of God and should guide us in all things."

Sir Wilhelm snorted, sending a spray of wine over his plate. "Surely you are not one of those Dissenters, Waite. The Church of England is the only true church."

The commander's jaw flexed. "Where, pray tell, Sir Wilhelm, does it indicate that in the Word of God? I have yet to read that passage." He gave the man a patronizing grin.

Sir Wilhelm squirmed in his seat and huffed in response.

"Well said, Mr. Waite." Grace fingered the top button of her gown, and Faith wondered if perhaps her piety wasn't simply due to a lack of air from the stranglehold her tight-fitting collars had upon her neck.

"You must forgive Grace," the admiral said. "She is overzealous in her faith, as her mother was." He dropped his fork onto his plate with a clank.

"I do not believe you can be overzealous in your love for God, Admiral."

Mr. Waite nodded toward Grace.

Faith let out a painfully ladylike sigh. *Wonderful, another Puritan in our midst.* "You do not know my sister, Mr. Waite."

Sir Wilhelm cleared his throat. " 'Tis best to leave God out of the affairs of men."

Grace cocked her delicate head. "Which would explain, Sir Wilhelm, why man has made such a mess of this world."

Hope frowned then pushed her plate aside and leaned over the table, drawing Sir Wilhelm's gaze to her chest—though obviously not the gaze she intended to draw, as her attention locked upon the commander. "What brings you to Charles Towne, Mr. Waite?"

"After Blackbeard's horrendous blockade of your city this past May, Parliament thought it wise to send some of His Majesty's ships to patrol the area." The commander nodded toward the admiral.

The admiral scowled. "The pirate attack was quite an event, I have heard. The poor citizens of this town held at ransom by a thieving pirate, demanding, of all things, medical supplies. And him holding Samuel Wragg, a member of the council, hostage and threatening to kill him. Absurd."

"I couldn't agree more, Admiral," Mr. Waite said. "Which is precisely why I have been sent here—to capture every pirate patrolling these waters and ensure they are hung by the neck until dead."

CHAPTER 4

The biscuit in Faith's mouth instantly dried, leaving a hardened clump that scraped across her tongue. Grabbing some water to wash it down, she leaned back in her chair, eyed Mr. Waite, and pressed a hand to her stomach, where the food she had just consumed began to protest.

"How exciting!" Hope beamed, clapping her hands. "A pirate hunter in our very own house."

"I am simply doing my duty, miss." Mr. Waite gave Faith a concerned look. "Are you feeling well, Miss Westcott? You have gone quite pale."

Faith nodded, gathered her resolve, and opened her mouth to say something witty, but her voice mutinied.

"I daresay." Hope placed a hand on her chest, her voice a soft purr. "I feel much safer knowing you are guarding our harbor from those vile creatures."

Sir Wilhelm lifted his glass in salute. "We proprietors do appreciate the presence of the Royal Navy to protect our interests in the province."

"We are pleased to be of service." Mr. Waite's gaze drifted over the ladies and landed on the admiral. "Did you say that you have another daughter back in England?"

Leaning forward, the admiral filled his glass of wine for the third time, nearly tipping it in the process. He slammed the decanter down with a thud. Faith cringed. Her father took to drinking only when something vexed him. And the combination was oft more explosive than powder and matchstick. "Charity, my only married daughter, remained in Portsmouth," he said.

Faith's ire rose along with a sudden pounding in her head. "Imprisoned in Portsmouth, you meant to say, Father." Instantly she wished she had kept her mouth shut—for once—for Father's face swelled like a globefish.

Mr. Waite raised a curious brow in her direction, shifting his gaze between her and the admiral. Faith sighed. She might as well continue what she had started.

"My sister was forced to marry a beastly man who stole the printing business Father had allowed her to embark upon. And. . ." She glanced at Hope, whose countenance had fallen. "And he was unfaithful." A clump of sorrow rose in Faith's throat. She grabbed Hope's hand beneath the table and squeezed against the clammy chill that clung to her sister's palm.

The admiral dropped his knife onto his plate with a loud clank. "And you know better than to speak of such things at my table, Faith."

Sir Wilhelm pointed his fork at her. "Forgive me for saying so, but your sister's husband could hardly have stolen a business that upon marriage became his by law. Besides, women have no sense for business, nor for the spending of money acquired from such ventures. These things are best left up to men."

"Here, here, good man." The admiral lifted his glass.

"And ofttimes a man is forced to seek"—Sir Wilhelm cleared his throat—"shall we say, diversions elsewhere when his life at home is unpleasant." He shrugged before chomping on a biscuit.

Faith shot to her feet, her chair scraping over the wooden floor behind her. Heat inflamed her face. Her fingers tingled, yearning for a weapon, any weapon. Her eyes landed on a pitcher of water. She grabbed it, squeezing her fist over the cool handle. " 'Tis to be expected, sir, only of scoundrels and savages," she said in as calm a voice as possible as she filled her glass. Then, setting the pitcher down in front of Sir Wilhelm—atop a serving spoon—she quickly withdrew her hand as the wavering container toppled over. A cascade of water spilled onto the table, gushed toward the edge, and flooded Sir Wilhelm's breeches before splattering onto the floor.

Springing to his feet, he stumbled over his chair, sending it crashing behind him. "Of all the. . . !" he screeched, reminding Faith of her parrot, Morgan, whenever something riled him.

"Faith!" Her father stood and directed the serving maids to assist Sir Wilhelm. Their shoes clomped over the wooden floorboards like a herd of cattle as they sped off, returning within seconds with towels. "Where is your head, girl?"

"It was an accident, Father." Faith lifted her hands in a conciliatory gesture then clasped them together before facing Sir Wilhelm. "My sincere apologies, Sir Wilhelm. I was not paying attention."

Sir Wilhelm scowled as he snatched a towel from one of the maids with a snap and dabbed at his sodden breeches. "Perhaps, Admiral, you should hire a governess to teach your daughters proper etiquette. Apparently, without their mother, their social graces have lapsed."

"It was an unintentional mishap, Sir Wilhelm," Grace said, ever the voice of calm propriety.

The admiral frowned. For a second, Faith thought he would defend his daughters, but then he grabbed his drink and plopped back into his chair.

After tossing the wet towel back to the maid, Sir Wilhelm adjusted his wig and took his seat. Mr. Waite held his hand to his mouth, and Faith sensed a smile lingered behind it. When his eyes met hers, a spark of playfulness danced across them.

"Sit down, Faith." Her father pounded his boot on the floor and pointed to her chair. "You have insulted our guest enough. If you cannot behave, I will insist you leave this room at once."

Faith sank into her chair, not wanting to leave her sisters to endure Sir Wilhelm's vile opinions without her protection. She squeezed Hope's arm and felt her quiver as a soft sob escaped the poor girl. A heavy weight of guilt pressed down upon Faith. Why had she resurrected such a horrid memory?

"Quit your sniveling, girl," the admiral barked at Hope. "We have guests."

Faith glared at her father. He knew very well what had upset Hope. Yet repeatedly he chose to hide behind the delusion of propriety. He could face battles upon the sea, witness men's legs being blasted into twigs, make snap decisions that changed the course of history, but he could not face what had happened to his own daughter.

"You must forgive my daughters, Mr. Waite." The admiral scratched his thick gray sideburns as the servants cleared the dishes from the table. "Since their mother died, they have not had proper female instruction."

"As you well know, Father"—Faith could not control the acrid bite in her tone—"I have taken that role upon myself. And I will continue to do so." She turned toward her sisters. "Although I know I can never take

Mother's place." She eased a lock of Hope's golden hair from her face and saw her mother staring back at her. Faith's heart warmed. "You look so much like her."

Hope smiled, her eyes shimmering.

"Your mother must have been an incredible woman." Mr. Waite's deep voice smoothed the ripples of distress radiating over the table. His warm gaze landed on Faith and lingered there as if he were soaking in every detail of her. "Possessing both beauty and piety." He smiled then looked down and began fidgeting with his spoon.

Faith took a sip of cool water, hoping to douse the heat rising within her at his perusal.

"She is in heaven now." Grace kissed Hope on the cheek.

"God shouldn't have taken her in the first place." Faith released Hope's hand. "We have more need of her here than He does in heaven."

"What you need, my dear, is a good husband to tame you," the admiral said, gulping down another swig of wine.

"I will never marry." Faith shook her head and gave her father a stern look.

The admiral huffed. "Don't be absurd."

Sir Wilhelm cleared his throat and exchanged a knowing glance with her father—a glance that sent dread crawling over Faith.

"If a woman can provide for herself," she said, "she needn't subject herself to the tyranny of a man who restricts her freedom and forces his every whim—"

"As I have informed you, my dear Faith," her father interrupted, his voice strained to the point of exploding, "should you ever find yourself in possession of so great a fortune, I have promised not to arrange a marriage against your will." The wrinkles at the corners of his eyes seemed to fold together as he stared at her.

"Then I hold you to our bargain." Faith squared her shoulders, daring to hope that she could indeed fulfill her end of it. "If I amass this fortune you speak of, you will force neither me nor my sisters into marriage?"

"Yes, of course." The admiral dabbed his mouth with the edge of the tablecloth. "But time runs out. With your mother gone and me so often at sea, I may have no choice but to ensure your future happiness. The sooner you are all married, the better."

"And pray tell, Miss Westcott, how do you intend to procure such a fortune?" Sir Wilhelm asked with a hint of sarcasm.

"I have started a soap-making business, which I can assure you will be quite successful." Faith stiffened her jaw and focused on her uneaten plate of food.

"Which I have yet to see any evidence of, I might add," the admiral said with a chortle.

Sir Wilhelm joined in his laughter, and Faith reached for her side where her cutlass normally hung but found only her beaded sash. Not that she would have stabbed the horrid excuse of a man, but it would have been amusing to see his face if she had tried. Instead, she rubbed her fingers over the smooth beads.

Grace leaned toward Faith, her mouth pinched in concern. "Marriage is a blessed union of God and should be honored."

With a sigh, Faith returned a gentle smile to her sister. Sweet Grace. So young and naive, but with such a heart of gold. Faith sometimes wished she had been born with so agreeable a nature. But alas, that was not to be. "It is a union not meant for all."

"Nevertheless," the admiral began, leaning back in his chair and folding his hands over his belly, "I believe I have been more than generous with you girls. In the five years since your mother...since your mother has been gone, you could have chosen any one of the fine young men clamoring for your attention in Portsmouth." He raised a cynical brow toward Faith. "All of them in possession of a good fortune, I might add."

"Oh pish, Father. They were naught but pompous bores."

The admiral shifted his inquiring gaze to Hope. "And you, my dear?"

"There were far too many of them. I simply could not choose." She waved her hand through the air.

Pursing his lips, he gazed at his youngest daughter. "What say you, fair Grace?"

Grace played with her fingers in her lap. "Like Faith, I do not wish to marry. The apostle Paul instructs that 'tis best to serve the Lord wholeheartedly without the distractions of a husband."

"Ah yes," the admiral sighed. "Grace's pursuit of holy living has kept many possible suitors far away, I am afraid. There's the rub, if you will." He shifted a stern gaze over his daughters. "I fear my only mistake has been in giving any of you a choice. Despite your fallacious opinions, I made a fine match for your sister Charity, a man of title and wealth. I only delayed in procuring the same for you because of your constant bickering and complaining."

"Father." Faith dropped her fork on her plate with a clang. "Despite his title and wealth, Lord Villement is naught but a—"

"Enough!" His roar echoed across the room, silencing all noise save the patter of rain on the window. Then, composing himself, he smiled at Mr. Waite. "So you see my dilemma?"

Sir Wilhelm's salacious gaze slithered over Faith. "Not so daunting a dilemma, Admiral, that a bit of parental discipline could not solve." Then, plunging the last bite of roast between his slimy lips, he patted his stomach. "Delicious."

The admiral poured himself another glass of wine and slowly sipped it as the maids came with pudding and tea. His eyes began to glass over. Shame instantly dissolved Faith's fury. She had upset and embarrassed her father again—and in front of guests. Perhaps it would be better if she excused herself, along with her sisters.

She pushed back her chair, the scrape of wood only adding to her annoyance. "Mr. Waite, you seem like a fine man—," she began, intending to apologize for her brash behavior.

"I am happy to hear it, Faith," her father interrupted. "Because I am making him guardian over you and your sisters until I return from Spain."

Mr. Waite set his teacup onto the saucer. "With all due respect, Admiral, I must refuse the honor, sir." He sat straight in his chair and met the admiral's gaze head-on.

"Refuse?" The admiral slowly rose, his face reddening, his tone filled with incredulity.

"Our guardian?" Faith could not believe her ears. "We do not need a guardian, Father. We have Lucas and Edwin. They can watch over us."

"I think it is a fine idea," Hope added, fluttering her lashes.

"Why ask a complete stranger?" A sultry grin spread over Sir Wilhelm's mouth as his gaze swept over Faith. "It is obvious he protests. I would be honored to protect the ladies in your absence, Admiral." He pulled a jeweled snuffbox from his pocket and snorted a pinch of dark powder up one nostril.

Faith shuddered.

The admiral loosened his white cravat. "Nay, you have far too many re-sponsibilities, Sir Wilhelm, plus your other involvement with this family."

"What involvement?" Faith demanded.

Mr. Waite shifted his stance and gave the admiral a level stare. "Admiral, might I suggest you choose from one of the local gentry? I am sure there are many willing and trustworthy young men."

The admiral snorted and shook his head, a frown marring his leathery skin. "Do you take me for a fool, Waite? I have searched far and wide through this forsaken outpost, but there is no one else I trust with the safety of my daughters save you." He scratched his thick sideburns and gave the commander such a look of disappointment that Faith nearly melted by proximity. But Mr. Waite held his ground, his eyes locked upon her father's, his stern expression unflinching.

"But I see you will let me down. Very well." The admiral waved a hand at Mr. Waite as if dismissing him.

Faith had to admit she felt relieved herself. The last thing she needed was a pirate hunter living at the house. But something was afoot between her father and Sir Wilhelm, and she intended to discover what it was.

❧

"Come in, Faith. Come in." Faith's father stood at the fireplace later that same evening, lighting his pipe from a stick he pulled from the coals. Mr. Waite had long since bid them all farewell and returned to his ship, and everyone else in the house had retired to their chambers. Sir Wilhelm rose from his chair and gave her a salacious look that nearly sent her scampering from the room. Instead, she took a few steps inside, keeping her distance from him yet staying close to the door should she need to escape. Her mind swam through a thousand reasons why her father had requested her presence in the drawing room after dinner, but now that she saw Sir Wilhelm, only one possibility—one dreadful possibility—surfaced.

The admiral rubbed his temples then glanced at Sir Wilhelm before taking a puff from his pipe. "I have some wonderful news for you, my dear." But the look on his face was not one of joy or excitement, but rather the look a parent gave a child when she was about to be punished. "Please sit down."

Faith threw back her shoulders. "I'd rather stand."

"I insist!" he bellowed, pointing with his pipe toward the sofa.

Lowering herself to the soft cushions, Faith tried to stop her heart from crashing against her chest. Across from her, Sir Wilhelm laid the back of his fingers to his nose and retook his seat, never letting his eyes leave her.

"Sir Wilhelm has made a most generous offer." Her father laid a hand on the mantel and smiled at Sir Wilhelm.

Faith clenched her fists in her lap and glanced out the door into the dark foyer, feeling like a condemned prisoner about to receive her sentence.

"He has asked for your hand in marriage."

A death sentence. The words sped across the deck of her mind, waiting for the final cannon blast to blow them into the water.

"And I have given him my approval."

Hit and sunk. Faith rose from the sofa slowly, methodically, trying to curb her fury. "I have not given *my* approval, Father," she spat through clenched teeth. "I will not be married off like chattel."

"You will do as I say!" He pounded his fist onto the mantel, sending a porcelain vase crashing to the floor.

Faith jumped and stared at the pieces of jagged painted glass littering the wooden planks like the shattered pieces of her heart.

"I know what is best for you." His voice lowered but still retained its fury.

Clasping her hands together, she faced Sir Wilhelm with as much civility as she could muster. "My apologies, sir, if my father has misled you. I do not wish to insult you, but I have no intention of marrying you or anyone else."

Tugging at his lopsided wig, Sir Wilhelm plucked out his handkerchief and fidgeted with it. "Admiral, I am surprised a man of your standing would allow such insolence in his home."

The admiral puffed out his chest until it seemed to double in girth. "Faith, I will have no more insubordination from you. It is already arranged. You will marry Sir Wilhelm."

Panic clambered up Faith's throat. Desperate for any reprieve, she willed tears to her eyes, hoping to soften his resolve. "Father, please reconsider. What of our bargain? I need more time."

The admiral's face swelled red. "Time for what, girl? All the time in the world will not grant you the fortune you need to remain independent. Besides, you are four and twenty, well past time for a proper union. In a few years, no man will have you. Or perhaps that is what you are hoping for?"

"I want to choose my own husband." Faith gave him her most innocent, pleading look—the one that usually pried through the crusty casing around his heart.

The admiral's harsh demeanor softened just a bit, giving Faith a flicker of hope. He took a puff from his pipe. "So you want to choose your own husband, is it?" He paused, and a hint of compassion flickered in his eyes. It was the look she'd often seen when her mother had been alive. "Fine. We shall compromise. Either you will find a suitable husband by the time I return from Spain, or"—he let out a sarcastic snort—"make a sizable profit from this soap-making business you claim to be running, or mark my words, you will indeed marry Sir Wilhelm."

CHAPTER 5

Tiny pellets of rain blasted over Faith, stinging her face like a hundred needles. Bracing her boots on the foredeck of the *Red Siren*, she yanked the tricorn from her head and allowed the saturated wind to tear through her tangled curls. She flung her arms out wide and closed her eyes, hoping to forget the events of the evening as a wall of salty air, spiced with the scent of rain and sea, crashed over her. While some people went to drink for comfort, Faith went to sea. The thunder and crash of massive waves, the endless horizon, and the freedom of the wind in her hair never failed to soothe her nerves. But for some reason, tonight she could not shake the sickly face of Sir Wilhelm from her mind or his licentious gaze slithering over her when her father had announced their betrothal. She shuddered.

Footsteps sounded beside her, and she turned to see Lucas. Water dripped from the corner of a hat that hid his eyes in its shadow. He smiled.

"I doubt we'll be findin' any ships worth pillaging on a night like this, mistress."

Faith gazed out over the swirling cauldron, dark, save for occasional strips of white foam illuminated by a half-moon that danced betwixt the clouds. Rain formed droplets on her lashes, and she brushed them dry. Lucas was right.

"Not that I mind none," he continued with a snort. "Ye knows I like the smell o' the sea far better than the smell of them stables."

"I suppose I just needed to think." Faith gripped the wet railing, stunned by the chill that ran up her arms. "But truth be told, it would have been nice to take a prize tonight."

"We done good so far, mistress. That cargo last month of silks and coffee brought us a fair price."

"But I need more." Faith slapped the railing. "Far more."

"I hear ye, mistress. But never ye mind. There's lots o' treasure to be had in these waters."

Lucas probably thought her greedy, but her father's announcement had only incited Faith's urgency. That her father was willing to marry her off to so foul a man as Sir Wilhelm was bad enough, but Hope would be next on his list, and then sweet Grace. Were all the admiral's daughters doomed to lives of abuse and misery? She would not stand for it. She had made a promise to her mother to take care of her sisters, and she refused to allow them to be sold off like prize horses to the highest bidder. She had yet to meet a man she considered worthy to marry—especially so-called Christian men.

Hypocrites, all of them.

Faith glanced at her first mate. Though enormous in size and much harsher in appearance than her father, Lucas Corwin was nothing like the admiral. He understood things like humility, compassion, and loyalty to family. "Thank you for sailing on such short notice, Lucas, and thank the men for me, will you?"

"Aye, they's happy to come." Lucas slapped the air with his hand. "All 'cept Grayson and Mac. I couldn't rouse them from their drink so quick." He snickered.

The loyalty of her crew astounded her. When they weren't out pirating, they spent their time gambling and drinking in town, waiting for her next call. Despite the humiliation of taking orders from a female captain, most of them had chosen to follow her from England to the colonies.

Lucas shifted his weight and fumbled with the hilt of his cutlass. "They's good men fer the most part. And they follow ye 'cause yer fair and ye don't hurt no one like most pirates. They's not after no killin'—just the treasure."

Morgan cawed from his post behind her. "Shiver me timbers. Shiver me timbers."

Lucas tugged his waistcoat tighter around him. "That bird be right 'bout one thing. It be so cold tonight, the timbers are quakin'."

Faith nodded as a blast of wind sent a chill through her sodden shirt. Unusually cold for August, to be sure. Not a good omen of things to come.

Lightning etched the sky in the distance, highlighting the wild dance of the sea—the lawless, tumultuous sea. How she loved it!

A sail cracked above them, and Lucas turned. "Reef the topsails!" he blared to one of the men before facing Faith again. "I thought we was caught fer sure when that cap'n showed up at yer house." He scratched his chin. "Don't knows why he didn't recollect me."

"You were bald four years ago. Remember, the lice?" Faith plopped her tricorn back on her head. "But fortune smiled upon us, for it seems he didn't recognize me either." She shrugged. "Or perchance he just plays with us. But thanks be to Go—the powers that be, that the man had the courage to turn down my father's request to be guardian over me and my sisters, or I fear we would be seeing much more of him."

Thunder drummed across the sky in an ominous echo of her statement.

"Yer guardian?" Lucas laughed.

"Yes, and not only that. The Royal Navy has sent him here to hunt pirates." She gave Lucas a sly grin.

He slapped his thigh. "Why, I'll be a pickled hen. God has a sense o' humor, after all."

"I doubt *God* has much to do with any of this." Faith grew somber.

The ship bucked, sending a spray of seawater over them. Faith shook the water from her waistcoat and adjusted her baldric. Dressing in men's clothing always made her feel more in control—a feeling she had come to crave more with each passing year.

"As soon as my father sails for Italy, we will take the *Siren* out as often as possible," she instructed Lucas, who nodded his head and gave her a mischievous grin.

Her father would be gone for at least six months. With a little luck and a lot of pluck, she and her crew could pirate these waters clean of all their treasures. But what to do with Mr. Waite? The last thing she needed was an HMS warship lurking about. He presented a problem indeed. He no longer appeared to be the half-witted lackey she had met five years before. Controlled and cordial, he carried himself as a man of honor. Strength and intelligence shone in his handsome blue eyes. She saw the way he looked at her. And she could not deny the tingle of warmth she felt in his presence.

Nevertheless, she must avoid him as much as possible. The less he knew about her and her family, the less suspicious he would be of her nighttime activities. Not that he would ever believe that the daughter of an admiral was a pirate. But she must play it safe in any case. She had come too far, accomplished too much to get caught now.

"Hard about, Lucas. Back to port," she ordered, eyeing the massive black clouds on the horizon. "For I fear a storm is on the way."

⁓

Dajon knelt before the wooden altar. A chill from the stone floor seeped through his breeches into his knees. Above him on the brick wall, the cross of Christ, his Lord, hung as a reminder of what the Son of God had sacrificed in his stead. He closed his eyes, shutting out the candlelight that illuminated the narrow brick Congregational church of his friend Rev. Richard Halloway. Dajon needed wisdom. He needed comfort, and he sought it from the One who never failed him.

Some time later, after he had poured out his heart to his Father, the scuffle of footsteps accompanied by baritone humming jarred Dajon from his meditation. He opened his eyes to see Rev. Halloway flipping through the pages of a book in the shadows by the communion table.

Clearing his throat, Dajon rose from the altar.

"Ah, my friend, you startled me," the reverend exclaimed as he came into the candle's glow, a wide grin on his ruddy face. He cast a glance behind him where the faint gleam of a new day brightened a window in the back of the sanctuary. " 'Tis early. What brings you here at this hour?" His bushy brows knit together.

Dajon shifted his weight and clutched the hilt of his sword. "I could not sleep."

"Something amiss?" The reverend led Dajon to a pew. "Sit. Tell me." He closed the book on his lap.

Dajon squinted at the title on the volume, unsure whether he should share his fears with his friend. "Richard Allestree's *Whole Duty of Man*?"

"Aye, have you read it?" The reverend lifted the book.

Dajon shook his head and sat beside him.

"I shall lend it to you when I am finished. It will strengthen your faith. But you did not come to discuss what I am reading."

41

Dajon squeezed the bridge of his nose. "I did not come to talk at all, only to pray."

The reverend patted him on the back. "Then you have already done what is most important."

Rev. Halloway's green eyes sparkled in the candlelight. The crinkle of his leathery skin and the gray flecks in his curly blond hair were the only things that gave away his age. He exuded a genuine concern that always pulled Dajon's darkest secrets out of hiding.

"Admiral Westcott requested that I act as guardian to his daughters while he is overseas."

The reverend let out a deep laugh. "Yes, the Westcott daughters. Newly arrived from England. I have heard men in town speak of their beauty."

"Then you know my dilemma." Dajon sprang to his feet and paced before the altar.

"You speak of Lady Rawlings?"

"Aye." A heavy weight entombed his heart as memories of a past life resurrected. "My answer was no, of course. But I fear my career will suffer for it. He doesn't understand my refusal. But what choice did I have?" Dajon released a heavy sigh.

" 'Twas a long time ago, Dajon."

"Not long enough."

The reverend slapped his hand on the pew. "When will you forgive yourself for what God has already forgotten?"

"How can I? It was my own foolish passion that caused her death." He gazed at the cross. "And I have vowed to God that I would never repeat that mistake."

"He has heard you. He knows your heart. And He will not give you a temptation you cannot resist."

Dajon sighed and gave the reverend a lopsided grin. "Have you seen Miss Faith Westcott?"

"If you mean the redhead, aye, I have." The reverend nodded. "I have taken notice of her as much as the good Lord allows."

"Even though I've just made her acquaintance, something comes over me when she is near. A flame that burns in my gut and befuddles my brain." Dajon plopped down on the pew again and propped his elbows on his knees. "I have the strange sensation that I have met her before, but I know that's not possible." He shook his head. "Of all the men under his command, why did the admiral have to ask me? I have spent the past four years making all the right choices, doing my duty to God and country."

"Perhaps that is why. That he trusts you with his most precious treasures—his own daughters—says a great deal about your character."

Dajon snorted. "If he only knew."

"You are not the man you once were." The reverend leaned back against the pew, the aged wood creaking beneath his weight.

"Perhaps. But it will be a long time hence before I can make amends for what I have done."

The reverend touched Dajon's arm. "You can never pay the price for what God has already paid, my friend."

"As you keep telling me." Dajon attempted a smile. "Nevertheless, I find I am not ready for such a temptation."

"If you were not, God would not have sent it your way."

Dajon clenched his hands together. "It matters not. I turned him down and now must suffer the repercussions to my career."

"Surely the admiral will not punish you for refusing such a personal favor?"

"You do not know him. He is not called the 'Iron Wall' for nothing." Dajon snickered. "No one who has ever come against him has walked away unscathed."

The door of the sanctuary swung open and crashed against the wall. A stiff breeze whipped through the narrow room, sending the candle flames flickering.

Dajon turned to see two uniformed men marching toward him. He stood. They saluted him, and the one closet to him held out a piece of paper. "For you, Mr. Waite."

Dajon took the paper and broke the seal. It was from Admiral Westcott. As he read, his blood turned to ice.

Mr. Waite,

My orders have come through, and I am to set sail immediately. I found your refusal to act as guardian over my daughters in my absence somewhat surprising and therefore have no recourse but to assume it was merely due to modesty on your part. As I am sure you are aware, I consider this task to be associated with the security of our grand and glorious nation, long live King George, in that it will afford me the ability to focus entirely on my duties rather than on the safety of my daughters. I must tell you my resolutions are firm, and therefore I place my daughters in your trustworthy charge. And I assure you that you shall find yourself amply rewarded when I return. Instructions have been left with Edwin Huxley, my steward.

Everything inside of Dajon screamed a defiant *No!* Yet there was no one present to whom he could protest—at least no one with the power to alter the path laid before him.

I did not wish to wake the girls, so I shall leave you the task of bidding them farewell in my stead. I trust you implicitly, Waite. But mark my words, I will hold you personally responsible for the safety and welfare of my daughters.

Signed this day, the 15th of August in the year of our Lord, seventeen hundred and eighteen,

Rear Admiral Henry Westcott

CHAPTER 5

Tap, tap, tap.

Faith shoved a pillow over her head and rolled over. "Go away."

Tap, tap, tap.

"Miss Faith. You got to get up now." Molly's voice filtered through the door.

Faith fought against the sleep that pressed her deep into the mattress, but then she decided nothing could be important enough to disturb it and allowed it to consume her again.

The door creaked open, and footsteps clicked across the room, followed by a blast of bright light as her curtains were drawn back. "Sorry to disturb you, but you are needed downstairs."

Morgan cawed from his wooden perch next to Faith's bed.

Straining to sit, Faith huffed and rubbed her eyes. "What time is it?" She held out her hand, and Morgan flew to her. "Where is Loretta?"

"Noon, young missy." Molly clamped her hands on her hips. "Far too late for a proper lady to be sleepin'. And I sent the chamber maid on an errand." Molly eyed Morgan. "And a proper lady don't live with no bird, neither."

"But I just retired to bed—" Faith snapped her mouth shut.

"I know when you got yerself to bed. You and that scrap dog Lucas out roamin' the streets all night doin' God knows what." She clicked her tongue. "Shame, shame, shame on both of you."

"It is not what you think, Molly." Faith swung her legs over the side of her bed while Molly sifted through her armoire. *It's actually much worse.* Faith smiled.

"It's not my business to think. I jest keep prayin' for you, and for Lucas, too." Molly broke into a song that sounded like a cross between an African

45

chant and a Christian hymn.

Blinking her eyes in an effort to keep them open, Faith stared at Molly as she selected a gown and undergarments and approached the bed. Two oval black eyes set in glowing skin the color of cinnamon stared back at her. Standing barely over five feet tall, the slender cook more than made up for her size with her determination.

Faith snickered. "Good heavens, what is the rush?" She set Morgan down on the blue satin coverlet.

"Heaven *will* be good, not that you gonna see much of it." Molly tossed a green silk gown, stiff petticoats, and a bodice onto the bed beside Faith. "And the rush is that handsome captain be down below awaitin' you."

"Mr. Waite? Why ever would he be here?" Faith jumped to the floor and tore off her nightdress, anxious to find out what the man wanted and to be rid of him as soon as possible before he ingratiated himself with her family.

Molly strode to the door, shaking her head. "Well, if I'd known that would get you up, I'd a said so in the first place."

After quickly donning her gown, Faith flew down the stairs, but then she halted at the bottom to thread her fingers through her hair and pat her eyes, hoping the puffiness of sleep had subsided. She held a lock of her hair up to her nose and drew in a deep breath. Lemons. She smiled. At least the lemon oil she had sprinkled through her hair masked the scent of the sea—something she knew the captain would smell in an instant.

Turning, she burst into the parlor, intending to make a grand entrance. But she was too late. Hope had already draped herself over poor Mr. Waite.

Grace sat stiffly on the sofa, while Edwin stood beside the admiral's desk, a sheaf of papers in hand.

Plucking Hope's arm from his, the commander turned toward Faith. His dark eyebrows rose as he straightened his blue coat and took a step toward her. The tip of his service sword clanged against the table, and he glanced down. But when he raised his gaze, his blue eyes met hers with such intensity that Faith's heart took on a rapid beat. She chided herself. She was supposed to be getting rid of him, not allowing his good looks and commanding presence to turn her insides to mush.

"Miss Westcott." He bowed, and a strand of his dark hair brushed against his cheek.

Her breath quickened. "Mr. Waite."

"Forgive me if I disturbed your rest." He grinned.

"Rest? Nay. I was reading." Faith waved a hand through the air and gazed off to her right.

"Our sister always sleeps half the day away," Grace said with disdain.

"Grace." Hope patted her silky golden hair, pinned up in a fashionable coiffure, and stared at her sister. "You should not say such things. What will Mr. Waite think of us?"

Mr. Waite shifted his stance, his black boots thumping on the wooden floor. "I will not keep you and your sisters long. I have come to extend your father's farewell and to go over my obligations with Edwin." He nodded toward the steward.

"Farewell?" Faith huffed. "So my father has fled in the night like a coward."

Darting to her, Hope clutched Faith's arm. "Can you believe Father left us without saying good-bye?" Tears glistened in her sister's eyes, and Faith's heart sank. It seemed her father's true love was and always would be the navy. "I am sure he had good reason." She offered her sister a weak smile.

Two black bags sitting by her father's desk caught Faith's gaze. Surely this pirate hunter was not planning to take up residence in their home? Had he not resolutely turned her father down? "Are we to assume, Mr. Waite, that you find yourself equally lacking in fortitude—so much so that you cannot deny my father's preposterous request?"

Mr. Waite gritted his teeth. "I assure you, Miss Westcott, I find the arrangement as displeasing as you do. But I fear I was given no choice."

"Ah." Faith raised one brow. "So he left without speaking to you as well." She flattened her lips. It certainly sounded like the kind of conniving tactic her father might employ. He had never been able to take no for an answer.

"He was called away suddenly." Mr. Waite's tone held no conviction.

"He could not wait a few hours?" Hope sobbed and crossed her arms over her lavender brocade gown—the one that brought out the gold sparkles in her hair and the deep blue in her eyes. "Sometimes I wonder if he loves us at all or simply wants to marry us off and be rid of the responsibility." She swiped a tear from her cheek. "I wish Mother were still with us." She hung her head, her voice tinged with sorrow. "We may not see Father for a year."

"Six months, in fact, miss," Mr. Waite interjected. "At least that is the time period he indicated to Edwin."

Edwin nodded in agreement from his position beside their father's desk.

Forcing back tears from her own eyes, Faith plucked a handkerchief from her pocket and handed it to Hope. "Father loves us in his own way, Hope. And Grace and I are still here. We will not leave you."

Grace rose to join them. "Faith is right. We will never leave you. And you know Father was never good at saying farewell." She eased a lock of Hope's hair from her face and smiled, her green eyes beaming with warmth and love.

Mr. Waite cleared his throat. "I have no doubt he was quite upset at having to leave so suddenly."

Faith cocked her head. "And all along, I was under the misunderstanding that good Christian men were not supposed to lie."

The captain snapped his blue gaze in her direction. " 'Twas merely my opinion, miss, and therefore cannot be judged as either false or true."

"Then should we expect to be assaulted with your good opinions on a regular basis?" Faith retorted. Perhaps if she were rude enough to him, he would leave.

"So as not to offend your *tender* sensibilities, I will attempt to keep my opinions to a minimum." He gave her a mock bow.

Tender. Of all the. . .

"The truth of the matter, Mr. Waite, is that we know our father far better than you do." Faith turned and stomped toward the bookcase, trying to mask her anger. "The Royal Navy is his life. I fear we have always come second."

"As Mother did as well." Hope twisted a lock of her hair around one slender finger until it appeared hopelessly entangled.

Grace stilled Hope's hand and began to untwine her hair. "Human love is fraught with shortcomings. Only God's love satisfies."

Faith snorted and waved off her sister's religious platitude as she turned to face them.

Hope eased the loose strand of hair behind her ear. "I have found no satisfaction in God's love."

Grace clutched her sister's shoulders. "You should not say such a thing! And you should not speak poorly of Father either." Releasing her, Grace took a step back, her conflicted gaze shifting between Faith and Hope. "We must honor him as God's Word says." Yet even as the words left her mouth, they rang hollow through the air.

Faith flung a hand to her hip. "It is hard to honor a man who intends to do the same thing to us as he did to our sister Charity. Can you deny that, Grace?"

Hope began to sob again.

Grace slid onto the sofa and shook her head. "I cannot deny that what he did was wrong, even cruel. But the Bible says we must honor him anyway." She sighed and clutched her gown, twisting it in her hands as if trying to make sense out of the pious rules she dedicated her life to following.

"And how can I honor a man I hardly know?" Hope swallowed and lowered her gaze. "Even when he is home, he seems to find no pleasure in us—only fault."

"Then why are you so distraught when he leaves?" Faith wrinkled her brow.

Hope glanced at Faith, a wounded look in her blue eyes. "Because I keep hoping that someday he'll grow to approve of me and maybe. . . maybe even love me."

Faith's heart shriveled. "Father will always be Father. But we will always have each other, and we have just as much love to give you as any father or mother."

"Even more," Grace added, and Hope's sobs slowly softened.

Faith's gaze landed on the captain. She had forgotten he was still standing there. His annoyed gaze wavered over them and then shifted to the door as though he wanted to make a dash for it and never return. What a handsome vision he presented, even in his flustered state—tall, broad shouldered, commanding in his blue navy coat. A bit of stubble peppered his strong jaw as if he had been too hurried that morning to shave.

"If you ladies would be so kind as to take a seat," he finally said then turned toward Edwin, who stood staring out the window, no doubt bored by what he often called the Westcott sisters' theatrical display. "Edwin, the papers, if you please." Mr. Waite held out his hand.

Faith eased onto the sofa where Grace had taken a seat. Hope slid next to her and squeezed her hand.

"So am I to assume, Mr. Waite, that you intend to become our guardian—despite your earlier protest?" Faith shot him a challenging look.

His sharp eyes locked upon hers. "It seems for the time being that I have been given no choice in the matter. However, allow me to assure you ladies"—he directed a stern gaze at each of them in turn—"you will no doubt find my methods of command no less strict than you are accustomed to."

Faith found her admiration for the man rising. Regardless of the difficult position imposed upon him by their father, Mr. Waite had no intention of shrugging off the responsibility as some men would have. Yet despite her regard for his integrity, it did naught to aid her plan to be rid of him. In fact, quite the opposite, especially if he intended to rule the house with an iron hand. For with their father gone so often, she and her sisters were not accustomed to discipline. And now was certainly not the time to start.

"Mr. Waite, surely you understand this is not your ship and we are not your crew. Are we to be flogged and made to scrub the deck whenever we misbehave?"

Hope giggled.

"If you do not misbehave, Miss Westcott," Mr. Waite said, perching on the edge of the admiral's desk and taking the papers from Edwin, "you will not have to find that out. Now." He shifted through the documents in his hand. "Your steward and I have gone over the admiral's wishes, and we are in complete agreement on every rule."

Edwin moved beside Mr. Waite, arms crossed over his chest, a superior look on his puffy face. But Faith knew how to handle him. It was this new intruder, this resolute captain, who gave her pause.

"Miss Hope," he began. "I will address you first since your father left specific instructions for you."

"He did?" Hope's eyes lit up. She scooted to the edge of her seat.

"It is your father's express order that you have no dealings with a"—the captain peered at the paper—"Lord Arthur Falkland."

Hope shot to her feet. "Impossible! I will not suffer it. Arthur—Lord Falkland—is my beau. We are courting."

"He is also a scoundrel, dear Hope. Everyone in town knows it." Grace twisted the button at the top of her throat.

"Nevertheless…,"Mr. Waite sighed, rising to his feet. "It is your father's desire that you not see him nor a Miss Anne Cormac." He broadened his stance as Faith imagined him doing when commanding his men aboard his ship. But to his obvious chagrin, it did not have the intended effect on Hope, for she began to sob, fisting her hands at her sides.

"Anne is a friend of mine, and if my father cared enough to stay home, he would know Lord Falkland to be a gentleman." She fell sideways on the sofa, and Faith threw an arm around her and glared at Mr. Waite.

The captain tugged his collar. "You may address this issue with the admiral when he returns. In the meantime, you will abide by his wishes or answer to me." He pressed that rebellious strand of hair behind his ear, and Faith suspected he wished he could restrain the three of them as easily. But she had to admit she rather enjoyed the pink hue rising up his face, the twitch of his lips, and the beads of sweat forming on his forehead. His eyes met hers, and he raised a brow as if he saw through her charade.

He flipped the papers in his hand. "Under no circumstances are any of you to travel this city unescorted. Lucas, Mr. Huxley, or myself, when I am not at sea, must be with you at all times whenever you leave this house."

"'Tis impossible." Grace shook her head defiantly, drawing the captain's shocked gaze.

Grace sat up straight and folded her hands in her lap. "My charity work takes me all over the city. Surely you know that when the good Lord calls us on a mission, we must go immediately. I cannot always wait for an escort."

"What happened to honoring our father?" Hope snickered.

Grace raised her pert nose in the air. "God's work comes first."

Mr. Waite sent Grace an indulgent, if somewhat stiff, smile. "I appreciate the divine nature of your work, Miss Grace, and I am sure Edwin or Lucas will happily accompany you whenever possible, but these are the standing orders, and they will be obeyed."

Shifting her gaze away, Grace sank back into the sofa.

"Or what, Mr. Waite—will you lock us in the hold of your ship?" Faith teased.

"If I have to, Miss Westcott." His lips curved in a sardonic grin. "And I would not test me on that if I were you."

～

The thumping of regimental drums began pounding in Dajon's head, cautioning him to conclude his business and be gone—back to the sanity of his ship. He flipped through the papers, determined to spout off the remaining rules without further interruption.

"All monies will be under my control," Dajon continued in a hurried tone. "Aside from necessities, which will be provided, please come to me or Mr. Huxley for anything you need."

"I daresay, Mr. Waite." Faith's lips twisted in a mocking grin. "We are big girls and can handle our own money."

"I care not for what you perceive you can and cannot do, Miss Westcott. It is only what you will do that concerns me." He threw back his shoulders and gave them all his sternest look.

Faith widened her eyes. "Do you never break a rule, Mr. Waite?" The pert look on her face was at once alluring and infuriating, and he nearly choked at the tantalizing hold it had upon him.

"Not if I can help it, Miss Westcott."

Intelligence shone behind her sparkling auburn eyes. Was she testing him? He marched to the fireplace and faced them with his most intimidating stare. Surely if he could command a ship full of men, he could control these three women.

Ignoring him, Hope turned toward her sister. "What about that new gown Father promised to buy me?"

"You have no need of another gown, Hope." Grace shook her head. "You should give the ones you have to the poor."

Hope gave her sister a scowl.

Dajon cleared his throat and raised his voice. "These are the rules. When I am not present, Mr. Huxley is in charge. Is that understood?"

Edwin pointed a jagged finger at the girls. "Mark my words. Your father will hear of every infraction."

Hope tossed her nose in the air. "I will not give my gowns to the poor and go about town wearing rags like you do, Grace." She stomped her foot.

Scooting to the edge of her seat, Faith took her sister's hand in hers. "Come now, Hope; of course you will not be forced to sell your dresses. Ladies, let us not forget we have a guest."

Hope eyed Dajon. "He is not a guest anymore. He is our new father—or might as well be. He is just like him."

Dajon dropped his gaze and rubbed the sweat from his forehead. He felt like a zoologist charged with taming a flock of screeching, fluttering jungle fowl.

A bird squawked somewhere upstairs, confirming his assessment.

When a knock sounded at the front door, he prayed it was the admiral returning home, having discovered his orders were in error.

"Pardon me." Edwin gave Dajon a look of pity and left the room as the girls continued arguing.

"Sir Wilhelm Carteret to see Miss Westcott," Edwin announced when he returned.

The white-wigged, sickly man slithered into the room with one hand on his hip, the other hanging in midair, and leered at Faith like a sly serpent.

A pained expression crossed her features as she rose slowly to her feet. "Sir Wilhelm, this is unexpected."

His eyes narrowed. "I heard your father left suddenly and thought you might need company, but I see Mr. Waite has beat me to it." He pursed his lips in a semblance of a grin and bowed toward Dajon.

"Sir Wilhelm." Dajon set the papers down on the desk, feeling as if he had been snatched from the lion's den. "You are most fortunate in your timing. My business here is finished."

Hope sprang from the couch and rubbed her temples. "Forgive me, but I feel a headache coming on." She nodded to Dajon and Sir Wilhelm and hurriedly made her way to the door like a rabbit under a hawk's gaze.

"I shall help you to your chamber, sister." Grace followed quickly on her heels, leaving a befuddled Faith in her wake.

Throwing back her shoulders, she faced Sir Wilhelm. "Mr. Waite has offered to take me for a stroll." She turned to face Dajon. "Have you not, Mr. Waite?"

Dajon could not mistake the pleading look in her eyes, nor the disgust he'd seen souring within them the moment Sir Wilhelm had entered the room. Did she hate this man so much that she preferred Dajon's company? He shifted his gaze between her urging glance and the rancor burning in Sir Wilhelm's eyes. By thunder, the last thing he needed was to prance about with this red-haired beauty on his arm. Yet the other two girls seemed to hold her in some esteem. Perhaps he could recruit her assistance in keeping order at home. Before he realized what he was doing, he agreed with a placating nod.

"Perhaps we can visit some other time, Sir Wilhelm?" Faith's sweet smile dripped with venom. "But do inform us ahead of time when we can expect your visit." She turned to Edwin. "Please take Mr. Waite's things to the guesthouse."

With a flutter of lashes and a smile that would melt any man's heart, Faith thrust an arm through Dajon's and pulled him into the entrance hall and out the door, leaving a rather disgruntled Sir Wilhelm behind.

CHAPTER 7

Faith shielded her eyes from the sun as she clung to the wobbling jolly boat. Up ahead, the dark hull of the HMS *Enforcer* swelled like a leviathan rising from the sea. Two bare masts towered over her as they thrust into the blue sky, contradicting her belief that sloops were purely single-masted vessels. Truth be told, this ship appeared more the size of a small frigate than a sloop. As they neared the hull, nine gun ports gaped at her like charred eye sockets from its side. That would put the ship's guns numbering at least eighteen—provided there weren't any more on deck—eighteen to the *Red Siren*'s sixteen. Still, not terrible odds if their paths should cross at sea.

Faith's gaze drifted to Mr. Waite, seated stiffly at the head of the boat. He smiled then returned his stern face to his crew as they rowed in unison over the choppy waves of Charles Towne Harbor. How she had managed to convince him to give her a tour of his ship, she could not fathom, but she hadn't been able to resist asking him, even if it meant she would have to spend more time with the man she had vowed to avoid. She could not deny that he had come in handy today as a diversion to Sir Wilhelm's slobbering attentions. And she could not expect to completely elude a man living at her home. Besides, since he clearly did not recognize her— or he would have had her arrested already—perhaps she could use Mr. Waite after all.

Nevertheless, excitement coursed through her at the chance to inspect one of His Majesty's Royal Navy ships. It certainly couldn't hurt to learn as much as she could about the ships that pursued her—something her father had never given her a chance to do. *"A navy ship is no place for a lady,"* she could still hear him say.

"Oars up!" one of the men shouted. The eight-man crew hefted their oars straight above their heads as the boat thudded and splashed against the ship's hull.

Faith glanced up at the planks of damp wood that rose above her like the impenetrable walls of an enemy fortress—impenetrable to obvious foes, not clandestine foes like her. For like a tiny white ant, she intended to bore her way through the ship, seek out its weaknesses, and devour it from within.

"Captain's coming aboard!" someone yelled from above.

After the men secured the jolly boat with ropes, a bosun's chair was lowered over the side.

Faith rolled her eyes. She had hoped to avoid this demeaning way men had devised to hoist women aboard ships—as if they were cargo. She could climb the rope ladder as well as any man.

But she couldn't tell that to the captain.

Mr. Waite rose and extended a hand to Faith. "I'm afraid this is the only way we have to bring you safely aboard, Miss Westcott."

"I am sure I will manage." She smiled as she settled into the swaying chair and grabbed the ropes on each side.

Mr. Waite gave the signal to hoist her aboard, and the baritone command "Heave, heave!" poured over the bulwarks as the ropes snapped tight and her chair rose.

"Side by side, lively now, men," another man yelled from above as the captain sprang up the rope ladder with the ease of a man who spent more time aboard a ship than on land.

As Faith rounded the top railing, dozens of eyes shot her way, but the crowd of sailors quickly resumed their forward stares. A line of men near the railing raised whistles and blew out a sharp trill as drums pounded behind her.

Mr. Waite grabbed the rail and jumped on board. "Atte-e-e-en-tion!" Every sailor removed his hat, and the captain responded by touching the tip of his.

"Welcome aboard, Captain." A young, uniformed officer with a thin mustache stepped forward just as Faith's shoes tapped the deck. Two seamen assisted her off the wobbling chair.

"Thank you, Mr. Borland," Mr. Waite replied as the rest of the crew dispersed to their duties.

Faith stood amazed at the formality and organization of the sailors, even at port.

"Miss Faith Westcott." Mr. Waite gestured toward her. "May I present Mr. Reginald Borland, my first lieutenant, as well as a good friend."

"At your service, miss." The young man bowed and allowed his narrow brown eyes to drift over her. Then, slapping his bicorn atop his sandy hair, he straightened his blue navy coat. A line of gold buttons ran down the center of each pristine white lapel, winking at Faith in the sunlight.

"Miss Westcott is my temporary ward," Mr. Waite explained, "and has requested a brief tour of the ship. Since we have no current orders to sail, I thought to oblige her."

"Very well, Captain." Lieutenant Borland offered a sly wink toward his captain before turning to leave.

Ignoring him, the captain extended his elbow toward Faith and led her down a set of stairs into the bowels of the ship. Men hustled to and fro but quickly snapped to attention when their captain passed. Dozens of gazes pierced Faith from all directions—even from deep within the shadows. Mr. Waite placed his warm hand over hers as they continued. The protective sentiment sent a spark through Faith that she immediately dismissed.

She had no need of a man to protect her.

"I am at a loss as to how to address you, sir," she said as they turned and proceeded down the aft companionway. "Are you not simply a lieutenant?"

Mr. Waite stiffened beside her and stretched out his neck as if pulling a cord tight. "Indeed, I am."

Pleased that she had flustered him, Faith grinned, knowing her expression was concealed by the shadows. "Yet my father calls you a commander, and your men refer to you as 'Captain.' "

"There is no formal rank between lieutenant and captain, miss. But because I am the commander of this ship, my men must call me Captain. You may address me as either Mr. Waite or Captain, if you wish."

Oh, how kind of you. Faith shook her head at the man's impudence as she examined the narrow hallway. Lantern light cast monstrous shadows across the low deckhead. With each flicker of the wick or rock of the ship, they altered shape and crouched, ready to pounce upon them—upon her.

Not that she hadn't seen a dark companionway on a ship before, but on this ship full of enemies, the shadows seemed more threatening—as if they knew what mischief she was about.

The captain showed her the master's cabin, clerk's cabin, and two storerooms before he approached a large oak door at the end of the hall.

"Allow me to show you the captain's cabin, Miss Westcott, and then I shall give you a tour around the top deck before I escort you home."

Faith blinked. "What of the rest of your ship, Mr. Waite? Surely I have not seen it all."

" 'Tis a big ship, miss," he said, reaching for the door handle. "Many areas are not fit for a lady to enter."

Faith let out a huff before she realized it and covered her mouth, pretending to cough. "I beg you to change your mind, Mr. Waite." She eased beside him, a bit closer than propriety allowed. "What have I to fear with you by my side?" She tried to flutter her lashes, but they felt like maniacal butterflies upon her cheeks.

"Have you something in your eyes, Miss Westcott?" The captain leaned toward her, a curious look wrinkling his forehead.

Faith lowered her shoulders and scowled. "Nay, but I beg you. I had my heart set upon seeing the entire ship, and now I find you were naught but teasing me."

She scrunched her lips into a pout as she had seen Hope do so often, but instead of swooning at her feet, instead of apologizing for being so obstinate, instead of offering her everything she wanted, the captain simply laughed and turned away. "Nay, my apologies, miss, but I fear your sensibilities are far too fragile."

My sensibilities? Good heavens. Faith's head began to pound. "My curiosity demands it, sir!" She hadn't meant to shout, but she had to do something to get this buffoon to show her his ship.

Releasing the door latch, Mr. Waite studied her curiously, his eyes narrowing as if he were plotting some battle strategy and she were but a chart laid out before him. "Very well, we would not want you to think me a tease, Miss Westcott, now, would we?" And though his tone was all politeness, the look he gave her was one of a cat about to devour a mouse.

The stench of mold, sweat, and urine assaulted her as he led her down a ladder, past the wardroom then down another ladder into the bowels of the ship. Flinging a hand to her nose, she coughed and took a step back.

Not that she wasn't accustomed to such smells aboard a ship, but this ship housed a lot more men than her small brigantine. And her crew didn't live aboard her ship for more than a day, whereas the men on an HMS warship were oft at sea for months. The captain lifted his lantern to reveal stacks of crates and barrels crowding them on all sides. The patter of tiny feet joined the creak of the wood.

"The hold, miss." He shifted his playful gaze her way. "And as we discussed, 'tis where I throw wards who misbehave." His lips curved slightly, and Faith longed to slap them back into a straight line.

"Watch your step, miss," Mr. Waite warned as a furry beast skittered across Faith's shoe.

She hated rats. Abhorred them, actually, and longed to kick the smelly rodent into the corner, but for Mr. Waite's sake, she let out a tiny yelp and flung her hand to her chest.

When she glanced up at the captain, a smirk sat upon his handsome lips.

He was doing this on purpose. He wanted her to faint dead away from the smells and the rats so he could prove he had been correct in his assessment of the softer gender. *The insolent, unchivalrous knave.*

"Had enough, Miss Westcott?" He gave her a smug look.

A storm began to brew within Faith.

"Why no, Mr. Waite. I have only just begun."

But she soon found she had misjudged her resilience, for the captain seemed intent on showing her the most atrocious parts of the ship: empty stalls that not long ago had housed animals from the crossing from England and still retained a stench that would knock a hardened farmer on his back; the bloodstained operating table and floors of the sick bay that seemed to hold the eerie screams of the dying; and the galley, complete with a bubbling pot of slimy gray stew that reeked worse than the animal stalls. Faith caught a glimpse of weevils digging tunnels through the biscuits laid out for the day, and she held a hand over her mouth and gulped down a clump of bile, ignoring Mr. Waite's smirk. Perhaps she wasn't the tough pirate she claimed to be. For in all her plundering, she had not seen much blood, nor had she been forced to house animals or even hire a cook for her crew. Since she couldn't be away from home for longer than a night, she chose her victims well. Never British vessels. Always small merchantmen, undermanned and undergunned. And not one of them had given her much resistance.

Mr. Waite held out his arm. "Perhaps you need some fresh air?"

As much as Faith would love to go above, she had yet to see the gun deck. But how to express an interest in such weapons without drawing suspicion? She nodded, knowing the cannons were housed on the level above them. "Perhaps we could begin our ascent."

As they made their way to the stairs, they passed a large room that spanned into darkness in both directions. Hammocks swung from the rafters like a school of fish swimming above tables that crowded a floor filthy with scraps of food and spilled grog. Snores and curses could be heard filtering through the room and bouncing off the moist hull.

"The *Enforcer* houses one hundred and twenty men," Mr. Waite announced proudly as he led her up the ladder.

And Faith believed at that moment she could smell every single one of their unwashed bodies. At least her crew kept themselves somewhat clean—albeit per her orders.

Clutching her skirts, Faith made her way up the creaking narrow stairs and glanced around the ship in awe. Though similar to her sleek brigantine in some ways, this sailing vessel was larger by comparison, and despite the squalor, everything in it, including crew and captain, operated together like a precise machine. But then again, Faith was no Royal Navy captain, nor did she ever intend to run her ship as if she were. Besides, the *Red Siren* could outrun this clumsy old bucket any day. She had nothing to fear.

Beads of perspiration slid beneath her bodice as they approached the gun deck, and she wondered how the crewmen endured this stifling heat below deck day after day. Turning, the captain gestured with his lantern toward another set of stairs. "Just one more flight, miss, and you shall find relief."

Faith offered him a sweet smile. "May I see the cannons first?"

"We call them guns when they are on a ship." He examined her, searching her eyes through the shadows. "I must admit, you are a far more resilient woman than I first surmised, Miss Westcott. Most ladies would have no interest in such deadly weapons."

She wanted to tell him she was not like most women. She wanted to tell him she had an obsession with cannons, with the round iron shot, the ear-deafening blast, the invigorating sting of gunpowder in the air. "I have an interest in many things, Mr. Waite."

"So be it." He nodded for her to precede him.

Faith scanned the gun deck, lined on both sides with nine massive cannons resting in their trucks, their muzzles pointed toward closed ports—twelve-pounders, by the looks of them. Stale smoke lingered in the air. She slid her hand over the cold iron as if it were a dear friend and glanced over her shoulder at the captain. "I never pictured them so large. They must be quite deadly."

"Yes, they can be." Mr. Waite scratched his chin and cocked his head curiously. "As you can see, we have eighteen here and two more on deck."

Twenty guns altogether. Faith made a mental note. "It warms a lady's heart to know she has a brave, strong captain like you protecting her home from pirates." The silly words sounded even more ludicrous lingering in the air between them, and Faith further embarrassed herself with yet another attempt to flutter her lashes.

Mr. Waite stared at her, confusion twisting his features.

She cleared her throat. "Have you killed many of the villains?"

"None as of yet. But rather than kill them, it is my hope to bring them to justice."

"Perhaps they would prefer to die at sea rather than hang by a noose." The words spat out of her mouth with scorn before she could stop them, but the captain didn't flinch. Only the slight narrowing of his handsome blue eyes revealed any reaction at all.

"Am I to presume you hold some fondness for these thieves?" He crossed his arms over his chest.

"Good heavens! Why, of course not." Faith sashayed to his side. She must be more careful. This man was not one to be easily duped. Faith brushed her hand over his arm and felt his body tense. "It must be dreadfully loud in here when you are at battle."

The heat between them rose like steam on a sultry day. The captain's gaze dropped to her lips and remained there for what seemed minutes before he cleared his throat and took a step back. "Yes, I fear you would find it intolerable."

Faith gave him a coy grin. *Intolerable? I can load and shoot one of these guns faster than most of your men can.*

The slight upturn of Mr. Waite's lips reached his imperious eyes in a glimmer. "You do not agree. I can see it in your eyes." His gaze flickered over Faith. Her body warmed under his intense perusal. She plucked out her fan and looked away.

Dash it all, the man sees right through me. "I do not often agree with the opinions of others, Mr. Waite. I prefer to hear the blast myself before I make such a determination."

"Indeed? Well, perhaps I shall fire one for you someday."

Or at her, most likely. She smiled.

He offered her his arm. "Shall we? I need to retrieve some papers from my cabin before I escort you home."

The captain's cabin reflected its master in every detail, from the methodical arrangement of the furniture to the disciplined stacks of papers atop his oak desk. Rows of alphabetically ordered books lined the shelves built into the paneled walls. Faith ran a hand along the bindings and glanced at the titles: *Campaigns during the War of Spanish Succession 1704-1711, Handbook for Seaman Gunners, Misconduct and the Line of Duty, Naval Ordinances, Regulations of the British Royal Navy. . .* Below them, all manner of religious books lay reverently side by side: the Holy Bible, its leather edges worn; John Hervey's *Meditations and Contemplations*; Milton's *Paradise Lost*. Faith scowled. Mr. Waite appeared to be as dedicated to his God as he was to his navy.

To the left of the shelves, an open wardrobe revealed pressed and pristine uniforms hanging in a row next to a dark blue frock with gold embroidered trim around the collar. Two pairs of polished boots stood at attention beneath them.

The captain sifted through papers on his desk before glancing at her. "Forgive me, Miss Westcott, I shall be with you in a moment. Please have a seat."

She ambled over to the other side of the cabin where several plaques, framed documents, and ribbons dotted the wall: a medal for "conspicuous gallantry and intrepidity at the risk of life and beyond the call of duty"; a meritorious commendation medal; combat action ribbons; a plaque signifying Captain Dajon Waite as a naval expert in the use of pistols, swords, and cannons. Faith stole a glance at him. Surely this was a man to reckon with upon the seas.

Not at all like the young sailor she'd encountered on the English Channel five years past. As soon as her men had surrounded him, he'd given up without a fight. Then she'd ordered Lucas to round up his crew and set them adrift in one of their own jolly boats while her crew transferred all their belongings and weapons to his bigger and better-equipped ship.

Mr. Waite's gaze met hers, and he gestured toward a chair. "So what is your opinion of my ship, Miss Westcott?"

"Your ship, Mr. Waite?" Faith flashed a grin. "I thought it belonged to England." She eased into the wooden seat. "Truth be told, I imagine her far too bulky to catch pirates."

"Indeed." He let out a deep chuckle that caused a warm flutter in Faith's belly. "Fine lined and well armed—a beauty upon the water. I assure you, she will encounter no difficulty in her task."

"You speak of her as you would a lover."

A red hue crept up the captain's face, and he returned to his papers.

"I suppose time will tell." Faith enjoyed her ability to embarrass him so easily. "But I thank you for the tour." As she gazed at the strong, commanding man before her, she almost welcomed the challenge of meeting him upon the sea—almost—for what did her experience compare with his? Ah, but what a grand opportunity to test her skill and her crew's against the finest of His Majesty's Navy. One more glance at the taunting display of medals adorning the wall and she shook her head, wondering at her sanity.

A rap on the door brought her to her senses, and the captain's deep "Enter!" filled the room.

The first lieutenant, Borland, marched inside. He glanced at Faith then faced Mr. Waite. "Pardon me, Captain, but I have a dispatch for you."

The captain extended his hand and snatched the paper, broke the wax seal, and scanned the contents before meeting his first lieutenant's hard gaze.

"May I inquire—" Borland cut off his words and cast a look of concern toward Faith.

Following his first lieutenant's gaze, the captain shrugged, dismissing Faith's presence as having no bearing in the secrecy of the matter.

"A Dutch merchant ship," Mr. Waite announced, "laden with pearls, arriving tomorrow afternoon. We are to rendezvous with her off Hilton Head Island just after noon and provide safe escort from there to our harbor."

Faith's heart thumped wildly as she glanced between the two men.

"'Tis good news, Captain," Borland said. "At least we shall finally set sail again."

Good news, indeed. Faith's gaze shot out the door. She must get home quickly and make plans.

The captain nodded. "Inform the men, if you please."

Borland started to leave then swung back around. "The pirate ship we have been seeking was spotted last night by a local fisherman."

Faith gulped.

"Very good." Mr. Waite nodded. "Then she has not abandoned these waters." He folded the paper neatly and tucked it in his pocket.

"Pray tell, what ship is that?" Faith hoped the tremor in her hands did not reach her voice.

Mr. Borland took her in with a look far too admiring for Faith's comfort. "A troublesome knave who has been plundering these waters for the past few months." He chuckled. "Some say 'tis a woman pirate."

"A woman pirate? Absurd." Faith rose to her feet. "These merchants who spotted her—him—no doubt had consumed too much rum. How can a woman be a pirate?"

The captain circled his desk and leaned back on the edge. "I assure you, they can." His brow darkened. "And it is my first priority to catch this blackguard, man or woman—this one they call the Red Siren."

CHAPTER 8

Dajon eyed the red-haired beauty walking beside him, her delicate fingers tucked into the crook of his elbow as he led her up to the main deck. A solemn mood had settled upon her after the discussion of pirates and treasure ships. No doubt the thought of battles and death upset her—or did it? Dajon perceived a strength beneath the swish of lace and the flutter of dark lashes she so frequently offered him. He could not shake the feeling she was hiding something.

Shame struck him. Although she had urged him to show her the entire ship, he should not have shown her the most repugnant sections aboard. He supposed he had been trying to humble her, but in reality his own pride had reared its ugly head, for he rather enjoyed watching her brazen demeanor slowly dwindle. Silently he repented, for she had obviously suffered under the sights and smells below, but surprisingly, no more than any man unaccustomed to them. In fact, she had moved through the ship with ease, not once losing her footing or cowering in the dark shadows. And her interest in the guns. By thunder, what a fascinating woman.

"Mr. James, prepare the jolly boat," he ordered one of the men standing by the capstan, sending the sailor into action as he shouted orders to the men around him.

As they waited, Faith gripped the railing and closed her eyes. Dajon watched the evening breeze slide its cool fingers through the loose curls adorning her neck, playing with each silky strand, and he found his own fingers aching to do the same. An overwhelming urge to kiss her forced him to tear his gaze away. What was he thinking? His orders were to protect this woman—protect her from letches like himself—a task made all the more difficult when she insisted upon flirting with him all day. Or had she? Perhaps it was simply his own wishful desires.

Oh Lord, give me strength, strength to resist such a tempting morsel laid before me, strength to stay upon the course I have vowed to pursue.

He dared another glance her way. The setting sun transformed her skin into shimmering gold, and Dajon swallowed. Surely this exquisite creature would not be interested in him. More likely, she sought the most convenient alternative to that lecherous Sir Wilhelm Carteret. Dajon flexed his jaw. He would not be so easily taken in by her feminine wiles. Forcing his gaze from her, he watched the sun fling lustrous streams of crimson, orange, and gold into the darkening sky as it sank behind a flowing sea of trees.

Faith smiled and flashed her auburn eyes his way. "Beautiful, is it not? God's creation—untamed and untainted by man."

"Am I mistaken then?" Dajon recalled the animosity toward God she had so blatantly expressed the night before. "You do believe in an almighty Creator?"

"I believe in Him, Captain. I simply do not believe He gives much thought to us, at least not as the Bible implies He does." Faith tossed her chin in the air.

Her declaration stirred both sadness and curiosity within him. "I am sorry."

"Do not be." She raised one brow. "I am not. 'Tis freeing, actually."

"Might I ask what made you give up on God so easily?" He leaned on the railing beside her.

"Easily?" She waved her hand in the air. "You would not understand. You have no doubt led a charmed life."

"Nay, I would not say so." Dajon glanced over the railing and saw the sailors climbing aboard the rocking jolly boat and loosening the ropes. Hardly easy. His life had been riddled with strife and heartache.

Mr. James approached and tapped the brim of his bicorn. "Ready, Captain."

"Very well." Over Mr. James's shoulder, Dajon saw Borland staring at them in a most peculiar way. The first lieutenant dropped his gaze and disappeared below hatches before Dajon could acknowledge him.

"Shall we?" He extended his arm toward Miss Westcott but found she had retreated toward the foremast, allowing two sailors carrying a barrel to pass by. A gust of wind struck the ship, flapping the slack sails and tousling the red curls of her loose bun. She offered Dajon a sultry smile that sent a spark through him. And something else—a memory triggered deep within him. He paused, trying to grab hold of it, but whatever it was evaded him. Perhaps it was her exquisite crimson hair—a rarity among women. He'd seen only a few ladies who had been graced with such an audacious color.

By the time they had rowed ashore and entered Charles Towne through one of the three gates breaching the massive rampart that circled the city, darkness had begun to descend. "My apologies, Miss Westcott, for keeping you out so late."

"I do thank you for showing me your boat, Mr. Waite," Faith replied as she took the lead, weaving around piles of horse manure that littered the dirt of Bay Street.

"Ship, if you please." Dajon rushed to catch up with her and offered her his arm.

Faith smiled but did not take it. "Of course. But there is no need to see me home. You must have preparations to attend to on board. I am quite safe within these walls."

"Aye, I do have a bit of work to do on my ship, but afterward, I'll be staying in the guesthouse per your father's request." Dajon glanced at the stone enclosure that blocked their view of the bay. "To find such a fortified city in the colonies, complete with moat and drawbridge, is quite astonishing." He fingered the hilt of his sword as they passed one of the port's taverns. "But with Spain's recent attacks and the Tuscarora Indian war, 'tis no wonder the settlers thought it worth the added protection. Not to alarm you, Miss Westcott." He grabbed her arm, forcing her to slow her pace. "But the wall is not impenetrable, and there are dangers lurking within the city as well."

"I realize, Mr. Waite, that you and my father have an arrangement, but any fool can see that it was forced upon you against your will. My father has a way of doing that to people." Faith halted and placed one hand on her gently rounded hip. "Believe me, there is no need for your constant watch. I have been caring for myself and my sisters since my mother died, and I will continue to do so."

His blood began to heat under her ungrateful and dismissive attitude. "You seemed to have need of me when Sir Wilhelm came calling." He gave her a sideways glance. "And when you begged so ardently to see my ship."

She stared at him with the look a spider might bestow upon a fly caught in her web. Finally, she let out a sigh. "My apologies. You have been most gracious." She offered him a smile that seemed to strain the muscles of her face.

However befuddled by the woman's teetering moods, Dajon felt he could not leave her without an escort. "It is unsafe for a woman to traipse through town alone." He cast a wary gaze around them. "Especially this one. And regarding your sisters—surely you do not expect to protect them against everything, Miss Westcott. There are some things best left in the hands of men, due simply to their physical strength and ability."

Her creamy face reddened, darkening the cluster of freckles on her nose. "No doubt another one of your grand opinions? Well, I, for one, have found that conjecture to be naught but a lie perpetrated by men to keep women in submission." Turning, she stomped forward as if she were trying to lose him and turned onto Queen Street. Music from a harpsichord chimed from a tavern to their left.

"Indeed?" Keeping pace with her, Dajon shook his head, baffled by her insolence, her independence, but most of all, her foolishness. No wonder the admiral worried for his daughters. This one in particular seemed to go out of her way to find danger. He chuckled.

Faith huffed and flashed a dark gaze his way. "I amuse you, Mr. Waite?"

"Amuse and confuse, miss, for not an hour ago, you played the temptress below hatches on board my ship, and now you play the shrew."

"Of all the. . .I did no such thing." Clutching her skirts, she picked up her pace and stumbled over a ladder. The boy perched on top ceased nailing a sign over a doorpost and clung to the wooden tips of the ladder for dear life.

. Dajon settled the tottering steps and gave the wide-eyed boy an apologetic shrug before turning to find the wayward redhead. A mob of workers had spilled onto the street from a two-story brick warehouse and joined a surging crowd of sailors and merchants who were headed toward the nearest tavern. Horses clopped by in every direction, weaving around the throng and spewing clumps of mud into the air from their hooves.

Faith was nowhere in sight.

Dread gripped Dajon. His first day as guardian and he had lost one of the admiral's daughters—at night, in one of the worst sections of town. The crowd became a muted blur in the encroaching shadows as Dajon searched for a flash of red hair. Barreling through the throng, he bumped into a well-dressed man in a fine ruffled cambric shirt, swinging a cane. A curled gray periwig perched atop his head.

"I beg your pardon," Dajon said.

The man clicked his tongue in disgust as Dajon dashed across the street before an oncoming coach. The horse reared, neighing in protest. Dajon jumped aside before the beast's hooves could pummel him. They landed with two thuds in a puddle, spraying mud through the air.

"Watch out, you bumpkin!" the driver yelled.

Dajon glanced down at the thick mud sliding down his white breeches then scanned the street once more. No sign of Miss Westcott.

His chest tightened.

Feminine laughter bounced into the night—familiar laughter. He rushed forward, parting the crowd. A tall man with a portly woman on his arm ambled unaware in front of him. The woman blubbered in laughter at something the man had said, and Dajon darted to the left to bypass them.

Up ahead, light from a crowded saloon spilled onto the street. Three men surrounded Faith.

Sweat broke out on Dajon's forehead. His mouth dried. He bolted forward when another couple stepped in front of him, blocking his way.

Over their shoulders, Dajon saw Faith say something to a burly man then nod in Dajon's direction. Two other men stood on each side of her, smirks on their grimy faces. Passersby quickly looked the other way and crossed the street. Why didn't anyone come to her rescue? Angling toward the right, Dajon sped past the couple and shoved his way through a mob of sailors, ignoring the curses they flung at his back.

Faith grinned before turning and strutting away.

Dashing past an oncoming carriage, Dajon rushed to catch up to her, but the three men who'd been harassing her formed a barricade of human flesh in his path.

The burly man lowered his thick brows and scowled. "The lady don't be wantin' ye followin' her, sailor."

One of the other men took a brazen step toward Dajon. "You navy boys think to be gettin' all the women." Though gangly, the man's frame rose far above Dajon's as he peered down his hawklike nose. Greasy strands of hair stuck to his forehead like tentacles. The stench of sweat and stale fish burned Dajon's nose.

The third man spit onto the ground, cast a glance at the retreating Faith, and returned a surly grin to Dajon.

A bawdy tune blasted over them from the tavern as some of its patrons crept out to watch the altercation. A few men stopped in the street and whispered among themselves. Dajon wondered whether he could count on their assistance or if they were merely assembling for the show.

"Three against one." The first man chortled. "Fair odds, says I."

"Let me pass at once," Dajon ordered the men. In the distance, Faith suddenly halted and swung about, but he could not see her expression in the shadows. Blasted woman. Had she instructed these men to delay him? Surely not. She could not be associated with these ruffians.

The burly man laughed. "Why don't ye go back to yer boat and leave the lady alone."

Dajon drew his sword and leveled the tip beneath the man's hairy chin. "Why don't you step aside and allow me to pass."

The man did not flinch. Not a flicker of fear crossed his steady gaze.

From the corner of his eye, Dajon saw Faith retracing her steps until she stood behind the men, hands on her hips. He wanted to warn her to stay back, but the men appeared to have no interest in her now.

Her eyes shifted to Dajon's. No fear, only annoyance burned within them. "I will have you know, gentlemen," she began in an insolent tone, "that this is the captain of the HMS *Enforcer*, and he is an expert in swordsmanship."

Dajon grimaced and lowered his blade. *What is she saying?* He did not relish a fight. These scoundrels would only take her words as a challenge, especially in front of the crowd forming around them. His palms grew sweaty as he tightened his grip on his sword.

The burly man let out a coarse laugh and slapped his thigh. The other man narrowed his flaming eyes upon Dajon and wiped the spit seeping from the side of his mouth. He eased one hand to his chest. "How are ye with pistols?"

Faith shifted her gaze between her crew and the captain. She'd meant only for them to delay Mr. Waite, not kill him. After she had instructed them to gather the rest of the men at the ship in the morning, her foremost thought was to hurry home, inform Lucas, and get some much-needed sleep, not stroll through town on the arm of the man who would put a noose around her neck if he knew who she was. Besides, the man gave her an unsettled feeling in her stomach, and she didn't like it—not one bit. The less time spent in his company, the better. But she should have realized her men could not resist taunting a commander in His Majesty's Navy.

The captain's eyes drifted to hers again, and in a flash, Bishop plucked a gun from inside his vest and pointed it at Mr. Waite before he could react. But the captain only glared at him—a confident, icy glare that sent a shiver down Faith's back. Her fear for Mr. Waite's safety suddenly shifted to a fear for her crew's.

In one swift motion, Mr. Waite yanked his pistol from its brace and pounded the handle on Bishop's gun, knocking it the ground, then he whipped his pistol around by the trigger and pointed it straight at the man's heart.

"I can handle a pistol as well," he said with an insolent smirk, cocking the weapon.

A cheer rose from the crowd as the three men stood with their jaws agape.

Mr. Waite wiped the sweat from his brow. "Now, if you please, I will be on my way."

Unwilling admiration surged within Faith as she watched the captain dispatch her hardened crew so quickly and with such skill. Without so much as a glance her way, he sheathed his sword, brushed by her men, who backed away from him, and took her arm. He tugged her through the crowd, his pistol still firmly gripped in his hand. When they were well away from the center of town, he housed it again then whirled her around to face him, seizing her shoulders.

"Of all the preposterous, dangerous things to do—wandering around the port at night without an escort." His gaze skimmed over her. "Are you hurt? No, of course you're not hurt." He snorted and released her. "Did you know those men?"

"Nay." She gazed up at him, barely able to discern his features in the darkness. A cloud moved aside, allowing moonlight to flood over him. Somehow the mixture of silvery light and sinister shadows made him appear far more dangerous than he did in full sunlight. Or maybe it was because she'd just witnessed him best three of her most skilled crewmen. And his height did naught but aid the impression. Rarely had Faith, who herself was taller than most women, met a man who towered above her.

"They seemed to know you." Suspicion sharpened his tone.

"I only paid them a shilling to delay you."

"To delay me?" Mr. Waite said. "They could have killed me."

"You handled them quite well, Captain. And besides, I returned as soon as I saw the situation escalate."

"To do what? Protect me?" He snickered and spiked a hand through his dark hair. "All you did was incite them further by telling them who I was."

"Nevertheless, I'm flattered that you were willing to engage them in order to escort me home."

Mr. Waite released a long sigh. "I do not wish to see you harmed. Regardless of your insistence that you can take care of yourself, Miss Westcott, I fear you do not understand the wicked intentions of most men."

Concern burned in his eyes—for her or merely for maintaining his position with her father? He took her hand in his, and the warmth and strength from his touch sent streams of assurance through her. She did not care for the unfamiliar sensation.

A salty breeze blew in from the bay and played with the wayward strand of hair dangling over his cheek. The muted sounds of music and laughter from town swirled around them then combined with the orchestra of leaves fluttering from beech trees that lined the avenue.

A horse and carriage clattered by, startling Faith back to her senses. "We should be going."

When they reached the Westcott home, the captain took Faith's elbow and led her up the stairs to the porch. "Quite an interesting evening, Miss Westcott."

She swung about. "I'm glad I amused you, Mr. Waite." She lowered her gaze to his muddied breeches and giggled. "But I see you have soiled your pristine uniform."

"A battle wound worth the pain for your sake." Amusement heightened his voice.

Faith eyed him curiously, finding surprising enjoyment in their repartee.

"I must return to the ship for a few hours," he said. "Afterward, I shall be in the guesthouse should you have need of me."

"And pray tell, why would I have need of you?"

Cocking a brow, he gave her a condescending look. "Simply promise me, Miss Westcott, that you will stay put and not go strolling through the streets at night again."

"You can hardly blame me for what happened," she snapped. "Good heavens, 'twas you who forced me onward with your insulting comments. I simply wished to return home in peace."

"What insulting..." He sighed and scratched his jaw. "In any case, you should not be so surprised if you draw the wrong sort of attention. Only unscrupulous women wander the streets at night."

"Why, Mr. Waite." She pressed a hand to her bosom. "I am quite overcome with your concern." She fluttered her lashes again but this time with every intent to appear as silly as she felt.

He broke into a grin as he lengthened his stance. "I daresay, Miss Westcott, you have me quite befuddled. I do not know whether you are trying to allure me with your charms or stab me with your words."

Faith cocked her head and considered which strategy she indeed preferred. "Perhaps both."

A wicked playfulness danced across his eyes. "Until tomorrow." He bowed, slapped his bicorn atop his head, and walked away.

Faith entered the house and slammed the oak door then leaned against it with a sigh. What was she doing? Her plan had been to get home as soon as possible, not engage in witty banter with a man who obviously found her company disagreeable. Not that she wasn't accustomed to that. Her tall stature, intelligent wit, and independent mannerisms never failed to keep suitors at bay. But what did she care?

Confusion trampled over the new feelings rising within her. At least her day had not been a total loss, for she had learned the whereabouts of a treasure ship, and that alone was well worth enduring the captain's company.

"And where have you been?" Edwin crashed into the room, wringing his hands.

"Why, you know very well, Edwin, I was with Mr. Waite." Faith sashayed into the room.

"He should inform me when he will have you home past dark," Edwin huffed.

"I shall be sure to tell him the next time I see him."

"Very well." The lines etched in his ruddy face deepened. "I should inform you that Miss Hope went missing most of the day as well."

Alarm knotted Faith's stomach, but she couldn't show Edwin her concern. No doubt the jittery steward would go running to Mr. Waite with the news. "I am sure she was here. Perhaps she was just avoiding you, Edwin. You worry too much." But Faith well knew her sister's propensity for wayward adventures—one that had become a perpetual thorn in Faith's side. While Faith risked her life to ensure a future for Hope, her sister was intent on destroying it. "Is she here now?" Faith's breath halted as she awaited his reply.

"Yes, miss."

"Then all is well."

Edwin released a big sigh that shook his sagging jowls. "I knew there would be problems." He turned on his heels and headed toward the back of the house. His whiny voice faded down the hallway. "I told the admiral. I warned him."

At the sound of footsteps, Faith looked up to see Lucas creeping into the entrance hall. "I wanted to make sure ye survived the day with the cap'n."

"That I did, Lucas." Winking, she grabbed the banister and whispered, "We set sail at dawn."

"Do ye know of a ship to plunder?"

Faith grinned. "That I do. A fair prize indeed."

With a mischievous twinkle in his eye, Lucas scrambled away.

Faith lifted her weary limbs slowly up the stairs. She must check on her sisters. She hoped they were tucked in for the night. She could grab only a few hours of sleep before she had to rise and make haste to prepare the *Red Siren* to sail.

For she must reach that treasure ship before Captain Waite.

CHAPTER 9

Darkness smothered Faith as she tiptoed down the stairs. Morgan's jagged talons clamped over her right shoulder, but he remained unusually silent. Clutching her simple linen dress with one hand to keep it from swishing, Faith crept downward, gliding her other hand over the delicately carved oak banister. Yet for all her efforts to move quietly, each step echoed a tune uniquely its own, creating an entire ensemble of creaks and groans by the time she made it down to the entrance hall. Breathless, she halted, listening for any stirrings above where Edwin and her sisters slept.

Guarding the far wall, the grandfather clock drummed a rhythmic *ticktock* that echoed the beating of her heart, yet she could barely make out its stately shape in the darkness. At just past three in the morning, she hoped no one would be awake and she could easily slip away unnoticed. For if she did not set sail by dawn, not only would she not be able to reach the treasure ship before Mr. Waite, but she would risk encountering him along the way. She headed toward the front door, not wanting to risk her normal exit from the back gardens, which could be viewed from the guesthouse where she hoped the captain was still deep in slumber.

As she thought of him, a smile tilted her lips. Today she would best the infamous commander by stealing the treasure he had sworn to protect right from under his handsome nose.

Faint voices reached her ears. Halting, Faith huffed and placed Morgan on the banister, cautioning him to remain. "I shall return shortly." She brushed her fingers over his soft feathers, and he leaned his head against her hand in reply. Then, making her way down the dark hallway, she slunk toward the back of the house, past the warming room, and out the back door, following the sounds drifting from the kitchen.

The muggy night air enveloped her like a swamp. Stars twinkled between the branches of a massive live oak that stood guard against the side fence. Up ahead, soft candlelight and hushed voices flowed through the open windows of the cooking room.

Faith knew she should leave and be about her business, but she thought she had recognized Hope's soft voice. And she could not imagine what her sister was doing up at so early an hour. Hastening into the kitchen, she allowed the swinging door to bump her from behind. A wave of warmth caressed her from the fireplace, where coals smoldered below a three-legged iron kettle. Hope sat at the table nursing a steaming cup of tea. Molly leaned against a baking shelf littered with wooden bowls and rolling pins, a scowl on her face and her hands on her hips.

Fear squeezed Faith's heart. "Good heavens, what is amiss?"

Hope's look of surprise at seeing her sister faded to one of alarm as her gaze shifted to Molly.

The cook shook her head. "Bad enough you kept me up half the night worryin' about you. Now you woke up your sister."

Faith took a step toward Hope, whose gaze immediately dropped to her tea.

Molly huffed. "I tell you what's amiss, Miss Faith. Your sister arrived home only an hour ago."

"I beg your pardon? At two in the morning?" Shock halted Faith as her gaze flitted between Molly and Hope. She had known her sister to venture out without permission before but never so late. "I checked on you. You were asleep when I retired for the night."

Hope's silence sent pinpricks of fear over Faith's scalp. She rushed to her sister's side. "Has someone hurt you, dear?" Horrid memories resurged as Faith knelt and examined her sister from head to toe. Hope wore her best dress—a low-necked French gown of royal blue silk, woven with gold thread—but nary a mark could be seen upon it—or on Hope for that matter. Faith pressed a hand over her heart to still its rapid beat.

"Never you mind, Miss Faith." Molly hiked her skirts up and tucked them into her waistband to avoid setting them aflame then grabbed a cloth and lifted the kettle from the fire. "She be all right, at least in body. In the head, I isn't too sure." She placed the pot on the serving table.

"Where have you been?" Faith demanded as anger replaced her fear.

Her throat went dry. "Or should I be asking with whom?"

Wiping a curl of golden hair from her forehead, Hope shrugged. "I assure you, dear sister, I was with Arthur and perfectly safe."

"Arthur? You speak of Lord Falkland?" Rising, Faith blew out a sigh and began to pace. "You call him by his familiar name after only a few months' acquaintance?"

"I feel as though I have known him all my life." Hope smiled, her eyes dancing.

Molly snorted.

Hope's brows drew together. "He loves me."

"Has he declared his love?" Faith threw one hand to her hip. "Has he approached Father for your hand as a true gentleman should, rather than risk your reputation by flaunting you about town at all hours of the night?"

"Not in so many words." Hope raised her chin. "And he was not flaunting me about."

Molly clicked her tongue. "Alls I know is, it's most unproper for a young lady to behave so. If your pappy knew—"

"Father is not here." Hope's icy gaze shot to Molly. "He is never here." She pressed a hand to her stomach. "If you must know, we were at the Sign of Bacchus."

"A tavern?" Faith could not believe her ears. She rubbed her eyes. She did not have time for Hope's petty defiance.

"'Tis not a tavern," Hope shot back. "Arthur refers to it as a club. They hold concerts, lectures, and balls for the most influential of high society. Everyone who is anyone spends her evenings at the Sign."

Faith had heard of the place. It was said to contain the finest collection of mahogany furniture in town. Original oil paintings of Henrietta Johnson, a local artist, lined the stairwell leading to the nineteen boarding rooms above. Of all the public drinking houses, it was by far the most polished in town.

"Perhaps so, but 'tis still a tavern and no place for a lady," Faith snapped, angrier with herself than with Hope. She must keep a closer watch upon her sister. "I suppose Anne Cormac was there as well?"

"Anne is a dear friend of mine. We share the same passions."

"What passions might those be? Defying your fathers? Associating with gamblers and rogues through all hours of the night like common trollops?"

Hope swallowed hard.

"And what do we know of Lord Falkland?" Faith tried to lower her rising voice. "Nothing, save his reputation as a philanderer and a swindler."

Hope sprang to her feet, her eyes welling with tears. "He is neither of those things. You do not know him. He is a gentleman. Full of passion and life." She swiped at a tear trickling down her cheek. "He tells me I am special."

Faith regarded her sister. *Of course he does, dear one. 'Tis what swindlers do.* Her heart wilted. Sweet Hope. Always the dreamer, always the romantic. Was it her past that forced her into such dangerous liaisons? Fear bristled over Faith. She might be able to protect her sister from these scoundrels, but how was she to protect Hope from herself?

Molly cleared her throat. "Would you like some tea, Miss Faith? Since you up and all."

"No thank you, Molly." Faith sighed. "I'm sorry you have missed your sleep. You should have awakened me when you discovered Miss Hope gone."

"I couldn'a slept anyways." Molly shrugged. "No sense in worryin' the both of us. I was about to alert Mr. Waite—it being his job and all—when Miss Hope come home."

The side door creaked open, and Lucas's tall frame filled the tiny entrance. His questioning dark eyes met Faith's then drifted to Molly and down to her bare ankles. He shifted his gaze. "Morning, Miss Molly, Miss Hope."

Flustered, Molly yanked her skirts from her waistband and allowed them to drop over her legs. Faith had never seen a Negro blush, but she was sure she detected a red hue upon Molly's otherwise flawless cinnamon-colored skin.

"Why, we might as well throw a party seein' as so many of us can't sleep tonight." Molly turned and began stacking a set of wooden bowls on the baking table.

"You're lookin' fine this mornin', Miss Molly." Lucas gazed at Molly's back as he twisted his hat in his massive hands.

Molly veered around and gave Lucas a snort. "Why, I'll thank you not to be lookin', Mr. Corwin." Her voice was caustic, but a hint of a smile danced on her mouth.

The grin slipped from Lucas's face as he ran a hand through the coils of his shoulder-length black hair.

Hope raised a brow. "You and Lucas are venturing out again?" Her words sent a jolt of surprise through Faith. "Yes, I have eyes," she continued. "I have seen you two run off in the middle of the night many a time. What I fail to understand is why 'tis so appalling when I do the same."

Faith balled her hands into fists. "First of all, Lucas is my escort. Secondly. . . 'tis none of your concern. I am the eldest, and you will listen to me."

Pain etched across Hope's gaze, igniting into anger. "If I must do as you say, dear sister, then I must also do as you do. Therefore, I shall go out at night whenever I please."

Faith ground her teeth together. How could she make her sister understand that what she did, she did for Hope? "There is a big difference between what I am doing and what you are doing." Faith averted her eyes as guilt showered over her. With their mother gone, her sisters looked to her to model how a proper, moral lady behaved. She had not realized until now just how closely they watched her.

And how deeply she was failing them.

"I am securing your future," she said simply.

"By running off in the thick of night to make soap, no doubt?" Hope smirked. "You must think me as dull witted as Father does."

"On the contrary, I find you to be quite smart. Perhaps a bit foolish at times." Faith exchanged a knowing glance with Lucas. "All I ask is that you trust me."

"And we best be gettin' to it, mistress." Lucas nodded, his eyes alight with urgency. "Time's a wastin'."

Wringing her hands, Faith glanced out the window, where the square shape of the stables across the yard emerged from the darkness. She had spent far too much time arguing with her sister.

Hope shot her tear-filled gaze to Molly. "Why do you not scold my sister as you do me, Molly?" Wrapping her arms about herself, she hung her head. "Why is everyone in this family against me?"

"Not my place to scold either of you. . .not my place." Molly tossed a rag onto the table and patted the knot of ebony hair at the nape of her neck. "I'm just worryin' for your safety, is all. But there's not much I can do if the both of you keep runnin' off at night." She shook her head.

"I haven't the time to discuss this now." Faith approached the door and turned to face Hope. "We shall talk more when I return."

"Forgive me, sister, if I do not believe you, for you rarely have time to visit with me anymore." The lines on Hope's face deepened, her eyes pleading pools that tugged upon Faith's heart.

"I must go." Faith forced out the words she knew would hurt her sister, but she had no choice. If she delayed even another minute, they would be too late.

Hope's eyes sharpened. "Perhaps I should discuss this with Mr. Waite? I am sure he has time to converse with me."

Lucas cleared his throat and gestured toward the door.

Faith tightened her lips to keep the anger she felt from firing out from them. "I wish you would not do that." But the pain on her sister's face melted her anger away. She held out a hand toward Hope. "Someday you shall see that all I want is what is best for you."

"You do not know what is best for me." Hope sniffed then took a step toward the door. "If you will excuse me, I am rather tired."

Faith laid a gentle hand on Hope's arm as she passed. "Promise me you will stay home until I return."

Hope nodded, her blue eyes rising to meet Faith's. Despite the tears, they held a sweet innocence tainted by a deep sorrow.

Faith placed a kiss upon Hope's cheek. "Sleep well."

Lucas held open the door as Hope edged by him and disappeared toward the house.

After she left, Molly pointed an accusing finger toward Faith. "You spoil that child."

"She has suffered more than either you or I could imagine." Faith swallowed the burning agony that had risen in her throat and turned to leave.

"She looks up to you, Miss Faith." Molly's sharp tone yanked Faith around again. "If you want to do right by her, be a good example."

"I *am* doing right by her. You will see, Molly." Faith glanced over her shoulder at Lucas, who was still holding the door ajar. They were late. "We must be—"

"I don't want to know where you two are off to." Molly shook her head. "Your family treats me well, pays me fair when most of my people ain't nothin' but slaves in this province. I thank you for that. And for the first time in my life, I feels like I'm a part of a family. So it's not my place to be tattling on you or Miss Hope. I don't want to risk being let go by the admiral. So alls I can do is pray for the good Lord to watch over you."

"I'll take proper care of her, Miss Molly. Don't ye be worryin' none," Lucas said.

"Don't be worryin', you say?" Molly smirked and planted her hands on her waist. "Why, you's just as bad an influence on Miss Faith as she is on Miss Hope. And a grown man, too. Shame on you."

"Let's away, Lucas." Faith nudged him, but his gaze was fixed on Molly, a devilish grin alighting his face.

"Now what's got you grinnin' like the cat that ate the mouse?" Molly asked.

"Only that ye noticed I'm a grown man."

"Any fool can see that." Molly flung a hand in the air with a huff. "Now be gone with you."

Lucas slapped his oversize hat on his head, tipped it at Molly, and disappeared out the door.

"If Edwin or the captain inquires as to our whereabouts when they arise," Faith said, "please tell them we have gone into town for supplies."

"Now you know I can't be lyin' for you. What would the good Lord think of that?" Molly grabbed a rag and tossed it over her shoulder with a disapproving glance.

Faith sighed. "Very well, then. Tell them whatever you wish." She turned and followed Lucas into the darkness.

Before Faith made it back into the house, a sweet hymn swirled over her from the kitchen. Each word of praise to a God Faith no longer spoke to jabbed at her heart.

Out the front door, Lucas disappeared into the shadows and soon returned leading two horses.

Faith whistled, and Morgan flew to her outstretched hand. She set the bird on the horse's back, then clutching her skirts, she mounted her steed, Seaspray, with ease and placed the parrot on the saddle horn. He screeched and flapped his wings, causing the horse to jerk. Grabbing the reins, she steadied the anxious beast until Lucas settled upon his.

The excitement of the coming adventure began to cloud out the disturbing altercation with her sister—for now. But Faith knew she had to address Hope's wayward ways soon, before the girl got herself into trouble.

"Let's be about that treasure, shall we?" She winked at Lucas and kicked her horse, and the two of them sped out the gate and down the lane.

They had not a moment to lose. Faith could not afford to trade broadsides with a British warship, especially one commanded by a highly decorated officer. Such a confrontation not only would result in her ship being sunk to the bottom of the sea but would no doubt leave both her and her crew dead.

CHAPTER 10

Planting her boots on the beakhead of the *Red Siren*, Faith crossed her arms over her chest and braced herself against the oncoming white-tipped swell. The turbulent seas reflected the raging of her heart as the ship bolted then careened over a huge wave. She shook her head, trying to dislodge the memories of the morning. She must concentrate on the task at hand.

After a twenty-minute gallop, she and Lucas had arrived at the bayou, where the *Red Siren* hid in an estuary, anchored safely amid fern and foliage. Her crew had already prepared the vessel with anticipation and welcomed her with greed-infested grins. In less than an hour, Faith had changed into breeches and waistcoat, navigated the ship through the narrow channel, and sent it spewing from the tiny inlet like venom from a snake upon the mighty sea.

A sinister grin played upon her lips. Mr. Waite expected to rendezvous with the treasure ship off Hilton Head in the afternoon, but Faith would meet up with the vessel long before then. By her calculations, the merchant ship would pass Tybee Island—nigh fifteen miles south of St. Helena—near midday, and the *Red Siren* would be there to give her a proper pirate greeting.

A gray haze broke the grip of darkness on the horizon and drove the black shroud back into the sky. Soon splashes of coral, saffron, and crimson dazzled the morning like jewels strewed above the indigo sea.

Closing her eyes, Faith relished the whip of the wind in her hair and the sting of the sea in her nostrils, but thoughts of her sisters intruded upon her peace. Terror drew her muscles taut. After all of Faith's hard work, after all the risks she had taken to protect her sisters from marriages to unsavory men, Hope threw herself at the most unsavory of them all.

Word about town was that Lord Falkland acquired and consumed women as frivolously as he did his wealth and in equally as shady a manner. And Lady Cormac—an ill-tempered woman of extreme impertinence—was rumored to be no lady at all but the illegitimate daughter of a local lawyer. What could Hope possibly find so alluring in such disagreeable company?

An arc of bright gold peeked over the horizon, sending a blanket of warmth and light over Faith, lifting her spirits. Depending on her success today, she might finally acquire enough fortune to meet, nay, exceed her father's condition for her and her sisters' independence. Not to mention free her from marrying Sir Wilhelm. How she would answer the admiral when he inquired as to the source of her sudden wealth, she had no idea, but her father never reneged on a promise. At last Faith would be able to stay home and keep a better watch on Hope—and on Grace as well, for truth be told, Faith's youngest sister put herself in no less danger than Hope when she ventured to the shady outskirts of town on her missions to feed the poor and the Indians. Only by the grace of God—no, purely by luck alone—she had not been kidnapped or murdered. Why, oh, why couldn't her sisters stay home and behave like proper young ladies?

The sails above Faith snapped as a gust struck them. She tugged her black velvet waistcoat tighter about her neck against the chill breeze.

Lucas appeared beside her. "All sails be unfurled, and we've caught a weather breeze, mistress. I reckon we'll be at Tybee afore noon."

"Thank you, Lucas."

The ship bucked again, sending a spray of bubbling foam over the bow. Salt stung Faith's eyes, and she examined her first mate.

She wouldn't be a pirate captain if not for him. When she'd rescued him from the streets of Portsmouth, starving and beaten, and convinced her father to hire him as their groomsman, she had no idea he had sailed on a pirate ship for four years under the dread pirate captain Samuel Burgess. When Captain Burgess was brought to Britain and convicted of piracy, Lucas and several of the crew managed to escape, but they faced a fate nearly as horrifying as the noose as they fought for scraps of food on the streets of London.

Lucas taught Faith everything she knew about sailing, navigation, firing a pistol, firing a cannon, even wielding a sword. Together they had stolen their first boat, a small fishing vessel anchored in the harbor at Portsmouth. With that, they began their pirating career and, with each successive conquest, acquired faster ships, until Faith had finally settled on this sleek brigantine—compliments of Mr. Waite.

When Lucas had refused to assume command of the crew, Faith slid into the role of captain with the ease of one putting on a glove. She seemed to have a natural ability to command, make quick decisions, and inspire the men.

Lucas squinted toward the sunrise, a dreamy grin softening his features. But Faith surmised piracy was not on his mind at the moment.

"Am I mistaken, Lucas, or do you fancy Miss Molly?"

The sun gleamed off his perfect white teeth. "Ye noticed?" He shook his head. "She be. . .she be. . .a rare blossom of a woman, to be sure." He shrugged. "But she shuns me, as ye saw."

"Nay, I am not so sure." Faith offered him a coy smile.

"Don't be teasin' me, mistress."

"Despite present appearances, I *am* a woman. And I sense that Miss Molly is not as repulsed by you as she pretends. Trust me."

Lucas scratched his head, his fingers tangling in the black hair that hung in thick wires to his shoulders. "Odds fish that I do find some comfort in that."

"Is she aware of your heritage?"

"That I be a half-breed? Nay."

"She may not know you have some Negro in you. The color of your skin could pass for a summer day's tan."

"D'ye think it would make a difference?"

"Perhaps. You should tell her about your past."

He scowled. "How my parents were murdered, how I's once a slave, how I run away and became a pirate?"

Faith snickered. "Well, perhaps you should omit that last part."

"Aye, to be sure. She be a godly woman, which is why she don't want to be hearin' about me past neither."

"It might soften her opinion of you." Faith blinked when she realized that she of all people was playing the matchmaker. Yet an undeniable spark crackled across the room when Lucas and Molly were together.

"What would a proper Christian woman like her want with a half-breed, half-witted, thievin' barracuda like me?" Lucas rubbed the back of his thick neck.

"Aye, but there is so much more to you than that, and you know it." Faith flashed him a knowing glance. "Besides, I have never seen you run from anything, Lucas. 'Tis why I'm glad you're my first mate. Fearless, adventurous. You risk your life every day on this ship, but you fear a woman who stands barely five feet tall?"

"Aye, that be about the way of it." He crossed his beefy arms over his chest, and they both laughed out loud.

"Sail ho!" Mac's deep voice bellowed from the crosstrees.

Yanking her spyglass from her belt, Faith raised it and scanned the horizon. Off their starboard beam, the coastline of the New World sped by in sun-kissed shimmers of emerald and honey. Up ahead, nothing but dark blue streaked with foam-crested waves extended to the horizon. "Where lies she?"

"Four points off our larboard bow!"

Shifting the glass to the left, Faith squinted and spotted the tips of two pyramids, dark against the rising sun. But as the ship grew larger, from her size and colors, she appeared to be naught but a French fishing vessel—too small to carry any fortune of note.

"Let her pass, men. She is not the one we want." She turned to Lucas. "Keep our British colors aloft and alert me when another ship approaches."

"Aye, aye, mistress."

Faith marched to the foredeck ladder then swerved about. "Have Kane check all the pistols and muskets and ensure they are working properly. And tell Bates to ready the guns."

Lucas nodded with a smile.

Three hours later, after catching parcels of sleep in between several ship sightings, Faith emerged from the companionway in a bouffant red-satin skirt, a gold-lace stomacher trimmed with pearls, and a cream-colored bodice that blossomed into double-ruffled sleeves. In one hand she carried a folding fan, in the other a flintlock pistol. A red silk scarf adorned her neck. They had arrived at Tybee Island, and she must dress appropriately for such important guests.

All gazes shot to her, and Morgan squawked a whistle.

With a roll of her eyes, Faith braced one hand on her hip and cleared her throat to allow her most imperious tone. It always seemed harder to command the ship arrayed like a child's doll.

"Prepare to go about!" she barked across the deck, sending the crew up into the shrouds. Plucking the spyglass from her belt, she scanned the coastline, nigh three miles off their starboard side. She must turn the ship around and maintain a leisurely course in the same direction their prey would be sailing, thus allowing their enemies to come alongside with ease when they took the bait.

She heard the familiar hollow thud of Lucas's boots approach.

"Hard to larboard, Lucas, but keep a slow pace." She lowered her glass and squinted at him in the sunlight. A strand of hair slapped her face, and she waved it aside.

With a nod, he swung about and began braying orders. "Ease down the helm! Let go the foresheets and headsheets!"

"Bring down the foresheets, bring down the foresheets," Morgan hooted as he paced upon his tiny perch.

The purling of the sea along the hull softened to a trickle as the ship slowed.

Lucas wiped the sweat from his neck. "Helm, bring her about. Raise tacks and sheets." Men scrambled like monkeys across the ratlines, shrouds, and yards that towered precariously overhead.

Faith gripped the railing as the ship veered to port, spitting a fountain of white foam off her stern. After further orders, the yards on the main and crossjack swung around together and braced up sharp on the new tack. Wind eased into the rising canvas, sending the ship skimming through the turquoise water.

Kane joined her at the main deck railing and spit off to the side. The rugged boy's dark gaze took in the expanse of sea before them. "When d'ye expect this ship o' yers, Capitaine?" He folded arms nearly as thick as his thighs across his chest.

"Anytime now. Not to worry, Kane." Faith had never regretted offering a position on her ship to the half-French, half-British seaman she'd found tied to a chain, scrubbing the deck of a French merchant vessel. Later she'd learned he'd been abandoned by his young mother on the streets of Bristol and, at the age of thirteen, press-ganged into the Royal Navy. Now barely eighteen, though his face remained boyish, he had grown into a very imposing seaman.

He flashed a playful grin her way. "I ain't worried none, Capitaine," he said in that peculiar accent of his that still held a trace of French. "Ye have a natural sense about ye when it comes to ships."

"Is the barrel ready to be set afire?" Faith asked.

"Just awaitin' yer order, Capitaine." He pressed both sides of his mustache.

They had not come across any ships of note on the passage south, so she had to assume the treasure ship would soon pass their way. One glance at the sun's position told her it was close to eleven o'clock. She hoped they wouldn't have long to wait.

But wait they did.

Another three hours passed in which no ships were seen save a small fishing vessel that gave them a friendly hail. Standing on the quarterdeck, Faith clutched the railing. The rough wood bit into her skin. Trickles of perspiration slid beneath her heavy gown as the sun, now beginning its descent in the sky, flung its fiery arrows upon them. But she doubted it was the sun that caused her to perspire. Her nerves knotted into balls with each passing second. *Where is that ship?*

"Don't be worryin' none, Cap'n," Wilson said behind her as he steadfastly manned the helm.

She cast him a measured smile over her shoulder. As stout a sailor as ever could be found and none more loyal, Wilson had stood at the ship's wheel for hours without complaint. "Have Strom relieve you, Mr. Wilson."

"Nay, I'd like to stay at me post, if ye don't mind."

Faith nodded with a smile and turned back around.

Lucas's tall figure loomed over one of the men below on the main deck as he assisted him in securing a rope on the belaying pin. The other pirates lingered about like powder kegs ready to explode. Some busied themselves playing dice, others cleaning their weapons. She allowed no drinking on her ship before a raid. Rum dulled the wits and slowed the senses, but the lack of it seemed to keep the men far too jittery.

Faith drew in a deep breath of crisp air, bringing with it the earthy scents of damp wood and tar. Oh, how she loved the smells of a ship!

Yet not even sailing upon her precious sea could loosen the dread that now fastened itself around her. Perhaps she was the one who had been duped. She took a quick scan of the horizon and bit her lip. Had the captain known who she was all along? Had he set a trap for her? Her legs numbed.

"Nobody's fool, nobody's fool," Morgan cawed from his perch on the mainmast just below Faith, his words echoing her own impression of Mr. Waite. She frowned at her feathery friend. "Whose side are you on, anyway?"

With a flap of his red and blue wings, he cocked his head upward and stared at her with one eye.

"A sail, a sail!" Mac shouted.

Shielding her eyes from the sun, she surveyed the horizon.

The dark silhouette of a ship bore down upon them.

CHAPTER 11

Pressing the spyglass to her eye, Faith focused on the brimming sails. A three-masted, square-rigged merchant ship rose and plunged over the agitated sea. Dutch and British colors flapped in the breeze over her foremast and mizzenmast. From her lines and size, she appeared to be a *fluyt*, a Dutch-designed ship built to hold a large cargo and a small crew.

But not built to house many guns. Faith grinned.

She focused on the larboard bow. The words *Vliegende Draeck* stood out in blue upon the tan hull. "The *Flying Dragon*," Faith whispered, snapping the spyglass shut.

"Light the fire!" she bellowed then scanned the crew. "Get below hatches and wait for my command."

Clutching her skirts, Faith leaped down the quarterdeck ladder and rushed to the railing, waving her cream-colored fan over her head.

Black smoke curled up from the barrel as several pirates dropped buckets into the sea and then hoisted them up, pretending to battle the flames.

Gripping the railing, Faith leaned over the side and knotted her face into a look of utter despair while shrieking pleas for help toward the merchantman. She made out the silhouette of the captain on the vessel's foredeck and the glint of sunlight off his spyglass as he studied her.

Veering slightly to larboard, the *Flying Dragon* turned and began its approach bow on.

Lucas smacked his lips. "Looks like ye've caught a big fish on yer hook this time, mistress."

"Aye, 'twas easier than I thought," Faith remarked out of the side of her mouth while maintaining her display of distress.

Ivory foam spewed upon the bow of the Dutch ship as she sped toward her trap. Then, suddenly, the creamy spray slunk back into the sea. The merchant vessel slowed. Down went her topgallants and mainsails until she took up a gliding position just outside the reach of the *Red Siren*'s guns.

Faith dropped her fan to her side with a huff. "Of all the nerve. Why does he not rescue me?"

Lucas chuckled and adjusted the captain's hat Faith insisted he wear during raids. "Mebbe he don't favor women."

"Perhaps *you* should drape yourself over the rail, then?" Faith scanned her crew. "Begin to lower the boats, men. And act more frantic. Quicken the fire! We need more smoke. And hurry it up there. Grayson, Strom," she barked at two pirates passing by with buckets in hand. They stopped and gave her sheepish grins. "You need to appear terrified, not like you are carrying water to a Sunday picnic."

"Sorry, Cap'n." Grayson's one remaining tooth perched like a yellowed pyramid among a desert of decaying gums. The portly seaman—with the shortest arms Faith had ever seen, reaching only to his waist—always made her smile. Strom, a gangly, shy youth with hair braided down his back, lowered his eyes under Faith's perusal and trotted after Grayson to fetch more water.

Faith turned to Lucas. "Perhaps 'tis you," she said, looking him up and down. "You do present a formidable figure." She handed him the spyglass. "Gaze at them and give them a friendly wave."

Raising the glass, Lucas perused the vessel. "She sits low in the water."

"That would be the treasure. 'Laden with pearls,' I believe, was the phrase the good Mr. Waite used. Pray tell, what is their captain doing?"

"He be talkin' with three of his crew, mistress—like he's decidin' what to do." Lucas lowered the glass and gave a friendly wave to the merchant ship. "I be thinkin' ye might 'ave met your match. This captain be smart. He takes no chances with so much treasure aboard."

"Of all the impertinence." Faith tossed her hands to her hips. "What sort of gentleman allows a lady to burn to death?" Shaking her head, she strutted toward middeck. "I suppose we shall have to go after him." The idea was not without its appeal, for she dearly loved the thrill of the chase. Besides, it could take several hours to plunder the ship once they caught her, depending on the amount of treasure in her hold. "Look, mistress, he sends a boat."

Faith spun on her heels and snatched the spyglass from Lucas. Ten men lowered themselves into one of the ship's longboats and shoved off.

"Good heavens, now what to do? When they discover our ruse..."

"Can I blow 'em out o' the water, Cap'n?" Bates, her master gunner, had popped up from the hatch and stood before them, a gleam in his twitching eyes.

"Fire the guns, fire the guns," Morgan screeched.

"Nay." Faith slapped the spyglass into the palm of her hand. "We shall take them hostage." She winked at Lucas, who gave her a sly loo in return.

"By thunder, I think that'll work, mistress."

"Never fear, Mr. Bates." Faith gave the gun master a reassuring nod. "If all goes well, you will put your precious guns to the test soon enough."

"Aye." Bates's gloomy expression brightened, and he turned and wobbled away on the block of wood that served as his right foot—a souvenir of the Queen Anne's War.

Within minutes the longboat slogged against the hull of the *Red Siren*, and Lucas beckoned the men upward. One by one they leaped over the railing, their cautious eyes roving over the ship. Some had swords sheathed at their sides, others with pistols stuffed in baldrics, but they did not draw them, perhaps lured into a deception of safety by the sight of so few sailors on board and Faith's sweet, innocent smile.

Silence seeped through the ship, interrupted only by the lap of the waves against the hull.

A man of no more than two and twenty, with a comely face and a pointed beard, bowed with a sweep of his plumed hat before Lucas. "My captain sends his regards and bids us assist you in putting out your fire, Captain."

Faith sauntered forward and placed her boot on a stool, drawing the attention of the men—partly, she assumed, because they had never seen a lady wearing boots and partly because she bared the curve of her shapely calf.

"I accept your assistance as well as your captain's regards." Faith grinned as she reached under her skirts and plucked a pistol from a strap around her thigh. "But I must insist you remain on board as our guests." She leveled the gun at the young merchantman as the rest of her crew drew and cocked their weapons.

A horde of pirates spilled from the hatches, curses firing from their mouths. They formed a barricade around the sailors before they could draw their weapons.

"Clap 'em in irons. Clap 'em in irons," Morgan admonished with a flap of his wings.

"Welcome aboard the pirate ship the *Red Siren*, gentlemen." Faith leveled a sardonic gaze upon them. Oh, how she loved saying those words and, even more so, watching the expressions of those who heard it from *her* mouth.

Shock, anger, and fear combined into a whirl of emotions that swept over the men's faces. Their shoulders slumped as they raised their hands into the air.

Faith ordered them bound with rope and wire and taken below, then she turned toward the Dutch ship. As expected, the capture of his crew had not gone unnoticed by the captain. Men darted across the deck in a mad frenzy as sails were raised to meet the wind.

"Hard to starboard, Mr. Wilson. All hands, up tops and gallants. After her!" she shouted.

The crew flew up into the ratlines as the ship veered to starboard. In moments, the white canvas caught the wind in a jarring snap that sent the *Red Siren* plummeting over the churning waves.

Faith marched to the foredeck as the ship pitched over a roller, spraying her with salty mist. "Raise our colors, if you please, Lucas." She tossed the command over her shoulder, knowing her first mate would not be far behind her.

Lucas repeated the order to one of the pirates nearby, sending him to the ropes. Soon, down came the white, red, and blue British Union Jack and up went the scarlet emblem of the *Red Siren*—a dark silhouette of a woman with a sword in one hand and pistol in the other set against a red background.

Gripping the railing, Faith surveyed her fleeing prey. Although the *Flying Dragon* had all her canvas spread to the breeze, she lumbered through the water like an overstuffed whale. Faith smiled, doubting such a heavily laden ship would live up to her name today.

Blocks creaked and spars rattled above her as they slung aweather and all sails glutted themselves with wind. Sunlight sparkled in clusters of diamonds off the azure sea, reminding Faith of the treasure she would soon possess—and the security it would provide her sisters. Excitement quickened her heart, along with an occasional twinge of fear. She expected no resistance, but there was always the chance someone would get injured. And although her crew had known the risks when they signed on with her, she doubted she could bear it if one of them took a fall.

Faith glanced at Lucas, who stood beside her—ever the rock of calm assurance. He winked then smacked his lips together in anticipation of the battle.

The *Red Siren* rose and swooped over the sea as they bore down upon the doomed Dutchman. Within minutes, they came alongside, matching her thrust for thrust through the choppy waters and positioning themselves within gun range.

"Lucas, have Bates fire a warning shot over their bow, if you please."

"Aye, aye, mistress." Lucas jumped down the foredeck ladder and disappeared below.

Soon the familiar command to fire echoed through the ship, and the vessel exploded in a thunderous boom that sent a violent shudder through her hull. Gray smoke enveloped them and stung Faith's nose. Coughing, she swatted it aside, anxiously peering toward the *Flying Dragon* to see the effect of their threat.

The merchant vessel did not lower her sails.

"Signal them to put their helm over," she roared over her shoulder to Lambert.

Lucas and Grayson joined her on the foredeck while Lambert scrambled aloft to lower and raise the fore topsail, but before he could signal the *Flying Dragon*, her answer came in the form of a volley from the demichasers at her stern. A hail of small deadly shot pummeled the deck, sending the pirates ducking for cover.

"By thunder." Grayson, who did not so much as flinch at the volley, scratched his coarse beard. "That cap'n sure's got some pluck."

"He's naught but a fool," Faith spat. She spun around to face her first mate. "Lucas, bring the prisoners up on deck and place them in plain sight."

He nodded.

"Then bring us in closer and ready the chain shot. If he wishes to make things difficult, I shall be happy to comply."

"Aye, aye, mistress." Lucas stormed away and fired orders across the ship.

Grayson shifted his bloodshot, droopy eyes her way.

Taking his thick, rough hand in hers, Faith squeezed it. "Next time we are fired upon, please protect yourself, Grayson. I would like you to sail with me for a while longer."

With a flash of his single tooth, Grayson's weathered face blossomed into a bright shade of red. "At me age, Cap'n, I'd rather be takin' me chances standing upright than break a bone droppin' to the deck." Chuckling, he ambled away.

Facing forward, Faith braced herself as the *Red Siren* pitched over a wave and angled to starboard. Salt water sprayed a cool mist over her, shielding her from the continual onslaught of the sun.

They must hurry. Mr. Waite would no doubt come in search of the treasure ship when she failed to make an appearance at their rendezvous off Hilton Head. Faith drew a shaky breath. She had no intention of facing one of His Majesty's warships, nor the battle-honored man who commanded her. After checking the pistol stuffed in her waistband, she clutched her skirts, barreled down the foredeck ladder to the main deck, and glanced at her enemy, nigh fifty yards abaft the *Red Siren*'s beam. Men huddled around a swivel gun mounted on her railing, readying it to fire. If Bates did not hurry, they might have to endure another barrage of round shot.

Lucas popped his head above hatches. "Waitin' on your command to fire, mistress."

"Whenever you have the shot."

No sooner had Lucas disappeared below than another thunderous blast rocked the *Red Siren*. Faith grabbed the capstan, closing her eyes against the acrid smoke. Even before it cleared, the distant crack of splitting timbers and the boom of falling wood confirmed their success. Dashing to the railing, Faith gazed toward the *Flying Dragon*, her shape taking form in the dissipating mist. Her foremast was shattered, and fragments of her yards and a tangle of cordage hung to the decks below.

Crowding around the railing, the pirates waited to see their enemy's response. Finally, the merchant vessel dipped her colors in surrender.

Huzzahs and shouts of glee rose from the pirates, and soon the *Red Siren* crashed alongside the Dutch merchant ship to grapple and board her. Faith moved the prisoners, hands still bound behind their backs, within view of their captain.

Then, standing with one boot upon the bulwarks, she cocked and pointed her pistol at the head of one of the prisoners—the young man with the plumed hat who had first spoken to Lucas. Sweat broke out above his upper lip where a slight quiver had suddenly taken residence. She longed to assure him she meant him no harm. But instead she yelled across the expanse to the merchantmen. "I will speak to the captain."

After muffled protests, a stout man with a barrel chest and a mop of brown hair detached himself from the group of sailors and marched forward. With legs spread apart, he crossed his arms over his chest and cast an anxious glance toward the young man at the barrel end of Faith's gun.

"I'm Captain Grainger." His polite nod belied the fury reddening his face.

"A pleasure, sir," Faith said. "Quarter will be granted and your men unharmed, Captain, provided you lay down all your arms and open your hatches. These are my conditions. I suggest you accept them."

"Give 'em no quarter," Morgan squawked from his post, drawing the captain's gaze.

With clenched jaw, Captain Grainger turned and surveyed his men before his dark eyes narrowed back upon her. "Very well. You have left me no choice."

"Excellent." Faith lowered her pistol and nodded to Lucas.

"Prepare to board!" Lucas bellowed as the men armed themselves and crowded at the railing.

The tiny crew of the *Flying Dragon* formed a trembling line of acquiescence as they threw their weapons in a pile.

After ordering two of her men to guard the prisoners, Faith clutched her skirts with one hand, her pistol in the other and led her boarding crew over the bulwarks and into the waist of the ship. She regretted not changing into her breeches, but there had not been enough time.

With a snap of her fingers, her crew jumped to the task of plundering—an undertaking at which they had become quite proficient. Within an hour, they had hauled up a mountain of chests, crates, and velvet boxes brimming with gold ingots, pearls, spices, and sugar.

Faith paced before the crew of the *Flying Dragon*, feeling their gazes scour over her and pierce her like grapeshot whenever she turned her back to them. But she was used to it. They no doubt suffered not only the shock of encountering a female pirate but also the humiliation of being captured by one.

A wave of guilt tumbled over her, but she shook it off as she always did. No one would suffer injury or loss by her actions save the pockets of rich merchantmen. And neither society nor God had provided any other way to save her and her sisters.

Lucas began directing the men to transfer the treasure aboard the *Red Siren*, and one by one, under straining backs and forceful grunts, chests and crates were hoisted over the bulwarks and stowed below in the hold.

Shielding her eyes, Faith glanced upward. As if mocking her, the sun took on a hurried pace in its descent. Sweat streaked down her neckline, and she tugged at her gown, longing for her billowing white shirt that allowed a breath of air against her skin. Removing her scarf, she dabbed at the perspiration and then tucked the crimson fabric into her belt. To plunder the entire ship would take far too long. Surely by now Mr. Waite would be engaged in a furious search for the missing treasure ship. She gritted her teeth and continued pacing, trying to calm her anxieties. But no sooner had the thought crossed her mind than a shout blared from the crosstrees of the *Red Siren*.

"Cap'n, a sail!"

CHAPTER 12

Swinging about, Faith marched to the railing and raised her spyglass. Surging pyramids of white canvas taunted her from the masts of a British sloop of war. The Union Jack stretched proudly atop the foremast, stiff in the afternoon wind. Close-hauled to the northerly breeze and listing to starboard under the weight of it, the ship bore down upon them at full speed.

"Blast!" Faith clenched her fists and stormed across the deck, scanning the pirates who had halted in their tracks.

"Who is she, mistress?" Lucas's normally rigid features crumpled into a frown.

Faith eyed the crates of treasure crowding the deck, ignoring the merchant sailors muttering as they cast hopeful glances over their shoulders toward the British warship.

Her crew had taken barely half the treasure. But there was no time. She glanced back toward the oncoming ship.

" 'Tis the HMS *Enforcer*," Faith hissed through clenched teeth. "Back to the ship, men!"

"But what 'bout the treasure, Cap'n?" Wilson complained.

"Aye, we can't be leavin' all this loot!" Lambert added sharply, the other pirates grunting in agreement.

Throwing her hands to her hips, Faith strutted toward her men. "Can you spend it whilst you dangle at the end of a noose, Mr. Lambert?"

Lambert's expression soured. The pirates' gazes shot toward the HMS *Enforcer* as its threatening silhouette loomed larger on the horizon.

"Ye 'eard the cap'n," Lucas shouted. "Unhook these grapnels and be gone wit' ye now. Back to the ship!"

Morgan's loud squawk shrieked over the decks of the *Red Siren*.

"Run fer yer lives! Run fer yer lives!" His urgent plea hastened the men as they clambered over the bulwarks, casting yearning glances toward the abandoned treasure.

"Lucas, free the prisoners. Quickly, and then prepare to unfurl all sail." Faith heard the squeak of panic in her voice as she stormed across the deck and assisted Bates, Kane, and Strom with the grapnels. She had no plans to find herself at the end of a noose either, nor to lose everything she had worked so hard to acquire. She glanced at Bates, who battled to pry loose a hook embedded in the splintered deck. "Best get over to the ship and ready the guns."

He rubbed his chin and gave her an understanding look and an "Aye" before he tottered toward the *Red Siren*.

Taking over for Bates, Faith struggled with the iron claw as the snap of sails buffeted her ears. When the last grapnel was freed, Kane and Strom tossed them over to the *Red Siren* and flew over the railings after them. The ships groaned as they began to pull apart. The freed prisoners stood beside Captain Grainger, glaring at Faith.

"Come aboard, mistress!" Lucas yelled at her from the railing, extending his hand to assist her across the wobbling bulwarks.

Faith shot one more glance at the oncoming British warship. Her stomach tightened. The sunlight glinted off the tawny lines of the vessel's sleek body, sharpening each detail. The gaping mouths of nine charred muzzles punched through her starboard hull in a threatening display of cannon power.

Dashing toward Lucas, Faith suddenly halted, spun around, and returned to the captain of the merchant ship. Plucking the scarf from her belt, she handed it to him—a scarlet banner fluttering in the breeze. He fixed her with a cold eye but did not take it. The jeering gleam in his eyes taunted her.

"Forgive me for cutting our visit so short, Captain," Faith said, hiding her rising fear behind an angelic smile. "But if you will do me one last favor and give this to the dear captain of the HMS *Enforcer*, with my compliments?"

With brows pinched, he hesitated, and from the look in his eye, Faith thought he intended to seize her. If it weren't for the *click* of several muskets cocking behind her, he might have done just that.

With a grunt, he grabbed her scarf instead.

"Come on, Cap'n. . .hurry!" Grayson yelled.

The ships began to separate as the wind caught the sails in a series of jaunty snaps.

Lifting her skirts, she darted to the railing then froze. The chasm between the ships yawned a gaping blue mouth that was now too far to traverse. Several pirates stared at her from the other side, fear sparking in their gazes. Two of them still held their muskets firm upon the merchantmen.

Suddenly the air reverberated with the thunder of a twelve-pounder.

Faith turned to see a jet of white smoke drifting above one of the *Enforcer*'s guns. The shot splashed into the sea just ten yards before their bow. Her breath caught in her throat.

Standing atop the crosstrees, Lucas tossed her a rope. She reached for it, but it fell just short of her grasp. Cursing, he hauled it back in.

Below her, the indigo water growled like the carnivorous mouth of a raging monster.

The *Red Siren* drifted farther away.

Faith gulped and thought about praying, but she knew God would pay her no mind, especially in these circumstances. She flexed her hands, trying to stop the tingling fear that numbed her fingers.

Lucas swung the rope again. This time she caught it. Clutching it, she took a running start and threw herself over the side. The rope snapped as her weight pulled it taut. The coarse fibers tore the skin on her palms as she flew through the air and swung her legs high.

Her boots thudded on the main deck of the *Red Siren*, accompanied by the cheers of her crew.

❦

Dajon stood at the quarterdeck railing, his first and second lieutenants flanking him, mimicking his stiff posture. He clenched his jaw and tried to still the fury boiling in his stomach and keep his steady gaze upon the Dutch merchant vessel—the ship he'd been assigned to protect, the ship that was now rubbing hulls with that thieving imp of a pirate.

"She's fleeing, Captain." One of the officers halted at attention on the deck below, where sailors hustled to their stations.

"Fire a warning shot across her bow."

"Yes, Captain." The man touched his hat and shouted an order down the companionway.

A moment later, a gun belched its iron shot in an ear-hammering blast, sending a tremble through the ship. A gust of smoke-laden wind blew over Dajon, stealing his breath.

" 'Tis like they knew exactly where she would be," Borland remarked.

"Indeed." Dajon pounded his fists upon the railing. What were the odds that this pirate would be in exactly the right place at the right time? Though many pirates cruised the known shipping lanes, they usually came upon their prey purely by accident and would go days, sometimes months without a conquest. Either this blackguard was extremely lucky, or he had been privy to some ill-gotten information. Dajon hated to consider that he had a traitor on board his ship.

He leveled his telescope upon the pirate ship. The captain had not heeded his warning, but Dajon had not expected him to. He had yet to see a pirate surrender. Most preferred a glorious death in battle to the humiliation of swinging from a noose. He scanned the *Vliegende Draeck*. Her foremast lay in a crumpled heap upon her deck, but it appeared she had suffered no additional damage. Even so, her speed would be severely crippled, and without his protection, she would be easy sport for the next roving bandit.

"Are you going after her, sir?" Excitement lifted the voice of Jamieson, his second lieutenant.

Dajon grimaced. Oh, how he wanted to. How he wanted to put that rapacious rogue in his place. After all, wasn't that what he had been sent to do on these colonial waters?

But he could not leave the merchant ship.

The pirate ship made a swift turn and promptly went about on a southern tack. Her captain had wisely chosen not to risk passing between Dajon's ship and the coast, where they might be trapped. Instead, she ventured out to sea. With her masts a crown of white canvas, she stuck out a rebellious tongue of white foam at him from her mouth at the stern.

"Captain?" A wild entreaty glittered in Jamieson's eyes.

Dajon snorted and clamped tight fingers over the hilt of his sword. Everything inside of him ached to give the command to pursue the villains, but his orders. . .

"Nay, Jamieson. With the wind on her quarter, she will be far too swift for us." Dajon heard the hesitancy in his voice, as if he were trying to convince himself of that, as well.

Borland twisted his greased mustache. "You should give chase, Captain. You may not have another chance."

Dajon leveled his brow as he scowled at the fleeing bandit. "I shall have another chance, Mr. Borland; you can wager on that. But for now, I cannot abandon the Dutch ship. I have orders to protect her."

Borland snorted.

"Begging your pardon, Captain," Jamieson said with a snort, "but it seems you are a bit late for that."

Dajon gritted his teeth. "We can yet redeem some of our honor, as it appears from the jumble of crates strewed about the deck of the Dutch ship, the pirates did not have time to take all the treasure."

The pirate ship tacked to larboard, catching Dajon's eye, and he raised the scope, focusing on the fleeing vessel. His heart leaped at the familiar lines of her hull, the point of her bowsprit, the way she glided through the water. He shifted the glass to the bow, where the words *Red Siren* flashed before him in bold crimson.

He knew that ship. It was the *Lady Em*—his father's merchant ship—he was sure of it.

Hot blood gushed through his veins.

Upon the foredeck, a woman in a red dress stood facing the wind. She wore a large floppy hat shoved so low on her head that neither her face nor even a strand of her hair could be glimpsed. As if sensing his scrutiny, she turned briefly and gave him a full navy salute before swerving back around. Yet he could not make out her face.

"By thunder!" Dajon whacked the spyglass on the railing. "Of all the gall!"

"What is it, Captain?" Borland asked.

" 'Tis my father's ship!"

Both officers gave him curious looks, and some of the sailors on the deck below halted and stared at him as if surprised by their captain's sudden outburst.

"That pirate sails my father's merchant ship—the same one taken off Portsmouth nigh five years ago." Dajon doffed his bicorn and wiped the sweat from his brow. Since he had not shared the humiliating story with anyone, he wasn't surprised by the incredulous gasps coming from his men.

"The great Captain Waite overtaken by a pirate?" Borland mocked. "I would never have thought it possible."

"Many ships have similar lines, Captain," Jamieson said. "How could you possibly recognize your father's?"

"Because regardless of the blasphemous name painted on her bow and the vermin that infest her, I would know my father's ship anywhere, just as I would know that woman pirate anywhere."

"A woman pirate, you say?" Jamieson gave a humorless laugh. "So the tales are true."

Borland grabbed the spyglass and held it to his eye. "Ah yes, there is a woman aboard her—a trace of a red dress upon the forecastle. Yet perhaps she is the captain's mistress."

"Nay, she is no mere mistress." Dajon pictured her insolent salute, and fury hammered through his head until he felt it would explode— fury at how she had beaten him five years before, fury at the agony he had suffered because of it, and fury that she still scavenged the seas with such arrogance—and in his father's ship! Intolerable. But—he felt a grin tugging at his lips—she had made a fatal error in bringing her band of brigands overseas to terrorize colonial waters.

For Dajon was no longer a man to be trifled with.

"We have no choice but to pursue her, Captain." Jamieson swore. "This insult cannot go unanswered. You must retrieve your father's ship."

Borland grinned. "So we have finally crossed paths with the famous pirate ship the *Red Siren*, and her captain is a woman, after all." A malicious satisfaction beamed from his eyes, giving Dajon pause. "A most exciting day."

Dajon stiffened his jaw. "Exciting" was the last term he would use. Every muscle within him twitched to give chase and bring the vixen to justice. But he must obey naval code. He must not allow emotion to rule over him.

Ever again.

"Bring us alongside the Dutchman, if you please, Mr. Borland."

Jamieson's disgruntled gaze darted first to Borland then to Dajon. "But, Captain, she is within our reach."

"Never fear, Mr. Jamieson. I have no doubt we have not seen the last of the *Red Siren*," Dajon said.

Borland turned and bellowed orders below, sending men up to lower topsails.

By the time the HMS *Enforcer* anchored keel to keel with the *Flying Dragon*, the *Red Siren* was but a speck on the horizon. As Dajon climbed into the longboat and gave the order to shove off, his neck and back ached from the tense rage that had spiked through him the past hour.

Once aboard the *Flying Dragon*, he adjusted his blue coat, threw back his shoulders, and marched over to take his verbal lashing from the captain.

"We thank you kindly for your swift assistance." The captain of the Dutchman smirked in obvious disgust. "Albeit too little, too late."

"Captain Waite, at your service." Dajon removed his hat. "We were told to meet you off Hilton Head, Captain. . . ?"

"Grainger."

"Captain Grainger." Dajon repeated the name between gritted teeth. "When you were not there, I made all haste to find you."

"Made haste or not, 'tis no matter to me. As you can see, you are too late." He waved a weathered hand over the barrels and crates still crowding the deck. "That pirate ran off with half my goods."

"And would have taken the rest if we had not arrived when we did," Dajon reminded him, hoping to put an end to the impudent man's accusations.

"Aye, I'll grant you that." The captain spit off to the side. "But she took most of me pearls—and the rare conch ones, to boot. They would 'ave brought a grand price."

"Conch pearls?"

"Aye, I had just ten of them. Rare pink beauties found only in queen conch shells."

Dajon turned, bumping into Borland, who stood beside him with a smug look of satisfaction on his face. A small band of ashen-faced sailors huddled around the mainmast beside a pile of frayed rope. "Do you need assistance with the injured?" Dajon asked the captain.

"There ain't no injured."

"None?" The revelation shocked Dajon. Pirates were a bloody breed, known to relish the violence they inflicted upon their victims.

"The scamps didn't harm a soul. They cared only for the treasure."

"Then you made no resistance?"

Captain Grainger shot his fiery gaze to Dajon. "If you're calling me a coward, then say it outright, and we'll settle it like gentlemen."

"I am calling you no such thing, Captain," Dajon said with as much sincerity as he could muster, although the idea of a duel, if only to release his frustration, was not without appeal.

"She had a bloody pistol pointed at my son." He nodded to the slight youth who stood by the mainmast rubbing his wrists. "What did you expect me to do? Besides, we were outnumbered."

"You did the right thing."

"I live for your approval, Captain." His mocking tone elicited chortles from his crew.

Ignoring him, as well as Borland who stood smirking beside him, Dajon continued, "The pirate captain was a woman, then?"

"Aye."

"Can you tell me what she looked like?"

"A beauty, if ye ask me," one of the sailors standing nearby piped up.

"Aye, she was winsome, to be sure." Grainger nodded. "A spitfire, that one." He shook his head. "A mass of red hair the color of copper, with the eyes of a dragon and the face of an angel."

Suddenly a vision of Faith flashed into Dajon's mind, but he tossed it aside. One troublesome redhead was enough for the moment.

"I suggest you store the rest of your goods below, Captain, and raise what sails you have left. I can assure you a safe voyage to Charles Towne from here."

"I should expect nothing less." Grainger thrust out his bristly chin.

Donning his bicorn, Dajon spun on his heel, anxious to be gone from the captain's insulting demeanor.

"She asked me to give you this, Captain." Grainger's voice halted him, and he turned to see the man flicking a red scarf through the air.

Grabbing the silky cloth, Dajon rubbed it between two fingers and eyed Grainger. "She said to give it to me specifically?"

"Aye, to the captain of the HMS *Enforcer*—with her compliments, I might add."

Dajon examined it again. The initials *R. S.*, embroidered in gold thread, decorated one corner. *Red Siren*. Resisting the urge to rip it to shreds, he crumpled the cloth in his fist instead. The insolence of this woman! Gripping the hilt of his sword, Dajon stormed across the deck. He would catch her. He would catch her and turn her over to the Vice Admiralty Court. Then she would no longer be a plague upon these waters—or a plague upon his life.

CHAPTER 13

Faith gave Seaspray a gentle nudge as they turned the corner onto Church Street. The huge round columns of the First Baptist Church shone like glassy pillars in the moonlight, making the first chapel built in Charles Towne look more like a Roman coliseum than a house of worship.

"Ye took in a fine haul today, mistress." Lucas gave an exhausted sigh as he eased his horse beside hers.

"Yes, a fine haul, indeed, Lucas." Faith tried to match his exuberance, tried to appreciate the wealth they had acquired, but frustration simmered deep in her belly over the treasure lost. After they had counted the plunder and divided it among the crew, Faith had dismissed the men, and she and Lucas had made several trips deeper into the wilderness with the remainder of the booty loaded on their horses. There they spent two backbreaking hours unloading the jewels, pearls, and spices inside a cave—piled atop the rest of the treasure Faith had amassed over the years.

She patted the small pouch hanging on her belt. She'd kept a few of the best pearls with her. Conch pearls. Very rare and very expensive. They would serve to remind her that she was nearly at her goal. Nearly. If only she could have finished the job today.

"Blast that Mr. Waite!" she hissed, twitching the reins to avoid a passing carriage.

"Aye, 'twas poor timin', indeed." Lucas smiled.

His stallion snorted, and Faith smiled at her first mate's ever-gleeful demeanor. How long had he sailed with her? Six years now?

"I fear I would be lost without you, Lucas. I do believe you are the only man I have ever trusted." Truth be told, he was also the only person who knew the whereabouts of her treasure. At first, she had hated confiding in him—hated trusting any man. But without his help, she would never be able to transport her plunder to safety.

An unusually cool breeze blew in from the bay, chilling the perspiration that had taken residence on Faith's neck. She prodded her horse onward, past a three-story, cream-colored house adorned with wrought iron balconies and a narrow piazza that stretched along the side of the building facing the sea to catch the prevailing breeze. She was still growing accustomed to the strange architecture in Charles Towne—so different from the Georgian-style houses back home with their hipped roofs, stone parapets, and massive porticoes in front.

"Ye saved me life, mistress. If ye hadn't rescued me from the streets and gave me a place to live, I'd be lying in me grave by now."

"Ah, but all that wealth must prove a tempting sight, does it not?" Faith regretted the words as soon as they left her mouth. Lucas had never given her reason to doubt his loyalty. To question it now was insulting at best. "Forgive me, Lucas." She rubbed the back of her neck. " 'Tis been a long day." And no doubt, the dangers and trials had weakened her faith—in herself and in him as well.

Lucas kept his gaze straight ahead. "Never ye mind, mistress. Ye knows how I feel. All the wealth in the world holds no lure for me—not if takin' it means hurtin' ye and yer sisters. Yer like kin to me now." He regarded her, flipping back his stiff black hair. " 'Sides, what would a half-breed like me do wit' all that treasure?"

Faith swallowed a burning lump of emotion. No man, not her father nor any relation nor suitor, had warmed her soul and earned her regard as much as this half-breed castoff of society. How poorly that spoke of the so-called Christian gentlemen she had known.

Exhaustion tugged at her shoulders. Even the horses struggled as they made their way through the dusty streets, past shops and houses and the curious eyes of the few citizens still lingering about at night. Faith kept to the shadows, thankful she had left Morgan snug in her cabin on board the *Red Siren*, for no doubt, his chattering presence would only draw more unwanted attention their way.

Another breeze wafted over her, carrying with it the scent of salt, fish, and pine. It danced through the loose strands of her hair, and Faith quickly pinned the wayward curls up behind her, drawing the gaze of two passersby. The gentlemen tipped their hats in her direction, and she lowered her chin, hoping they would not recognize her in the dim lantern light. It was bad enough that one of the Westcott daughters roamed the streets at night; two would cast an indelible tarnish on the family name.

Turning down Broad Street, Faith eased her horse toward Meeting Street, where a drawbridge in the inner wall led to Johnson's covered half-moon, over the moat, and then over another drawbridge to the outside of the city. The early citizens, terrified by the many Indian and Spanish attacks, erected the strong double wall, yet already parts of it were being dismantled as the city outgrew its boundaries. Her house was one of those that sat outside the fortification.

Home. She could almost feel the comfort of her warm, soft bed and hoped Edwin had given up on her arrival and retired early with his ritual sip of brandy. She did not feel up to another one of his rattling lectures. Nor did she wish to confront Mr. Waite. Certainly he would still be occupied in securing the *Flying Dragon* at port. With a head start and a fair wind, she had no doubt beat him home, even with the extra time required to store her day's plunder.

Faith made her way outside the wall and then turned Seaspray down Hasell Street, through the open gate, and up to the front porch of her house. She slid off her mount, her boots crunching on the gravel, and handed Lucas her reins. But lights flickering through the windows crushed any hopes of an inconspicuous entrance.

No sooner had she opened the door than a blinding light struck her in the face.

"Where have you been, Miss Faith?"

Taking a step back, she shielded her eyes and pushed the lantern aside to reveal the quivering jowls and tremulous gaze of Edwin.

"Forgive me, Edwin, I did not intend to be so late. Lucas and I were delayed in town."

"Delayed? By what, I might ask? At nine o'clock at night? This is insufferable. What am I to do? And with Mr. Waite gone, too? I had no one to turn to...."

With a huff, Faith allowed Edwin his tirade, praying that without interruption it would run its course and falter for lack of opposition.

"And Miss Molly telling me nothing, and Miss Grace gone all day as well—"

Faith's breath halted in her throat. "Did you say Grace was gone?"

Edwin wrinkled his nose and fixed her with a dark gaze. "Never fear. She arrived in time for supper."

Faith sighed. No doubt her sister had been on one of her charity runs, but Faith would have to speak to her nonetheless. "And Hope?"

"She is home." Edwin rubbed his forehead and began to sway.

Faith clutched his elbow, fearing he would fall. "Edwin, please take a seat." Leading him to a chair, she forced him into it and snatched the lantern from his hand, placing it on the table.

"You do not know what I have endured today," he whined, clutching his heart. "This disobedience is not to be borne, not to be borne, I tell you."

"Edwin, quit your fussing. I was not without escort." Faith blew out a sigh. "Are we not all home and safe now?"

Edwin nodded, blubbering out a sigh.

"You worry for naught." Faith made her way to the stairs and gazed down the dark hallway, hoping to catch a glimpse of the guesthouse through the back window. Nothing but black. She faced the steward. He wrung his hands together like a wet rag, and Faith felt sorry for the man.

His proud eyes rose to meet hers. "You must promise not to be out so late without informing me."

"Of course. But I am too utterly spent to quarrel with you further," Faith said. "Did Mr. Waite arrive yet?"

Edwin shook his head and snorted. "Most unbefitting a guardian, if you ask me."

"You heard my father. His obligations are first and foremost to the navy."

"Perhaps Sir Wilhelm would be more suited for the job. He called upon you several times today."

A chill stiffened her back. "Indeed? Several times?" Thankful she had missed the slimy proprietor, she worried at his persistence, which, if not rewarded, would surely cast suspicions on her activities.

"Yes, twice. He was most concerned for you." Edwin rose and snatched the lantern. "And most disagreeable when I could not inform him of your whereabouts."

"He is a disagreeable man, regardless." Faith placed a hand on Edwin's arm. "Now off to bed with you. Have your brandy and sleep well. You do look pale."

He snorted.

"Everything will appear more cheery in the morning—you shall see."

With a click of his tongue, Edwin grabbed the banister. Faith silenced her giggle as she watched him ascend the stairs, muttering all the while.

Darkness blanketed the entrance hall. Only the sound of Faith's shallow breathing, the ticking of the grandfather clock, and the rustle of leaves outside the windows stirred the silence. She glanced to her right. An open door led to her father's study, where, if he were home, he would no doubt be sitting, smoking his pipe and reading by the warm fire. Now a dark chill seeped from the room and crept over her, reminding her of his absence. Even though they often quarreled, she missed him. She knew he loved his daughters in his own way, but she had come to accept the fact that he loved the sea more. When her mother was still alive, she had filled their home in England with warmth and love. Without her, emptiness haunted every room. Perhaps that was why Hope and Grace sought comfort elsewhere. Faith sighed. If she could seize just one more prize as wealthy as the *Flying Dragon*, she would be able to change not only their fortunes but the shroud of gloom that hovered over this house as well.

Plucking the pins from her hair, Faith shook her head and exited the back of the house, noting the absence of the usual sliver of light beneath the kitchen door. Molly must have retired early. 'Twas no wonder. The poor woman got up at four o'clock each morning to gather the eggs, haul the water, and rekindle the fire.

The door swung away beneath her hand, and the ensuing puff of air from the kitchen, redolent of fresh bread and beef stew, swirled over Faith, sending her stomach grumbling with longing for the supper she had missed. Moonlight spun a silver web across deep shadows as Faith groped her way to the table in search of a candle.

Her fingers bumped into something hard and warm. Hot breath flowed over her.

Jumping back, she screamed at the dark silhouette looming in the shadows. "One more step and I'll slice you!" She reached for the cutlass that no longer hung at her side and then turned to flee. But strong hands grabbed her arms and swung her around.

"Be still, woman, 'tis me." The deep, masculine voice reverberated in the room.

Fear and rage crashed over Faith. Horrifying memories wrestled against her reason, and she thrashed against his grip. She pounded her fists on his chest, but his solid frame did not budge.

"Calm yourself, Miss Westcott. There's naught to fear." His grasp was firm but gentle as he pulled her toward him. He smelled of leather and salt.

Yet her panic made his words sound like unintelligible mumbles. Drawing a deep breath, Faith rammed her knee into his groin.

Instantly, he released her. "Great guns, woman," he moaned as his dark body folded in half.

"Mr. Waite?" Faith took a step back and caught her breath.

"Aye," he gasped. "What is left of me."

Embarrassment flooded her. Then anger took its place at her exposure of her fear—her weakness—in front of him. "You scared me half to death, Mr. Waite! 'Tis what you get for slinking around in the dark." As her eyes adjusted to the dark, she grabbed the candle, now visible on the table, and lit it from the embers still smoking in the fireplace.

The captain's dark hair hung around his face. His breaths came in deep spurts as he leaned over, hands on his knees.

When she approached with the light, he lifted his gaze, and despite the pain in his eyes, a slight smirk played on his lips. With obvious difficulty, he eased himself upright then pressed the wrinkles from his blue coat. The tip of his service sword clanged against the table. "Perhaps next time, a warning shot would suffice?"

"You'll get no warning from me." Faith sent him a fiery gaze. "Not when you come upon me unawares in the dark." She noticed her red scarf poking from a pocket inside his waistcoat, and she suppressed a grin. Twice she had bested him today, yet somehow the second time did not hold the same thrill as the first. If she had known it was the captain, she certainly would not have attacked him. She had no desire to hurt him, and though he tried to hide it, the grimace on his face betrayed his pain.

"Have a seat, Mr. Waite, and I shall fetch you some tea." She started to turn, but once again, he grabbed her arm.

His heated breath, tinged with liquor, drifted over Faith, sending the candle flickering between them. Dark eyes perused her as if memorizing every inch of her face. Desire and admiration intermingled in their depths, and an unusual flutter rose within Faith's belly. Wayward strands of his hair grazed the stubble on his cheek. A smudge of dirt stained his tousled collar, and his blue coat hung unbuttoned over his wide chest—so unlike the kempt, orderly captain.

He reached up. Faith flinched but remained anchored in place, not wanting him to see his effect upon her.

" 'Tis obvious I frightened you terribly, Miss Westcott. Please accept my apologies." He brushed a finger over her cheek.

A warm flush surged through Faith. She snatched her arm from his grasp and turned away. "Frightened?" She waved a hand through the air. "Nonsense. You merely surprised me." She bit her lip. She must remember that Mr. Waite was not only a man—something she doubted she could ever forget—and therefore not to be trusted, but her enemy as well.

But such an enemy. With her back to him, Faith grinned, hoping to turn the tables and have a bit of fun. "Beg your pardon, Mr. Waite, but do I smell a hint of alcohol about you?"

She heard him expel a deep breath. " 'Twas a difficult day." The frustration in his voice stung her conscience.

She swerved around and placed a hand to her chest. "I daresay I am shocked, Mr. Waite. I would never have expected a godly man such as yourself to partake of the devil's brew."

"I have a sip of port on board my ship when the occasion calls for it," he replied with confidence. The tiny upturn of his mouth and the playful look in his eyes let her know he was not a man so easily ruffled by her barbs.

She longed to make some sarcastic comment about the occasion that had caused his annoyance. But the way his intense gaze drifted over her sent her insides quivering in a warm pool, and she just stood there, locked in the hold of his blue eyes.

Forcing herself to look away, she set the candle down, fetched a handful of tea leaves, and tossed them into a pot on the table. Shame weighed upon her. She was not some weak female who swooned over the attentions of a man—albeit a most handsome, honorable man.

No, no, no. Not just a man but an enemy—an enemy who stood between her and her goal of plundering one more treasure-laden ship, an enemy who stood between her and the safety and happiness of her sisters. Anger flared within her, melting her passion and igniting her determination.

Dajon watched Faith retrieve two china cups from the cupboard. Her curls cascaded in a crimson waterfall that poured to her waist. He swallowed a lump of desire. What a paradox this woman was. She reminded him of a wildcat: independent, cautious, yet when her claws were not drawn, soft and vulnerable. She had been truly terrified of him in the dark, though he had tried to console her both with his words and his touch. What had happened to her to cause so frantic a reaction?

What was happening to him?

Years ago, he had sworn that the only woman he would ever need would be the ship he sailed upon, for after what happened with Marianne, how could he trust himself with the safety of another lady? His promise had not been difficult to keep—until now.

As he watched Faith cross the room, a picture of femininity yet carrying herself with the confidence and command of a captain at sea, he longed to know everything about her.

"Pray tell, why were you wandering about in the dark anyway?" She placed the cups on the table.

Dajon drew his sword and laid it across a bench before he eased into a chair. "I seem to have forgotten to eat today. I was searching for a lamp when I heard you come in."

"Why did you not alert me to your presence?" She eyed him guardedly. Then, turning, she grabbed a cloth and folded it around the handle of a kettle that hung over the few coals still simmering in the fireplace.

Dajon's gaze swept over her as she knelt, her curves alluring beneath the simple dress she wore. "I thought you might be a robber." He flinched under the prick of his conscience. Truth be told, the minute she had entered the room, he could not take his eyes off her silky skin, the way the moonlight shimmered over it and reflected a glittering red halo around her hair.

Until she had kneed him in the crotch, of course.

Lifting the kettle, she poured the warm water into the pot on the table. As she did, her leg brushed against his, and she jumped, sending her hair spilling past Dajon's face.

The aroma of salt and smoke filled his nose, and he leaned back in the chair, wondering why she did not perfume herself with lilac or rose oil like other women he had known. Suspicion brought his mind to full alert. He narrowed his gaze upon her.

"What ails you now, Mr. Waite? Did I hurt your leg as well?"

"Your hair smells of the sea." He folded his hands over his stomach.

A hint of alarm flickered across her face. She stirred the pot, lifted it, and tipped it over Dajon's cup. "Lucas and I had business at the port today." Her hand trembled, spilling the liquid onto the table. "Oh, good heavens." Setting the pot down with a clunk, she dabbed the puddles of tea with a cloth.

"Aye, so Molly told me early this morning." Dajon lifted his cup. "Must have been important to force you to rise before the sun." He took a sip of the tea, hoping its warmth and her answer would dissolve the ridiculous notions that now filled his head.

"Most important." Faith shifted away and returned the kettle to the hearth. "I had to purchase supplies for my soap business."

"Quite a few supplies, I would imagine, to have taken the entire day to procure, for it seems we both arrived home at the same time this evening."

"Whatever do you mean? I have been here for hours," she retorted without facing him.

"I beg your pardon, miss. When I saw Lucas bedding down two horses in the stable, I assumed. . ."

Faith spun around and flung one hand to her hip. "You assume too much, Mr. Waite." Her gaze flitted down to his pocket, where he'd stuffed the pirate's scarf. "And did you escort your treasure ship to port safely?"

"Yes. Thank you for your concern. The ship is anchored safely in the harbor as we speak." He set down his cup.

With a smirk, she shifted her gaze away.

"But I see you have taken notice of my souvenir of the day's adventures." Withdrawing the scarf, Dajon rose and extended it to her. Since she had lived in Charles Towne for more than two months, perhaps she could give him a clue as to the identity of the owner.

Her face paled, giving him pause.

She lowered her chin and cleared her throat. When she raised her gaze, a different woman lurked behind those auburn eyes. Gone was the hard sheen, the defiant glare, and in its place, a seductive innocence glimmered.

Snatching the scarf, she fingered the initials and rubbed the silk between her fingers. "A lady admirer. Why, Mr. Waite, I had no idea." She turned her back to him. "And all along I thought"—a tiny sob escaped her—"well, I thought you had some affection for me."

Taken aback by her sudden change, Dajon's voice cracked, and the words he had intended to say faltered on his lips. He rubbed the bridge of his nose, where an ache from an old injury rose to haunt him. Had he been absent so long from courting rituals that he no longer recognized a lady's intentions? By thunder, Faith was unlike any woman he had known, to be sure, but he could not be that daft.

Dajon circled her. Placing a finger beneath her chin, he lifted her gaze to his. "I do not know the lady who owns it. I thought perhaps you might recognize it."

"Me? Why, anyone can tell by the bold color that it clearly belongs to some trollop. What would I know of it?" She lifted the scarf and dabbed at her moist cheeks.

Suppressing a chuckle, Dajon leaned and peered intently into her eyes.

"What are you doing?" she snapped.

"Trying to see if there are two of you in there." He grinned and then furrowed his brow. "The transformation is so swift and unpredictable, I know not which of you to expect, vixen or enchantress."

Batting her tears away, she glared at him, and behind her eyes burned a fury and determination matching that of any brigand he'd ever seen. Thrusting the cloth in his hand, she turned her back to him, flinging her hair behind her in a fiery cloud.

He lengthened his stance. " 'Twas a gift from a pirate—a *lady* pirate—prowling the Carolina seas." Dajon leaned down and drew a whiff of her hair. Smoke, salt, and a hint of lemon. "Her hair is the same color as yours." Since her back was still turned, he took the liberty of caressing a lock between his fingers, enjoying the silky feel and delighting in the way the curl sprang back when he released it. "Odd that she has only made her presence known these past few months. I daresay she appeared about the same time you arrived here in Charles Towne." Why did he enjoy taunting her so? Perhaps because the ache still burned in his groin where she had kneed him. Perhaps because he enjoyed the banter of her sharp wit and the way the freckles on her nose scrunched together when she grew angry. Because even the thought of an admiral's daughter being a pirate was absolutely ludicrous. An impossibility.

She wheeled around, her thick strands slapping his side. "There are many women with red hair in these colonies, Mr. Waite. It is not a crime. And tales of women pirates have been tantalizing the ears of these adventurous pilgrims for years."

"See, now the vixen has reappeared," he teased, noting the fury burning within her eyes.

"Why are you being so cruel? Is it because I kicked you?" She huffed. "Edwin told me you were still away, and I thought I was all alone." Her voice softened as she inched closer to him. 'Tis frightening to be a woman without protection."

Visions of Faith handling herself fearlessly with the ruffians on the street shot through Dajon's mind, followed by her declaration that she could take care of herself and her sisters without him. But as he felt the heat from her body close to his and as her lemony scent swirled beneath his nose, Dajon had difficulty forming a rational thought from the memories. "I must say, I do prefer the enchantress."

She lifted her head and shifted her misty eyes to his. Her sweet breath puffed upon his chin like an aphrodisiac as her gaze swept over his lips.

Heat stormed through Dajon, weakening his reason and his defenses. The heady pull of her was too much to resist. He lowered his lips to meet hers.

No.

He halted. She was toying with him. He was sure of it. *Lord, help me. I have not the strength to resist her without You.*

A blast of indignation shot through him. What was he doing? He pulled away and crossed his arms over his chest. "Forgive me."

Faith cocked her head. A spark of victory flashed in her eyes. Dajon took a forceful step toward her again and leaned down, his mouth inches from her ear. "You play a dangerous game, Miss Westcott." Then, righting himself, he scoured her with his gaze. "I suggest you not offer yourself in so tempting a manner. Next time, I may well accept your invitation." He gave her a mischievous grin and bowed.

She narrowed her eyes.

Turning on his heels, Dajon grabbed his sword and stomped from the room. A blast of cool air struck him, reviving his reason. He cursed himself for being so weak. Allowing two ladies to get the best of him. He could not let it happen again.

CHAPTER 14

Faith rose early the next morning, determined to spend time with her sisters. With a yawn, she entered the dining room, lured there by their bickering voices.

"Oh, do come in, dear." Hope gestured for Faith to sit in the chair beside hers as the aroma of tea, strawberry jam, and toast danced around her, nudging her stomach awake.

Grace peeked at her from behind *Meditations and Contemplations* and smiled before resuming her reading. "Rising before noon? Whatever is the occasion?"

"Would you care for some tea, Miss Faith?" Miranda, the serving maid, curtsied in her direction.

"Yes, thank you." Ignoring Grace's remark, Faith took the seat next to Hope as Miranda filled her porcelain cup. Fragrant steam swirled off the hot liquid as rays of the morning sun set the silverware, fruit, and china glittering in vibrant colors against the white cotton tablecloth.

"Pray tell, where were you all day yesterday, Faith?" Hope set down her toast and formed her lips into a tiny pout. "With Grace gone as well, I was left with naught to do but sit and read. I wrote Father a letter." She swallowed and lowered her gaze. "Not that he will respond."

"It pleases me to see that you kept your promise and stayed home." Faith drew a slice of toast from the serving plate.

"I fail to see why I was forced to remain here when both you and Grace were free to roam wherever you wished."

Closing her book, Grace set it beside her plate. "I was delivering food to the settlers on the Ashley River. I asked if you would accompany me, but you refused."

"Why would I want to traipse through fields and forest, ruin my gown with mud and filth, and risk being attacked by savages?" Hope said with a huff.

"Perchance to help those in need?" Grace raised a pious brow. "Maybe if you thought of someone else besides yourself, you would not be in so disagreeable a mood all the time."

"I am not disagreeable." Hope turned up her nose and dropped a lump of sugar into her coffee with a plop. "Lord Falkland says I am the kindest and most charming woman he has ever known."

At the mention of Lord Falkland, fear resurged to gnaw at Faith. She determined to discuss the rogue with Hope later, but for now, she turned to her other sister. "Which reminds me, Grace. You are fully aware of Father's rules about leaving the house unescorted."

"Are you not bound by the same rules?" Grace flashed her green eyes at Faith, accusation burning within them.

"I was with Lucas yesterday."

"Mrs. Gibson accompanied me." Grace took a bite of her toast and set it down as if the matter were closed.

"'Tis not the same thing, and you know it. Mrs. Gibson, although a sweet, godly woman, cannot protect you in the event of some misfortune."

Grace brushed her feathery raven bangs aside and gave Faith a look of scorn. "You can hardly assume to govern us when you are never home. You're as bad as Father is."

Faith winced beneath the sting of Grace's words. She bit her lip to keep from spewing an angry retort. She was nothing like their father. While he went to sea for glory and adventure, ignoring his family at home, she went to sea to better their futures, doing her best to spend as much time with them as she could.

Hope slouched in her chair. "Where were you? You said we could talk when you returned."

"Forgive me. I was delayed." Faith laid a gentle hand over Hope's. "I promise we will talk today."

"Your promises mean nothing." Hope snatched her hand from beneath Faith's. "Grace is right. You are never here. And with Mother gone and Father always away, I feel as though I am not only an orphan but an only child." Moisture covered her sapphire eyes, and she turned away.

Faith stirred cream into her tea, the silver spoon clanging against the porcelain cup as if tolling her guilt. How could she make her sisters understand that her many absences were for their benefit—that their welfare and future were all that consumed her energies and time? Yet she could not let them in on her secret. Grace would be so appalled that she might even turn Faith over to the authorities—albeit to cleanse her from her iniquity. And Hope would only use Faith's pirating as a free license to pursue her own scandalous activities.

Faith clanked her cup down a little too hard and proceeded to butter her toast as if she were sharpening her cutlass.

She risked her life over and over for her sisters, and this was her reward.

Grace sighed and raised one brow. "If you are expecting Faith to be here for us, Hope, you will only face disappointment. For even when she is here, she sleeps half the day."

Faith forced down her anger and smiled. "Why don't we spend the whole day together, just the three of us? How does that sound?" Perhaps she could appease both her own guilt and her sisters' need for her company all at once.

Hope broke into a beaming smile. "That would be lovely."

Happy to have mollified her sister, Faith glanced out the window. The golden flowers of the Carolina jasmine waved in the morning breeze as they clung to a trestle. The pink and violet blossoms of dogwoods and magnolias that had sparkled across the city like jewels early that spring had faded in the latter months of the summer, replaced by coral honeysuckle and sea myrtle, delighting Faith in the variety of unusual flowers that graced this untamed wilderness. She had come to love the beauty of this land and could see her and her sisters settled happily here once their fortune was secured.

Only one person stood in her way.

And as if she could conjure him up by her thoughts, Mr. Waite strode by the window in his blue uniform.

Hope's gaze followed him across the paned glass. "He is so handsome, is he not?"

"I suppose." Faith tried to still the sudden thump of her heart. She sipped her tea, hoping its warmth would sooth her nerves, but instead the acidic taste bit her tongue. In all the discord, she had forgotten to add sugar.

"I thought your affections were for only Lord Falkland," Grace snickered.

"They are, of course." Hope gave her a coquettish smile. "But there is no harm in admiring, is there?"

Grace chuckled. "You are incorrigible."

Faith felt the captain enter even before his baritone voice filled the room like a symphony. "Good morning, ladies."

Hope giggled, and Grace shot him a playful smile.

Mr. Waite harrumphed. "Did I miss something?"

Faith heard his boots shuffle on the wooden floor as she dropped two lumps of sugar into her tea. His warm breath wafted down her neck.

"Good morning, Miss Westcott." The scent of lye tickled her nose. The man obviously kept himself as clean on the outside as he did on the inside.

A heated flush rose from her belly and set her face aflame at the memory of their encounter last night. "Good morning, Mr. Waite," she said without turning, for she was certain her face must be as bright as the red apple that perched atop the bowl in the middle of the table.

His piercing gaze locked upon her as he rounded the table, flung his coattails out behind him, and took a seat across from her. His hair, pulled and tied behind him in a queue, reminded Faith of the color of the roast coffee filling Hope's cup.

She had hardly been able to sleep the entire night. Every time she had started to drift off to a much-needed slumber, the memory of his lips so close to hers kept jolting her awake. The unfairness of it. What was wrong with her? She had thought to tease him, but instead she was the one whose passions had been stirred.

And why was he staring at her now as if he knew her darkest secrets?

Hope twirled a lock of her golden hair. "I trust you slept well, Mr. Waite?"

"Magnificently, thank you." His blue eyes slid to Faith, a smile flickering within them.

Was he mocking her?

"You look lovely this morning, Miss Hope," the captain said as he waved away Miranda and poured himself some tea. Steam rose from the hot liquid in an exotic dance that mimicked the heat radiating within Faith.

Hope flashed him a girlish smile.

"And you as well, Miss Grace." Mr. Waite poured cream into his cup.

"Why, thank you, Mr. Waite. If you don't mind my saying so, 'tis nice to have a Christian gentleman around the house."

"I am finding your home to my liking as well, Miss Grace." He grabbed a slice of toast, spread some jam upon it, and shoved it into his mouth, tearing off a bite.

"My sister has just promised to spend the entire day with Grace and me." Hope's voice lifted with excitement. "Perhaps you could join us?" She tapped Faith's leg beneath the table.

Faith kicked her sister in return. The last thing she wanted was to spend the day with Mr. Waite.

"Ouch." Hope flinched and leaned down to rub her ankle.

"She has? What a grand idea." The captain smiled as if he hadn't noticed anything unusual and brushed the crumbs from his pristine white lapels. "But are you sure, Miss Westcott, you have nothing more pressing to attend to?"

Faith smiled and tried to hide the agitation brewing in her stomach. "Of course I don't. What could you be referring to?"

"Nothing, I assure you. It seems some urgent matter always steals your time away from home." Mr. Waite finished his toast and rubbed his hands together. His strong jaw flexed with each chew as his playful blue gaze flickered over her.

"How would you know? You have been here no more than a few days."

"And yet you are never here."

Faith tightened the corners of her mouth for a moment to keep from spewing angry words at him. When she recovered sufficiently, she smiled sweetly. "I am here now, Mr. Waite."

"Indeed." He sipped his tea and grinned. "And what pleasure I find in your company."

"Can we go to the park?" Hope asked.

"After we attend church." Grace stirred her tea then set down her spoon with a soft clang. "It is the Lord's Day."

"Oh pshaw. Why must we always go to church?" Hope's shoulders slumped.

Grace frowned at her sister and twirled the button on her collar. "Can you not give God back one hour of your time for all He has done for you?"

"What has He done for me?" Hope crinkled her nose and patted her perfectly styled hair. "I am stuck here in this horrid town. Mother is gone. Father is always away, and I am forbidden to have any fun at all."

"Things are not always as they seem, Miss Hope." Mr. Waite plucked an apple from the bowl. "You have plenty to eat, a comfortable home, beautiful clothes, and your health. These are gifts from God. Many do not have such luxuries." He chomped on the apple.

Grace nodded in approval and cast a matronly look toward Hope.

"Faith does not attend church," Hope quipped and tilted her head.

Faith shuffled in her seat. Her sister's mouth always ran wild like a storm at sea.

Mr. Waite raised a brow.

"She stopped attending shortly after Mother died."

"Indeed?" Sorrow tainted his voice.

"It was Mother's wish that you both attend church regularly." Grace rubbed her thumb over the handle of her teacup. "She begged me to ensure that all of us maintained our faith in God." Her voice cracked. "It was most important to her, but neither of you have listened to me at all."

Hope rolled her eyes. "Perhaps if you did not look down upon us from your high and lofty pedestal, we would."

"I do not—" Grace snapped then pursed her lips. "Oh, never mind." Releasing her teacup, she sat back in her chair.

Mr. Waite cast a disapproving glance over them all.

"I am afraid I do not share your faith in God, Mr. Waite." Faith took a bite of her toast. "And it would seem neither does my sister." The jam, however, soured in her mouth, and she swallowed it with a gulp.

"So you have told me. Yet you have not denied His existence. Perchance church would be a good place to hear from Him again?"

If she wanted to hear from God, Faith longed to respond, but she did not wish to incite another argument with Grace. Instead, she remained silent, thankful when she heard Edwin's uneven gait behind her.

"Sir Wilhelm," the steward announced as he halted beside Faith. The bags beneath Edwin's eyes hung lower and darker this morning, no doubt because of his incessant worrying. But Faith refused to concern herself with the skittish steward. Her sisters provided her with enough stress, and to make matters worse, she must now deal with this pompous bore, Wilhelm.

Closing her eyes, Faith wondered what the infernal man could possibly want.

Mr. Waite dropped his apple to his plate then stood, scraping his chair over the floor, and bowed. "Sir Wilhelm. A pleasure."

Yet there was no pleasure to be found in the captain's gaze. Faith saw only wariness in his blue eyes as he took in the Carolina proprietor. Well, at least Mr. Waite was a good judge of character.

"Mr. Waite," Sir Wilhelm replied, his look of surprise quickly replaced by one of disappointment that tugged on his pasty white skin. "Here again, I see."

"I am afraid I do reside here for the time being." Mr. Waite gestured for Sir Wilhelm to take a chair.

Ignoring him, Sir Wilhelm briefly nodded toward Hope and Grace before his sunken brown eyes fixed on Faith. "Miss Westcott, you are the picture of beauty this morning."

Faith flashed a curt smile but quickly faced forward and fingered her half-eaten toast. *Oh, please go away.*

" 'Tis a glorious day, and I have come to inquire whether you and your sisters would do me the honor of joining me on a carriage ride through the country."

Silence struck the table as if a mighty blast of wind stole all their voices and blew them away.

"A splendid idea, Sir Wilhelm," Mr. Waite said, breaking through the shroud of discomfiture. "I was about to escort Miss Hope and Miss Grace to church. But I believe Miss Westcott is available." He raised his sarcastic brow her way. "Are you not?"

The cad. Faith wanted to strangle him but instead forced her lips into a pert smile. "Why, no, Mr. Waite, you misunderstood me. I have every intention of attending church with my sisters today." She gazed up at Sir Wilhelm. "Please accept my apologies, but as you can see, we have plans."

Mr. Waite widened his eyes. "I have a grand idea. Perhaps Sir Wilhelm would like to join us?"

⁓

Faith shifted on the hard pew as a bead of perspiration made its way beneath her gown. It took a wayward course down her back, twisting and turning before finally being trapped by a fold of her dress. She wondered if it was due to the summer heat or the fact that she had not stepped foot in a church in over seven years.

Mr. Waite sat smugly beside her. She longed to grind her elbow into his side. How dare he use her hatred for Sir Wilhelm to manipulate her into coming to church! To make matters worse, the buffoon had accepted Mr. Waite's invitation to join them and took up valuable space on her right, space she would have preferred anyone else to have taken, even the miscreants down by the docks. There was something grotesque about the man—the sickly smell of him, the way he looked at her that made her stomach shrivel in nausea. And she was not one easily overcome by queasiness.

Her sisters sat on the other side of him, Hope staring into space as if wishing she were anywhere else but here—Faith could well understand her sentiment—and Grace with gloved hands clasped around the Bible in her lap, waiting in anticipation of worshipping a God who surely would neither hear nor care.

Sir Wilhelm slid closer to her until his arm touched hers. She flinched and shifted away, only to bump into Mr. Waite. Heat from his body shot through her until further drops of perspiration slid down her back to join the wet blotch she was sure was forming on her gown.

The captain flashed her one of his charming smiles but made no effort to move aside.

This was going to be a long service.

A rugged, stocky man with sandy hair that seemed to spike out in all directions approached the lectern. He wore normal street clothes of breeches and waistcoat rather than the long flowing robes of the Anglican priests, and Faith assumed he was a simple attendant until he opened a Bible and began to read aloud. Never in all her years of attending church had she seen any priest like him. A simple, humble man. Even when he glanced across the crowd, naught but love beamed from his gaze, instead of the condemnation and vainglorious snobbery she had often witnessed in the eyes of the priests back home.

Above him a large wooden cross hung upon a brick wall, framed on each side with long narrow windows. The sight of it sent a twinge of shame through Faith, making her feel suddenly tainted inside, unworthy. Swallowing hard, she shut out the passage he read—something from the Gospel of Matthew about seeds—and instead focused on a rather handsome man sitting in the front row who kept glancing over his shoulder at Hope.

The square brick building that encircled the fifty or so parishioners was much smaller than St. Philip's, where her father and her sisters usually attended. The crude furnishings and lack of decorations made it seem more like a rustic barn than a place of worship. The scents swirling around her of aged wood, mold, dirt, and tallow only confirmed her assessment.

Still, Faith could not shake the sweet Spirit permeating the place, evident on the faces of those who listened with rapt attention to the reverend's passionate reading:

" 'But he that received the seed into stony places, the same is he that heareth the word, and anon with joy receiveth it; yet hath he not root in himself, but dureth for a while: for when tribulation or persecution ariseth because of the word, by and by he is offended.' "

Offended? Had she become offended at God? Confusion tore through her. Perhaps she had. But who wouldn't be offended when the almighty God, the one Being who had power to do or allow whatever He wished, had sentenced her sister Charity to a lifetime of misery, had allowed Hope to endure an unspeakable horror, and had taken their mother from them at so young an age—the only parent who truly loved them. Yes, Faith was indeed offended.

Determined to block out the convicting words, she gazed over the small building, amazed that a church without the beauty of stained glass, without the ivory pillars and gold-inlaid altar, without the incense and white robes could stir more passion within her than she had felt in years.

And she did not care for it one bit.

On her left, Mr. Waite sifted through the Bible in his lap as if it were a delicate treasure he had just found in the hold of his ship. To her right, Sir

Wilhelm began to snore, eliciting giggles from Hope, which were quickly stifled by Grace's stern look of admonition.

The reverend continued: " 'The Son of man shall send forth his angels, and they shall gather out of his kingdom all things that offend, and them which do iniquity; and shall cast them into a furnace of fire: there shall be wailing and gnashing of teeth. Then shall the righteous shine forth as the sun in the kingdom of their Father. Who hath ears to hear, let him hear.' "

All things that offend, eh? Perhaps God was as offended with her as she was with Him. The only difference was that He had the power to cast her into a fiery furnace. Would He really do such a thing when all she was trying to do was save her sisters? Withdrawing her handkerchief, Faith dabbed at the perspiration on her neck. Perhaps He would. She really didn't know God anymore.

Maybe she never had.

She thought about saying a prayer to Him here in this holy place that seemed so filled with His presence. She thought about it, but the words wouldn't form in her mind. She gazed up at the wooden cross that symbolized the ultimate sacrifice of a Man, claiming to be God, who had come down to earth to save His children from their wickedness.

Her wickedness.

Instead of the guilt, the condemnation Faith expected to feel, a strong sense of love drifted over her like a cloud on a hot summer's day. It settled on her and soothed away the rough edges of her nerves. Closing her eyes, she basked in the peace. A gentle call, open arms, the flap of angel wings cooled her in the stifling church. She breathed deeply, longing to give in to it, longing to let go of her fears, her frustrations—her fight.

No!

Everything inside of her screamed in defiance. She would not serve a God who had allowed such suffering in her life.

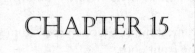

CHAPTER 15

Dajon had expected Faith to be uncomfortable at church, especially at a church where the powerful Word of God was read out loud, but certainly not as discomfited as she appeared. The poor woman could barely sit still. Her eyes flitted about the church as if she were seeking any possible means of escape. Sigh after sigh poured from her mouth, and tiny groans escaped from deep within her. At one point, she had closed her eyes and seemed to finally settle down, but then she jerked suddenly as if she had been stabbed. Now her breathing sounded like that of a seagull with its beak full of fish.

Rev. Halloway's sermons could certainly be convicting, but Dajon had not anticipated quite so strong a reaction. A breeze wafted in through the open window, teasing him with the scent of lemons. He drew it in like a sweet elixir, the aroma reminding him of Faith's glowing auburn eyes, her rosy plump lips, and the tiny freckles that adorned her nose. With her arm brushing against his, he found it difficult to focus on what the reverend was saying—or on anything else for that matter. Shifting slightly away from her, he tried to shake off the heated daze. Not since Marianne had a woman affected him so ardently. Opening his Bible, he searched through it for words of strength.

Father, please help me. Do not let me fail You again.

After the service, Faith sprang from her seat and snapped her gaze to the back door as if plotting her path to freedom. But before she could make a dash for it, Dajon grabbed her arm.

"Leaving so soon?" he teased. "Come, I would like you to meet Rev. Halloway."

A look of dread sparked in her eyes as if he had asked her to meet God Himself. "Truly, there is no need." She tugged from his grasp.

"But I insist. He is my dear friend, and I know you will find him most amiable."

Faith looked at him as if he were an annoying bug she longed to squash.

"I would love to meet him," Grace chirped from their right as people began to flow out the front door.

Hope pointed at Sir Wilhelm, still sitting in the pew, his eyes shut, his chin snuggled amid the folds of his waistcoat. Deep breaths fluttered between his lips. She tugged on her sister's sleeve with a giggle. "Should we wake him?"

"Of all the irreverence." Grace shook her head. "Of course, wake him."

"No. Please do not." Faith reached out a hand toward her sisters and shook her head then eyed Dajon with the same warning.

He scratched his chin. "Well, I suppose we could let him sleep a bit longer—while you meet Rev. Halloway, that is."

"Yes, yes, by all means, introduce us to your friend." Pulling her skirts close, Faith inched past the snoring man.

Dajon stifled a chuckle at the lengths she went to, to avoid her intended.

"Rev. Halloway, may I introduce the Westcott ladies, Miss Faith Westcott, Miss Hope Westcott, and Miss Grace Westcott."

The reverend nodded toward all the ladies, but his gaze remained on Faith. He smiled and then cast a sideways glance at Dajon.

Dajon gritted his teeth, hoping Faith had not noticed their exchange, but the moment her narrowed eyes met his, he knew that she had. She faced the reverend. "And how long have you known Mr. Waite, Reverend?"

"Ah, just this past month." He folded his hands over his prominent belly. "Did you care for the sermon, Miss Westcott?"

"Forgive me, Reverend." Faith shifted her stance and tucked a lock of hair behind her ear. A tiny purple scar marred the golden skin of her neck. In the shape of a half-moon, it curved upward like a smile just below her left ear. Dajon didn't remember seeing it before. An odd scar for a woman.

"But in all honesty," she continued, "I found my mind distracted with other matters."

Although at first taken aback by her forthrightness, Dajon could not help but appreciate her candor. While most people hid the truth behind the excuse of propriety, this lady spoke her mind without fear of consequence. Quite refreshing, indeed.

Dajon watched Rev. Halloway's reaction curiously but was not surprised when he saw naught but humor and love beaming from his friend's gaze.

Grace clicked her tongue and clutched her Bible to her chest. "You are all rudeness, sister." She turned to the reverend. "It was an eloquently spoken word of truth."

He laughed. "Eloquent? I doubt it. But filled with truth—now that I'll agree with."

The reverend tilted his head toward Sir Wilhelm, still asleep in the pew. "Seems your friend shares your view of my sermons, Miss Westcott."

Her mouth quirked in disgust. "I assure you he shares none of my views." She smiled at the reverend.

Faith liked his friend. Dajon found himself oddly pleased at that discovery.

"And you." Rev. Halloway turned toward Hope. "Are you of the same opinion?"

Hope glanced down, obviously unsure how to respond, and a moment of awkward silence settled upon them, conveniently interrupted by the approach of Mr. Mason.

Tanned from many hours working outdoors, Nathaniel tossed his brown hair out of his face and halted next to the reverend, but his gaze drifted over Hope in obvious admiration.

"Ah, Nathaniel." The reverend gripped the young man around the shoulder and shook him good-naturedly as a father would a son. "Ladies, may I introduce my ward, Mr. Nathaniel Mason."

Hope raised her nose. "We have met."

His gleeful expression sobered. "Yes, down at the docks."

"You are building a boat or some such thing." She shrugged and glanced away.

"A merchant brig, miss," Nathaniel corrected, lengthening his stance.

"Nathaniel is skilled at carpentry and shipbuilding," Rev. Halloway said proudly. "He has great plans to own his own merchant fleet someday."

Hope coughed and fingered the lace trim on her sleeves. "Can we go for a stroll in the park now?"

Annoyance flamed within Dajon at the sight of his friend being slighted in such a manner. Truth be told, by the standards of society, Nathaniel was not a man to be noticed. Born to a street harlot who died soon after, he grew up as an orphan on the streets of Charles Towne until Rev. Halloway took him in and raised him as his own son. But the boy—man now, for he was nigh five and twenty—possessed the kind spirit of a parson. Dajon had tried to enlist him as his ship's carpenter, but Nathaniel had plans of his own.

"In a moment, Hope." Faith adjusted her flowered hat, drawing Dajon's attention to the tiny scar on her neck. Most curious. He longed to know the cause of it.

"Shall we go?" She faced him, saw the direction of his gaze, then quickly bowed her head. Tugging on a lock of hair, she pressed it over the scar.

"Holy Chesterfield, is the service over already?" Sir Wilhelm thundered from behind them, staggering to his feet and wiping the drool from his chin.

❧

A wall of August heat struck Dajon as he escorted the ladies from the church onto Meeting Street.

Sir Wilhelm wiggled his way beside Faith and offered her his arm as he squinted against the bright sun.

She pretended not to notice and instead placed her fingers inside the crook of Dajon's arm. He patted them and glanced down at her, delighting in the way the sunlight sparkled like embers through the curls spiraling from her bonnet. He knew he had only Sir Wilhelm to thank for her attention, but at the moment, he would accept it any way it came.

Dajon drew in a deep breath, hoping to calm his passions, and instantly regretted it. A foul odor hung over the small town. Since most of the settlers were afraid to venture outside the city walls for fear of Indians, garbage and sewage piled up in the streets, not to mention the reek from the many animals that were slaughtered for meat. It reminded Dajon of the smell deep within his ship.

Snapping open his snuffbox, Sir Wilhelm inhaled a pinch of powder into each nostril as if that would mask the stench. "We should return for my carriage. I will not be seen traipsing around town like commoners."

"But we are commoners, Sir Wilhelm." Grace hurried her pace to step beside him, still clutching her Bible to her chest. "All of God's creatures are equal in His sight."

Ignoring her, Sir Wilhelm withdrew a handkerchief and dabbed at the sweat upon his brow.

"Why don't you go back and retrieve your carriage, Sir Wilhelm?" Faith tossed a glance in his direction. "We will wait for you here."

Dajon chuckled, but when Faith squeezed his arm, he quickly disguised it with a cough.

But Sir Wilhelm did not take the bait. Instead, he eased the cravat from his neck and whimpered something about the infernal heat.

Hope blew out a sigh that stirred the golden curls dangling on her forehead. "Can we not go to the park now?"

"That is where we are going, my dear," Faith responded.

As they proceeded past the massive white steeple of St. Philip's, Dajon looked up to see Borland barreling toward him.

The young lieutenant halted and came to attention. "Captain." His gaze scoured over the ladies. "I *thought* I would find you at church."

Dajon flinched. Was that disdain tainting his voice?

"You are needed on the ship at once."

Dajon's first thoughts were of the Red Siren, or perhaps another pirate, Stede Bonnet, one of Blackbeard's associates—a villain Dajon was determined to catch and one he'd heard frequented these waters. "Bonnet?"

"Nay, Captain. Word is he is still holed up in a cove somewhere north of here." Mr. Borland threw back his shoulders and puffed out his chest, no doubt for the ladies' benefit. "And Vane has not been sighted either."

"Oh, pirates, how exciting." Hope flung a hand to her bosom. Borland flashed a smile her way.

Dajon glanced around at his entourage. "Mr. Reginald Borland, may I present Sir Wilhelm Carteret. Mr. Borland is the first lieutenant aboard my ship." He followed with all the introductions, noting the way Borland's gaze lingered far too long upon each lady.

Hope stepped forward and extended her hand, offering the young lieutenant a flirtatious grin.

Sir Wilhelm dabbed the back of his neck and adjusted his white periwig. "Mr. Waite's first lieutenant, eh, Mr. Borland? How do you find the position?"

A church bell tolled in the distance.

Borland shifted his boots on the gravel. "It is good to be led by so great a commander." He flashed a grin.

"But would you not rather be a captain yourself?" Sir Wilhelm asked.

"Someday I shall, I hope." Borland still did not meet Dajon's gaze.

"Mr. Borland is a great seaman." Dajon slapped him on the back. "He has already passed the lieutenant's exam. It is only a matter of time before he is promoted, I am sure."

A carriage approached on their left, spewing up dirt and manure, and Dajon gestured for the ladies to move to the side of the road. The men followed as the *clip-clop* of the horses faded.

"Indeed? You have served in His Majesty's Navy for some time, Mr. Borland?" Sir Wilhelm continued to press poor Borland with his questions, giving Dajon pause. The man was up to something. But what?

"Since I was thirteen, sir. The captain and I joined together." Borland glanced at Dajon, and within his warm smile lay the friend Dajon had come to love as a brother. Fond memories sped through him of those early years when they had both run away to join the navy.

"And you, Mr. Waite?" Sir Wilhelm shifted his beady gaze to Dajon.

"I have served eleven years altogether. I took a leave from service after six years to join my father's merchant business but then returned to the navy five years ago."

"Did you not find the merchant business to your liking, Mr. Waite?" Sir Wilhelm asked.

Dajon gazed at the dirt-encrusted cobblestones and swallowed down a lump of bad memories. "I did not, sir."

"Hmm. A master and commander already, Mr. Waite. Quite impressive, is it not, Mr. Borland?"

Dajon studied his friend, expecting to see his approval, his agreement, anything but the stone-faced expression he wore. He shifted his stance before giving Sir Wilhelm a forced smile. "Quite."

Then, raising his chin, he nodded toward Dajon. "We must go, Captain. An important post from the Admiralty has just arrived."

"Of course." Dajon turned toward the women. "I fear I must leave you ladies in Sir Wilhelm's capable hands." His attempt to conceal a smile faltered, invoking an angry glance from Faith.

"I am sure we can find our way home, Sir Wilhelm." She turned to the man and waved him on in dismissal. "You must have far more pressing matters to attend to."

"Nonsense. I will not stand for it. It would be my utmost delight to escort you home." He proffered his elbow.

"But I thought we were going to the park," Hope whined, stamping her foot.

"If you will excuse me for a moment." Faith tugged on Dajon's arm, leading him to the side. "You will not leave me alone with this man." She ground out the words as if they sliced her lips.

"Why, Miss Westcott, I had no idea you cared so much for my company." He gave her a mischievous grin, noting the scowl she returned. "But. . ." He cocked his head. "I suggest you get used to Sir Wilhelm, for I fear the fortune you expect to make from your soap business will not be sufficient to care for you and your sisters. I have yet to see you make a single bar."

He winked at her and walked away.

As he made his way down the street with Borland marching at his side, his thoughts shot to the red-haired beauty he had left fuming behind him. Alarm made his skin bristle as another red-haired woman filled his mind. This one no beauty but a vixen, a murderer, a thief—the Red Siren. He must capture this woman pirate, whoever she was, and bring her to justice. But how?

A trap.

Yes, of course. He would spread information throughout town about the location of a treasure ship—a ship whose hull overflowed with jewels, a ship the Red Siren would not be able to resist. Then he would lie in wait and see if she took the bait.

CHAPTER 16

Closing the front door on Sir Wilhelm's appalled, bloated face, Faith blew out a sigh and leaned back against the oak slab.

"I'll be in my chamber," Grace shouted as she bounded up the stairs.

Sweeping the bonnet from her head, Hope giggled. "You shouldn't treat your betrothed with such disregard." A playful gleam danced across her eyes.

"He is not my betrothed, and I simply refuse to spend the day with that imbecile. 'Twas bad enough we were forced to endure his escort home—thanks to Mr. Waite." Insufferable man.

"But a headache? Could you not think of something more believable?"

Faith huffed and rubbed her temples, where a dull burning had formed. "Truth be told, the man does give me a headache." She laughed, and Hope joined her.

"Now we have the rest of the day to spend together." Hope's eyes lit up. "What shall we do?"

Yanking the pins from her hair, Faith ran her fingers through her curls, freeing them from their tight bindings and giving herself a minute to think. After Mr. Waite's skeptical taunt, she knew she had no choice but to devote her afternoon to creating at least the illusion of running a successful soap business. The man was pure exasperation! His suspicions were ruining her plans. But what to do with her sister? "I have just the thing." She forced a smile. "Why don't you help me make soap?"

"Make soap with you?" Hope snapped. "Why would I want to do that? 'Tis smelly and dirty."

"Come now, I assure you it will be enjoyable." Faith slid her arm inside Hope's and smiled. "And you can tell me all about what is going on in your life."

"No." Hope jerked from her grasp and backed away. "You promised to take me for a stroll in the park. You promised we would spend the entire day together, not slave away in some hot, sweaty kitchen."

"I can hardly take you to the park without proper escort. You have Mr. Waite to thank for that." Faith snorted. "And I fully intend to spend the day with you. That is why I am asking for your assistance."

"I should have known." Hope tugged on a lock of her hair and shook her head. "I should have known you would not follow through with your promise. Once again I find you are not to be trusted." She clung to the carved banister in the entrance hall, her chest heaving beneath her violet muslin gown.

Anger stormed through Faith. *Spoiled girl.* "Not to be trusted? How dare you? Why, I am doing this all for you. You and Grace."

"For me, you say?" Hope's laugh took on a caustic tone. She waved a hand back toward the kitchen. "This is not for me nor for Grace. You are doing this for yourself, and you know it. At least be honest about that." She sniffed and raised the back of her hand to her nose.

The words stung Faith in a place so deep within her heart that they left her speechless. She didn't know whether to scream or to cry. Finally, she inched toward Hope, giving her a soft, playful look. "We will have fun, I promise."

Hope's sapphire eyes glossed over with tears. "You are doing this for yourself, and you know it," she repeated, her accusing words echoing in Faith's ears like one of Morgan's shrill parodies.

Faith longed to tell Hope that she would love nothing more than to spend a day in town strolling through the park, enjoying her sister's company as if they were a pair of giddy schoolgirls. She wanted to tell her that her ruse of soap making was merely a cover for the real fortune Faith was acquiring on Hope's behalf.

But she didn't. All she said instead was, " 'Tis your choice. I must make soap. If you choose to join me, I would be most pleased. If not, you can hardly blame me for not spending time with you."

Daggers of fury shot from Hope's eyes as she spun on her heel and ran upstairs. The slamming of her chamber door boomed across the house like an ominous gong. Why did it seem that the harder Faith tried to help her sisters, the greater a mess she made of everything?

Sir Wilhelm Carteret crept into the corruption of his mother's sickroom. Though Miss Westcott had played the timid devotee today, he sensed a true regard, perhaps even affection, growing within her toward him. A pure lady, one inexperienced in the world, would certainly be somewhat frightened at the prospect of marriage—and in particular, the marriage bed. He grinned. That would explain her hesitant and even diffident behavior toward him, to be sure. He squeezed his nose against the miasma of stale breath, sweat, and disease that had taken residence within and now assailed him. A sickly moan reached his ears, and he swerved on his heels, suddenly rethinking his visit. But he must procure his mother's approval of the match before he pursued Miss Westcott further. And he knew that wouldn't be an easy task.

"Willy, is that you?" The cracked voice split the thick air in the room.

"Yes, Mother, 'tis I." Sir Wilhelm tensed and trudged toward the oak bed at the center of the dismal chamber.

"What are you doing sneaking around in the dark? Light a lamp and come forward." She hacked a moist cough before continuing. "So much like your father. He always was a rat who preferred the darkness."

Retrieving a lamp from the walnut desk, Sir Wilhelm thrust a stick of pinewood into the glowing embers in the fireplace and lit the wick. The fire, which his mother insisted be kept burning day and night despite the weather outside, kept the master chamber both stifling and filled with smoke. Sir Wilhelm strained for a breath of fresh air as he approached the bed, the lantern casting an eerie glow over the walnut desk and chairs that guarded the base of the window and a vanity squeezed into the right corner. Wilhelm rounded a velvet divan and tripped over a pewter basin that protruded from beneath the bed. It was well past emptying, and vile contents of the chamber pot sloshed over his left ankle. Beside it, a bitter vapor wafted from a glazed apothecary bowl full of the physician's latest mixture of herbs intended to cure his mother. A thin sheet of sunlight sliced through an opening in the heavy curtains and landed on the spilled contents of the chamber pot.

Setting the lantern on the bed stand, he sniffed and peered down at the swollen, pasty pallor of his mother's face. She had once been quite comely, but age and sickness, in addition to her constant disagreeable spirit, had sapped her beauty long ago. Dark, hollow eyes shot to his, ever spewing their venom wherever they landed.

On second thought, perhaps she had never been beautiful.

"What have you been about, Willy? I trust you have been down to the House of Assembly as I instructed. You need to ensure the proprietor's voice among these barbaric settlers." She struggled to sit, flinging out a shaky hand for his assistance. "There are rumblings of dissent—especially among those who call themselves the Goose Creek men. They want Carolina to become a British colony. Can you imagine? Then where would we be?"

Wilhelm reached behind his mother and assisted her into a sitting position, holding his breath against the stench of death that clung to her these past several years. "We would still have our landholdings, Mother."

Lady Eleanor Carteret, daughter of the Earl of Devenish, married to the son of Sir George Carteret, one of the original proprietors of the realm of Carolina, squared her shoulders and lifted her regal chin in the air as if her bed were the throne of England. But her breath came in short gasps, and she collapsed on the pillow behind her, breaking the facade of superiority that had more times than not sparked fear in all those around her.

"Land without power is meaningless. There is plenty of land in this new world for everyone." She pointed a crooked finger at him. "Power is what will secure our interest and our future."

Wilhelm turned his head and sneezed, his nose burning in the infested room.

She gestured to a mug on the bed stand. "Hand me my elixir and tell me your news of Parliament."

Wilhelm grabbed the mug, took a whiff, and nearly gagged at the pungent odor, then placed it in his mother's trembling hands. He held his nose. "What is that putrid stench?" He plucked his snuffbox from his pocket.

" 'Tis the medicines Dr. Kingston has prescribed for me. With these and the weekly bleedings, he guarantees my full recovery." She took a sip, sending the loose skin of her face folding in on itself.

"He will guarantee anything as long as you pay him." Wilhelm sniffed a speck of powder then slumped his shoulders, allowing the calm

139

sensation to filter through him.

"Enough of that. Tell me what is happening in the council."

"I did not attend today. I had some business at Admiral Westcott's home."

"Pray tell, what business? Unless you have overcome your seasickness and plan on following in your grandfather's grand footsteps." She scrutinized him. "Not that you could. I fear you are not made of the same stout material."

"Admiral Westcott has been called to Italy, and. . ." Wilhelm ran a hand under his nose.

"Quit sniffing and be out with it!"

He straightened his back. "He has promised me his daughter Faith's hand in marriage when he returns."

"As wife? Finally. I thought you would never draw the eye of a decent lady. Now perchance I will see grandchildren before I die."

Wilhelm fidgeted with a wrinkle in the sheets by his knee.

"Although an admiral's daughter is certainly beneath your station, I suppose a man like you cannot be too particular." His mother pushed a spike of her wiry gray hair behind her.

Wilhelm shifted the muscles in his back beneath his mother's insults. He should be used to them by now, but for some reason, her words always hit their mark. "Regardless of her lineage, I assure you, she is a fine match. Beautiful, intelligent, strong. You would like her."

"Perhaps." Closing her eyes, she leaned back onto the mound of pillows. "But it would have been nice to see you joined with a lady of your own class. Especially after all I have done for you. Ensuring your place in Parliament and among the lord proprietors instead of your Uncle Phillip. Do you realize the risks I took? The powerful people I crossed?" She coughed and held her chest as if she were taking her last breath. "Without me you would be nothing but a sniveling incompetent. You know everything I have done—everything I ever do—is for you." A tear escaped her eye and weaved a crooked trail around line and wrinkle.

"I know, Mother, and I am eternally grateful. I owe you everything." Without her strength, her brains, her devious plots, his uncle Phillip would have taken over as head of the Carteret family.

Yet he tired of the invisible chain that held him locked to her, as if the umbilical cord had never been severed. It sickened him as much as empowered him.

Lady Eleanor huffed. "Nevertheless, I will be pleased to see you married." She looked away. "But you must promise to attend Parliament and follow my instructions to the mark. The future of this family depends on you."

Wilhelm squeezed his mother's hand. "I will, Mother; I promise." Yet no sooner did his hopes rise upon the wind than thoughts of Captain Waite shot them down.

"Now what ails you, Willy?"

"I fear there is another suitor who might divert Miss Westcott's affections from me."

"How could any woman choose another over you?"

Wilhelm had wondered the same thing himself, but after the past few encounters with Captain Waite and Miss Westcott, it seemed obvious the girl was far too innocent to understand the crafty manipulation and venomous charm of the commander.

"I daresay, then." His mother gave a haughty snort. "She is not as wise as you make her out to be. Dismissing your affections. Upon my word, 'tis unheard of. Who is this suitor?"

"A commander in the Royal Navy, a callow, ignoble fellow."

"A lowly commander? What do you expect from an admiral's daughter? She is not worthy of you." She waved her bony hand through the air. "Let her go."

"I cannot, Mother. I must have her. I have never wanted anything so badly."

True to form, his mother took his hand in hers. "There, there, Willy. There, there. You shall have her, then. No woman dares to shun my dear Willy."

"What am I to do, Mother?" Having accomplished his goal, Wilhelm pushed back from her aged, decaying body. "I cannot force her affections."

"Perhaps not, but you can rid yourself of the competition."

Wilhelm was pleased to see that his mother's desires ran along the same twisted lines as his own. "But how?"

"We must eliminate him by cunning. Dig up his skeletons. Everyone has something reprehensible in his past. Find his and expose it for all to see."

She gripped his hand, her fingers like icy claws. "Ruin the man. Destroy his career." Her eyes narrowed into the cold slits of a hawk hunting its prey. "Do whatever you have to in order to get what you want."

CHAPTER 17

Running her sleeve across her moist brow, Faith stirred the thick cauldron of lye and pork fat boiling in a large kettle atop the fire. She'd had no idea making soap could be so difficult and tedious. A sweltering August wind steamed in through the open door and, joining with the heat from the fire, transformed the kitchen into a giant furnace. She felt like a Sunday goose being roasted alive. As she continued to stir the bubbling fat, the muscles in her arms burned with a searing pain that matched the growing agony in her heart over the argument she'd had with Hope earlier that day.

But now as Faith laid down the greasy ladle and patted her neck with the hem of the stained apron hanging at her waist, she found the task anything but enjoyable, and she supposed she couldn't blame Hope for not wanting to partake of this noxious mess.

She lifted a strand of her curly hair to her nose and cringed. The stench of lard saturated her. Grabbing a ribbon from the table, she tied up her thick tresses and took a step outside for some fresh air.

Shielding her eyes from the bright sun sinking behind the oak trees that lined the fence, Faith watched Lucas brush down a horse across the way in the barn. When he glanced her way, she smiled, and he returned the gesture.

Closing her eyes for a moment, she allowed the slight breeze to cool the fiery skin of her neck and face before she returned to the kitchen.

Staring at the gurgling brew, Faith hoped she had put in the right amount of lye, or the soap would not harden correctly. From what she had learned from the ladies in town, soap making was an exact science and took years to perfect, and from the looks of things, it would indeed take her that long before she could produce one decent batch of soap. All her prior attempts had ended in a foul-smelling puddle of slop, not fit to wash the cutlery with, let alone a person. Last month she'd been forced to send Lucas on a two-day journey to Beaufort to buy soap from one of the soap makers in town so she could sell it here in Charles Towne as her own. But she could not afford to be without Lucas for that long again, not when she was so close to acquiring the fortune she needed. Oh, why had she not chosen some other craft like perfume making or quilting?

A deep chuckle sounded from the door. "So ye truly is tryin' yer hand at soap, mistress?"

Faith flung a flustered look over her shoulder at Lucas, whose large frame shadowed the doorway. "The ever-suspicious Mr. Waite dropped his glove of challenge upon me today. I had no choice but to accept."

"He did, did he?" Another hearty chuckle bubbled through the room like the aroma of her fatty stew.

"You find that amusing?"

"Aye, to see the"—he glanced both ways behind him—"notorious pirate captain the Red Siren covered wit' grease and smellin' like a rancid pig, all due to a simple comment from Mr. Waite. Aye, I do find it amusin', the power he holds over ye."

Faith spun around. "He holds no power over me." She tossed the ladle onto the table. Brown sticky globs splattered across the surface. Faith wiped the sweat from the back of her neck. "Other than the noose, I suppose." She gave Lucas a sassy look. "And it will be your neck, too, if we are caught. Perchance then you might not find it so amusing?"

The grin on Lucas's mouth did not falter.

Faith blew out a sigh, relieving her tension. "How else do you expect me to prove to the man where my fortune comes from when it suddenly appears?"

He shrugged. "Seems to me such a man would never buy such a ludicrous tale anyway."

Faith sank into a chair with a huff. "I fear you are correct. But I must at least make a pretense of producing some soap, whether he buys the tale or not."

She batted at a pesky fly that must have found her new scent alluring. "But how else to convince him?"

"All he be knowin', mistress, is that the Red Siren be a lady with red

144

hair." He cocked his head. "That don't prove nothin'."

"Good heavens, that is it." Faith shot to her feet. "I know exactly how to divert any suspicions he may have of my even remotely being the Red Siren."

Lucas's brow furrowed.

Outside the window, Molly strode by the kitchen, hoisting a basket of vegetables atop her head. Following Faith's gaze, Lucas watched her over his shoulder until she disappeared into the house.

Faith cocked her head and grinned. "No doubt, she'll be coming here soon to cook supper."

"I knows."

"Why don't you stay and talk to her, Lucas?"

"She don't want to be talkin' none to me, mistress." Disappointment tugged the corners of his mouth downward.

"I would not be so sure." Faith grabbed the ladle and shuffled back to the boiling pot.

"Oh, saints preserve us. Whatever is that smell?" Molly's voice sliced through the steamy room, and Faith turned to see the tiny cook push past Lucas and explode into the room like a firecracker.

Faith shook her head. How could so much energy be contained in such a small package? "I am making soap, if you must know."

"Not in my kitchen, you're not." Molly set her basket down on the table and threw a hand to her nose.

"Where else do you suggest?"

Lucas stood just inside the door, his gaze taking in Molly as if she were the queen of some exotic land.

Following Faith's glance, Molly turned to the large groomsman. "What you grinnin' at, you oversize fool?"

"I's grinnin' at you, Miss Molly." Lucas crossed his arms over his chest.

Molly's tongue went uncharacteristically still as if the heat in the room had melted it. She stared at Lucas dumbfounded, the attraction between them like a grappling hook pulling one ship to another and neither able to prevent it. "Well, stop it before I wipe that smile off yer face," Molly shot back.

"Good day to ye, then, Miss Molly." Lucas nodded and headed out the door.

"Good day, Mr. Corwin."

Faith gave Molly a crafty look.

"Now don't you be grinnin' at me, neither." Molly began unloading her vegetables onto the table. Ripe tomatoes, green beans, okra, carrots, and summer squash.

Faith's mouth watered at the sight. She had not eaten since breakfast that morning. Resuming her stirring, she wondered why the expected froth had not appeared in her mixture. Flies began to swarm around it as if it were naught but bubbling horse manure. It certainly smelled as if it was. "My soap is nearly done boiling, Molly. Then I shall pour it into the frames and be out of your way."

"I dunno who you trying to fool, Miss Faith, but you ain't made a bar of soap in your life."

"Perhaps, but there is a first time for everything." Faith smiled, remembering the complete look of adoration on Lucas's face when he had looked at Molly. Swinging around, Faith laid down her ladle and wiped the sweat from her brow with her apron. A first time for soap making and a first time for love. "I do not know if I should speak of this or not."

"Then don't." Molly directed a stern glance her way. "I ain't in for no gossip."

"It isn't gossip." Lucas would certainly be furious, but she hated to see these two precious friends of hers lose out on something wonderful—something meant to be—due to pure stubbornness. She might as well just blurt it out. "Lucas is sweet on you."

Silence, save for the crackle of the fire and the hum of insects, settled over the room.

Molly did not look up, but a slight quiver in her bottom lip gave her away.

"Mr. Corwin? Hogwash. I won't be hearin' talk like that."

"Come now, surely you have noticed the way he looks at you."

"He looks the same way at the horses." Molly laughed.

Faith threw a hand to her hip. "He is handsome, strong, healthy, and a good worker, Miss Molly. He would make a fine husband."

"Husband?" Molly flinched, and the whites of her eyes widened against the encroaching darkness. "By all that is holy, what d'you think yer doing—matchmaking? You who swears never to marry unless you're forced to. I declare, I never thought I'd see the day."

"I just think you two would make a good match, 'tis all."

Molly's expression sobered. She set down the squash and eased into a chair. "I tells you, Miss Faith. I seen a lot of pain in my life. And it all comes from caring 'bout people."

Faith took a chair beside the cook and gave her an understanding nod. After all, hadn't all of Faith's pain come from things that had happened to those she loved? But it suddenly occurred to her that she really knew nothing about this woman whom she had grown to care for these past months.

"Molly, tell me about your past." Though her voice was soft and pleading, Faith worried her words came out more as an order than a request.

Flinching, Molly straightened her back then gazed at the floor.

As a servant would beneath a harsh command.

A servant, not a slave, for the admiral paid her well for her position. But Faith considered Miss Molly more a friend than a servant. Did Molly know that? Or did the shackles of slavery bind her heart from ever giving itself freely to anyone in authority over her? "You may tell me only if you wish." Faith laid her hand over Molly's. "We are friends."

Molly raised her gaze and smiled. "I was torn from my ma and pa when I was jest ten, Miss Faith." Her smile faded. "Sold as a slave to a landowner in Barbados. A kind family. But by the time I was sixteen, the mistress o' the house got it in her head to be jealous o' the way her husband was lookin' at me. So they sold me."

"How awful." Faith swallowed. The idea of slavery repulsed her. She could not imagine anyone finding it acceptable, let alone civilized. Yet how different was slavery from what had happened to her older sister, Charity?

"Sold me to a vicious sugarcane farmer on Jamaica, a spiteful man, miss," Molly continued. "He did things to me I'd rather not say."

Faith grasped both of Molly's hands and squeezed them. "The only way I survived was by makin' friends wit' the other slaves. They became like family to me." Molly raised her moist gaze to Faith. "But then one day, I watched my owner beat my dearest friend to death for stealin' a banana from a tree. So's I ran away. Left the only people I loved, once again." She shuddered beneath a quiet sob. "That's when I met up with the Franklins.

They brought me here to the colonies and taught me to cook. But more important, they taught me 'bout the Lord. That's when I gave my life to Jesus. 'Tain't been the same since." Her sudden grin quickly faded. "But o' course, they both got killed in the Indian wars."

Faith closed her eyes against the burning behind them and swallowed. How could this slight woman have endured so much agony in one life? And yet, oddly, she still clung to a faith that spoke of the goodness of God. Perhaps it was all she had left to cling to—this hope of a caring God, a hope that would surely shrivel beneath the next disaster.

"You see, Miss Faith, everyone I've ever loved been taken from me. I can't stand the pain no more. The only One who will never leave me is Jesus, but I ain't attaching meself to no one else—no man 'specially."

Faith could understand Molly's fear of getting close to Lucas, but she knew her first mate. He would never hurt Molly, would never betray her. Faith forced down an unseemly chuckle at how absurd, though true, her approbation was of a man who was a good groomsman but a better pirate.

"Molly, I am so sorry." She gave the cook's hand a squeeze. "I had no idea you had suffered so much."

"Not yer fault, miss." Her dark cheeks flushing, Molly withdrew her hand and stood. She stomped across the room, grabbed a knife from a counter, and began chopping the heads off carrots as if they represented her ex-owners.

Faith laid a gentle hand on her arm, stopping her. "But I beg you, do not deny yourself love and happiness out of a fear born from other people's cruelty."

A skeptical look crossed Molly's face, but she said nothing.

"Should you not be trusting God?" Faith asked with all sincerity then suddenly cringed. Where had that come from? God had certainly not proven Himself trustworthy in her own life and especially not in Molly's.

Molly laughed then, a warm, hearty chuckle that filled the room. "Well, mercy me, do you hear yerself, Miss Faith? 'Tain't no hope for that batch of soap, but there may be hope for you, after all."

⌒

Holding a lantern, Faith knelt in the kitchen by her soap crates to investigate the vile brew's progress. It was well past midnight, and she couldn't sleep. Perhaps it was because of the unusually strained atmosphere at supper that night that stretched across the dining room like a rigid spar. With both of her sisters angry at her, Faith had done her best to ease tensions with light chatter and whimsical jests, but to no avail.

Perhaps it was her fear of the noose, brought on by the captain's suspicion of her piracy. Or perhaps it was that she was beginning to realize, as she examined the molten slop in the crates, that she had no idea how to make soap.

"Confound it all, what is that smell?" Mr. Waite's deep voice startled Faith. Springing up, she faced him, one hand subconsciously reaching for her cutlass, which, of course, was not there. Instead, she flung the hand to her breast.

"My apologies, Miss Westcott, I saw the light and wondered who might still be awake at this hour." He bowed and sauntered into the room, looking ever so dashing in his blue uniform.

" 'Tis twice now I have caught you wandering about in the kitchen at night."

"I could say the same of you, Miss Westcott." He raised his nose and took a whiff, his forehead wrinkling. "But the last time we met here, the aroma in the room was much more pleasant. Methinks I should be relieved that I missed whatever was served for supper."

" 'Tis not supper you smell, Mr. Waite, but the batch of soap I made today." Pride lifted her voice, false as it was.

"Indeed?" He approached, the hint of a smirk curving his lips.

Stepping aside, she gestured toward the wooden crates filled with her greasy concoction and prayed Mr. Waite knew no more about soap than she did.

He leaned over them but quickly shrank back as if someone had punched him. "I do hope you intend to add scented oil, Miss Westcott, or I fear you've created the cure for overpopulation."

"How dare you?" Faith stormed. "I have already scented them. What you smell is all part of the curing process." She had no idea why they continued to emit such a foul odor.

His boots scuffed over the floor behind her. Warm breath heated her cheek, and she winced at her own stench. She had soaked in a hot bath for hours—Molly had insisted on providing oceans of hot fresh water in hopes of removing the smell—and scrubbed her skin and hair until they were squeaky, but for some reason, the abhorrent odor still clung to her.

But why did she care what Mr. Waite thought?

"New perfume, Miss Westcott? I believe I may not succumb so easily to your charms tonight." He took another whiff and then withdrew slightly.

Faith spun around. "Believe me, Mr. Waite, when I tell you that I have since regretted that moment of insanity last evening when we nearly . . .we nearly. . ."

He grinned. "Then you have nothing to fear from me."

Faith studied his eyes, those crisp ocean blue eyes that seemed to hold as many secrets as the depths of the sea.

Does he know? Is he toying with me?

He hid his feelings well behind a wall of sarcasm and wit. Her gaze drifted down to the strong lines of his jaw shadowed with a hint of evening stubble. One lock of hair hung over his left ear, and she wondered if under his facade of obedience and dutifulness there didn't exist a streak of rebellion just like this one mutinous strand.

Her heart took on a rapid pace as he returned her stare with equal intensity. Yes, there was more to this man than he revealed. Something untamed, something dangerous lurked behind his eyes—eyes that were now fixated upon her lips. He swallowed—the long, hard swallow of a man dying of thirst.

Truth be told, Faith's throat had gone dry as well. A flush of heat blasted over her, though the coals in the fire were naught but embers now. What was wrong with her?

Nevertheless, she would not back down from this man, whatever game he was playing.

He cocked his head slightly and grinned—not his usual sardonic playful grin, but a warm, tender one. Then, reaching up, he caressed her cheek with his thumb and cupped his hand around her jaw.

Faith closed her eyes beneath the heady sensations that swirled through her.

When she opened them, his lips hovered over hers.

"I thought I had naught to fear from you," she whispered.

"I thought you had forsaken your insanity."

He drew closer, and Faith found herself suddenly wishing he would either arrest her or kiss her. Either way, this madness would end.

"Miss Faith! Miss Faith!" Edwin's shaky voice snapped her back to reality. She jerked away from Mr. Waite.

Edwin barreled into the kitchen, his belly quivering.

"What is it, Edwin? Whatever is the matter?" She darted to him, alarm spiking through her.

" 'Tis Miss Hope," Edwin managed between gasps.

"Hope?" Faith had checked on her not three hours past, and she had been fast asleep. "Is she sick?"

"A man came to the door." Edwin's gaze flitted between Faith and Mr. Waite.

"What man? What of Hope?" Faith grabbed his shoulders and shook him.

"A friend, a footman from the Brewton home." Edwin plopped into a chair.

Mr. Waite came alongside Faith. "What did he say, man? Spit it out."

"Miss Hope is in trouble."

Faith could make no sense of his jabbering. "In her chamber?"

"Nay, miss." Edwin glanced up at her, a look of hopelessness tugging at his eyes. "Downtown at the Pink House Tavern."

CHAPTER 18

Pressing his handkerchief to his nose, Sir Wilhelm strutted into the dark, sooty room of the tavern. A stout man with greasy hair coiling around his shoulders bumped into him, his tankard of ale sloshing over the sides. "Look out where yer goin'," he slurred.

Sir Wilhelm pushed the man aside and wiped his handkerchief over his velvet waistcoat where the lout had touched him. "How dare you, you vile sot. Don't you know who I am?" Sir Wilhelm offered the man a vision of his profile as he adjusted his periwig, but the sailor simply gave a derisive snort and went his way.

Of all the. . . Sir Wilhelm huffed. This was precisely the reason he never graced these filthy havens with his genteel presence. His mother had been right. Commoners never appreciated the immense responsibility of those in authority nor that the freedoms they enjoyed were only by the sacrifice and grace of their lords. How could they, with such miniscule, narrow brains?

Sir Wilhelm sniffed, his nose burning against the rancid alcohol and body odor that seeped through the air like a fetid fog. As he peered across the shadowy room, littered with indescribable rabble, bloodshot eyes gave him cursory glances before returning to their ale. Why, dressed as he was in black velvet breeches fringed in gold, white satin shirt, and fur-trimmed waistcoat, surely even these miscreants recognized nobility. At least the proprietor of this devil's haven should greet him and lead him to the best seat in the house—he glanced over the crumb-encrusted, liquor-saturated, marred tables and scrunched his nose—if there were such a seat.

He tossed his nose in the air. The devil take them all. Could they not tell he had money to spend—more money than the whole lot of them put together? Hesitating, he longed to turn on his leather heels and storm out. That would show them. But he had heard that Mr. Waite's first lieutenant, Mr. Borland, frequented this vulgar alehouse, and he must speak to him. If Sir Wilhelm's intuition was correct—as it usually was—he might find an ally in Borland.

Sir Wilhelm took another step, holding one hand aloft, and scanned the filthy faces. He had hoped to arrive sooner, before the entire building crawled with vermin, but he had crossed paths with Miss Hope and that pretentious peacock Lord Falkland. Why Mr. Waite allowed the young girl to roam the streets at night with such objectionable company, Sir Wilhelm could not understand. From the looks of her, she had already imbibed too much alcohol. He supposed he should have stepped in and escorted her home, but alas, the admiral had not chosen him as guardian. Instead, he had chosen that nincompoop Waite, and the admiral would have to pay the price for his stupidity.

In the far corner, a blur of blue navy coats crossed Sir Wilhelm's vision. Starting toward them, he weaved among the tables, careful not to touch anything—or anyone—but angry voices slithered out like snakes nonetheless, sinking their insulting fangs into his conscience.

"Look, gents, if it ain't our proprietor. Have ye come down from yer castle to the mire to visit the peasants?" one man trumpeted.

"Where were ye when we needed ye?" another man taunted. "When the Yamasee attacked and stole all our food?"

"Ain't you supposed to be protectin' us and not stealin' our money and land?" a doxy spat at him, the mounds of her breasts quivering above her tight-fitting bodice.

Ignoring the taunts, Sir Wilhelm kept his eyes straight ahead, his gaze above the squabbling riffraff. He and the other proprietors had done all they could to protect the settlers against the massive Indian attack. But what were they supposed to do in face of such a savage enemy? Unappreciative louts!

Mr. Borland turned as Sir Wilhelm approached the table. Setting his mug down, the young officer rose and brushed the crumbs from his coat. "Sir Wilhelm, how good to see you." Lines formed between his narrowed eyes. No doubt he was surprised to see Sir Wilhelm in such a debased place.

Sir Wilhelm nodded in greeting as relief lifted his shoulders. Finally, someone who offered him the respect he deserved.

"Sir Wilhelm Carteret." Mr. Borland gestured toward his friends, who had also stood. "May I present Mr. Copeland and Mr. Willis."

"Sir Wilhelm is a descendant of one of the original proprietors of Carolina," Borland added.

The men bowed. "A pleasure, sir," Mr. Copeland said.

Sir Wilhelm nodded in agreement then faced Mr. Borland. "May I speak with you alone? 'Tis a matter of grave importance."

"Of course." He turned toward his friends, raised his brows, and jerked his head to the right.

Frowning, they grabbed their mugs, nodded toward Sir Wilhelm, and shuffled away.

"Won't you have a seat, Sir Wilhelm?" Mr. Borland gestured toward a chair beside his and then snapped his fingers at a barmaid across the room. "A drink, perhaps?"

"Thank you." Sir Wilhelm flapped his handkerchief across the chair, scattering the noxious crumbs. But upon further inspection of the seat, laden with globs of unidentifiable origin, he spread out the cloth and sat upon it. "It is I who shall buy you a drink, Mr. Borland, if you'll allow me." He eyed the near-empty mug of ale in front of the man. "Perhaps some rum?"

Borland's grin told him the lieutenant enjoyed his liquor. Perfect. A couple of glasses of rum, and Sir Wilhelm would have the man agreeing to anything.

The barmaid arrived with one hand on her bounteous hip and a look of boredom that her painted lips failed to disguise. Sir Wilhelm plucked a shilling from his pouch and dropped it into her sweaty hand. "Bottle of rum, if you please, and keep the change." The shiny gold lit a greedy fire in her blue eyes. Like flies to the light, these rustics could be controlled with a simple coin. Sir Wilhelm shook his head as she scampered away.

"Begging your pardon, sir, but what brings you here?" Mr. Borland sat back in his chair and folded his hands over his stomach, drumming one set of fingers over the other.

Sir Wilhelm noted the glaze covering Mr. Borland's eyes and gave him his most congenial smile. "I believe we have a common interest."

Borland cocked his head and narrowed his gaze. "I cannot imagine what that could be."

The barmaid returned with an open bottle of rum and two glasses, and Sir Wilhelm quickly poured some into Borland's glass and slid it over to him.

"It concerns your commander, Mr. Waite." Sir Wilhelm wrinkled his nose against a new foul odor wafting his way as he tipped the bottle to his own glass.

"Ah...yes. The great Mr. Waite." Borland gave a sardonic chortle and reached for his rum. "What do you wish to do, give him another medal, have a parade in his honor, or perhaps appoint him to Parliament?" He took a swig.

Sir Wilhelm grinned. Just as he had suspected. "Have another drink." He poured another shot into Borland's cup.

Borland grabbed it, tossed it to the back of his throat, then set the glass down. "I don't mean any disrespect, sir, 'tis just that Dajon—I mean Mr. Waite and I do not always agree on things." He twisted his thick sandy mustache between two fingers and stared at his empty glass.

The sounds of the tavern surged around Sir Wilhelm like a hundred ignorant voices pounding in his head. He rubbed his temples. How did people relax in such a place? Even before the thought left him, the crash of a table, the blast of insults, and the smack of fist to face sounded from the front door as a fight broke out. Borland peered through the haze toward the commotion.

"Mr. Waite has cheated you out of promotions that should have been yours, has he not?" Sir Wilhelm drew Borland's attention back to him.

Borland snapped his gaze back, grabbed the bottle, and poured himself some rum. He shrugged.

"No need to reply. I have keen eyes for this sort of thing." Sir Wilhelm plucked out his snuffbox. "And I can also tell a man of worth when I see one. A man with the wits and courage to command." Taking a pinch of the black powder, he sniffed some up each nostril then snorted against the burn. "And a man who is none of those things."

Borland's dark gaze wandered over Sir Wilhelm like a bird in flight trying to find a place to land. His lips wrinkled in a half smile.

Sir Wilhelm sighed. "You, sir, are the one who should be in command of the HMS *Enforcer*, not that ninny Waite." Withdrawing another handkerchief from his waistcoat, he wiped the rim of his glass—only God knew if they ever washed these things—and took a sip. The liquor sped a burning trail down his throat, instantly warming his belly. "Let me guess. He is the type of man who sidles up to the Admiralty like a trollop to a plush merchant—just as he did with Admiral Westcott."

Borland swayed and raised his glass. "But what is it to you, if I may ask?" His wavering cup finally found his mouth, and he took a sip.

A string of foul curses muddied the air behind Sir Wilhelm, and he cringed. The sooner he could leave this place, the better. " 'Tis only that I am a man of justice, as well as a proprietor who wishes our city to be protected by the best man possible. Truth be told, I would sleep far better knowing you were in charge."

Borland leaned his elbows on the table. "Well, what's to be done about it?" he slurred, shrugging again.

"Come now, Borland. You must think like a leader, like a commander." Sir Wilhelm slapped him on the back, nearly toppling him. "Pray tell, how do you confront an obstacle, Mr. Borland?"

"I remove it."

"Precisely!"

Mr. Borland labored to his feet, wobbled, then clung to the edge of the table and thrust his face at Sir Wilhelm. "What are you suggesting, sir? I will do no harm to Dajon. I have called him friend for far too long."

"Harm? Nay, of course not." Sir Wilhelm scrunched his face into what he hoped was a look of complete abhorrence. "Sit down, Borland, if you please." He stood and eased the man down into his chair then wiped his hands with his handkerchief.

Sir Wilhelm reluctantly took his seat again. "All I am suggesting is that we *persuade* Mr. Waite to break some naval code or rule—something that will do him no more harm than to get him dismissed."

Mr. Borland threw his head back and let out a loud chortle that drew the gaze of the crowd around them. Placing his elbows on the table, he leaned toward Sir Wilhelm. "You do not know Mr. Waite, sir. He would never break a rule."

Disgust soured in Wilhelm's mouth. "Egad, he's not God, Borland. Perhaps that is why you cannot defeat him. You think he is some divine being. But I assure you, he is human like you and me."

Hot air blasted in from the open window. The light from the flame flickered across Borland's inebriated expression, twisting his features into a tortured snarl. Sir Wilhelm snorted. How did these navy officers manage themselves in battle?

"He has weaknesses, has he not?" Sir Wilhelm held two fingers to his nose.

From the other side of the room, the eerie sound of an aged fiddle screeched a ribald tune that grated over Sir Wilhelm like the talons of a huge bird. *What is his weakness, lad? Tell me before I go mad in this place.*

Swirling his glass, Borland stared inquisitively into the rum as if it contained the answer to the question.

"Aye." He finally nodded and lifted his gaze, a hazy gleam in his eye. "He has a weakness for the ladies, I am told. Some tragedy from his past involving a woman."

A slow grin spread over Sir Wilhelm's lips. Since Mr. Waite had only recently arrived from England and no one knew of him here in the colonies, Sir Wilhelm had dispatched one of his men overseas to gather what information he could on the good Mr. Waite's past. From the sounds of it, he would not be disappointed with the results. Power surged through him, strengthening him. Things were going better than expected. He leaned toward Mr. Borland. "Pray tell, what is the consequence for an officer in His Majesty's Navy for, say. . .ravishing a woman?"

Borland shrugged. "Depends on the woman, I suppose. If she were a lady, possibly death. If she were a trollop, most likely no charges would be leveled. But if she were a decent woman, an officer could be cashiered."

"Cashiered?"

"Dismissed in disgrace."

"Perfect." Sir Wilhelm adjusted his periwig and leaned back in his chair. Borland belched and shook his head. "Again, sir, you deceive yourself. Mr. Waite would never commit such an act." He slumped in his chair.

Sir Wilhelm gritted his teeth. How long must he spoon-feed this buffoon? "Do you want command of the ship, or do you not, Mr. Borland?"

"Even with him gone, there is no assurance I will be made commander." Borland drummed his fingers over the ale-sodden table.

Sir Wilhelm raised one eyebrow, feigning patience. "You forget to whom you speak, my dear sir. My grandfather was the comptroller of the navy. My family still has the ear of the Admiralty."

Mr. Borland raised his shoulders. His glassy eyes locked on Sir Wilhelm's. "But why would you do this for me?"

"As I said, I would sleep much better with you patrolling the coast."

Borland nodded, his expression lifted with hope, but then his smile suddenly sank. "Still, we must get him to do the deed, and I assure you, he will not."

Sir Wilhelm huffed. "I can assure you, it matters not what Mr. Waite does or does not do."

Borland's inquisitive gaze met his. A slick smile alighted upon his lips and spread until it seemed to take over his face.

After glancing around them, Sir Wilhelm laid his handkerchief on the table, placed his arm over it, and leaned toward Borland. "Now this is what we shall do."

CHAPTER 19

"Confound it all." Dajon stormed from the kitchen out into the yard still shrouded in darkness. The scent of rain stung his nose, soon stolen by the smell of horses and sweet hay emanating from the stables. Thunder rumbled, sending energy crackling through the air like a cannon about to fire.

Faith's footsteps pounded after him. "The Pink House? Do you know the place?"

Yes, he knew the place, but he had no intention of informing her that it was the most nefarious tavern in town.

Turning to her, he gripped her shoulders and gave her his most confident look. "Never fear. I'll wake Lucas and take him with me. I assure you, I will bring your sister home safely."

"What sort of place is it?" A mixture of fear and anger raged in her eyes, and he longed to ease her pain, to replace it with the joy and admiration he'd seen in her gaze just minutes ago.

"Please do not worry, Miss Westcott." Releasing her, Dajon headed toward the servants' quarters above the kitchen.

"Mr. Waite, I demand you answer me." She marched after him.

Dajon halted and faced her. "It is no place for a lady. That is all I will tell you." A look of frantic despair marred her comely features, softening Dajon's harsh manner. He eased a lock of hair from her face then shook off her bewitching spell and swerved back around. "Go in the house. I will handle this."

"I will do no such thing!"

"I do not have time for your insolence." He entered the small brick house and took the stairs two at a time, praying she would listen to him but all the while knowing she would not.

Minutes later when he dashed into the stables, a sleepy Lucas on his heels, he found a lantern hanging from a hook on the wall and Faith saddling the second of two horses.

"I thank you for your assistance, Miss Westcott, but now I must insist you go into the house."

"She is my sister, Mr. Waite." She cinched the final strap beneath the horse's belly. "I suggest you stop wasting time arguing with me."

Dajon squeezed the bridge of his nose, where a dull pain began to burn. Impudent woman. He had a difficult enough task ahead of him without adding another female to protect.

"I'd let 'er come if I was you, Mr. Waite," Lucas said, leading another horse from its stall. "She can fend fer 'erself."

"Not where we are going." Images of Marianne lying limp in his arms, blood spilling from her mouth, stormed across his vision. He would not bring another lady into a dangerous situation.

Faith adjusted the bit in the horse's mouth and threw her hand to her hip. "You may be accustomed to having your orders obeyed aboard your ship, Captain, but this is not the HMS *Enforcer*, nor am I one of your crew."

Withdrawing a handkerchief, Dajon dabbed at the sweat on his throat then twisted the cloth into a knot, longing to stuff it into her sassy mouth.

"If you leave without me, I shall follow you anyway. Isn't it better I ride under your protection than all alone?"

Fuming, Dajon turned and assisted Lucas with the final horse, realizing he had lost the battle. "You will do what I say when we get there, or mark my words, I shall tie you to a tree if I must in order to keep you out of trouble. Do you understand?" He snapped his gaze to her.

"Yes, sir." She saluted him stiffly then lifted her skirts and swung onto her horse.

As they galloped through the dark streets, Dajon's fears stung him like the tiny pelts of rain that sliced through the night sky. He wondered in what condition he would find Hope. Foolish girl. Had she gone there alone? If so, it would be unlikely she remained unscathed. In fact, it was more likely that she had been robbed of her purity, along with her money, and then tossed into a ditch.

And what of Faith? He glanced at her as she galloped beside him, as at ease upon a horse as she seemed strolling in the garden. Though fear tightened the corners of her mouth, courage and resolution held them in a thin line. He had never met a woman like her. So different from timid, sweet Marianne.

On the other side of Faith, Lucas kept a steady pace, as if the two had ridden in haste side by side many times before. The sight alarmed Dajon. The more he became acquainted with Faith, the more he could see the markings of a pirate within her: commanding, confident, rebellious, and greedy. Not a greed for gold, but for whatever would purchase freedom for her and her sisters. He nearly laughed at the thought. Impossible.

Great guns, he'd almost kissed her tonight—again. Her allure was intoxicating—too heady for him to resist. And that frightened him the most.

His hair had loosened from his queue, and he shook it free, allowing the rising wind to clear his head. He mustn't think of Faith now nor the Red Siren. He must focus on saving Hope, no matter what danger she had thrown herself into.

He tugged back the reins as they passed through the city gates then turned onto Meeting Street. The fetid odors of the city surrounded him, along with the eerie chime of an off-key violin accompanied by devilish laughter. Lightning carved a craggy spike across the dark sky as if warning him of impending danger.

Evil was afoot this night. Dajon could feel it.

He could feel it in the sharp hairs bristling across his neck, in the chill rippling down his back. He could feel it in his spirit.

His thoughts shifted to the only One who possessed the power to protect them from such unseen forces, and he chided himself. Why hadn't he thought to pray for Hope sooner?

Father, please protect Hope. Please let no harm befall her. Keep the villains from her and watch over her until we arrive.

When he raised his gaze, it was to Faith's curious stare.

"Who were you talking to?"

Thunder growled in the distance, announcing a storm. "I was praying for your sister."

"Humph." She nudged her horse into a trot.

161

Faith thrust her nose in the air but did not respond. Angry voices blared in the street ahead of her. They had not seen a soul since entering the city, all asleep at this hour save for the men down by the docks, the miscreants of the sea who spent their coins on idle pleasures and boastful brawls. In that way, she certainly differed from her pirate compatriots.

Narrow houses sprang up on both sides of the street. Two- and three-story stone structures originally built to house families but now transformed into filthy bordellos. Scantily clad women of all shapes and sizes spilled from the door and windows of one of them as if the house could not contain them all. Men with mugs of ale in hand hung on the trollops like ill-fitting shawls.

Drunken eyes shot toward the trio in the street, and for the first time that night, Faith found comfort in riding between the captain and Lucas.

A flash of lightning drew her gaze to a pink building up ahead.

The Pink House.

Faith swallowed and tried to quiet the pounding of her heart.

Mr. Waite raised a hand to slow them. The horses' hooves clicked over the narrow cobblestone street like the ticking of a clock counting down their demise.

The captain turned in his saddle. "Miss Westcott, I beg you. Allow Lucas to escort you home. Mullato Alley is no place for a lady at night."

So this was Mullato Alley—the most perilous district in town. She had thus far managed to avoid traveling this way, and now she knew why 'twas spoken of in hushed tones. But no matter her fear, no matter her disgust, she must think only of Hope and of bringing her sister home safely. Faith took a deep breath and threw back her shoulders. "My sister is here somewhere, Mr. Waite. Therefore I will stay. She will no doubt need me when we discover her whereabouts."

The captain grunted but said nothing more.

Terror stiffened each nerve within Faith as they proceeded to the Pink House. Men brawled openly in the street. Angry shouts and curses burst through the night like pistol shots. To her right, a ring of boisterous sailors, shouting and thrusting their fists in the air, had formed around two others engaged in a sword fight. The clank of metal on metal rang across the street in ominous tones. Somewhere a gun fired.

What had lured Hope down to this ungodly place? Hadn't she had enough of lecherous men? Faith shivered beneath a rising swell of fear for her sister's safety. An unusual desire to pray gripped her—an urge to appeal to a force outside herself, for as she looked around at the violent depravity consuming the alley, she could not imagine any of them escaping unharmed.

The captain's gaze locked upon the Pink House. Concern tightened his features, and beads of sweat glistened between his eyebrows. She turned to Lucas. "Give me one of your pistols."

Mr. Waite shot her a curious look.

"I know how to shoot it. Never fear." She knew she had just given him more fuel to feed his suspicions, but she couldn't concern herself with that at the moment. In light of what she saw before her, she realized it was not just Hope's innocence on the line but her very life.

Gripping the weapon, Faith stuffed it in the belt on her gown, finding a small measure of relief at being armed again. Now if she just had her cutlass.

As the captain led them around the side of the Pink House, where several horses stood tethered to a post, Faith tried to ignore the lewd comments tossed her way, tried to allow them to pass over her like the wind rising upon the oncoming storm, but she could not. Instead of disgusting her, however, they only pricked her ire. How dare these men fling such foul, degrading suggestions toward a lady, or any woman for that matter?

At least the captain and Lucas's presence seemed to keep them at bay. No doubt most were too inebriated to follow through with their obscene threats anyway.

Mr. Waite dismounted and held out his hand to assist her from her horse. "I apologize, Miss Westcott, for the insults you are forced to endure, but I fear if I were to attempt to defend your honor for each one, I would be engaged in battle the entire night."

" 'Tis quite all right, Mr. Waite." Faith took his hand, glad for the warm strength that enveloped hers, and hopped to the ground. "I believe I can suffer through it for my sister's sake."

"You are a brave woman." He gave her an admiring look then plucked his pistol from the inside of his coat, primed it, replaced it, and nodded toward Lucas.

Without asking, he placed Faith's hand firmly on his arm. "Stay close to me," he ordered as the three of them rounded the building and slipped through the front door.

The stink of ale, tobacco, and human sweat assaulted Faith. She held her breath against the onslaught and tried to focus. The tavern was a swaying mass of inebriated humanity stretched in every direction. In the right corner, a plump woman perched at a harpsichord banged out a bawdy tune, while a skinny man attempted a vain accompaniment with his violin. An off-key ballad rose from a mob clustered around them, their mugs of ale raised toward the rafters.

A loud thump startled Faith, drawing her attention to a table at her left where two men arm wrestled. A crowd circled them, placing bets. Angry card games exploded with insults and threats from every corner. Women snuggled upon men's laps and cooed into their ears. A narrow staircase led upstairs, its wood creaking under the continual passage of its patrons to whatever wickedness loomed above.

Mr. Waite tensed beside Faith as he scanned the room. Hope was not here, at least not in this part of the tavern.

Some of the patrons fired seething glances their way as they muttered to their companions.

Faith felt his eyes lock upon her long before she saw him.

A man wearing a plumed captain's hat, leather jerkin, black waistcoat, and cocky grin stared at her from a table in the corner. He sat back in his chair with his arms folded across his thick chest. A motley group—his crew, no doubt—sat with him.

A pirate.

His gaze scoured over her as if she were tonight's supper then shot to Captain Waite and narrowed.

"Have ye come to arrest me then?" His eyes dropped to the three gold buttons lining each of Mr. Waite's cuffs. "Lieutenant, is it? Ha." He snorted, his spit splattering onto the table. "They send a mere lieutenant to arrest the great Captain Vane." The men surrounding him erupted into a round of drunken cackles as every hazy eye in the place shot to the trio.

So this was Charles Vane. Faith had heard of his brutality—how he tortured and murdered the crews of his captured vessels, how he never abided by the pirate code and cheated his own crew out of their share of the plunder, and how he had arrogantly snubbed the offer of pardon given by the governor of the Bahamas by setting a French ship aflame and destroying two Royal Navy ships. As she took in his grotesque physique and the pure evil simmering in his gaze, she felt as if a thousand bugs crawled down her back, the sensation made all the more disgusting by the shame of her association with his kind. Averting her eyes, she scanned the room once again for any sign of Hope.

Mr. Waite returned the man's stare and waited until the chortles silenced.

"Ye come here with a mere woman and a slave?" the pirate continued his verbal joust.

Lucas grunted and gripped the hilt of his sword.

The pirate's eyes shifted to the groomsman's threatening gesture, and a wicked sneer played upon his lips.

Mr. Waite raised his brows. "I'll be happy to arrest you if you wish, Mr. Vane," he said nonchalantly, "but I am afraid I have not heard of you."

Faith elbowed the captain and sent an anxious glance his way. Surely he knew who this vile man was. 'Twas sheer folly to antagonize such a volatile beast.

The pirate's face exploded in a purple rage. "Not heard of me?" He shot up, his chair thumping to the floor. The crowd shrank back. "I've plundered o'er twenty ships in these waters." He flung a glance over his men to receive the expected grunts of approbation, even as he slid his hand within his waistcoat.

The captain remained steady and relaxed beside her as if he were talking to a mere servant. Either he was mad, or he possessed more courage than she had ever seen.

"You must be quite proud of yourself, Mr. Vane, but alas, I care not." Mr. Waite gazed off to the right as if the exchange bored him. "We have come in search of a lady."

"Well, ye ain't gonna find a lady in here," blared a man's voice above the noise of the crowd, eliciting a barrage of chortles.

The pirate fumbled within his coat. Faith knew he went for his pistol.

She knew he would have already drawn it if not for the alcohol tugging on his reflexes. Lucas shifted his stance, his fingers stretching beside his own weapon. Faith clutched the handle of her gun. Her moist palms slipped over the cool metal. Why didn't the captain do something?

The laugher abated, leaving a deadly silence in its wake.

A slow smile crept over the pirate's lips. He plucked his pistol from inside his waistcoat. The cock of a dozen pistols snapped through the room like firecrackers—Faith's and Lucas's and the captain's among them. She hadn't even seen Mr. Waite draw his.

Mr. Vane aimed the dark barrel of his pistol at the captain's heart. His grin faded.

The captain did not move, his own weapon trained upon the pirate.

Eight men surrounding Vane leveled their pistols upon the trio, while only their three returned the threat. A maze of deadly steel crisscrossed before them, ready to fire in a lethal explosion.

Fear as she'd never known before dug its claws into Faith and kept her frozen in place.

There was no way out of this. They were all going to die.

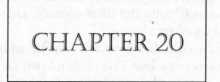

CHAPTER 20

Faith gazed at the dark, gaping holes of at least twenty pistols leveled upon her heart and thought this as good a time as any to make peace with a God she had ignored for years. Mr. Waite grabbed her hand with his free one and tried to pull her behind him.

She did not budge.

Though the chivalrous gesture warmed her, better to die alongside her companions than after they had been pummeled with bullets and dropped to the floor at her feet.

Oh God, if You are there. . . .I know I haven't spoken to You very much. . . but please help us—for the captain's sake. He's a good man.

From the corner of her eye, Faith spotted a woman in a formfitting purple gown saunter over to Vane. Her brown hair, tied behind her like a man's, curled down her back. Two brace of pistols were slung across her chest.

"Settle down, Charlie." She sidled beside him and gave him a sultry grin. "I know this woman." She winked at Faith. "They mean you no harm. And besides, since when have you ever allowed a navy pig to stir your ire?" She waved a jeweled hand through the air. "Ignore him. He is nothing."

"Anne." Faith lowered her pistol and stormed toward the woman she now recognized as Hope's friend.

"Miss Westcott," the captain hissed urgently behind her.

Vane's glazed eyes flickered briefly to Anne then to Faith, before fixing again on Mr. Waite. His pistol wobbled. Grabbing his mug, he gulped down another swig of ale, foam beading on his mustache, and then switched the weapon to his other hand.

"Do you know where Hope is?"

A spark of alarm flitted across Anne's confident expression. "She did not return home?"

Faith shook her head.

Facing Vane again, Anne placed a hand on his arm holding the gun. "Put the pistol down, Charlie. Pay them no mind. Do we not have better things to do?" she cooed into his ear.

"Gone wit' ye, woman. Leave me be!" Vane jerked her hand away and gave Mr. Waite a venomous look. "Yer outnumbered, sir. Surrender or die."

"I plan to do neither, Mr. Bane," the captain huffed. "But how about this? I will—"

"I said me name was Vane, not Bane!" the pirate interrupted in a spasm of fury. He sent a scathing glance over the room, silencing the few who had dared to laugh.

"Vane, Bane, whatever." Mr. Waite shrugged. "As I was saying, I will not arrest you on the condition that you tell me where our lady friend is to be found. Agreed?" The muscles in his jaw flexed, but Faith could see no other indication of unease in his staunch demeanor.

"I've got me a better idea," Vane snarled. "I'll kill ye where ye stand and take the fine lady ye brought wit' ye fer meself."

Laughter rumbled through the foul air just as a blast of thunder roared outside.

Raindrops struck the roof, at first sounding like tiny footfalls then growing in intensity until the reverberation of pounding drums filled the whole tavern.

A chill slithered over Faith.

Mr. Waite cast a wary glance at her, motioning her to step away from Anne.

She did.

He nodded toward Lucas.

Faith's heart took on a frenzied beat. What was he planning?

He faced Vane. His stern gaze and rigid stance contained all the energy of a lightning bolt about to strike.

Vane snickered and tightened his finger around the trigger of his pistol.

Instantly the captain booted the table that stood between them. Mugs of ale and bottles of rum shot through the air, crashing into pieces against walls and floor and showering the crowd with shards of glass and drops of liquor.

Vane stumbled back. His pistol fired.

Guns exploded.

Faith ducked.

A man grabbed her arm and dragged her from her feet. Twisting, she kneed him in the groin then regained her balance and waved her gun across a circle of men descending upon her.

Lucas tugged her beside him. He shot one man in the leg, dropped his gun, and drew his cutlass.

The man screamed and clutched the wound.

Sword tips bristled at them from every direction.

"Halt or I'll kill him!" Mr. Waite's voice thundered through the room.

Silence, save for the pounding of the rain, descended upon them.

Mr. Waite marched toward Vane, his pistol leveled at the pirate's shocked face. Vane raised his own weapon and gave a sideways grin at the smoke curling upward from the barrel. He tossed it aside with a clank.

"Tell your men to lower their weapons," Mr. Waite commanded. "Or I swear by the love of all that is holy, I will blast what's left of your brains all over the wall."

The pirate's upper lip twitched. A look of insolent defiance burned in his gaze. Faith knew that look. He wasn't going to comply. He would risk his death rather than suffer shame in front of his men.

Without warning, Anne rushed to his side, raised a pistol, and whacked the handle down on Vane's head. His eyes rolled upward before he crumpled to the ground in a heap.

Murmurs rumbled through the crowd of onlookers, their mouths agape, but Anne turned to face them and threw her hands to her hips. "Go about yer business, ye sotted dogs," she yelled as loudly as any man. "He just needs a wee bit of sleep, 'tis all."

Tension spiked through the room. Faith tried to contain the heavy breath that threatened to burst through her chest. Then, one by one, the men began to laugh. Coarse chortles soon chased out the hostility as the sailors slowly dispersed.

Anne tilted her pretty head toward the captain. "I couldn't let you kill him. I've grown quite fond of him, you see."

Mr. Waite lowered his gun. "Are you well, Miss Westcott?"

"Yes, I'm fine." She turned toward Anne. "Where is my sister?"

Anne finished giving instructions to Vane's crew to attend to him, then she grabbed Faith's arm. "She was here an hour ago." She gestured for Mr. Waite and Lucas to follow her then led them to the back of the tavern. "I saw her leave through the back door into the garden. I assumed she went home." She glanced over the three of them, concern warming her cold, hard eyes.

"How could you leave her alone?" Faith asked.

"I am not her guardian. She came here of her own accord."

"But you are her friend." Faith jerked from her grasp. "She's not strong like you are."

Anne flinched and narrowed her eyes. "She's more like me than you may think." She allowed her gaze to wander over Faith. She grinned. "And from the looks of you, you are, as well."

Faith ground her teeth. She might be a pirate, but she was nothing like this depraved strumpet.

Was she?

Anne glanced at Mr. Waite and Lucas. "Who are your friends?"

The captain nodded. "Mr. Waite, commander of the HMS *Enforcer*."

Faith gestured toward Lucas. "And this is Lucas, my first—my groomsman," she stammered.

"Your first groomsman, eh?" Anne snickered then pushed aside the massive oak door that led into the back garden. "Like I told you, she went this way about an hour ago."

"Alone?" the captain asked.

"Aye, as far as I could see."

"Did she say where she might be heading?"

"Not to me." Annie cocked her head and grinned, allowing her sultry gaze to drift over Mr. Waite.

The captain brushed past her, grabbing Faith's elbow as he went. "Thank you, Anne. That will be all." He dismissed her as if she were one of his crewmen.

Lucas squeezed by her, as well, eyeing her with caution.

Anne scowled before she released the door and stomped back into the tavern, muttering something about pompous naval officers.

Lightning flashed, illuminating the porch in stark grays and whites before snapping it back into darkness. Two lanterns swaying on poles offered little light over the dismal scene. Rain pounded the slanted covering above them. Droplets squeezed between the wooden slats. One of them slid down Faith's gown, weaving a trail of unease down her back as she scanned the shadows for Hope.

The captain released her elbow and took her hand in his. Lucas came alongside them. Together they took a step forward. Weeds reached up between the cracks of cobblestone and clawed at their feet as they made their way to the edge of the porch and stopped, peering out into the shadows. A brick wall enclosed the small garden, if one could call it that. Thistles and brown shrubs littered the area. A massive tree stood in the center, a cracked stone fountain at its base. Though most of the patrons had gone inside out of the rain, some remained splayed across benches and over the cobblestones in such a drunken stupor that they were oblivious to the raindrops splattering over them.

Faith gulped as a metallic taste rose in her throat. Hope was nowhere in sight.

Thunder shook the sky as they stepped from beneath the overhang. Drops of rain pelted Faith's skin. An eerie ballad snaked through the moist air like a witch's chant. A radiance flickered from beyond the tree.

Mr. Waite squeezed her hand. "Never fear. We shall find her, Miss Westcott." He led her around the trunk and down a path.

Faith's gaze shot to a far corner of the garden where a lantern burned. No, 'twas not a lantern but a fire, a pillar of fire nigh two feet tall. The flames burned bright despite the lashing rain and wind.

Mr. Waite headed for it.

With their backs to the fire, a group of men hunched together against the rain. When they weren't hoisting bottles to their mouths, they belted out a sinister trill that sent chills over Faith.

> *Oh devils, we call ye*
> *Out from yer graves.*
> *Give us yer power;*
> *We are yer slaves.*

Faith snapped her gaze back to the fire. A shadowy figured huddled just beyond it.

Hope.

Faith yanked her hand from Mr. Waite's and dashed toward the corner. Hope curled into a ball against the brick wall, drenched and shivering.

"'Tis Hope," she yelled over her shoulder, sidestepping the fire and kneeling beside her sister.

"Hope?" She touched her arm, cold as ice. Faith gulped. "What have they done to you?" Hope's eyes fluttered, but she did not open them. A moan escaped her lips. A hundred heinous scenarios crept through Faith's mind. "Not again, Lord. Not again."

"Heaven help us." Mr. Waite stepped around the flame, slid his arms beneath Hope, and hoisted her effortlessly into his arms.

The fire disappeared.

Faith's widened eyes met the captain's. She shifted her gaze to the spot where the fire had been and then to Lucas, who stood frozen in place, the whites of his eyes fixated on the missing flame. No wood, no smoke, nothing to indicate a fire had just burned there. The ground beneath it was not even charred. Faith placed her hand over the spot.

Moist, cold soil met her fingers.

"There she be!" one of the drunken men shouted, arousing the others from their ballad. The mob rose and clambered toward them.

"We've been lookin' fer that lady!" bellowed a slovenly fellow in front, pointing his bottle at Hope.

"Aye, she just disappeared," another commented, and the men grunted in unison.

Faith glanced at Mr. Waite but could not make out his features in the shadows. She wiped drops of rain from her lashes and stood.

Two of the men drew their swords. "We saw her first. She's ours."

Lucas swerved to face them and slowly pulled out his cutlass. The metal against sheath rang an eerie chime across the yard. Yanking her pistol from her belt, Faith aimed it at the mob and counted the dark, swaying heads.

Ten.

Ten to three. And Mr. Waite with his hands encumbered beneath the weight of Hope's unconscious body.

"She does not belong to you," the captain said with all the authority of a king.

"To the devil wit' ye, sir. I'm givin' ye a fair warning. There be powers at work here that ye best be heedin'."

"I agree with you gentlemen," Mr. Waite replied, his tone so calm and steady it astonished Faith. "There are indeed powers at work here. But if I were you, I'd be careful which ones I associated with."

Malefic chortles filled the air as lightning shot a fiery dagger across the sky, flashing a spectral glow over their faces.

Faith swallowed. A chill struck her as if a wall of ice passed through her.

Evil was here.

A malevolent force tugged upon her, weighing her down with dread and hopelessness.

She shook the rain from her face and tried to steady her wobbling gun. What did Mr. Waite hope to gain from this derisive repartee? It would take more than mere words to disarm these men and the wickedness that empowered them.

The captain took a bold step forward, clutching Hope more tightly to his chest. "This woman is not yours. She belongs to God," he roared, "and in the name of Jesus Christ, the Son of the living God, I order you to stand down."

Thunder boomed. The ground shuddered.

The men shrank back as if a broadside had struck them in the gut. Although their eyes narrowed and their jaws tightened, they made no move toward Hope.

Mr. Waite turned and marched across the garden toward the back exit.

Faith glanced over her shoulder as she ran next to him, expecting the villains to give chase. Behind her, Lucas ran backward, his sword brandished toward the band of cursing men.

Mr. Waite kicked open the iron gate. It squealed on its hinges and slammed into the brick wall.

Faith followed him around the side of the tavern where they'd left their horses. One final glance over her shoulder told her the men had not moved an inch.

Grabbing her arm, Lucas pulled her away from the sight.

Mr. Waite halted amid the row of horses and wheeled around.

Faith touched his arm. "What is it?"

"One of our horses is missing."

"Hey, you there." A slurred voice echoed through the alleyway. "Ain't ye the strangers that bested old Charlie?"

Mr. Waited snapped his eyes toward Faith. "We've no time. We shall make do with two. Lucas, mount up, and I'll hand you Miss Hope."

"Aye, aye." Lucas untied the reins, swung onto the horse, then leaned down to receive Hope. She moaned as he grasped her and laid her across the saddle in front of him.

"Hey, I told ye to stop!" A crowd of men formed at the head of the alley. "Are we gonna let this bilge-sucking navy dog come down to our territory an' make a fool o' poor Charlie? Let's teach 'im a lesson."

Groans and "ayes" bounced off the brick walls.

Faith lifted her pistol and stepped out from the horses. "Stay back, or I'll drop you where you stand."

"Ouch now." The man snickered. "Did ye hear that, gents? The lady's gonna shoot us."

He and his companions fell into a fit of laughter.

Lucas backed up his horse and leveled his own pistol upon them.

The captain took a running leap and jumped onto his steed then held down his hand for Faith.

She hesitated, shifting her eyes between him and the crowd. One well-aimed shot by these villains at their fleeing backs and all would be lost. Perhaps she should remain and keep them at bay until Mr. Waite and Lucas could escape with Hope. Perhaps it was the only way to ensure her sister's safety.

"Are you coming? Or do you plan to take on these ruffians by yourself?"

Though she couldn't see his face, she envisioned the sardonic curve of his lips.

"Trust me. I will get you and your sister home safely. Now, please." He stretched out his hand farther even as the horse clawed at the mud, perhaps sensing the impending danger.

Trust. Her chest tightened. Placing her life and the life of her sister in someone else's hands made Faith's stomach constrict so tightly she felt it would explode into a thousand pieces. But she had little choice at the moment. And Mr. Waite had not let her down thus far.

Stuffing the pistol in her belt, she took his hand, and he hoisted her up before him and grabbed the reins.

The men recovered from their gaiety. "Hey, where ye runnin' off to, ye cowards?" One of the men took a step forward and plucked out his sword. "I'm challengin' ye to a duel, ye spineless son of Neptune's whore."

Mr. Waite twitched the horse's reins and faced the man. "Another time, perhaps?" He gave the horse a swift kick in the belly, sending the steed galloping down the alley straight toward the mob.

CHAPTER 21

The drunken men formed an oscillating row. Dajon sped straight for them, intending to run them down if he had to. But at the last minute, they jerked aside, some tumbling to the ground, others scrambling for their fallen pistols. Dajon bolted ahead. He did not look back.

A barrage of cracks and pops split the night air.

A bullet whizzed past his ear.

Dajon jerked the reins to the right and then the left, weaving a chaotic path down the street, dodging the volley of bullets. Lucas galloped beside him doing the same, one arm holding Hope in a fierce grip.

Lightning cracked the sky in a fork of brilliance, casting an eerie gray flash over the buildings that lined the road. Laying propriety aside, Dajon wrapped his arms around Faith's waist and pressed her back against his chest, then they lunged around the corner down Meeting Street. The thud of horse hooves in the mud matched the furious beat of his heart. Thunder bellowed above them as if war in heaven had broken out right over their heads. Faith jumped, and he gripped her tighter as he cast a quick glance over his shoulder. No one followed.

Easing the horse to a trot, he wiped the sweat from his forehead with his sleeve before returning his hand to Faith's waist. Lucas drew up alongside him and cast a glance his way, his expression lost in the shadows.

"Hope." Faith beckoned to her sister, reaching her hand across the distance between them, but no response came from the dark mound bounding at their side.

"She be all right, mistress," Lucas said. "Her breathin' be steady. And I ain't seen no blood."

Faith released a sigh. Her shoulders drooped slightly. Dajon brushed the curls from her cheek and leaned toward her, intending to offer her a word of comfort. Instead, his gaze landed on the black shape of a pistol clasped tightly between her hands.

Reaching around her, he touched her arm. "Give me the pistol, Miss Westcott. 'Tis over now. You are safe." Yet he wondered if she gripped the weapon out of fear—or anger. Truth be told, none of her behavior that evening had portrayed an ounce of fear—and certainly none of the trembling, swooning, or outright panic one would expect of a lady in the face of such danger and debauchery.

She hesitated for a moment then flipped the pistol in the air, catching it by the barrel, and handed it to him over her shoulder, handle first.

Like an expert marksman.

Dajon stuffed it in his belt and swallowed against the horrifying revelation rising in his throat.

He pulled back on the reins, slowing the horse to a walk as they approached the city gates. Visions of Faith storming into the tavern as boldly as she would her own parlor and then standing her ground in a room full of drunken villains, pirates, and ruffians blasted across his mind. Not just standing her ground, but drawing her weapon, demanding her sister's return. Why, she had not even blinked at the lewdness and profanity surrounding her. What sort of lady was she?

A pirate lady.

No. He could not believe it. He would not believe it.

Through the city gates, Dajon turned the horse onto the dirt path to Hasell Street, searching for an explanation for Faith's behavior, any explanation besides the one that kept shoving its way to the forefront of his mind. Perhaps her father had trained her in arms. Perhaps she'd been forced to defend their home in the past. No. He knew Admiral Westcott. He would never allow one of his daughters to behave in such an improper and audacious manner.

She wiggled in the saddle and pulled away from him. "You do not have to hold me so tightly anymore," she shot back over her shoulder.

He leaned toward her ear. "Enjoying yourself too much, perchance?"

"I'm sure many women succumb to your infinite charms, Captain, but I am not among them." Dajon chuckled but kept a firm grip upon her. "I am deeply wounded, Miss Westcott. After all we've been through, 'tis only that I wouldn't want you to fall."

"If you don't control those hands, it won't be me who falls from this horse, Mr. Waite." She shuffled in the saddle again, and the movements of her body against Dajon sent a surge of heat through him. He released her momentarily and cleared his throat. What was he doing? The last thing he needed was to entangle himself with a woman, especially an admiral's daughter—and especially this particular woman who had far too many secrets stowed under hatches.

But Miss Westcott. Never had he encountered such a lady, such a dichotomy of charm and venom all wrapped up in a curvaceous, fiery parcel.

He leaned toward her, longing to savor the moment of her close proximity—one that he doubted would ever come again. But the stench of that awful soap bit his nose, overpowering her normal sweet, lemony aroma. He huffed. Certainly the lady knew no more about soap making than he did.

She flipped her hair behind her, swatting him in the face with the fetid strands, and glanced toward Lucas and Hope. "I do thank you, Mr. Waite." Her voice had softened, had even taken on a penitent tone. "My sister appears unharmed, at least on the outside. I thought surely all was lost when we entered the tavern and she was nowhere to be seen."

" 'Twas my pleasure. I am only glad we arrived in time." Dajon glanced at the groaning petite form in Lucas's arms. "If you and your sisters would simply follow the rules, you could avoid putting yourselves in such danger. That is what rules are for, Miss Westcott—for your own safety and the safety of others."

She gave a most unladylike snort. "I fear your task as our guardian has been much more than you bargained for, Mr. Waite. Perhaps you now wish to reconsider?"

His task? Surprisingly, neither Dajon's obligation to the admiral nor the consequences to his career had even penetrated his decisions tonight. He had acted only out of fear for Hope's safety, and in particular, out of his strong desire to alleviate Faith's distress. When had he begun to care for this family? And more important, when had he begun to put his career, his very life on the line for them?

Surely, Lord, this unselfish act will pay off a portion of my past debt.

He felt a shudder course through Faith. "I fear for what my sister endured before we arrived."

Dajon remained silent. He knew all too well the wickedness that went on in those nefarious dens. As he envisioned the fiendish group of men that had surrounded Hope, he loathed to think what they had done to her, what they had planned on doing. Certainly even more evil had been afoot than ravishing a young woman.

But the Lord had shown up strong! The strange fire, the presence of God that had protected Hope. A surge of faith lifted Dajon's spirits. "Never fear, God was with your sister the whole time, even before we arrived."

A brisk wind swirled, shoving dark clouds aside and allowing the glow of a half-moon to shine upon them.

Faith shook her head.

Lucas cleared his throat. "Beggin' yer pardon, sir, but what exactly did happen back there? I ain't seen nothin' like that before."

"That, Mr. Corwin, was the mighty hand of God."

"But the fire—it jest disappeared."

"Amazing, wasn't it?" Dajon still found it hard to believe himself. Yet how could he deny what he had seen? It reminded him of the pillar of fire God had sent to protect the people of Israel as they traveled across the wilderness. Excitement sped through him.

"And those men couldn'a see Miss Hope till the fire was gone." Lucas's normally hearty voice quivered slightly.

"And the ground was cold and wet beneath the flames after they disappeared," Faith added, awe softening her normal confident tone.

"Aye." He smiled.

Lucas shifted in his saddle, adjusting Hope in his arms. "And those men—they stopped. They didn't chase us after ye commanded them in the name of Jesus to stand down."

"The name of Jesus has been placed 'far above all principality, and power, and might, and dominion, and every name that is named, not only in this world, but also in that which is to come,' " Dajon said, quoting from Ephesians. He felt a tingling sensation throughout his body.

Faith stiffened against his chest.

"God exists," Lucas announced incredulously.

"That He does, Mr. Corwin. That He does."

"I am sure there is another explanation." Faith's sharp tone bit into Dajon's joy. The Lord had rescued one of the Westcott sisters from evil, but the other was still locked in a dungeon of disbelief. *Lord, if this miracle cannot convince her, what will?* Without God, she would forever be wandering through life searching for something that could not be found.

Dajon nudged the horse, prodding him into a trot. Tonight God had used him to do battle against evil to save Hope. And he was more determined than ever not to allow those same wicked forces to keep Faith from the Lord.

⟞

Faith sat on the edge of the bed and rubbed her sister's hand. As soon as they had arrived home, she'd instructed Lucas to carry Hope into Faith's chamber, where she could sit with her until she awoke. Faith considered waking Grace but thought it wiser to allow her sister to rest. No sense in all of them being exhausted on the morrow. So with the chambermaid's help, Faith had undressed Hope, searched for wounds—finding none, not even a drop of blood—and then clad her in a nightgown and wrapped her among the blankets on her bed. Though Hope had fluttered her eyes briefly during the commotion, she had not regained consciousness. And that thought alone terrified Faith more than anything. Something dreadful must have happened to cause her sister to remain ensconced within the dark places of her mind.

Laying her face in her hands, Faith released the tears she'd withheld all evening, allowing them to flow down her cheeks and drip off her chin one by one onto the down quilt. It was all her fault. If she had just spent the day at the park with Hope like she had promised, they would not have fought, and Hope would not have ventured out into the night.

Faith glanced at the blurred shape of her sister lying on the bed. "I'm so sorry, my dear, sweet Hope. Please forgive me." She squeezed Hope's hand then swiped the tears from her own cheeks. No time for crying. From now on, Faith would do better. She would spend more time with her sisters, even if it meant forgoing her sleep.

Releasing her sister's hand, Faith rose and walked toward the window. She clenched her fists then leaned on the ledge, allowing the moonlight to drench her in a wash of silver. If she could plunder one or two more treasure-laden ships, she might have enough to approach her father. Then she would have all the time in the world to spend with her sisters, to protect them, to guide them.

She glanced across the yard where Spanish moss on a red cedar swayed in the breeze. Below, Molly's prize vegetable garden guarded the side wall, framed by purple larkspur, wild geranium, and tall evening primrose, its strong, sweet scent permeating the night air. The storm had passed. Tomorrow would be a beautiful day. Perhaps a new start? She opened her mouth to speak. Then slammed it shut. What was she doing? She had been about to pray—to thank God for saving Hope and to plead with Him for the soundness of her sister's mind and heart. She lowered her gaze to the chipped white paint around the window. Hadn't she prayed at the tavern during a moment of despair, and hadn't God answered her prayers? But why would He, when she had turned her back on Him long ago?

No, 'twas Mr. Waite. 'Twas his prayer God answered. And only his. Yet that would mean God did care for His children—at least some of them.

"Though you have left Me, I have never left you."

Tears surged into her eyes. She shook her head. *No. You've allowed too many tragedies, too much pain. I cannot trust You. I will not.*

"I love you."

A tap sounded on the door, and Faith brushed her tears aside before whispering, "Enter," thinking it must be the chambermaid or perhaps Molly come to scold her for their dangerous escapade.

The door creaked open, and the hollow thud of boots sounded on the wooden floor. She turned, her heart skipping a beat.

The large frame of Mr. Waite filled the doorway. "Forgive me, Miss Westcott, I know this is most improper, but I cannot sleep and thought to check on Miss Hope. May I?"

Swallowing her sorrow and guilt, Faith squared her shoulders. "Of course. Please come in."

He glanced toward the bed and crossed the room. No navy coat hid his broad chest—a chest that stretched his shirt like a full sail under a mighty wind. His breeches were haphazardly stuffed into black boots. His dark hair hung loosely about his collar, and a day's stubble peppered his chin.

Faith's breath halted as he stepped into the moonlight.

181

He nodded toward the bed. "How is she?"

A rush of heat sped through Faith. She took a step back. "I don't know. She has not awakened."

"Were there. . .were there wounds?"

"Nay." She crossed her arms over her stomach, hoping to still the beating of her heart. "Not on the outside, anyway."

He nodded as if he understood. Faith tightened her jaw. As if he could possibly understand the internal wounds of a woman.

"I've sent for the doctor," he said. "There must be a reason she is still benumbed."

"She has been like this before." Faith glanced out the window, feeling her guard weakening before the outpouring of this man's concern.

The captain cocked his head curiously.

"This is not the first time she has been accosted by licentious knaves, Mr. Waite." He blinked then glanced toward the bed. When he returned his gaze to hers, sorrow stained his otherwise clear blue eyes.

Feeling suddenly weak, Faith sank onto the window ledge. Did this man care about Hope, about her? She studied him, searching for a hint of duplicity but finding only sincerity burning in his gaze. Yet nobody cared for anyone unless there was personal gain. He wanted something. But what? She let out a sigh. No matter. He had saved Hope. And for that, he did not deserve to be scorned.

"Forgive me, Mr. Waite. 'Tis just that my sister has suffered much."

"I'm sorry. There is much evil in the world." Without warning, he reached out and took her hand.

His warm fingers enclosed hers protectively. Faith knew she should jerk from his grasp, but the comforting strength of his touch filled a need long unmet. "Evil in the world? Aye. But in your own household?" Faith gritted her teeth against a flood of emotion.

Mr. Waite continued to caress her hand, but he made no reply. He leaned against the wall framing the window, so close to her she could smell the sea upon him. The salty fragrance settled over her nerves, untying the many knots formed during the night's harrowing venture.

Should she tell him? She longed to pour out her heart to this man. Hope moaned from the bed, drawing both their gazes momentarily.

Faith glanced out the window. "My older sister, Charity, is married to a ruthless, cruel man, Lord Herbert Villement. Not only does he mistreat Charity—severely—but he set his wicked eyes upon adding all her sisters to his harem." She shot a fiery gaze his way. "He claims to be a godly Christian man."

Mr. Waite stopped caressing her hand; his fingers stiffened.

Faith swallowed. " 'Twas Hope he set his sights upon first. Possibly because I refused to acknowledge his lewd suggestions, and Grace"—she gave a wry laugh—"sweet Grace's piety no doubt disturbed the demons lurking within him. Hope has always been such a flirt, you see." She glanced at Mr. Waite, his dark gaze locked upon her as he listened with interest. "All of it harmless in her innocence and youth. Poor thing. She longed for approval. Still does, I suppose." Faith retrieved her hand and stood, not wanting the comfort to assuage the anger of her memories. She gazed at the shadowy form on the bed. "Papa never appreciated Hope. He finds her ignorant and flighty, and she and Mother were so much alike that they squabbled over everything." Faith let out a pained laugh. "Hope never knew how much Mother truly loved her." Faith's eyes burned, and she pulled her hand from his and stepped into the shadows.

He crossed his arms over his chest, his dark silhouette like a sturdy ship on the horizon.

Faith clasped her hands together. "We tried to avoid our new brother-in-law as much as we could. His salacious dalliance masked behind polite discourse was not lost on us as he must have assumed. But as family, he had access to our home whenever he wished." Her stomach soured as visions of him bursting through their front door shot through her mind, hat and cane in hand, licking his lips in a ravenous grin. "Which was often—usually whenever Father was away and Charity was, of course, home unwell. 'Twas no wonder she had a perpetual headache." Faith snorted and grabbed her throat, trying to dissolve the clump of pain that had taken residence there.

The captain's knuckles whitened as he grabbed the window ledge. Still, he said nothing. He took a step toward her.

Faith held up a hand to stay his advance. She did not want his comfort, his sympathy. She must finish her story. She must let it out, or she feared it would explode within her like the backfiring of a ship's gun.

"One evening, Mother and Grace had gone to the city. Papa was at sea, and most of the servants had been dismissed on holiday, leaving Hope and me alone in the house. I heard her scream."

The same chill that had stabbed through Faith that night stabbed through her now. Wrapping her arms about her chest, she shut her eyes against the image that was forever engraved in her mind.

"By the time I stormed into Hope's chamber, he was donning his pantaloons and spewing foul curses toward her as she lay on the bed." Tears fought their way to the forefront of Faith's eyes, but she willed them back with her fury.

A gentle touch on her arm startled her. She jumped and snapped her eyes open to see the captain's tall figure beside her.

"She was but seventeen," Faith sobbed.

Moonlight glimmered off the hint of moisture covering Mr. Waite's gaze. His nostrils flared, and a tiny purple vein began to throb on his forehead.

Faith stepped away from his grasp. "Then Lord Villement came after me."

CHAPTER 22

"Lord Villement came after you?" Dajon's stomach convulsed. He tried to say something, wanted to say something to comfort Faith, but when he opened his mouth, all he found on his tongue was an anchor chain of angry curses.

"Aye." Faith's voice was but a whisper. "He pinned me to the floor by the fireplace, grunting over me like a beast."

"Did he. . .did he. . ." Dajon could not form the words, much less the thought.

She lifted her gaze to his, but the shadows hid her expression. "I grabbed the poker and stabbed him in the leg." She spat the words so quickly and with such finality that it sounded as if there could be no other ending to the dreadful story. But her bunched fists at her sides and the stiffness of her shoulders as she moved to the window told a different tale.

"I threatened to pierce the other leg and would have if he hadn't fled from the house in agony."

Dajon blew out a sigh and raked a hand through his hair. At least Faith had been spared. The moonlight doused her in a halo of silver, highlighting her stiff posture and making all the more noticeable the shudder that now ran through her. He moved closer, longing to take her in his arms, to protect and soothe her. Would she welcome his embrace? Or would she fear him—a man alone in her chamber?

As if in answer, she whirled around and faced the window.

He halted. "I'm sorry."

"It was a long time ago." She snorted and waved a hand through the air. "I have tried to care for both my sisters since, but I fear I have failed miserably. At least Father brought us to the colonies—away from our brother-in-law—but if he forced Charity to marry that cad, will he not do the same to us—marry us off to the first man who comes knocking on his door? Like that vile Sir Wilhelm? I cannot let that happen again." She swayed as if her legs would give way beneath her.

Dajon started toward her again, but she instantly crystallized, her posture rigid. "You take on too much. It is not your job to protect and provide for them."

She shot him a hard glance. "Who, then? You? My father? No. Mother handed me that baton on her deathbed. Not that I wouldn't have gladly taken it anyway."

Anger tightened every muscle in his back. "Surely your brother-in-law was punished?"

Leaning against the wall beside the window, Faith hugged herself but remained silent.

"Did you not report him to your parents?"

She flung her hair over her shoulder, the moonlight setting it aflame in shimmering red. "Yes. Mother was horrified, but what could she do? It was his word against Hope's. Who would believe a seventeen-year-old girl over a lord? Father dove into his usual denial of any problems with his girls and refused to believe the event had ever taken place. Charity believed us, but fear of her husband kept her silent. So naught was ever done." Faith huffed. "Women are of little import. Certainly not enough to make a fuss over."

"Perhaps in some circles, yes. But *I* do not believe so." Anger and sorrow wrestled within Dajon's gut. It was unfathomable that this cretin had gotten away with such a heinous crime. And heartbreaking to witness the effects of it upon both Faith and her sister. And the villain claimed to be a Christian. No wonder her faith had dwindled.

"If I had been there, I assure you the man would have been punished." He inched closer to her.

"Well, you weren't there, were you?" Faith snapped. "And neither was your God. Apparently He thinks as much of women as society does."

Dajon winced. "I am here now." He touched her arm, and when she didn't move away, he pulled her closer to him.

She stiffened, but then slowly her shoulders sank. She gazed up at him, her glistening auburn eyes only inches from his. "You are here only on my father's orders."

He brushed the back of his fingers lightly across her cheek, enjoying the way she closed her eyes beneath his touch. "Do you really believe that is still my only reason?"

Her lashes fluttered against her cheeks like ripples on a calm sea. She opened her mouth then shut it as he continued to caress her skin. He placed a gentle kiss upon her forehead and allowed his gaze to wander down to her full lips. They quivered slightly.

Was she inviting his kiss?

He licked his own lips, forcing down his passion, forcing down his longing to explore that sassy mouth of hers with his own.

He ground his teeth together, fighting an urge that threatened to crash over him like a powerful wave.

Lord, I need Your strength.

What was he doing?

Faith was vulnerable, upset, and alone with him in her bedchamber. To take advantage of this moment would be incorrigible. Besides, she had suffered enough under the care of men, and Dajon did not trust himself not to add further pain by his own affections, no matter how genuine.

Gathering every ounce of God-given resistance, Dajon released her shoulders. "You are wrong about God, Miss Westcott. He highly esteems women. His love for them is evident throughout the scriptures."

She snapped open her eyes. Was it surprise, disappointment, or perhaps both that flashed from their depths?

Touching a lock of her hair, he fingered the silky strand, unable to resist at least that small token. Their flight through the rainy night seemed to have cleansed it, leaving it fresh and enticing. "You must not blame God for everything bad in this world."

She jerked away and plopped down on the window ledge. "Why not? Is He not sovereign? Can He not snap a finger and do whatever He wishes?"

The overwhelming passion of only a moment ago seeped from Dajon's body as quickly as if a keg plug had been pulled. "Aye, He can. As He did tonight." Dajon raised a brow and crossed his arms over his chest. At all costs, he must rein back the itch to touch her again. "Did He not save your sister?"

Faith snarled. "Perhaps, but why tonight and not five years ago?"

"I do not know. But I do know this"—he leaned toward her—"He has never left you or your sisters."

Faith shook her head stubbornly.

With a sigh, Dajon stepped toward the bed. No wonder she blamed God; no wonder her faith had faltered.

But Hope. His gaze took in her sleeping form on the bed. "I don't understand why your sister continually throws herself in the path of danger. It is as if she is begging for a repeat of her harrowing past. She must listen to her father—to me." He shifted his gaze to Faith, who stood and stared out the window, fingers gripping the sleeves of her gown.

She spun around and threw her hands to her hips. "Adhering to the dictates of men has only caused her pain. She had broken none of your God's rules when she was ravished by our brother-in-law. Naught was broken save her heart and her innocence. And no rule can ever heal the damage done to either of those."

Dajon tucked his hair behind his ear, searching for a way to help her understand that rules were made to protect people—both God's rules and man's—and all too often, broken hearts were the result of broken rules. "You think me a rule follower, but I have not always been so."

"You? The pious Mr. Waite. Broke a rule or two in your day, have you?" She sashayed over to him, her eyes flashing in the candlelight. "Told a wee lie, perhaps, or neglected to read your Bible ten times a day?" She snickered.

Dajon shuddered. Did he appear so saintly, so sanctimonious? Had he become so good at hiding his true self behind a shield of divine rules that no one thought him human? "Nothing quite so harmless, I assure you. I have a past I am not proud of. I have hurt others. . .caused great harm because of my own foolishness."

"I find that hard to believe." Faith ran her hand over the smooth wood of the bedpost and gazed at her sister.

Dajon wanted to share his sordid past with her, if only to convince her he was as fallen and sinful as anyone else. But he thought better of it. Her hatred of men's treatment of women meant she would not react well to his woeful tale. "I have since found great security in the rules of God and forgiveness in His love."

She darted an icy look his way. "And I have found that regardless of whether you follow God's rules, He does not protect you."

Dajon felt as if a twenty-pounder sat upon his chest. He placed his hand over hers on the bedpost and felt her tremble. "I wish I could take your pain away."

She faced him, her eyes narrowing, but did not remove her hand from beneath his. "Why would you care? What is it that you really want, Mr. Waite?"

A good question. What did he want? How could he tell her when he didn't quite know what he wanted? He allowed his gaze to wander over her face, her skin as lustrous as a pearl, her fiery eyes so full of life, the cluster of freckles on her pert little nose that darkened when her ire was pricked, and those plump lips begging for attention. Taking her hand from the post, he brought it to his lips and placed a kiss upon it, all the while keeping his eyes locked upon hers.

She tilted her lips in a gentle smile—a genuine smile devoid of the tough facade and sarcasm. Dajon's heart swelled under the warmth of it.

And he knew. He knew at that moment that he cared for her. As much as he fought it, as much as he denied it, he was enchanted by this brazen, redheaded, stubborn spitfire of a woman.

"I see you have no answer, Mr. Waite?" she quipped. "Well, what should I expect from a—"

Dajon brushed a thumb over the sleek line of her jaw, silencing her. Relishing in the softness of her skin, he tipped her head toward him and placed his lips upon hers. Why he gave in to the impulse, he couldn't say for sure. Perhaps it was to still her insolent tongue. Perhaps he could no longer resist her, or perhaps it was because she'd asked what he wanted, and truth be told, all he wanted was to kiss her.

She sank into him, receiving his kiss with equal passion. He lost himself in the feel of her, the softness of her lips, the smell of her breath, the warmth of her curves next to him. He felt as though his whole body was aflame and drinking her in was the only way to put out the fire. She reached up and ran her fingers over the stubble on his cheek and moaned.

Releasing her lips, Dajon reluctantly withdrew, kissed her cheek, and folded her in his embrace. He ran his fingers through the curls cascading down her back.

Then, as if another person took over her body, she yanked away from him and gave him a fierce look. "How dare you!"

Dajon flexed his jaw then grinned. "You asked me what I wanted, did you not?"

"Aye, but I did not ask for a demonstration."

"I heard no complaints."

"How could I protest with your mouth smothering mine?"

"Perhaps I mistook the moan you uttered as one of ecstasy instead of dissent? You should be more clear in your intentions." Dajon could not help but laugh.

"Allow me to be absolutely clear now, Mr. Waite." Faith stormed toward the door and flung it open. "Please leave. You have shown me what you want. 'Tis naught but the same thing every man wants."

"Great guns, woman, do you really believe me to be so base?" Dajon approached her. " 'Twas more than passion that ignited that kiss." He halted and sighed. Arms crossed over her waist, she would not look his way. " 'Twas more than passion I felt from you." He eased his fingers over her lips, still moist from his kiss. She did not move. Nay, perhaps he was fooling himself into hoping she returned his ardor. But still she allowed his touch. Her chest rose and fell rapidly; for a moment, he thought she would soften, but she batted his hand away and retreated in such haste that she stumbled over a small table by the door. It wobbled on its thin legs, sending something atop it to the floor with a thud.

Click, click, click. A round object spilled from a small pouch and bounced over the wooden planks.

"What have we here?" Dajon bent and picked up a tiny glimmering bead and held it up to a nearby candle. Alarm pricked his scalp and shot his heart into his throat. He shifted it to his other hand and examined it more closely, not ready to acknowledge what he saw.

It was a pearl. A rare conch pearl.

CHAPTER 23

Dajon stomped through the soggy streets of Charles Towne, ignoring his dark surroundings and the muddy water that splashed over his leather boots and up onto his white breeches. It had been nearly a week since he had seen Faith, nearly a week since he had discovered the conch pearls in her chamber. Unable to face the conclusion the pearls forced upon him, he had avoided her altogether, sneaking home late at night after everyone had retired and rising well before dawn.

Between two fingers of his right hand, he ground the tiny pearl, attempting to crush it and cast the powder into the rising wind—scattering its existence. Perhaps then he could silence its screaming accusation—that Faith, the lady he'd vowed to protect, the lady he had come to love, was also the pirate he must now bring to justice.

But the stubborn jewel would not submit to his pounding fury. It remained strong and round and shiny, like a cannonball shot straight through his heart.

Though she had pretended innocence and swore she had obtained the precious pearls in England, Faith had been unable to hide the guilt shriveling the features of her face. Dajon had charged from her chamber, out of the house, and off into the night to quell the rising storm within him. In his haste, he had forgotten to give her back the pearl. Now, after carrying it around with him for a week, he longed to toss it into Charles Towne Bay where no one would ever find it.

But he could not.

Duty. Duty and honor called to him from every corner. They had been his only friends these past four years. Faithful friends who had never let him down, friends who had restrained his wild streak—kept him safe in God's will where he could no longer hurt himself or anyone else. They would not forsake him now unless he abandoned them. And he had no intention of doing so. The pearl was evidence. One more bread crumb along the path to capturing the Red Siren.

Yet with each step down that path, Dajon's boots weighed like anchors, tugging at his feet and pulling down his heart along with them.

Why? Why, oh Lord, does it have to be her?

Dajon swallowed hard and clenched his fists as he turned another corner, paying no mind to where he was heading but instead allowing his nose to guide him to port. He had spent most of his evenings sauntering about town, waiting until after midnight to return to the Westcott home. Tonight, however, time had become lost amid the confusion in his mind, and it was far too close to dawn to risk disturbing Faith and her sisters. He would spend what was left of the night on his ship. Perchance there he could make sense of the astonishing evening last week: the miraculous rescue of Hope, Faith's intimate disclosure of their sorrowful past...

The passionate kiss they had shared.

And the pearl burning his fingers like a red-hot coal.

The depravity that filled the streets only a few hours ago had dwindled into an eerie silence, broken only by the distant lap of waves against the docks. A blast of hot air struck Dajon, carrying with it the smell of fish and manure and the pungent scent of the rice swamps just outside town. Removing his bicorn, he wiped the sweat from his brow and wondered why he had ever thought trading the cool weather of England for this torrid bog was a grand idea.

A woman's scream split the heavy air, jarring Dajon.

Scanning the surroundings, he realized he had wandered into a pernicious section of town by the docks off Bay Street. Shops and warehouses interspersed with taverns rose like ghost ships on each side of him.

Dajon froze, listening for another scream. Above him, thick clouds churned over a half-moon, flinging bands of light across the scene. He took another step. The click of his boots echoed down the deserted street like the cocking of a pistol. A moan sounded. Dajon jerked to the right. A drunken man sprawled on the porch of a house.

Another scream shot across the street, followed by a whimper.

Plopping the pearl into his pocket, Dajon bolted toward the sound, rounding the corner of a warehouse and dodging down a narrow pathway.

Another yell for help sped past his ears. Drawing his sword, he barreled toward the end of the alley. He squinted into the darkness and saw the jumbled shapes of two men hunched over someone on the ground. The lacy edge of a petticoat fluttered between their feet.

"You there! Stand down. Get off her!" Dajon dashed toward the men. They stole a glance at him over their shoulders then scampered away like rats down the alleyway before he could reach them.

For a moment, Dajon thought to pursue them, if only to teach them a lesson, but the tiny moan from their victim brought him to her side.

"Are you all right, miss?" He reached down to assist her off the muddy ground, and she flew at him, her arms encircling his back in such a tight grip, his breath burst from his throat.

"Thank you, sir. Oh, thank you for saving me, kind sir."

"Are you injured?" Dajon laid down his sword and tried to pry the woman off him, but she clung to him like a barnacle on a ship.

"I don't know. I am so overcome with fear." Her high-pitched voice rang insincere in his ears, but he shook it off. Fear did odd things to people.

"Can you stand?" Dajon supported her back. "Let me help you up, and we shall see if you are hurt."

Once on her feet, the woman released him and entered a swoon. He caught her before she toppled back to the ground. A cloud parted, flooding the alleyway with moonlight, and dark green eyes the color of a tropical sea gazed at him as if he were the only man in the world. The scent of sweet peaches swirled about his nose, chasing away the foul odors of the city. Her breasts rose and fell with each surging breath in the low-cut bodice. Long ebony hair fluttered in the breeze like silk.

Dajon swallowed.

Taking a step back, he cleared his throat and searched for his sword. "You appear to be unharmed, miss."

Retrieving his weapon, he sheathed it and found his eyes drawn to her again. She gave him one of those smiles that women give men across a room to entice them: a mixture of innocence, feminine dependence, and a hint of steamy dalliance.

Heat flared through Dajon even as every muscle tensed within him. He looked away. "You shouldn't be out alone so late at night, miss."

"I know." She sighed. "It was unavoidable, I'm afraid. And I was on my way home when those two beasts. . ." Pausing, she threw her hand to her chest as if to still the beating of her heart then raised it to wipe a tear from her eye.

Dajon touched her arm to offer some comfort. Truly, she seemed quite distraught. "You are safe now."

"Aye, thanks to you." She placed her hands on his blue coat, her fingers exploring his muscular chest. "What would I have done if you hadn't come to my rescue?"

" 'Twas my pleasure, miss." Dajon gripped his sword and stared off into the nebulous shadows of the night, anywhere but into this woman's sensuous green eyes.

"Perhaps I can repay you for your kindness?" She snuggled up beside him and fingered the gold buttons on his coat.

Dajon smelled danger. It wasn't the harrowing kind of life-threatening danger brought on by swords and guns and evil men. It was a delicious kind of danger, the kind of danger a man could lose himself in for days, only to emerge a skeleton of the man he had been, sullied and damaged beyond repair. It was the kind of danger, however, that was almost worth it.

Almost.

Lord, my God and my strength, was all Dajon could think to pray.

He clenched his jaw and allowed his gaze to wander over the woman's voluptuous form. "I thank you for your offer, miss, but I am otherwise engaged."

The woman's eyes grew wide beneath a furrowed brow. She flinched as if he had struck her. "You dare to turn me down?" Her tone carried no anger, no wounded sentiment, just pure incredulity at his rejection. 'Twas obvious she had never received one before.

God, why are You allowing this temptation now? Dajon tightened his grip on the hilt of his sword and rubbed his fingers over the cold silver. Had the week not held enough trials for one man to endure? Now this? His greatest weakness flaunted before him? He nearly laughed as he stared at one of the most alluring females he had ever seen, burrowing next to him and all but handing herself to him as if he were the king of England.

Certainly she was no real lady. Possibly a trollop or perhaps some nobleman's mistress. Who would know if Dajon spent some time with her? What harm would it do? By thunder, he could use some comfort after the shock and dismay of discovering the pearl in Faith's chamber.

Dajon squeezed the bridge of his nose. *No. Lord, I promised to follow You—to abide by Your laws.* A surge of strength leveled his shoulders.

With a cordial grin, he took her hand from his arm and released it. "Truly, you are quite lovely. Irresistible, to be sure. I would, however, prefer the honor of escorting you safely home."

Her green eyes filled to glistening pools. She shook her head. "You are a true gentleman, sir."

Footsteps sounded.

Whisking tears from her cheeks, the woman's breathing took on a rapid pace. The lines on her face tightened.

Dajon snapped his gaze down the dark alleyway as the footsteps drew nearer, but before he could draw his pistol, the lady began pounding his chest and screaming, "Get off me! Help me! Help me!"

Seizing her arms, Dajon shook her. "What are you saying? Have you gone mad? Calm yourself, woman."

She took a step back and clawed at her gown until it tore down the front, revealing her undergarments beneath.

Forgetting about the oncoming footsteps, Dajon stared aghast at her as she pummeled him again with her fists.

"What's this?" A stern voice boomed into the alleyway, and a dark figure rushed toward Dajon and shoved him to the ground. Drawing his sword, the man leveled the tip upon Dajon's chest.

The woman gasped and held her gown together as if a sudden rush of propriety had overcome her.

"Margaret, who is this man? Was he accosting you? I'll run him through right here!"

Dajon struggled to rise, but the man's blade kept him on the ground. He shifted his disbelieving gaze from the woman—Margaret—who continued to feign hysterics, to the man, a large fellow with the gruff face and haggard clothing of a dock worker and the hands of a trained swordsman.

The realization that he had been duped swallowed Dajon like a sudden squall at sea.

What could be the purpose? Surely everyone knew a lieutenant in His Majesty's Navy had no wealth to speak of unless it had been inherited.

He ground his teeth together then eyed the woman with the same look he gave one of his crew when he knew the correct course to take. "Miss, I beg you to tell this man the truth."

A variety of emotions passed over her face like waves on a beach, temporarily disturbing her pristine features: from anger to confusion to remorse to sorrow. Her lips puckered then flattened as her eyes flickered between the men.

Finally, her shoulders lowered, and she released her torn dress. "Nay, brother. He has done me no harm. In fact, quite the opposite." Sorrow alighted upon her features. "He has treated me more like a lady than any man I've ever known."

The anger in the man's dark eyes intensified under a flash of confusion. He gazed back and forth between Miss Margaret and Dajon; then, with a shrug of his shoulders, he sheathed his blade and held out his hand. "My apologies, sir. My sister often finds herself in, shall we say, delicate situations with men." He chuckled.

Grabbing his hand, Dajon stood and brushed off his coat. "I have no doubt."

"I am Henry Wittfield." He gestured toward the woman. "The unfortunate brother of Mrs. Margaret Gladstone."

"Dajon Waite, commander of the HMS *Enforcer*, at your service." Dajon nodded, still stunned by the odd events.

Henry turned to Margaret. "Your husband is worried about you."

She blew out a sigh and grabbed his arm. "As always, brother. Now let's be gone." She tugged on him as if she couldn't get away fast enough.

"Good night to you, sir," Mr. Wittfield said over his shoulder as Margaret hauled him from the alleyway without a single glance back at Dajon.

Retrieving his fallen bicorn, Dajon plopped it atop his head and stared up at the half-moon that had lit the outlandish scene like a stage light pouring down on a ghoulish comedy act. Even as a cloud overtook the glowing orb and shrouded Dajon once again in darkness, even as the cold mud now soaked through his breeches, even as the stink of refuse returned to sting his nose, he was thankful God had given him the strength to resist the sumptuous Mrs. Gladstone.

꧁

Borland tapped lightly on the captain's door. He had heard Dajon return just before dawn, and from the sound of his pounding boots and the slam of his door, he assumed all had gone according to plan. Now, unable to wait another moment, he risked disturbing the captain's sleep with some minor detail of the ship.

He tapped again.

"Enter," the gruff voice laden with sleep bellowed, and Borland pushed aside the oak slab. As he scanned the room, he spotted Dajon sitting on the edge of his rumpled bed, head in his hands.

"What is it, Borland?" Dajon rubbed his eyes.

"Henderson wants to know if he should grease the masts today, Captain."

"You woke me for that?" Dajon gave a disgruntled snort.

"My apologies, Captain. It *is* after eight bells, but I see now you had a rather late night." He delighted to see the dark, swollen splotches beneath Dajon's half-open eyes. "Is everything all right, Captain? Did you encounter some mischief last night?"

"Whatever would make you think that?" Dajon stood, annoyance hardening the lines in his jaw.

"You slept in your uniform. 'Tis unlike you to be so untidy." Borland took a tentative step toward him and pointed at his breeches. "And you're covered in mud." Truth be told, he'd never seen Dajon in such a state of disarray, and that could mean only one thing.

Sir Carteret's plan had worked.

Dajon slogged to his desk. "I had a most eventful evening."

Excellent. Borland could almost hear the constable and his men—or better yet, the marines—marching across the deck to arrest Dajon. He could almost see himself obligingly having to assume command of the ship as they dragged Dajon away.

"Eventful, sir?"

Fisting his hands on his waist, Dajon stared out the window. "Aye. But nothing I couldn't handle, I assure you."

Egad. Nothing he couldn't handle. Mrs. Margaret Gladstone, who was both the wife of a rich tradesman—a silversmith—and a woman in possession of less-than-sterling morals, had been the perfect lure. The only thing that bothered Borland was why the authorities had not been alerted last night as soon as the woman's brother caught Dajon in the reprehensible act.

No bother. It would happen soon enough, and finally the great Dajon Waite's luck would run out like so much seawater through a deck scuttle. Then Borland would assume the command he should have been given long ago. Justice would be served at last.

"Borland. . .Borland?"

Borland snapped his focus back to Dajon, who had turned to face him with a quizzical look. "Yes, Captain."

"I said to tell Henderson to proceed in greasing the masts, if you please." He rubbed the stubble on his jaw. "Now will that be all, or do you have some other pressing emergency?"

"No, Captain. That is all." Borland shifted his boots, unable to force himself to leave without trying once more to discover what had occurred last night. "Are you sure all is well? You seem distraught, Captain. Perhaps I can help."

Dajon eased out of his crumpled coat and tossed it onto a chair with a huff, but when he faced Borland, the harshness in his eyes had softened. "You are indeed a good friend, Borland. I thank you for your concern." He approached and clasped Borland's forearm then released it with a sigh. "But it seems I must bear this particular burden on my own."

A pinprick of guilt prevented the grin that strained to rise upon Borland's lips. He could manage only a nod as he reminded himself that his so-called friend had stolen what was rightfully his. Saluting, he turned and dashed out the door before Dajon's friendly demeanor did any more damage to his resolve for justice.

⥿

Dajon stared at the thick oak door long after the echo of its slam had faded. Mr. Borland was behaving rather oddly. Whatever had gotten into the man? Had he taken up grog so early in the morning? After the events of last night, Dajon wondered if the whole world had gone mad. Rubbing the back of his neck, he walked to the stern window that looked out upon Charles Towne Harbor. Ships of all sizes, ranging from schooners to brigantines to merchant frigates, rocked in the bay, their decks a flurry of activity as men loaded and unloaded merchandise before the heat of the day made the work unbearable. Off in the distance, Shute's Folly Island floated upon the water like an alligator's eye surveying its surroundings. Beyond it, James and Sullivan's Islands formed the entrance to the port of Charles Towne, protecting it from the ravages of the Atlantic.

But also providing an excellent point of entry for pirates—big enough for a large ship to sail through, but small enough to form a blockade and hold the city hostage. Which was precisely what Blackbeard had done not three months earlier.

Dipping his fingers in his waistcoat pocket, he pulled out the shiny round pearl, hoping to pull out a pebble instead, a lump of coal, anything but the conch pearl—hoping he had only dreamed that he'd found it in Faith's chamber. But there it perched betwixt his dirty fingers, winking at him in the sun's rays that beamed in through the paned window. Amazing how one little jewel could turn his life into a pool of bilge.

He tossed it in the air and caught it then dropped it back into his pocket. He had already set in play his plan to trap the notorious Red Siren. And now he must pray—pray with all his heart—that the villain was not Faith Westcott. Gripping the window ledge, he squeezed the rough wood until his knuckles whitened. If he was forced to arrest her, what would happen to her sisters? Her father? Not to mention to Faith herself?

She would be hanged.

All convicted pirates were hanged.

Something solid like a ball of tangled rope stuck in his throat, nearly choking him. How could he go through with it?

He slammed his fists down on the ledge. A splinter jabbed his skin.

Yet how could he not?

Four years ago, he'd vowed to live his life for God and country and nothing else. He would not make another mistake based on foolhardy emotions.

CHAPTER 24

Faith dropped another lump of sugar into her tea and offered the silver bowl, stacked full of sweet clusters, to Hope, sitting beside her on the flowered settee. Her sister shook her head then continued to stare down at the cup of coffee cradled in her hands. It had been a week since the traumatic incident at the Pink House, and although the doctor had pronounced Hope physically well, she had not been her usual exuberant self since. In fact, neither a single complaint nor critical remark had escaped her mouth, not even a plea to go shopping or attend a party. Sad to say, Faith preferred the old petulant Hope to this shell of a woman.

"Grace, have you any plans today?" Faith turned toward her other sister, who sat straight backed in the Queen Anne upholstered arm- chair, sipping her tea.

"Am I permitted to have plans?" Grace tilted her head, her voice carrying a sarcastic sting.

A light breeze stirred the curtains that flanked the open french doors leading out to the veranda. Faith caught the scent of the sea and took a deep breath, shifting in her seat. Oh, to be out upon those vast, carefree waters instead of sitting in this stuffy room with her equally stuffy sisters. She had thought spending the morning with them in the drawing room would be a good start to a cheerful day together, but she found their humors had not improved overmuch since yesterday.

Faith had remained home the entire week, not daring to take her ship out after Mr. Waite had discovered the pearl in her chamber. Unfortunately, she'd been forced to endure Sir Wilhelm's company on two separate occasions: first when he'd come to inquire after Hope's welfare, and second when he'd intruded on their dinner to invite Faith to a concert at Dillon's Inn. Both times she had ushered him quickly out the door, spouting excuses of ill health and dour humor. But she knew the man would not be put off forever.

However, during her time at home, Faith had been able to keep a stricter eye upon her sisters and spend much-needed time with them, as well as curb their foolish ventures into dangerous territory.

But from the tight expression souring Grace's face, she doubted her sister had been pleased with Faith's constant attentions.

Setting her cup down on the silver service tray with a clink, Grace pressed the folds of her plain muslin skirt. "I had planned to deliver a basket of fresh peaches and bread to the Baker widow. She has four children to feed, you know."

Faith clenched her jaw and felt a knot form in her stomach. "But if I understand correctly, her home is far outside the city walls. Nearly at the Ashley River."

Hope looked up from her coffee. "There have been several Indian attacks there of late." Her monotone voice belied the danger in her statement as she stared into the empty space of the room.

"Indeed, Hope." Faith laid a gentle hand on her arm but kept her firm gaze upon Grace. "And that is precisely why you will not go."

Grace smoothed the side of her raven hair as if a strand had dared to come loose. Which never happened, of course, because she kept them all drawn so tightly in a bun that Faith often wondered if that wasn't the reason her expression seemed so rigid.

Grace's green eyes snapped toward Faith. "It has been most pleasant having you home, Faith, but Father did not leave you as caretaker over us."

Hope glanced out the window as another breeze swirled through the room. "No. He left Mr. Waite."

"Where *is* the glorious Mr. Waite?" Grace smirked. "Perchance you have scared him off, Faith?"

"I have no idea." Faith fingered the lacy trim on her blue cotton gown as the tea bit her stomach. Pressing a hand over her complaining belly, she glanced at the intricately carved crown molding then at the Dutch floral oil paintings her mother had collected that decorated the violet walls, trying to avoid both of her sisters' imperious gazes.

"I should rather suppose navy business keeps him away." But she knew better. She had learned from Lucas that Mr. Waite had spent every night in the guesthouse, always leaving before dawn. Clearly he'd been avoiding her. She pictured the look on his face when she had told him— lied to him—about the pearls, how his brows had pinched together, how his eyes had widened, and how a look of disbelief and sorrow had passed through their blue depths. Most likely he had spent the week gathering the evidence he needed to arrest her. But what proof could he find?

Her ship.

Perhaps he had discovered her ship—or rather *his* ship. Still, he would have no way to link the vessel to her. Lucas had traveled there twice this past week to feed Morgan, and the *Red Siren* had been anchored in the same spot, seemingly undiscovered.

A pang of guilt made her shift in her seat. Guilt for the lies she had told, guilt for the life she had chosen. What was wrong with her?

"Clearly he is quite taken with you, Faith." Grace gave her a smile that revealed a bit of sauciness beneath her prudish exterior.

"Absurd." Setting down her cup, Faith jumped to her feet. "Pure rubbish." She strolled to the window and looked out upon the gardens below where Molly's purple bougainvillea climbed the white fence that guarded the side of the house. "He merely looks out for us as instructed by Father." Then why did she feel a sudden elation at Grace's statement? No matter. Even if Mr. Waite had felt some affection for her, it surely would have suffocated by now beneath his growing suspicions.

"Regardless, I owe him my life," Hope said.

"You owe God your life," Grace retorted. Faith swung around just in time to see Molly enter with a tray of biscuits and another kettle of tea. She nodded toward the cook, who set the tray down on the mahogany table in the center of the room. The buttery smell of the biscuits danced beneath Faith's nose even as her stomach lurched at the thought of eating.

She headed back toward her sisters. "Grace is right. 'Twas a miracle if ever I saw one." And although Faith still had a difficult time believing exactly what she had seen, she could not deny it, either.

Hope set her cup down beside the tray. "It was no such thing. Mr. Waite rescued me."

Molly clasped her hands together. "I beg your pardon, Miss Hope, if you'll forgive me for interrupting, but Mr. Corwin can't speak of nothin' else." Her eyes widened. "How there was a shield of light in front of Miss Hope and how those ruffians couldn't even see her until Mr. Waite arrived. Then how they was held off by some force while you got away. Why, I never seen Mr. Corwin so excited. He's behaving like he's just been made governor of Carolina."

Hope snickered.

"But you, Miss Faith"—Molly shook a long slender finger at her—"you shouldn't have been there at all. A lady in such a place. The shame of it."

"If your God can protect Hope," Faith said, her voice a bit more caustic than she intended, "then He can protect me as well, can He not?"

Molly snorted. "He can do what He wants, I suppose. And you should be thanking Him that He kep' you safe. But the both of you best be staying out of such places, or He may not the next time."

"God always protects me when I journey to do His will." Grace straightened her back and clasped her hands together in her lap. "However, if you're out of His will, no wonder you found yourself in harm's way." The sanctimonious look on her face suddenly collapsed into folds of confusion. "Yet..."

Hope scowled at her sister. "Then why, pray tell, did He protect me, Grace?"

"I thought you insisted He did nothing of the kind?" Grace smirked.

Narrowing her eyes, Hope collapsed into the settee with a huff. "I'm still not saying He saved me. I'm simply pointing out that your conjecture is flawed."

Faith eased beside Hope. Her sister had not relayed any of the details of that night to anyone, despite frequent prodding. In fact, this was the first sign of emotion she'd exhibited in a week, and despite the argumentative nature of Hope's words, Faith was happy to see the old Hope come back to life.

Molly grabbed the tray of empty cups. "All I kin say is, it thrills me to know that the Almighty is still active and powerful and kin save us even from our own follies."

"He is the same yesterday, today, and forever." Grace laid a hand on Molly's arm and smiled.

"That He is. I kin see that now. And Mr. Corwin is starting to see things different as well." Molly winked at Faith as if they shared a secret, but Faith wanted no part of this holy alliance. If Lucas decided to follow such an untrustworthy God, then he had best do so on his own time. Turning, Molly began humming one of her conscience-grating hymns as she exited the room.

Faith sighed. She must take the *Red Siren* out. One more good raid, one more shipload of plunder and she would be able to care for her sisters properly, hire protection for Grace—an army if she had to—and Hope would no longer have to vie for the affections of such wretched men as Lord Falkland.

Yet why did she have the nagging feeling that no amount of wealth would be enough to tame her two sisters?

As if in answer to Faith's question, Hope crossed her arms over her chest. "When can I see Arthur. . .Lord Falkland?"

"I beg your pardon." Faith gave her sister a scorching look. "Is he not the one that got you into that mess at the Pink House? He abandoned you. Don't you remember?"

"How do you know that?"

"Your friend Miss Cormac told us."

"You spoke with Anne?" A strange expression of shock fringed with humor danced over Hope's face. "I wouldn't believe her. She rarely tells the truth."

Why Hope would befriend someone who was devoid of honesty was beyond Faith, but that was another issue. "She had no reason to lie. Lord Falkland left you all alone in that heinous tavern to be ravished and God knows what else. You cannot deny he was the one who brought you there."

Hope begrudgingly nodded but would not meet Faith's gaze.

Faith took her hand in hers. "Please, dear. You must see what type of man he is. He doesn't love you."

"He does love me." Hope jerked her hand away. "You don't know him. 'Twas unavoidable. He was called away on a matter of great urgency." Her eyes glistened with tears.

"Could he not escort you home first?"

"He asked Mr. Ackers to do the honor."

"And who, pray tell, is Mr. Ackers?"

"A loyal friend of Arthur's." Hope swallowed and gazed down at the Chinese rug warming the floor at their feet.

"And why did this Mr. Ackers not escort you home?"

"I don't know. He disappeared."

"Disappeared? Of all the. . ." Fury exploded within Faith, sending sharp pains into her belly. She wanted to drag one of her cannons to this Lord Falkland's home and blast it to rubbish. "Seems your Lord Falkland invokes no more loyalty among his friends than a thief in a room full of magistrates."

" 'Twas Mr. Ackers who left me." Hope's lip quivered. Tears slid down her cheeks. "I didn't know what to do."

Faith wanted to tell her she shouldn't have been there in the first place, but instead, she plucked a handkerchief from her pocket and handed it to Hope. "If it weren't for Mr. Waite—"

"And God," Grace interjected.

"I loathe to think what could have happened to you," Faith continued.

"What difference does it make?" Hope swiped at her tears. "I'm already sullied." Leaning forward, she dropped her head into her hands.

Faith's heart crumbled into ashes. She glanced at Grace, who returned her agonized gaze.

Rising, Grace approached them and sat on the other side of Hope. "You are not sullied in God's eyes."

"God is not here," Hope muttered. "And He does not have to live in a society that allows men to dominate women and then holds the women accountable for the outcome."

Faith waited for Grace's usual retort; instead, tears flooded her sister's eyes, and she put her arm around Hope, saying nothing.

Truth be told, Faith couldn't agree more with her sister's assessment, but what was to be done about it? It was the way of things. Wealth was their only salvation, and until she could garner enough of it, she must stop Hope from destroying what was left of her life. "Nevertheless, I insist you stay away from Lord Falkland."

Hope raised her glassy eyes to Faith. "You cannot order me about. I will see whom I choose to see." No anger tainted her tone, no defiance, no desperation. She had simply uttered the statement as fact.

A chill iced Faith's bones. Rebellious, stubborn girl! How could she make her see the error of her ways before it was too late? "I assure you, Lord Falkland will cause you naught but pain. Why do you insist on destroying yourself?"

"The good Lord may not come to your aid next time, Hope." Grace brushed a honey-colored lock of hair from Hope's face.

"I care not." Shrugging from between her sisters, Hope rose and took a deep breath. "How many suitors do you see lining up at our door? I'm two and twenty already. And I love Arthur. . .Lord Falkland. He may not be perfect, but he loves me and he has enough wealth to keep me happy."

Faith stood, feeling every muscle tense. Enough of this defiance. If she had to, she'd put her sisters under guard to keep them from harm.

Oh, Mother, I'm trying so hard to protect them, but you didn't exactly give me much to work with. "Hope, you will not—"

Edwin appeared in the doorway, his face even paler than usual. "Mr. Waite to see you, miss." His droopy eyes darted around the room. "He has two gentlemen with him."

"Gentlemen? Officers? Are they in red uniforms?"

"One of them is, miss."

She coughed, gasping for air, and then held a hand over her aching stomach. Had he come to arrest her? She scanned the room looking for a place to hide and then realized how ridiculous that was.

"Edwin, please tell him I'm not feeling well. In fact"—she glanced at her sisters with a pleading look—"tell him we are *all* not feeling well."

"Very well, miss." With a sigh, Edwin left, but no sooner had he disappeared than a scuffle sounded in the hall and Mr. Waite's deep voice bounded through the room.

"Not feeling well? All three of you?" He marched into the room as if it were the deck of his ship. He leveled a hot and loaded gaze straight at Faith.

CHAPTER 25

Dajon patted Faith's gloved hand and gently tucked it in the crook of his elbow. He could still feel the tremble in it even after an hour of strolling downtown. He had certainly expected some reaction from her after the traumatic night they had shared last week, especially after their passionate kiss. But he hadn't expected the complete horror that had shot from her eyes when he had entered the drawing room with Borland and Cudney on his heels. He had only thought to bring the marine at the last minute, as a way to gauge her guilt. And, unfortunately, her reaction had weighed heavily on the scales of iniquity—a pirate's reaction if ever he saw one.

All color had drained from her face. Even the peach of her lips had transformed to gray. Her chest heaved like the swells of a summer squall upon the sea. What other explanation could be offered?

"I thank you, Mr. Waite, for your kind offer." She looked up at him and smiled, her auburn eyes a sparkling mixture of unease and playfulness. "I do admit I feel much better out in the summer air. And my sisters needed an outing more than I, I'm afraid."

"My pleasure, Miss Westcott. I had no idea you have been indisposed."

"Just a bit of fatigue. Nothing to be concerned about." She plucked out her fan and fluttered it through the air.

He glanced at Hope on the arm of Borland as the two of them strolled down the lane. "Your sister seems much improved."

"Yes." Faith lowered her lashes. "She has been melancholy this past week. Only today has she returned somewhat to herself." She sighed and allowed a tiny grin. "Although I'm not altogether sure I am ready for the return of her peevish attitude."

Dajon chuckled, but Faith sobered instantly. "I must beg your forgiveness, Mr. Waite, for my burdening you with our family affairs that night."

"Never fear." Dajon patted her hand again. "You can trust me to keep your confidence."

"I am in your debt, sir." She gave his arm a squeeze that reached up to warm his heart.

Grace, her hand stiffly on Cudney's arm, came alongside him. "We have missed your company, Mr. Waite." She gazed at him with green eyes framed by lashes as thick as a virgin forest. With her petite, curvaceous figure and ebony hair, she possessed an exotic beauty that rarely peeked out from behind her rigid exterior.

"How kind of you to say, Miss Grace. I'm afraid I've been quite busy on board my ship." He eyed his marine, marching beside her. The man's stiff mouth and glazed eyes indicated he wasn't particularly enjoying Grace's company. Perhaps she had been expounding to him the dangers of sin as they strode along.

"Thank you for inviting us to the festival," Grace continued. "My sister was becoming quite the magistrate, forbidding us even to leave the house."

"She was, was she?" Dajon studied Faith, who was fanning the air about her as if swatting away the conversation. "The lady who rides a horse better than most men, enters dangerous taverns in the thick of night, and fires pistols with deadly accuracy? That lady?"

"Yes, exactly." Grace giggled. "She holds us to a far higher standard than herself, it would seem."

"Indeed."

Faith snapped her hard gaze to her sister. "The things I do are for your protection and are quite different from putting oneself in danger's way for naught."

Grace frowned. "I would hardly call feeding the—"

"Nevertheless," Dajon interrupted, hoping to ward off another mind-hammering argument between the sisters. "It is I who should thank you, Miss Grace, for the pleasure of your company." He grinned. With a lift of her nose, she and Mr. Cudney proceeded ahead to join Hope and Mr. Borland.

Dajon had been pleased to discover that the citizens of Charles Towne had planned a small festival celebrating the return of the summer's crops after much of their plantings had been destroyed by the Yamasee Indian raids the previous year. Local artisans agreed to display their wares on the street while musicians entertained passersby. The small event provided the perfect opportunity to invite the Westcott ladies out for a pleasurable day, as well as the perfect distraction for Dajon's real purpose—to bait Faith with the news of the arrival of a merchant ship.

But as he allowed his gaze to sweep over her smooth skin, kissed pink by the sun, her fiery curls dancing in the breeze around the half-moon scar that adorned her graceful neck, even the cluster of freckles atop her nose, he wondered how he could be so deceptive to such an extraordinary woman. He swallowed, gazing at her moist lips, remembering the soft feel of them on his own, her hunger, her passion, her need for him. Shifting his eyes away, he prayed for a cool breeze to blast over him and revive his reason.

But what choice did he have? He had to know the truth, even if it killed him. And somehow today, as Faith walked beside him, clinging to his arm as if she belonged there forever, he knew that it just might.

~

Faith adjusted her flowered straw hat, longing to tear it from her head and shake her hair loose in the breeze. Beneath the grueling August sun, her head felt like a poached egg. Or maybe it was the feel of Mr. Waite's strong arm beneath her hand that caused her to overheat. More than likely, it was the trembling that still coursed through her body. For she had thought for certain when he had marched into their drawing room, marine in tow, that he had procured enough evidence to arrest her.

Turning down Queen Street, she felt a salty breeze waft around her. She took in a deep breath, noting Mr. Waite did the same. He loved the sea as much as she did. At least they had one thing in common. But their similitude stopped there.

The blasted man was taunting her. She knew it.

She shouldn't have accepted his invitation. But as she heard Hope's laughter and saw Grace examining an Indian basket, she knew her sisters had needed a carefree day of amusement.

Perhaps it would be Faith's last one with them.

Perhaps Mr. Waite was simply luring her close enough to the half-moon bastion so when he arrested her he wouldn't have far to throw her in the Watch House prison. Her mouth went dry even as another trickle of perspiration slid down the back of her dress.

When they turned down Bay Street, the cobblestone avenue exploded in a cacophony of sounds and movements. Ladies decked in gay colors, on the arms of men in their finery, flitted across the path to examine shop wares displayed in front of the stores. Music frolicked down the street from a small band positioned under the shade of a hickory tree. Harpsichord, violin, and flute harmonized together in a lively tune.

As they wove their way through the clamoring crowd, they passed exquisitely carved furniture made from oak, mahogany, pine, and cypress, oil paintings from local artists, the latest fashions, shoes, silk fans, musical instruments, and gold and silver jewelry. A variety of languages filled the air, most of which Faith recognized: Dutch, German, French. Charles Towne attracted people from all over the world looking for freedom and a new start in a fresh land, and this day every one of them seemed to be strolling about on Bay Street.

Up ahead, a French trapper and his Indian wife bartered with a shop owner over some pelts flung across his arm. Long matted hair framed his face and swayed across his back as he spoke. Behind him, his wife, wearing dirt-smudged furs, kept her gaze on the ground. Yet not three yards away strolled a man and lady decked in silk and lace—the finest fashions of London society. Faith doubted she would ever grow accustomed to the extreme contradiction of this wild land.

A curricle clomped toward them, and Mr. Waite ushered Faith from its path, placing himself between her and the street. A woman, donned in a silk ruffled gown and white powered wig, gave Mr. Waite an appreciative smile from its seat as they passed.

"Are you enjoying yourself, Miss Westcott?" He leaned down to whisper in her ear. The scent of leather and lye swirled about her nose and quickened her breathing. "You seem a bit tense." His lips curved in that sardonic grin that always sent her heart pounding.

Faith dared to glance into his sharp blue eyes, down to his strong jaw, and over to his dark umber hair pulled behind him. She could understand why he attracted feminine admiration. She averted her gaze before she gave him the satisfaction of seeing her own admiration.

"I fear I am still not quite myself, Mr. Waite, but I am happy to see my sisters enjoying themselves."

Faith closed her eyes, longing to drown out all the sounds around her, save the lap of the bay upon the quays. She took in a deep breath. There it was: the salty smell of the sea hidden among the odor of horse and sweat and city refuse. She could hardly wait to sail upon its mighty waves again where no problems, no guilt, no fears assailed her. Only peace.

That feeling of peace quickly diminished, however, when Faith opened her eyes and saw the Watch House up ahead. She froze, drew a shaky breath, and forced herself onward. The sounds of the city faded into a muddled clamor as she strolled past the ominous building, her hand still clenching Mr. Waite's arm. Unable to avert her gaze, she stared at the circular stone tower that protruded in a semicircle into the bay, a citadel guarding the city's entrance. The brick Watch House loomed just before it. Faith couldn't help but wonder how many poor souls were imprisoned within.

Oh God, please don't let me become one of them.

Good heavens. She was praying again. Yet even as she made the silent plea, she tripped over one of the cobblestones and barreled forward.

Catching her arm, Mr. Waite stayed her fall. "Are you all right, Miss Westcott?"

"Yes, forgive me." His hand touched the small of her back, sending a flame of heat up her spine. She jerked away from him. "I wasn't paying attention."

"You seem a bit unnerved today, miss." The captain shifted his daring blue eyes between her and the Watch House.

"I am concerned for my sisters. Forgive me. I am not very good company."

"That could never be the case." He gave her a sincere smile.

As they continued onward past the Watch House gates, Faith's heart took on a more relaxed beat.

He must not have any evidence against her. He'd probably forgotten all about the pearl, and she had been worried for nothing.

As they passed one of the docks, the wooden frame of a ship projecting from an open warehouse drew Faith's attention. Several men scampered about, and the pounding of hammers and the scrape of saws filled the air.

Faith had never seen a ship being built before, and she stopped, lifting her hand to shield her eyes from the sun. A familiar figure hefting a large piece of wood onto his shoulder emerged from the warehouse, shouting orders to one of the men.

"Is that not the man we met in church?"

Mr. Waite snapped his gaze toward the open warehouse. "Ah yes." He raised a hand to his mouth. "Mr. Mason," he called.

Mr. Mason squinted in their direction then dropped the log from his shoulder and waved. He started to move toward them but froze as if he saw a ghost. Following his gaze, Faith found it had locked upon Hope, who stopped beside her.

Grabbing a cloth from a bench, Mr. Mason mopped the sweat from his face and neck then tossed it aside and approached them.

After nodding his greeting toward Mr. Waite, Faith, and the others, he turned toward Hope. "Good day, Miss Hope." He swiped a hand through his brown hair and drank her in with his gaze. His moist cotton shirt clung to his arms and chest, revealing strong muscles beneath.

Hope huffed. "Whatever are you doing out here in the hot sun like a common laborer?"

His grin fell slack. "I fear I *am* a common laborer." He jerked a thumb over his shoulder. "I am building my third merchant ship." He rubbed his stubbled jaw and crossed his thick arms over his chest.

"Mr. Mason's other two ships are no doubt upon the seas at this moment," Mr. Waite commented. "Someday, Mr. Mason, I fear you will be a wealthy man."

"All I want is to be able to take care of myself, Mr. Waite." Mr. Mason glanced at the captain, then his eyes quickly shifted back to Hope. "And a family someday."

"Still." Hope raised a haughty brow. "Can you not hire someone to do this menial work?"

"I prefer to work alongside my men and make sure the job is done correctly, if that's acceptable to your ladyship." He gave a mock bow.

"Why should I care? I simply do not see the point of getting so filthy and sweaty." A deep shade of red crept up Hope's face.

"Work is good for you, Miss Hope. It gives you something to occupy your time other than pleasing yourself." Amusement flickered in his dark eyes. "You should try it sometime."

Grace giggled, and Faith found herself enjoying the banter between Hope and this common man. She had never seen her sister quite so befuddled, so abashed. Normally Hope would have dismissed the man instantly and walked away, yet there she stood, as mesmerized with him as he seemed to be with her.

"How dare you?" Hope's jaw tightened. She tore her gaze from his, as if waiting for his apology, waiting for him to grovel at her feet as most men did.

"You are the one who stopped to converse with me."

"I did no such thing."

"Yet here you remain." He grinned.

"I shall remedy that immediately, sir." She grabbed onto Mr. Borland's hand. "Come along, Mr. Borland."

With a shrug of his shoulders, the lieutenant followed behind her like a horse-drawn carriage.

Faith and Mr. Waite said their good-byes as Mr. Mason returned to his work, chuckling as he went.

"At last a man who sees beyond our sister's beauty," Grace commented with a chortle.

"Indeed." Faith squeezed Grace's hand. "He is extraordinary at that."

"What an impertinent, rude man." Hope sneered when they caught up to her and Borland.

"I thought him quite charming," Faith teased.

"You would think—"

"Ah, there is Mallory's Tea Shoppe," Mr. Waite interrupted. "I hear they serve an excellent lemonade." He gestured to a small, quaint shop to their right. The wide front porch was furnished with white tables and chairs. "Shall we refresh ourselves, ladies?"

Grace nodded with a smile, and Hope's eyes lit up. "Why, yes. That sounds delightful."

After everyone was seated with lemonade in hand, Mr. Waite rose, scraping his chair over the aged porch floor. "If you will excuse me, ladies. I saw someone inside I need to speak with." He cast a knowing look toward

Borland. "I shall only be a minute."

An awkward silence ensued in his absence.

Faith studied Mr. Cudney, whose posture reminded her of a backstay under a stiff wind. What was his purpose among them if not to arrest her? Surely not to socialize. He seemed as out of place as a priest on a pirate ship.

"Mr. Cudney, may I ask how long have you been a marine?"

"A little over two years, miss." His brown eyes met hers with a brief smile then skittered away.

"And do you serve on only His Majesty's ships?"

"Yes."

"The marines fight as infantry aboard the ship," Mr. Borland said. "They carry out guard duties, suppress mutinies, and enforce regulations."

"I see." Faith knew that, of course, but smiled at Borland nonetheless.

"You must be very courageous." Hope rested her head in one hand and cooed in Mr. Cudney's direction. A red hue that matched the color of his uniform marched up the poor man's face.

"Speaking of courage," Mr. Borland began, stroking his moustache and clearing his throat. "We shall need courage like his to protect the *Lady Adeline* sailing in from Martinique day after next."

"Protection from what?" Grace asked, taking a sip of her lemonade.

Faith pressed her cool mug between her hands, the tantalizing scent of lemons swirling about her nose, and willed her expression to remain placid as she listened to Borland's response.

"From pirates, miss, of course, as well as other villains upon the sea."

Grace fingered a button at her high collar. "May God have mercy on their wicked souls."

Frowning at her sister, Faith ignored the unusual guilt needling her heart.

The *Lady Adeline*. A merchant vessel that needed guarding. Precisely the opportunity Faith had been awaiting. But how could she find out more without giving herself away?

"Pray tell, Mr. Borland," Faith said, twirling a lock of her hair non-chalantly around her finger, "what is so special about this merchant vessel that you believe it to be the target of pirates?" She took a sip of her lemonade, the sour taste curling her tongue.

"Only that she carries a cargo of Spanish gold stolen in a raid. Worth a fortune, I'm told."

Faith coughed and nearly spit the lemonade from her mouth. "So Mr. Waite will be at sea the day after next?"

"Aye, in two days. We are to meet the ship midmorning off St. Helena Sound but should return to port before sunset." He leaned toward her, a sly look gleaming in his eye. "I suppose 'tis acceptable to relay this information to you and your sisters. Your father is an admiral, after all." He sat back in his chair and straightened his coat. "Is there something you expect you'll need Mr. Waite for day after tomorrow?"

"Nay." Faith waved a hand through the air. "I just wondered in case my sisters and I require an escort into town."

Grace's brow wrinkled. "We can simply ask Lucas or Edwin. You venture into town with Lucas all the time."

"Not that we'll be permitted to go out anyway," Hope added.

The door opened with a creak, and Mr. Waite returned and plopped down beside Faith.

Taking another sip of lemonade, she avoided his gaze. Her heart soared at this fortuitous information. She must return home as soon as possible to make plans for what might be her very last pirate raid.

"Mr. Waite?" A man dressed in a fine ruffled shirt, breeches, and silk hose took the steps up to their table and nodded toward the captain. "Are you Mr. Waite, the commander of the HMS *Enforcer*?" he asked with exuberance as he removed his hat.

"Yes, I am." Dajon stood and took his outstretched arm.

Grinning, the man shook Mr. Waite's hand over and over as if trying to loosen his bones. "I have been searching for you, sir."

"And you are?" Mr. Waite pulled his hand free.

"I am Mr. Hugh Gladstone, a man greatly in your debt." He straightened his velvet crimson jacket.

Mr. Borland's normally tanned face blanched as white as the table. He fidgeted with his mug of lemonade and avoided glancing at the two men as they spoke, and Faith wondered at his sudden agitation.

"Gladstone." Mr. Waite rubbed his jaw. "The name is familiar to me."

"You saved my wife, Mrs. Margaret Gladstone, from great danger last night, did you not?"

"Your wife." Mr. Waite's eyes sparked in recollection, and he shifted his stance. "Yes, of course."

"She informed me how you came upon those ruffians attacking her in the street."

Mr. Waite nodded then led Mr. Gladstone a few yards to their right, uttering, "If you'll excuse me," over his shoulder as he went.

But Faith kept her ear pointed in his direction and her eyes on Borland, who squirmed in his seat as if sitting upon hot coals.

"And you fought them off bravely and saved her reputation and quite possibly her life," Mr. Gladstone was saying.

Mr. Waite cleared his throat. "Any gentleman would have done the same."

"Ah, that is where you are wrong, sir. Many would not have been bothered. Especially with a woman about town so late in the evening." He leaned toward the captain. "They would not have suspected her to be a virtuous lady."

Faith glanced at Mr. Waite. With hands clenched behind his back, he lowered his gaze to the white planks of the porch deck. His brow glistened with perspiration.

Mr. Gladstone's voice lowered to a whisper. "My wife takes laudanum for a painful ailment and ofttimes wanders off at night."

"I am sorry to hear that."

"She has nothing but good things to say about you, sir. How you behaved the gentleman and risked your own life for hers."

Mr. Borland sipped his lemonade but then began hacking as if it contained sand.

Glancing his way then back at Mr. Gladstone, Mr. Waite responded, "It was nothing, I assure you. Now if you don't object, I must be—" He turned to leave.

"Might I offer you a reward?"

"There is no need." Mr. Waite halted and gave the man a sincere look. "But do take good care of your wife, Mr. Gladstone." His voice held a hint of warning.

"That I will, sir." The man planted his hat atop his head and shook Mr. Waite's hand again before he barreled down the stairs. "You are a hero, sir. A true hero!" he yelled as he dashed off.

By the time Mr. Waite had returned to the table, Mr. Borland was a fuming pot of angst. Was he so competitive with his captain that any noble act on Mr. Waite's part caused such a violent reaction?

Nonetheless, Faith found her own regard for Mr. Waite billowing within her. Truly this man respected women—all women. Even those with less-than-scrupulous behavior. Even those most men would give no notice to unless they sought a night's entertainment.

She faced him, wanting to express her regard, but the ruddy hue creeping up his neck and the way he tightly gripped his mug indicated his discomfort with the topic.

"Lord Falkland!" Hope nearly jumped from her chair, tossing her hand to her mouth. She stood for a moment, staring down the crowded street. Her eyes locked upon something in the distance. "Arthur!" Clutching her skirts, she darted from the table, toppling her chair behind her.

The captain rose and gave Faith a level gaze. "Stay here," he ordered and then stomped after Hope. But she had never been good at obeying commands, especially when it came to her sister's welfare. Dashing past him, Faith ignored his call to her and pressed her hat upon her head as she tried to catch up with Hope. Straining to see past the throng of people and horses, she finally spotted the source of Hope's despair.

Lord Falkland sauntered down the street, decked in a ruffled lace shirt, damask waistcoat, tight-fitting breeches, and a fashionable bicorn, with a beautiful woman on his arm.

"Hope, wait," Faith cried after her sister.

Falkland nudged his hat up and gazed toward the commotion. When he saw Hope, his eyes snapped wide, but they quickly narrowed. With the grace of a serpent, he patted the woman's hand, whispered in her ear, and sent her on her way; then he turned with open arms toward Hope. "Hope, my dear. A pleasure to see you looking so well."

Hope halted before him just as Faith reached her and grabbed her hand, tugging her away from the cur. But Faith quickly realized she didn't have to keep Hope from him. Hope stood stiffly in place, eyes plump with tears, shock freezing her features into tight little lines.

Falkland lowered his arms. "Something bothers you, my dear?"

"Who is she?" Hope's voice carried the tone of a condemned prisoner.

"Who?" Falkland tapped his cane on the street and brushed a speck of dirt from his sleeve.

Faith eyed the man with disdain. Here before her pranced another vain fop who not only cared nothing for her sister but took advantage of Hope's desperate need for love. Not the first time in her life, Faith longed to be a man so she could pound the sneering grin from his face. Her hand curled. She just might attempt it anyway.

"Oh, you mean Mrs. Blackwell." Lord Falkland feigned innocence. "Her husband imposed upon me to escort her to the festival. He is ill with the fever, poor fellow."

"Her husband?" Hope's voice lifted a bit, and she loosened her grip on Faith's hand.

"Yes, dear. You can't be jealous, can you?" He took her other hand in his and raised it to his mouth, placing a kiss upon it.

And in that moment, watching the exchange between Falkland and her sister—the devotion and adoration beaming from Hope's eyes, the flicker of victory and dominance burning in Falkland's gaze—Faith knew.

She knew her sister had given herself to this foul beast, heart and body.

"Why haven't you called on me?" Hope pouted and glanced at him from beneath her lashes.

"I heard you were ill, my dear."

"She was ill because of you," Faith hissed.

Falkland shifted his dark, lifeless eyes to her. "Good day to you, Miss Westcott. You are always a picture of beauty."

"And you, sir, are always a picture of chicanery."

"I beg your pardon?" he huffed and ran a finger over his slick eyebrows.

Mr. Waite joined them, crossing his arms over his chest. "Lord Falkland, I assume?"

"Yes, and you are?"

"Mr. Waite. I am guardian to these ladies."

"Indeed." Falkland glanced at a passing carriage as if bored with the conversation.

Mr. Waite took a forceful step toward him, towering over the man. "And as their guardian, I must insist that you stay away from Miss Hope."

Hope gasped and clung to Lord Falkland's arm. "He will not."

Lord Falkland patted her hand like a condescending parent then plucked it from his arm. "You may insist what you like, sir, but I believe the lady has made her choice."

"The lady"—Mr. Waite stepped in front of Hope, pushing her behind him—"is not safe in your company. Any man who escorts a woman to a place like the Pink House then abandons her is not fit to be entrusted with the care of dogs."

Hope struggled to weave around Mr. Waite, but Faith grabbed her arm and held her in place.

"How dare you!" Lord Falkland tapped his cane into the dirt, sending a puff of dust into the air. "I'll have you know that the lady begged me to go to the Pink House. She rather enjoys that sort of atmosphere—the drinking, the gambling, the, shall we say, interesting clientele. Don't you, dear?" His snakelike eyes peered around Mr. Waite and slithered over Hope.

Hope's forehead wrinkled, and she stared back at him as if he had slapped her. Faith circled an arm around her shoulders and drew her closer. "She does not enjoy associating herself with the same squalor that you do, sir, and she suffered greatly for your negligence."

"I left her in the care of a friend." Lord Falkland raised a hand and examined his nails.

"Your friend abandoned her." The veins in Mr. Waite's neck began to throb, and a strand of his dark hair flicked over his jaw in the stiff breeze. "Do you realize the danger you put her in? Do you realize what almost happened to her?"

"What is she to you?" Falkland's dark gaze shifted between Mr. Waite and Hope. "Ah yes. Now I see. You wish a piece of her for yourself."

Mr. Waite raised his fist and slugged Lord Falkland across the jaw. His lordship floundered like a fish on a dry deck. His cane flew through the air, and he landed with a thud upon the stone street.

Gasps and "Oh mys" shot in their direction, and a crowd gathered to watch.

Faith couldn't help the grin when Mr. Waite caught the silver-hilted cane as it careened to the ground and pointed it at Falkland.

"You are never to see Miss Hope Westcott again. Do I make myself clear?" He flung the fancy stick at Falkland, whose face was already swelling into a sweaty red mass.

"No!" Hope jerked from her sister's grasp and dropped beside Lord Falkland, kissing his jaw where he'd been hit.

Brushing her aside as if she were a mere annoyance, he stood, wiped off his breeches, and straightened his shirt. "How dare you strike me!" Falkland rubbed his jaw and then lifted it in the air. "Do you realize who I am, sir?"

"No, but I recognize *what* you are," Waite said.

A mixture of pride and relief lifted Faith's spirits.

"Rest assured, Mr. Waite," Falkland twisted from Hope's clawing hands, "you may soon find yourself called out."

"I await the pleasure." Mr. Waite bowed.

Faith laid an arm around Hope's shoulders and tried to pry her away from Lord Falkland's side, but she stomped her foot as if planting it firmly in the ground. She turned her glassy eyes to Mr. Waite. "You cannot keep us apart."

"Never fear, my dear," Falkland announced to Hope, but his piercing gaze remained on the captain. "I *will* see you again. You can be sure of that."

"Do not try me, your lordship." Mr. Waite gripped the hilt of his service sword.

"And I will see you in irons if you dare to strike me again."

With a mocking nod toward Lord Falkland, Mr. Waite took hold of Hope's arm, pulling her from the vile man.

After sending Mr. Borland and Mr. Cudney back to the ship, which was but a few minutes' journey from where they were, Mr. Waite escorted Faith and Grace as they dragged a sobbing Hope back to the house. When Mr. Waite had returned to his ship, and as soon as Faith had seen Hope tucked safely in bed within her chamber, she sought out Lucas and found him in the stables.

He glanced up at her, his initial grin fading beneath what must have been a look of urgency on her face.

"What's wrong, mistress? Ye look like yer loaded and primed and ready to fire."

"Just some trouble in town with Hope, but Mr. Waite handled it." She leaned against a wooden post and smiled. "In fact, I spent the entire day with the commander." She raised her brows. "Which made it the perfect day for the Red Siren to have attacked some poor merchantmen at sea. Grayson and Strom?"

He nodded.

"Tell them to proceed first thing in the morning."

CHAPTER 26

Gripping the taffrail, Dajon gazed over Charles Towne Bay, watching the cream-capped swells coming in from the sea like white ruffles on an indigo shirt. Twenty ships anchored in the harbor; one other Royal Navy ship, the HMS *Perseverance*, a forty-four-gun ship, had recently arrived from Portsmouth, and the rest of them were merchant and trading ships. He knew because earlier today he'd examined each one in great detail through his spyglass.

Anything to take his mind off Miss Faith Westcott.

Yet he still could not shake the strange events of yesterday from his mind. Faith's unusual nervousness, the constant bickering of her sisters, the odd but entertaining exchange between Mr. Mason and Hope, and then the coup de grâce—the infuriating encounter with Lord Falkland. Dajon had to admit that spending the day with the Westcott ladies had been anything but dull. Chuckling, he shook his head, but his grin quickly faded along with the late afternoon sun. The trap had been set.

His insides felt like a lead weight that threatened to drag him to the bottom of the sea. If his suspicions were true, tomorrow he would capture Faith, the notorious Red Siren, and be forced to turn her over to the Charles Towne authorities.

To be hanged.

And no matter how hard he tried to forbid the maddening woman entrance to his thoughts, she barged in anyway, over and over again, proclaiming her many worthwhile qualities—all of which he adored: her independence, her pluck, the fire in her auburn eyes, the depth of love she had for her sisters, her courage, those red curls, and her determination that spoke of deep passions within. He had never known a woman like her and probably never would again. The only thing missing was her love and devotion to God, something he hoped to remedy by a closer association with her—that was, if she wasn't the Red Siren.

But he knew he must prepare himself for the worst possible outcome. He had to be strong. He had to do the right thing.

He gulped as a slow burn seared behind his eyes.

He had to do his duty.

Below him, on the main deck, his crew scampered to and fro, following his orders to ready the ship. Curses and laughter tumbled through the air, as well as the pounding of a hammer in the distance and the scampering of bare feet upon the yardarms above him.

Clenching the railing, he felt the bite of a splinter on his palm, but it did not compare to the sharp pain in his heart.

Oh Lord, I have followed You these four years. I have obeyed all Your commands and never faltered. Please do not test me in this. Please do not let Miss Westcott and the Red Siren be one and the same.

"Captain." Mr. Jamieson's high-pitched voice intruded from behind.

Dajon tightened his grip but did not turn around. "Yes."

"Two merchant sailors to see you, sir. They have some information."

"Of what nature?"

"About the Red Siren."

Releasing the railing, Dajon swung about to see two gruff-looking men standing behind Mr. Jamieson, hats in hand. "What about the Red Siren?" Dajon asked.

The elder of the men stepped forward, his spindly gray hair forming a ring around his sunbaked face. "Captain Milner at yer service, sir." He gestured to his companion. "And this here's Landers."

Dajon nodded and examined the men as Jamieson took his leave. Where Captain Milner was broad and stocky, Landers was slight and short. They smelled of fish, sweat, and salt, and their stained, faded silk waistcoats indicated a failed attempt at noble attire. Seamen, to be sure. Milner looked down and turned his hat around and around as if pondering what to say next. Was that a slight tremble in his hands?

"Yes, yes. Spit it out, man." Dajon's voice shot out louder than he'd intended. "What have you to tell me?"

Captain Milner's gaze snapped to his. "We hear yer hunting pirates. In particular, a lady pirate that goes by the name the Red Siren."

223

"That is correct." Dajon fisted his hands on his waist.

"Well, we came across her yesterday, we did. Or rather, she came across us." He chuckled at his own joke, and Landers snickered behind him.

"The Red Siren attacked you?" Dajon raised his eyebrows, not daring to hope what he'd just heard was true.

"Aye, sir, that she did." Milner gazed off to the right. "Fired upon me ship then grappled and boarded us."

Dajon's breath formed a ball in his chest. "Yesterday, you say?"

"Took most o' our cargo, too. Spices, coffee, chocolate, and sugar."

"Cursed pirate." Landers spat to the side.

"What time yesterday?"

" 'Twas near midday, methinks." Milner glanced over his shoulder at his companion.

"Aye, midday." Landers nodded, but he wouldn't meet Dajon's gaze. "I remember 'cause the sun was right o'er me head."

Dajon rubbed his jaw and eyed the men. Strange fellows, these two, but then again, if they had truly been attacked and boarded by a pirate crew, that would be enough to unnerve anyone.

"Can you describe her?"

"Who?" Landers asked.

"The Red Siren, you dim-witted sluggard," Captain Milner shouted over his shoulder then grinned sheepishly at Dajon.

Milner tapped his finger against his chin. "Aye, she was short." He gazed to the right again as if trying to remember. "Fat. Aye, quite plump she was. She had red hair, but it seemed more brown than red when she came up close." He grinned and nodded.

"Aye, she had an ugly scar that ran 'cross her forehead." Landers slid a finger above his brow.

"It weren't her forehead." Milner turned and slapped him with his hat.

"Yes, it was," Landers hissed through gritted teeth, glancing at Dajon.

But Dajon cared nothing about the scar. He had heard enough to convince him.

Faith was not the Red Siren!

Not only had she been with him yesterday during the pirate attack, but she looked nothing like the person these men described.

Dajon felt as if he'd just been released from a long imprisonment in a dark dungeon.

God had answered his prayer.

Thank You, Lord.

Dismissing the merchants, he leaped down the quarterdeck ladder then down the companionway to his quarters. After washing his face and donning fresh attire, he took a cockboat to shore and started for the Westcott home. As the sun set beyond the tangled forest that bordered the town, Dajon felt as though daylight was just rising within him.

He must see Faith. He must apologize to her for his ludicrous suspicions. And he must tell her. . .must express to her something he thought he'd never say, let alone feel for another woman in his life. He must tell her that he loved her.

⁂

Faith eased her fingers over the horse's soft neck and leaned her forehead against his face. Snorting, the horse pricked his ears toward her.

"Oh, Seaspray, would that I were a simple horse like you, without a care in the world." She sighed and reached up to rub the other side of the horse's neck. Seaspray—named for the steed's cream-colored coat—had taken Faith back and forth to her ship on many an occasion and was one of the few privy to her dual identity. Somehow it made her feel as though they were best friends.

Seaspray licked his lips as if agreeing with Faith's thoughts and then jerked his head back to gaze at her. The gentle glow from a single lantern hanging on a hook filtered over them, and Faith thought she saw a flicker of understanding in the horse's eyes.

Unable to sleep, she had crept down to the stables, where she often came to find comfort among the horses. 'Twas where she had come to know Lucas back in Portsmouth. There the stables had become an escape, a place of refuge from the troubles that plagued her home, and she had passed many pleasant hours helping to care for the horses—that was before she found a much better sanctuary upon the sea.

Grabbing a bristle brush, she began stroking Seaspray's thick mane, her mind drifting to the merchant ship she planned to plunder tomorrow. Forcing down a nagging twinge of guilt, she allowed a flash of exhilaration to charge through her. The chase, the danger, the mighty sea. She loved it all and couldn't wait to be on her ship again. Perhaps that was why sleep had eluded her. Or maybe 'twas a certain captain who kept her thoughts and heart ajitter.

A shuffle sounded behind her in the dirt. She instinctively reached for her sword, but her hand floundered over the soft folds of her nightdress. Gripping the brush with both hands, she spun around, aiming it at the intruder.

Mr. Waite, one boot crossed over the other, leaned against the stable door frame, a sarcastic grin on his handsome lips. "What are you planning to do with that? Scrub me to death?"

"If I have to." She grinned in return but then, realizing her state of undress, dropped the brush and pulled her robe tighter around her.

Mr. Waite's gaze soaked her in as if she were a dying man's last drink. But the look within his blue eyes carried no malice, no lust, nothing to give her pause. Quite the opposite, in fact. It was a look that sent her belly quivering and her pulse racing. His loose umber hair grazed the collar of a fine cambric shirt that was open at the neck. Black velvet breeches rode low upon his hips. It was the first time she had seen him without his uniform, and she swallowed and lowered her lashes, gazing at the dirt floor, lest he see the attraction in her face. "May I help you with something, Mr. Waite?"

"Forgive me for startling you." His boots rustled in the straw as he moved closer. "I looked for you earlier, but Molly said you had retired."

"Yes, still a bit of fatigue, I'm afraid." Faith slid one foot nonchalantly through the dirt, not caring if her silk slipper got soiled. Truthfully, she had heard him come home but found she could not face him—not knowing what she must do on the morrow. Deceive him. Defy him.

Defeat him.

Why did the idea of outwitting the Royal Navy suddenly cause such discord within her when it never had before? Daring a glance at him, she knew the answer. It wasn't the Royal Navy she was battling this time. It was this honorable, courageous, kind man before her. And the thought made her stomach curl in on itself. She averted her gaze, knowing that if she stared too long into those blue eyes filled with affection, she might not be able to go through with her plan.

But she had to. For her sisters. Especially for Hope. Now more than ever, they were in far more desperate need of the independence that wealth would bring them.

"Then you must be feeling refreshed after your rest?"

"Nay, I couldn't sleep." She nudged a tuft of hay with her toe.

"I fear you have infected me with that disease." His deep chuckle bounced off the wooden walls and landed on her like a warm blanket. Why was he being so cordial? Had Grayson and Strom spoken with him? Had he given up his suspicions of her?

He leaned against the nearest stall. The tantalizing scent of leather and the sea swirled around her and sent delightful needles down her spine. She took a step away from him.

"I must admit to something, Miss Westcott. And I hope you shall find it as amusing as I and will not become cross with me."

Leaning over, she picked up the brush and set it on a stool. Good heavens, what did he intend to tell her? That he knew who she really was? Surely that would not be in any way amusing. "There is no need, Mr. Waite. I assure you." She flicked her hand through the air.

"Oh, but I daresay there is." He touched her arm. "I owe you a sincere apology." Sorrow shone from his eyes.

"There could be nothing you have done that requires it." Faith gripped the edges of her robe and expelled a nervous breath. *Except perhaps the way you make my heart burst and my belly flutter whenever you are near. Except perhaps that I am a pirate and you are a pirate hunter sworn to bring me to justice.*

Clasping his hands behind his back, he turned and took a few steps away from her, his movements lacking the usual confidence she'd come to expect. "'Tis the funniest thing, actually. For quite some time now...well, actually for just a few weeks, I. . ." He turned to face her and rubbed the back of his neck then gave her a sheepish look. "I. . ."

"You what, Mr. Waite?"

"I thought you might be the Red Siren." He blurted the words that crackled with both embarrassment and relief.

The needles of pleasure she'd experienced only a moment ago transformed into jabs of panic. Did he know? Was he testing her?

He began to laugh, and she joined him, holding her stomach and bending over in feigned hilarity. "Me? A pirate?" she chortled.

Seaspray tossed his head over the stall and snorted, nodding as if confirming Mr. Waite's suspicion.

Throwing a hand to her throat to hide the furious throb in her veins, Faith nudged the horse back into his pen. "You teased me about it once, but I thought it mere sport."

"I am ashamed at having ever entertained such a ridiculous notion." Mr. Waite raked a hand through his hair then approached, taking her hand in his. "I came to beg your forgiveness."

"Why, there's naught to forgive, Mr. Waite." Faith tugged her hand away and gripped the railing. "You've made me laugh, and that is enough."

"I do feel quite dreadful about it, really."

"You shouldn't." Faith snapped her gaze to his, unable to halt the booming tone of her voice.

Mr. Waite flinched, and she hoped she had not given herself away. But how could she accept his apology when he had done nothing wrong, and she, everything?

❧

Dajon studied her, trying to make sense of her odd reaction. Unpredictable. It was one of the things he loved about her but also a constant source of frustration. Where he assumed she would have been horrified, even furious at his assumption, she waved it aside as if it were naught but a jest. Her response, in fact, aligned more with guilt than with innocence.

But no.

Not only did he have the testimony of the two merchants, but he'd sent some of his crew into town to verify their story. And, indeed, tales of the *Red Siren* attacking a small merchant ship just off Charles Towne were circulating around the city's taverns.

Flinging her red curls over her shoulder, she brushed her hands over the horse's face, her gaze turned from his. When he'd first seen Faith standing there so serenely, whispering to the steed, her white robe shimmering in a halo of light and her hair a cascade of glittering red, he could have remained where he was and watched her all night. And when she'd turned to face him, threatening him with the brush, he'd longed to take her in his arms. And now that the wall of suspicion had been toppled between them, he must tell her how he felt.

"There is something else."

She raised her eyes to his.

"It may seem untoward, even improper, after confessing my rather ludicrous and disparaging suspicions, but I. . ."

Should he tell her? Hadn't he sworn off women after what had happened with Marianne? Hadn't he vowed to God never to put himself in a position to bring harm to another by his own foolish passions?

Why did You bring this precious lady to me, Lord? Why have You allowed me to feel such overwhelming affection for her?

"Yes, Mr. Waite?" The freckles on Faith's nose clumped together under a pert wrinkle.

Dajon brushed the back of his hand over her cheek, relishing the silky feel of her skin and the way she instantly closed her eyes. Perhaps he had learned. Perhaps by God's grace, Dajon had changed. Perhaps God had deemed him ready again.

"Surely you have no doubt as to my intentions, Miss Westcott."

Her lips parted, and she released a tiny sigh as he continued caressing her cheek.

"If your father were here, I would speak to him, but alas. . ."

Her eyes popped open as if she'd just been awakened from a dream. "What would you need to discuss with my father that you cannot discuss with me?"

"Surely you know." Placing a finger beneath her chin, Dajon raised her gaze to his. Her auburn eyes shone with a moist luster that bristled with desire, admiration, and something else. Was it fear? Frustration? He knew she feared depending on any man, but surely she could see that he was different.

"It would be my honor if you'd allow me to—"

"Please say no more." She tore her gaze away and clasped her robe.

"Court you, Miss Westcott." He stepped closer until there was but a breath between them. "I confess, though I have discovered you are no pirate, you have quite plundered my heart as if you were."

"Please." She jerked away. "You do not know what you are saying."

"On the contrary, it is the only thing I seem sure about of late." Dajon wiped the moisture from his brow, confused once again by her reaction.

A battle seemed to rage within Faith's eyes. One second they sparkled with affection and admiration; the next they stabbed him with defiance and determination. Her jaw tightened, and she swallowed. Dajon had realized that her distrust of men might give her pause when he declared his affections, but he hadn't expected such resistance.

"It can never be," she said sharply and turned to leave.

He grabbed her arm, unwilling to see her go, unwilling to give in to the agony clawing at his heart.

"Release me." She struggled against his grip.

"Tell me you feel nothing for me, and I will."

She bent her knee as if to kick him, but this time he saw it coming and pressed himself firmly against her.

Dajon grasped her face in his hands and pressed his lips against hers. He hadn't planned to kiss her. He had simply wanted to calm her down, simply wanted her to stay, but when she instantly melted into him, he claimed her mouth as his own and kissed her with all the passion that had been building up in him since the day he met her.

When he released her, they stood in silence, their heavy breaths mingling in the air between them.

"I have my answer then," Dajon said, placing a kiss on her forehead.

With a horrified gasp, Faith ripped herself from his arms and fled into the night.

CHAPTER 27

Perched high upon the foreyard, Faith clung to the mast with one hand and a halyard with the other. She thrust her face into the wind, allowing it to blast away her doubts, her fears, and, in particular, her thoughts of Mr. Waite. Curling her bare toes around the yardarm, she spotted Lucas nigh eighty feet below, giving orders to the crew, looking more like a speck of dirt tossed by the wind than a commanding first mate. She loved it up here among the topsails. If she closed her eyes, she could imagine herself a bird, soaring over the vast ocean, unfettered, unhindered—free at last.

"You are most fortunate, Morgan," she said to the red and green macaw balancing on the backstay beside her.

"Gentlemen of fortune, we are, we are," he squawked, making her smile.

Off the larboard side, the rising arc of a brilliant sun poked over the dark line of the horizon. Exhaling a puff of gold, maroon, and copper upon the dark waters, it set the waves aglow with the breath of dawn. She smiled at the matchless beauty of creation. Nothing but wind and sparkling waves as far as her eye could see.

She was home.

Then why did she feel so unsettled?

It was that blasted Mr. Waite. He confused her. He frustrated her.

He delighted her.

She brushed her fingers over her lips. Why had she given in to his kiss? Yet stopping it would have been akin to stopping a cannon from firing after the powder had already been lit. Even now with the chill morning wind swirling about her, her body warmed at the thought. But her passion quickly drowned beneath a wave of guilt. There he had stood declaring her innocent of piracy and announcing his affections for her, and all the while she was about to plunder a ship she had learned about only through him.

But this would be her last time. And though a sudden mourning came over her at the death of her adventurous life upon the sea, she knew the risks were far too high to continue. But then, maybe then she could entertain thoughts of a possible courtship with Captain Waite. Possible, yes. The thought surprised her. Though she had sworn never to depend upon a man, never to marry, this man, this Captain Dajon Waite, might just be a man worth altering her plans for.

Climbing down the ratlines with ease, Faith dropped to the wooden planks below and then marched across the main deck of the *Red Siren*, allowing her bare toes to caress the moist wood as she went. She adjusted her baldric about her chest and leaped up the quarterdeck ladder— something she could never do without the freedom breeches afforded her. Planting her feet firmly on the hard deck, she gave a quick nod to Wilson at the helm before facing the ship's bow as it rose and plunged through the choppy sea.

Morgan soon followed, alighting upon his usual perch on the mainmast.

Taking the ladder in one leap, Lucas positioned himself beside her and scratched his thick dark hair. "And where are we to be expecting to find this treasure ship, Cap'n?"

Faith tugged on the black bandanna she'd tied atop her head and tried to ignore the lack of fervor normally present in Lucas's voice. "Since Mr. Borland let it slip that they were only to protect her from St. Helena Sound onward, I expect the *Lady Adeline* to arrive off Port Royal sometime this morning." She cast him a sly grin. "We should pass her any minute."

"And what's to ensure that Captain Waite won't be passin' our way as well?"

Faith glanced at her first mate, but he kept his gaze upon the sea. "He would have no reason to come this far south."

Lucas huffed and gripped the railing.

"What is it, Lucas?"

"Seems to me yer takin' a big risk." He scratched his head. "Mr. Waite is no fool."

"Aye, I'll grant you that. But he has no further reason to suspect me.

Any information Borland disclosed would be considered safe within my feeble feminine mind." She chuckled, but Lucas did not join her. In fact, he rubbed his leathery skin and shook his head.

"Our plan worked, Lucas. You should be pleased."

" 'Tis not that."

"What, then? Where is your usual zeal, your excitement? We are about to give chase and plunder some unsuspecting merchant." Faith gripped the hilt of her cutlass.

"Seems to have lost its allure as of late, Cap'n." Lucas's jaw flinched, and he gazed down at the crew ambling over the deck. "Seems almost wrong to be stealin' so."

" 'We plunder and pillage and pilfer and prey.' " Morgan repeated a pirate's ballad from his perch, only increasing Faith's rising shame.

She felt as if the ship had been struck by a twenty-pounder and was taking on water. Lucas had always been so strong, her stalwart first mate, her faithful partner. Side by side, they had plundered the seas, amassed a fortune, defeated foes. "Please do not tell me you have suddenly grown a conscience." She could not keep the irritation from her voice nor the increasing weight of loss from her soul.

His glance carried both pain and excitement. "It jest be that I ne'er thought there be a God before. An' now I think He exists. . .an' He might even care about me."

"Well, you'd best put that thought out of your mind." Faith crossed her arms over her chest. "You will only be disappointed." Yet hadn't she entertained similar thoughts recently?

Lucas said nothing, only watched the foam spray over the bow of the ship as the orb of the sun rose above the horizon.

"You've allowed that strange event, miracle, whatever it was at the Pink House to befuddle your mind," Faith hissed.

Lucas gave her one of his playful grins. "Nay, I've been speakin' to Miss Molly and to Mr. Waite."

"Oh, now I understand." Faith blew out a sigh. "The God-fearing duo has turned my first mate into a jellyfish." Frankly, she was surprised her sister Grace hadn't joined in the mind-altering conversion.

"Yellow-bellied jellyfish, yellow-bellied jellyfish," Morgan chirped.

Shaking the wind from the coils of his hair, Lucas only smiled.

Faith studied the curve of his lips, and a sudden hope lifted the heaviness from her. "Ah, you almost had me fooled." She pointed a finger his way. "You're just doing this to win Molly's affections, aren't you?"

Lucas shook his head. "Nay. You know me, Miss Faith—I mean, Cap'n. Becoming one of those religious sorts be the last thing I'd be doin', especially for a woman. No matter how remarkable she be."

The first mate glanced at the sails flapping in the breeze before them. "Mac, brace in the foreyard," he yelled across to the man climbing up the foremast rigging.

"What of your past?" Faith asked, blinking back her shock. "What of your slavery, the murder of your parents? Are those the actions of a loving God?"

"Aye, I'll admit I used to think that way." He nodded then leaned on the rail and met her gaze. "But I can't deny what I've seen, what I've felt."

"Felt?"

"Aye, Cap'n. I've been talkin' to God." Lucas's eyes sparkled. "An' methinks He's talkin' back."

"Good heavens." Faith shifted her gaze to the tumultuous waves. Anywhere but into those joy-filled eyes. "What have they done to you?"

"Whate'er it is, I like it, mistress." Lucas lengthened his stance and crossed his arms over his thick chest. "Methinks I like it a lot."

Morgan paced across his perch, bobbing his head up and down. "Mush fer brains. Mush fer brains."

"There you have it. Even Morgan can see the truth." She nodded toward the bird with a smile, but Lucas only shook his head and gazed out upon the sea.

Faith huffed. Of all the people in the world to have fallen for such a hoax, Lucas would have been her last guess. He'd suffered far more pain and loss in his life than she could ever imagine. How could he so easily surrender to a God who had allowed all that to happen?

Temporary madness. With time, hopefully, it would pass.

"Well, you have my word, Lucas: If you help me take in a good haul today, I shall never impose upon your newfound holiness for such a vile act as pirating again."

"I will hold ye to that, Cap'n." He grinned. "For it will surely please me more than anything to see you out o' this life as well."

"A sail, Cap'n!" Kane yelled from the crosstrees.

A slow grin crept across Faith's lips even as exhilaration raced through her veins. "Let's be about it then, Lucas. Once more for old times' sake."

⁓

Slamming his logbook shut, Dajon rose from his desk, flung on his frock, and headed up on deck. This was the day he would catch the notorious Red Siren. After discovering—much to his utter glee—that Faith was not one and the same, he had propagated the news of the *Lady Adeline* all over Charles Towne, ensuring all the sailors who traveled these waters knew of the incoming merchant ship and her valuable cargo. Surely word would reach the pirate.

Climbing up the companionway ladder, he emerged onto the deck to a blast of wind and spray that only increased his exuberance. Perhaps now he could keep his mind off the alluring and frustrating Faith. A sharp twinge from an old injury pinched his nose, and he squeezed it, hoping to force down the pain and the memories along with it. Marching across the deck, he gazed upon the morning mist dissipating over the water. If only the fog of confusion hovering in his mind would dissipate so easily.

Faith returned his affections. He knew it. Her body, her voice, her eyes, and especially her lips—a sudden warmth spread through him as he remembered her sweet taste—everything displayed her passionate ardor, everything save her words and the way she had dashed from his embrace. But why?

While only partially aware of his crew's salutes and "Good days" as they passed, Dajon watched the golden sun arise from its bed of blue to start anew its journey across the sky.

Fear. That was what he'd seen in those auburn eyes. But of what?

Of men. From her past, no doubt—from the horrible things that had happened to her sisters. And all from the same loathsome ruffian.

Dajon clenched his jaw. The man should be flogged and then keelhauled for what he'd done to these ladies, to this family.

The ship bucked over a rising swell, and Dajon braced his boots on the slippery deck. The jolt seemed to loosen a hidden truth within him. Had Dajon revealed his ardor for her too soon? Had he been too harsh, too passionate with his kiss? Perhaps that was why she had fled. Gripping the main deck railing, he squeezed it and vowed to be more careful, gentler, more patient. He must prove his trustworthiness to her, no matter how long it took. For Miss Faith Westcott was a lady well worth the wait.

Leaping up to the quarterdeck, he took his position beside Borland.

"Sailing trim, Captain, southeast by south," the first lieutenant stated without glancing his way.

"Very good, Mr. Borland. Any moment, then." Dajon clasped his hands behind his back. They had already passed St. Helena Sound. The pirate ship could turn up anywhere now.

The warmth of the sun caressed his left cheek while the wind slapped the other, reminding him of Faith's ever-changing moods. By the powers, was she never far from his thoughts?

He glanced at his first lieutenant, standing beside him as stiff as a marine, eyes locked on the point of the ship's bow, his jaw rigid and his fists bunched. Dajon had never seen him quite so tense before.

"Did you sleep well, Mr. Borland?"

"Aye, sir." His tone pricked Dajon like icicles.

Perhaps he was frightened about the upcoming battle. But no. They'd been in many skirmishes before, and Borland had always been the epitome of bravery. "Are you unwell, then?"

"No, Captain."

"Very well." Dajon conceded to the man's foul mood, supposing he didn't want to discuss whatever vexed him. "When we have the ships in our sights, lower the topgallants, if you please. We must give this pirate time to shed her snake's skin and reveal her true colors."

"Will she not be able to tell the *Lady Adeline* is a decoy?" Mr. Borland said, although the effort seemed to exhaust him. "I have heard she's a clever pirate."

"Never fear, Borland. I have ensured that the *Lady Adeline* appears in every way a true merchant ship. I even had her loaded with ballast so she sits low in the water."

Mr. Jamieson joined them, his face alight with anticipation.

"Once she raises her colors and fires a shot, then we have her," Dajon continued.

"Very exciting." Jamieson rubbed his hands together and then adjusted his bicorn. He faced Dajon with a look of concern. "Will it not be difficult to arrest a lady?"

Dajon's mind filled with visions of the arrogant, brash woman who had stolen his father's ship from him five years ago, leaving him to return home in disgrace. "This is no woman. 'Tis naught but a callous thief housed in a female body, as devoid of conscience and decency as any other pirate." He gripped the cold silver of his sword. "No, I have no qualms about escorting this lady to the noose."

A dark cloud appeared on the horizon, threatening to cast a shroud of gloom on the promise of a bright day.

"Besides, gentlemen, if all goes well today, we will catch a pirate." He lifted his voice, trying to cheer up his friends. "And not just any pirate. One who has been pilfering these waters for months. Certainly that will shed a favorable light on us back at the Admiralty."

"On you, Captain." Borland finally met his gaze, though the glint in his eyes was anything but friendly. It reminded Dajon of a flaming linstock. "It will shed a light upon only you."

"Nonsense, Borland." Dajon gave a half chuckle, unsettled by the hostility in his friend's gaze. "You know I shall report all of our efforts in the success."

Borland's face twisted as if he were stifling a sharp retort, but he returned his gaze to the sea and said no more.

"Sail ho!" The cry came from above them.

"Where away, Mr. Gibson?" Borland yelled.

"Off the larboard bow, sir. Three points."

"Hold up there!" Gibson bellowed again. "Two sails now, sir."

Dajon plucked out his spyglass and pressed it to his eye. Two ships, indeed. Too far to know who they were for sure, but one swiftly bore down upon the other.

It had to be the *Red Siren*.

"Ease the helm, Mr. Borland. Away aloft and trim the sails. Let's take her in slow." Dajon slapped his glass into the palm of his hand and grinned as Borland repeated his orders to the crew.

"The last thing we want to do is scare her off."

≈

"Shouldn't ye be changin' yer clothes, Cap'n?" Lucas asked as he strapped on his cutlass.

"Nay, I tire of hiding behind ruffles and lace." Faith poured priming powder from her horn into the small pan in her pistol, careful not to spill any. "Today I will plunder this ship dressed like a pirate—a true pirate."

Lucas grinned. " 'Tis fittin' fer yer last time."

Then, as if noting the gleam in her eye, he added with a raised brow, "It *will* be yer last time, Cap'n?"

"Don't you be pointing that pharisaical eye toward me, Lucas." Faith cocked her head and gave him a sideways glance. "You forget I know you too well."

A blast of wind stole his warm laughter as the *Red Siren* split the waves with each thrust of her bow.

Bracing her boots, Faith leveled the glass on her eye. "Besides, see how low she sits in the water? Heavy cargo." She lowered the glass and winked at Lucas. "Methinks there be gold in that ship." But when her first mate's stern eye did not falter, she conceded, "Yes, Lucas, this will be my last time, I assure you."

Scanning the horizon, she saw no other sails besides the merchant ship, the words *Lady Adeline* painted in black upon her bow, French colors flapping upon her mainmast. Only two swivel guns guarded her deck. No gun ports appeared on the hull. Defenseless and as out of place upon these violent seas as a lady in a brothel.

And with all her gold for the taking.

At the thought of stealing this unsuspecting merchant's gold, a weight of shame tugged upon Faith. She winced and furrowed her brow. Was this newfound godliness of Lucas's contagious? Good heavens, she hoped not.

The *Red Siren* surged and plunged over a wave, spraying glittering white foam over the bow. Shaking it off along with her guilt, Faith studied her prey. "Odd. Surely she spots us. Why doesn't she run?"

"Their cap'n seems to be loadin' his swivels." Lucas smacked his lips. "Methinks he is unsure whether we are friend or foe."

"We have not hailed them as either," Faith yelled over the crashing waves. She wrinkled her brow. "But his swivels? Against our sixteen guns? Either he is a fool, or he is completely mad."

Flinging her hands to her waist, Faith marched across the quarter-deck to the railing and gazed down upon her crew readying for battle. The ship creaked and moaned as it forced aside each opposing wave, fighting its way to its victim. White canvas cracked above her like a whip, prodding the ship forward.

"Should I raise our colors, Capitaine?" Kane yelled from the main deck.

Shielding her eyes from the sun, Faith gazed up at the Union Jack bristling in the breeze. "Not yet, Mr. Kane. They appear to be unaware of the danger."

Yet Faith was the one who felt a sudden unease prickle her skin. They would be on the ship in minutes. With so much gold aboard, why did she not at least make a run for it? Swinging about, spyglass to her eye, she scanned the horizon once again. Nothing but azure sea streaked in sparkling white.

"Orders, Cap'n?" cried Bates. The master gunner's twitching eyes met hers from below.

"Lucas," she yelled over her shoulder. "Shorten sail. Down tops and gallants."

Lucas repeated the orders, sending men into the main shrouds and scrambling aloft.

"All hands about ship!" Faith boomed from the quarterdeck railing. "Prepare to board. Mr. Wilson," she bellowed to the man at the helm, "lay me athwart her larboard side."

"Aye, aye, Cap'n." The barrel-chested pirate turned the wheel.

Faith glanced back at Bates. "When we come alongside her, fire a warning shot across her stern, if you please, Mr. Bates."

"Aye." The man gave her a toothless grin and waddled off.

"Let's make our intentions known, gentlemen." Faith drew her cutlass and held it over her head. "For the gold!"

"Aye, fer the gold!" the men echoed and then hurled hearty boasts and curses toward the merchant ship now only fifty yards away.

Jumping down the ladder, Lucas halted at the main deck railing and stared at their prey. Faith joined him and followed his gaze to the sailors buzzing about their swivels as if trying to figure out how to fire them. Her first mate scratched his thick hair.

Minutes later a thunderous blast shook the ship and sent a ripple through the water. Acrid smoke curled from the *Red Siren*'s gun port, and a splash sounded where the shot plunged harmlessly into the sea beyond the *Lady Adeline.*

The crew of the merchant vessel skittered across the deck in a frenzy but soon lowered their colors in a signal of surrender.

"Something's amiss, Cap'n." Lucas frowned. " 'Twas far too easy fer a ship carryin' a fortune."

Faith knew he was right. She knew she should hoist sail and flee while she had the chance. But she couldn't. Too much rode upon this last venture. Besides, when would she have another opportunity at such wealth?

Just one more haul. Just one more.

Against every instinct within her, she turned to Lucas. "Then let's take her quickly and be gone," she snapped.

As the band of blue narrowed between the ships and Faith's crew readied the grappling irons, the merchant captain stood amidships and gazed her way. He cupped his hands. "Ahoy, from whence came ye, and what do ye want?"

Bracing her fists at her waist, Faith yelled in reply, "Good quarter will be granted to you, sir, if you lay down your arms, open the hatches, and haul down your sails."

A grin took root and began to spread upon the captain's lips. And before it reached the corners of his mouth, sheer terror struck Faith.

"Cap'n, off our stern!" Lambert's normally steady voice quaked from the crosstrees.

Her heart turned to ice, and she knew before she even turned. She knew what she would see.

The HMS *Enforcer* plunged toward them, white foam exploding off its bow.

~

"We've got her now!" Dajon snapped his spyglass shut, excitement bristling his skin. "Took the bait like the greedy shark she is."

He turned to Borland, who stood beside him at the quarterdeck railing. "Unfurl the topsails and gallants."

Mr. Borland repeated his command, sending the crew aloft. Soon the *Enforcer*'s sails caught the wind in a sharp snap, sending the ship skimming over the rolling swells at top speed.

Fierce wind clawed at his bicorn, and Dajon shoved it down on his head and clung to the railing. Frothy dark water swept over the deck and rolled out the scuppers. The sharp scent of salt and fish tore at his nose as they raced to get windward of the pirate.

"She's raising her sails, Captain," Jamieson said, lowering his glass.

"She'll not catch the wind in time." Dajon crossed his arms over his chest. "Ready the chain shot, if you please, Mr. Jamieson."

"Yes, sir." Mr. Jamieson stormed off and dropped below deck to inform the gun crew.

"Beat to quarters. Clear the deck for battle," Dajon instructed Borland, who bellowed his commands to the crew.

The shrill sound of a whistle screeched through the air, and the crew scrambled over the deck, clearing away barrels and crates, stowing equipment below hatches, and arming themselves with musket and sword.

Spyglass to his eye, Dajon scanned the *Red Siren*—his father's ship. A fire brewed in his belly at the sight of it. At last he would have it back.

Though the pirate crew furiously tugged at the furled sails aloft, they would not loosen the canvas in time. He would be on her in minutes. His gaze shifted to the Union Jack. She had not raised her pirate colors. But no matter—she had clearly come alongside the merchant vessel to plunder it.

And this would be her last time.

They were nearly within firing distance, and Dajon gave the order to lower sails.

The *Red Siren*'s gun ports flung open in an attempt, he assumed, to scare him off, making him snort. "She's brazen. I'll give her that."

The *Lady Adeline* had already drifted away and was hoisting sail rapidly in order to escape the impending battle.

"Run out the guns, fire a warning shot, and then signal her to surrender," Dajon commanded.

The thud of port hatches striking the hull reverberated through the ship, one after the other, followed by the clanks of gun trucks grating over the deck. The thunderous boom of a cannon shook both ship and sky, and Dajon peered through the smoke toward his enemy. Would she surrender or put up a useless fight that would surely end in bloodshed?

"She lowers her flag, Captain," Mr. Borland announced with a grin.

Huzzahs erupted from his crew.

Dajon nodded in satisfaction.

"Lower the cockboat, Mr. Borland. Let us pay a visit to the infamous *Red Siren*. Shall we?" He slapped his friend on the back and stomped down the quarterdeck ladder.

"Aye, Captain."

As the boat thudded against the wet hull of the *Red Siren* and rope ladders were tossed over the rail, Dajon rose in the wobbly boat and adjusted his navy coat. He squared his shoulders and gazed up at the dark hull of his father's ship. Pride rippled through him. He had caught the *Red Siren*. He had done his duty and protected the colonial waters and the citizens of this land from the ravages of this vexatious pirate.

Thank You, God, for this victory, he silently prayed, hoping that this courageous act would somehow atone for at least one of his past sins.

Leaping over the bulwarks, Dajon landed with a thud onto the deck, followed quickly by Mr. Borland and ten marines. He scanned the ship, seeing nothing but a crew of scurrilous pirates staring at him, scowls dripping from their faces.

"Your arms, gentlemen. Toss them in a pile, if you please." He gestured toward the center of the deck.

Slowly they complied, each one slogging toward middeck, flinging their weapons onto a growing heap of metal and their curses toward him and his men.

"Now where, pray tell, is your captain?" Dajon allowed his eyes to travel over the crew, shooting each man down with his imperious gaze. "Has she scurried below decks like the coward she is?"

A tall, dark man emerged from the shadows beneath the foredeck ladder. "She has no wish to see you, Mr. Waite." The familiar voice struck Dajon before the face registered in his brain. Even then, it took a minute before Dajon found his breath.

"Lucas." Dajon's jaw hung slack, and for a moment, he thought it would loosen and drop to the deck at his feet. "What in God's. . . What are you doing here?"

"Never mind, Lucas." A feminine voice swirled in the air like a siren's call, and a woman, dressed in breeches and a white flowing shirt, crossed with baldric and pistols, stepped out from behind Lucas. The floppy hat perched upon her head hid her face, and Dajon's heart crashed through his ribs at the sight of her.

She sauntered toward him and pulled out her cutlass.

Instantly the muskets of all ten marines leveled upon her. She snickered. "Frightened of a woman? *Tsk-tsk.*" She shook her head. "I would request a new batch of marines if I were you, Captain."

A hint of a smile played under the shadow of her hat.

She handed the hilt end of her sword to Dajon. "With my compliments, Captain." The scent of lemons joined the salty breeze and spiked him like a dagger. His pulse throbbed in his neck. He tried to move, but his boots felt as though they were bolted to the deck.

A green and red parrot flew down and landed on the capstan. "Clap 'er in irons. Clap 'er in irons."

The lady lifted her chin and slowly raised her gaze to his. A tiny scar in the shape of a quarter moon taunted him from her neck. Beneath the shadow of her hat, eyes the color of mahogany met his with a look of determination—and sorrow.

CHAPTER 28

Faith paced across the floor of her cabin, her boots pounding over the wooden planks like the ominous beat of drums preceding a hanging. She gazed at the thick oak door imprisoning her and knew a marine stood guard just outside.

What a fool I am.

Raising a hand to her mouth, she gnawed her nails and stomped toward a case of books on the starboard side of the cabin before swerving and retracing her steps. Sunlight streaming in from the stern window wove a forked trail around her desk and chairs, and she hesitated to step into it, fearing the virtuous light would scorch her wicked pirate skin.

Mr. Waite had set a perfect trap, and she'd fallen for it like a hungry fish led into a shark's cave. So greedy, so desperate to reach her goal, she'd ignored the warnings, the churning in her gut, the trepidation that prickled down her spine, even Lucas's uneasiness.

And now look where she was. Trapped. Caught.

Doomed.

All was lost. Everything she'd worked for. Everything she'd hoped for.

She spun on her heel and retraced her steps again, the pounding of her boots over the wooden floor jarring her nerves like a judge's gavel.

She froze. Her crew would be imprisoned. They'd be hung. It was all her fault. She wiped the sweat from her neck. What had she done? Lucas had warned her against going on this final raid—had not wanted to go himself. Now he would die because of her foolishness, and he and Molly would never have a chance to share their love.

Faith clenched her fists and took up her pace again. And her sisters. What would become of them?

She couldn't shake the vision of the captain's face from her mind. He had not known it was her until that moment. She could tell from the horror and pain that shot from his gaze when he saw her, like daggers piercing deep within her heart.

He'd grabbed her cutlass and tossed it into the sea. The sharp steel formed an arc of spinning light glittering in the sun's rays as it flew through the air. Then the churning waves of the sea reached up to grab it and pull it below, swallowing it up in darkness.

The end of her pirate career.

Then without saying a word, Mr. Waite had ordered his marines to take her below. Although she could hear the rustling of movement above her, she had no idea what he was doing.

Or thinking.

Footsteps approached, the door blasted open, and in walked Captain Waite. Faith froze.

"Leave us," he ordered the marine who had stepped in after him. Then turning, he slammed the door shut. A blast of salty sea air wafted over her—her last breath of freedom.

The captain didn't look at her. Didn't speak to her. Instead, he stomped to her desk, sifted through her charts and books scattered atop it, then gazed across the room, his eyes skipping over her as if he feared looking at her might infect him with some disease.

Faith pressed a hand to her chest. She felt as if a grappling hook had clawed her heart in two. He hated her. And how could she blame him?

He swallowed hard. Tossing his bicorn on the desk, he finally lifted his gaze to hers. "So." He waved a hand across the room. "You are indeed a pirate. The Red Siren, in fact." He picked up a stack of maps from the desk and then slapped them back down. "You must be proud of yourself."

"No, I—"

"All this time," he said through gritted teeth. "While you were fluttering those thick lashes at me and playing the coquette."

"I never—"

He held up a hand, his face a boiling cauldron. "Enough of your lies!" he yelled, and Faith flinched. She'd never seen him so angry before.

"Teasing me. . .playing me for a fool." He raked a hand through his hair, loosening a strand from his queue, then stormed toward her—a six-foot-one, two-hundred-pound cannonball fired her way.

Taking a step back, Faith held his gaze. Halting inches from her face, he rubbed a harsh thumb over her lips, forcing her back, then he jerked his hand from her mouth. "Kissing me. Vixen," he spat the word and turned from her.

Faith lowered her gaze, battling the tears burning behind her eyes. A drop of sweat etched a ragged path down her back.

"And those two men up on deck, Milner and Landers. . .or whoever they are." He faced her once more, and his fiery gaze incinerated her. "You had them lie to me, play the part of poor plundered merchants." He gave a derisive snort. "And all the while they were part of your crew. Great guns, woman, have you no shame?"

Faith opened her mouth to reply, to tell him that no, she had no shame—at least not until recently, not until she had fallen in love with him, not until God had miraculously saved her sister, and not until this moment when the realization flooded her that her continual running away from God had brought naught but disaster in her life. But Dajon didn't give her the chance to say any of those things before he began ranting again.

"Stealing? Thieving and God knows what else." He pounded his fist on the desk, sending the maps, lantern, pen, and coil of rope quaking. "How many men have you killed, maimed while you plundered their ships?"

"I have hurt no one."

His gaze locked with hers, pain screaming from his blue eyes. And she knew immediately that she had indeed hurt someone—someone very dear to her.

"What will your father say?" The captain tore off his frock and tossed it into a chair. It slid from the seat and crumpled into a pile on the floor, but he didn't notice. Instead, he gripped the hilt of his sword and resumed the pacing Faith had ceased.

"I—" she began.

"It will ruin him. Do you know that?"

Of course she knew that. Her father's welfare and especially that of her sisters had been all that consumed her thoughts these past five years.

"And your sisters? What is to become of them? You thought to protect them, but all you have done is secured their ruin. No decent man will have them now."

A burning lump of sorrow stuck in Faith's throat. A weight as heavy as a thousand cannonballs fell upon Faith, threatening to crush her. She'd only meant to save them, to give them the freedom to choose a decent husband or none at all, but in the end, she had caused just the opposite.

"Dajon." She took a step toward him and dared to use his Christian name, but the searing gaze he gave her told her to stay where she was.

The ship careened over a wave, its wooden hull creaking in protest.

"I saw no other way. My mother left them in my charge." A black cloud swallowed up the sunlight beaming into the cabin, only adding to the gloom settling over Faith. "I could not allow what happened to Charity happen to them."

"So you took to piracy?" Mr. Waite's brow wrinkled into folds of disgust, then he gave a cynical shrug. "Of course, a most logical choice for a proper British lady."

A spark of anger overtook her remorse. "How else was I to acquire a fortune to secure our future? Pray tell. Enlighten me, Captain." She tossed her hair over her shoulder. "I won't even inherit my father's estate. That will go to that foul beast, Lord Villement."

Dajon blew out a sigh and stomped to the bookcase.

"Are you aware that this is my father's ship? This"—he pounded on the bulkhead—"was *my* cabin." He arched a contemptuous brow.

Faith nodded.

"Then you knew it was me all along?"

Thunder rumbled in the distance.

"From the moment I saw you." Faith untied the bandanna and tugged it from her head. "You are not a man easy to forget."

He snorted. "Do you have any idea what you did to me that day?" His jaw flexed. "Besides stealing my father's ship and all his cargo?"

A dark red hue exploded on his cheeks and spread throughout his face. He folded his arms across his chest, his fists tight wads of fury.

"I was thrown from the family business—disinherited." His voice was as sharp as the point of a sword. "I spent a year. . .I spent a year doing things I'm not proud of—things that ruined many lives."

Faith gulped and wrung her bandanna into a tight cord in her hands. "I'm sorry."

He faced her with a sneer. "Now you're sorry? But not sorry enough to stop pirating these waters when you knew I was responsible for keeping them safe, eh? Not *that* sorry."

"This was to be my last time."

"Ah. . .of course." He grinned. "Well, as it turns out, it will be."

Dajon drew his sword and placed it on the desk then leaned back upon the worn oak. "Once again you are determined to shame me." He crossed one boot over the other.

"This time the shame is mine, Captain."

"Indeed." His gaze met hers, and she sensed a softening within the piercing blue.

"What was I to do? What choice did I have?" she said.

"Perchance, Miss Westcott, to trust God. Did you consider that?"

"Hardly," Faith scoffed and eyed the lantern swinging from the wooden beams above her as she tried to rouse her usual fury toward the Almighty. But at the moment, the only anger she felt was toward herself. "Trust God? After my mother died trying to give my father the son he wanted? After my sister found herself imprisoned in a hellish marriage? After my other sister was ravished and ruined? No, sir. I decided God was not handling things very well."

"And I see you have done so much better."

She lowered her gaze beneath his sardonic glare. The truth of his words began to chisel a trail through her stony resolve. No, she had done a far worse job. Every step she'd taken away from God, everything she had tried to do in her own power had only made things worse. Her relationship with her sisters had suffered due to her absences. And consequently, without proper feminine guidance, Grace kept placing herself in terrible danger and Hope continually threw herself at disreputable men. All while Faith spent her nights scouring the seas, trying to amass a fortune that now seemed suddenly. . .

Quite worthless.

She'd hurt her sisters, she'd hurt this honorable man before her, she would ruin her father and their family reputation, and at the end of it all, she would be hanged.

Her legs began to feel as fluid as the sea beneath the ship, and she shuffled to one of her padded chairs and fell into it, dropping her head into her hands.

"Oh, God, forgive me." Why had she not seen it until now?

Until it was too late.

Dread and shame swallowed the last of her pride, the last of her rebellion, but she would not allow her tears to flow. Not for herself. She didn't deserve them.

No sound came from Captain Waite. Perhaps he waited for her to spend her sorrow before he locked her in the hold below and escorted her to the Watch House. He was a gentleman, after all. But she had to know one more thing. Taking a deep breath, she sat up and found his gaze scouring over her. "Pray tell, Captain, if God is so loving, if He loves us so much, why did He allow all those horrible things to happen to my family?"

Dajon shook his head. The tight lines on his face had smoothed, and the gleam had returned to his eyes. "I do not know. The world is a wicked place. People can be very cruel." A shaft of sunlight broke through the clouds and swirled around him, framing him in sparkling specks of dust.

Faith gripped the arms of the chair, wanting to rise but unsure if her legs would cooperate. She'd heard this explanation before, but still, it brought her no satisfaction. "But He's God. He can stop them. He can protect us."

"Yes, He can." Dajon nodded and rubbed his jaw. "But perhaps He has other plans. Maybe He allows things to happen that will lead us in a different direction, or bring us closer to Him, or strengthen our character. We do not know. That is where trust comes in."

"Trust?" Faith snickered. "When everything is crumbling down around me?"

"Aye. That is what trust is. 'Tis easy to trust when all is well." Dajon shoved the strand of hair behind his ear, gripped the edge of the desk, and leaned toward her, urgency sparking in his gaze. "Trust that His Word is true, Miss Westcott, that He loves you, that He is with you, 'that all things work together for good to them that love God' and then see what He can create out of life's worst calamities."

The truth of his words hit Faith like a refreshing wave, but regret and agony soon followed in its wake. "That's not difficult for someone like you who loves to follow rules."

His deep sarcastic chuckle bounced across the room. "Not difficult you say? I fear you do not know me very well."

"Still, I do not know if I can simply sit by when tragedy strikes and do nothing when 'tis within my power to change things."

Dajon approached and gripped the arms of her chair, staring down at her. "But don't you see? You have never really had the power to change anything—except to make things worse."

Faith gazed up at him. A loose coil of hair grazed his stubbled chin. The smell of lye and leather teased her with the scent of a man she knew now she could never have. She longed to throw herself into his arms, to seek the strength and protection she knew she'd find there. . . if only for a moment before he led her away. A moment she would cherish forever.

No longer able to bear the look of pity and sorrow in his eyes, she tore her gaze from his. Once admiration had filled them. Affection—perhaps even love.

Oh God, forgive me.

The stomping of footsteps sounded from above. They were coming for her.

She must prepare herself to accept the consequences of her foolish actions—the consequences she deserved.

≈

Dajon jerked from the chair and took a step back, watching as Faith stared at the wooden planks above her head. Rising, she threw back her shoulders and stepped into a beam of sunlight that set her hair aglow and her skin shimmering.

Dajon gulped.

The fear, the rage, the defiance in her eyes had fled, replaced by remorse and defeat.

"Dajon. . .Mr. Waite." She raised her chin. Such bravery in the face of such defeat. He'd known navy captains with less fortitude. "I have wronged you greatly. I have wronged my sisters, my father, everyone I care about. I know it means naught to you, but I *am* truly sorry." Her auburn eyes glistened, but she kept her tears captive. "I realize now that I blamed God for all the wrongs in my life, instead of believing what I knew deep down to be true of Him."

Silently Dajon thanked God for giving him the right words to help her understand, to help her see the truth of what she'd done. Though he hated to see her so distraught, a crest of admiration rose within him at her quick and humble repentance. But what to do with her now? Agony strangled him at the thought of what he knew he must do.

She let out a small sigh then continued: "I cannot change what I've done, but. . ." She swept a hand through the air. "You have your ship back now, and you have caught your pirate. You shall have your revenge for the pain I've caused you."

"Revenge? By the powers, woman, do you think that is what I want?" Dajon gripped her shoulders, fighting the urge to pull her into his arms. Instead, he turned, stomped to the desk, and plucked a feather pen from its holder. Her lemon scent, the heat from her body, and the submissive appeal in her eyes were driving him mad, but he must keep a clear head. He must not allow his sentiment to cloud his judgment.

Oh God, what am I to do?

The sunlight disappeared as quickly as if God had blown out a candle, and rain pummeled the deck above like the sound of a thousand boots— boots that marched across his heart, that marched to arrest Faith. He began plucking tiny barbs from the pen. If he turned her in for piracy, she would be hanged. How could he bear it? Yet she seemed repentant, remorseful. If she vowed never to pirate again, what good would come of her death? But oh, the harm that would come of it. Her father ruined, her sisters' lives destroyed.

He didn't know what to do. *Help me, Lord. Please.*

Rules and law. They had been his friends for many years. God's law and man's rules. He had vowed to follow both. Whenever he strayed from them in the past, he'd hurt others—people he loved—just as Faith had done. Crimes should be punished, or wickedness would become the rule.

But what of grace? The soft voice, barely an utterance, rose above the pounding rain.

"Captain Waite," Faith said from behind him, her voice devoid of life. "Let us get this over with. I cannot bear it another minute."

Neither could he.

Dropping the pen, he spun around and marched toward her with nothing on his mind but to grab her and hide her away where no one would ever find her.

She flinched at his threatening approach but met his gaze.

He halted. Great guns, she truly thought he hated her. He snorted, shaking his head.

"Do what you must do." She held out her hands so he could bind them.

He took her hands in his. "Dear lady. . ." Releasing her, he rubbed his eyes. "I can't believe I'm saying this." He snapped his gaze back to hers. "But I understand your reasons. You're clearly mad, but I understand."

"Then what has you so vexed?"

"The position you have forced upon me."

"The position, Captain, is to your favor, for you will be hailed a hero for catching the infamous Red Siren." The breath of a smile that lifted her lips instantly dissipated.

"I care not about that if it means I must lose you." There, he had said it. He had said what had been rending his heart in two. He had said the very thing that defied everything he believed in.

"I don't understand." She pressed a hand over the baldric crossing her chest.

"Take your ship back to wherever you keep it." Dajon grabbed his sword and sheathed it. "By the way, where *do* you keep it?"

A white sheen covered Faith's rosy face, and she gaped at him as if he were the ghost of Captain Morgan come back to life.

"Never mind." He huffed. "I don't want to know."

"You're not arresting me?" She blinked and seemed to be having trouble finding air around her. "But your men. They saw me."

"Mr. Borland may have. But you still had your hat on, remember? I doubt anyone else recognized you."

"But if the Admiralty discovers this?"

"I'll be court-martialed and executed."

"Nay, I won't take that chance." Faith flung out her wrists again.

"You will because I will not see you hang." Dajon grabbed one of her hands even as he forced back a smile. Not only was the lady truly repentant, but it would seem she returned his affections as well. "Do you understand me?"

She tugged her hand away. "No, I do not. You will arrest me at once."

"I give the orders on this ship now." He flashed a superior grin. "And

I will do no such thing."

"Look what I have done to you. Stolen your ship, disgraced your name, caused you so much pain." Her face was a knot of confusion.

"Can you be so daft?" He eased a finger over her soft cheek. "You can navigate a ship, play the pirate, ride a horse, fire a pistol, and probably wield that cutlass I tossed into the sea, but you cannot recognize love when you see it."

"Love?" She gasped.

"Yes. 'Twill most likely be the death of me, but I love you, Faith. I cannot help myself." He cupped her chin and caressed her cheek with his thumb.

She closed her eyes. Her chest rose and fell rapidly as if she were running from some unknown danger. One tear escaped the fringe of her dark lashes, then she sank into him.

Entwining her within his embrace, Dajon wished he could always keep her safe in his arms, but keeping this woman safe would be like trying to catch the wind in his sails and hold it there forever. Weaving his fingers through her curls, he leaned his head atop hers and released a sigh.

She gazed up at him, her sparkling eyes shifting between his. The freckles on her nose begged for attention, and he placed a gentle kiss upon them. "Might I say, you look quite ravishing in breeches," he whispered.

She moved her lips closer to his. "I'll wager you say that to all the pirates you catch."

Pressing her against him, he captured her mouth with his, feeling her heartache, her will, her pain dissolve into him. Heat seared through him. He yearned for more of this tantalizing woman, more of her heart, more of her soul, more of her body. Releasing her before he gave in to his desire, he caught his breath. Then, noticing the tears streaming down her cheeks, he kissed them away. "Please don't cry."

"Dajon, I can't allow you to do this." She shook her head, swiping at her tears and backing away from him. "I will not risk harming another person I love for my own mistakes."

"There is no risk. No one need know of this. You never raised your flag and didn't board the ship. I'll tell the men we made a mistake. You are merely searching for a lost relative."

"But what of Borland? What of the *Lady Adeline*? Clearly the captain knew what I was about."

"Borland is a friend. He will keep silent. And the *Lady Adeline* is even now on her way to Jamaica."

"It is too risky." She swallowed. Her jaw tightened.

Dajon gripped her shoulders and gently shook her, hoping to shake loose the sudden fog that had befuddled her brain. "Do you wish to die at the end of a noose? Do you wish to see your sisters miserable, your father ruined?"

"Of course not." She pulled away from his grasp. "But neither do I wish to see any harm come to you." Her eyes flooded with tears again.

"This is the only way." Dajon held out his hand. "Faith, please, trust me. I promise all will be well."

Taking his hand, she leaned her head on his chest.

"Very well, I concede. But not for me. I deserve no better than the noose for what I've done. But for my sisters and my father."

"Good girl." Dajon brushed his fingers through her hair.

He held her back from him. "But you must promise me."

"Anything."

"Promise me you will never pirate again."

"Oh, Dajon, I assure you, that is an easy promise to keep."

CHAPTER 29

Leaping from the cockboat, Borland stomped down the wooden dock, feeling it quake beneath his angry march. Raising the collar of his frock against the rain that blasted across his path, he headed toward his favorite tavern.

He needed a drink. A good, long, strong drink.

Anything to squelch the incessant howling in his head. Egad, Miss Westcott was the Red Siren. As soon as he'd heard her voice, as soon as he'd watched her flounce across the deck to Captain Waite, as soon as he'd seen that tiny thread of red hair dancing across her neck, he knew. Yet the captain had the audacity to set her free.

Borland should be overcome with joy.

He would not have to do a thing. This woman, this pirate, would be Dajon's undoing. The event could not have gone better if Borland had spent years planning it—and even then, he could never have conceived of such a fortuitous outcome.

Rain stung his cheek. He lowered his chin and folded his arms across his chest before darting across the muddy street. The screech of jarring wheels and the irritated whinny of a horse jolted him from his thoughts.

"Watch where yer goin', ye bird-witted laggard," the driver of the buggy yelled before flicking his reins and continuing onward.

Thunder roared an angry admonition as Borland plodded forward, the mud clawing at his boots like demons dragging him to the underworld.

Pulling from their grasp, Borland trudged up the stairs of the Blind Arms alehouse and shook off the eerie feeling that he had somehow escaped a perilous ending.

A ribald tune floated through the open window upon flickering fingers of candlelight, beckoning him inside. Borland doffed his bicorn and slapped it on his knee, licking his lips as the smell of ale wafted over him.

"Mr. Borland!" shouted a familiar voice from within the pounding rain.

Peering through the darkness, Borland made out a fashionable calash as it lumbered through the mud and stopped before the tavern.

A footman, with coat dripping and hair plastered to his face, jumped down from the driver's bench, placed a box step in the mud, and held an umbrella aloft as Sir Wilhelm Carteret emerged from the enclosed carriage. He stepped uneasily onto the box then dashed beneath the porch as if the rain would somehow melt him.

"Sir Wilhelm." Borland nodded, annoyed at the delay to his evening's drink. "What may I do for you, sir?"

Sir Wilhelm's lips flattened into a haughty line as he clutched Borland's arm and dragged him to the side. "Why have I not heard of Mr. Waite's arrest?" Sniffing, he raised a hand to his nose. "Mrs. Gladstone refuses to see me."

Borland ripped from his grasp. "You haven't heard then?" He snorted. "Mr. Waite didn't take the lovely Mrs. Gladstone up on her offer, as I informed you he would not."

Sir Wilhelm growled. "That matters not. The brother should have caught them in an embrace, and her word would seal the captain's doom."

Borland drew a shaky breath of the rain-spiced air and tried to quell the searing fury in his belly. "Nay, I fear the lady was so smitten with the chivalrous Mr. Waite that she reneged on our agreement and hailed him her rescuing knight." Borland waved a hand through the air in a royal gesture.

"Gads! I cannot believe it." Sir Wilhelm turned and gripped the railing then snapped his hands from the soggy wood. "This is inconceivable." He swung about, his white periwig slightly askew.

"Aye, and her husband trumpets the captain's praises all about town, even offered him a reward." The vision of Mr. Gladstone all but bowing down to worship Dajon etched green trenches of jealousy in Borland's mind.

Captain Waite's never-ending good fortune.

Sir Wilhelm gritted his teeth. "I must get the blasted man out of the

way! Surely you know of some other way—anything that will ruin him."
He pounded the air with his fist, lace flopping at his wrist.

Yes, Borland did indeed know of a way to ruin Mr. Waite. He longed
to tell Sir Carteret. The juicy news perched on the tip of his tongue and
heralded its call so loudly Borland was sure Sir Wilhelm would hear it.
But he snapped his mouth shut. He could not do it.

Not yet.

Dajon would not only be ruined. He would be executed.

Borland felt like Satan himself holding the cursed apple. But if he
offered the vile fruit to Sir Wilhelm, 'twould be the great Captain Waite
who would fall—not only fall but die as well—and while Borland longed
to take back from Dajon what was rightfully his, he was not ready to cause
the death of his longtime friend.

He slid a finger over his moist mustache and gave Sir Wilhelm a look
of defeat. "No, I told you. Captain Waite is perfect."

Sir Wilhelm sneered and waved a hand in dismissal. "Not as perfect as
you think. There is another way." His thin lips spread in an insidious grin.
"I received some very interesting news from London today." He patted his
waistcoat pocket and turned to leave.

"News of Dajon?"

"Of his past," he shot over his shoulder.

"Enough to discredit his naval service? Or more?"

Sir Wilhelm swung about. "Nay, but enough to discredit him with Miss
Westcott." Carteret flicked his eyebrows then climbed into his carriage.

Borland's shoulders sank. If Sir Wilhelm only knew the weapon
Borland held, he would no doubt pay handsomely for its possession. Then
not only would they both be rid of the infuriating Captain Waite, but
Borland would be a wealthy man, as well as the commander of the HMS
Enforcer. How could any man pass up such an opportunity? Besides, it
was his duty to report Dajon to the Admiralty. If he didn't and didn't do
it quickly, then he, too, would face a court-martial for withholding the
information.

But to inform Sir Wilhelm would mean a certain death sentence for
Dajon. And Borland needed to exhaust every other means to discredit his
commander before he resorted to such dire measures.

The footman snapped the reins, and the calash lumbered down the street. Borland watched until darkness enveloped the retreating coach before he ducked into the tavern.

He needed that drink now more than ever.

❧

A daring ray of sunlight peeked through a crack in the heavy curtains hanging in Faith's chamber. Pushing aside her coverlet, she slid from her bed and darted to the window. She'd hardly slept at all and had lain in bed the last hour waiting for the sun to rise. Grabbing the curtains, she flung them aside, allowing the morning sun to wash over her, cleanse her, warm her. It was a new day.

A new life.

A tingling sensation radiated from her heart, bringing with it such peace and love as she had not known before. It was the presence of God. She knew because she had felt Him all night long as she spoke to Him from her bed.

"Oh Lord, I have been so foolish. But You never left me."

Moisture filled her eyes, and she closed them as she knelt on the wooden floor and bowed before the holiness, the power, and the love of a God who, even though she had given up on Him, had never given up on her. Tears spilled down her cheeks, plopping onto the floorboards below like sparkling diamonds. She released a tiny chuckle. These tears of joy, tears of submission, were far more beautiful than the worldly jewels she had sought to obtain.

Though she still could not understand the reason behind all her family's tragedies, somehow now deep within her, she knew. She knew God was in control, and His love for them, His desire for their best, had prompted all that had occurred.

"I thank You, Lord. I thank You for saving me from the noose, though that is surely what I deserve—and far worse. I thank You for saving Hope and for keeping all of us safe in Your arms."

Rising, she pulled on her robe, opened a drawer of her dressing chest, and began flinging out petticoats, ribbons, frilly caps, and scarves onto the floor. It had to be here.

Then she saw it hidden among the folds of a chemise. Her Bible.

Grabbing it, she hopped onto her bed and opened it, tracing her fingers over the holy pages. How long had it been since she'd read it? Six, seven years? Even then, it had not made much sense to her. Yet oddly, she had kept it safely tucked away all this time. She flipped a few pages, and her eyes landed on a scripture in Psalms: "Though I walk in the midst of trouble, thou wilt revive me: thou shalt stretch forth thine hand against the wrath of mine enemies, and thy right hand shall save me. The LORD will perfect that which concerneth me: thy mercy, O LORD, endureth for ever: forsake not the works of thine own hands."

Yes, God had revived her, had preserved her life. Not only hers but her sisters' lives as well—even in the midst of terrible trouble.

But not your mother's life. The subtle whisper slithered into her mind even as a chill overtook her.

Faith bit her lip. True, her mother had died, but perhaps taking her home was a form of saving her. Perhaps physical death was not the most important thing God desired to save them from. Besides, her mother was the most pious woman Faith had ever known. Surely she did not lament the glorious place where she now resided.

And God hadn't said her family would encounter no trouble, only that He would save them through it. Glancing down at the verse again, Faith locked her gaze upon the phrase "The LORD will perfect that which concerneth me." God had a purpose for her, a plan, a reason for everything that happened. But she had stopped trusting Him. Stopped believing that He cared. And sailed off on her own course.

She gently closed the book. "Oh Father, help me to trust You no matter what calamities may befall me or my family."

Her thoughts sped to her mother again, and renewed sorrow burned behind her eyes. Yet despite the pain, God had worked everything to the good. He had brought her Dajon.

Dajon. Thoughts of him bubbled within her like new wine. Honorable, God-fearing, kind, strong, brave—a million adjectives swept across her mind, each one proclaiming his virtues. Not only was he all those things, but he respected women as well—a rarity among the cads she and her sisters had encountered of late. And he was honest. He would never deceive her, never hurt her, never hurt anyone. She hadn't known men like him existed. If she had, perhaps she wouldn't have been so opposed to marriage. Surprise sent her head spinning. Surprise that the thought of marriage had even occurred to her, let alone made every inch of her shiver with joy.

Perhaps Dajon was the answer to her problems. A God-sent answer. A union with him would provide the protection and support she needed—they all needed—giving her time to find proper suitors for her sisters. Not to mention that she would no longer be obliged to marry Sir Wilhelm when her father returned.

Yet she knew the price Dajon had paid to release her. The cost of going against everything he believed in: truth and duty and obedience. Not to mention the risk he took with his own life.

Truly, he must love her.

～

"Good morning, Hope, Grace. Isn't it a lovely day?" Faith floated into the dining room, anxious to see her sisters, anxious to express her affection for them, to tell them that things would be different, that now all would be well. She was met by the tantalizing scent of oatmeal, honey, sweet cream, and orange marmalade. Her stomach rumbled.

Hope, modishly dressed in a cotton lavender gown trimmed in silver lace, gave her a curious glance before returning to her coffee.

"Hope, let me see you." Faith clutched her hand and pulled her to standing, then she studied her sister's sweet features, the golden gleam in her hair, her thick dark lashes surrounding sapphire eyes. Had Faith ever really seen her before? Had she ever really looked at her as anything other than a nuisance? "Such a lovely lady you've become." She hugged her, but Hope was so stiff it felt as though Faith hugged one of the masts on her ship.

When she pulled back, Hope's face had contorted into confusion.

Faith gulped. Was it so unusual for her to express affection to her sisters?

"And Grace." Faith skirted the table in a swish of lace, but her sister flinched and backed away, looking at Faith as if she were the devil himself.

Ignoring her, she took Grace's hand in hers and squeezed it. "Such constant faith in God. What an inspiration you are to us all."

Grace exchanged a glance with Hope then frowned at Faith. "Oh my.

Tell me you haven't taken up that vile devil's brew—and so early in the morning?" She rose and began sniffing around Faith's mouth.

"Nay, something far better." Faith squelched her rising frustration and turned to stare out the window.

"Miss, would you care for some tea?" the serving maid chirped behind her.

"Yes, Miranda, thank you." Faith took her seat, and after the maid had poured her tea, she plopped two lumps of sugar into the steaming liquid.

Sipping the sweet, lemony tea, she enjoyed the warm trail it made down her throat and into her belly. "Things will be different around here," she began, raising her voice in excitement. "I shall be home more often. We shall attend to our studies—art, literature, science—take up the pianoforte, perhaps. Make Father proud."

Hope blinked. "Whatever has come over you? Are you ill?" She pressed the back of her hand to Faith's cheek then waved it through the air. "Please do not make any more promises you never intend to keep."

Faith sighed, feeling as if the sugar had turned to lead in her stomach. She placed a gentle hand on Hope's arm. "Forgive me for being such a horrible sister, will you?" She glanced at Grace. "And you as well? Can you both ever forgive me?"

Footsteps sounded behind her. "What's this about being a horrible sister?" Molly set a tray of cakes down on the table.

"Call the doctor, Molly. I fear some savage fever has captured our sister's brain," Hope said in all seriousness.

Molly leaned over to examine Faith. "Something different about you for sure. A glow, a brightness in yer eye." She straightened her stance. "Well, whate'er has gotten into you, I hope it stays."

"God has gotten into me." Faith grinned.

"God, did you say?" Molly clapped her hands. "The Almighty Hisself? Well, praise the Lord. Jest what I've been praying for."

Grace cast a hopeful glance toward Faith. "Truly?"

Faith gave her a reassuring nod.

Hope dropped her cup into her saucer, the clank echoing through the room. A look of horror marred her face. "Now what is to become of me? I am surrounded."

Faith and Molly laughed.

"Sir Wilhelm Carteret to see you, Miss Westcott," Edwin announced from the doorway.

Carteret. He was the last person Faith wanted to see. Now or ever.

"Escort him to the drawing room, Edwin. I shall be there shortly." She stood, straightening her gown. "Not even Sir Wilhelm will dampen my mood today," she promised her sisters. But as she made her way to the drawing room, her father's ultimatum hit her in the chest like a boarding ax. Unless Dajon proposed, she would be forced to marry this buffoon when Father returned. And although she believed Dajon loved her, she had no idea of his true intentions.

Whom are you trusting? echoed an inaudible voice within her.

Herself again. Faith hung her head. Slipping back into her old ways so soon. *Forgive me, Lord.* She said a silent prayer as she entered the drawing room and barely glanced at the odious man.

"Sir Wilhelm."

"Miss Westcott," he said in greeting. Taking her hand, he placed a warm, slobbering kiss on it.

Faith suddenly wished she had donned her gloves. Snatching her hand away, she took a step back and wiggled her nose at the smell of the pungent starch Sir Wilhelm lavished upon his wig.

He seemed to be waiting with anticipation for her to say something—such as how good it was to see him or to what did she owe the honor of his esteemed visit—but she just stood, hands clasped before her and brows raised.

"Well, you're no doubt wondering the reason for my call." He cleared his throat and adjusted the cravat abounding in waves of white silk around his neck. "I feel we should become better acquainted. We are, after all, betrothed." His thin, pale lips spread into a catlike grin.

The tea in Faith's stomach churned into a brew of repulsion, and she pressed a hand to her belly, hoping its contents would stay put. "I fear you cannot claim that victory yet, Sir Wilhelm. Not until my father returns."

"Victory, ah, yes. It would indeed be so for us both."

Faith scratched beneath her collar, feeling a sudden rash creep up her neck. "Do not presume, sir, to assess my feelings in this matter."

"I make the presumption, Miss Westcott, based on any woman's delight at the prospect of so favorable a future—especially a lady with no title or fortune to call her own."

"I may not have title or fortune, but I have a heart and a will to marry whomever I wish."

"Pshaw!" Withdrawing an embroidered handkerchief, he flapped it through the air. "Women do not have the capacity to make their own decisions, which is why these arrangements are best made between men."

Faith bunched her fists, digging her nails into her palms. "Sir Wilhelm, I do not wish to be impertinent, nor do I wish to offend you, but I must inform you that I am opposed to this match and will do everything in my power to prevent it from occurring."

Sir Wilhelm's face blanched an even whiter shade than Faith had thought possible. But then his mouth curved in a sly grin. "Ah, you play the coquette with me. So charming." He took her hand in his, intending to plant one of his slobbering kisses upon it again, but Faith snagged it back.

"I assure you, sir, I am playing no game." She grimaced as anger tightened every muscle within her. This man's bloated opinion of himself had surely swallowed all of his reason.

"You will feel differently, dear, when we are married." His slimy gaze perused her from head to toe as if imagining the event.

"We will never be married," she spat through gritted teeth.

"I realize your aversion to the union, Miss Westcott." Sir Wilhelm flung a hand through the air and left it hanging there as if waiting for some token. "A certain timidity is to be expected among genteel ladies. But I assure you, with my fortune and position, you will be most happy."

The mélange of angst and fury in Faith's stomach nearly boiled over. "As I have said, I seek neither your fortune nor your position, sir, and I fear I must by good conscience inform you that I would rather broil over a savage fire than marry you." She hated to be cruel, but in the face of such arrogant presumption, she had no choice.

Sir Wilhelm swept back the long white curls of his periwig and straightened his silk waistcoat as if preparing to speak to an assembly. "'Tis that Mr. Waite, isn't it?" His congenial tone turned caustic. "You prefer a poor commander with no wealth or title? Foolish woman," he hissed and snapped his gaze from hers before he took up a slow pace across the room.

"He treats women with dignity. Respect." Faith crossed her arms over her chest. "Something you would do well to observe and learn from."

Spinning on his heel, Sir Wilhelm faced her, his snakelike eyes narrowing. "Perhaps this will change your mind." He reached inside his coat and pulled out a stack of papers, unfolding them with a flap of his hands. "I have discovered that your esteemed Mr. Waite is not who he appears to be."

Sir Wilhelm's confident tone sent a twinge of fear through Faith. "What madness is this? Would you stoop so low, sir, as to slander another man's name?"

"Slander, Miss Westcott, or reveal the truth?" The mole by his right ear seemed to throb with each vile word he spoke.

Faith tore her gaze from it and rubbed her arms. Unease prickled over her, the unease of impending attack, an intuition she'd honed during her years at sea.

Sir Wilhelm gave a satisfied smirk. "It pains me to tell you that not five years ago, your priestly Mr. Waite was involved in quite the scandal outside Brent."

"Scandal?" Faith planted a hand to her waist and blew out a sigh. "Really, Sir Wilhelm. This is beneath even you."

"See for yourself."

Snatching the papers from his hand, Faith began perusing them, only half listening to his vainglorious drivel.

"Seems your pious captain was known to be quite the coxcomb in his time. Apparently had an affair with a Lady Marianne Rawlings—a married woman." Faith felt his piercing eyes lock upon her, but she did not look up.

The words before her blurred into squiggly lines.

"When she was found with child, he killed her to cover up the sordid event."

Killed. With child. The words scrambled in the air around her just like the sentences did on the page now quivering in her hands. Other words joined them in her memory—words spoken by Dajon in confession of a sordid past.

Scanning the legal document, obviously from a barrister, Faith tried to focus. *Mishap. . .Mr. Dajon Waite and Lady Rawlings involved in a carriage accident. . .Slick roads. . .The Lady Rawlings and her unborn child died from injuries.*

Everything inside of her screamed a defiant *No!*

It couldn't be true. Not Dajon.

He wouldn't have an affair with a married woman. He wouldn't dispose of her and their child as if they were inconvenient trifles.

"Treats women with dignity, did you say?" Sir Wilhelm withdrew his snuffbox and snorted a pinch into each nostril. "Now you see, my dear, since you must find a suitable husband before your father returns and Mr. Waite obviously falls short, you will have no choice but to marry me."

CHAPTER 30

Dajon led his horse down Hasell Street toward the Westcott home. Well past midnight, no need to hurry. Everyone would have retired by now. After he'd watched the *Red Siren* sail away, the HMS *Enforcer* had encountered a foundering merchant ship, taking on water through a rotted hole in her side more rapidly than she could pump it out. He and his crew had spent the rest of the day and part of the night assisting them with a temporary patch and then hauling them into port. After he'd spent the night on his ship, he'd awoken to pressing business from the Admiralty that had stolen his entire day and most of his evening.

It had taken every bit of his will to remain at his tasks, to not drop everything and dash off to see Faith—to see how she fared after her harrowing capture and release, how her renewed faith was settling in, and where her true feelings toward him lay.

He thanked God that no one else on the ship, aside from Borland, had actually seen Faith. No one else knew her true identity. Her flag had not been raised. The *Red Siren* painted on the hull had not been visible from the side they boarded, and she had fired only one shot, a warning shot he easily explained away as the means of an inexperienced captain's daughter to get the merchant ship's attention.

The marines had been quite satisfied with his explanation of mistaken identity. The distraught captain's daughter had only been searching for her missing father after the poor man had been abducted and forced into slavery aboard a ship by a vindictive merchant in payment for an exorbitant debt he owed.

No one recognized Lucas. No one knew Faith, save Borland, and Borland was Dajon's lifelong friend, his partner, his confidant. He accepted Dajon's promise that Faith had vowed never to pirate again.

Then why did guilt continually churn in Dajon's gut? *God, forgive me for my lies, but I did not know how else to save her.*

Daring a glance into the black sky, he hoped for some sign of absolution. Nothing but dark clouds broiled over a sliver of a moon. *Lord, no harm was done. In fact, quite the opposite—a known pirate has repented. Then why do I feel like You have abandoned me?*

Regardless, Dajon could not imagine having taken any other course. Because the only other course available was one that led to Faith's neck in a noose.

Agony choked him at the thought, and he took a deep breath of the night air, fragrant with earth and jasmine. A vision of Faith in breeches and waistcoat stormed through his mind.

A pirate.

He smiled. By the powers, what an incredible woman. He yearned to see her, to take her in his arms, to express his sincere devotion to her; it would have to wait until morning, though, for no doubt she had retired hours ago.

Dismounting, Dajon led his horse through the back gate of the Westcott house. He nodded at Lucas and handed him the reins. "Good evening, Lucas, or good morning, rather. My apologies for keeping you up so late." The air hung like a heavy curtain around them. Not a breeze, not a whisper of wind stirred the thick folds of humidity.

Lucas grunted and took the reins. Unusual for the normally cheerful groomsman, but then, Dajon had caught him at piracy. Perhaps he was concerned for his future. "Never fear, Lucas, I have no intention of arresting you for your part in Miss Westcott's piracy. She explained that your participation was only to assist and protect her and that you have no desire to pirate again."

Lucas shifted his stance but said not a word.

Trying to determine his mood, Dajon peered at him, but the groomsman's features were lost in the shadows. Even the outline of his hair blended into the ebony night.

"Never mind," Dajon said. "We shall discuss it later. I'm spent and wish to retire."

Lucas didn't move.

A thick silence waxed between them. Dajon drew in a deep breath of air burdened with the smell of horseflesh and human sweat. An uneasiness, borne from many battles, pricked his fingers, causing them to grip the hilt of his sword and peer into the darkness surrounding them.

"You may lead him to the stables, Lucas. I am home for the night."

Lucas cleared his throat. "Forgive me, Mr. Waite, but I can't be doin' what ye ask of me."

Before shock could settle in, the snap of a twig and the crunch of gravel drew Dajon's gaze toward the house, where a form appeared out of the darkness. A curvaceous form in a light-colored gown that swished when she walked.

Faith.

He took a step toward her in expectation.

"That will be all, Lucas. Leave the horse where it is." Her harsh tone froze Dajon in place. "Mr. Waite will be leaving shortly."

Dajon gave a humorless laugh. "What are you saying? I have only just arrived." Removing his bicorn, he dabbed at the sweat on his forehead. By thunder, 'twas a muggy night. Perhaps the soggy air had somehow seeped into Faith's brain, befuddling it.

Dropping the reins, Lucas hesitated, shifting his weight back and forth, but one look from Faith sent him shuffling away.

"Why are you awake at this hour?" Dajon asked, beginning to believe that he wouldn't like her answer at all. He held out a hand, hoping she'd take it and relieve him of the fear that now prickled his scalp.

But she did not. Instead, she turned, took a few steps, and positioned herself by his horse. Was that a sword strapped to her side? "I must protect my sisters."

"From whom, pray tell?"

"From you."

Dajon took a step back, as if an icy wall of water had crashed over him. Peering into the darkness that seemed to stretch for miles between them, he searched for her eyes but could only make out two simmering black coals.

Fear gave way to anger. He had done naught to deserve this ill treatment. "What has gotten into you? Yesterday—"

"Yesterday, I thought I knew you," she snapped and crossed her arms over her waist, where Dajon thought he saw the dark shape of a pistol shoved into her belt.

Knew me? Dajon swallowed, sending what felt like lead pellets into his stomach. The hoot of an owl echoed across the garden. Dajon had the odd feeling the bird was somehow warning him to flee. "Miss Westcott, if you'll forgive me, I am in no mood for games."

"I'm not the one playing a charade."

Dajon bunched his fists. Nothing was making sense. It was as if he had walked into a playhouse where one of Shakespeare's tragedies was being performed. Only he was up onstage. "Whatever are you talking about? And why do you all of a sudden feel you need to protect your sisters from me? I have done you no harm—in fact, quite the opposite."

She snorted. "Unfortunately, Lady Marianne Rawlings cannot claim the same."

All hope, all joy drained out of Dajon, soaking into the ground beneath him. Only an empty shell of shame and horror remained. Now he understood. "Who told you?"

"Sir Wilhelm."

Ah yes. Dajon should have seen it coming, should have told Faith the truth, but he longed to bury his past forever in the hope that he could forget it as well.

"Tell me it's not true." Faith's stalwart voice broke in a slight tremble.

The owl repeated its eerie call from somewhere above them. No more lies. He would tell no more lies tonight. "I cannot deny it."

She flinched and stepped back, bumping into his horse, who protested with a snort. "Though I am truly thankful for all you've done, I must ask you to leave immediately and never come back." Grabbing the reins, she held them out to him.

Sweat slid behind his collar and down his back—putrid beads of shock, of pain, of remorse. But he could not leave. "Your father left me in charge, Miss Westcott. I cannot abandon my post."

"My father did not know what kind of man you are."

"Perhaps, but I thought *you* might have discovered that truth these past weeks."

"As I said, you play a good charade." The venom in her voice stung every nerve within him.

"I still cannot leave you and your sisters unprotected." He may have lost Faith. He may have lost her love, he may never recover from the gaping hole in his heart, but he still had a duty to perform. "So if you'll permit me." He grabbed the horse's reins and felt her flinch when their fingers brushed. Was she frightened of him or simply repulsed? He started for the stables. "I promise I shall make every effort not to offend you with my presence."

"Which you will find quite easy since you no longer reside here." Faith's seething voice scraped over him, but he stepped around her, leading the horse toward the flickering light in the stables.

The swish of a sword being drawn sliced the thick air. Something sharp pricked his back. "Not another step, Captain."

He slowly turned to face her, just as a cloud eased away from the moon, revealing her tear-stained face. The silver glint of the sword formed a bridge between them, and he wished it were that easy to span the painful gap that now threatened to separate them forever.

"Are you going to kill me, Faith?"

"I will do what I must to keep my sisters safe from men like you."

"You know I would never harm you or your—"

"I don't know anything anymore!" she shouted. Her sword wavered.

In her state of mind, he wouldn't put it past her to run him through. He didn't know exactly what Sir Wilhelm had told her, but if it was anything close to the truth, she now believed him capable of forcing himself upon a decent lady—a married lady at that—stealing her away from her husband and home in the middle of the night, only to have her killed along with their child.

As the point of her sword etched a quivering trail across his chest, he reached for his own sword and drew it in one quick swoop. He batted hers from her hand and onto the ground with a clank that sounded muddled in the humid air.

Faith gasped. Backing away from him, she plucked out her pistol, cocked it, and pointed it at his chest. "Please leave," she sobbed.

Until now he'd heard only the anger in her voice, the spite, but now he heard the pain, like a wail of anguish piercing through the air and into his heart. He had hurt her terribly, and the thought gutted him as if she had indeed run him through with her sword. "Very well. I will leave." Turning his horse around, he faced Faith. "If it means anything at all to you, I am truly sorry." He headed for the gate.

She sniffed. "I suppose you'll turn me in for piracy now."

"Why?" He shrugged and halted. "Nothing has changed. You will not go back on your vow to quit?"

"No."

"Then I have no reason to turn you over to the authorities." He could only pray to the Lord that she wouldn't turn away from God, as well. "Besides, I still love you."

Dajon mounted his horse in one leap and grabbed the reins. He risked one more glance at the woman he'd grown to love and admire. She held the pistol out before her, leveled upon his heart. Did she really believe he would hurt her? The thought sank him to the depths of the sea. "If you need anything, you know where—"

His words faltered on his lips.

The owl gave his eerie hoot for a third time, announcing Dajon's exit back into shame and regret.

Nudging his horse, he rode off into a darkness so thick, so black that he truly believed it would never be light again.

◆

"Why we goin' to the ship?" Lucas asked, bringing his horse alongside Faith's.

"I told you. I have to clean it out. Get all of our things removed. Bring Morgan home. 'Tis not my ship anymore." Faith adjusted her straw bonnet against the rising sun. "I must return it to Mr. Waite."

The thought saddened her. The *Red Siren* had been a faithful friend these past five years. Her ticket to the sea, to wealth, to freedom. But that was all gone now. Perhaps Mr. Waite would have allowed her to take the ship out upon the seas now and then, once she proved to him her pirating days were over—and after the name *Red Siren* was scraped from the hull, of course—but that was no longer an option.

She now longed to be rid of anything associated with Mr. Waite. "I still have a hard time believin' he let ye go like that," Lucas said as the trail narrowed and they entered a thick patch of trees.

Beams of glittering morning sun streamed through the forest like ribbons of hope, transforming the leaves of hickories and sweet gums into sparkling emerald and their barks into columns of amber. It appeared more like a magical forest from a fairy tale than a Carolina woodland.

Faith huffed. Just like her short-lived romance with Mr. Waite. Destined to live only in a storybook where endings were always happy. Not in real life where they never were.

As if mimicking her faltering mood, the air thickened around her with the earthy, pungent smell of rotting wood and dank moss. Something stung her neck, and she slapped a mosquito.

Lucas struck his arm where another blood-sucking beast had landed. "An' especially after ye near run 'im through with yer blade last night." He snickered.

Faith made no reply as the events of the night drilled through her mind for the thousandth time. So enraged at Mr. Waite's betrayal and the revelation of his true character—or lack thereof—her only thought had been to put as much distance between the loathsome man and her sisters as she could. She hadn't considered that he held the power to throw her in prison, not until after she'd pointed the pistol at him.

Why had she confronted him? Perhaps deep down, despite the proof stamped upon documents now littering her drawing room floor, she hoped it wasn't true—that Dajon. . .Mr. Waite would deny the allegations, would offer some explanation. But when he hadn't, when he had only confirmed her biggest fears, she flew into a rage. She would rather see him dead than harm her sisters.

"The day is young, Lucas. Mr. Waite could be alerting the authorities about us as we speak." The daunting thought had occurred to her even before she'd opened her eyes that morning. She wanted to believe Mr. Waite would stick to their bargain, she wanted to believe he was a man of his word, but she'd been trusting a man she no longer knew. Dread consumed her. It was as if Faith, her sisters, and her father were lined up before a loaded cannon and Mr. Waite stood nearby, holding the linstock that would set off the blast.

A bird the color of a turquoise sky flitted across their path, chirping a cheerful tune, followed by several of his friends. Faith envied their carefree life.

"Mr. Waite'll not be turnin' ye in." Lucas loosened his neckerchief then used it to dab the back of his thick neck, revealing the pink tip of a scar beneath his shirt. Faith cringed. She had never gotten used to seeing the molten stripes marring her friend's back. Yet even after being nearly whipped to death as a boy, Lucas now allowed God to give him hope for the future.

"The man loves ye; any fool can see that," he said.

"The only fool here is me." Faith dipped her head beneath an over-hanging branch. "For I believed Mr. Waite was the God-fearing man he claimed to be. A man like him is incapable of love."

They rode side by side in silence. Only the clump of their horses' hooves over the sandy trail and the orchestra of birds and buzzing insects accompanied them.

The faint snort of a horse sounded, and Faith grabbed her pistol. Lucas did the same. They both scanned the thicket of trees then shot a glance behind them. Nothing. Not many people dared to venture into the backwoods surrounding Charles Towne, especially with all the Indian attacks recently. Most likely a trapper or a lone Indian, neither of which would be a threat to them.

Returning her pistol to her baldric, Faith tugged on the leather straps, hoping for a breeze to ease inside her cotton gown and cool her searing skin.

Lucas shifted in the saddle and stretched his broad back. "I's praying fer you, mistress. An' fer Mr. Waite."

"You need not bother, Lucas," she retorted. "Mr. Waite was a man of prayer, a man of faith, but he turned out to be naught but a scoundrel who preys on the affections of innocent women." Faith's heart shriveled even as she said the words. "Just like all men." Then she bit her lip and glanced at Lucas. "Yourself excluded, of course."

Lucas flashed a set of pearly teeth that matched the whites of his eyes. "Why, thank ye, mistress. But whate'er Mr. Waite done, 'twas a long time ago, eh?"

"Aye."

"Thanks be to God that He not only forgives but forgets the sins o' our pasts."

"Only if we repent of them." Faith slapped another mosquito and wondered for the first time if Mr. Waite had been sorry for his actions.

Not that it would matter to Faith.

Lucas scratched his hair. "Seems to me Mr. Waite ain't nothin' like this man you done heard about."

True. Mr. Waite had proven himself to be naught but an honorable, God-fearing man these past few weeks. A clump of moss hanging from an almond pine grazed over Faith's shoulder as she tried to brush away thoughts of the man's admirable character. He was a swindler. That was all.

"Perhaps. Perhaps not," she said. "But I cannot forget the abuse of an innocent woman. Not after what has happened to Charity and to Hope."

"God changes people. He already be changin' me, mistress."

Faith studied her first mate, groomsman, and longtime friend, unable to deny the new lightness in his bearing and hope in his eyes. "I must forbid you to spend any more time with Molly—or Miss Grace, for that matter." She gave him a playful grin. "I find I prefer the old nefarious Lucas"—she deepened her voice—"first mate on the pirate ship *Red Siren*, than this charitable, high-spirited optimist." They both laughed.

Lucas grew serious. "I just hoping ye don't lay blame fer Mr. Waite's failings on God." Concern warmed his dark eyes.

Did she? No. She knew that would be pure foolishness, for that would thrust her right back where she started, blaming God for everything wrong in the world and in her life. Truth be told, God had never left her or her sisters. He had more than proven that with His miraculous rescue of Hope. Then what Faith had felt in the cabin of her ship when Dajon had confronted her, what she had felt in her chamber—the very presence of God, the love, the hope, the forgiveness that had blanketed her—was more real than anything she had known. In fact, it seemed to be the only reality she could count on anymore.

"No, Lucas. I fear that I, too, have been forever changed."

They rode the rest of the way in silence, battling the insects and the heat, and finally emerged onto the lagoon where the *Red Siren* floated in the midst of a glassy pool fringed in green moss and algae. The bare masts of the ship thrust into the sky, blending with the myriad trees surrounding them. No one would see the ship unless he happened to emerge right at this spot, and even then the anchor chain was bolted by a hefty lock that would forbid it to be raised. So far, the ship had remained safe.

After dismounting, Faith assisted Lucas in uncovering a nearby canoe, and then together they paddled out to the ship and gathered her flag, Morgan, some of her books and charts, a small chest of doubloons and rubies, and the silver swept-hilt rapier she'd captured from a French privateer. By the time they made it back to shore, the heat rose like steam off the tepid swamp.

As she and Lucas silently loaded her things into packs they had slung over their horses, Faith swallowed down the sorrow clogging her throat and avoided gazing at her ship. This might be the last time she would ever see it and definitely the last time she would call it hers, the last time she would march across its decks as they rose and fell over the tumultuous waves, the last time she would be in command. She didn't regret her change of heart. She knew now that what she had done was wrong, but it didn't seem to dull the pain of loss she felt—not only the loss of her ship but the loss of Mr. Waite.

A harsh scuffle sounded behind her, followed by a thud and a gurgle.

"Avast! Head for the shoals! Head for the shoals!" Morgan squawked from his perch on the saddle horn.

Gripping the handle of her pistol, Faith swerved around to see a beefy man, his thick arm clamped around Lucas's neck, pointing a knife at his throat. Her first mate's pistol lay useless on the dirt by his feet, and the fear flickering in his eyes seemed more for her than for himself. The beast of a man behind him slowly widened his mouth into a grimy, yellow-toothed grin.

In an instant, Faith had her pistol cocked and pointed at the intruder, but before she could utter her ultimatum, the sound of footsteps scraped across her ears. She spun her weapon in the other direction. The gun nearly fell from her hand when Sir Wilhelm Carteret emerged into the clearing. His periwig perched atop his egg-shaped head, slanted precariously as if at any minute it would slide off. Powder-muddied sweat oozed from beneath it onto his forehead and down his bloated, reddened cheeks.

"Load the guns! Load the guns!" Morgan screeched, and the flap of his wings filled the air as he, no doubt, headed for the safety of the trees.

Coward.

"Well, well." Sir Wilhelm placed one hand on his hip and the other in midair. "I daresay, what a surprise, my dear." His pretentious gaze combed over the *Red Siren*.

"You followed me," Faith spat as she tried to surmount her shock and plot her next step.

"You can't say I didn't warn you. I told you that you would pay for your refusal and your insolent behavior. Did I not?"

"I will shoot you where you stand." Faith's finger itched over the trigger, longing to put an end to this miserable man's life, while at the same time knowing she could not take another's life, even when her freedom and her very life were at stake.

"Nonsense. You will do no such thing." He smirked and gestured toward Lucas with a nod of his head. "Not unless you wish to see your slave here die." He loosened his cravat from his neck and flapped it through the air, trying to banish the swarm of gnats enamored with his wig.

Faith dared a glance at Lucas. A line of blood marred his bronze neck, but his eyes carried more annoyance than fear.

"He is not my slave. He is my friend."

"No matter." Sir Wilhelm waved a hand of dismissal toward Lucas. "You will put down your weapon, or I will order my man to slit his throat."

Faith studied Sir Wilhelm's icy gaze and knew he meant it. He would kill Lucas and get away with it. Lucas was a Negro and a pirate, after all. Releasing the cock, Faith tossed the pistol to the ground.

Sir Wilhelm's thin lips broke into a malicious grin. "So—you are indeed the notorious Red Siren? I am all astonishment." He nearly giggled with glee. "This is most fortuitous." His normally dull eyes blazed with a hard, calculated look.

Ignoring the fear and nausea spinning in her stomach, Faith planted her fists on her waist. "What is it you want?"

"Hmm." Approaching her, he took her hand and rubbed his clammy, cold fingers over hers. "You know what I want." He leaned toward her, inundating her with the stench of snuff and starch. "You will marry me."

Yanking her hand from his, Faith retreated. "I will not."

"Then I shall be forced to turn you in for piracy."

CHAPTER 31

Faith plopped down onto the moist floor, laid her head against the rough brick wall, and brought her knees to her chest. In this far corner of her cell, tucked in among the shadows, she could escape the licentious gazes of the other prisoners. Their ogling had begun to grate on her nerves like acid on an open wound. Grasping a handful of straw, she shoved it beneath her bottom, both to soften her seat and to shield her from the damp stones. An archway of bricks formed the ceiling above her, upon which hung a lantern whose flame was often extinguished, enshrouding her in the nightmarish gloom of the Watch House dungeon.

The dismal cage had been her home for a week, and she could no longer smell the human waste, fear, and death that thickened the air around her. That was not a good sign. She wondered if she would also grow accustomed to being imprisoned within these dank walls, but if her fellow inmates—who had obviously been here longer than she—provided any clue by their constant complaining and cursing, she would never get used to losing her freedom.

Her only joy was the remembrance of Sir Wilhelm's face when she'd informed him that she'd rather hang for piracy than become his wife. He had bent over so violently that she thought he was going to choke on his own vile spit. His periwig flew to the ground, leaving naught on his head but a bald, heat-prickled scalp.

After he had composed himself and covered his fury with a veneer of unruffled arrogance, Faith had convinced him that she would go with him peaceably if he would release Lucas unharmed. She had watched his beady gaze flicker between her and Lucas—who was still being restrained by Sir Wilhelm's henchman—and knew he realized what she already had. That Wilhelm was not man enough to contain her without his man's help.

After the henchman had withdrawn the knife from Lucas's throat, Faith had ordered her reluctant first mate back home with the admonition that he send for her father and take care of her sisters until the admiral returned. The assurance of her faithful friend's loyalty had been the only beam of light in the otherwise dark, hopeless void that continued to close in around her with each passing minute.

Thoughts of her sisters and their precarious futures bombarded Faith in her loneliest hours. With her imminent demise and their father returning from overseas, they would no doubt find themselves married off to the first suitors who would accept them before further scandal racked the family. A sob rose to her throat, but she refused to release it. She deserved her fate. Her sisters did not deserve theirs. She longed to see them one last time, if only to apologize for her foolish actions. Why hadn't they come to see her? Perhaps ladies were not permitted in the dungeon of the Watch House. And as she listened to the depraved conversations and fiendish threats of the men around her, Faith could understand why.

But no word, either?

Nothing from Lucas or Edwin—or Dajon. Not that she expected to see the captain after the malicious way she had thrown him from their home.

Much to her deep chagrin, the only visitor she'd had was Sir Wilhelm, who had come to call upon her twice with the same proposition. If she married him, she would be released and exonerated of all charges, and he would take care of her and her sisters for the rest of their lives. All her problems would be solved with one simple yes. Just one yes seeping through her lips but, oh, the bitter taste.

She had begun to pray—to plead with an invisible God, to humble herself before His power and majesty and ask for guidance. It felt odd, even scary at first, asking for help, relying on someone else, trusting someone else, but the more she prayed, the more she relished the companionship of her heavenly Father.

And she had felt God telling her to trust Him—that He had another plan, a better plan, and for once, she resisted taking charge of her own life. Only now as her faith dwindled along with her strength, she wondered if she had made the right choice.

I know You forgive me, Lord. I'm trying to do the right thing now. Is it too late for me? Is it too late for my sisters? Please do not punish them for my sins. Please protect them and provide godly men to be their husbands who will love them and cherish them.

She swiped away a tear before it slid down her cheek. No more crying. Perhaps she had strayed too far into the wickedness of this world, done too many bad things to be redeemed. But surely it was not too late for her sisters.

She heard the jailer before she saw him. The scrape of his bare, impotent foot over the stones had become an omen of bad tidings. Soon he emerged from the shadows carrying a bucket that seethed with the odor of animal fat and rotten eggs. Sweat gleamed atop his head, which was as big as a melon, while greasy strands clinging loosely to its sides swayed with each step. Halting, he gaped at her with the permanent grin of a hungry alligator.

"Here's yer grub, missy. Come an' get it."

"Just push it beneath the bars, if you please, Gordon."

"I'll thank ye to be callin' me *Lord* Gordon, like I told ye to."

A chuckle erupted from the cage beside hers, and Gordon pressed his face up to the rusty iron bars of her cell and whispered, "If ye be nice t' me, thar's privileges I can do fer ye to make yer stay more agreeable." Lust dripped from his bloodshot eyes.

A shudder of disgust gripped Faith just when she thought she had no more left. "I thank you, *Lord* Gordon, but I'd rather be flogged and tossed to the sharks."

Wicked chortles bounced through the air.

His eyes narrowed. "That can be arranged, ye high an' mighty wench," he growled as he dipped the ladle into his bucket of slop. But instead of pouring it onto her plate, he dumped it into her chamber pot, sitting just inside the bars. "Enjoy your meal." He laughed and slogged off, a wake of obscenities spilling from his lips after him.

But Faith had grown cold to those as well.

"Scorned ye again, old Gordie," one of the prisoners chortled.

Faith turned off the sound of the men's vulgar grumblings as Gordon made his rounds. Soon he dragged himself back in front of her cell and, with a reluctant grunt, gave her the news that she had a male visitor.

A visitor? Sir Wilhelm had already seen her earlier in the day. Faith dashed to the bars. *Lucas*. It had to be. Perhaps with word from her sisters. Faith's heart swelled. It would be so good to see a friendly face.

But it wasn't a friendly face that appeared a few minutes later lumbering down the tower steps—at least not friendly any longer. Mr. Dajon Waite, donned in a disheveled uniform, took the last step and headed toward her, his boots clomping over the stones. Gordon withered under the captain's imperious gaze, and he scampered away before Mr. Waite's blue eyes shifted to Faith's.

Backing away from the bars, Faith gripped the folds of her filthy gown as anger, fear, and—to her surprise—joy waged a fierce battle within her at the sight of him. "Come to gloat?"

He snorted. "Hardly." Anguish burned in his gaze. "I would have come sooner, but Sir Wilhelm's scrawny arm is more powerful than it appears."

Faith nodded. Indeed. The gaunt man and his noble connections did wield a mighty sword among Governor Johnson and the assembly. Her wisp of faith dwindled yet again. Who could stand up to such a powerful man?

Dajon approached the bars. Gray shadows clouded the skin beneath his eyes. His dark hair grazed his collar. He spiked a hand through the unruly strands and then scratched the stubble littering his chin. Faith wasn't sure which of them looked worse.

He swiped a lock of hair behind his ear and met her gaze in a hold so intense that she could feel his passion, his torment—his love—span between them like a sturdy plank, drawing her near.

Suddenly his past made no difference to her. Her heart had lodged in her throat when he'd entered the room and had remained there. She loved him—no matter what he'd done. Her stomach coiled into a knot as she fought the urge to run to him, to touch him, to feel his comforting strong hands on hers, but instead, pride allowed her to say only, "Why have you come?"

He swallowed hard and looked away. "To see how you are doing."

"So you see"—she swept a hand over her cell as if she were showing him her parlor—"I'm quite comfortable."

He frowned, and she chided herself for being so caustic.

"Faith." He took a step toward her. "I have sent a dispatch to Bath up north. Governor Eden harbors sympathies toward pirates wishing to reform. He has granted the King's Pardon to many who have sworn to change their ways."

Hope, an emotion Faith had abandoned during the week, sprang to life. "Why would you help me?"

"You know." The intense look in his blue eyes said more than enough.

He still loved her.

Hoots and coarse jests blasted over them. Dajon gazed down the row of gloomy cells, but the prisoners only increased their vile banter. "I'm sorry you have to hear such lubricity."

Faith raised a shoulder. "I have learned to ignore them."

"It may take a month to arrive, but I have sent my recommendation along with the urgent request." Dajon spit the words out quickly, as if doing so would help speed the process. "My position in His Majesty's Navy should carry some merit with the governor, who appreciates our presence in the colonial waters."

"But what of Sir Wilhelm?"

"His powerful arm does not stretch as far as Bath, thanks be to God."

Sweat broke out on his forehead, and he wiped it away with his sleeve then shrugged off his waistcoat and draped it over his arm. His damp shirt clung to his muscled chest. Power exuded from him, an angry, pent-up frustration that knifed into the air all around him. His jaw tensed.

Faith gazed at him in awe. She'd done naught but deceive him, lie to him, force him to risk his life and his career, and then nearly shoot him, and here he stood, his eyes filled with love as he tried to save her life.

"There is one problem," he continued, drawing in a deep breath. "Sir Wilhelm is rushing your trial through the courts. He could possibly have you convicted and. . ." Dajon's gaze did not falter, though his voice did.

"Hanged." Faith swallowed.

Dajon clasped a bar with one of his hands. "Before the pardon arrives."

Wicked laughter shot off the brick walls. "Aye, afore too long, we all be dancin' the hempen jig."

Dajon gripped the hilt of his sword and stared into the dungeon as if he intended to slice the prisoner's throat. Slowly he returned his frenzied gaze to hers. "Sir Wilhelm has many powerful allies."

The hope that had risen within Faith dissolved and fell into her stomach like an anchor. "Then rest assured, he will have his way."

⚓

"I won't allow him." Dajon leaned toward her, not caring when the iron bars bit into his skin. He would not watch the woman he loved die.

Not again.

The pardon would arrive in time. It had to. But as he gazed at Faith, her red curls flaming around her face, her auburn eyes still simmering boldly beneath a shroud of defeat, he wondered for a brief moment if she would indeed abide by its conditions.

"He found you at the *Red Siren*?" Dajon hated to ask, but he had to know if she had planned on pirating again—if the news of his past had driven her so swiftly back to her old ways.

"Aye, with my colors in hand." Faith gave a sardonic smirk, then her eyes widened. "I wasn't taking the ship out, Dajon, if that's what you're thinking."

The sound of his Christian name on her lips—even with a hint of spite—flowed over him like honey.

"I was only removing my things," she added. "To return the ship to you."

Rubbing the sweat from the back of his neck, Dajon studied her. Her steady stance and the pleading sincerity in her eyes convinced him that, for once, she told him the truth. "I believe you."

"So easily." She shook her head and lowered her lashes. "When I wouldn't even allow you to explain your actions to me."

"I hope you'll allow me to do so now."

"It matters not. All is lost." She turned her back to him and wrapped her arms around herself. A sob rippled down her back.

"Your opinion of me matters a great deal." Dajon rattled the bars, longing to rip them from their moorings and go to her, take her in his arms. But his outburst only brought a cloud of dirt raining down upon him and a cacophony of chortles from the other prisoners.

"After you stole my father's merchant ship. . ." He cleared his throat at the memory, finding it hard to believe he loved the same woman who had ruined him that day. "I was banished from the family business."

Turning around, Faith met his pained gaze with hers, but she said nothing.

"I fell in with some bad sorts—wealthy, titled bad sorts, that is. I took up gambling, drinking, carousing." Flashes of those sordid memories burned trails of guilt and remorse across his mind. His throat constricted. "Then I met Lady Rawlings. Her husband, Lord Rawlings, was a cruel, abusive man who beat her frequently."

"Much like Charity's husband." Faith's voice came out barely above a whisper.

"Perhaps worse." Anger still flared in his belly at the remembrance of the man's brutality.

"Our acquaintance was quite innocent in the beginning, I assure you. For a time, we seemed to flow in the same circles, same country dances, same balls and playhouses. Her sweet spirit and innocence drew me to her, especially after the sordid company I had grown accustomed to keeping." Dajon hesitated, unsure how much of the affair to disclose to Faith. Would she turn from him in disgust? No matter. 'Twas time to lay out the details before her and let her decide.

"When I discovered her horrendous predicament at home, it only served to draw me closer to her, to comfort her and help her. But what could I do?" He shrugged. "I had no business being with her. She was married, and I had nothing to offer her—but my love."

"Ah, ain't that sweet." The man in a cell kitty-corner from Faith's clung to the bars and thrust his deathly pale face toward them.

Ignoring him, Dajon eyed Faith, trying to assess the effect of his tale, but she stood riveted in place, nothing but concern beaming from her gaze.

"When I discovered she was with child...our child"—Dajon lowered his voice to a whisper—"we planned to run away together. But Lord Rawlings learned of our plot and chased us. The roads were slick." Dajon jerked back from the bars, hoping to dislodge the vision of Marianne's lifeless body in his arms. "You know the rest," he choked out.

A familiar pain seared through his nose, and Dajon reached up to rub it. When the carriage had careened off the road, overturned, and plummeted into a ditch, his nose had been smashed. The haunting ache was a constant reminder of his failure to care for the woman he loved. He deserved much worse.

Now Faith knew the truth. Dajon braced himself for her reaction. But much to his surprise, Faith rushed to the bars and reached out a hand toward him. He gripped it like a lifeline and drew close to her. Placing a gentle kiss upon her fingers, he cringed at the red marks marring her delicate skin. The hint of lemon battled against the dungeon's fetid smells and made its way to his nose.

He sighed and raised his gaze to hers, afraid of what he might see, but no condemnation shot from her eyes, only compassion and concern. "I did love her, Faith, or at least I thought I did. But I see now how every step I took was wrong. Everything I did went against God's plan, His law, and because of my disobedience and stupidity, I caused her death—and the death of our child." Renewed agony threatened to strangle him, and he swallowed against the burning in his throat.

"I'm so very sorry, Dajon." Reaching through the bars, Faith pressed her other hand over his heart. The warmth and tenderness of her familiar touch soothed him like a healing balm. Her auburn eyes enveloped him with a kindness he didn't deserve. "I thought you were no better than my sister's husband or Sir Wilhelm—or most of the men I've met—but I see now that you meant only to save this lady, to protect her."

"A lot of good I did her." Dajon snorted. "I suppose I've been trying to make up for it ever since, to pay some sort of penance."

"But don't you see?" Faith's voice lifted. "You can never pay the price. None of us can. I have realized that in the long hours I've spent down in this dungeon."

Dajon brushed a finger over her cheek, still as soft as silk. She closed her eyes beneath his touch. "Very wise for one so newly returned to God."

She opened her eyes and smiled. "He and I have had much to discuss this past week."

"Aye and He's been speaking with me as well. I now see that adhering to a list of rules just for the sake of following them does not please God. Nor does it atone for any past sins. Jesus has already done that on the cross."

Faith smiled. "And how did you come to this grand conclusion?"

"When I set you free." He uttered a low chuckle. "The guilt of breaking a rule ate at me day and night, but at the same time, I knew deep in my gut that it was the right thing to do. It was then that I realized God does not concern Himself so much with rules as He does with us. Doing what's right will then flow naturally out of our relationship with Him."

Tears filled her eyes, and she leaned her forehead on the iron bars. "I cannot believe I've been such a fool."

"We have both been fools." Dajon brushed a cluster of matted curls from her face. His stomach tightened. "These blasted bars." He jerked them again, longing to hold her, to wipe away her tears, to steal her away from this horrid place.

"Don't bother. I've tried." She forced a smile then lowered her voice to a whisper. "But please, tell me you are safe. No one knows that you let me go?"

"Only Mr. Borland."

"And you trust him?"

"Aye. Although we had a bit of a falling-out last week." The hatred and fury on Borland's face during their argument had shocked Dajon. Borland had wanted to pursue Stede Bonnet, a pirate known to be holed up in Cape Fear, but Dajon had deferred to a local hero, Colonel Rhett, who had volunteered to bring him in. Dajon couldn't very well run off and leave Faith alone in prison, her future so uncertain. Borland had not agreed and had defiantly resisted until Dajon had been forced to pull rank and silence him. It was the first time Dajon had noticed Borland's fervent ambition.

"It was nothing." He shook the memory from his head, preferring to drown it with happier times they had spent together. "We have been friends for years."

Faith's lip quivered. "Dajon, I could not bear it if harm came to you because of me."

"I love hearing you say my name." He swept his thumb over her still-rosy lips.

"I am serious." She frowned.

Gripping her face, he drew her near, brushing his mouth against hers. He felt her tremble.

"Dajon," was all she said.

He consumed her lips with his, ignoring the ribald howls from their audience.

Cold, hard fingers of iron bit into his cheeks, forbidding him to have more of her.

Dajon pulled away. "I love you, Faith," he whispered between thick breaths.

"And I you, Dajon." When her eyes lifted to his, they brimmed with all the admiration and love he'd only seen glimpses of before.

He eased his hands onto her shoulders and nudged her back a step. "How are you truly?" he asked, eyeing her soiled gown, torn and tattered around the hem, the mud stains on her neck and arms, and the abrasions on her hands and her sunken cheeks. How remarkable that he still found her ravishing. "You've not been eating."

She lifted her nose in the air. "That stench you smell?"

"Aye."

"That's supper, I'm afraid."

Dajon raised a brow. "I see. I shall sneak down some decent food."

"Don't bother. I'm sure I shall be relieved of this place soon enough, one way or another." She bit her lip. "Any word of my sisters?"

"You forbade me to see them, remember?" he teased, but when worry creased her face, he grabbed her hand again. "Never fear. I have inquired of Lucas. They are worried sick about you, but all is well."

Her expression tightened, and she shifted her shimmering eyes to his. "Dajon, if I. . .if the pardon does not. . ." She took a deep breath. "Please take care of them." She squeezed his hand. "Promise me you will."

"I am going to get you out of here." Dajon brought both of her hands to his lips and sealed his vow with a tender kiss. "That's the only promise I will make."

Trouble was, he didn't know if it was a promise he could keep.

CHAPTER 32

Borland paced across the elaborate drawing room of the Carteret mansion. His boots clicked over the tile floor to the rhythm of the brass clock that mocked him from atop the fireplace. He had been ushered here nearly a half hour ago by a rather pretentious butler, who had admitted him only as a result of Borland's volatile persistence. Though Borland had sent several posts during the past week to Sir Wilhelm, the pompous halfwit had made no response nor any attempt to contact him. A frustrated anger sizzled within Borland for being ignored by a man who, no doubt, thought he had no further use for him.

Sir Wilhelm would certainly be surprised to find out differently today.

As Borland passed through the streams of sunlight flowing in through two french windows, he eyed the exquisite jewel-encrusted cornices above them, the gilded sconces lining the wall, and the collection of Ming vases displayed on a bureau by the entrance. He clicked his tongue. A waste of wealth on a buffoon like Sir Wilhelm.

Heading for the marble fireplace, Borland's boots thudded over the Chinese carpet at the room's center as he weaved around a velvet settee and a pair of elaborately upholstered chairs. Above the mantel, an oil painting of what must have been Sir Wilhelm's grandfather, Sir George Carteret, glared down at Borland with the same supercilious arrogance of his grandson. Yet behind those oppressive dark eyes burned a wisdom and strength conspicuously absent in Sir Wilhelm.

A rabid sweat broke out on Borland's neck. What was he doing? Could he truly betray his lifelong friend?

Friend, indeed. What has he ever done for you? A chill slithered down Borland's spine.

Memories of the argument with Dajon last week replayed in his mind, rekindling his fury. He could still envision Dajon's red, fuming face when he had turned to Borland and yelled, "Enough! I am the captain, and you will obey my orders," forcing Borland to relent, to submit, and finally to admit. . .

That Dajon was his captain, not his friend.

Perhaps they had been friends once, but those days were long gone. And if Borland were to consider Dajon by rank alone, then his captain had made a terrible mistake. Allowing the Red Siren to slip from his grasp was bad enough, but then to refuse to chase after Stede Bonnet when he had been spotted so close to Charles Towne was beyond incorrigible. By refusing to do his duty, Dajon had in effect caused his entire crew to miss out on the glory, the praise that the capture of a pirate would bring them back at the Admiralty. And for what? A trollop—a pirate wench, at that!

Borland blew out a snort. He would show the mighty Dajon Waite who the real captain of the HMS *Enforcer* should be.

Guilt stabbed his gut, twisting and turning its blade until he could almost feel the pain. But what else could he do? He threw back his shoulders. It was his duty to report the captain. And if he was going to command one of His Majesty's ships, he'd have to learn to make tough decisions.

Even if it cost Dajon his life.

But no. He would not let it get that far. And that was why he needed Sir Wilhelm. That and the considerable fortune he knew the man would hand over for the information Borland possessed.

"Sir Wilhelm." The butler's drone buzzed into the room from the arched doorway, announcing the entrance of his master as if he were the king of England himself. Sir Wilhelm floated into the room on a puff of stale air and gave Borland a cursory glance before plopping down onto the settee as if coming downstairs had completely exhausted him.

"Devil's blood. What is it, Mr. Borland? You know I am a busy man."

Borland gritted his teeth. Pity he needed this vainglorious nitwit to carry out his plans. "I have sent you several urgent posts. Did you not receive them?"

"Of course." Sir Wilhelm adjusted the lace that drooped about his sleeves. "I cannot be bothered with every minor correspondence."

Borland grabbed the back of one of the chairs and nearly punctured the fabric with his violent grip. "I have information which may greatly aid your cause."

Sir Wilhelm's brows flashed upward with interest. "And pray tell, what cause is that?"

"Your quest for the red-haired Westcott lady." Borland crossed his arms over his chest, feeling some of the man's power drift his way. "I hear she is about to be hanged."

"Yes." Sir Wilhelm shifted his gaze, but not before Borland saw the anger and bitterness fuming in his eyes. "What is your news?"

"It concerns Captain Waite."

❦

Something scampered over Faith's arm. With a start, she jumped to her feet and swiped at her soiled gown. A cockroach skittered away beneath the straw. Shuddering, she gripped her arms. She knew she should be used to the bugs by now, but for some reason, the huge cockroaches still made her skin crawl. Filthy, tormenting beasts—like demons from hell.

She glanced at the sludge and refuse littering the murky dungeon, felt the heat sear her skin and the reek sting her nose. Hell. Perhaps this was it, after all.

But no. Yesterday a bright light had pierced this sepulcher. Dajon had come to see her. And surely God would not allow an honorable man like him to visit a damned place like hell.

It was near midday. She knew because the heat became unbearable at this hour and the air so thick with fetor that she gasped for every breath. She'd given up on her pacing and had succumbed to a moment's sleep, a near impossibility in her nest of bugs and rats.

A jangle of keys, a crank of a lock, and the scrape of a door opening, followed by the sound of footsteps, perked her ears. Was *Lord* Gordon coming with another proposition? Making her way to the bars, she strained to see the bottom of the stairway, daring to hope she had another visitor, longing to see Dajon again or perhaps Lucas or her sisters.

The thump and scrape of Gordon's limp foot on the wooden stairs grew louder until finally the jailer emerged into the dim lantern light, followed by the shiny buckled shoes, white stockings, and velvet breeches of a stylishly attired man. Bile rose in Faith's throat. Sir Wilhelm again. No doubt seeing if she'd had enough of this place and would agree to his proposal.

When he approached her cell, the eyes that met hers did not contain the usual pleading conceit but instead beamed with a victorious confidence most unnatural for the silly, diffident man.

Faith's throat went dry. "What do you want?" she huffed, backing away from the bars lest he try to touch her. Odd that she now found her cage a refuge instead of a prison.

"Me, want?" He snickered. "Why, I believe 'tis you who will be wanting something from me."

Uneasiness pricked the back of Faith's neck. "Never."

Sir Wilhelm turned to Gordon, who casually leaned against the stone wall across the way. "Leave us."

Scowling, the jailer shuffled back up the stairs, dragging his foot behind him.

Withdrawing a handkerchief, Sir Wilhelm held it to his nose. "Still so brave, so spirited after living in this muck for days." Was that a twinge of admiration in his gaze? He coughed and tugged upon his cravat. "However do you stand this place?"

"Somehow I find it preferable to your company." Faith retreated into the shadows, hoping that if he couldn't see her, he would give up his quest and leave.

Hideous laughter echoed through the dungeon, and Sir Wilhelm turned and stared down the row of cells before shifting his cold brown eyes back to her. "Would you find the death of your precious Mr. Waite preferable to my company?" The corner of his thin lips lifted in an exalted smirk.

Alarm fastened onto Faith like a leech. "What nonsense is this?" She fisted her hands on her waist, bracing herself against this desperate cur's lies.

He leaned toward the bars. "I know that your illustrious captain caught you before I did." His whisper hissed over her like a snake. "And that he let you go."

All remaining strength drained from Faith's legs. They began to wobble. Ambling farther into the shadows, she leaned against the wall for support, not wanting Sir Wilhelm to see her fear. Gathering her wits, she responded in her most unruffled tone, "He did no such thing. And besides, what does it matter to you?"

"Nothing." He adjusted his wig and jumped when a cockroach scurried by his shoes. The folds of his face contorted in disgust as he watched the insect dart away. "It matters naught to me. In fact, Mr. Borland intends to have his captain arrested soon."

The realization struck Faith as violently as if the ceiling of the dungeon had crashed down on her. *Mr. Borland has betrayed his best friend. But why?* "Mr. Borland?"

Sir Wilhelm grinned, obviously detecting the crack of alarm in her voice. "Yes, you remember, my dear, Mr. Waite's first lieutenant—the man standing upon the deck of your ship, the *Red Siren*, when he and Mr. Waite boarded her?"

Faith pressed a hand against the wall. The craggy stone scraped her raw skin. So Borland had told Sir Wilhelm everything. A chill overtook her, even in the tepid heat. It made no sense. "If Mr. Borland intends to arrest Dajon. . .Mr. Waite, then why hasn't he done so already?"

"Mr. Borland and I have an arrangement." Sir Wilhelm blew his nose into his handkerchief then scanned above him with wary eyes, no doubt looking for flying insects. Faith prayed for a sudden swarm to nest in the man's elaborate wig.

Pushing off the wall, she crept toward the row of iron bars, longing for them to disappear so she could use her remaining strength to throttle the beast.

Sir Wilhelm tugged off his cravat and blotted the sweat covering his brow. The white, sickly skin of his neck matched the ghostly pallor of his face. A tuft of grizzly black hair peeked around his lapel as if looking for an escape. "You will marry me in two days," he announced, the tone of his voice leaving no room for argument.

"And if I don't?"

"Then I fear Mr. Borland will arrest Mr. Waite for treason." Sir Wilhelm waved his handkerchief through the air. "And as you know, he'll be court-martialed and executed."

Faith approached him, ignoring the way his gaze slithered over her and the resultant brew of disgust churning in her stomach. Something still didn't make sense. "What is in it for Borland?"

"Let's just say Mr. Borland is a much wealthier man today than he was yesterday." His eyes glinted with cruel delight.

Would Mr. Borland betray his captain for money? Perhaps. The greed for wealth and power often drove a man—or a woman—to malevolence. She cringed at her own guilt.

Oh God, what am I to do?

"You have two days to ponder my proposal. Otherwise, I fear Mr. Waite shall meet an untimely death. And I know you do not want that on your conscience along with everything else." Withdrawing his snuffbox, Sir Wilhelm snorted a pinch into each nostril then stared at her. A shameless grin angled over his mouth, and he extended his hand through the bars.

Faith retreated beyond his reach—at least for the moment.

He snapped back his hand. "Never fear. I can wait. It shall make our union all the much sweeter."

Faith longed to respond, to tell him that if he ever took her as wife, it would be anything but sweet, but her love for Dajon stilled her tongue.

Twisting on his heel portentously, he sauntered toward the stairs then swerved back around. "Oh, and by the by, I've given strict orders forbidding Mr. Waite to call upon you again. Although I *have* permitted your sisters to visit. Perhaps that will soften your opinion of me and give you more reason to consider their futures rather than just thinking of your own." He snickered and began his ascent. The stairway soon swallowed him up, along with his bestial laughter. Faith wished he would disappear from her life just as easily.

But before she had a chance to fully absorb the implications of Sir Wilhelm's threat, the thumping of footsteps sounded on the stairs, and much to her delight, behind Gordon, Lucas's burly body descended. And following him, Molly, Hope, and Grace emerged in the darkness. Sunlight from above filtered down upon them, highlighting their colorful gowns and glowing cheeks—like a grand parade filled with all the people she loved.

Faith's heart nearly burst through her chest. It was by far the most wonderful sight she'd seen in quite some time.

"Faith!" Hope gathered her skirts and dashed to the cell, thrusting her hands through the iron bars and grabbing her by the shoulders. Tears streamed down her sister's reddened cheeks.

Grace slid beside her and clutched the rods, a frightened look pinching her face.

Lecherous comments assailed them from deep within the dungeon. Hope's eyes widened, and Faith felt her sister's tremble through her hand. A crimson blush stole over Grace's ivory skin.

"Ignore them. They can't harm you." Faith took Hope's and Grace's hands in hers. Grace's eyes locked upon Faith's, but strength beamed from behind her anxious look.

Faith gave an appreciative nod to Lucas and Molly standing behind them.

Darting a frenzied gaze over Faith's cell, Hope raised a hand to her nose. "Oh, Faith. Pirating?"

" 'Twas quite lucrative." Faith cocked one penitent brow, hoping to alleviate her sister's distress with a bit of levity.

"I'm sure. But the Red Siren. Mercy me." Grace shook her head, but instead of giving Faith the expected disapproving glare, her eyes filled with tears.

"Lucrative but wrong." Faith let out a jagged sigh. "Very wrong. I didn't mean to hurt you, Grace." She glanced at Hope. "Nor you, sweet Hope."

"I didn't want this for you." Grace swallowed. "I've tried so hard to keep us all from any pain. How often have I told you that bad things happen when you disobey God?" Grace shook the bars as if trying to force home her point. "Look what happened to Mother, to Charity."

"Whatever did they do wrong?" Hope swiped a tear from her cheek and frowned at her sister.

Grace flattened her lips, her green eyes etched with sorrow. "You know Mother was not, shall we say, the most virtuous woman in her youth, and Charity. . .how oft did she have trouble telling the truth?"

"Oh, bah. I care not. I think being a pirate would be exciting." Hope sniffed then snapped her gaze to Faith. "Why didn't you tell me? I could have joined you."

"That is precisely why I didn't tell you," Faith shot back, but her slight smile soon faded beneath a wave of shame—shame for her, shame for her sisters, shame for their family. She released their hands and looked away. "No matter what you think of me, I was doing it for you—for us."

"Yes, Lucas explained." Grace leaned her head on the bars. "I'm so sorry that you believed you had no other recourse. I had no idea the burden you bore for our welfare—what you must have gone through to try to ensure our future. Please forgive me."

"You bear no blame, sweet Grace." Faith brushed a black curl from her sister's face.

A baby rat scampered across the stones by Hope's shoes, and she screamed and jumped back. "Oh my. How do you stand it in here?" She sobbed. "All that time when we thought you had abandoned us, you were risking your life for our welfare."

"Please do not make it a noble venture," Faith huffed.

"But we could have helped you." Hope reached through the bars again and brushed a reassuring hand over Faith's arm. "We could have worked something out together." She smiled at Grace. "We are sisters, after all."

"Yes, we are." Faith took Hope's hand in hers. "What I should have done is trusted God to take care of us."

Grace smiled.

"Can you both ever forgive me?" Faith asked, sorrow clawing at her throat. She wished more than anything she could go back in time and make things right. Do the right thing. Make the right choices. Save her sisters all this pain. But she couldn't. "I've made quite a mess of things."

"Of course we forgive you," Grace said, and Hope nodded.

Foul insinuations followed by fiendish chortles pierced their ears, and Faith bit her lip, angry that her sisters must endure this for her sake. Yet one more harmful consequence of her stupidity.

She gazed at them. Perspiration dotted Grace's upper lip, and Hope, like a precious flower, seemed ready to wilt at any moment.

"You mustn't stay long. 'Tis quite beastly down here, I'm afraid." As much as Faith longed to see her sisters, she could not force them to bear a punishment fit only for her.

"Nonsense." Hope squared her shoulders. "If you can endure it for this long, then we can surely abide it for a few minutes."

Faith blinked at her sister's sudden bravery. Reaching through the bars, she grabbed Grace's hand, too, and brought both sisters close.

Grace's tender gaze swept over Faith. "Your gown is in tatters. And you look so thin. How much longer must you stay here?"

"What will happen to you, Faith?" Hope's voice was strained with fear. "They hang pirates." New tears forged trails down her cheeks. "First Mother, now you. I cannot lose you both." She broke out into sobs, and Grace released Faith's hand and swung her arm over Hope's shoulder.

"We can pray, Hope. We *will* pray."

"Oh, what good will that do?" Hope snapped the words out between wails.

Grace continued to console her, tears filling her eyes.

As she watched her two sisters suffer for her mistakes, Faith wished the ground would suddenly open up and swallow her alive. *Oh, Mother. I'm so sorry. I have failed you. I have failed my precious sisters, and most of all, I have failed God.*

She battled against the tears burning behind her eyes.

They need me, Lord. They cannot endure another loss. It cannot be Your will that I hang. Please, Lord, save me. Not for my sake, but for theirs.

But perhaps God had already given her a way out. If she married Sir Wilhelm. . . Releasing Hope, Faith pressed a hand over her roiling stomach. Truth be told, she deserved to live out her days with the odious man for the pain and suffering she had caused.

Faith shifted her gaze between her sisters. "Listen to me. You aren't going to lose me. Do you hear?" Faith shook off a quiver of repulsion at the thought of becoming Sir Wilhelm's wife. "I shall be out of here in two days."

"Truly?" Hope sniffed.

"Aye. I promise, and we will all be well taken care of."

"I don't understand." Grace furrowed her delicate brow. "How is that possible?"

"Governor Johnson will issue me a pardon," Faith said, trying to use a confident tone. No need in upsetting them further by telling them it was Sir Wilhelm who would procure it.

"Ye ain't gettin' no pardon, missy!" a dark voice bellowed. Lucas started toward the other cells as if he could silence the men, but then he suddenly stopped.

"Ye'll be hangin' wit' the rest of us," the man cackled like an old hen.

"I fear he's right. Governor Johnson hates pirates. And after what Blackbeard and his crew did to this town, he has vowed to hang every single one of them he catches," Grace said.

"Never mind about that." Faith tossed her hair over her shoulder, trying to hide her own apprehension that even someone as powerful as Sir Wilhelm could squeeze a pardon out of Robert Johnson. Hoping for a diversion, she gestured for Lucas and Molly to come closer. Their intertwined hands separated as they took up places on each side of her sisters.

"Aye, Cap'n." Lucas nodded then peered into her cell. Repulsion and agony burned in his gaze. "I should be in there wit' ye."

"Oh, good heavens, Lucas, what good would that do?" Faith sighed then shifted her smiling eyes between him and Molly. "Were you holding Miss Molly's hand?" She knew what she had seen, and the prospect it posed delighted her.

Lucas flashed a gleaming white smile that brightened the dingy dungeon.

"They are courting," Hope interjected, dabbing her cheeks with a handkerchief. "Isn't it marvelous?"

Faith swept her gaze to Molly, who had lowered hers and was shuffling her shoe against the stone floor. "Molly, I do declare, what happened to your fear of caring for anyone—especially a man?"

Molly shrugged one shoulder and smiled. "When I see you turn to trusting God after all you been through, I figured I needed to start trusting Him, too." She cast an adoring look at Lucas, which he quickly returned. "An' I always had a soft spot for reformed pirates."

"Well, at least one good thing has come out of all this mess." Faith forced a smile. "I am most pleased."

Facing Lucas, she grew serious. "How are things at home?"

"I sent a dispatch to the admiral. I don't know when he'll get it, but I's sure he'll be comin' home when he does. Everything else is fine." Lucas cast a sideways glance at Hope that gave Faith pause.

Faith studied her two siblings. "Have they behaved, Lucas?"

Hope's expression sank.

"Miss Hope's done run off wit' that Lord Falkland a couple of times, mistress. I can't seem to keep an eye on her all the time," Lucas replied, folding his hat in his hands.

Faith snapped her gaze to Hope. "Hope, why? Why do you throw yourself at a man who will only use you?"

"He's leaving, Faith." Hope's blue eyes swam.

"What do you mean?"

"He sets sail tomorrow for England."

"The sooner the better." Molly snorted.

"He won't take me with him. I love him, Faith." She dabbed her eyes with her handkerchief. "I thought he'd make me an offer of marriage before he left."

Faith clenched her jaw. "The man is a scoundrel, Hope. He cares for no one but himself."

"You are wrong." She stamped her foot. "He promised to marry me when he returns."

"Oh, he did, did he?" Faith's heart sunk at the naiveté of her sister. The ruffian would most likely never return, and Hope would either wallow in grief for years or find comfort in the arms of the next man who smiled her way. But at least Faith wouldn't have to worry about Lord Falkland anymore.

"Remember, Hope, how God protected you from those scoundrels at the Pink House?"

Hope did not raise her gaze.

"Perhaps He is doing the same thing now," Faith continued, praying the Lord would reveal His love and mercy to Hope as He had done with Faith. "Perhaps He is protecting you by sending Lord Falkland away."

"If He is, then He is cruel," Hope said in a sharp tone that sliced through Faith's heart.

Retrieving her arm from around Hope, Grace tucked a loose tendril of her sister's hair behind her ear. "How can you discuss something so trivial as Lord Falkland when our sister is locked up in a dungeon?"

"She inquired of me," Hope snapped with a pout. "And besides, she said she would be pardoned in a few days."

"That's right," Faith said. *Freed from prison one day, only to be chained to a madman the next.*

Hope coughed and drew her handkerchief to her nose. "The smell in here."

"You should leave. It isn't good for you to be down here." Faith turned to Molly. "Please take my sisters upstairs. I need to speak with Lucas for a moment."

"No, I don't want to leave you," Hope pleaded.

Faith forced herself to smile. "I'll see you in a few days."

"She'll be jest fine, Miss Hope." Molly began to lead Hope away. Grace swallowed hard and flashed a wavering grin toward Faith before turning to join them.

"Grace." Faith tugged on her sister's arm, halting her. "If something goes wrong. . .I mean with the pardon. . ."

Grace's green eyes became glistening pools. "Please don't say it."

"Promise me you'll take care of Hope. She will need your strength."

Grace nodded as a tear escaped her lashes and sped down her cheek. "You will get out of here. I know it."

"Pray, Grace. Please pray."

"I'll be prayin', too, Miss Faith," Molly said over her shoulder as she led both girls to the bottom of the stairway.

"Lucas, I need you to get a message to Mr. Waite for me."

"Aye."

No matter what Faith's future held, she must warn Dajon. "Please inform him that Mr. Borland is not his friend. He has told Sir Wilhelm that Mr. Waite let us go free."

Lucas's dark brows rose, and alarm burned in his eyes.

"Mr. Waite is in danger," Faith said.

"But Sir Wilhelm, don't he want the cap'n out of his way? Why don't he and Borland just have him arrested?"

"Because I have made a bargain with them to prevent it."

Lucas gave her a puzzled look. "What sort of bargain?"

Faith ground her teeth together, barely able to spit out the words. "I have promised to marry Sir Wilhelm."

CHAPTER 33

Dajon leaped up the foredeck ladder and charged across the wooden deck, making his way to the bow of the ship. Anger tore at him, ripping his self-control to shreds. He had to calm himself before he faced Borland, or who knew what he might do. He thrust his face into a blast of salty air. A metallic scent bit his nose, a sharp smell that made his skin crawl and permeated the air with a feeling of unease.

Friend. Some friend, indeed. He snorted, clutching the railing as the HMS *Enforcer* lunged over a rising swell then slapped the back of the wave, showering him with warm spray. He shook his head, scattering the droplets onto the railing, where they shimmered like diamonds in the moonlight.

Two of his crew lazed nearby, but one steely gaze from him sent them hustling away. He needed to be alone. He had to think. He had to patch the wound from Borland's treachery, and then he had to decide what to do with the rat.

After Lucas had delivered Faith's message, Dajon had tried to visit her, but upon being prevented from doing so, he had weighed anchor and headed directly out to sea. He'd always heard the voice of God more clearly when he coursed through the vast, untamed ocean, and he hoped that would be the case tonight. If not, he feared he'd be forced to follow through with his original impulse of strangling Borland and then tossing his lifeless body to the sharks.

God, help me. Is there any pain worse than the betrayal of a friend? Then he remembered how the Lord had been betrayed by all His dearest friends—those who had sworn their love and loyalty to Him. *How did You bear it, Lord?*

"*Forgive.*" The word floated on the breeze, weaving around the strands of his hair.

Dajon shook his head and doffed his bicorn, tossing it to the deck. *I don't know if I can.*

Booted steps clumped over the deck, but Dajon didn't turn around. He clenched his jaw and prayed it wasn't Borland. He'd been avoiding the man quite successfully and hoped to continue to do so for a while longer.

"Captain." The voice spiked over him—one that used to lift Dajon's spirits but now only clawed at his heart. "What brings us out upon the waters this fine night? News of a pirate nearby?" Borland planted his boots firmly on the deck beside Dajon and crossed his arms over his chest.

A blast of hot wind, laced with salt and fish and betrayal, tore over Dajon, and he lengthened his stance and stared at his first lieutenant. The wind played havoc with the coils of Borland's sandy hair, tugging them from his queue. He wouldn't meet Dajon's gaze. In fact, Dajon couldn't recall the last time he'd seen the playful camaraderie that had often danced across his friend's brown eyes.

Blood surged to Dajon's fists. How dare the man even speak to him after what he'd done? But here he stood, feigning a friendship that had probably never existed and all the while betraying Dajon's confidence. "Why, Borland?"

Borland flinched, and the side of his mouth quirked, but otherwise he remained still. "Why what, Captain?"

Dajon grappled the hilt of his service sword, longing to draw it and end this charade. "No more games."

Borland's jaw tightened. "I see you are not quite yourself tonight, Captain." He turned to leave. "I shall speak to you at another time."

Seizing him, Dajon twisted him around. "You will speak to me now."

Borland's eyes flashed with a fury that startled Dajon. "Very well." He tugged his arm from Dajon's grasp as if he detested even his touch. "What is it you wish to discuss?"

The ship bucked, forcing both him and Borland to grab the rail. Dajon took the time to draw a deep breath to restrain his rising fury. "Why did you betray me?" he growled through gritted teeth. "And to that ninny Sir Wilhelm?"

Borland's eyes darted about wildly before they met his, fear skipping over them, but then a cold sheen swallowed up the fear and his body stiffened. "I was doing my duty."

"Your *duty?* You agreed that if Miss Westcott abandoned her piracy, we would allow her to go free."

"No," Borland snarled. "*You* agreed to that. I merely listened and obeyed." He shifted his gaze back to the sea. "Which is all I ever do."

Shocked by the hostility firing from his friend's eyes, Dajon stared out over the churning black sea that spanned to an even darker horizon. The moon illuminated crystal foam upon the waves and frowned at him as if she disapproved of the goings-on below. He wished she would fling some light upon his current situation, for no matter how far back he searched, Dajon could think of no time he had mistreated Borland or any of the other men on his crew. "You do what I say because I am in command." Dajon spoke with grave deliberation.

"Yet in doing so, you ask me to risk not only my career but my life." Borland dared to laugh. "Our friendship does not extend that far."

Dajon clenched his jaw, wondering if their friendship extended any further than Borland's self-interest. "You know very well that if I were caught, I would never divulge to anyone that you had any knowledge of what I did." Dajon gripped the railing. "Nevertheless, you should have informed me of your true feelings instead of placating me with lies."

Borland crossed his arms over his chest. " 'Twas my responsibility to turn you in. A captain who does not abide by the articles of war should not be in command of one of His Majesty's ships." He flicked the hair from his face and gazed out upon the sea. "Yes, perhaps this ship needs a new commander."

The hull of the ship creaked and moaned in protest, and it took every ounce of Dajon's control not to slam his fist into Borland's jaw. "Jealousy? That's what this is about?" Dajon roared. "You envy my position—is that it? After all these years?"

Storming to the foremast, Dajon punched it, but all he did was cause searing pain to shoot through his fingers and into his wrist. Shaking his burning hand, he faced Borland, who remained a rigid bulwark.

"Then our friendship has been naught but a pretense." Dajon returned to his side and thrust his face toward him.

"Not always."

"When did you begin to hate me so?" Dajon gripped the roughened wood of the railing.

"When you received command of this ship over me—with fewer years' service and no connections. Egad!" Borland gave Dajon a scorching look. "You even resigned for two years and then came back, like the prodigal son expecting a lavish party upon your return."

"And you the faithful son," Dajon muttered, cursing himself. He'd never considered that his friend might be envious of his promotion, never once thought Borland would be anything but happy for his success. "I have been a fool to trust you."

"You don't understand, Dajon. You never have." Borland shot him a look of disdain and thrust out his chin. "If I do not make a success of myself in the navy, I will be a disgrace to my father, my entire family. It is what they expect of me."

Watching the Union Jack flapping on the bowsprit, Dajon tried to recall his friend's history. Borland came from nobility—a second son, not in line to inherit the family fortune but nobility nonetheless—and from a long line of naval captains. "I did not ask for the honor, Borland."

"No, of course not." Borland's voice burned with sarcasm. "The great Dajon Waite, praised for his heroic encounter with a Spanish flotilla off Càdiz that prevented a resurgence of hostilities. Pure rubbish, I say. I was there right beside you, but did I receive a command?" His fists clenched as if trying to squash the memory.

"So you send me to my death."

"No." He slid his dark eyes over to Dajon. "My intent was to simply have you removed from the navy." His upper lip twitched beneath a slick mustache.

Fury rampaged through Dajon, shattering all control. Gripping Borland's stiff collar, Dajon thrust a fist into his stomach. Borland folded with a groan and stumbled back.

"Treason is an offense punishable by death," Dajon said through clenched teeth, landing another blow on Borland's jaw, snapping his head to the side. Then, clutching his coat, Dajon shoved him toward the bow and hauled his limp body precariously atop the railing.

Borland gripped Dajon's hands, trying to detach them from his neck. His eyes exploded with terror as he glanced below him at the raging water.

"Do you think me so vile as to have you killed to further my own career?" he squeaked.

Dajon tightened his grip and jerked Borland's head farther down toward where the bow of the ship crashed through the ebony water in a frothy, raging V. Only the weight of Dajon's body prevented the man from tumbling into the water. Just one inch to the left, just one shove and Dajon would be rid of this menace forever. Without his testimony, Dajon would live and Faith would not have to marry Sir Wilhelm.

"Forgive as I have forgiven you."

The words splashed over him along with the salty spray of the sea, but Dajon shook them off.

"Sir Wilhelm promised me you will not be executed." Borland clawed at Dajon's fingers, his face as ashen as the moonlight that spilled over it.

The muscles in Dajon's face knotted into tight balls. His fingers began to ache. Fury urged him onward. Fury and the pain of betrayal, of being played for a fool. He could not remember a time he'd ever been this angry, a time when he wanted to kill.

A beaming spire of white light lit up the eastern sky. The sharp sting of electricity hung in the air, sending the hair on the back of Dajon's neck spiking. His breath grew ragged and deep as he remembered the pillar of fire—God's pillar of fire—that had saved Hope. A fire of grace. For Hope had done naught to deserve it. In fact, quite the opposite.

"Please, Dajon," Borland begged, his eyes sharp with panic, his hands clamping over Dajon's wrists as if they were his only lifeline.

Grinding his teeth, Dajon held him farther over the edge, trying to fight the rage that took control of him.

Lightning flashed again, this time closer, and Dajon wondered why there was no thunder, no clouds. A chill crawled over his skin. His hands no longer ached. His muscles bulged with strength. And he knew all he had to do was release the squirming wretch and Borland would tumble into the sea.

God's grace. A free gift of forgiveness for a debt that could never be paid. Like Dajon's debt. Like Borland's. The Almighty had lavished His grace upon Dajon; who was he not to do the same for his enemies?

"You insolent buffoon." Dragging Borland's stiff body back over the rail, Dajon released him.

Stumbling backward, Borland gripped his throat and tripped over a hatch coaming.

Dajon drew his sword and pointed the gleaming tip at Borland. He no longer intended to kill him, but certainly God would allow him this small satisfaction of seeing his friend continue to squirm. "Sir Wilhelm exaggerates his power. I'll grant you, the jingle-brained man has some authority here in Carolina where his grandfather was one of the eight lord proprietors, but his word carries no weight with the Admiralty. He could no more stop an order of execution from a court-martial than he could stop the recent Indian raids or Spanish attacks."

Shock followed by a sudden realization passed over Borland's expression as he wavered over the deck, trying to regain his balance while avoiding Dajon's blade.

Angry waves slapped the hull, reaching white fingers onto the deck as if they were yearning for the prey that had escaped them. Instead, they spit their salty spray over the two men. Dajon gazed into the night sky, clear save for the sparkle of stars and the glimmer of the moon. The lightning had vanished. Had he only imagined it, or was it some wicked force tempting him to commit murder?

Shaking off the frightening thought, Dajon lifted Borland's chin with the tip of his sword. "And look what you have forced upon Miss Westcott. Now she'll have to marry that feeble knave." Dajon grimaced, nauseated at the thought of that man's slimy hands touching Faith.

Borland straightened his coat and threw back his shoulders as if hoping to regain his dignity. Or perhaps he'd seen the bloodlust dissipate from Dajon's eye and no longer feared his fury. " 'Tis a better fate than the noose. Besides, that she would resign herself to marry such a maggot to save you is quite noble."

Dajon raised one brow angrily. "Except you and I both know that I shall be arrested as soon as she is wed."

Borland shrugged. "That was the plan." He eyed Dajon's blade. "But I beg you to believe me—I thought you would lose your commission, not your life."

Dajon studied his first lieutenant, wondering if that were true, if there was a scrap of decency left in the friend he once knew. "It matters not anymore."

"You can run." Borland swallowed and stared at Dajon pleadingly. "Change your name; lose yourself in the colonies or, better yet, the West Indies. A man can make a fortune as a privateer, I'm told."

"Only during wartime or else be hanged as a pirate."

"Never fear. I'm sure we shall declare war on France or Spain soon enough." Borland chuckled.

Dajon blew out a harsh breath. When disaster had struck his career so long ago, he'd run away, away from his family, away from God. "Nay. I'm tired of running." He lowered his blade and waved it toward the ladder. "Get out of my sight."

Borland eased away, keeping his eye on Dajon, before turning and making haste for the ladder. But suddenly he halted and turned around. "What will you do?" No anger, no hatred stained his voice, just curiosity.

"Why, turn myself in, of course." Dajon sheathed his sword, the sharp hiss of metal sealing his decision. "First thing in the morning. Then"— despite his dire future, he allowed himself a speck of joy that reached his mouth in a grin—"I shall send word to Miss Westcott that she no longer need marry Sir Wilhelm."

⌘

Borland shook his head, trying to dislodge the water in his ear. Perhaps he had misheard his captain. "Turn yourself in?"

Dajon crossed his arms over his chest but said nothing.

Borland inched his way back toward him, certain that his captain no longer intended to kill him. There had been a moment, a brief moment, when Dajon had held Borland over the railing that he could not claim such confidence.

But now the rage had fled, replaced by a calm, sincere resolve. "But why? Why submit to certain death?"

"What is it to you?" Dajon faced the sea.

"But you can still save yourself."

"I told you, I will not run away."

Borland peered at his friend inquisitively. Perhaps Dajon had not thought things through. "Surely you realize that if you leave, Sir Wilhelm will no longer have a card to play in this mad scheme of his. Miss Westcott will not have to marry him. And you'll be free to live out your life."

"And you'll be free to assume my command at no expense to your conscience, eh?" Dajon's sharp gaze bit into Borland. "Isn't that it?"

Shifting his eyes away, Borland recoiled in shame. Dajon was right. After all the trouble Borland had caused, he still thought only of himself.

"Nevertheless, you are correct." Dajon released a sigh and gripped the railing. "I have betrayed my country. I allowed a known pirate to go free. And I will not run, nor will I abandon Miss Westcott in her greatest hour of need."

Borland searched his mind for some other plausible explanation, some other reason for which a man would willingly die, certainly not for honor and duty, and certainly not for a foolish woman. "There will be other women, Dajon. You attract them like sailors to grog."

Flinching, Dajon frowned. "None like Miss Westcott, I'm afraid."

Sentimental fop. "This is madness, Dajon. You have been bewitched. Regardless, you still won't have her. You'll be dead, and if she doesn't marry Sir Wilhelm, she will soon join you."

The *Enforcer* dipped over a swell, nodding in agreement. Milky froth leaped onto the deck and swirled about Borland's boots like the confusion in his mind.

"Perhaps." Dajon tore off his waistcoat, draping it over the rail. "Or Sir Wilhelm will relent at the last minute, or the King's pardon I've requested will arrive in time." He shrugged. " 'Tis in God's hands. At least she will not be forced to marry a man she abhors just to save me. Because there will be no saving me. But if she is hanged"—Dajon winced as if the thought pained him—"then you are correct. We will be together in a far better place."

Wiping the sweat from his neck, Borland suppressed a chuckle at his friend's foolhardy faith. "Don't tell me you truly believe that."

"With all my heart," Dajon replied without hesitation, his tone neither defensive nor patronizing. "I took my eyes off eternity for far too long and put them upon rules, regulations, and things of this world. But no more."

"But are you not relying on your rules again by turning yourself in?" Fear squeezed Borland until sweat began to form on his brow. If he couldn't convince Dajon to run, the captain's death would be on his hands forever. He doubted he could live under the weight of that guilt.

Scanning the dark, churning sea, Borland wondered at the existence of so grand a God-King that men would willingly die to follow Him. "So am I to believe that God wants you dead?"

"I don't know. But I do know this." Dajon shot him a confident gaze. "He doesn't want me to run."

"You stand ready to turn yourself in for treason, willing to be executed, and for what? To follow the leading of this unseen God." Borland grunted and shifted his boots over the damp wood. A bell tolled, echoing over the deck, followed by another, announcing the change of watch.

Crazy, sanctimonious fool. Turning, Borland began pacing across the deck, trying to make sense out of something that could not be made sense of. He halted at the edge of the forecastle and studied Dajon. His captain stood tall and strong, gazing out over the ocean as though deep in conversation. A peaceful power exuded from Dajon that drew Borland back. When he reached his side, the captain glanced his way.

Borland lowered his gaze. "How can you bear to be near me?" he asked, rubbing his sore neck, remembering that only a moment ago, Dajon indeed hadn't been able to bear it. "I am the reason you find yourself in this predicament. I am the reason you will die."

A flash of anger sparked in Dajon's eyes but quickly dissipated. "No, Borland. I must admit I was angry at your betrayal, but truth be told, I broke the law and I deserve my punishment. What's done is done. In the end, I'm no better than you."

Borland swallowed a burning lump in his throat. "How can you say that? You're the most decent, honorable man I know." He shook his head and followed Dajon's gaze to the onyx sea. A sudden calm had overtaken it. Only a slight rustle stirred the black liquid. The frown of the moon reflected off the dark waters as a large fish broke through the mirror with a crystalline splash. A dolphin, perhaps. A breeze tickled the angry sweat on his neck and brow, and Borland lowered his shoulders. Peace settled over him, but it was more than peace. It was a knowing.

"I can't do it." His voice rent the stillness of the night.

Dajon glanced his way.

"I won't testify against you." Borland locked his gaze upon his captain's. "I've told only Sir Wilhelm. It's his word against mine. I will simply tell the court I have nothing to say in the matter."

Dajon's eyes narrowed as if he pondered whether he could trust him.

Borland ground his teeth together. "I don't blame you for your mistrust. What I have done is far too ghastly to forgive. But I now see that my indomitable pride, my envy, and my selfishness have led me down this vile trail. And I find I detest the direction they have taken me."

"Sir Wilhelm will still bring charges." Dajon tore his gaze away.

"No doubt. But without witnesses, what can he do?"

The captain tightened his lips. "That would depend on whether the Admiralty Court would believe him or not." He flashed a disbelieving smile at Borland. "A moment ago, I wanted to kill you."

"And a moment ago, I had a plot in place to kill you." Borland cocked a conciliatory brow.

"And you say there is no God." Dajon clutched the back of Borland's neck and tossed him back and forth.

"Careful with the neck, Captain."

Dajon released him, and both men grew silent for a moment.

"We should tell Miss Westcott immediately," Borland said. Grabbing Dajon's coat and hat, he handed them to his captain.

"Sir Wilhelm forbids me to see her."

"Then I will go."

Dajon scratched his jaw. "Nay. Find out when the wedding is to take place." A slow smile stretched across his lips. "I have a better idea."

CHAPTER 34

"Great guns, Mr. Jamieson. Where are all the cockboats?" Dajon scanned the empty braces perched atop the deck then glanced over the port side as Borland dashed toward the stern and leaned over the taffrail.

"None here, Captain—sir!" Borland yelled.

"Who took them out?"

"Midshipman Salles took one out, sir," Mr. Jamieson offered.

"Yes, but who else?" Dajon spiked a hand through his hair. "I gave no one else permission to leave the ship." He glanced up at the smoldering sun now halfway across the sky and swiped the sweat from his brow.

He must get to shore. He had only an hour before Faith would marry Sir Wilhelm. Alarm gripped him, squeezing hope drop by drop from his heart. Everything, his entire future and that of Faith's rested solely on his perfect timing.

Fisting his hands on his waist, he scanned Charles Towne port, nearly a mile from the ship. Nothing but indigo waters, stirred only by passing ships and diving pelicans, separated him from reaching his dreams.

Borland approached on his left. "I don't understand it. All the boats have disappeared."

~

Faith slid her silk shoes up the stairs of the brick courthouse, the clank of the irons around her ankles ringing a death knell with each step she took. Reaching up, she tried to wipe the perspiration from her neck, but the chains binding her wrists forbade her. On each side, deputies of the assembly gripped her elbows and assisted her onward. If she wasn't so distraught, she would laugh at all the fuss they were making over one small woman.

But she was a pirate, after all.

And after assessing the slight men beside her, she'd decided they were wise to use such precautions. Freed from these chains and with a cutlass in hand, she had no doubt she could dispatch them with ease.

But regardless, she wouldn't dare attempt it. Not with Dajon's life on the line.

Would she never see him again? The pain of that possibility stabbed her deep in the gut. What had he done when Lucas had given him the news of her decision to marry Wilhelm? Perhaps he had gone to Bath himself to speed up Governor Eden's pardon. She had no way of knowing where he was, no way of informing anyone of the abominable event about to take place. After Lucas, Molly, and her sisters had left, Sir Wilhelm had prevented anyone from calling upon her again.

Two giddy girls shuffled along behind her, fussing over the lacy trim around her hem and waist.

"Oh, Miss Westcott, you do look so beautiful," one of them said.

"Beautiful. I so love weddings," the other girl chirped, reminding Faith of Morgan's meaningless squawking.

She longed to spin around and ask them if they did not see the chains that bound her feet and hands but thought better of wasting her energy. They were naught but young girls, with no more brains than begonias, hired by Sir Wilhelm to prepare her for this loathsome farce of a ceremony.

Choking down a rising clump of disgust, Faith took the final step, the silk of her emerald gown swishing over her stockings. Neither her warm sudsy bath, nor the beautiful gown now adorning her, nor the string of pearls at her throat had been able to remove the filth of the dungeon from her skin.

Or the repulsion of marrying Sir Wilhelm from her heart.

One of the deputies shoved aside the massive oak door, and a blast of mold, human sweat, and decay assailed her.

She swallowed, hesitating as her legs seemed to melt. The deputies tugged on her elbows, but snatching them from their grasp, she stepped inside of her own free will. She would not be led like a condemned prisoner to her death. She had made her choice.

Faith took another step inside, and the girls scrambled to get by her and take their places at the front. The door slammed shut, showering Faith with dust from the rafters and locking her in a vault from which there was no escape. As her eyes became accustomed to the dim interior, the form of Sir Wilhelm took shape like a specter at the far end of the room. He stood before a long, upraised judge's table dressed in all the finery of his class. Turning to face her, he licked his gaunt lips as a grin slithered over them. Beside him, a man dressed in a fine cambric shirt and a richly embellished velvet waistcoat and breeches eyed her with suspicion. A priest, wearing the flowing white robes of the Church of England, stood at the front, sifting through the pages of a small book.

Sir Wilhelm beckoned her forward like a snake into his coils, sunlight glinting off his jeweled fingers. The deputies nudged her from behind. Her chains scraped over the wooden floor as she glanced out the window to her left. A wooden platform broiled in the hot sun, two nooses dangling lifelessly in the windless day. No doubt Sir Wilhelm had planned the ceremony within sight of her alternative.

Pompous half-wit. Little did he know she would gladly put the noose around her own neck rather than marry him. 'Twas only thoughts of Dajon that kept her feet moving toward a fate worse than death.

Oh God, help me. I know I deserve this and far worse. But if there's any way in Your mercy to rescue me while sparing Dajon and my sisters, even if by my death, please come to my aid.

Faith inched ahead, praying for a breeze to whip in through the window, but the air remained tepid, static as doldrums at sea. No movement, not a single wisp stirring. Dead, like her heart.

Keeping her face forward, she finally reached the front.

"Miss Westcott, may I introduce Judge Nicolas Trott." Sir Wilhelm gestured toward the finely dressed man beside him.

Trott. Faith had heard of the man. An Anglican priest, descended from a highly influential British family, he was known for his lack of mercy and his particular hatred of pirates.

With an arrogant snort, he perused her.

Sir Wilhelm retrieved a paper from his coat and waved it before her face. "On Judge Trott's recommendation, Governor Johnson has graciously given me your full pardon."

How she longed to snatch the document and stuff it into his pretentious mouth.

The judge snapped a quick glance her way as if staring at her too long would infect him. "I trust you'll not be pirating again, Miss Westcott."

"I trust I'll not be doing anything pleasurable ever again, sir."

A hint of a smile lifted the judge's lips.

Perspiration streamed down Faith's back, drawing the silk close against her skin. Somewhere in the distance, a bell tolled. Sir Wilhelm took his spot beside her, rubbing his arm against hers. Disgust swept over her like raw refuse, and she stepped away.

The young girls giggled with delight from their seats, oblivious to the nightmare playing out before them.

Faith glanced over her shoulder at the thick wooden door holding her captive, the deputies flanking each side. Oh, that Captain Waite would come barging through those doors and whisk her away from this madman, but she knew that would never happen. He probably had no idea this marriage was even taking place, and if he did, to halt it would mean his certain death.

As if reading her mind, Sir Wilhelm leaned toward her with a sneer. The smell of starch and stale breath curled in her nose. "Looking for your Mr. Waite, perchance? Hoping for a heroic rescue, my dear? Even if he knew about the proceedings, I've arranged for him to be detained today. We wouldn't want our blessed nuptials to be interrupted, now, would we? Besides, if he dares show his presumptuous face, I'll have him arrested on the spot." He brushed a speck of dirt from his waistcoat as if it were Dajon himself.

Regardless of the man's omens of doom, a spark of hope lit within Faith. Dajon was still free—and alive! And that speck of knowledge gave her the courage to continue.

She thrust her hands toward him and rattled her shackles. "Do you suppose you could unchain me for the ceremony, Sir Wilhelm, or am I to be kept in irons our entire marriage?

A lecherous fire glinted in his eyes. "If it keeps you forever mine."

"All the chains in the world will never accomplish that, sir."

With a curse, he snapped his fingers and called for one of the deputies.

After her chains were removed, Faith flexed her ankles and rubbed her aching wrists, sure they were red beneath her pristine gloves.

"We are ready, Reverend." Sir Wilhelm faced the priest, who had been observing the odd proceedings with both interest and disapproval. For a moment, Faith hoped he would not agree to perform such an obvious mockery of the sanctity of marriage, but all hope was dashed when he adjusted his red sash and said, "Very well. Let us begin."

Dajon pulled himself out of the bay and crawled onto the wharf. He stood and shook the water from his hair. Wiping the drips streaming down his face, he eyed the dock men and sailors who stood slack jawed, gaping at him. He had no time to explain to them why he'd just emerged from the harbor like a fish from the water. Instead, he bolted down the dock, weaving around crates and barrels and clusters of men, ignoring the hollers and yelps that followed in his wake—and the curse when he accidentally bumped one man into the water.

"My apologies!" he yelled without looking back.

Barreling past the docks, he charged onto the street and was nearly trampled by a pair of geldings pulling a carriage. He waved off the driver's rather obscene expletive and shielded his eyes from the sun. There in the distance, the bricks of the courthouse shone bright red against the other brown buildings. He dashed down the crowded street, ignoring the sharp rocks scraping over his bare feet, and prayed harder than he ever had.

Just a few more minutes, Lord. Can You hold them up for just a few more minutes?

" 'Dearly beloved, we are gathered together here in the sight of God, and in the face of this congregation, to join together this man and this woman in holy matrimony, which is an honorable estate, instituted of God in the time of man's innocence, signifying unto us the mystical union betwixt Christ and His church. . . .' "

The priest droned on, reading from *The Book of Common Prayer*, and Faith's legs transformed into squid tentacles beneath her. She stumbled backward, and Sir Wilhelm gripped her around the waist and drew her near, imprisoning her against his languid body, only further increasing her nausea.

313

" '. . . is not by any to be enterprised, nor taken in hand, unadvisedly, lightly, or wantonly, to satisfy men's carnal lusts and appetites, like brute beasts that have no understanding.' "

Brute beasts? Faith dared a glance at Sir Wilhelm, wondering if he recognized himself in those words. But he stared ahead, a supercilious smirk planted on his mouth.

" 'I require and charge you both, as ye will answer at the dreadful day of judgment when the secrets of all hearts shall be disclosed, that if either of you know any impediment, why ye may not be lawfully joined together in matrimony, ye do now confess it.' "

The priest paused, looked up from his book, and glanced around the room. His gaze took in the deputies guarding the door, the frivolous girls squirming with excitement in their seats, and Judge Trott, who retrieved a pocket watch from his waistcoat and looked at the time with a sigh.

No one uttered a word. No one came to her rescue.

Sir Wilhelm tightened his grip around her waist, and she suddenly felt as though she were chained to an anchor, sinking deeper and deeper into a bottomless sea.

The priest's searching gaze then passed over Sir Wilhelm and landed on Faith. He raised his brows as if encouraging her to respond.

Lowering her gaze, Faith bit her lip then clenched her jaw and held her breath—anything to keep the words blasting forth from her mouth that yes, she knew of an impediment to this marriage. She knew exactly why they should not be lawfully joined together. *Joined.* A shudder ran through her, and she pressed a hand over her rebelling stomach.

But for Dajon's sake, she remained silent.

Casting an anxious glance over his shoulder, Sir Wilhelm waved a hand through the air. "If you please, Reverend. We are in a hurry."

Giving Sir Wilhelm a look of annoyance, the priest cleared his throat and resumed his reading.

"Sir Wilhelm Carteret, wilt thou have this woman to be thy wedded wife, to live together after God's ordinance in the holy estate of matrimony? Wilt thou love her, comfort her, honor and keep her, in sickness and in health, and forsaking all others, keep thee only unto her, so long as ye both shall live?"

Sir Wilhelm opened his mouth and said something, but his answer was drowned beneath the enormous thud of the door crashing open behind them.

Wheeling around, Faith squinted at the tall figure standing in the doorway, her eyes adjusting to the light that blazed behind him. Water dripped from his breeches onto the wooden floor like droplets of hope.

"I hope I'm not too late for the wedding." Sarcasm rang in his deep voice.

Dajon.

Faith's heart leaped and then took on a frenzied beat, stealing her breath away.

Sauntering toward them, Dajon shook water from his cotton shirt. His blue eyes were riveted on her, laughter and love sparkling within them.

Sir Wilhelm thrust his pale face into the reverend's. "I said, *I will.* Now carry on."

Dajon tore Sir Wilhelm's hand from Faith's waist and pushed himself between them. He swiped a hand through his wet hair, its dark ends dripping onto his shirt. The wet fabric clung to his muscled chest still heaving from exertion. He smelled of the sea and of salt and life.

He winked at Faith, and a warm, peaceful sensation flooded through her, quickly extinguished by her fear for his life. "What are you doing here?" she whispered through clenched teeth. "They will arrest you."

Ignoring her, he turned toward the priest. "I protest this union, Reverend."

"Finally." The reverend snapped his book shut and folded his arms over his robes.

"I order you to continue." Sir Wilhelm's rabid gaze shot over them and then locked onto the reverend as if he would devour him whole.

But the priest simply shrugged as if the situation were out of his control.

"Deputies, arrest this man at once!" Sir Wilhelm ordered the men standing guard at the now open door, then he glanced at Judge Trott, who stood to the side watching everything with a stern yet detached gaze.

A sickening wave of dread washed over Faith. She had done everything to prevent this very thing from happening. *Why, God? Please help us.*

"On what charge, may I inquire?" Dajon asked in a tone that bespoke no fear of the answer.

"Treason." Sir Wilhelm threw back his shoulders and faced the judge. "Judge, this man willingly allowed this pirate to go free."

"Indeed?" Judge Trott rubbed his chin, seeming to be more amused than appalled.

"Yes, I have a trustworthy witness from his ship. His own first lieutenant."

Faith studied Dajon, his body a statue. Not a tremble passed through him. No fear shot from his clear eyes. In fact, he stood nonchalantly as if he were awaiting his breakfast. She grabbed his hand and squeezed it, and he raised it to his lips, locking his gaze upon hers—a sultry, playful, dangerous gaze.

"Is this true, sir?" Judge Trott shifted his stance.

"That Sir Wilhelm has a trustworthy witness?" Dajon released her hand and cocked a brow at the judge. "Or that I let this lovely pirate go free?"

Judge Trott grunted. "Never mind. This is a matter for the Admiralty Court. I shall ensure they are assembled as soon as possible."

"Pray don't trouble yourself, Your Excellency." Dajon bowed slightly. "The witness Sir Wilhelm speaks of cannot seem to recall the incident. But it doesn't matter. . . ." He cast a sly glance at Faith. "I resigned my commission yesterday to the commander in chief aboard the HMS *Perseverance*."

Faith gasped. Dajon's career meant everything to him. She could not believe he would willingly resign.

Dajon shrugged one shoulder. "You may speak to him yourself, if you wish."

Judge Trott plucked his watch out again, eyeing the time. "Very well. Very well." Returning the watch to his pocket, he eyed Sir Wilhelm. "Unless this lady protests, I believe this wedding is canceled." He tilted his head at Faith and awaited her response.

She could hardly believe her ears. Was this truly happening, or was she dreaming? She dared not move for fear of waking up.

"Indeed, I do not, sir," Faith said.

Sir Wilhelm barreled toward Judge Trott, his eyes alight with fury. "But, sir. I insist you arrest this man."

"Do you have some other charge to make against him?"

Sir Wilhelm's face turned purple as he sputtered curses and shot his fiery gaze over the room.

"Then this matter is closed." The judge released a heavy sigh. "Now if you will excuse me, I have far more pressing business to attend to." He started for the door.

"Then I insist you hang this woman for piracy." Sir Wilhelm's quivering, frantic voice bounced off the brick walls and screeched through the room like a wail from a badly tuned violin. He pointed his bony finger at Faith.

She clung to Dajon's wet arm and swallowed, knowing well this man's vengeance was not beyond watching her die.

Dajon laid his strong, warm hand over hers.

Judge Trott spun on his heel, his face puffed out in exasperation. "Egad, man. She has been pardoned."

Sir Wilhelm plucked the paper from his pocket, holding it up for all to see. Then, gripping it between his fingers, he started to rip it, but Dajon was on him in a second and snatched it from his hand. "Thank you. So kind of you."

Judge Trott turned and marched from the room, his deputies in tow.

Sir Wilhelm faced them, his face contorted into a sickly knot, his eyes afire with hatred. For a brief moment, it seemed as if he contemplated charging Dajon, but he must have seen the futility of such an action, for he remained in place.

"You have not seen the last of me." He spat and wiped the saliva from his chin.

"To my utter despair," Dajon replied.

Sir Wilhelm turned and marched from the room, flinging a chain of foul curses over his shoulder.

Faith fell into Dajon's arms. The moisture from his shirt soaked into her gown like a refreshing ointment. "Is this really happening?" She leaned back and gazed up at him. "I cannot believe you came for me."

He took her face in both hands and shook his head. "How could you ever believe that I would not?" He kissed her forehead, her nose then placed his lips on hers.

Heat inflamed her belly, threatening to overtake her, but feeling the reverend's eye upon them, Faith pushed from Dajon's embrace and threw a hand to her hip.

"What took you so long? I nearly married that buffoon." She glanced at his powerful physique, all the more evident through his wet attire. "And why are you all wet?"

" 'Twas such a hot day I thought I'd swim into port instead of taking a boat." He chuckled, a playful gleam in his eyes. "And I had to wait until I was sure Sir Wilhelm had procured your pardon, which I knew he must do before you wed."

"Will there be no wedding?" the whining voice of one of the girls asked. Embarrassment flushed over Faith. She had forgotten the silly girls were still present.

Dajon cocked a brow and gazed at Faith then at the reverend, who had remained before the judge's bench like a pillar of aplomb, a look of satisfaction on his face.

Faith's breath kindled anew, sending her chest heaving. Once again her legs wobbled beneath her.

Dajon took her hand in his and gazed down at her, his blue eyes so assured, so true, so loving.

"Miss Westcott, will you marry me?"

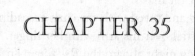

CHAPTER 35

Leaning on his elbow, Dajon gazed at the beauty sleeping beside him. Sunlight streamed in through the stern window, setting her curls sparkling in an array of red, orange, and gold. Dark fringes of lashes shadowed her golden cheeks, and a tiny cluster of freckles danced upon her nose. Stirring, she moaned and snuggled close to his chest. The scent of lemon and lilies danced around him, reminding him of the glorious night they'd spent in each other's arms. He allowed his gaze to wander down her creamy neck, across her bare shoulders, and down to where the coverlet forbade his eyes to go farther. He couldn't believe she was his wife.

Thank You, God. Thank You for this precious gift.

The ship rocked over a wave, shifting the sun across her eyelids that she slowly fluttered open. When she focused on him, a delicate grin adorned her lips. "Good morning, husband."

"Good morning, wife." He brushed a thumb across her cheek.

Reaching up, she ran her fingers through his hair and then allowed her hand to boldly caress his shoulder, then the muscles in his arm, then over to finger the hair upon his chest.

His body warmed. "I'm real, I assure you." He grabbed her hand and kissed it.

"I would never have believed I could be so happy." She shifted her shimmering auburn eyes to his. "Yesterday I faced either the noose or Sir Wilhelm's bed—both equally repugnant." She smiled, but then a flicker of sorrow pinched her features. "I had lost all hope. And now here I am, not only freed from those hideous fates but the wife of the most wonderful man I've ever known."

The snap of a sail sounded above them, followed by the creak of the hull.

"And I'm at sea." Her eyes widened with glee, and she sat up, holding the coverlet to her chest. "And I'm on my ship"—she gave him a measured smile—"*your* ship, I mean."

Dajon chuckled and toyed with the curls cascading down her back.

Faith traced a trail over his arm with her finger. "What a grand idea to spend our wedding night aboard the *Red Siren*. I'm so glad you brought her to port."

"After I resigned my commission, I must admit I felt naked without a ship to command." Dajon caressed the silky skin of her back, his mind and body shifting to the soft feel of his beautiful wife.

Leaning down on her elbow, Faith frowned, the mirth of only a moment ago drained from her face. "I can't believe you did that for me. You love the navy. Your career—it meant so much to you." She lowered her gaze and began to pick at a loose thread on the coverlet.

Placing a finger beneath her chin, he raised her eyes to his. "Truth be told, as soon as I began to understand the enormity of God's grace, I realized I didn't need the navy to redeem me from my past sins." He shrugged.

"But you love the sea as much as I do."

A lock of her hair fell over her shoulder and grazed the bed. Dajon twirled it between his fingers. "You gave up your seafaring career as well, did you not?"

"Career?" She giggled. "If you can call it that, but aye, I did. For the Lord."

"Then perhaps He has other plans for us upon the sea." He pulled her down beside him, showering her neck with kisses until she pushed him away, laughing.

The tiny purple scar below her left ear caught his eye. He traced the half-moon with his finger. "Where did you get this?"

"In a sword fight." She gave him a sassy look.

"Of course." Dajon laughed. "I know I should be horrified to discover my new wife is a swordsman"—he cleared his throat—"or swordswoman, but somehow I find it quite enticing."

A challenge sparked in her eyes. "Perhaps we can try our hand at swordplay someday."

"Perhaps, but I fear you are not a woman accustomed to defeat."

"Nay and why would that change?" One side of her mouth curved in a grin.

"Speaking of pirating." Dajon thought better to change the subject before she challenged him to a duel. "What of all the treasure you've stolen?" He raised his brows.

Faith held a finger to his lips. "The Lord has already shown me what I am to do."

"Indeed?"

"Since I cannot return the wealth to its proper owners, I shall give it all to charity—to the poor, to those in need."

"What about providing for your sisters and their future?"

"I won't deny I'm a bit uneasy about it." Faith sighed. "But I need to trust God. I know He has a plan for all of us—a good plan—if we will only trust and follow Him."

Dajon smiled, feeling the warmth of her statement spread down to his toes.

"All save this ship, that is." She gave him a sideways smile. "I have returned her to her rightful owner."

"Nay."

"What do you mean? The *Red Siren* is yours."

"I am giving her back to you. . .as a wedding present."

She shook her head. "I don't deserve such a gift. Not after I stole her from you."

"You stole my heart, too." Dajon brushed a thumb over her cheek. "And I'm giving that back to you as well."

Her eyes moistened. "Then I vow to take good care of both." She pulled him down and met his lips with hers. For a moment, Dajon lost himself in her taste, squeezing her closer, his body heating.

As if completely unaware of her effect upon him, she pushed him back. "What shall we do with the ship? Merchant or"—her voice sparked with excitement—"privateer?"

Dajon chuckled. "Only in wartime, my little pirate, or we shall be right back where we started."

"Oh, very well. But we shall command her together." Faith folded the top of the coverlet and patted it with finality.

"Together?" Dajon cocked a brow. "Nay, my love. I never share my command."

Her lips leveled in a satisfied smirk. "Well, 'tis time you begin, my husband."

"Having such a notorious pirate for a wife should prove quite interesting." He rubbed a thumb over her lips, longing to kiss them again.

She kissed his finger and smiled. "We should return home soon and tell my sisters the good news. They must be worried sick about me."

"Yes, we shall." Dajon crept closer. "But 'tis far too early."

Faith ran her fingers over the stubble on his cheek and frowned.

"Why the sad look?" he asked.

"I am too happy for words. What if I am only dreaming?"

"I assure you, you are not." Dajon brushed her curls from her forehead. "But perhaps I need to prove it to you."

"And how do you intend to do that?" Her tone held a challenge.

He gave her a roguish grin.

She smiled at him in return, her gaze beaming an invitation.

And Dajon lowered his lips upon hers to accept it.

EPILOGUE

Faith pushed open the front door of the Westcott home and nearly ran over Edwin. He stumbled backward, his bloodshot eyes rounding like saucers.

"Miss Westcott. What. . .where. . .how?"

Dajon entered behind her and led the tottering steward to a chair beside the grandfather clock. "There, there, man. Have a rest. I assure you we are not ghosts."

Edwin slid into the seat. "But you were in prison."

"I am aware of that, Edwin. Now, if you please, where are my sisters?" Excitement rippled through her. Faith gripped the banister and peered upstairs. At nearly one o'clock in the afternoon, everyone should be up and about.

"In the drawing room, I believe," Edwin stuttered, withdrawing a handkerchief and dabbing his forehead.

After closing the door, Dajon proffered his arm with a smile. "Shall we?"

Gripping his elbow, Faith allowed him to lead her up the stairs. She still couldn't believe that the extraordinary man beside her was her husband, and she couldn't wait to share the news with her sisters.

"Miss Faith! Miss Faith!" Molly's high-pitched voice pulled them back to the bottom of the stairway. The cook sped down the hallway, her muslin skirts flailing behind her. "I thought I heard yer voice." Her eyes landed on Dajon, and she halted. "Oh, Mr. Waite. Warms my soul to see you." She caught her breath as her gaze shifted suspiciously between them, then she darted to Faith. "How did you get out of prison, Miss Faith?" She reached up as if she wanted to hug her but hesitated. Throwing her arms around her, Faith embraced Molly, and they both broke into a jumbled mix of sobbing laughter.

Pulling away, Faith held her at arm's length. "I have much to tell you."

Grace's soft footsteps upon the stairs drew Faith's attention. Her normally glowing skin seemed pale in the light coming in through the back window. Dark smudges tugged on her glassy green eyes. Clutching a book in hand, she inched her way down to Faith as if she didn't quite believe what she was seeing.

The back door slammed, and a thud of boots sounded before Lucas barreled into the foyer, hat in hand and smelling of hay and horses. His eyes shimmered as a beaming smile took over his mouth.

"Lucas!"

"Miss Faith. How did ye—"

Grace flew down the remaining stairs and into Faith's arms, stopping Lucas's question in midair and nearly knocking Faith over. "Praise be to God. I'm so glad to see you."

"And I you, sweet sister." Faith squeezed her then took a step back. "You're trembling." She took both her hands in hers. "Everything will be okay now. I am free."

"Free," Molly repeated. "Why, heaven be praised!" She clapped her hands together.

"I have such good news to share. Where is Hope?" Faith started for the stairs. "I want her to hear this, too. Is she in her chamber?"

A sullen silence struck the room. No one's eyes met hers.

Dajon took her hand as if he sensed something was amiss. "Where is Miss Hope?" His question flung into the room like a net and hung waiting for an answer to fill it.

Grace stepped forward. "She left a note in her chamber yesterday morning."

"What did it say?" A sweat broke out on the back of Faith's neck.

Grace's bottom lip quivered even as her eyes pooled with tears.

"She has stowed away aboard Lord Falkland's ship heading to England."

DISCUSSION QUESTIONS

1. The story of Faith Westcott is taken from the parable in Matthew 13 where a farmer sows seed that falls on rocky soil and when the sun comes up, the new plant gets scorched and it withers because it had no root. What were the things that happened to Faith that caused her to get scorched? Can you understand how things like that could cause someone with shallow faith to turn away from God? Why? Describe this type of shallow faith.

2. Have you ever suffered a tragedy or tragedies in your life that made you question God's love or even His existence? Describe what happened.

3. What was the result in Faith's life when she tried to take matters into her own hands? What was the effect on her life? On her sisters? On her father? On Lucas? Did things get better for Faith or worse? Describe.

4. What happened that finally brought Faith to an understanding that God still loved her and longed for her to return to Him?

5. Can you list any good things that came as a result of the tragedies in Faith's life? How about in your own experience with tragedy?

6. What did Dajon struggle with the most in his walk with God? What did he hope to accomplish in the navy?

7. Is it easier for us to do good works to make ourselves worthy of heaven or to accept God's free gift of grace? Have you struggled with your own battle between works and faith? If so, describe what you have learned. What is the difference between faith and works, and how are they related?

8. What made Dajon realize that no amount of good deeds could make up for his sins? What conclusion did he come to about good deeds as they relate to following the Lord?

9. What was Reginald Borland's goal in the story? Have you ever been jealous of someone else's success? Even a friend? What happened that helped Reggie to see himself for who he truly was?

10. Although she was a godly woman, what was Molly's biggest fear? What helped her to get past that fear?

11. At the beginning of the story Lucas is an atheist. Do you remember why? What happened to convince him there is a loving God? Have you ever seen a miracle? Do you believe God still uses miracles as evidence of His Word to save the lost?

12. Of the three sisters, who could you most relate to and why?

the Blue
ENCHANTRESS

Charles Towne Belles / Book 2

DEDICATION

To anyone who has ever felt worthless and
unloved and who has sought to obtain
value through the lies of this world.

He also that received seed among the thorns is he that heareth
the word; and the care of this world, and the deceitfulness of riches,
choke the word, and he becometh unfruitful.
MATTHEW 13:22

CHAPTER 1

St. Kitts, September 17-18

"G entlemen, what will ye offer for this rare treasure of a lady?" The words crashed over Hope Westcott like bilge water. "Why, she'll make any of ye a fine wife, a cook, a housemaid"—the man gave a lascivious chuckle—"whate'er ye desire."

"How 'bout someone to warm me bed at night," one man bellowed, and a cacophony of chortles gurgled through the air.

Hope slammed her eyes shut against the mob of men who pressed on three sides of the tall wooden platform, shoving one another to get a better peek at her. Something crawled over her foot, and she pried her eyes open, keeping her face lowered. A black spider skittered away. Red scrapes and bruises marred her bare feet. When had she lost her satin shoes—the gold braided ones she'd worn to impress Lord Falkland? She couldn't recall.

"What d'ye say? How much for this fine young lady?" The man grabbed a fistful of her hair and yanked her head back. Pain, like a dozen claws, pierced her skull. "She's a handsome one, to be sure. And these golden locks." He attempted to slide his fingers through her matted strands, but before becoming hopelessly entangled in them, he jerked his hand free, wrenching out a clump of her hair. Hope winced. "Have ye seen the likes of them?"

Ribald whistles and groans of agreement spewed over her.

"Two shillings," one man yelled.

Hope dared to glance across the throng amassing before the auction block. A wild sea of lustful eyes sprayed over her. A band of men dressed in garments stained with dirt and sweat bunched toward the front, yelling out bids. Behind them, other men in velvet waistcoats leaned their heads together, no doubt to discuss the value of this recent offering, while studying her as if she were a breeding mare. Slaves knelt in the dirt along the outskirts of the mob, waiting for their masters. Beyond them, a row of wooden buildings stretched in either direction. Brazen women emerged from a tavern and draped themselves over the railings, watching Hope's predicament with interest. On the street, ladies in modish gowns averted their eyes as they tugged the men on their arms from the sordid scene.

Hope lowered her head. *This can't be happening. I'm dreaming. I am still on the ship. Just a nightmare. Only a nightmare.* Humiliation swept over her with an ever-rising dread as the reality of her situation blasted its way through her mind.

She swallowed hard and tried to drown out the grunts and salacious insults tossed her way by the bartering rabble. Perhaps if she couldn't hear them, if she couldn't see them, they would disappear and she would wake up back home, safe in Charles Towne, safe in her bedchamber, safe with her sisters, just like she was before she'd put her trust in a man who betrayed her.

"Egad, man. Two shillings, is it? For this beauty?" The auctioneer spit off to the side. The yellowish glob landed on Hope's skirt. Her heart felt as though it had liquefied into an equally offensive blob and oozed down beside it.

How did I get here? In her terror, she could not remember. She raised her gaze to the auctioneer. Cold eyes, hard like marbles, met hers, and a sinister grin twisted his lips. He adjusted his tricorn to further shade his chubby face from the burning sun.

"She looks too feeble for any real work," another man yelled.

The sounds of the crowd dimmed. The men's fists forged into the air as if pushing through mud. Garbled laughter drained from their yellow-toothed mouths like molasses. Hope's heart beat slower, and she wished for death.

The gentle lap of waves caressed her ears, their peaceful cadence drawing her away. Tearing her gaze from the nightmarish spectacle, she glanced over her shoulder, past the muscled henchmen who'd escorted her here. Two docks jutted out into a small bay brimming with sparkling turquoise water where several ships rocked back and forth as if shaking their heads at her in pity. Salt and papaya and sun combined in a pleasant aroma that lured her mind away from her present horror.

Her eyes locked upon the glimmering red and gold figurine of Ares at the bow of Lord Falkland's ship. She blinked back the burning behind her eyes. When she'd boarded it nigh a week past—or was it two weeks?—all her hopes and dreams had boarded with her. Somewhere along the way, they had been cast into the depths of the sea. She only wished she had joined them. Although the ship gleamed majestically in the bay, all she had seen of it for weeks had been the four walls of a small cabin below deck.

The roar of the crowd wrenched her mind back to the present and turned her face forward.

"Five shillings."

"'Tis robbery, and ye know it," the auctioneer barked. "Where are any of ye clods goin' t' find a real lady like this?"

A stream of perspiration raced down Hope's back as if seeking escape. But there was no escape. She was about to be sold as a slave, a harlot to one of these cruel and prurient taskmasters. A fate worse than death. A fate her sister had fought hard to keep her from. A fate Hope had brought upon herself. Numbness crept over her even as her eyes filled with tears. *Oh God. This can't be happening.*

She gazed upward at the blue sky dusted with thick clouds, hoping for some deliverance, some sign that God had not abandoned her.

The men continued to haggle, their voices booming louder and louder, grating over her like the howls of demons.

Her head felt like it had detached from her body and was floating up to join the clouds. Palm trees danced in the light breeze coming off the bay. Their tall trunks and fronds formed an oscillating blur of green and brown. The buildings, the mob, and the whole heinous scene joined the growing mass and began twirling around Hope. Her legs turned to jelly, and she toppled to the platform.

"Get up!" A sharp crack stung her cheek. Two hands like rough rope clamped over her arms and dragged her to her feet. Pain lanced through her right foot where a splinter had found a home. Holding a hand to her stinging face, Hope sobbed.

The henchman released her with a grunt of disgust.

"I told ye she won't last a week," one burly man shouted.

"She ain't good for nothing but to look at."

Planting a strained grin upon his lips, the auctioneer swatted her rear end. "Aye, but she's much more stout than she appears, gentlemen."

Horrified and no longer caring about the repercussions, Hope slapped the man's face. He raised his fist, and she cowered. The crowd roared its mirth.

"One pound, then," a tall man sporting a white wig called out. "I could use me a pretty wench." Withdrawing a handkerchief, he dabbed at the perspiration on his forehead.

Wench. Slave. Hope shook her head, trying to force herself to accept what her mind kept trying to deny. A sudden surge of courage, based on naught but her instinct to survive, stiffened her spine. She thrust out her chin and faced the auctioneer. "I beg your pardon, sir. There's been a mistake. I am no slave."

"Indeed?" He cocked one brow and gave her a patronizing smirk.

Hope searched the horde for a sympathetic face—just one. "My name is Miss Hope Westcott," she shouted. "My father is Admiral Henry Westcott. I live in Charles Towne with my two sisters."

"And I'm King George," a farmer howled, slapping his knee.

"My father will pay handsomely for my safe return." Hope scanned the leering faces. Not one. Not one look of sympathy or belief or kindness. Fear crawled up her throat. She stomped her foot, sending a shard of pain up her leg. "You must believe me," she sobbed. "I don't belong here."

Ignoring the laughter, Hope spotted a purple plume fluttering in the breeze atop a gold-trimmed hat in the distance. "Arthur!" She darted for the stairs but two hands grabbed her from behind and held her in place. "Don't leave me! Lord Falkland!" She struggled in her captor's grasp. His grip tightened, sending a throbbing ache across her back.

Swerving about, Lord Falkland tapped his cane into the dirt and tipped the brim of his hat up, but the distance between them forbade Hope a vision of his expression.

"Tell them who I am, Arthur. Please save me!"

He leaned toward the woman beside him and said something, then coughed into his hand. *What is he doing?* The man who once professed an undying love for Hope, the man who promised to marry her, to love her forever, the man who bore the responsibility for her being here in the first place. How could he stand there and do nothing while she met such a hideous fate?

The elegant lady beside him turned her nose up at Hope, then, threading her arm through Lord Falkland's, she wheeled him around and pulled him down the road.

Hope watched him leave, and with each step of his cordovan boots, her heart and her very soul sank deeper into the wood of the auction block beneath her feet.

Nothing made any sense. Had the world gone completely mad?

"Two pounds," a corpulent man in the back roared.

A memory flashed through Hope's mind as she gazed across the band of men. A vision of African slaves, women and children, being auctioned off in Charles Towne. How many times had she passed by, ignoring them, uncaring, unconcerned by the proceedings?

Was this God's way of repaying her for her selfishness, her lack of charity?

"Five pounds."

Disappointed curses rumbled among the men at the front, who had obviously reached their limit of coin.

The auctioneer's mouth spread wide, greed dripping from its corners. "Five pounds, gentlemen. Do I hear six for this lovely lady?"

A blast of hot air rolled over Hope, stealing her breath. Human sweat, fish, and horse manure filled her nose and saturated her skin. The unforgiving sun beat a hot hammer atop her head until she felt she would ignite into a burning torch at any moment. Indeed, she prayed she would. Better to be reduced to a pile of ashes than endure what the future held for her.

"Six pounds," a short man with a round belly and stiff brown wig yelled from the back of the mob in a tone that indicated he knew what he was doing and had no intention of losing his prize. Decked in a fine damask waistcoat, silk breeches, and a gold-chained pocket watch, which he kept snapping open and shut, he exuded wealth and power.

Hope's stomach twisted into a vicious knot, and she clutched her throat to keep from heaving whatever shred of moisture remained in her empty stomach.

The auctioneer gaped at her, obviously shocked she could command such a price. Rumblings overtook the crowd as the short man pushed his way through to claim his prize. The closer he came, the faster Hope's chest heaved and the lighter her head became. Blood pounded in her ears, drowning out the groans of the mob. *No, God. No.*

"Do I hear seven?" the auctioneer bellowed. "She's young and will breed you some fine sons."

"Just what I'll be needing." The man halted at the platform, glanced over the crowd for any possible competitors, then took the stairs to Hope's right. He halted beside her too close for propriety's sake and assailed her with the stench of lard and tobacco. A long purple scar crossed his bloated red face as his eyes grazed over her like a stallion on a breeding mare. Hope shuddered and gasped for a breath of air. Her palms broke out in a sweat, and she rubbed them on her already moist gown.

The auctioneer threw a hand to his hip and gazed over the crowd.

The man squeezed her arms, and Hope snapped from his grasp and took a step back, abhorred at his audacity. He chuckled. "Not much muscle on her, but she's got pluck."

He belched, placed his watch back into the fob pocket of his breeches, and removed a leather pouch from his belt. "Six pounds it is."

The silver tip of a sword hung at his side. If Hope were quick about it, perhaps she could grab it and, with some luck, fight her way out of here. She clenched her teeth. Who was she trying to fool? Where was her pirate sister when she needed her? Surely Faith would know exactly what to do. Yet what did it matter? Hope would rather die trying to escape than become this loathsome man's slave.

As the man counted out the coins into the auctioneer's greedy hands, Hope reached for the sword.

CHAPTER 2

"Seven pounds." Nathaniel Mason charged toward the platform, shoving his way through the unruly throng. "Seven pounds." Even as he bellowed the amount, he wondered if he had lost his mind. That was over half of the coin in his money pouch, and he needed all of it to purchase his supplies for the return trip to Charles Towne.

The stout man on the platform beside Miss Hope swung about and glared at Nathaniel as if he were naught but an annoying bug. His hand froze in midair, a gold coin clenched between his stubby fingers. "What is the meaning of this?"

The auctioneer's eyes glinted with greedy amusement as he doffed his tricorn and swept it through the air with a bow of deference. "Seven pounds from the gentlemen in the blue waistcoat. Do I hear eight?" He raised a questioning brow toward the man beside him before surveying the grumbling mob.

"I wouldn't pay eight pounds fer me own mother!" a man in front of the crowd cackled, eliciting squawks of laughter from all those around him.

"Eight." The red-faced man continued to count out his coins into the auctioneer's open pouch as if no opposition could prevent him from carrying out his task.

Shoving through the horde of sweaty, cursing men, Nathaniel leapt upon the platform. "Nine pounds," he shouted above the clamor and allowed his gaze to brush over Miss Hope.

When he'd first seen her from across the street where he'd been arranging with a merchant to load the man's goods aboard ship, his heart had plunged like a stone into his boots. Though the woman resembled Miss Hope in hair and color of skin, he could not believe it was the lady he knew from Charles Towne—not so far from the safety of her home, not in such slovenly condition, and certainly not being sold as an indentured servant. But as he approached the throng, he recognized the familiar golden hair with a hint of red, and those glistening eyes the color of the Caribbean Sea that had mesmerized him back home.

And his heart had rammed into his ribs.

How had she come to such dire straits? *Kidnapped.* The word blasted through his thoughts. 'Twas the only explanation. White women brought a handsome price in the islands, where they were in short supply. And Miss Hope's particular beauty would lure many a slave trader to steal her from her home, take her far away where no one would know her, and sell her to some lonely, desperate plantation owner. In these savage lands, most people looked the other way at such injustices. The last time he'd seen her, she'd been strolling down the streets of Charles Towne attired in a fine taffeta gown, her arm entwined around that of a marine.

And if he recalled, tossing her snooty nose in the air at him as well.

Like she always had. Belittled him. Ignored him. Treated him as though he were dung on the street.

You owe her nothing.

But now those crystal blue eyes locked upon his as if he were her only lifeline in a storm threatening to drown her beneath its waves. Dirt smudged her face and neck. Dark circles tugged the skin beneath her eyes. Her hair hung loose in tangled nests upon a stained and tattered gown. "Mr. Mason." She managed to whisper his name, and that one whisper held all the desperation and pleading he needed to continue.

"The lady is mine, sir." The rotund merchantman gave Nathaniel a cursory glance. "I have already made a bargain with this man, and as you can see I am sealing it with my payment."

"Aye, let 'im have her," a lanky man from the crowd barked at Nathaniel. "Garrison ain't had no lady in years."

Laughter roared across the mob like a sudden thunderstorm, and the merchantman's face blossomed in a mad dash of crimson. He shot the man a vicious glare before continuing to count his money.

"Me vote goes t' the young sailor," another shorter man bellowed. "He looks like he's been out t' sea far too long an' needs a wench t' warm his bed." He surveyed the chortling mob. "Who'll care to place a wager on him?"

An onslaught of bets saturated the air like a tropical downpour.

Nathaniel shoved his way between Mr. Garrison and Hope, guiding her behind him, and faced the auctioneer. "Is the auction closed, sir?"

"Nay." The man grinned. "Not as long as the bidding continues." He wiped spittle from his chin. "Truth be told, I may get to my drink early today."

"Then I believe the last offer was nine pounds." Nathaniel reached for his money pouch.

"Ten." Mr. Garrison waved Nathaniel off and snapped open his pocket watch. "Best that or leave."

Nathaniel glanced over his shoulder at Hope, whose moist eyes sparked with fear, then out on the bay where his ship rested idly in the turquoise waters. He'd come to St. Kitts to fill her hold with tobacco, sugar, cotton, rum, herbs, and salt—a shipload of cargo to take back to Charles Towne. He had lined up willing merchants and farmers, and if all went well, he stood to pocket a huge profit for his trouble. Enough to purchase another ship for his burgeoning fleet.

His gaze settled back on Hope. Tears now spilled from her eyes, winding slick trails through the dirt on her cheeks. "Please help me, Mr. Mason."

Facing forward, Nathaniel swallowed a lump of emotion he could not describe. He doffed his hat and wiped the sweat from his forehead. "Eleven."

It was all he had.

"Twelve." The man uttered the word without hesitation and scratched beneath a wig as stiff as his resolve. He shot an annoyed look at Nathaniel. "I intend to have her, sir. I suggest you stand down." He snapped his watch shut and returned it to his pocket.

Nathaniel rubbed his eyes. *What should I do, Lord?* He couldn't leave this lady in the lecherous hands of these men, but he had nothing else to offer. Nothing, except his. . . Nathaniel snapped his gaze back to his ship—the ship he had built with his own hands, the ship he had spent four years working as a carpenter to pay for and another year to build.

He clutched his side where an old wound began to burn.

What is the value of a ship compared to a human life?

The auctioneer tapped his boot on the wooden platform. "Can you best the offer or not, sir?"

A burst of blood rushed to Nathaniel's head. His lungs collapsed under the weight of what he knew he must do. He gasped for breath amidst the air saturated with the stench of human sweat and the sting of rain. He faced the auctioneer, avoiding Miss Hope's desperate eyes. "I offer. . .I offer you my merchant brig," he spit out the words before he changed his mind, then he clenched his fists, not believing the words still hanging on the wind.

The auctioneer's eyes widened, and he studied Nathaniel as if to ensure he was not mocking him, but Nathaniel knew not an ounce of humor would be found on his expression.

"Which one is it?" The auctioneer gazed out upon the water.

"'Tis the two-masted brig, there in the center, by the East Indiamen." Nathaniel pointed toward the pride of his fleet as his heart sank. "The one with the blue cross painted on her stern. I built her myself."

"Ah yes, I see. She's a beauty." The auctioneer slapped Nathaniel on the back. "I'll take her." He poured Mr. Garrison's coins back into the man's hand, then glanced at Miss Hope. "Though I daresay I fear I am getting the best of our bargain." He chuckled.

A collective gasp shot from the horde of men, followed by renewed profanity and further feverish wagers.

Mr. Garrison squeezed his hands over the clanking coins and thrust them toward the auctioneer. "I do protest, sir. He cannot offer his ship. This is unheard of." His cheeks budded in patches of purple and red, and his dark eyes darted between the three of them like grapeshot searching for a victim.

Nathaniel couldn't move his feet. Every part of him seemed numb save his pounding heart and the odd buzzing filling his head. Had he just sold the *Blue Triumph*, his best merchant ship?

And for a woman who did naught but spurn him at every turn.

She wasn't spurning him now. The taut lines in her face had softened, and she smiled up at him with thankfulness and admiration.

He tore his eyes from her. He must think. He could still change his mind. Save his ship and walk away. He clenched his jaw, then his fists, until his nails bit into his skin. Maybe the pain would return his senses to him. He released a long sigh, hoping it would stifle the sinking feeling that dragged upon his heart. It didn't.

Of course there was no other choice. *O God, give me a way out.*

The auctioneer faced Mr. Garrison. "Counter the offer, sir, or I suggest you take your money and leave."

"I am not authorized. . .I mean to say, I cannot. . ." he blubbered and removed a handkerchief to dab the sweat from his neck. After firing one last angry glance their way, he turned and waddled down the stairs, cursing his way through the laughing rabble.

Groans emanated from the men who had lost their wagers as the clank of coins rang through the humid air.

Miss Hope clutched Nathaniel's arm with a grip that said she would not easily release him. A month ago such attentions would have pleased him, but under the present situation, nausea bubbled in his gut.

The auctioneer swatted at the crowd to dismiss them. "Be gone with ye. I'm done for the day."

Cursing, the men dispersed while Nathaniel begrudgingly made arrangements with the auctioneer to transfer the ship to his care.

CHAPTER 3

Hope could not stop trembling. Her whole body shivered as if she were in the midst of an icy winter on the shores of Portsmouth. Yet it was anything but cold in the stagnant sweltering air of the tiny room into which Mr. Mason had thrust her over two hours ago. Where had he gone?

Hugging herself, she lay back on the lumpy bed and stared at the wooden beams of the ceiling. Once they must have been smooth and beautiful, but now they were marred and stained—just like her, worn out and impure. The sounds of bells ringing, horses clomping, and people chattering reached her through an open window that allowed not a hint of a breeze to enter. In the tavern below, men quarreled and laughed as they took to their drink while some sotted fool hammered out a morbid tune on a harpsichord.

She longed to cry, to let out all the horror of the past few weeks, but she found she could no more force her tears to come than she could will herself to stop shaking.

A vision of the lewd throng of men reaching out for her with coins in their filthy hands seared across her mind. Squeezing her eyes shut, she tried to erase the scene, but instead, the flabby face of the merchantman who had nearly purchased her penetrated her thoughts until her stomach soured.

But she had been delivered.

She could scarce believe it, and in particular, she could scarce believe the form in which her deliverance had come. Not in Lord Falkland, a gentleman and the man who had claimed to love her, but in Mr. Mason, an uneducated commoner—a man she had done her best to avoid in Charles Towne.

The door to the chamber slammed open, and Hope sprang from the bed. Mr. Mason marched in, tossed a brown bag into the corner, and slammed the wooden slab behind him. Without glancing her way, he stormed to the window and gazed out as if he wished he were anywhere but here with her.

"What is that?" She pointed toward the large bag and leaned on the bed before her wobbling legs gave way beneath her.

"All I have left of my ship." The fury in his voice jarred her.

Though she had thanked him over and over after they'd left the auction block, he had barely spoken two words to her. He hadn't offered her any comfort, hadn't reassured her all would be well like a true gentleman would have.

She couldn't blame him. He had paid a high price for her redemption.

"I am sorry for your loss, Mr. Mason."

He grunted.

"I owe you my life."

Again, a grunt.

"Are you to be angry with me forever?" She used her sweetest voice, the one that melted most men's hearts.

Finally, he turned to face her, arms clenched so tightly across his chest that his muscles bulged beneath his shirt. He had removed his waistcoat—another thing a gentleman would never do in the presence of a lady—and only a linen shirt covered the wide expanse of his chest. Hair the color of dark walnut curled at the edge of his collar. A muscle twitched in his strong, stubbled jaw, and his dark eyes reminded her of a panther about to spring.

Spreading the folds of her torn skirt around her, she lowered her head, unsettled by another wave of familiar fear rising within her. "You were much kinder back in Charles Towne."

He snorted. "Back in Charles Towne, I hadn't lost five years of hard work." He rubbed the back of his neck, plopped down in a chair by the window, and closed his eyes.

A gust of wind sent the tan curtains framing the window into a feathery dance and brought a moment's relief from the heat. Hope grabbed her mass of tangled hair and lifted it off her back, allowing a whiff of air to cool her heated skin and hopefully ease her taut nerves. She eyed Mr. Mason. Once again, she found herself at the mercy of a man's good graces. Considering the last time had not turned out so well and that this man harbored animosity toward her, she could not stop her body from trembling.

When he opened his eyes, Hope sighed in relief to see the harshness of a moment ago had softened. Placing his elbows on his knees, he leaned forward. "You have no doubt suffered greatly, and my thoughts have been for my own loss. Please tell me, Miss Hope. What happened to you? What brought you here to St. Kitts, and worse yet, to that auction block?"

"Is that where I am?" Hope shrugged. "I've been locked in a cabin aboard Lord Falkland's. . ." She paused and swallowed against the pain rising in her throat. "Ship for two weeks."

He scratched his jaw. "Lord Falkland. Is he not your beau? You and he were the talk of Charles Towne."

Hope squeezed her lips together. Tears burned behind her eyes, yet still they would not fall. "Apparently, I was mistaken."

"How did you come to be on his ship?" His low, sympathetic tone comforted her.

"I hoped to surprise him." Grabbing a tangled lock of hair, Hope flattened it between her thumb and forefinger. "And surprise him I did. He—and his wife."

Mr. Mason's brow wrinkled. "Surprise him." He said the words slowly as if he were analyzing them for some hidden meaning. Fidgeting in his chair, he examined the floorboards beneath his boots. When he lifted his face, veins pulsed in his reddened forehead.

"Fire and thunder." He shot to his feet. "You intended to run away with him." His incredulous shout boomed off the walls of the tiny chamber.

Hope winced at his sudden outburst. "Yes, we were betrothed—not officially, that is—but he promised to marry me when he returned"—sobs crowded in her throat, causing her words to jumble—"and I thought he was simply trying to protect me from an arduous journey by forbidding me to join him."

Mr. Mason paced like a caged animal, hands fisted at his sides.

"Fire and thunder!" he bellowed again, raking a hand through his hair. "Do you mean to tell me you brought this on yourself?"

Hope swallowed. "How was I to know he was a cad, and married, and that he would hand me over to the captain to do with me as he wished?" Outrage burned anew in her chest at Lord Falkland's betrayal. Outrage and agony. Biting her lip, she dared a glance at Mr. Mason, who had taken up his pacing again, and she feared she'd lost her only friend in this godforsaken outpost.

His tanned complexion exploded in crimson while the knuckles of his fisted hands turned white. "Do you realize the price I have paid for your licentious affair?"

Hope's stomach folded in on itself. Yes, she did, at least as much as she could understand. Couldn't the man see she was trying to apologize? His cruel words stung her. It was not the first time her association with Lord Falkland had been referred to in such a lewd manner, but it did naught to lessen the pain. "We loved one another."

"Yes. I can see that. 'Tis what a man does with the woman he loves, sells her off as a slave to another." He gave a derisive snicker.

"How can you be so cruel? My heart is crushed beyond repair." Placing a hand on the bedraggled coverlet, Hope leaned her weight upon it and lowered her chin. "I wish I were dead."

He snorted. "If you intend to kill yourself, I wish you had done it before today so I wouldn't have been forced to forfeit my ship to save you."

Surely he was mocking her, yet not a trace of amusement rang in his deep voice. "Am I not worth more than a boat?"

"A brig, if you please, and one that did not come easy to me, as most things have come for you."

She snapped her eyes to his, her jaw tightening. "You think what I have endured has been easy?"

Halting, Mr. Mason folded his arms across his chest. "Nay, I think you are a foolish girl with foolish dreams who hasn't a care for the effect her choices have on others."

Hope shot to her feet, ignoring the pain spiking up her calves. She didn't know whether to be angry at his vicious affront or fall to the floor in a heap of despair. She'd never met a man with so little sympathy for a lady in distress. "I thought you were a Christian."

"'Tis the Christian in me that saved you from that vulgar merchant-man. So I'd be thanking God, if I were you. But the man in me will not toss vain flatteries and sentimental comforts where they aren't deserved." He ran a hand through his wavy hair and turned to gaze out the window as if she weren't worth his time.

Her heart crumbled. How much rejection could one lady endure? "Since you find my company so objectionable, I will relieve you of any further obligation." The last thing she wanted to do was accept help given out of some false sense of religious obligation—especially from a man who obviously hated her.

Hope took careful steps across the wooden floor so as not to catch another splinter in her already bloody feet. "Truly, I do thank you for all you've done, Mr. Mason." Behind her, she heard his boots shuffling across the floor, but he made no move to stop her. What did she expect? He owed her nothing, while she owed him everything. Yet with each step, her knees melted. Slowing her pace, she began to sob as a million frightening scenarios scrambled across her mind of how she would make it back home to Charles Towne unprotected and all alone.

As she reached for the door handle, her head grew light, and she blinked to clear her vision. All her strength seemed to drain from her. She turned the handle. Boot steps pounded over the floor behind her, and a warm hand covered hers. She looked up at Mr. Mason, but his gaze had dropped to her bloodied feet. Cursing, he hoisted her up in his arms and carried her to the bed, setting her gently upon it.

When he sat beside her, an overwhelming urge to seek comfort and safety in the arms of a man overcame her and she fell against him. The scent of wood and tar and man cradled her, and tears finally began to flow down her face.

He stretched an arm around her shoulder. "All is well now, Miss Hope." The hesitant tone of his voice belied the assurance of his words.

Regardless, she snuggled into the warmth of his body that surrounded her like a shield, releasing a torrent of tears. Ashamed, she clung to him, not wanting him to see what was surely her swollen, red face.

He patted her arm as someone would a pet dog—a dog that might bite him. Was he that repulsed by her? "Never fear. You are safe now."

Safe. Was she truly safe? She had feared for her life for so long, she doubted she would recognize the feeling. But here, sheltered within this man's strong arms, a hint of its comfort rose within her.

Gently pushing her away, he peered down at her injured feet. His jaw tensed. "I did not realize you had been wounded."

She swiped the tears from her cheeks, encouraged by his kind display. "What is to become of me, Mr. Mason?"

Bolting off the bed, he swerved to face her, the hard glint returning to his eyes. "Never fear. I intend to return you to Charles Towne, Miss Hope. I've arranged for us to travel on a ship, the *Lady Devon,* tomorrow at sunrise. She heads for Kingstown, where I expect my other ship to arrive in a few weeks."

Hope drew in a deep breath of relief and allowed it to soften the rapid beat of her heart. "You are too kind, Mr. Mason. But I thought you had no money left?"

"I do not. I have signed on as a navigator to pay for our passage."

"I see." Hope bit her lip, realizing the depths this man had fallen because of her. "But you have another ship?" At least she had not completely ruined him.

"Aye, and we can sail her from Kingstown to Charles Towne and have you home within a fortnight." He stood, allowing his gaze to wander over her for what seemed like an eternity.

But not before Hope saw a speck of longing in his eyes. She sighed, relieved to see she still could affect a man even in her disheveled condition. She might need to secure this man's affection in order to get home safely.

CHAPTER 4

Nathaniel reached out to assist Hope as she tried to jump from the oscillating bosun's swing. Clutching her waist, he lifted her toward him and set her down as gently as he could. She winced when her feet touched the deck.

Her scent of honey and sunshine swirled around him, and his body heated despite the morning chill—despite all his efforts otherwise. She raised her sapphire gaze to his, brightened further by the smile curving her lips. Clearing his throat, Nathaniel picked up the brown bag he had dropped in order to help her. Even as angry as he was, even now knowing her lack of virtue, her close proximity still affected him like it had back in Charles Towne. What was it about her that made him so weak?

"Thank you, Mr. Mason, but I don't see why I must be brought aboard ship as if I were a crate." She brushed dirt from her green muslin gown that, though stiffened and splayed by the various undergarments ladies were required to wear, did naught to hide her bounteous curves.

"'Twould be improper and dangerous for you to climb the ropes above the sailors, miss."

With a huff and not an ounce of embarrassment at his comment, she shielded her eyes from the sun and gazed toward the docks of St. Kitts jutting from the small town like tongues ready to receive their daily food. Beyond the ramshackle buildings and waving palms, the island swooped to form a huge mountain blanketed in mossy green. Over the hill in the distance, a darkening sky gave Nathaniel pause.

"Barbaric place," Hope spat out, jolting him from his admiration of the small island's beauty. But how could he blame her after what had nearly happened to her in this tiny port? Though exhaustion tugged upon her face, her smooth pearly skin, no longer smudged with dirt, shimmered in the morning sunlight that also set aglitter her bouquet of golden curls pinned atop her head. No one would recognize her as the filthy, rag-clad woman auctioned off yesterday in the town square. And although she held her pert little nose high in the air, shame still seemed to weigh down her shoulders. She observed the bustling deck, seemingly unaware of the appreciative glances thrown her way from every man aboard—or was she? Something in her expression, the slight uplift of her lips, the lofty slant of her brow, told him otherwise.

When Nathaniel had tapped on her door that morning, she had opened it with such force, he thought she would barrel right into him. The mixture of shock and delight beaming on her face took him by surprise. Had she thought he would abandon her? Like Lord Falkland? Like her father? Like how many other men in her life? But he had been far too angry to spend any more time in her presence, so after he arranged for her bath, a fresh gown, and a meal, Nathaniel had sought his night's rest elsewhere. Perhaps he should have at least informed her. She had been through a harrowing experience—by her own doing to be sure—but he was a Christian, a man of God, and she needed his comfort, not his anger, nor his contempt.

Angry voices drew his attention up on the quarterdeck, where a group of sailors crowded around the man Nathaniel assumed to be the captain. One crewman kept pointing toward the eastern sky while the others grunted their agreements laced with foul exclamations. The captain planted his fists upon his waist and responded to his men, and although Nathaniel couldn't make out his words, the man's rigid stance and the fury reddening his face said more than enough.

A muscle twitched in Nathaniel's jaw. Word among the seamen at port was that, although Captain Conway was new to the Caribbean, he had already acquired a reputation as a cruel, overbearing man, and few but the most desperate signed on to his crew.

A net full of barrels hauled by ropes rose over the side of the ship and hovered in midair, and Nathaniel quickly guided Hope out of the way toward the railing. "What type of ship is this, Mr. Mason?" She squinted into the sun perched atop the green crest of the island. "A merchant brig." He tightened his jaw and scanned the choppy harbor.

"Like your ship," she said in a voice thick with guilt as she stared down at the moist deck.

Yes. Then he spotted her—his brig, the *Blue Triumph*. Jeweled waves danced against her hull as she rocked in the bay. An ache formed in his gut. He supposed he should be pleased Hope felt some remorse, but Nathaniel could summon no joy at the thought. It would take him years to recover from the loss, and that meant more years before he could realize his dream of owning his own merchant fleet.

"I am truly sorry, Mr. Mason." Her eyes shone with sincerity. "I made an awful mess of things and have cost you a great deal. You have been nothing but kind and done more than most gentlemen would." She laid a hand on his arm. "When we return home, I'm sure my father will offer some recompense for your loss."

Tugging his arm from beneath her hand, Nathaniel ignored the spark that shot through him at her touch, even as he doubted her declaration to be true. Admiral Westcott's reputation spoke of a gruff, commanding man who was as tight with his fortune as he was in running his ships.

Taking a step back from her, Nathaniel forced his thoughts to her less redeeming qualities. She was a sly one—a charmer. Like a coquettish fox, luring men into her den, skilled in the art of female attraction. Perhaps that was what had drawn him to her in Charles Towne. There, he had thought her a virtuous woman. But a proper lady would not sneak aboard a man's ship with the intention of running away with him, regardless of whether she thought they were betrothed and he was unmarried. Nay, a woman like that was certainly no longer chaste. A woman like that was too much like his mother.

However sincere her apology, Nathaniel had no intention of allowing his anger to dissolve. Yes, he could forgive her—as was his Christian duty. But forget? Forgetting such a horrendous infraction was far beyond his ability and bordered on the divine. And he was not God.

A gust of wind from the west crashed over them with the smell of fish, salt, and sweat, and Hope raised a hand to her nose and lifted her gaze to a family upon the quarterdeck. A man dressed in silk stockings, black velvet breeches, and an elaborately embroidered waistcoat stood beside a woman who was fretting over her young daughter. Hope's gaze locked upon the little girl, and she smiled for the first time since Nathaniel had seen her on the slave block.

Behind the couple stood Captain Conway, arms locked across his chest, surveying the loading of the ship. A young, light-haired gentleman standing beside him leaned to whisper in his ear. The man's gaze landed on Nathaniel and Hope as he spoke to the captain, and the gleam in his eyes sent a ripple of unease down Nathaniel's back.

The commanding shouts of officers drew Nathaniel's attention back to the main deck where amidst the sailors scrambling to follow orders, a small group of passengers—satchels, and valises in hand—scurried across the deck. Several crewmen followed behind them. One by one, they slid over the railing and climbed down to a waiting boat.

The captain marched to the quarterdeck railing and thrust a fist in their direction. "Begone with you, then. Leave, you yellow-livered cowards." He let out a wicked chortle. "We have no need of your kind."

Nathaniel reached out and grabbed one of the departing crewmen, a young boy with shaggy brown hair and red splotches on his face.

"Why are you leaving?"

"A hurricane, sir." He gestured toward the angry sky in the east. "Headin' this way."

"You don't know for certain," Nathaniel said. "Most likely, 'tis just a summer storm."

"Mebbe, but I ain't takin' me chances. Not for the likes o' Cap'n Conway." Fear sparked in the young boy's brown eyes, and he hurried off after his companions.

Nathaniel eyed the thick clouds piling atop the horizon. By sailing this time of year, they risked facing one of the monstrous storms, but many a year passed in which none occurred. He glanced at Hope, whose attentions had shifted to the handsome, light-haired man who'd been speaking to the captain but who now marched across the deck issuing orders and sending looks of interest her way. Nathaniel huffed. He needed to get her settled in her quarters below—away from the eyes of unsavory men. He needed to escort her safely home. And the sooner the better. His inquiries at port had told him there would not be another ship bound for Kingstown for two weeks. And that was far too long to wait on the whim of a possible storm.

A loud *crack* pierced the air followed by the snap of twine and the groan of heavy crates. "Look out below!" someone yelled.

Nathaniel shot a quick glance above him, dropped his bag, grabbed Hope's arm, and yanked her out of the way.

Slam! The crunch and crack of wood shot across the deck. A jarring impact shook the brig. Hope leaned into him, her chest heaving. "Oh my!"

Atop the spot where they had just stood lay the shattered pieces of several crates. Clothing, jewelry, spices, and coffee spilled from the splintered cavities. Ale chugged onto the deck from a cracked barrel. Nathaniel said a quick prayer of thanks. If he hadn't looked up in time, both he and Hope would have been crushed. He spotted the edge of his brown bag beneath a massive box, and a muscle knotted in his chest.

"Thank you, Mr. Mason. You have saved my life once again." Hope raised a hand to her forehead and laid her head on his shoulder. "I feel faint."

Nathaniel flinched at the feel of her soft curves pressed against him, but he feared if he moved aside, she'd swoon to the deck and he'd be forced to take her in his arms.

The young man Hope had been watching with such interest shouted obscenities at the sailors manning the ropes. His cropped sandy hair flopped in the breeze as he marched across the deck, shifting a harried gaze over the broken crates and pieces of rope littering the deck. His eyes settled upon Nathaniel, then Hope, and he charged toward them.

"My apologies, sir, miss. Are you both unharmed?"

"Yes. I believe so." Nathaniel eased Hope away and brushed the dust from his waistcoat. "However, my dunnage was not so fortunate. I believe it has suffered an early death."

The young man clicked his tongue and stared at what remained of Nathaniel's bag. "I hope it contained nothing of value."

Just everything I had left of my ship. Nathaniel grimaced and gave Hope a curt smile. Since he'd met her yesterday, he'd lost his ship, nearly his life, and now everything else he carried on his journey: clothing, his prize spyglass, his mother's locket, his ship's logbook, among other valued mementos—all in his efforts to save her. If he believed in such things, he might think she was a woman of bad fortune.

"Mr. Gavin Keese." The young man extended his hand to Nathaniel. "I'm the second mate." He glanced at Hope, admiration glinting in his eyes.

"A pleasure, Mr. Keese. I am Nathaniel Mason, the navigator." Nathaniel grabbed his hand and gave it a strong but friendly shake.

"Aye, good. Then we shall be working together. As you can see, many of the crew have abandoned the ship in fear of a little storm." His features wrinkled in disgust. "Which has left the remainder a bit overwrought, I'm afraid. No doubt the cause of this mishap." He shifted his admiring gaze back to Hope. "And this is. . . ?"

Nathaniel ground his teeth together. "Forgive me. May I introduce Miss Hope Westcott." He forced a smile.

With a gentlemanly bow, Mr. Keese placed a kiss upon her ungloved fingers. Hope gave him a coy smile that would have melted even the most zealous priest.

Several seconds—which seemed like long minutes—dragged by in which Mr. Keese and Hope's eyes and hands remained locked in a lingering, playful dalliance.

The biscuit Nathaniel ate to break his fast that morning began to rebel in his stomach. He had assumed the burden of escorting Hope safely home, but he had neither the time nor the inclination to deal with any more of her troublesome liaisons. Grimacing, he fought back the urge to step between Hope and her new admirer. Instead, he cleared his throat. "I must check in with the captain."

"Good. I shall keep Miss Hope company until you return." Mr. Keese's blue eyes never left hers. "If that's acceptable with her, of course."

She smiled her approval, both of them ignoring Nathaniel.

Growling, he stormed off to report to the captain, who ordered him to show Hope to her stateroom and get to work.

Nathaniel returned and proffered his elbow once again. "Shall we?"

"Nay, I'm quite comfortable here." She waved at him, engulfed in laughter at something Mr. Keese had said.

"I thought you were feeling faint."

"It seems to have passed," she said in a lighthearted tone but did not meet his eyes.

Mr. Keese scratched the sable-colored whiskers on his jawline. "Alas, I fear I must be about my work as well, Miss Hope." He kissed her hand again. "But I'm sure we shall see each other soon."

"Yes, I'm sure we will." Hope watched the young man saunter away before she took Nathaniel's arm with a sigh.

Disgust simmered in his belly as he assisted her down the companionway ladder. "Perhaps you should avoid playing the coquette until you return to Charles Towne." He intended to keep the sarcasm from his voice, but it rang clear in the narrow hallway.

"Coquette? Why, I was doing no such thing." She released his arm. The ship rolled and she bumped into the bulkhead. Rubbing her elbow, she continued beside him. "I was simply being kind to Mr. Keese."

Kind indeed. Nathaniel led her through the dim hallway to the forecabin, where he was told the women were staying. "Most men will not attribute your attentions to mere kindness, Miss Hope." He halted at the door. "Ah, here we are."

"And pray tell, what will they attribute them to?" Her words fired at him like musket shots.

Nathaniel wiped the sweat from the back of his neck and leaned toward her ear. "Perchance it was this *being kind*, as you call it, that has caused the mess in which you currently find yourself."

She shot her gaze up to his, bumping his chin with her forehead. Light from a nearby lantern hanging on the deckhead filtered down upon her, revealing moist, fiery eyes. "If you are implying I am some trollop who throws herself at any man who comes along, you are mistaken. Lord Falkland and I loved each other, or at least so I thought." She lowered her gaze and rubbed her forehead. "I would have married him. . . if. . .well, never mind. I do not have to explain myself to you, nor stand here and bear your insults."

"I'm afraid you do, at least until I am able to escort you home."

Hope opened her mouth to reply but slammed it shut and looked away.

Opening the door to the forecabin, Nathaniel ushered her inside and closed the door before she thought of a sassy retort. Turning, he stomped down the hallway and back up on deck. Gazing out upon the dark boiling sky, he tried to shake away all thoughts of Hope. Harrowing or not, her experience of the past few weeks had obviously not changed her. When confronted with the first handsome man who offered her attention, she had all too soon resumed her flirtatious ways. Perhaps God had prevented their acquaintance in Charles Towne for that reason.

Yet why was Nathaniel still so drawn to her?

Why, Lord?

When she was everything he didn't want in a woman. Without God, without morals, and unwilling to take a good look at herself and see her need for change. The decorous reputation he worked so hard to obtain would only suffer should he entangle himself with such a woman. Nathaniel rubbed his aching side and stiffened as a gust of wind struck him. What if they did encounter a hurricane? He prayed he'd made the right decision. Yet he could not fathom adding another two weeks to his time with Hope. Facing a storm at sea seemed preferable to spending any more time with her than necessary. Women like her caused nothing but problems, heartache, broken lives. . . .

And orphaned children.

CHAPTER 5

Removing her shoes from her bandaged feet, Hope plopped onto one of the beds built into the bulwarks. A sharp pain shot up her back. Lifting the thin feather mattress revealed naught but solid wood beneath. Even imprisoned aboard Falkland's ship, she'd been given a real bed.

Falkland. Arthur.

Her heart felt like a lead weight at the thought of him. Leaning over, she rubbed her burning eyes, trying to barricade any further tears from falling. The smell of rotting wood and some foul odor she could not identify wafted around her, permeating her skin and making her feel filthier, more unworthy than she already did. She brushed a wayward tear from her face. Would the pain ever go away?

Flirting with Mr. Keese had softened it, at least for a moment. It helped to know other men appreciated her beauty and charm, even if Lord Falkland had not. Without much sleep and even with puffy red circles beneath her eyes from crying half the night, she still could turn a gentleman's head.

All save Nathaniel. What a perplexing man. Whenever she began to think he had succumbed to her charms, he would turn away, donning an impenetrable shield against her coquettish darts.

She huffed. Why on earth did she care? Though he had proven himself to be an honorable man, he was naught but a commoner, a tradesman. Why would she want him?

Why would he want me? Used goods, soiled, and worthless.

Nathaniel had rescued her out of his Christian duty. Whenever he looked at her—which he made every effort to avoid doing, as if he could catch some disease from her—disapproval burned in his gaze.

Rising, Hope stepped to the tiny window and gazed out at St. Kitts.

Workers, merchants, and sailors buzzed about the small town like ants. A chill swept over her at the thought she could right now be at the mercy of that hideous merchantman.

If not for Nathaniel Mason.

Anguish seeped through her. All she had ever wanted was to find a man who would truly love her, marry her, and give her a brood of children. She loved children, their sweetness, their innocence yet untainted by the cruel world. She had often dreamed of someday opening an orphanage in Charles Towne—a place where unwanted children would be loved and protected, a place where they could enjoy the sweet childhood she never had. Lord Falkland had wanted children—at least he had told her as much, but now she wondered if anything he had said had been true.

She let out a sordid chuckle and swiped a tear from her cheek. Who did she think she was? Women like her didn't run orphanages. Only decent, virtuous women like her sister Grace were entrusted with the care of innocent children.

Peering through the salt-encrusted stains on the window, Hope watched as everything on the tiny island twisted and distorted like some maniacal nightmare—just like her life. How had she ended up in this place? Where had things gone so drastically wrong? She had thrown herself into the arms of a man, given herself away in the hope he would love her and marry her. And her wanton, foolish behavior had nearly cost her everything. But now she had a second chance. She would strive to improve herself—to become a true virtuous lady, strong and brave like her sister Faith, and honest and pure like her sister Grace. Then she would capture the heart of a true gentleman, and then, maybe then, this agonizing emptiness within her would be filled.

The door swung open, and in walked a tall girl in a plain cotton gown, valise in hand. When she saw Hope, her face lit with a huge smile. "Oh, forgive me for intruding." She glanced around the room. "I believe I am staying in this cabin, too. I am Abigail Sheldon." She placed her things on the middle cot and untied the ribbon beneath her chin before removing her bonnet.

"Hope Westcott." Hope returned her smile.

Hair the color of chestnuts spilled from Miss Sheldon's pins. "'Tis windy aboard ship." She attempted to tuck the loose strands back in place.

Sparkling hazel eyes reached out to Hope with more clarity and innocence than she had seen in a long while. A cheerful peace cascaded around the young girl like a refreshing waterfall, and Hope liked her immediately.

"I suppose we are the only two unattached females aboard," Miss Sheldon said as the ship swayed, forcing her to hold onto a beam for support.

"Indeed? I hadn't realized." Hope found it surprising she wasn't the only lone woman. Most ladies wouldn't dare travel unescorted, unless they were the type who entertained men for profit.

The snap of canvas and the pounding of sailors' feet above deck filled the room. They would soon set sail, and Hope would once again be at sea. Only this time, she sailed home to the safety of her sisters' arms instead of into an unknown tempest. This time, she sailed farther away from Lord Falkland—Arthur—instead of traveling to a wedding she realized now would be played out only in her dreams.

He sold me as a slave. She could not deny the truth blaring like a trumpet through her mind, but the sound had not fully penetrated the wall around her heart. She could not allow it. Not yet. For she feared it would drive her utterly mad.

"Miss Westcott. Miss Westcott."

Hope gazed at the young girl smiling down at her. "Forgive me. My thoughts were elsewhere."

"I was saying that I believe the only other woman aboard is a Mrs. Hendr—"

Instantly the door opened and the modishly dressed lady Hope had seen earlier on deck entered the room, a small girl, no more than six years old, in tow.

"Ah, there she is. I was just telling Miss Westcott we are the only three women aboard. Well, four, if you count your daughter." Miss Sheldon knelt and smiled at the girl clinging to her mother's dress. Red curls spiraled from beneath a straw bonnet, and wide blue eyes glanced their way before she snuggled into a fold of her mother's skirt.

The poor thing looked petrified, and Hope longed to scoop her into her arms and reassure her all would be well.

The woman waved her silk fan about her face and sighed. "I wanted to stay with my husband, but the captain doesn't permit couples together on the ship, though I cannot imagine why, and now Miss Elise and I must lodge with two perfect strangers." Her blue eyes widened as her gaze flicked between Hope and Miss Sheldon. "Oh, do forgive me. I am quite distraught. I'm not good at traveling. Elise has not been away from home, and I fear she's caught one of those hideous tropical fevers. Can you feel her skin? Does she feel warm to you?" She pushed the hesitant girl closer to Miss Sheldon and closed the door behind her.

Hope's head spun with the woman's constant chattering, but aside from her unbridled tongue, she was quite lovely. Close to Hope's age, if not a few years older, she carried herself with a lofty urbanity expected of her station. Her flawless creamy skin was crowned with a fashionable coiffeur of hair the color of mahogany. A crimson overgown sat graciously upon her exquisitely laced bodice, which ended in a trim of flowered embroidery. The young girl, dressed no less stylishly, allowed Miss Sheldon to touch her face.

"Nay, Mrs. Hendrick. She feels quite healthy to me."

"My goodness, thank you, but I am sure she is not well. Come, Elise, you must rest." The mother assisted her daughter in taking off her shoes and helped her climb onto a cot. "You can never be too careful." Plopping beside the child, she waved her fan about her as if she could swat away the heat and the foul smell saturating the cabin.

"Forgive me, I am Mrs. Hendrick, and this is Miss Elise Hendrick." She eased a lock of her daughter's hair from her brow, and the girl smiled up at her mother, then uttered a hushed "Pleased to meet you" in their direction.

"Abigail Sheldon." Miss Sheldon gave a quick curtsy.

Hope nodded at Mrs. Hendrick. "Hope Westcott."

"Well, I suppose 'tis good to have female companionship aboard this vessel, especially with so many unseemly men on board. I mean"—Mrs. Hendrick leaned toward them as if she had a grand secret to share—"you would not believe the way I was ogled over when I first arrived. Upon my word, it was most frightening, but at least I have a husband to watch over me." She huffed and eyed the door. "Where is that man with our things? Faith, but 'tis hot in here, and so small. How shall we manage? I cannot believe William has allowed me to suffer so."

"I'm sure we will all get along splendidly." Miss Sheldon brushed the feathery strands of hair from her forehead and gave Mrs. Hendrick a look of confidence.

Hope felt none of the same assurance. The woman had naught to complain about. They all suffered under the same conditions. At least Mrs. Hendrick had a husband, a child, and obviously plenty of wealth. Hope had nothing but the dress on her back and her torn chemise and stained corset beneath it. She had lost everything: her dignity, her reputation—and her heart.

"*All by your own doing.*" The gentle voice eased over Hope's conscience as her throat burned with sorrow. It was true. She deserved her fate.

A loud *crack* sounded from above, and the ship lurched. At last they were departing this uncivilized island.

Mrs. Hendrick regarded both Miss Sheldon and Hope with a curious eye. "How did you ladies come to be traveling alone?"

Miss Sheldon wrung her hands together and stepped to the door before turning to face them. Her eyes moistened and she seemed to be having trouble speaking. "My parents were killed recently," she blurted out in a strained voice.

"Oh, my dear, I'm so sorry." Mrs. Hendrick dashed to her and grabbed her hands.

Hope swallowed and thought of her own mother—of happier times, of feeling protected, loved, and cherished—feelings long since buried beneath the soil of Portsmouth, along with her mother. "I, too, lost my mother."

Miss Sheldon whisked a tear from her cheek and smiled. "Then you understand."

Plucking a handkerchief from her pocket, Mrs. Hendrick handed it to Miss Sheldon. "If I may be so bold, what happened to them?"

"They were killed in a slave uprising in Antigua last month." Miss Sheldon bowed her head.

"Oh my. How horrible." Mrs. Hendrick placed an arm around the girl's shoulders. "What was your family doing on such a savage island?"

"My parents were missionaries with the Society for the Propagation of the Gospel in Foreign Parts," Miss Sheldon managed to utter between sobs.

Mrs. Hendrick's face contorted. "Indeed. How nice." Releasing Miss

Sheldon, she took a step back. "Have you no other relations? Are you all alone?"

"Nay, 'tis only me left." Miss Sheldon accepted the handkerchief Mrs. Hendrick offered and dabbed her cheeks, where despite the sorrow etching slick trails down her skin, a glow still emanated. "Me and God, that is."

Mrs. Hendrick patted her stylish coiffeur and sat back down beside her daughter, who had lain down and closed her eyes.

Hope sighed. She had hoped she and Miss Sheldon could become friends, but once the pious girl discovered Hope's marred past, she would most likely have nothing to do with her.

The brig groaned and creaked over the rising swells as it no doubt made its way out onto the open sea. Placing her hand over her stomach, Mrs. Hendrick directed her curiosity upon Hope. "And you, Miss Westcott?"

Hope flattened her lips and grabbed a lock of her hair. Her story was as far removed from Miss Sheldon's as a bishop's from a trollop's, and she knew the telling of it would bring her neither credit nor sympathy from these two particular women. "I shall not bore you with the tale, Mrs. Hendrick. Suffice it to say I am on my way home to Charles Towne where my family awaits me."

"But a young lady traveling alone? Are you not afraid?"

"There is a gentleman who travels with me. He is a member of the crew."

"A relation?"

Though tempted to lie, Hope knew Mr. Mason would not confirm her deceit. But she so dearly wanted these ladies to like her, to approve of her, befriend her. She could use a friend right now, someone who would understand the pain of a broken heart. "Merely an acquaintance who rescued me in a great time of need." She braced herself for the sanctimonious looks of disapproval.

"How romantic." Miss Sheldon sniffed and offered Hope a faint smile.

"I assure you it is not." Hope gazed out the tiny window, where all she could see from her bunk was clear blue sky.

"'Tis most unseemly." Mrs. Hendrick gave a ladylike snort and stared at Hope as if she were naught but an annoying rodent—the same look

Hope had received a thousand times from the proper ladies of Charles Towne, a look that made her feel like manure on the street, fit only to be trampled upon.

She supposed she deserved no better.

Averting her gaze before they saw the moisture fill her eyes, Hope knew it would do no good to try to defend herself to this woman. She had tried before with Mrs. Hendrick's type and never gotten anywhere. Once these so-called genteel ladies made up their minds about a woman's virtue, nothing would dissuade them.

Hope lay down on the bed with a *clunk*, giving up her dream to finally have a friend. She never seemed to measure up in other women's eyes. Either they were jealous of her or they thought her too crude or too wanton or too far beneath them. The scorching looks and disdainful attitudes they shot her way never missed their mark as they might suppose. She felt every one of them like a sharp blade in her heart.

Men were a different sort of animal. Hope rarely had problems befriending men. They adored her, they lavished gifts upon her, they made her feel special. And besides, they were far more interesting than most women she knew, save for her sister Faith.

Hope squeezed her eyes shut, wishing she could shut out the world around her as easily, or at least the two women in her cabin. Or should she? Perhaps stowed away in quarters no bigger than a necessary room with two constant reminders of her inadequacies was indeed a fitting punishment. One she could make the best of. She could learn from these women. Learn how a proper lady behaves. Start afresh and prove to everyone on this ship that she was as virtuous as any true lady.

Excitement jolted through her, and she sat up. No one knew her past here. She could change—she *would* change. And when she returned to Charles Towne, she would prove her new character to everyone—first to her sisters and then to those who had shunned her. Then, maybe then, she could catch the heart of a gentleman, open up an orphanage, and fulfill her life's dream.

CHAPTER 6

"Miss Westcott, you are looking quite lovely this evening." Captain Conway's gaze took in Hope as if she were a sweetmeat. With a flip of his coattails, he took his seat at the head of the table laden with more food than Hope had seen since she had begun her foolish escapade aboard Falkland's ship nigh on two weeks ago. A steaming platter of roast pork perched in the center between two flickering candles. Bowls of plantains, mangos, rice, corn, and biscuits spread across the wooden table, their sweet and spicy scents rising to join in a melodious aroma. Hope's stomach lurched in anticipation.

"Why, thank you, Captain." She gave him a curt smile but looked away, not wanting to encourage his attentions. Circling the table, Nathaniel sat across from her, a scowl on his face.

When he'd come to escort her and Miss Sheldon to the captain's quarters for dinner, Hope had been elated—on one account to be freed from the stifling cabin and on another because her stomach had been growling like a wild beast all afternoon. But it was the pleasant way her heart leapt when she had opened the door to see Nathaniel's handsome face that gave her pause.

Pushing aside the uncomfortable reaction, she'd happily taken his arm, while Miss Sheldon clutched the other, and he had escorted them both to dinner as if they were going to a ball.

"Thank you for the invitation, Captain." She felt Mr. Keese's eyes upon her from his seat to her right, but placing her hands in her lap, she ignored him. "Surely you do not feast like this every night?"

Captain Conway fingered his pointed gray beard. "Nay, miss, especially when we've been long out to sea." Pockmarks marred his sun-blistered skin that looked as thick as a cowhide, and although the gray hair strewn

361

throughout his head told a tale of a hard life at sea, his lively bronze-colored eyes revealed a much younger man within.

Over his shoulder, through the stern window, Hope noticed the sun sinking wearily behind the ebony horizon, waving glorious ribbons of crimson, gold, and copper onto the choppy sea in its evening farewell.

A pudgy, well-dressed man burst into the room, grumbling his apologies, and took a seat to the right of the captain.

"Ah, now that we are all here," the captain announced, "may I introduce Mr. Herbert Russell." He gestured toward the man, who nodded with a grunt. "And beside him, Major Harold Paine."

The stiff man, dressed in a red military coat crossed with a white baldric, slid a finger over his thin mustache and narrowed his eyes over the guests.

"Then, Mr. Mason, my new navigator." Nathaniel gave a cursory glance around the table before his gaze locked upon Hope's and remained there. An emotion she could not determine brewed within them, and she squirmed beneath his perusal.

The captain continued. "Miss Abigail Sheldon, I believe?"

"Yes, Captain." Miss Sheldon smiled.

Turning in his chair, Captain Conway nodded to the dashing man at his left. "Mr. William Hendrick." Hope leaned forward to study Mrs. Hendrick's husband, the man she'd seen on deck earlier. Still attired in his stylish garb, he barely acknowledged the introduction, nor anyone else in the room for that matter, as he poured wine into his glass from a pewter decanter.

"Beside him, Mr. Gavin Keese," the captain continued. "My second mate on this journey." Mr. Keese nodded toward everyone then grinned at Hope, a sparkle in his eye.

"And finally, the lovely Miss Hope Westcott."

Hope smiled as sweetly as she could at all the guests, searching for some kindness, some approval in their eyes. Back in Charles Towne, her inappropriate deeds and those of her sister Faith had put a stain on their family's reputation. But here among these strangers, Hope could start anew. And what better way than with a military officer, a captain, and two wealthy businessmen—obviously gentlemen all. She longed to be treated like a lady, not like a stained handkerchief to be used and tossed aside.

Not like Falkland had treated her.

"A fine spread, Captain." Mr. Russell rubbed his hands together, his eyes gleaming as he examined the banquet.

"For our first night at sea, and with such important guests, I could think of no better way to start our journey." Captain Conway poured wine into his glass. "Besides, 'twould be a crime indeed to have two such lovely ladies on board and not enjoy their beauty."

A red hue crept up Miss Sheldon's face as the captain shifted his eyes her way.

"Indeed," Mr. Keese agreed.

"Speaking of beauty, where is your wife, Mr. Hendrick?" the captain asked the modish man on his left.

"She is not well." He sipped his drink. "You know how women cannot handle the sea."

"I'm sorry to hear of it."

Hope bit her lip. *Cannot handle the sea, indeed.* She wanted to correct him—to inform him that if he tore his eyes from his drink, he might see two healthy women seated at the table with him, but she thought better of it. No sense in stirring up trouble, especially for poor Mrs. Hendrick. Hope had left her casting her accounts into her chamber pot, and although Miss Sheldon had wanted to stay and care for her, Mrs. Hendrick would have none of it. Nor would she allow Hope to take Miss Elise to dinner.

The ship bucked over a wave. Creaks and groans filled the room, and plates shifted on the table. Hope gasped, and Mr. Keese placed his hand on hers beneath the table and winked. The warmth of his skin and his playful dalliance lifted Hope's spirits, and she longed to encourage his affections—if only to ease the agony wrenching at her heart. Instead, she snatched her hand from beneath his and looked away.

"Shall we begin?" The captain reached for a plate of steaming rice.

"Should we not bless the food, Captain?" Miss Sheldon asked.

Nathaniel's stiff lips finally cracked in a smile as he nodded approvingly at Miss Sheldon. They exchanged a glance that sent uncomfortable needles prickling across Hope's chest, befuddling her mind as to the cause. She took a sip of wine.

"Of course. Of course." The captain blew out a snort and stared at his plate. "God in heaven, bless this meal and keep us safe on our journey. Amen." He said the prayer with such rapidity, it seemed he feared the food would vanish before he finished.

"Amen," Miss Sheldon and Nathaniel said in unison.

Soon bowls and platters were passed, and they all piled the savory food onto their plates. Hope spooned the tasty pork, corn, and rice into her mouth as fast as ladylike decorum would allow. She had not had a meal like this since she left Charles Towne, and her stomach sang in thanksgiving with each bite. Succulent, moist, and spicy, the pork reminded Hope of Molly's cooking back home. Home. Part of her missed it terribly—the security, the love of her sisters—but part of her dreaded going back, dreaded the memories of Lord Falkland on every corner, dreaded the accusing whispers behind her back, the ruined reputation she dragged behind her like a cannonball on a chain.

But for now, she was far from home, enjoying the attentions and admiration of reputable men. Helping herself to more wine, she forced a smile. Her sister Grace would never allow her to indulge so at home.

Nathaniel stabbed a chunk of pork. "Captain, I hear you are new to the Caribbean. If I may ask, where did you sail before?"

"I sailed a run between Boston and Liverpool for many years." He pushed his food around with his fork.

"What brings you south?" Nathaniel leaned back in his chair.

"I grew tired of the cold seas and North Atlantic storms," he mumbled. A momentary glimpse of sorrow burned in his eyes before their gleam returned. "And word is there is a fortune to be made here in the West Indies. Mr. Russell, here, knows all about that." The captain slapped the back of the man sitting to his right. "Don't you, Herbert? He's found his pot of gold trading on these seas."

Mr. Russell smacked his moist lips together, sending his pendulous jowls swinging. "Quite so. Quite so. Currently, I am on my way to purchase land in the Carolinas."

"Indeed?" Hope said. "I am sailing to Charles Towne, Mr. Russell. My family resides there."

"Then we shall see much of each other, my dear. I hear the land is plentiful and well suited for rice and indigo."

"You are correct, sir. Plantations and farms are springing up everywhere, and the town itself is growing so rapidly they are being forced to knock down the walls enclosing it for lack of room."

"So I have heard." He grinned. "A perfect time to purchase land in these burgeoning colonies." Mr. Russell plopped a chunk of pork into his mouth, chewed it to satisfaction, and then faced the man beside him. "Major Paine, pray tell, inform us of the happenings on the Leeward Islands."

The major straightened his already rigid posture and set down his fork, sprinkled with rice. "As you know, the lieutenant governor is sick with malaria. Hence I am traveling to England to convince Whitehall to instate me as the new governor should he die." He glanced around the room as if looking for admiration.

Mr. Keese chuckled. "Sink me. The poor man's shoes will still be warm when you snatch them from his body."

Miss Sheldon brushed her hair from her forehead. "Heaven forfend, Major. We should pray for the lieutenant governor's recovery instead of planning for his demise."

"Well said, Miss Sheldon." Nathaniel dropped a slice of mango into his mouth and gave the young missionary a look of approval.

Another sting of discomfort struck Hope. Without thinking, she leaned close to Mr. Keese—so close she could smell the sea in his hair—and asked him to pass the corn. Their shoulders brushed, and his eyes glinted with interest, but when she glanced back at Nathaniel, he covered a yawn with his hand and looked away.

Fisting her hands beneath the table, Hope chided herself for her behavior. A proper lady did not draw so close to a man. Why had she done it? She flattened her lips. This task of transforming into a genteel lady was not going to be as easy as she first assumed.

Hope rubbed her brow, trying to still the dizzying effects of the wine and make sense out of her unusual reactions to Nathaniel. Honorable, God-fearing Mr. Mason. He reminded her of Captain Waite, her sister's beau back home.

Major Paine's jaw stiffened. "Of course I pray night and day for the man's recovery, but in the best interest of England and due to the distance, the transfer of power must be done promptly, or chaos will rule on these islands."

"Aye, and we wouldn't want chaos to rule." Mr. Keese's eyebrows arched mischievously.

"Indeed, sir, we would not." Major Paine huffed and adjusted his black cravat. "I hope, Mr. Keese, that despite your insolence, your loyalties lie with England."

"I am loyal to none but myself." Mr. Keese shrugged and scooped a spoon of rice into this mouth.

"I have heard pirates say as much."

"Indeed? Then I am in good company."

Major Paine scratched beneath his white periwig and slowly rose to his feet. "You implicate yourself with those vile blackguards, sir?"

Hope's breath quickened. Was there to be a duel? Right here in the captain's cabin? Raising a hand to her throat, she eyed Mr. Keese, who sprang to his feet as if he didn't have a care in the world.

Pressing an open palm toward Mr. Keese, Nathaniel stood and leveled his other hand toward the major. "Ignore the boy, Major. He is clearly jesting with you and means no harm. Do you, Mr. Keese?"

Before he could answer, the captain bellowed. "Aye, Mr. Mason is correct," he said, a crumb flying from his mouth as he waved a biscuit toward the major. "I know the boy's father. A good Dutch merchant. His mother is from Southampton. Mr. Keese is an excellent seaman and is loyal to whomever he sails with, but he is no pirate."

The major sat down with a growl. "A man should know how to control his tongue."

Mr. Keese took his seat. A daring gleam shone from his eyes.

"More wine, Miss Westcott?" He held the decanter and began filling Hope's cup before she could answer. Charming, brave, and adventurous, Mr. Keese was every woman's dream. If he possessed wealth and land, he could have his pick of ladies, but for now, his attentions had the glorious effect of soothing her broken heart. The difficulty was, she had no idea how to respond to them without being unseemly. He continued pouring wine, caught up in her gaze, and splashed some of the red liquid onto the table.

"Oh, forgive me." He chuckled.

"Truly understandable with such a charming lady at your side," the captain chortled as he grabbed another biscuit from the tray.

"And what about you, Mr. Keese?" Hope asked, taking a sip of her wine. The warm liquid slid down her throat, setting her belly aflame and her head into a daze. "How did you come to be traveling on board this ship?"

"My father was in the Dutch West India Company, miss. He brought my mother and me to Curacao ten years ago. Sooner than I could walk, I learned to sail." He chuckled. "And when I was of age, I left home to seek fortune and fame. I am on this ship because the opportunity presented itself to me and I took it."

Mr. Hendrick leaned forward to glare at Mr. Keese as if he were a commodity unworthy of his purchase. "To procure either, you must have a plan and the forbearance to carry it out. I sense neither in a man so brash."

"Begging your pardon, sir, but I have acquired some fortune. Not enough fame as of yet, but I carry a shipload of adventures in my pocket"— he patted his black doublet—"enough to stir a man's soul for quite some time."

Major Paine snorted. "A man without discipline is a man without honor."

The ship lunged in a creaking protest, sloshing water from the top of a pitcher and spraying rice kernels over the table like sand. The brass lantern in front of Nathaniel teetered, and he grabbed it, steadying it before it fell. Light shimmered across his brown eyes—eyes that seemed to pierce right through Hope—offering a challenge. A flood of warmth swept over her beneath his gaze. Or perhaps it was simply the wine.

"Well, I, for one, find that type of life exciting," Hope declared, knowing full well she was not suited to such a reckless existence. It was her sister Faith who relished the unknown, who lived for each daring escapade.

"I am sure you will discover fortune and fame are overrated, Mr. Keese." Miss Sheldon's soft tone held neither pretentious accusation nor pious reprimand, but was said as simply a matter of understanding.

Mr. Russell belched while Mr. Hendrick turned to face the young girl, a smug look on his handsome face. "Easily said coming from someone who clearly has neither."

"What a cruel thing to say." Hope's voice blared louder than she intended. Still, she could not let the pompous man insult such a sweet lady.

Nathaniel directed a hard gaze toward Mr. Hendrick. "Apologize to the lady at once, sir."

"'Tis no matter." Miss Sheldon suffered the insult with a grace that seemed to sweeten her face—if that were possible. She swept a reassuring gaze over Hope and Nathaniel before turning to Mr. Hendrick, whose face had purpled at Nathaniel's command. "I assure you, Mr. Hendrick, I know of what I speak. My parents possessed great wealth in England, in addition to land. They gave up their worldly possessions to become missionaries."

"Perhaps, Miss Sheldon." Mr. Hendrick stifled his anger beneath another swig of wine. "But a lot of good it has done them. I heard they were murdered by the very people they were hoping to convert."

Miss Sheldon lowered her gaze.

"Enough," Nathaniel barked. "Can you not see the lady is still distraught over the loss of her parents?" A vein pulsed on his forehead.

Envy burned within Hope. She could not recall any man coming to her defense so vehemently, not even her father—and certainly not an honorable man like Nathaniel. A sudden desire to become worthy of the esteem of such a gentleman welled within her. If she could capture his regard, especially since he knew of her past, then surely that would be proof she had achieved the status of a proper and virtuous lady.

The captain slammed down his glass. "Calm yourself, Mr. Mason. Mr. Hendrick is my guest. But"—he pointed a finger at Mr. Hendrick— "I insist you treat all my guests with respect while you are on board my ship, sir."

Mr. Hendrick waved a hand through the air. "Egad. Cool your humors. I meant nothing by it." He took another gulp of his drink as Nathaniel fastened his glare upon the peevish man.

Captain Conway turned toward Miss Sheldon. "I do hope you'll forgive the outburst, Miss Sheldon. I fear the company is not what you are accustomed to. Please tell us what brings you aboard my fine ship."

Miss Sheldon's smile had returned. "I am traveling to Kingstown. A family friend, Reverend Hickman, has offered me a place to stay and a chance to continue my parents' missionary work there among the natives and slaves."

"Quite admirable." Nathaniel's eyes reflected astonishment as well as admiration. He scratched his jaw and looked at Hope as if comparing her to this holy, pristine, selfless angel beside him.

But of course there was no comparison.

Instead of enduring the disappointment she knew she'd find on his face, Hope watched the last traces of light fade from the horizon as darkness hovered over the sea like a bird of prey.

The food soured in her stomach, and she took another sip of wine.

"Not sure you can save these savage Indians. They are far too ignorant to understand the complexities of Christianity," Mr. Russell commented between shoving forkfuls of food into his mouth.

"The Christian message is not complex, sir," Nathaniel said, "but easy enough for a child to understand and embrace."

"Are you a religious man, Mr. Mason?" The captain shoved his plate aside and settled back in his chair.

"I was raised by a reverend, but I would consider myself more God-fearing than religious."

Hope flinched. She knew Nathaniel had been reared by Reverend Halloway, but God-fearing? Truly, he and Miss Sheldon were a perfect match.

Mr. Hendrick huffed. "There is no money in God's work. And a man is nothing without wealth and land. When I began my own business at age eighteen, I had nothing, not a shilling to my name. Now I own a fleet of merchant ships and a plantation on St. Kitts. Respect, power, and freedom." He cocked a condescending brow. "That's what money can buy you, sir."

"It cannot buy you freedom, Mr. Hendrick," Mr. Keese remarked, and Hope wondered why he dared to cross the man again. "Freedom you must take at your own risk. Money and land, they hold you captive, while I am free to go and do whatever I want." He gave the man a sarcastic smirk.

"'Tis my wife who holds me captive, sir," he countered with a chuckle as he poured himself more wine.

The man's disparaging remark about his wife made Hope's skin crawl, and she hoped the alcohol spoke for him and his careless words did not reflect his true opinions.

"But pray tell, Mr. Mason, what is your business?" he asked.

"I am a merchant as well. I own two ships or, rather, one now." He huffed but did not look at Hope. "I built them myself."

"Built, you say? Odd's fish." Captain Conway wiped his mouth with his sleeve. "Incredible feat. But how did you lose your ship?" He seemed to be holding back a chuckle.

Nathaniel hesitated as his somber gaze flickered over Hope, renewing her guilt. "An unfortunate circumstance."

"Humph. Any captain who loses his ship deserves his fate. Makes me wonder if you are fit to navigate."

"I assure you, I am quite capable." Nathaniel's jaw tightened. "I have captained my own ships for years and intend to find another to replace the one I lost as soon as possible."

The captain's brow grew dark and his eyes locked upon Nathaniel. "And how, pray tell, do you intend to replace it?"

"I will either purchase one or build another." Nathaniel shrugged.

Captain Conway shifted in his seat and pressed a fat thumb over the worn table. "I run a tight ship, Mr. Mason, and my crew is loyal to me." Spit shot from his mouth at the last sentence, and his eyes simmered, making Hope wonder if his statement were true.

"I have no doubt, Captain." Nathaniel regarded him curiously.

"Rest assured, sir, we are less than adequately manned." The captain picked up his glass. "And I will expect you to do more than a navigator's duties."

"I believe you'll find my work to your satisfaction, Captain." Nathaniel's calm, methodical tone belied the stiffness of his jaw.

"Very well." The captain tipped his glass and downed the rest of his wine. Then his glazed eyes widened and shifted between Hope and Nathaniel while a slow grin crept over his lips. "I believe you are escorting Miss Westcott home, Mr. Mason, are you not?"

"Aye, Captain."

"And how did you come to be in need of escort so far from home, Miss Hope?"

Cringing, Hope stared at her lap, searching her wine-clouded mind for an explanation that would not mar her standing with these people. "'Tis a long, arduous tale, Captain. Suffice it to say, I took the wrong ship, ended up at St. Kitts abandoned, and Mr. Mason graciously offered to escort me home."

"Do you know the man?"

"Yes, we are acquainted from Charles Towne."

"I am a friend of the family," Nathaniel offered, finishing the last bite of pork from his plate.

Major Paine clicked his tongue, while Mr. Hendrick snorted. "I'll wager."

Hope's heart melted at their accusing looks of disdain.

"I assure you our relationship is quite respectable," Mr. Mason added, as if he just realized the implications of his words.

Innocent fool.

"Respectable enough to have sold your brig to purchase the young lady?" The captain snickered and exchanged a knowing glance with Mr. Keese. Gasps burst through the cabin.

Hope felt as if she'd crashed into a cold, hard brick wall.

Mr. Keese's chortle transformed into a cough, which he hid behind his hand.

"Sold a ship to buy a woman?" Mr. Hendrick held his glass of wine in midair as if too shocked to know what to do with it.

"Ah, that explains it, then." Major Paine's eyes lit up.

"And what would that be, Major?" Hope asked sharply, wondering what other sordid details were to be disclosed about her.

"Yes, quite curious. I wondered what the man was doing," Major Paine announced to the whole table with a chuckle.

Hope directed an angry gaze his way. "Whatever do you mean?"

"Outside your door last night."

Shaking her head, Hope wondered if the man had consumed too much wine.

As she had.

She tried to fixate on his expression, but the red and white of his uniform blurred into a bloated pink stain drifting over his face.

"You didn't know? My word. He slept outside your door." Major Paine pointed to Nathaniel. "I thought perhaps you two had a lover's spat." Chuckles rumbled over the table—chuckles directed at her, at her virtue. "Now I realize he was protecting his investment."

Hope stared at her plate of food, stunned. All through the night, she'd wrung her sheets into knots, fearing Nathaniel would either come in and collect his due or abandon her altogether. Instead, he had sacrificed a decent night's sleep by guarding her door like a true gentleman.

"Respectable, eh? I'd say she'd had enough for one night and tossed him out." Mr. Hendrick scoffed.

"I beg your pardon." Hope sprang to her feet then wobbled and clung to the table to keep from falling. Tears swam across her already fuzzy vision. "How dare you?" For once she didn't deserve these people's scorn. For once she had done nothing wrong. At least nothing they knew about. But perhaps they could smell her shame like a festering wound. Perhaps she would never be healed of it.

She glanced over the muted shapes at the table, searching for an ally, a champion, but she couldn't focus on anyone's eyes. She thought she saw Nathaniel rise from his seat, she thought she heard his deep voice bellow in her defense, but all she heard in the end was her shoes clomping over the wooden deck as she dashed from the room.

CHAPTER 7

Hot wind tainted with the scent of salt and wet canvas buffeted Nathaniel as he stormed up the companionway ladder. Fear rippled down his back. He had already knocked upon the forecabin door looking for Hope, but Mrs. Hendrick's feeble voice squeaked from the other side, insisting she was alone. He knew Hope had partaken of too much wine. He knew she was distraught. What he didn't know was what she might do in that condition. He hoped nothing foolish. Yet he had a sense, in the brief time he'd known her, that Hope gave rule to her emotions over her reason far too often.

Silly, selfish girl. She reminded him of flotsam tossed to and fro upon the sea at the mercy of whatever winds happened to cross her path. How could anyone control such an erratic creature? Why should he care? He sighed. Perhaps God meant for him to help her. But how could he help her without losing himself so deeply in her charms that he would never find his way out?

Scanning the deck, he examined every dark shadow, finding only barrels, ropes, and a few sailors well into their cups. He nodded to the night watchman and leapt upon the quarterdeck where the helmsman pressed a steady hand upon the wheel. Their eyes met, and in the gleam of the lantern hanging at the mainmast, the man gestured ahead to the foredeck where Nathaniel made out a dark figure standing at the bow of the ship. The shadow of another figure hovered nearby, causing his heart to jump. Was someone harassing Hope?

He barreled down to the main deck, then jumped up the foredeck ladder and marched toward the bow. But as he approached, the second figure dissipated, leaving Hope standing alone. A night wind lumbered over him, heavy laden with her sobs. Nathaniel halted and rubbed his eyes, aching from lack of sleep. No doubt the reason for the strange apparition.

He eased beside her.

She flinched and swiped at her wet face. "What are you doing here?"

"You left so suddenly. I. . .I wanted to make sure you were. . .well."

She gazed at the dark, churning sea and closed her eyes. Her moist face shimmered in the light of a half moon. "I am quite well, Mr. Mason. Go back to your party."

"Who was here with you?"

"No one. I am alone, as you can see." Then, turning toward the sea, she offered a sad, forlorn smile. "The water looks so enticing, does it not? I had the strangest urge to throw myself into it a minute ago." She shook her head as if trying to wake from a nightmare. "I don't know why."

A chill slithered down Nathaniel. He said a quiet prayer of thanks he had arrived when he had.

The fetid odor from the head pricked his nose. He coughed. "Miss Hope, the stench here is not fitting for a lady. Allow me to escort you back to your cabin."

Her red-rimmed eyes teetered over him as if looking for a place to land. "'Tis exactly where I belong, then."

The ship rose over a swell, sending a warm, salty spray over them. But instead of cringing like most ladies, Hope spread her arms out as if she wished she could take flight. She stumbled, and Nathaniel readied his hands to catch her, but she caught her balance and stood like a wild bird with wings outstretched enjoying the wind in her feathers.

"Miss Hope, you shouldn't be—"

"There's something beautiful about the sea, isn't there? Something almost magical." She staggered. Nathaniel tossed his arm out behind her, but she clutched the railing again and smiled. And in that smile, beyond the fear, beyond the facade, beyond the pain, beamed an innocent little girl.

A protective yearning clutched Nathaniel's throat.

"Aye, the sea can be soothing at times." Nathaniel scratched his chin and gazed out over the dark waters. The wind had eased into a light breeze, yet the ship rocked above massive swells that had grown higher since earlier that day. "But I've spent enough time upon it to know it carries many hidden dangers, as well."

Her frown returned. "I suppose you are correct. Nothing is as good as it seems."

"They were wrong to impugn your character, Miss Hope. Many men, even good men, can be quite crude in their assumptions." Yet even as he said the words, he wondered if something beyond the men's lewd opinions had caused her present distress.

"Their crude assumptions were not incorrect, Mr. Mason. As you well know." Squeezing the remaining tears from her eyes, she drew a shuddering breath and stared down at the white V of foam slicing through the ebony waters.

"The past is in the past." Nathaniel uttered the only thing he could think to say, but deep down, he wondered if it were true. His mother's past, his past, haunted him day and night.

"You are wrong, Mr. Mason. The past follows us like a dark cloud." She tugged upon a loose strand of hair at her neck and scanned the black line of the horizon, though her eyes seemed to stare far beyond it.

"Then start right now to ensure a better past follows you." Precisely what he intended to do—to remove the stains his mother had left on him, on his life, to pull out from under the shame, the poverty, until the past was so far behind him he could no longer see it, could no longer smell it.

She snickered. "I wish it were that easy. Perhaps it is, for someone like you."

"You know nothing of me." The wide expanse of molten charcoal horizon broken only by random silver braids seemed to whisper of a dark hunger. He sensed her torment, evidenced by a small sigh, and turned to face her.

"I know enough." She tightened her lips. "You are the type of man who rescues foolish girls by selling half of all you own in the world. You're the type of man who sits outside a lady's door at night, forfeiting your sleep to protect her after she's ruined your life."

A tear slid down her cheek, and though he tried, Nathaniel could not resist wiping it away with his thumb. Then, easing his fingers down, he caressed her delicate jaw, astonished at the softness of her skin. A shard of desire shot through his belly. It sickened him. Was he so much like his mother he couldn't resist a simple temptation? He dropped his hand and took a step back. "Any honorable man would have done no less."

She gave a little smile. "I am not so sure, Mr. Mason." Stumbling, she gripped the railing again as a blast of wind struck them—oddly, from the west—freeing more of her curls to wave like ribbons of gold behind her. "I had thought. . .I had wanted. . .I wanted to know what it felt like to be treated like a respectable lady." She sniffed. "At least for a time."

Nathaniel swallowed against the burning in his throat. He didn't want to feel sorry for this woman, didn't want to care. She had brought all her trouble, including the way people treated her, upon herself. *So much like his mother.* But this woman's tears seeped into his heart, penetrating the hard crust of his childhood and softening a part of him that longed to take her in his arms—longed to comfort her. "Of what import are their opinions?"

"Of great import." She took in a deep breath.

Nathaniel flinched, realizing the hypocrisy of his question when he himself had sought for years to cast off the shroud of dishonor from his past and emerge into respectful society. "You need no one's approval save God's," he said as much to himself as to Hope.

Her sad, hollow chuckle was snatched away on the wind. "I fear I lost His approval a long time ago."

"Perhaps you lost His approval of your behavior but never His approval of you." A spark of purpose flickered within Nathaniel. Maybe he had been sent to help this woman, after all.

She snorted. "Spare me your religious exhortations. I've heard them all from my sister Grace."

Grunting, Nathaniel crossed his arms over his chest. How could he help someone who refused to be helped? But for now, he must calm her down and get her below before she lost her balance and fell into the sea, or some sailor came across her alone. Anger knotted in his gut at the position she once again had thrust upon him. Perhaps a change of subject would get her mind off her present woes. "Speaking of your sisters, they must be quite worried about you by now. Wasn't your sister Faith locked in the Watch Tower Dungeon?"

The ship plunged over a rising crest, showering them once again with warm, salty spray. Tiny beads of water sparkled over her face, neck, and the rising swell of her bosom, drawing his eyes to a place he had avoided glancing at all night. Coughing, he jerked his gaze back to the sea and rubbed the sweat from the back of his neck. The wind died down again. Yet the waves increased. A prickling of unease chittered down Nathaniel's back.

"Yes. Faith was awaiting trial," she finally said.

"And you left without discovering her fate?" Nathaniel hadn't intended his voice to sound so accusing, but he knew the Westcott sisters were close, and he couldn't imagine one of them leaving another one in danger.

She waved a hand through the air. "She assured me she would receive a pardon. Besides, Lord Falkland was to set sail, and I had no choice."

Nathaniel examined her, wondering if she could be so selfish as to leave with her sister's fate unknown. Or perhaps she had been so besotted with that buffoon Falkland that she had gone temporarily mad. Most likely a bit of both.

Her features hardened. "Don't look at me like that. I love my sisters, and I know they love me. I knew Faith would be fine. She always is." The ship thrust into the next roller, and Hope wobbled and gripped the railing. "I have never fit in with my sisters. Grace is so good that I don't believe she's ever had a vile thought in her life, and Faith is so strong, so brave, so much like our father. There's naught she cannot do if she puts her mind to it." She sighed. "Then, there's me."

Nathaniel grimaced, growing tired of the woman's self-pity. "I am sure God has gifted you with your own special talents." Though he suspected she'd been too preoccupied with carnal pursuits to find them.

"So I've been told." Releasing the railing, she tilted her head to the side and waved her hands over her voluptuous form, a coy smile upon her lips. "This, apparently, is the only gift I have to offer."

The ship jolted, sending Hope stumbling sideways. Nathaniel flung himself in her path, and she fell against him, her warm body molding to his.

His breath caught in his throat. She lifted her face and giggled. The sweet aroma of wine swirled around him. Her sapphire eyes glowed in the moonlight with an innocent pleading that seemed at odds with her libertine behavior.

His heart ran a race in his chest. He glanced at her inviting, parted lips and searched frantically for the anger he harbored against her. Where was it when he needed it most? Gathering his resolve, he gripped her arms, nudged her back a step, and cleared his throat. "It is not all you have to offer, Miss Hope." He tried to speak with firm authority, but his voice, low with passion, belied his statement.

She dropped her head on his shoulder and nestled closer, obviously as unconvinced by his statement as he was. Her golden hair, blowing in the breeze, tickled his nose and smelled of honey.

Lord?

Easing her hands up his arms, she gripped his muscles as if she absorbed strength from them, then she tipped her head up. Her warm breath caressed his chin as she brushed her fingers over the stubble on his jaw. A hot wave crashed over him, and he struggled for a breath of control.

Then her lips pressed upon his.

His limbs went numb as he gave in to the sensations roiling through him. She tasted of wine and mango, and he grew hungrier for more of her. How many times back in Charles Towne had his eyes drifted down to her full, moist lips, and how many times had he dreamed of how they would feel against his? Now as they caressed his cheeks, his chin, his head grew light and his senses reeled, and he knew in that one moment he could either lose himself completely or save himself forever.

Would it be so bad, to take the path his mother had trodden?

God help me.

No! He could not, would never. Pushing Hope away, he tried to catch his breath.

"What is it?" Shock heightened her voice.

"I cannot do this." Shame assaulted him at his behavior, his lack of control. Throughout the years, he'd resisted many women's flirtations, desiring to keep himself pure for his wife, wanting to do things right. But the way this beauty flung about her charms with ease and gave herself away so freely reminded him of exactly where he'd come from. A place to which he had vowed never to return.

She backed away from him, the simmer of passion fading from her eyes, replaced with sorrow, and then a hard sheen. "You asked what my talents were."

"I didn't ask for a demonstration." Nathaniel flexed his jaw, his lips still burning from their kiss.

"I heard no complaints."

"Why do you throw yourself at every man you meet?"

Her expression crumpled. "I don't want to. I'm trying not to." She gave him an angry pout and shook her head. "I don't know." Her shoulders sank. "I made a vow today to change."

"Try not drinking so much wine."

She shot him a fiery gaze.

"And flirting with Mr. Keese. You barely know him."

"I'm trying."

"Try harder."

She bunched her fists. Her mouth tightened. "Well, perhaps you should try not to accost a lady whilst she is all alone in the dark when you knew she had imbibed much wine. 'Tis most improper." She flung a hand to her breast and smirked. "What did you expect me to do?"

"I did not accost you. I *grabbed* you because you were about to fall." Nathaniel raised a brow. "Next time I shall allow you to tumble to the deck."

She stomped her foot and wobbled, but when he reached out to steady her, she snapped her arm away. "Don't touch me, or I'll scream and bring the crew swarming to my rescue."

Nathaniel laughed. "And what would they rescue you from?"

"From taking advantage of my distress and wine-befuddled senses."

"Despite the wine, I believe you knew exactly what you were doing." He narrowed his eyes. "An art you have perfected over the years, no doubt. But I do not intend to be your next victim."

"Victim! Pah. Go back to your lady, Miss Sheldon. You two are perfect for one another."

Miss Sheldon? Ah, the lady was jealous. The realization delighted him far more than it should have. "Perhaps, but that is none of your affair."

The ship lunged, sending white foam over the bow and onto Hope's shoes. She tossed her arms out to her sides to keep her balance.

"The seas roughen. I'll escort you back to your cabin." Nathaniel held out a hand.

"I don't need your help. Leave me be." Swinging around, she stomped back to the rail.

379

Any final drops of desire spilled from him onto the deck like the foam now bubbling around his boots, laughing at him—laughing at the control it had over him. Reason returned, and with it, anger at her defiance. "In your condition, you'll most likely fall overboard, and I don't feel like a swim tonight."

"Then leave me be and let me drown." She waved a hand behind her.

"You are a spoiled brat."

"And you are a pretentious brute."

The ship bucked again. Hope lost her balance and tumbled backward. Nathaniel reached out for her at first but then jerked his hands back. She thumped to the deck, her skirts billowing out around her, and began to sob.

With a huff, Nathaniel hoisted her in his arms. She writhed against him, shoving and punching him as Nathaniel took the foredeck ladder and then the companionway ladder below. Finally she slumped against his shoulder and released a quiet sigh.

Lord, why have You put this lady in my life?

She was the type of woman he abhorred. And he had done the exact thing she needed least of all. He'd given into her advance out of purely physical desire—like every other man in her life. How could he have done such a thing? When he had strived to maintain godly self-control his whole life, strived to eradicate any licentious tendencies inbred within him. But he knew one thing. Hope needed help, she needed healing—she needed God. And he was the last person to give her any of those things.

Lord, take away my anger and my desire for this woman and send her someone who can lead her to You.

Yes, he must keep his distance from the tantalizing Hope and return her to her home as soon as possible. And that's just what he intended to do.

"Here we are." He set her down at the door to the forecabin. "Promise me you'll stay in your cabin." He peered down at her.

"Forgive me, Mr. Mason." She hiccuped. "It would seem I am a source of constant trouble for you." Raising a hand to her forehead, she rubbed it. "I don't feel too well."

"Then I suggest you go to bed."

"I really am not well." She wobbled, and her face blanched.
Clutching her arms, Nathaniel steadied her.

Hope's eyes widened. She flung a hand to her mouth then bent double
and lost the contents of her stomach all over his boots.

CHAPTER 8

Hope drew in a deep breath of salty air, rubbed her throbbing temples, and closed her eyes for a moment against the mad rush of frothy water dashing against the hull of the brig. The gurgle and slap of the sea agitated the churning in her stomach, and she pressed a hand over the complaining organ. Above the crisp horizon, dark, wispy clouds hung like vultures ready to devour what was left of a clear morning. A multitude of sounds crashed over her: the snap of the sails, the sharp twang of rope, the creaks and groans of the brig, and the commands of the officers ordering the seamen to their tasks.

And she wished everything and everyone would simply *stop. . . making. . .noise.*

Adding to her affliction was the shame of the prior evening: the insults and looks of derision from the other passengers at dinner, her overindulgence of wine, and her encounter with Nathaniel—most of which she could not remember.

But she remembered enough.

Had she really lost her dinner upon his boots? She cringed and stared down at the choppy water. Perhaps it wasn't too late to toss herself into the sea, after all. Better that than to face Nathaniel after her drunken theatrics. *And their kiss.* She brushed her fingers over her lips, still tingling with the memory. Some lady she was. Throwing herself at the man like a common hussy. When she'd vowed to change. To be different—better.

But truthfully, she had no idea how to effect such a transformation. She needed the attentions she received from men as much as she needed food for her body. They fed an insatiable hunger within her. But like any good meal, the satisfaction they brought never lasted long, and soon she was starving again.

Turning, Hope averted her eyes from the rolling sea that only increased her queasiness. From the other side of the brig, Miss Sheldon waved and smiled as she wove her way through the working crew toward Hope. Some of the sailors stopped to wipe the sweat from their brows and allowed their gazes to follow after the young lady. Though taller than most women, Miss Sheldon glowed with an innocent beauty that reminded Hope of a fresh spring morning, and her behavior matched the propriety with which she carried herself. Perhaps Hope could elicit her help. Perhaps Miss Sheldon could teach Hope how to be a real lady.

"Good morning, Miss Hope." She grinned and tugged her bonnet further down atop a bounty of chestnut curls. "Where is your hat? This sun is merciless."

Hope tugged on a loose curl, torn from its pins by a blast of wind, ashamed she could never keep her hair secured in a befitting style. Always a rebellious strand or two would break free and flutter about with each shift of the breeze. "I seem to have forgotten it below."

"Shall I retrieve it for you?" Miss Sheldon's caring tone gave Hope a start, but she politely declined. She deserved a far worse beating than the fiery rays lashing down upon her.

Miss Sheldon's brow wrinkled and she touched Hope's arm. "Are you ill? You appear a bit pale."

Hope wanted to tell her that her mouth was as dry as a desert, her stomach a brewing caldron, and her head engaged in a battle, but it had all been her doing, and she deserved no sympathy. "Nay, I am fine."

With a look of genuine concern, Miss Sheldon slid beside Hope and turned to face her. "I am so sorry the men distressed you last night. It was incorrigible of them to make such accusations." A smatter of freckles on her forehead—the only mar on her otherwise creamy white skin—crinkled into a tiny blotch.

Hope urged a smile to her lips. *If you only knew the truth, you'd not be standing here beside me.* Or would she? Miss Sheldon's eyes carried not a hint of judgment or condemnation.

The captain emerged from below, tipped his hat at Hope and Miss Sheldon, then planted his boots on the deck and his fists on his hips as he surveyed his kingdom. Hope swallowed a lump of disdain. 'Twas the pompous captain who had broached the topic of Hope and Nathaniel's relationship last night. And he'd done so on purpose. In fact, as he glanced her way now, raising his eyebrows at her, he seemed to be gloating in his victory.

Hope shifted her attention to Mr. Keese, standing tall upon the quarterdeck. He had nodded at her earlier when she'd come on deck, but he'd made no effort at conversation. The smirk on his face had said quite enough. Beyond him, lazing upon a barrel beneath the shade of a sailcloth strung over his head, Mr. Hendrick sipped a drink, unconcerned with his sick wife below.

Movement caught her eye as Nathaniel emerged from the stern of the brig with cross-staff, divider, and chart in hand. Her heart lurched. She hadn't seen him come on deck, and of course he hadn't made his presence known to her. Why would he? Laying his instruments across a table beside the helm, he glanced over the brig. Their gazes met. Hope looked away, unable to bear the disapproval she knew would be upon his face.

Captain Conway swerved about. "You there! Mr. Mason. Attend the weather topsail braces."

Despite herself, Hope turned back toward Nathaniel.

He glanced up at the white sails fluttering under a light wind then back down at his captain. His jaw stiffened, then he stomped down the quarterdeck ladder and headed toward the foremast to do the captain's bidding.

Never once glancing her way.

"Mr. Mason seems quite the gentleman." Miss Sheldon's gaze followed him.

Hope's heart cinched at the girl's appraisal. Shrugging it off, Hope watched as Nathaniel marched across the deck, unavoidably admiring the way his tan breeches clung to his narrow waist and muscular thighs. How could she fault Miss Sheldon for her attraction to him? He truly was a gentleman: kind, quick-witted, and chivalrous. He deserved someone like Miss Sheldon—a sweet, godly woman. But somewhere deep within Hope sparked a longing to prove to him she could indeed change, that she could become a proper lady despite her abhorrent behavior last night.

Miss Sheldon's hazel eyes sparkled. "He seems quite taken with you."

Hope blinked. "I fear you are mistaken, Miss Sheldon."

"Call me Abigail, please."

"Abigail, I assure you his kindness toward me stems from his godly principles alone. I would say we are naught but mere acquaintances."

Hope's gaze once again locked upon Nathaniel as he tore off his waistcoat, dropped it to the deck, and flung himself into the shrouds. His white shirt flapped in the breeze, and the muscles in his arms bulged as he climbed the ratlines up the foremast.

Miss Sheldon giggled. "Hmm, I see."

A burst of heat stormed up Hope's neck. Tearing her eyes from Nathaniel, she shifted her attention back to the captain, who glared up at his new navigator as if he were a Spanish infiltrator.

The brig crashed over a turquoise wave, and Hope glanced aloft again to ensure Nathaniel had not lost his footing. But the man continued his climb with the ease of a hardened sailor until he was no more than a dark shadow at the top of the mast.

"Why is the captain sending Mr. Mason aloft? Is he not the navigator?" Hope asked.

Abigail shrugged. "I suppose because the ship is inadequately manned."

Standing beside the captain, Mr. Keese winked at Hope. She looked away, not wanting to encourage him further. And although she noticed the glances shot toward her and Abigail from all around, she must not encourage any of them either. Did Abigail notice the attention she drew? A sweet, trusting innocence beamed from her face, an innocence Hope knew she would never reclaim.

If only she could.

"Abigail, have you ever had a suitor?"

"Oh, heavens, no." She blushed. "There was neither the opportunity nor any available gentlemen on Antigua, I'm afraid."

"Surely you see the way men admire you."

"I try not to, Miss Hope." She gave her a sideways glance. "They admire only what they see on the outside, a beauty that fades and has nothing to do with who I am." She turned to face the sea. "What a glorious day!" A gust of wind pressed her modest cotton gown against her thin frame, making her appear all the more frail and delicate, belying what Hope was beginning to realize—that this woman was anything but weak and dainty.

Hope ran a hand across the back of her neck, wiping away the droplets of perspiration. Clutching her fluttering gown, she pondered what Abigail had said. Hope had not considered the admiring looks she received were something to be shrugged away, meaningless and flighty. Yet she found Abigail's words sparking through her mind, igniting her reason as a lantern in a dark room.

Hope smiled at her new friend. So much like her sister Grace, yet so different in many ways—more approachable, less judgmental. Yes, Hope could learn much from this pious, strong woman. She must spend as much time with her as she could. Perhaps observing Abigail's saintly mannerisms would teach Hope to behave accordingly.

A sail snapped, and Abigail tipped her hat up, her hazel eyes sparkling with admiration. Nathaniel stood precariously on the fore top-yard. "My word, but he's brave. I would die of fright up there."

A hint of coquetry tinged her voice, and Hope's exuberance of a moment ago shrank like the topgallant Nathaniel furled above. Even if she could learn to be a lady, even if she could put her past behind her, how could she ever compare with someone like Miss Sheldon?

The crown of a flowered straw hat appeared at the top of the companionway, and Mrs. Hendrick clambered onto the deck from below. Her daughter, Elise, gripped her mother's hand and, with wide eyes, surveyed the brig. Hope thought she saw a shudder pass through the small child as she enfolded herself in her mother's skirts, and Hope longed to assure her all was well despite the clamoring activity across the deck. But the scowl Mrs. Hendrick directed toward Hope stopped her. Gripping her stomach, the poor woman made her way to the railing, her face as white as the canvas that sped the brig on its course.

"Mrs. Hendrick. How do you fare this morning?" Abigail reached out to assist the woman. "And you, Miss Elise?"

The little girl smiled as Mrs. Hendrick gripped the railing like a lifeline and moaned.

"Can I get you something to eat?" Abigail placed a hand on the woman's back.

Another moan. She leaned over the railing and closed her eyes. "Thank you, but I fear I won't be eating for quite some time."

"I'm glad you came above deck as I suggested. The fresh air will do you good." Abigail took in a deep breath and held down her hat beneath another rush of wind.

Hope smiled at Elise, and the girl giggled in return, hiding in her mother's skirts. But even amidst her nausea, Mrs. Hendrick managed to cast a warning glare at Hope and take a step away from her as if she were afflicted with some dread disease.

Blinking back the burning behind her eyes, Hope looked up to see Mr. Hendrick glance their way, but he resumed his conversation with Major Paine, who stood beside him, arms across his chest.

Hope's blood boiled. The man seemed completely unconcerned with his wife's plight. Next to him, Major Paine kept nodding at some grand wisdom the pompous man no doubt graced upon him, but his slit-like gaze locked upon Hope. A grin slithered over his thin lips.

Nathaniel dropped to the deck with a *thump* and started for the quarterdeck ladder.

"Mr. Mason, stow those barrels below," the captain hollered, pointing to a cluster of four casks beneath the foredeck.

Halting in his tracks, Nathaniel narrowed his eyes upon the captain. He shifted his stance, and his lips twitched as if he battled to keep them closed. Finally, his chest heaved a sigh, and after a curt nod, he turned on his heels and headed toward the barrels, the clenching and unclenching of his fists the only indication of his inner turmoil.

Patches of sweat stained his white shirt, and he grimaced as he hefted the small drum onto his shoulder. Hope bit her lip. It was because of her Nathaniel wasn't the one giving the orders. It was because of her he was forced to work so hard and be humiliated by a man with half his brains. For the first time in her life, Hope began to realize how her witless actions affected others. Had they affected her sisters, too? Her father?

Abigail's gentle touch on Hope's arm startled her. "I must go below. I promised to bring some food and water to a sick sailor. Can you look after Mrs. Hendrick?" She nodded toward the groaning woman leaning over the railing.

Hope shook her head and started to tell Abigail the woman would surely protest, when Mrs. Hendrick, in a severe tone, saved her the effort. "There is no need. I shall be fine."

Hope shrugged. "I shall try," she whispered, "but only for you."

Abigail smiled and turned to leave, and as Hope watched her disappear below on her errand of mercy, she wondered how someone became so caring and selfless. Perhaps there was something missing from Hope, after all, some part of her heart God had forgotten to insert, for she could barely garner an ounce of sympathy for the suffering woman at her side—especially in light of the woman's contempt for her.

The brig bucked, sending Mrs. Hendrick toppling, and Hope reached out, caught her by the waist, and steadied her against the railing. Elise clung to her mother and began to whimper.

"You're with child." Hope could not hide the surprise in her tone.

"How did you know?" Mrs. Hendrick looked down at her belly in horror.

"I felt the tender mound when I touched you just now."

"Well, I'll thank you to keep your hands to yourself," she hissed and glanced down. "Elise, stop your fussing. Mother is sick. Be a good girl."

"I can care for Miss Elise if you'd like." Despite knowing Mrs. Hendrick would never allow such a thing, Hope couldn't help but offer. She would gladly risk another cruel rejection for the chance to comfort the small, frightened girl.

Mrs. Hendrick gave a ladylike snort.

Which Hope understood as a no. "How many months along are you?"

"Seven."

"Seven? I would have never guessed. You are so tiny."

A smile, the first one Mrs. Hendrick had graced upon Hope, quickly faded from her lips. "Mr. Hendrick detests plump women, so I must try and keep my weight down."

"Surely he understands you carry his child?"

"He is a man and does not bother himself with the details of childbearing."

Hope's jaw tensed. "It is not good for you. The baby needs nourishment."

"What do you know of it?" Mrs. Hendrick snapped and shot her icy blue eyes toward Hope. "How many children have you carried?" She paused and allowed her gaze to scour Hope. "Or perhaps you do know."

"How could I? I have never been married." Hope swallowed a lump of shame.

"Humph." Mrs. Hendrick glanced at her husband and adjusted the hat ribbon tied beneath her chin. She lifted her graceful nose and cultured eyebrows, but sorrow seemed to tug upon her high cheekbones and lustrous skin. Facing the sea, she held her stomach, and her face grew pale again.

Hope gazed across the endless ocean, its waves suddenly calm as if some invisible hand pressed down upon them. An eerie silence enveloped the brig, muffling even the occasional creak of wood and shout of the crew's voices. The wind ceased, and Hope rubbed the perspiration from her neck and watched as wisps of black clouds spread their talons across the horizon.

"Eleanor!" A loud growl rumbled across the deck. "Come hither, Eleanor!" If possible, Mrs. Hendrick's face grew even paler.

"I must speak to my husband." Mrs. Hendrick grabbed Elise by the hand. "If you will excuse me."

"Mother. May I stay here?" Elise tugged on her mother's skirts.

"No Elise, come with me."

"But Father is always so angry. Please let me stay."

"I will watch her for you, Mrs. Hendrick." Hope braced herself for the woman's rebuff while at the same time offering her an encouraging smile.

Mrs. Hendrick shifted her gaze between Elise and Hope, her face in a pinch as if Hope had asked if she could throw her daughter to the sharks.

"What harm could possibly come to the girl?" Hope raised her brows.

"Very well. But I shall have my eye on you." Mrs. Hendrick wagged a finger in Hope's face before lifting her satin skirts and trudging up the quarterdeck ladder.

Finding a small crate in the shade of the foredeck, Hope sat and hoisted Elise into her lap, grateful to be able to take her weight off her sore feet. Nestling her face into the girl's red curls, Hope breathed in the deep scent of innocence. Children always smelled fresh and pure—as if the cruel stench of the world had not yet been able to stick to them. "Are you afraid of the ship?"

Elise nodded, her wide blue eyes staring up at Hope's. "A little bit, but

Father says never to be afraid of anything."

A gust of wind wafted over them. Elise's curls slapped Hope's face, and she brushed them aside, thankful for the sudden reprieve from the stifling heat. "I think it's okay to be afraid sometimes."

"You do?"

"Yes. But not of this brig. I know there are many men running about and lots of loud yelling, but each is doing his job." Hope straightened the lace on Elise's sleeves. "Do you know what that job is?"

The girl shook her head.

"To get you safely to Kingstown."

"It is?" She glanced up at Hope with excitement.

Another blast of hot wind swept over them, fluttering Elise's skirts.

"So you see, there is nothing to fear," Hope announced, settling the fabric. "Except that this wind will whip our skirts off, I suppose." They both giggled.

A loud shout from the quarterdeck drew their attention. "Blast it all, woman!" Mr. Hendrick's booming voice echoed over the brig.

A shiver ran through Elise, and she began to finger the fringed tips of the lavender sash around her waist. "Are you afraid of your father, Miss Hope?"

Hope glanced at the red-faced man who had retaken his seat and was waving his wife away as if she were an annoying gnat. A deep sigh escaped Hope's lips, if only to curb the anger rising within her and the memories that resurfaced. Growing up, Hope had often been frightened of her own father, and that fear did naught to foster the secure haven in which every child should be raised and nurtured.

"Men can be scary sometimes. They're big, and they have deep voices like bears." She dug her fingers like claws into Elise to tickle her, hoping to get her mind off her parents.

Elise's giggle halted in a shriek as her mother grabbed her arm, tugged her from Hope's lap, and stormed below without a word, dragging the poor girl behind. Hope's last glimpse of the child was a flurry of red curls and wide, pleading eyes.

She rubbed her arms against a sudden chill despite the rising heat of the day, and stood. Stepping toward the railing, she clutched the hard wood until her fingers hurt. Children—and women—forever doomed to be at the mercy of those in power over them. Thoughts of her own childhood shoved their way into her mind. Her innocence stolen at so young an age. Her trust forever crushed.

Distant thunder growled, and the wind ceased again as if someone had opened and shut a door. The sea rose in mountainous swells like hump-backed monsters beneath a sheet of turquoise. The ship rocked. A black shroud consumed the entire horizon and sent out spindly fingers across the sky toward her as if intent on dragging her back into the swirling void. She trembled. A sense of evil and foreboding gripped her—a feeling that something or someone wanted to possess her, a feeling she'd had before, most recently at the Pink House Tavern in Charles Towne. Then, she had been rescued by Mr. Waite and her sister Faith. But now, who would save her?

Swerving around, Hope glanced over the deck. Two sailors nearby tying knots in ropes gaped at her with leering grins. Upon the quarterdeck, Major Paine's eyebrows lifted in invitation. The captain gave her a saucy smirk. Hope turned back around. Better to face the storm than the lecherous gazes of these men. She knew they took such liberties because they thought her wanton. She'd received the same looks back in Charles Towne once her relationship with Lord Falkland had seeped through gossiping lips across town.

"Good day, Miss Hope." Mr. Keese appeared beside her, tipping his bicorn and startling her.

"Good day, Mr. Keese." Hope tried to keep her tone free of any sultry invitation.

"You are looking lovely today, I must say."

"Please, sir, I wish you would not." She stared at the swirling water below.

His head jerked back as if she'd punched him. "It pains me you slight my compliment."

Hope faced him. Strands of loose sandy hair flapped in the wind, and a wild, inviting look beamed from his dark blue eyes. "Forgive me, Mr. Keese. I meant no offense. And I do thank you for your kindness." After the vulgar way the crew eyed her, not to mention Major Paine's bawdy glances, the perpetual smirk on the captain's mouth, and Mrs. Hendrick's insulting manner, Mr. Keese's kindness soothed Hope's wounded heart like salve. Surely it wasn't wrong to accept such attentions as long as she did not encourage them.

"I assure you this voyage would be pure drudgery without you, Miss Hope." One side of his mouth curved in a handsome smile.

"I am sure you would manage, Mr. Keese." Though Hope tried to squelch it, a grin lifted her lips as well.

"But life is more than managing, is it not, Miss Hope?" He took her hand in his, enveloping it with his strength and warmth. But no. She hardly knew him. It wasn't proper. She snagged it back and instead folded her hands together and stared at the oak planks of the deck by their feet.

A jagged streak of lightning crossed the dark sky, followed by a low roll of thunder. The brig rolled over a churning mound, and Mr. Keese put a hand on her back—she assumed to keep her from stumbling. When her eyes met his, no passion simmered within them. Just a friendly, playful gleam as if he were toying with her. Removing his hand, he coughed into it and grinned.

"Regardless of what you may think, Mr. Keese, I am not the strumpet the others on this ship assume me to be." She bit her lip. *Or at least I am not any longer.*

Mr. Keese scratched his whiskers and shrugged. "I rarely give much credence to the opinions of others."

From the untamed glimmer in his eyes and the confident way he carried himself, Hope knew he spoke the truth. She envied him. "'Tis an admirable quality, Mr. Keese." The brig pitched over another wave, and Hope gripped the railing. "I believe you and Miss Sheldon are my only friends on this voyage."

"Not Mr. Mason?" He cocked a brow.

"Least of all him." The sting of rain filled her nostrils. She brushed the hair from her face and glanced over the unusually calm sea lurking between the swells rippling in from the southeast. "I find most of the crew stare at me as if...as if..." Thunder rumbled, and she raised her voice over the din. "As if I am extending an open invitation to share my company at any time."

"You are, are you?" Nathaniel's guttural voice stormed between them. "How fortunate for you, Mr. Keese." He nodded toward Mr. Keese with a smile that belied the simmering in his dark eyes.

Hope rubbed her sweaty palms together and swallowed the burning lump in her throat. Throwing her shoulders back, she intended to explain, but Nathaniel's face was as stiff as a sail at full wind, and her words faltered on her lips.

"May I speak to you a moment?" he said without emotion.

"You misunderstand, Mr. Mason." Hope eyed Mr. Keese with a lift of her brows, encouraging him to come to her aid.

"I shall remember your invitation, Miss Hope." Mr. Keese took her hand and planted a kiss upon it. A playful grin twisted his lips before he marched away. Why was he playing a charade? Why didn't he explain the context of her statement to Nathaniel? Hope bunched her fists.

Nathaniel dabbed the sweat from his brow with his handkerchief then ran a hand through his moist hair. "I believe your meaning was clear, Miss Hope. The only thing I have misunderstood is your desire to change."

Hope huffed. Defeat settled in like an old familiar friend. She pressed a hand over her still-bubbling stomach.

"You're not going to be sick again?" He gave her a sideways smile. "I've not got my boots on to protect me this time."

Hope glanced down at his large tanned feet. "I hope you can forgive me, Mr. Mason. Regarding my behavior last night, I...I am quite overcome with shame."

He cocked his head and studied her with dark inquisitive eyes the color of coffee. Flecks of gold sparkled from within them like flickers of hope until the sun disappeared beneath a cloud and stole them away.

Hope's gaze dropped to his lips. A warm sensation fluttered in her belly, and she quickly looked away. What was wrong with her? It wasn't like she hadn't kissed a man before. Just not one who hadn't invited it. Just not a decent, honorable man like Nathaniel.

"I came to warn you to go below, Miss Hope." He crossed his arms over his sweat-soaked shirt and stiffened his jaw. "That is, when you are finished with your playful dalliances above."

"I wasn't engaged in any playful dal—oh, what is the use?" Hope waved a hand through the air.

He nodded toward the horizon. "There's a fierce storm brewing, and I fear the deck will become most unsafe in a short time."

"Thank you for the warning, Mr. Mason."

"Mr. Mason!" Captain Conway bellowed. "Quit dawdling and get back to work, or I'll send you below to pump out the bilge."

Nathaniel closed his eyes and pressed a hand over his left side. With a quick nod her way, he turned and stomped away.

Hope spun to face the storm again. A vicious tempest was brewing indeed. Both within her and without. Her every attempt to behave like a lady had failed miserably. Not by any fault of her own, but by the presumptions of others. Nathaniel in particular. How could she change if all those around her had already made up their minds as to her character?

CHAPTER 9

The brig heaved forward, and Nathaniel braced himself on the bulkhead to keep from tumbling down the hallway. The muscles in his arms and back throbbed. He hadn't worked so hard in years, not since he'd been a carpenter aboard old Captain Harley's ship. Known for running his merchantman stricter than a ship of the line, Captain Harley had always had difficulty manning his voyages. But Nathaniel had been young, in desperate need of work, and eager to learn how to sail. In that latter regard, he owed old Harley a huge debt, for the man took him under his tutelage and taught him everything he knew.

Captain Conway was a different animal. His harsh and unyielding command served no discernable purpose other than to exasperate and demean the crew. And he harbored an extra measure of ill will toward Nathaniel. Perhaps he resented Nathaniel's experience as a captain and feared he would attempt a mutiny. Ludicrous.

The brig canted, groaning like an old woman under the strain, and Nathaniel slammed into the bulkhead, careful not to drop his lantern. Thrusting it out before him, he followed the shifting circle of light through darkness as thick as molasses. He must make his way down to the hold, where he had heard Miss Sheldon was tending a patient.

Gripping the rough wood of the railing, he crept down the ladder as another wave jolted the brig and nearly sent him flying.

Outside the thick hull, the storm pummeled the merchantman with waves as high as a building and gusts of wind strong enough to blow a man overboard. The warning signs had been evident ever since they'd set sail from St. Kitts three days ago: the huge swells rolling in from the southeast, the calm winds interspersed with wild gusts from all directions. The signs of a hurricane—the most feared storm on the Caribbean. He had tried to warn the captain to seek shelter as soon as possible, but to no avail. The stubborn man kept insisting it was naught but a summer squall, that he'd encountered many a storm before in the North Atlantic, and that he'd be dead in his grave before he'd cower before the wind and waves. His eyes had taken on a wild glow as if some wicked force possessed him, and he kept shouting something about his wife and thrusting his fist in the air, cursing at the black clouds.

The man was clearly unsettled, which explained his brutal treatment of the crew but did naught to ease Nathaniel's fears of what would happen should they enter the hurricane's path.

At least Nathaniel had convinced the captain to sail south out of the storm's path before the worst of it hit. And the captain, per Nathaniel's request, had also brought down the topgallant yards and masts, strapped them to the deck, and secured storm lashings on the guns.

With these measures taken, they might well be out of danger by morning. But the ride throughout the long night would be tumultuous at best. Which was why Nathaniel must escort Miss Sheldon back to her quarters. Down in the hold, she could be crushed by cargo loosened by the storm. The sick crewman shouldn't be down there, either, but Captain Conway had insisted he remain as far from the rest of the crew as possible so as not to spread whatever disease ailed him.

Thunder growled like a ravenous monster, shaking the brig from truck to keelson, and Nathaniel hurried downward. As he took the last step, the ship lurched, and he tripped. Tiny paws skittered over his bare feet, and he kicked the beast aside. The stench of moldy grain and human waste assaulted him. Bracing his feet over the wobbling deck, he turned left and followed the flicker of a small light in the distance.

"Miss Sheldon," he bellowed, wending his way toward the light. "Miss Sheldon!"

"In here." A female voice screeched through the roar of the storm.

Pushing the door aside, he entered a tiny room crammed full with crates, barrels, and sailcloth. A cot protruded from amidst the clutter in one corner. Upon it lay a gaunt man shriveled into a ball, his bony white face a sunken frame of death. Miss Sheldon sat on a crate beside him, lantern in one hand and wet cloth in the other. She turned and gave Nathaniel a weak smile, her eyes moist with tears. The man moaned, and she dabbed the cloth on his forehead.

Dousing his lantern, Nathaniel approached, feeling his own blood drain from his face. He recognized the stench of death, one he'd witnessed many times before—an ugly, cruel force that knew no mercy. An icy chill stabbed him, shoving away the suffocating heat that had enveloped him since he'd descended below deck. "Is there no one but you with medical knowledge aboard the ship?"

"Nay, the captain's wife used to administer medicaments, but word is she remained behind in St. Kitts with some relations." Miss Sheldon's voice strained with sorrow.

"I don't blame her. The captain probably ordered her to haul barrels all day, as well."

She glanced his way, a glimmer of approval in her eyes. "You handle his harsh treatment well, Mr. Mason. With a humble spirit."

He chuckled. "I do not feel very humble."

The sailor moaned and smacked his lips together, and Miss Sheldon soaked her cloth in a bucket of water and squeezed droplets into his mouth.

The brig jerked to larboard. Miss Sheldon held on to the cot, and Nathaniel, still holding his lantern, threw his back against a stack of teetering crates to keep them from falling. "I've come to escort you back to your cabin, miss. 'Tis not safe here in the storm." He steadied the boxes and nodded toward the sailor. "And regardless of what the captain says, we should take him along as well."

The angry sea pounded against the hull with the roar of a broadside.

She shook her head. "The captain will not permit it, and I will not leave him." Facing the sailor, she dabbed the cloth on his neck. "There, there. It will be fine."

Nathaniel rubbed his eyes, stinging from salt, and squatted beside the bed. Admiration welled within him at the woman's selflessness.

A few strands of brown hair had loosened from her pins and waved across the back of her neck with every movement of the ship. And though her figure was hidden beneath a plain cotton gown buttoned all the way to her neck, her modest attire did not distract from her beauty.

How different she was from Hope. He had enjoyed seeing the two of them conversing so easily two days ago. Complete opposites standing together on the deck, laughing and chatting as if they'd been friends forever. But then who wouldn't want to bask in the joy and peace and acceptance flowing around Miss Sheldon like a morning breeze? Like her parents, she would no doubt make a great missionary. He sighed. But not him. Instead of drawing people to God's love, Nathaniel seemed to push them away.

"I understand your concern for him, Miss Sheldon, but this is more than a summer storm, and we aren't even in the thick of it yet. You risk your life by staying here."

Where most people would have expressed some alarm at his statement, Miss Sheldon's peaceful countenance remained as composed as if he'd just told her there was no sugar for her tea. "You are most kind to come down here for me, but I'm not leaving."

Nathaniel grunted. If he so desired, he could hoist her over one shoulder and the sick man over the other and haul them wherever he wished.

The sea roared against the hull, threatening to chomp down on the sodden wood with its sharp waves and break through to grab them at any moment. The brig pitched by the bow and plunged downward, knocking Nathaniel to his knees and Miss Sheldon from her crate. Steadying the lantern that teetered precariously in her hand, he assisted her to her feet. "We should not have a lantern lit. I insist you come with me at once, or I'll—"

A loud moan broke through the roar of the storm. The sailor's eyelids flew open and his gaze shot around the cabin—surprisingly clear for one so ill—and finally locked upon Nathaniel. Terror screamed from his face. His pale lips quivered. "They are coming for me."

Nathaniel knelt beside the man. "Who is coming for you?"

"The dark shadows. The dark shadows. Don't let them take me." His gaze flickered about the cabin again as if he could see monsters in the corners.

A chill slithered up Nathaniel's spine. He glanced across the tiny room. Light from the lantern cast eerie, shifting shadows over the bulkheads. Perhaps in his delirium of death, the poor sailor thought they were real. Then why did the hair on the back of Nathaniel's neck stiffen? And why did a chill envelop him where there should be only heat?

Miss Sheldon's wide eyes met Nathaniel's as she lowered herself back to her crate. She patted the sailor's forehead with the cloth. "Shhh, Mr. Boden. You are merely feverish."

The pungent smell of decay shrouded Nathaniel, and he grabbed the man's trembling hand, hoping to offer him some comfort. Soft, icy flesh gripped his. "He has no fever."

The brig lurched, and Nathaniel clung to the cot, which seemed to be the only thing not shifting in the room.

"He did a moment ago." Miss Sheldon touched the man's neck and frowned. "I don't understand."

Before Nathaniel could remove his hand, Mr. Boden squeezed it with more strength than Nathaniel would have thought possible from so feeble a man. "Are you the preacher?" he asked, his voice cracking with desperation.

"No. I'm not." Nathaniel cringed as the truth of his own words twisted through him like a knife. How could the son of a harlot be a preacher?

Mr. Boden writhed on the straw cot, clenching Nathaniel's hand in a viselike grip. "Don't let them take me."

"Shh, Mr. Boden. No one is going to take you anywhere." Miss Sheldon pressed down on his shoulders, trying to calm him, but he bolted and bucked so violently, she stumbled backward.

Sweat streaked down Nathaniel's back. An impossible blast of frigid wind whirled through the enclosed space, freezing his sodden shirt stiff. His heart thudded in achingly slow beats as if this ghostly breeze had the power to freeze a man solid. Evil was in this room—the same evil he had often felt as a child in his mother's chamber.

And he knew exactly what he had to do.

Bowing his head, he prayed for God's direction and His protection, then gripped Mr. Boden's shoulders. "They won't take you," he said. "Look at me."

Sweat poured off the man's forehead, beading into icy crystals. His chest heaved, and his thin lips faded to a pale blue.

"Look at me, Mr. Boden."

His desperate gaze fixed on Nathaniel. Labored breaths whistled in his throat as he settled back onto the cot. "Help me. Please."

Nathaniel laid a steady hand on the man's chest. "I cannot. You must put your trust in the Son of God. Call upon the name of Jesus."

Mr. Boden began coughing, choking, gasping for breath. He thrashed over the cot. The brig vaulted, toppling Nathaniel and Miss Sheldon. A deep wail roared through the ship as if the sea screamed its fury that it could not breech the hull.

Mr. Boden calmed, his gaze focused on the deckhead above him.

Nathaniel placed two fingers on his neck. "His pulse is weak."

"Jesus," the sailor whispered through wet, trembling lips. He let go of Nathaniel's hand. The terror in his gaze fled, replaced by a soothing peace. He released a long, heavy sigh, and his body stiffened.

Nathaniel held his breath, half expecting the fury of the unnatural cold to take them all in its grip. The icy chill that had consumed the room vanished. In its place, a sweet scent swirled past Nathaniel's nose. "Thank You, God," Nathaniel muttered, his voice raspy.

Tears pooled in Miss Sheldon's eyes. "You did it."

"I did nothing."

Thunder boomed. The brig pitched forward. Nathaniel grabbed her arm to steady her and held the lantern with his other.

She glanced at Mr. Boden, a peaceful look on his face. Wiping his forehead, she placed a kiss upon it. "I've been speaking to him most of the day about heaven and hell and turning himself over to God, but he wouldn't listen. Then you stomp in here and reach him in less than a minute."

"'Twas God, not me." Nathaniel still couldn't believe ushering the man into heaven had been that simple.

Miss Sheldon swiped away a tear. "Perhaps I do not have my parents' gift of spreading the gospel, after all. I wonder if I will be any use in Kingstown."

If we make it to Kingstown. Nathaniel stood, bracing his feet, and wondered why the waves seemed to be growing in size and intensity instead of lessening. "I'm sure you'll be a wonderful missionary." Truthfully, he hadn't the time to discuss it at the moment. He must get on deck and determine their course. He held out his hand. "Will you come with me now?"

She gazed at Mr. Boden. "Should we leave him?"

"He is no longer here."

"Of course." She smiled.

Holding her lantern with one hand, she clung to Nathaniel's arm with the other as he led the way out into the hold. Spotting a pile of ropes, he grabbed them from atop a crate and carried them up the ladder.

His heart squeezed in his chest as he approached the door to the forecabin. He'd managed to avoid Hope for two days, the storm having kept her below. But he couldn't face her. Not yet. Anger still simmered within him over the way she had offered an open invitation to Mr. Keese to spend time with her whenever he wished. A most inappropriate thing for a lady to say to a man she'd just met.

"Here we are, Miss Sheldon." Nathaniel halted, taking the lantern from her. "Tell the other women to tie themselves to their beds." He plucked a knife from his belt and held it out to her, along with the ropes.

Nodding, she took them and disappeared within, not an ounce of fear on her face.

Nathaniel dashed up the companionway ladder. Why didn't his heart jump when Miss Sheldon was near? Why did it leap only for Hope—a woman who reminded him too much of his mother? Yes, she had vowed to change, but his mother had made similar promises—none of which she had kept. And he doubted Hope would either.

But at the moment, he had more important things to worry about. From the way the ship lurched and vaulted beneath the growing waves, it appeared Captain Conway had changed his mind about heading south. If so, it would be too late to change course. Nathaniel must convince him to seek shelter before the full force of the hurricane struck. The merchantman would sail close to Puerto Rico, and with luck they could find a safe harbor among the bays on the south side of the island.

If they did not, and Captain Conway insisted on running before the wind, Nathaniel feared they all would die.

CHAPTER 10

The brig heaved to and fro like a seesaw. Hope clung to her bedpost, refusing to allow her surging fear to drive her to panic. The raging storm outside, coupled with Abigail's conspicuous absence, had coiled Hope's nerves into a tight ball.

The door burst open, and Abigail rushed into the cabin, bundles of rope in one hand and a knife in the other. With her back she forced the door shut against the buffeting wind, then squinted into the shadows.

"Oh, finally, there you are." Mrs. Hendrick cackled from her bed, where she and Elise hugged the wooden frame for dear life. "Where on earth have you been? Wandering around a ship full of men in the middle of the night is no place for a lady, especially during a storm." She squeezed Elise tighter to her chest. "And leaving us here with no word as to what is happening above. Where is my husband? He shouldn't leave Elise and me here alone. I hope he hasn't fallen overboard. We are beside ourselves with fright. I can't imagine what he's doing. No doubt he has taken to his brandy again, as he always does."

Hope rubbed her ears, which buzzed from hours of Mrs. Hendrick's incessant complaining. At one point, Hope had even considered going to find Mr. Hendrick and dragging the negligent husband to his family, or better yet, staying with him in whatever quiet haven he had found for himself.

The brig quivered beneath the growl of a massive wave, and Abigail leapt to her cot, gripping the wooden side as the cabin pitched. She tossed a bundle of ropes to Mrs. Hendrick. "I am sure your husband is fine, Mrs. Hendrick," she shouted over the storm. "No doubt he's strapped himself in somewhere. Which is what we need to do, as well."

Abigail handed one end of a long twine to Hope. "Mr. Mason

instructed us to tie ourselves to our beds," she shouted.

"Mr. Mason?" Hope's stomach soured. So that explained where Abigail had been all this time, as well as the shimmer of fading lantern light Hope had spotted in the hallway before Abigail had closed the door. Of course Nathaniel had not stopped long enough to inquire after Hope's welfare.

"This is madness," Mrs. Hendrick whined from across the cabin.

Hope peered toward her but could make out only the outline of her body and the small shadow of her daughter perched on her lap. The woman held the rope out before her as if it were a snake. "How am I supposed to tie myself and Elise up with this?"

"I will help you, Mrs. Hendrick," Abigail shouted over the crash of waves; then she faced Hope. "I was caring for a sick patient in the hold, and Mr. Mason came to escort me back to the cabin."

Hope grimaced as she peered through the shadows, trying to determine if the young girl's expression matched her gleeful tone, but the darkness mottled her features. "How can you sound so peaceful and happy during such a violent storm?" Hope's loud voice sounded surlier than she intended.

Abigail didn't seem to notice. She continued tying one end of her rope to her bed frame as casually as if she were latching a horse to a hitching post. "The most marvelous thing happened below." Her loud voice rose musically.

Something wonderful. Below? With Mr. Mason? Hope clutched the wooden frame as the ship vaulted over a wave and then tumbled downward, sending her heart tumbling down along with it. No woman sounded so peaceful, so happy in the midst of such a fearful tempest. Unless a man had expressed his ardor for her, or worse—kissed her.

But before Hope could inquire what wonderful thing Abigail referred to, thunder exploded in a series of enormous cracks and growls. Angry waves rammed into the hull. Their punches reverberated like a massive gong.

Abigail clambered over to where Mrs. Hendrick slumped in a puddle of despair, fumbling with her rope. "Mr. Mason said the storm worsens and it isn't safe to be unfettered."

"Oh my, I knew it. I knew I shouldn't have ventured on this trip with William," Mrs. Hendrick wailed. "This is all too much. Too much. I cannot bear it. We are all going to die."

Gripping the bulkhead, Hope hoisted herself up and tried to peer out the window. The maelstrom outside the tiny glass oval writhed in an undulating vision of raging black clouds one second and a hissing caldron of white-capped water the next. She braced her feet, mesmerized by the ferocity of the sea. Fear clawed her throat like none she had ever known. What if she were to die in this storm? She would never see her sisters again. She would never see her father again. But most of all, she would never have the chance to put her past behind her and become a true lady.

A massive wall of water thrust from the sea and loomed over the brig, curling into a fist. Two flashes of lightning shot from within the churning water, sparks from demon eyes. Flinging a hand to her mouth, Hope stumbled back from the window. A roar of thunder shook the tiny merchantman. Talons of ebony water snatched at Hope. She screamed. The watery claws slammed against the window. The glass rolled as if it had melted, and a ripple sped through the cabin bulkhead. Hope collapsed to the deck. Her heart thrashed in her chest. A spike of pain jolted up her back.

"What is it?" Abigail yelled from Mrs. Hendrick's berth.

Hope stared at the window. A shiver ran down her as she struggled to her feet. The brig bolted and tossed her onto one of the cots. She yanked the quilt over herself, attempting to hide from the evil presence. The same evil that had sought her on deck earlier. The same evil that had nearly consumed her back in Charles Towne and before that in Portsmouth—a dark, maniacal power that had followed her from England to the colonies. It followed her still.

Even hidden beneath the quilt, Hope couldn't escape the window's prying eye. She drew a shuddering breath and dropped to the deck, crawling over to assist Abigail.

Elise huddled beside her mother, clinging to her waist. When she glanced up and saw Hope, her eyes widened, and she dashed into Hope's arms. Embracing her, Hope rubbed her back, trying to still the girl's trembling. "Shhh. Don't be afraid."

"Please stay still, Mrs. Hendrick. We shall be safe." Abigail fought with the tangle of rope.

"How can I stay still?" Mrs. Hendrick continued her tirade. "The ship jumps like a grasshopper. Why must I be tied up? What if the ship sinks? How shall we escape then? Oh, where is my husband? He is never around when I need him. Will you go find him?" She lifted her pleading, moist eyes to Abigail.

"It is not safe." Loosening the rope, Abigail swung it around Mrs. Hendrick a second time. "I assure you, we will all be fine right here. And I have a knife should we need to free ourselves in a hurry."

Mrs. Hendrick's sharp gaze landed on Hope. "Get away from her, Elise. Come here!" She motioned for the little girl to return to her then pressed a hand over her stomach. "Oh, my poor baby."

Prying Elise from her arms, Hope clutched the little girl's shoulders and leaned toward her ear. "You must be strong for your mother. She needs you." Nudging her toward Mrs. Hendrick, she gave Elise a reassuring smile.

The girl took her place beside her mother, who threw an arm around her and pressed her close. Abigail looped another rope around Elise, then tied both of them to the bed frame.

Turning, she grabbed Hope's arm and scrambled back to her bunk. "Tie yourself up, Miss Hope."

The growl of the storm grew louder, deeper, angrier, as if they were surrounded by a thousand warriors bellowing their battle cries.

Hope laid a hand on Abigail's arm. "How bad is the storm, really?"

Abigail shifted her gaze above. "By the look on Mr. Mason's face when he left, I suggest you pray, Miss Hope. Pray as hard as you can."

⤳

Nathaniel clung to his lifeline and thrust headlong into the raging wind as a giant swell toppled over the stern of the brig and swept him off his feet. The bow of the vessel dove, and he gripped the rope with all his strength. A cascade of water pummeled him as the ship darted headfirst down a mountainous wave. His feet scrambled over the near vertical deck, seeking a hold. The brig slammed back level again. He must make his way to the foredeck and convince Captain Conway to take shelter in one of the nearby islands.

He struggled to his feet. His hands burned. His eyes stung. And the wind struck him with the force of a hundred fists. He shivered, shaking off the water that ran from his waistcoat like ale from a spigot. Wiping his face, he squinted up at the helm, almost hoping—God forgive him—that Captain Conway had been swept over with the last wave. But he made out a blurred, bulky shape clutching the wheel and thrusting a fist into the air. Wild, haughty laughter ricocheted over the ship like some villain's in a playact.

Above Nathaniel, the oscillating dark shapes of two sailors clung to the foremast, their arms and legs circling the wooden pole in frozen terror as they tried to obey their captain's command to raise the storm canvas. But as the mast swung like a pendulum over one side of the brig and then the other, all they could do was hang on for dear life. Several other men huddled across the deck, gripping the capstan, the railings, the ladders, or anything else solid they could latch onto as they waited for the next surge to strike.

And strike it did. Like a raging sea monster, the water lifted the ship up by the stern, rolling beneath it until the bow pointed toward the swirling clouds. Diving to the deck, Nathaniel grabbed the hatch combing, grateful he had convinced the captain to lash relieving tackle onto the tiller, for he feared the wheel wouldn't last much longer under this stress. Even so, if the rudder smashed, they'd be without steering ability. And steering was the one thing they needed right now.

Nathaniel struggled to his feet. Lightning flung white arrows toward the foundering merchantman, casting a ghostly light over the vicious seas that had been hidden behind the curtain of night. Thick gray mounds of water rose from the ebony caldron, their mouths foaming in search of victims. Fear squeezed Nathaniel's chest. A sense of pure evil pricked the hair on his arms. The same evil he'd felt below deck earlier. A relentless, hellish force. Only this time, it seemed all-encompassing and more determined than ever. A living, breathing entity that focused all its maniacal intent upon swallowing the tiny brig.

Nathaniel closed his eyes and tried to voice a prayer of protection, but the only word he uttered was a name—the name of the only One who could help them. "Jesus." Shaking the terrifying vision from his mind, he made his way to the quarterdeck ladder, shoving his arms against the blasts of wind as he went. His legs ached from trying to keep his balance aboard the teetering deck. Salt stung his eyes as an explosion of thunder deafened him. They were in the thick of the storm. He must convince the captain to keep the thrust of wind on the starboard quarter or the brig would broach and offer her vulnerable side to the oncoming swells.

If that happened, all would be lost.

Nathaniel lugged himself up onto the quarterdeck and turned his face from the wind to catch his breath. The captain gave him a cursory glance, then the lines in his face flattened as he strained to pull the wheel to larboard. Mr. Keese clung to the binnacle by the railing. When the second mate saw Nathaniel, he released his grip and forged toward him, reaching him as a wall of water cascaded over them. He rubbed his eyes and glanced at Nathaniel, frustration and rage burning within them.

"We must convince Conway to steer to starboard!" Nathaniel yelled into his ear.

Mr. Keese nodded and leaned toward him. "I have already tried. He refuses to listen." Water poured off his nose and chin onto Nathaniel's shirt.

Jerking his lifeline over the quarterdeck railing, Nathaniel stumbled around Mr. Keese and approached the captain. Bracing himself beside the man, Nathaniel turned his face from the wind so he could speak. "Captain, you must steer her to starboard. Keep the wind on her starboard quarter!"

"I do not take orders from you, Mr. Mason!" The captain shouted without so much as a glance his way.

"This is a hurricane, sir. I've been in one before. It is the only way to break free of it."

"Coward. 'Tis but a squall. I know what I am doing." Captain Conway bellowed into Nathaniel's face, rum heavy on his breath. "A storm like this took my first wife from me. But I'll not let it get the best of me again!" He shrieked, a sinister, depraved laugh like a man just escaped from an asylum.

Nathaniel's heart stopped as the realization struck him that the captain had gone mad.

Conway glared at him. "Go tie the additional shrouds to the mainmast like I ordered you, or I'll have you locked up below with the women!" He waved Nathaniel off, resumed his clamp on the wheel, and let out another blood-chilling laugh. "No storm gets the best of Captain Conway!"

Fury sent blood rushing to Nathaniel's fists, and he longed to smash one into the foolish man's jaw. If he did not, the captain's stupidity would kill them all. *God, what do I do?* But he already knew. Lives were at stake: the sailors, the women below—Hope.

He glanced at Mr. Keese, who remained at the railing, watching the altercation. Keese gave a nod of agreement—a nod between two men who knew what must be done. Nathaniel drew the extra knife he kept strapped to his side while Mr. Keese crept toward them along the railing. They would not harm the captain, simply relieve him of his duty.

The wind howled as if protesting his decision. Lightning flashed. The sharp smell of electricity filled the air. The brig jerked violently, sending Nathaniel and Mr. Keese toppling to the deck. Gripping his lifeline, Nathaniel pulled himself toward the quarterdeck railing and wrapped his arms around it. A mountainous swell forced the vessel upward toward the sky and tossed it as if it were a toy in a child's hand, then plunged it back onto the raging waters in a vicious spin.

An eerie silence consumed the merchantman as if the storm were pausing before the final crushing blow. Nathaniel clambered to his feet, coughing and spitting water. A towering swirl of black death rose over the starboard side. The ship had broached and now faced the storm with its broadside bared to the wind.

Captain Conway stood aghast, staring at it as if he just noticed the true ferocity of the storm.

Mr. Keese shook his head at Nathaniel and flattened himself on the deck.

"Hold on!" Nathaniel bellowed and grabbed the railing.

Lord, please save us. Please save Hope and everyone on the ship.

He squeezed his eyes shut as a wall of water crashed over him. The salty shroud enveloped him, clawed at him, sucking the life from him. Something solid rammed into his chest. He swallowed water. Choking, coughing, gasping for breath. His lifeline tugged him and flung him like a doll through the swirling mass. Darkness pulled on him, drawing him into its black void. His rope went taut, then slack, then taut again. He flailed his limbs, seeking any foothold. Salt burned his eyes, his nose, his throat—like acid. Terror consumed him. Not only the terror of dying, but the terror of dying so young—before he had a chance to prove himself, before he had a chance to serve God.

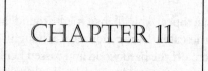

CHAPTER 11

Nathaniel's hand struck something solid, and he clung to it. The sea receded. He heaved for air, spewing water from his lungs. Grasping the capstan, he struggled to his feet and glanced over the brig. Though naught but a lifeless hull, she was still afloat.

The sharp crack of wood split the air—a loud *snap* followed by eerie creaks and groans. The mainmast toppled over as if some giant executioner had taken an ax to it. Through a salty haze, Nathaniel saw blurred figures of the remaining men scrambling to escape the falling timber. The mast pounded into the angry sea with an ominous *boom*, crushing the bulwarks and hurling walls of water into the air.

A web of rope and splintered wood covered the deck. What men had survived hunched together in groups, some cursing, some murmuring prayers. The mainmast and spars hung off the starboard side, suspended by a tangle of ropes that used to be the shrouds, halyards, sheets, and braces.

Another wave rose off their starboard beam. Lightning flashed. Captain Conway clung to the quarterdeck railing, his face a deathly shade of gray.

The surge struck, crashing over Nathaniel. Watery claws groped for him and tried to drag him overboard. He gripped his lifeline, ignoring the burning pain in his hands. The heavy mainmast tugged upon the brig, pitching it on its side and threatening to pull it into the ocean's depths.

The wave passed. Nathaniel scrambled to his feet. "Men, get your axes! Cut the mast adrift before it smashes through the hull!"

Thunder roared. The brig lurched to larboard, then tumbled downward. Grabbing his knife, Nathaniel joined the half-dozen men chopping away at the ropes and halyards. If they didn't cut the mast free in time, they would surely sink.

⁓

Hope clutched the ropes Abigail had tied around her chest. The brig pitched and sent the cabin listing sideways. Though she braced her feet, the force swept them off the hard wood and tossed her body in the air. Her shoes fell off. Her throat went dry, and her heart felt like it would crash through her chest. Surely they would capsize and all drown beneath the convulsing waters. The rough twine bit into her fingers and pressed into the skin on her arms and chest. Pain shot through her. She slammed her eyes shut and prayed for deliverance—prayed for the first time in years. She didn't want her legacy to be one of debauchery and wantonness.

Give me a chance, God. Give me a chance to change.

The brig leveled again, then began to teeter back and forth as if riding upon some mammoth's back. Thunder boomed and pounded on the hull in a deafening roar.

Mrs. Hendrick screamed—yet again—and Hope opened her eyes. Abigail's thin form lay sprawled across her cot, and in the distance, the dark shapes of Mrs. Hendrick and Elise huddled on their bed.

Hope wondered how Nathaniel fared. And Mr. Keese. Were they still on deck manning the brig, or had they gone below to ride out the storm? She couldn't even think of the alternative—wouldn't allow herself to think of it.

Releasing the rope, she rubbed her eyes, aching from stress and lack of sleep. A loud *crack* echoed through the cabin. The crunch and snap of wood sent an icy quiver through Hope. Screams blared from above. Something massive struck the brig with a jarring *crunch*. The vessel lurched to starboard, then canted back and tumbled in the other direction. The ropes scraped over her skin. Hope knew enough about ships to realize they had just lost a mast—a death sentence for a ship in a storm. She glanced at Abigail, whose wide eyes met hers with a knowing look. Whenever the roaring of the storm had subsided, Hope had heard Abigail praying, pleading for God's mercy and the eternal salvation of all on board.

"Never fear, Miss Hope. We will survive." Abigail smiled.

"I am not so sure," Hope yelled over the thunderous blast of another wave striking the brig. She clutched her ropes as the cabin jolted forward and back, sending her teeth clamping into the flesh of her lower lip.

"God told me," Abigail shouted with the confidence of an admiral of the line. She turned to Mrs. Hendrick. "We shall live through this, Mrs. Hendrick. Calm yourself."

Mrs. Hendrick let out a fearful wail.

Slowly, the roar of the storm lessened as if the beast retreated beneath Abigail's declaration. The bellowing thunder grew more distant. Waves ceased slamming into the hull, though the brig still swayed like a pendulum.

Tearing apart the knots on her ropes, Hope shoved them aside and stood to peer out the window, ignoring Abigail's warning. Through the streaks of water on the glass, she saw naught but darkness, save for an occasional foamy crest atop a distant swell.

The cabin door crashed open. Hope swerved to see Nathaniel's dark form, water streaming from his clothes. Relief eased through her taut nerves. She could not see his face or his expression, but she could feel his eyes upon her. "Untie yourselves and come on deck immediately," he commanded in a voice cracking from strain. He dashed to Abigail to help her with her ropes. "See to Mrs. Hendrick," he shouted to Hope, giving her no time to ponder the jealousy surging within her.

"What's happening? What are you doing?" Mrs. Hendrick cried. "Where is my husband? Don't touch me." She slapped Hope's hand as Hope fought to loosen the knots of her rope.

Though Hope would love nothing more than to untie Elise and leave her mother bound—and gagged—she continued to untangle the web of twine around them both.

"Make haste. There isn't much time." Nathaniel's commanding voice stung with a sense of urgency, hurrying her fingers. He assisted Abigail from the cot, then guided her toward the door. As soon as Hope had freed Mrs. Hendrick and Elise, he ushered them out as well. Grabbing Hope's arm, he led her down the hall behind the others.

Hope emerged from the companionway ladder to a blast of warm salty water that stung her eyes. She rubbed them and glanced across the deck. Above her, the clouds parted, forming a burgeoning circle of clear sky and allowing the light of a half-moon to blanket the vessel in an eerie glow. Severed timbers marked the spot where the wheel had stood. The mainmast was gone, broken off at the level of the bulwarks, its stump a cluster of bristling spikes. Where once the brig had been an ordered assembly of scrubbed and polished oak and brass, now it was naught but a dripping mass of splintered wood and a tangle of rope. Captain Conway sat on the quarterdeck, clinging to the railing, his face a mask of horror.

Hope's heart clamped. Without the mainmast, without steering, they were helpless against the next major swell.

Over the starboard side, Mr. Keese and two sailors hoisted the only remaining cockboat into the agitated waters. The ship vaulted and Nathaniel clutched Hope's arm. She glanced up at him. His dark hair matted to his head and dripped onto his sopping waistcoat. Water beaded in his lashes, but the look of concern he gave her sent her head whirling. "Are you harmed?"

"Nay." She shook her head. "What is happening? Was it a hurricane?"

"It *is* a hurricane." He scanned the brig, his eyes narrowed in concentration. "We are still in it. In the center." The lines of his face tightened, and he swallowed hard. Hope had no idea what he had been through, but she knew by the intense look in his eyes and the stiffness of his shoulders that he believed he now carried the responsibility for every life on board.

Mrs. Hendrick's hysterical sobbing drew their attention to the railing, where Abigail tried to console her.

Nathaniel faced Hope again and took her hand in his. Despite the moist chill on his rough, blistered skin, his firm grip comforted her. "We must get everyone into the boat."

The boat? She glanced across the endless expanse of swirling dark waters. "But where will we go?"

"An island, there in the distance." He gestured over his shoulder to where a gray mound rose from the sea. Land? It appeared to be naught but another menacing cloud bank sitting on the horizon.

Hope trembled and bit her lip. "Leave the safety of the brig?"

"It is not safe anymore." He raised a commanding brow. "Will you trust me?"

Hope gazed into his eyes and saw confidence and assurance within them.

Releasing her hand, he cupped her chin and stroked his thumb over her cheek. "I need you to be strong and help the others get into the boat."

Warmth radiated within her belly, spreading out like a soothing hot tea, temporarily smothering her fears. *He wants my help?* How many times in the face of danger had she behaved as hysterically as Mrs. Hendrick? Surrounded by strong sisters, Hope had found it too easy to be the weak one, the needy one.

But her sisters weren't here.

Squaring her shoulders, she drew a deep breath. No matter what terrors she faced, she longed to be strong for Nathaniel. For the first time in her life, someone needed her—and not just anyone, but an honorable gentleman—and she determined not to disappoint him.

She nodded, and he withdrew his hand, leaving her suddenly chilled.

Boots thudded over the slick wood, and Mr. Hendrick emerged from the hatch. "Is the storm over?"

Behind him, Mr. Russell lumbered onto the deck and slipped when his high-heeled leather shoes skidded across a puddle. Major Paine, who followed behind him, grabbed his arm before he fell.

"Oh, William." Mrs. Hendrick dashed to her husband, dragging Elise behind her. The brig pitched over a roller, and she tumbled into him.

"Confound it, Eleanor, what is all the fuss?" He grabbed her shoulders and held her at arm's length, then released her and brushed his velvet coat.

"What do you mean, 'all the fuss'?" Her voice cracked. "You left us alone during the storm without a word. Poor Elise was frightened half to death, and we didn't know whether you were dead or alive. Is that any way to treat. . . ?"

As Mrs. Hendrick poured her complaints onto her husband, Nathaniel sped toward the bulwarks and glanced down. "Steady now, men, steady." He turned toward Mr. Keese. "Go below and gather some lanterns, steel and flint, and weapons, if you please." With a nod, Mr. Keese disappeared down a hatch.

Beyond Nathaniel, clouds as thick and black as giant bears rose on the horizon. White lightning spiked through them. Thunder growled. Hope drew a shaky breath and clasped her hands together to keep them from trembling. The hurricane would soon return as Nathaniel had predicted. Bracing her bare feet on the moist deck, Hope made her way to where the Hendricks were still engaged in a quarrel. Nathaniel's booming voice echoed behind her.

"We can make it to the island, but we must leave immediately!"

Wind blasted around Hope, stinging her nose with the sharp smell of rain and salt. A light mist began to fall, and she hugged herself against the chill.

"Mr. Mason!" Captain Conway bellowed from the quarterdeck, where he seemed to have regained his senses and clambered to his feet. "What in the blazes are you doing? I ordered you to raise storm sails on the foremast."

Swerving around, Nathaniel glared up at the captain. "We must leave the ship at once, Captain. The rudder is disabled, the wheel is crushed, and the mainmast gone by the board."

"Are you mad? I will not leave my ship! The storm is over, as you can plainly see." Conway waved his hand toward the sky.

Halting, Hope glanced up to see that the patch of clear sky of only a moment ago was narrowing under the advancing circle of dark clouds. A gust of wind swirled her skirts around her legs as tiny drops of rain began to fall. Her palms grew moist.

Nathaniel shook his wet hair from his face. "The storm is far from over. This is merely the center of it. We must leave at once before the winds pick up again."

"What do you take me for? A dull-witted landlubber?" The captain leaned over the railing and pointed his finger at Nathaniel. "Is this some ploy to take over my ship? I knew you were a mutineer when I first laid eyes on you. Kreggs, Hanson." Captain Conway yelled at two sailors standing by the capstan. "Arrest this man at once and take him below."

Hope shuddered. Surely they wouldn't lock up the only man who was doing anything to save them.

The two men braced their bare feet over the rocking ship, looking like drowned lynx, but much to her relief, made no move to obey their captain.

Nathaniel gestured for Major Paine and Mr. Russell to approach the railing, then shot a stern gaze at Captain Conway. "Captain, I do not want command of your brig. In fact, I am trying to leave it, and I advise you to do the same. When the storm recommences, it will be far worse than what we've thus encountered." He glanced across the remaining crew. "We must all abandon ship."

"You will do no such thing!" the captain roared, his face a bloated gray in the dwindling moonlight. "No one leaves my brig."

The two sailors the captain had ordered to arrest Nathaniel came and stood by his side. "We're wit' ye, Mr. Mason."

Nathaniel smiled. "Mr. Kreggs, go below, if you please, and gather anyone who wants to join us." With a nod, the sailor darted off as Mr. Keese leapt onto the deck from a hatch, a large bundle in his hand. He took his stand beside Nathaniel.

Mrs. Hendrick's sobbing brought Hope's attention back to the task at hand. The woman clutched her husband's arm as Elise stood shivering by her mother's side. Hope longed to offer the little girl the comfort her mother neglected to give.

"We should go with them, William," Mrs. Hendrick whined. "Better to be on solid land than out here at sea."

Mr. Hendrick snorted. "Surely the captain knows far better than these"—he waved a hand in their direction—"these common sailors."

"But for Elise, for the baby." Mrs. Hendrick placed a trembling hand on her belly.

"Mr. Hendrick, please come with us," Hope pleaded.

"And why should I listen to the likes of you?" His mouth slanted sideways toward a strong jaw that would have made him handsome if he weren't such a swaggering peacock.

"Because Mr. Mason is telling the truth."

Thunder rumbled, and Hope glanced at the mushrooming black clouds swirling toward them. She gulped and tried to steady her rapid breathing and the pinpricks of fear traveling down her spine. Why was she helping these people who clearly hated her when all she wanted to do was make a mad dash toward the cockboat and reach the safety of land?

She pressed a hand to her neck to ease her racing pulse. She did it for Nathaniel, she reminded herself.

A wall of rain-laden wind slapped her with such force it turned her head to the side and stung her cheeks. Gulping for air, she braced her bare feet over the sodden wood as another wave lifted the brig.

Hope reached down and lifted Elise in her arms. "Come with us, now, Mrs. Hendrick. For Elise's sake. For your baby's sake." She held out her hand toward the blubbering woman.

"Oh, very well." Mr. Hendrick grabbed Elise from Hope's arms and ushered his wife toward the railing. "Infernal woman. Now you shall cause me to lose valuable time and precious cargo."

Hope shook her head, wondering if the man harbored any affection for his family at all.

Barreling down the quarterdeck ladder, the captain halted before Nathaniel and reached for his sword, but thankfully, the storm had stolen it from him, leaving an empty scabbard in its place. "I will not stand for this! Pure villainy, I say, pure villainy!" His hard, cruel eyes scoured the remainder of his crew. "The tiller can be repaired, and we have the foremast. You will not leave this ship!"

Nathaniel rubbed his left side and cast a quick glance at the agitated black sky, then over the remaining crew. "We must depart now!" His deep growl rolled over the ship, competing with the distant thunder. He faced the captain. "Or we will all die."

"Perhaps you didn't hear me, Mr. Mason." Captain Conway seethed. "No one leaves this ship without my permission."

"We are not your prisoners, Captain. The foremast is weakened. It will not last long when the storm returns. I beg you, sir. Leave the brig while you can."

Captain Conway's pockmarked face seemed to collapse. He glared over the lifeless deck, his fiery eyes seeking an ally. His gaze landed on a skinny man with a pointed beard sitting on the foredeck ladder. "Nichols, I command you to arrest Mr. Mason at once!"

Mr. Keese drew his pistol and pointed it at Conway. Nichols didn't move.

The captain laughed. "The powder's wet."

"I reloaded and primed it." Mr. Keese grinned.

"Enough of this." Nathaniel laid a hand on Mr. Keese's arm and eased the gun down. "We are leaving, Captain, with or without your permission." He spun on his heels. "And we will take anyone who wants to go with us."

A group of ten sailors huddled beneath the foredeck. Three more leaned over the railing, watching the proceedings with interest. Was that all that remained of the crew? Hope cringed at the realization that most of them had been swept out to sea.

The captain spit to the side. "Then begone with you all. You'll not last long on that tiny speck of land." Turning, he leapt up the quarterdeck ladder and took his spot where the wheel once stood.

The brig rose and plunged over a wave, and Hope wobbled as she made her way to Mr. Russell, who had remained glued to the capstan ever since he'd emerged from below. Terror sparked in his wide eyes. "Come, Mr. Russell. Time to leave." She placed her hand on his arm and guided him toward the bulwarks.

Kreggs bounded up from the hatch. Another sailor followed him.

Peering over the railing, Mr. Russell glanced at the tiny cockboat rocking in the foaming water and rubbed his thick hands together. Another swell slapped against the hull and lifted the brig. Mr. Russell's jowls quivered and his face turned white. "I cannot leave the ship. All my cargo is aboard. It is worth a fortune. I cannot leave the ship." His narrow eyes flitted about the deck like a nervous sparrow.

Hope laid her hand on his arm. "Is your life not worth more than gold, Mr. Russell?"

"If you stay here, you will lose both," Nathaniel said as a crack of thunder split the air. "Now let's be gone." He cast a wary glance at the black swirling clouds. A blast of wind slammed into them, stealing Hope's breath. She rubbed the sleeves of her wet gown.

"Don't listen to them, Mr. Russell. I will get you safely to Kingstown," the captain bellowed from the quarterdeck. "There, I intend to charge you, Mr. Mason, with the theft of my cockboat."

"You may come back and retrieve it any time you wish, Captain. I am only borrowing it. "Now, everyone, let's away! We haven't much time."

"Who is with us?" Nathaniel bellowed, leveling his gaze over the remaining crew.

One of the sailors dispatched from the crowd and stood beside him.

"Are you going, Major?" Nathaniel's gaze landed on Major Paine, who, wringing his wig in his hands, had up to now stood silently by the foredeck.

The major's gaze shifted from the brewing tempest on the horizon to the captain and then fixated on Hope. "Since I am in authority here, I cannot in good conscience leave these single ladies in the hands of such unscrupulous men." Approaching the railing, the major swung his legs over the bulwarks and lumbered down the ropes.

Mr. Keese approached Hope and proffered his hand. "May I assist you, Miss Hope?"

"Thank you, Mr. Keese, but I believe I shall wait until everyone else is aboard."

She tugged on Mr. Russell's arm. "I beg you, sir."

Nathaniel cast an approving glance her way that sent a wave of warmth through her, despite the cold wind.

A large swell rolled beneath the ship, tossing the cockboat against the hull with a *thud* as two more sailors climbed down to take their seats.

"We must hurry!" Nathaniel yelled.

"Mr. Russell?" She shouted over the rising wind and gave him her most pleading look.

Shaking his head, he backed away. "I cannot leave my cargo."

Hope's stomach clenched as a Bible verse her sister Grace often quoted floated through her mind: *"For what is a man advantaged, if he gain the whole world, and lose himself?"*

Nathaniel held out his hand. "Your turn, Miss Hope."

Taking his hand, she lifted her soaked skirts and eased over the bulwarks. Gripping the rope ladder, she clumsily made her way down as it flapped against the brig, scratching her fingers and crushing her knuckles against the hull. Numb with fear and pain, she wondered if she could descend another inch, when strong arms grabbed her waist and lifted her into the boat. Thanking Mr. Keese, she took a seat beside Abigail, noting the playful gleam normally present in Mr. Keese's eyes had dulled. That sight alone frightened her more than anything.

"Last chance, Captain. Mr. Russell," Nathaniel's booming voice came from above. The tiny boat rolled over a massive wave and slammed into the hull. Mrs. Hendrick screamed.

"You'll pay for this, Mr. Mason!" Captain Conway shouted in reply.

Lightning blazed across the sky as Nathaniel slid down the rope ladder and plopped into the boat, taking a seat beside Hope.

"Shove off, men!" Nathaniel shouted. "And row. Row as hard as you can."

Using the oars to push the boat from the brig, the crew plunged them into the water and grunted as they fought against the force of the powerful waves.

Hope gripped the edge of the boat as the tiny vessel leapt and vaulted over the sea, lifting her from the thwarts and slamming her down onto the hard wood. Waves of pain shot up her back. Nothing but black ink surrounded them, slick deadly liquid that surged in hungry mounds.

Water crashed over the sides of the boat, drenching them. The wind tore Hope's hair from its ribbons and pins. The saturated strands whipped through the air and stung her face. Perhaps it hadn't been a wise choice to leave the brig, after all. She could no longer see the ship. Would they make it in this tiny boat? She could feel Nathaniel's body heat beside her, the thrust of his muscular thigh against hers as he shoved his oar into the water over and over again. He glanced her way. "We shall make land, Miss Hope." The confidence of his words gave her a measure of solace.

Black, monstrous clouds engulfed the moon and stars, stealing his face from her view and the warmth from her heart. He plunged his oar back into the raging waters.

The rain began. Drops the size of grapes pelted them, stinging Hope's skin.

Abigail slid her hand into Hope's and squeezed it, and Hope leaned on her shoulder, drawing strength from the peace that draped around the young girl like a warm cloak.

Wave after wave pummeled them. Hope's wet gown clung to her. She shivered beneath the constant assault of the wind. Thunder opened its mouth and roared above the tiny craft.

Foamy fingers reached for her from atop the giant swells. Hope squeezed her eyes shut. An icy malevolence gripped her.

The boat lurched, then pitched, then wrenched up on its side. Muffled screams blared over the roar of the waves as the craft toppled, tossing Hope into the sea. She gasped for air. Swirling water enveloped her, muting the growl of the storm above. She kicked her feet, her arms flailing.

Her gown tangled around her legs, and she began to sink.

CHAPTER 12

Water filled Nathaniel's mouth, his ears, his nose. The raging of the storm grew faint, muted by the gurgling and bubbling around him. Thrusting his hands through the water, his lungs burning, he broke through the surface and heaved for a breath of the saturated air. A wave crashed over his head. Squeezing the water from his eyes, he scanned the liquid darkness. Cries for help blared at him from all directions. To his right, part of what remained of their boat floated on the crest of a wave. The Hendricks, their daughter, and two sailors clung to it for dear life. Wheezing, Major Paine gripped a barrel as it rose atop a massive wave. In the distance, Abigail and two more sailors hugged another section of the boat. Mr. Keese swam up to him.

"Where is Miss Hope?" Nathaniel shouted.

Gavin shook his head as another swell took him out of Nathaniel's view.

Nathaniel dove into the dark churning waters, driving his hands out before him. He kicked his feet. Deeper and deeper. Salt stung his eyes. Dark shadows like giant sea monsters rose to greet him from the depths.

Hope. God, help me find her. Don't let her die!

Terror sped through him at the thought of losing her, propelling him deeper. His chest burned. Panic closed his throat. He whipped his arms about, slicing through the liquid wall. He must reach her. Then his hand struck something solid yet soft. She floated through the water as if she had willingly sacrificed her life to the ravenous storm.

Hope.

He grabbed her waist and sped toward the surface. When they broke through, her head bobbed lifelessly against his shoulder. "No!" he screamed, heaving for a breath. *Lord, please.* Pressing her against his chest, he paddled through the violent swells toward the sound of waves crashing on the shore.

His feet struck sand. Struggling to rise, he hoisted her in his arms and carried her to the beach, gently laying her in the sand. She did not move. He turned her on her side and gripped her by the waist, lifting her from the ground. "Come on! Come on! Don't die on me. Spit it out!"

Her body flopped like a dead fish in his grasp. Sorrow choked in his throat and burned in his eyes. Releasing her, he sat back, panting. He clenched his fists and began to pound the sand, rage and agony searing through him.

Then she coughed. He looked up. Her body convulsed. Grabbing her, he held her as she spewed lungfuls of water onto the sand.

"Thank You, God. Thank You."

Hope gasped, sobbing, and fell into his arms.

Nathaniel dug his toes into the cool sand, saturated from the night's storm. *Hurricane, not a storm.* One of the most vicious he'd encountered. He rubbed the blisters on his hands and gazed across the troubled sea. Angry waves pummeled the shore. Lightning sparked from black clouds retreating on the horizon. Behind him, water drip-dropped from the leaves of palms and ficus trees—tears shed for those who had fallen prey to the deadly storm.

Bowing his head, Nathaniel thanked God for delivering them. Although the hurricane had tried to drag them all to the depths of the sea, by God's grace, it had not entirely succeeded. He also thanked God the cockboat had overturned so close to the island. Only Nathaniel, Mr. Keese, and one of the sailors knew how to swim, but the three of them were able to find and tow the cockboat's passengers to shore.

As Nathaniel shivered in his damp clothes, the glow of the sun peeped over the gray horizon as if trying to determine whether it was safe to rise and shed its light on another day. The golden orb must have liked what it saw, for it rose a little higher, chasing away the clouds with its bright rays and eliciting a cacophony of chirps and twitters from the tropical forest behind him.

"Did you not get any rest, Mr. Mason?" Abigail's cheerful voice startled him. The folds of her salt-encrusted skirt made a grating sound as she plopped down in the sand beside him.

He smiled at her apparent ease with her natural surroundings, but then again, she had no doubt dwelt in rustic conditions most of her life.

"Not much rest, no." He had woken to find Hope fast asleep in his arms. Heat had swept through him as his body tensed. Ashamed at his reaction, he had slipped quietly away.

Abigail stretched her arms above her. "As soon as the wind died down, I must have dozed off. 'Twas advantageous you found that cliff to shelter us. However did you see it in the dark?"

Nathaniel picked up a shell and squinted at the rising sun. After ensuring everyone was safely ashore, he'd known he must protect them from the torrential rain and thrashing wind. But where to go? If they stayed on the beach, a surge of seawater could snatch them back into the rabid ocean. If they hid in the forest, the trees could topple and crush them beneath their weight. But as the ferocity of the waves increased, he chose the former and led them into the dense thicket.

He shrugged. "I felt the wind lessen as we neared and knew, whatever it was, it had to be large and sturdy."

"You're very wise, Mr. Mason. I doubt any of us would be alive without your quick thinking."

Throughout the long night, they had huddled in groups, bracing against the rough cliff wall to avoid being blown away. Fists of wind punched them. Arrows of rain stabbed them. Nathaniel had engulfed Hope in his arms to shelter her from the onslaught. She had clung to his chest throughout the night, trembling, but uttering not a word.

She had been so strong aboard the brig, helping Mrs. Hendrick and her daughter onto the cockboat and then pleading with Mr. Russell. Although terror had burned in her eyes, she had waited until the last minute to leave the brig, and not once had she given in to her fears and blubbered like Mrs. Hendrick.

Nathaniel tossed the shell into an incoming wave, and it splashed into the swirling water. Hope's strength had surprised him. When he'd asked for her help, his intention had been to keep her calm and thus avoid the problem of two hysterical women. But she had accomplished much more than that.

He glanced at Abigail as she stared out upon the ribbons of sunlight winding their way across the deep blue waters. The warm golden fingers seemed to have a soothing effect upon the waves, stroking away the tension caused by the storm. Nathaniel released a sigh and soaked in their warmth, his own muscles easing from the stressful night.

Abigail had been naught but calm and peaceful throughout the storm, putting his own fears to shame. Then as if contradicting his unspoken praise, she shivered and gripped her arms. "There was something. . . something different about that storm."

Nathaniel rubbed his eyes, still stinging from salt. Indeed. A storm like none he had encountered.

Abigail wiped a strand of tangled hair from her face. "Something evil, a wicked presence. Did you not feel it?"

He nodded, relieved he hadn't gone completely mad. "Aye, I did. It seemed to have a purpose, a deep hatred aimed directly at us."

Drawing her knees to her chest, Abigail wrapped her arms around her legs. "Perhaps we angered the forces of darkness when you saved the ill sailor in the hold."

"God saved him, you mean."

"Yes." She smiled and brushed dried salt from her stiff gown.

"Or perhaps something or someone wants to stop you from going to Kingstown," Nathaniel offered.

"I assure you I am no threat to the enemy."

"No threat, you say?" He chuckled. "Aren't you going there to be a missionary like your parents?"

"I am not so sure." She began fingering the sand. "May I speak freely, Mr. Mason?"

"Of course."

"My parents spent their lives spreading the gospel to the descendents of the Arawaks and Caribs on Antigua. And what did they get for it? Murdered." She looked away. "No, not just murdered, sliced to pieces in their own bed." Her voice cracked. "I cannot shake the sounds of their screams from my ears or the vision of their mutilated bodies from my mind. Why did God allow that to happen? I know He loved them. They gave up everything for Him. And they were butchered for it." She gazed out to sea and bunched fistfuls of sand in her hands.

Nathaniel's gut wrenched. He wanted to tell her God must have had a reason. He wanted to tell her things would work out for good. But the words seemed so condescending in light of what she had suffered. "I don't have the answers, Miss Sheldon, but please don't give up on God."

She gave him a half smile. "I'm not giving up on Him. I know He loves me. But I don't know if I can make the same sacrifice my parents did. It frightens me, Mr. Mason, frightens me more than anything."

A band of waves pounded the shore, sending a misty spray over them. "Yet you were so calm through the most violent storm I've ever seen."

Abigail squinted toward a massive plank of wood floating atop an incoming wave. "The wind and rain don't scare me. Drowning at sea doesn't frighten me." One side of her mouth tilted upward in a smile. "Being hacked to pieces does. Besides, God told me we would survive the hurricane."

"Indeed?" Nathaniel eyed the streaks of honeyed gold cast by the sun on her brown hair, amazed at her courage, saddened by her fear, and suddenly envious of her open communication with God. How long had it been since he had heard a word from the Almighty? All the more reason why she should continue her work for Him. "Then surely God will give you the same assurance in your missionary work."

The freckles on her forehead scrunched together. "My parents had assurance. They believed God would protect and bless them for their sacrifice."

Above them a clear patch of blue pushed the dark clouds aside. "Do you think they feel blessed and protected where they are now?"

She flattened her lips, gave him a sideways glance, but said nothing.

The birds continued their cheerful chorus behind them as the full sun rose above the cloudy horizon. The petulant waves calmed to tumbling rollers depositing debris above arcs of bubbling foam.

"What does it matter?" She chuckled. "We are stuck on this island and, from all appearances, will not be going anywhere soon."

Nathaniel raked a hand through his hair—sticky with salt. If he didn't meet up with his other ship in Kingstown soon, Captain Grainer might set sail without him. A spindly crab skittered across the sand by his feet, then plunged into a tiny hole. "Never fear. The island has fresh water and a good anchorage. I'm sure a ship will come along soon."

"What do we do in the meantime?"

"We survive. I will build shelters and gather food, and we will pray for God to deliver us in His good time." Nathaniel had been formulating a plan since he'd arisen hours before. In the predawn glow he had seen bamboo, plantain, and palm trees aplenty on the island—great for making a sturdy shelter. Once he crafted a suitable hut for the ladies, he could set about finding all of them food to eat.

Abigail laid her hand on his arm. Dark lashes framed her glimmering hazel eyes. She smiled. "You are a godsend, Mr. Mason."

Returning her smile, he ignored the heat rising up his neck. Why couldn't he be attracted to a woman like Abigail? Innocent, pure, godly, devoting her life to others. Yet as becoming as she was, he could conjure nothing more than thoughts of friendship. It was Hope who made his blood heat, his thoughts jumble, his stomach flip. Why was he drawn to such an unprincipled, wanton woman?

Nathaniel released a heavy sigh, wondering whether he would ever free himself from his past.

CHAPTER 13

A dull ache throbbed behind Hope's eyes. She rubbed her temples and tried to form a rational thought. The hurricane. The brig damaged. Nathaniel. The cockboat. Water, an ocean of water surrounding her, filling her, weighing her down. Sinking. Peaceful and dark. Then strong hands grabbed her. Pulled her toward the surface. Gasping for air. Waves crashing all around her. Muscular arms surrounding her. Her feet dragging over sand, solid land. A bad dream.

A nightmare.

She shot up and opened her eyes. Her chest heaved and beads of perspiration slid down her neck. A muted blur of green and brown coalesced into trees and branches and clustered foliage. Pressing her hands against the sandy soil, she struggled to rise. Her legs wobbled, her feet hurt, and the throb in her head turned into hammering. Stumbling, she reached behind her. Her hand scraped over something sharp and cold. She gazed up. Above her, a craggy cliff towered beyond the treetops.

Where was she? How had she gotten here?

The sound of snoring drew her attention to a scatter of people lying about the filthy ground, sound asleep. Mr. and Mrs. Hendrick lay to her left—he with his back to his wife, while she cradled little Elise in her arms. Hope smiled, relieved to see the young girl alive and well. Mr. Keese, Major Paine, and several sailors lay off in the distance. But no Nathaniel. No Abigail.

Hope froze. Her throat constricted. Had they drowned?

Forcing herself into action despite the thumping in her head, she brushed aside the thick foliage and forged through a tangle of green. Drops of water sprayed over her from the ruffled leaves. The musky smell of moist earth enveloped her. Insects began to swarm around her head like

426

the thousand terrifying thoughts buzzing through her mind. If Nathaniel had drowned in the hurricane, who would escort her to Charles Towne? Who would protect her? And Abigail, her friend, her first real friend, gone before they had a chance to form a lasting bond? Following the sound of the crashing surf, she swatted aside a maze of vines and burst onto the beach.

There on the sand, watching the sun rise, sat Nathaniel and Abigail. Abigail's hand lay on his arm in a familiar touch. She smiled and they chuckled together like old friends.

Or lovers.

Hope's heart plummeted. She swallowed and tried to control her breathing, all the while ashamed at her reaction. She should be thrilled to find her friends alive, not burning with jealousy at their close association. Besides, all she sought was Nathaniel's approval, his admiration. Certainly not his love. She cringed. Was she so desperate for the attention of every man that she would deny these two godly people a happiness they both deserved? She bit her lip. What would a proper lady do in this situation? She would squelch the churning in her stomach and be the perfect picture of grace. Hope had set out to prove she could change, and change she would. Besides, what madness had befuddled her brain? Nathaniel would never grant his affections to a woman like her, for in so doing, he would deny the very essence of what made him a true gentleman.

Real gentlemen did not consort with women like her.

Chiding herself, she slogged through the moist sand and came up beside them.

"Miss Hope." Nathaniel jumped to his feet, brushing sand from his breeches. His strong jaw twitched as his intense gaze scoured her. A breeze wafted over them, tossing his wavy hair across his forehead and flapping his soiled linen shirt, giving her a peek of his muscular chest.

Hope's breath quickened again. She lowered her eyes toward her tattered, filthy dress and the strands of matted hair coiling over her shoulder and longed to sink into the sand beneath her. What a wretched sight she must present. Her state of disrepair compared with Abigail's beaming beauty forced a renewed surge of jealousy.

Abigail rose and took Hope's hands. "I told you we would survive."

Swallowing, Hope tried to gain control of her emotions. She greeted her friend with a smile. "Yes, you did. But I believe you said God would save us, not Mr. Mason." She cast a sarcastic glance his way. "Unless, of course, they are one and the same?" Which would explain Abigail's attraction to him, but certainly not Hope's.

He shifted his bare feet in the sand and cocked his head. "Nowhere close, I assure you, Miss Hope, but God can use the most unlikely people to accomplish His tasks."

"You are far too humble, sir, as I am sure Miss Sheldon would agree. No doubt she has been expressing her deepest gratitude to you this morning for saving her." Hope gave him a caustic smile.

He narrowed his eyes.

Abigail released Hope's hands and brushed a fringe of hair from her forehead. "Indeed. I do find Mr. Mason's humility refreshing."

"Hmm." Hope laid a finger on her bottom lip. "A worthy quality to be sure. And one that you possess as well, Miss Sheldon. 'God resisteth the proud, but giveth grace to the humble.' Is that not correct?" Dash it all, what was wrong with her? Why did her insides feel like they were all tied up in knots?

Nathaniel folded his arms across his chest. "I am pleased you know your Bible."

"I know enough of it. But I am sure Miss Sheldon knows far more than I, don't you, Miss Sheldon?" Hope raised an inquisitive brow toward Abigail, whose expression had crumpled in confusion.

Oh fodders. Hope knew she was behaving like a jealous schoolgirl, but the conflicting jumble of emotions swirling within her forbade her to stop. Perhaps she should leave before she made a complete nincompoop of herself.

"Forgive the interruption. I'm sure you two have much to discuss about God. . .redemption. . .sacrifice. . .or whatever holy matters you people find interesting." Hope swerved about, but Nathaniel clutched her arm. Instead of the anger she expected to see on his face, a slow smile spread over his lips. She bunched her fists.

He knows I'm jealous.

Releasing her, he took a step back. Dark stubble peppered his jaw, making him look dangerous. But it was the warm yearning in his eyes that truly frightened her. "Please don't leave, Miss Hope. We have much to discuss."

Her head began to pound again, and she rubbed her temples. She had set out to behave like a lady and had failed miserably—once again. "Forgive me. I must be tired."

"We have all endured a harrowing experience." Abigail approached Hope, her voice soft and brimming with kindness. So unlike Hope's sister Grace. Where Grace would have chided Hope for her inappropriate behavior, Abigail showed her naught but mercy.

Drying salt began to chafe the skin beneath her sleeve, and Hope scratched her arm. She deserved the irritation and far more for her ill-mannered conduct. Visions of the roiling dark waters pulling her down to the ocean depths seized her mind. She trembled. But strong hands had clutched her from a watery grave just in time. She raised her gaze to Nathaniel. "'Twas you who pulled me from the water."

His half-cocked, sensuous smile set Hope's stomach aflutter.

Further memories of the night surfaced: the dash into the shelter of the forest, Mrs. Hendrick's screams, the pelting rain. "And you who. . ." *Held me all night against the raging wind and rain.* His eyes locked upon hers, and something burned within their depths—desire? No. She was quite familiar with that look. This was something far deeper. Heat stormed up her neck and face, shocking her. She hadn't blushed in years—had thought she was far beyond blushing like an innocent schoolgirl. She turned aside and met Abigail's cat-like grin as the young woman shifted her gaze between her and Nathaniel.

"Who what?" Abigail asked.

"Never mind." Backing up, Hope lowered herself onto a huge boulder and dabbed the perspiration from her brow. Though the sun sat merely a handbreadth above the horizon, its searing rays had already begun to cook the tiny island. "Where are we?"

Nathaniel peered into the distance. "From my last calculation, one of the many small islands near Puerto Rico."

Leaves thrashed, and Major Paine and Mr. Hendrick emerged from the web of green.

"Here, here, Mr. Mason." Mr. Hendrick's red hair gleamed like fire in the sunlight. "We have survived your hurricane, it would seem."

Nathaniel nodded. "'Twas not my hurricane, but yes, God has been gracious to us."

Major Paine straightened his wrinkled red waistcoat. Blotches of mud stained his white breeches, and his boots squished as he walked. The periwig that normally sat atop his head was nowhere to be seen. In its stead, long, stringy brown hair flayed in a chaotic display about his shoulders. A sword hung at his side. He scanned the horizon. "Humph. Well now, look at the mess you've gotten us into."

Hope shook her head, stunned by the man's attitude.

"Would you prefer to have remained on the brig, Major?" Nathaniel's playful tone carried a hint of challenge.

"Aye, I would have." He ran his fingers through his hair, attempting to form some style out of the wayward strands. "No doubt she's made anchor at Kingstown by now."

Nathaniel frowned as he scanned the shoreline that stretched to the north and ended in a jumble of rocks.

Shielding her eyes from the sun, Hope followed his gaze to the debris scattered across the beach: buckets, wooden planks, sailcloth, barrels—the same barrels, from the looks of them, that Nathaniel had bound together on board the merchantman.

Nathaniel released a heavy sigh. "I fear you are mistaken, Major."

Mr. Keese burst onto the beach and marched over to them, rubbing his eyes and spraying sand into the air with his bare feet. Stains and rips marred his tan breeches, and his wrinkled shirt hung loosely about his hips. Seemingly undismayed by his tousled appearance, he winked at Hope and took a stance beside Nathaniel.

Ignoring him, Mr. Hendrick turned toward Nathaniel. "What do you mean, sir?"

"I mean 'tis plain the brig sank." Nathaniel spoke calmly over the distant crash of waves.

"Egad, I do not believe it." Mr. Hendrick and the major stared at him aghast.

"The sea has spit up the evidence, as you can see." Nathaniel waved a hand toward the debris.

The two men peered down the shoreline. Mr. Hendrick fingered his beard while Major Paine stooped to pick up a chunk of wood. Flipping it over, he examined it then tossed it down. "This could be any ship."

"Those barrels"—Nathaniel pointed to a group of casks shifting atop the incoming waves—"are the same ones I tied together on the brig before we left."

Mr. Hendrick snorted. "They could have been swept overboard."

"Aye, I suppose, but the sailcloth, the planking, the shattered remains of crates tell another tale." Nathaniel gestured to the debris. "All from a ship sailing close to this island during the storm."

"Poor Mr. Russell." Hope's chest tightened as the realization of his words sank in. "And the captain and all those men."

Abigail sat down beside her and squeezed her hand.

"Not like we didn't warn them." Mr. Keese gazed out to sea.

"So, there will be no ship returning for us." Mr. Hendrick planted his hands on his waist and gave an incredulous huff.

"Not anytime soon." Nathaniel shook his head.

Hope eyed the belligerent men. Why weren't they thankful to be alive? They should be grateful to Nathaniel for his quick thinking. She released a puff of shame. Yet had she been grateful when she had first encountered Nathaniel that morning?

Major Paine's face reddened. "What shall we do? We can't stay here." He glanced across the beach in disgust, then strolled over to where Hope and Abigail sat. "The ladies will not survive in this wilderness." He swatted a mosquito that landed on his arm.

Hope doubted the major would fare too well either.

"I know a bit about living under these conditions." Nathaniel eyed the major. "We will make the women comfortable, seek food and water, and wait until a ship sails by."

"Balderdash. That could take months." Major Paine placed a hand on Hope's shoulder as if staking his claim. "We must get the women off this savage place as soon as possible."

Hope squirmed from beneath his touch and shifted closer to Abigail. Didn't the man realize he would be at the bottom of the sea if not for Nathaniel?

Abigail squeezed her hand as if sensing Hope's unease. Her expression glowed with peace even amidst the squabbling. How could she sit there and allow these men to behave so ungraciously toward Nathaniel, especially in light of her obvious affection for him? Perchance that was how ladies were supposed to behave—quiet, demure, submissive. Hope sighed. Would she ever be able to comport herself in such a manner?

Nathaniel leveled a hard gaze upon the major. "And how do you propose to get us off this island?"

"We shall build a raft." He wagged a hand as if he could conjure one from thin air.

Mrs. Hendrick stumbled onto the beach, Elise beside her. Two sailors followed in her wake. She held a hand to her forehead. Her elegant coiffure had collapsed into a chaotic jumble like the vines she emerged from. Her lips were as white as her face, save for dark blotches beneath her eyes. Abigail dashed toward her and took her arm, leading her to the boulder beside Hope.

The two sailors stretched, glanced out to sea, then joined the group behind Mr. Hendrick.

Mrs. Hendrick shifted as far away from Hope as the rock would allow even as Elise climbed into Hope's lap. Planting a kiss on the girl's cheek, Hope snuggled against her, enjoying her warm, soft feel before Mrs. Hendrick would inevitable pull her away. But the woman heaved a sigh of exhausted resignation and looked the other way.

Giving his wife a cursory glance, Mr. Hendrick pulled a pocket watch attached to a chain from his waistcoat and snapped it open. Water dripped from it onto the sand, and he slammed it shut with a frown. "Yes, I daresay, a raft is the way to go, Major. It cannot be too far to Puerto Rico."

"You will never make it." Nathaniel said with the kind of authority that comes from deep within a man and not bestowed on him by others. "In case you haven't noticed, 'tis the season for storms. And this island lacks the materials to build a craft sturdy enough to withstand another squall."

"But you *claim* to be a shipbuilder, sir. Do you not?" Mr. Hendrick dropped the watch back into his pocket. "Surely you can construct a suitable raft. Besides, we may not encounter another storm for months."

"Are you willing to risk your life and the lives of these women on pure conjecture, sir?" Nathaniel swatted at a bug hovering by his head and released a grunt of frustration as if he wished he could do the same with Mr. Hendrick. "Nay, our best chance is to make ourselves comfortable until a ship arrives, seeking fresh water and fruit. I know this island. It is one of the few blessed with an abundance of both and is well known among the local sailors."

Hope eyed Mr. Hendrick and the major. Their expressions stiffened in unyielding arrogance. Blood throbbed in her aching head. "Even if you build a raft, and even if you make it to Puerto Rico, isn't that island in the hands of the Spanish?" She eased a lock of Elise's red hair behind her ear as all eyes shot to her.

Seagulls squawked overhead as if laughing at the ridiculous altercation below.

Nathaniel's brows rose, and Mr. Keese crossed his arms over his chest and grinned.

"My dear lady." Mr. Hendrick shifted his mulish jaw and laid a finger upon his chin, reminding Hope of a common gesture of Lord Falkland's. Why had she not noticed before its demeaning intent? "I have sailed these seas for a decade. And not to impugn Mr. Mason's knowledge, but I am quite capable of getting us safely off this island." He chuckled. "And since when do we cower before a few inept Spaniards, eh, Major?"

"Quite right." The major thrust out his narrow chin. "Enough of this nonsense. I am the highest authority here, and I say we build a raft."

Nathaniel pressed a hand on his side as if a sudden ache had arisen. "You may be the second in command of the Leeward Islands, Major, but you hold no power here. By all means, build your raft, but my first priority is our survival and the protection of these ladies."

The major's face turned a deep shade of maroon. His mouth opened and shut as if he were unable to respond.

Mr. Hendrick came to his aid. "Surely the ladies would be better cared for under the authority of a man who is used to commanding and making wise decisions."

"And where would we find such a man?" Mr. Keese grinned and scratched his whiskers.

"Enough of your impudence, sir." The major found his voice and gripped the hilt of his sword. "I issue the orders here, and I'll have you and your friend gagged and tied to a tree if you do not comply. Mr. Hendrick is correct. The ladies should be under our protection, not that of common sailors. It is our duty as gentlemen." He placed his hand once again on Hope's shoulder, slid it down to her elbow, and attempted to tug her from her seat.

Handing Elise to her mother, Hope jumped to her feet and jerked from the major's grasp. "Mr. Mason saved all of our lives last night!" A swarm of shocked gazes landed on her. "And I, for one, intend to place my trust in him." She licked her dry lips and felt the major's appraisal slithering over her.

Nathaniel's eyes widened.

The major sauntered over to stand beside Mr. Hendrick. "Ah yes, I forgot about your arrangement with Mr. Mason. Not worked off the full price he paid for you yet? Is that it?" He snickered.

Nathaniel released a massive sigh and shook his head as if resigning himself to an action he detested. "And you, sir, have insulted Miss Hope yet again. Something I told you at dinner I would not tolerate."

He had? Hope blinked. She had run from the captain's cabin too fast to hear such a chivalrous defense.

The major rubbed his thumb over the silver hilt of his sword. Nathaniel and Mr. Keese were unarmed.

The two sailors stood a few yards away, watching the altercation with amusement.

Hope's throat went dry. Perspiration slid down her back.

Nathaniel took a bold step toward the major. He narrowed his eyes. "Apologize to Miss Hope at once."

The major shifted his glance from side to side as if he would retreat, but then he threw back his shoulders, drew his sword, and leveled the tip beneath Nathaniel's chin.

CHAPTER 14

Unflinching, Nathaniel eyed the pompous man. The tip of the major's sword pierced the skin beneath Nathaniel's chin, sending a trickle of blood down his neck. Nathaniel had dealt with this type of man before—a man bent on gaining power no matter the cost.

Behind him Hope gasped, and at his side Mr. Keese made a move toward them, but Nathaniel lifted a hand to ward him off. There was no sense in anyone else getting hurt.

"I shall give you one chance to lower your blade and apologize to Miss Hope, Major." Nathaniel spoke slowly through his teeth so as not to disturb the sharp point digging into his chin, making sure, however, his tone carried the threat he intended. Though he assumed the major had been trained in swordsmanship, Nathaniel doubted the man would make the same assumption of a poor merchantman.

The major's dark eyes widened as a flicker of uncertainty, perhaps fear, flickered across them. His sword trembled, its tip scraping Nathaniel's skin, confirming his suspicions—the man was a coward.

Major Paine thrust out his pointed chin. "And I shall give you one more chance to submit to my authority." A burst of wind sent the gold fringe of his epaulet flapping against his shoulder, mocking the severity of his challenge.

Mr. Hendrick moved to stand behind the major, a supercilious grin upon his face.

"As you wish." Nathaniel snapped his gaze to the sea, feigning a look of surprise. The major flinched and glanced in the same direction, and in a lightning-quick move, Nathaniel struck the major's blade with his forearm and shoved it aside. Major Paine stumbled backward, and Nathaniel grabbed a fistful of sand and flung it into his eyes.

The major roared a foul curse, slammed his eyes shut, and began waving his sword out before him. Dodging the riotous swipes, Nathaniel darted to the major's side and snatched the weapon from his hand with ease.

The major ground his fists against his eyelids, growling like a wounded bear, then bent over, hands on his knees, and spit a string of obscenities onto the sand. "My eyes. My eyes. You've ruined my eyes."

Nathaniel flicked the hair from his face and caught his breath, happy he had dissolved the situation without injury. "'Tis just a bit of sand, Major. You will recover."

"Scads, Major." Mr. Hendrick rushed to his friend and helped him up. "Quit blabbering like a fool."

Shaking off Mr. Hendrick's grasp, Major Paine narrowed his streaming eyes upon Nathaniel. "You shall pay for this affront."

Nathaniel chuckled and wiped the sweat from his forehead. Though he would like nothing more than to challenge the man to a rematch, he had more important matters to deal with than feeding his pride and belittling the major. Turning, he tossed the sword, hilt first, to Mr. Keese, who caught it with a wink, then pressed the tip into the sand and leaned on the silver handle.

Hope's wide blue eyes, beaming with admiration, caught Nathaniel's gaze. A rush of warmth flooded him, and he tore his gaze away, returning his focus to Major Paine.

"Now, apologize, if you please."

"I meant no insult to you, miss," Major Paine whispered to the sand beside his feet.

"Very well. You may have your sword back, sir, when you promise to behave." Nathaniel grunted. "We are all stuck on this island for the unforeseen future, and we can best survive if we cooperate."

The major shifted his shoulders as if trying to regain his dignity. "You may do as you wish, Mr. Mason, but I intend to build a raft and leave this savage place as soon as possible. With or without you." He puffed out his chest and glanced first at the ladies, then behind him at the sailors. "Who is with me?" Water streamed from his reddened eyes.

Mr. Hendrick clapped a hand on the major's shoulder. "You can count on me." He peered around Nathaniel toward his wife. "I have no intention of living under these barbaric conditions until a ship happens along. Absurd! Come along, dear." He crooked a finger toward his wife.

With a groan, Mrs. Hendrick labored to her feet, took Elise by the hand, and joined her husband.

The major raised a brow toward Hope and Miss Sheldon, pasting on what he perhaps assumed was the alluring smile of a courtier, but instead it made him look more like a court jester.

Turning, Nathaniel faced the ladies, stepping aside to give them a pathway toward the major should they desire to go with him, but neither made a move.

The two sailors ambled over to stand behind Nathaniel.

The major's crimson face broke out in a sweat. Swerving on his heels, he marched away, kicking up sand as he went. Mr. Hendrick gave them all a haughty look, grabbed his wife and child, and followed after him.

～

Nathaniel plunged into the forest, hacking his way through the vines and branches with his sword in one hand and swatting them aside with a bucket in the other. If Mr. Keese hadn't gathered a bundle of weapons from the ship and passed them around in the cockboat, they'd be defenseless. Of course, Nathaniel had not carried a weapon on his person earlier in the day when Major Paine had decided to make himself king of the island. But then, a swordfight was the last thing Nathaniel had expected.

He wouldn't make that mistake again.

He slashed through a moss-covered branch, venting some of his anger. Tie him to a tree, indeed. If Major Paine had succeeded with his plan, they all would be lost. For he doubted the man knew how to survive in the tropics, let alone how to make a raft seaworthy enough to sail to Puerto Rico. Drawing a deep breath of the moist, earthy air, he pushed aside a thicket of ferns. He knew he was supposed to love his fellow man, but how did one love such a portentous mongrel?

And Mr. Hendrick was no better. For some reason, Nathaniel had expected more of him. Surely a man of Mr. Hendrick's position and accomplishments should possess some measure of wisdom and benevolence. Yet he conducted himself with no more judicious civility than that dunderhead, Paine. A vision of the blundering look on Major

Paine's face when Nathaniel had dispatched with him so quickly filled his mind. He grinned.

But a gentle nudge within put a halt to his thoughts. *Lord, forgive my pride.*

Still, both men had made their position clear. And that position was in direct opposition to Nathaniel. He grunted. Not only must he protect and provide for the survivors of the storm, but now he must battle an enemy camp.

Nathaniel stopped to catch his breath, and the buzz and whine of insects filled his ears. He waved them off, forming the only hint of a breeze in the stifling forest. Sweat streamed down his back, and his shirt, which had just begun to dry after the storm, grew damp again.

Major Paine's peevish face filled his vision, and he slashed through another leafy branch and forged ahead. All his life, men of position and power had looked down their haughty noses at him—the son of a trollop, a pauper, a poor merchantman—assuming he had no more brains than he had money. All his life, he'd fought against their disdain, their disfavor, trying to prove his value, his ability, his intelligence. And wasn't he well on his way? He had built two ships of his own, and if he hadn't been forced to sell one. . .

His thoughts drifted to Hope, and he tried to conjure up further anger to fuel his expedition through the tangled forest, but the vision of her tossing her pert little nose in the air as she stomped away from him and Miss Sheldon cooled his humor.

Jealous. Why did the thought delight him so? Birds chirped overhead, and he gazed up at their bright colors: red, purple, and blue—stark against the dark green canvas. Beautiful, colorful creatures, just like Hope, creatures that drew all admiring eyes their way, creatures who basked in the attentions they received. No, Hope wasn't jealous of Miss Sheldon. No doubt she was simply envious of any attentions not tossed her way.

The gushing sound he'd been listening for reached his ears, and he slashed his way toward it, finally bursting into a small clearing. A cascade of white, silky water spilled from a cliff nigh ten yards high into a large pond of liquid emerald. A pristine image of the myriad trees and colorful flowers reflected off the pond as if proud to display God's creation back to heaven. Amazed at the beauty of the Creator's handiwork, Nathaniel dropped to his knees and scooped handfuls of the liquid to his mouth and then splashed it over his head and neck and eased it over the blisters on his hands. At least they'd have plenty of fresh water to drink.

He sat for several minutes, breathing in the musky smells and relishing his time alone. The rustle of leaves reached his ears.

"Mr. Mason!"

He jerked around at the sweet sound of his name on feminine lips. An "ouch" chirped from a cluster of giant fig leaves, which then parted, and Hope stumbled into the clearing.

She glanced over the scenery and let out a sigh of delight. "'Tis like paradise." She looked at him, then bit her lip. Eyes as blue as the sea gripped him, and Nathaniel sensed that just like the sea, they covered a depth no one suspected. Her golden hair the color of the sun fell to her waist in a mass of tangled curls. She shifted her bare feet over the sandy soil and fingered the torn lace dangling from her neckline, in a futile attempt to put it back into place.

She appeared like a fallen angel, who against all odds had fought her way into heaven. Shaking the image, he tried to quell the sudden beating of his heart and turned to face the pond. He perched on a boulder under the pretense of stretching his legs "What are you doing here?" he said a bit too harshly. "'Tis not safe for you to be wandering about." Fire and thunder, the last thing he needed was to be alone in the forest with this enchantress.

"Why did *you* come here, then?"

"To find fresh water." He grabbed the bucket and dipped it in the pond. "You could have gotten lost."

Her soft footsteps approached.

"Oh pah. I followed your trail. 'Twas quite clear. Besides, I knew you were hurt." She pointed to the streak of red on his shirt where he'd shoved aside Major Paine's blade. "And I. . ." She looked down. "I thought I'd tend to your wound."

He stared at her creamy skin tinted pink from the morning's sun. "Why?" He could think of no rational reason she would struggle through the bugs and vines to dress a scratch on his arm—no reason save the one that frightened him the most.

A flicker of pain accused him from her eyes. "You were injured defending my honor. It's the least I can do."

"You don't owe me anything." He set the full bucket between them, water sloshing over the sides.

"I owe you everything, Mr. Mason." She glanced his way, then swerved around. "I owe you a ship, for one thing; my life, for another." He heard the tearing of fabric. "And now I owe you for standing up to that bully, Major Paine." He thought he saw her shudder before she faced him. "I do not trust him." She angled around the bucket and knelt beside him, two strips of cloth in hand. "Nor Mr. Hendrick. Their behavior toward you was inexcusable."

She dipped one cloth into the bucket and wrung it out. "Now let me see your arm."

"It is quite well, I assure you." Nathaniel inched away from her, not at all pleased with the way his body suddenly heated. He should be angry with her, furious. She'd caused him nothing but grief since the day he'd seen her on St. Kitts. He wouldn't even be on this island if not for her. And now he'd be forced to do the one thing he sought to avoid the most. Spend more time with her.

Birds fluttered and squawked overhead as though warning him about something.

"I promise I won't bite." Her eyes sparked with playfulness.

Her lips angled slightly in a pert little smile. He licked his own, remembering the kiss they'd shared on board the merchantman. Her lingering look suggested she had remembered it, too. "I'm not so sure." He grinned.

She blinked and glanced away as her cheeks reddened. "If you're referring to our kiss, I assure you it will not happen again."

Her words plummeted to the bottom of his gut.

"I am determined to change, Mr. Mason. Now, are you going to let me tend to your wound, or have I floundered through this swamp for no reason?"

Nathaniel gazed at the determined look on her face and decided the sooner he complied, the quicker they could part company. He pulled his shirt over his head and tossed it to the ground.

Hope's gaze lingered on his chest, and she fumbled with the cloth.

He shot her a playful look. "Have I offended you?"

"Of course not. 'Tis not like I haven't seen a man's bare chest be—" She slammed her mouth shut and dabbed the cloth on his wound. "Well, you know what I mean."

Yes, he did. And the reminder poured a bucket of cold water onto his simmering passions. She was a woman who toyed with men like playthings, a woman familiar with the intimate affections of men.

A woman not to be trusted.

She dipped the cloth into the bucket again, then squeezed it and finished cleaning his cut, the features of her face pinched in concentration.

Swatting at an annoying fly, she grabbed the dry cloth and wound it around his arm. "You were brave today. I've not seen anything like it. Not many men would have handled things so well with a sword pointed at their neck."

"It was nothing." Then why did his chest surge at her praise?

"Nevertheless, I find great comfort knowing you'll be looking out for us until a ship arrives."

Nathaniel's breath took a sudden leap into his throat. Was she flirting with him? After she'd announced her determination to change? He stared at her. But she remained focused on his arm, wrapping his wound with care, seemingly unaware of the effect her words had on him, not to mention how his skin heated each time her fingertips brushed across it. Purely a physical reaction to a beautiful woman. That was all. Nothing more.

"Why have you really come out here?" he asked, hoping to dissolve the mist of allure that hovered around her.

She gave a ladylike snort, crossed two ends of the cloth together, and tightened his bandage into a knot.

"Ouch." Pain shot up his arm, and he jerked away.

"That should take care of it." She struggled to her feet, hiding her face from him. "Good-bye, Mr. Mason."

Nathaniel grabbed her hand before she could turn away. Tears swam in her eyes. Perhaps she *had* come to help him out of the kindness of her heart. He was a cad. He should apologize but changed the subject instead. "You stood up to them well."

"Who?" She jerked from his grasp and turned her back to him.

"Major Paine and Mr. Hendrick." Nathaniel stood. His arm burned, and he rubbed his wound. It hadn't pained him before Hope had attended it.

"Not very ladylike, I suppose." She huffed.

"Ladylike or not, I appreciated it." Hope may not be a saint, but she had spunk, to be sure. Nathaniel's mother had been unable to stand up to anyone—had allowed men and women alike to abuse and take advantage of her. But not Hope.

"Truly?" She swerved about, and her hand slammed against his wounded arm.

He winced and let out a ragged breath.

"Oh, I am so clumsy. Please forgive me, Mr. Mason." She reached out to touch him, but he backed away, his arm still stinging.

When the pain subsided, he drew in a deep breath. True concern burned within her blue eyes, and an overwhelming urge to protect her rose within him. She exuded a charm, an appeal that transcended her beauty. Coupled with her ill reputation, it made her easy prey. He saw the way Major Paine looked at her, not to mention Mr. Keese's playful flirtations. He must protect her and provide for her—if she didn't kill him first. He grinned. A weight settled on his shoulders like none he'd known before. Many years had passed since he'd been responsible for the welfare of another. Not since caring for his mother as a young boy.

And that hadn't turned out well at all.

"Shall I see to your chin?" She reached up to touch him, but he jerked away. "Nay, it's fine." He doubted his body could handle any more of her close ministrations.

"I don't have the plague, Mr. Mason." She blinked and dropped her hand to her side. "You treat me in the same manner as Mrs. Hendrick does."

"That is not my intention. It's simply that. . .well. . ." Nathaniel rubbed the back of his neck. "I've suffered more misfortune these past five days than I've suffered in several years."

Her brow puckered. "And you're saying it's my fault?"

"There was my ship, of course."

"I suppose you're still angry about that." She kicked the sandy soil.

"I'm trying not to be."

"Try harder." She mimicked the same words he'd said to her back on the merchantman when she'd announced her efforts to behave. "Besides, I told you my father would give you another."

"Hmm. Then, I was nearly crushed by a bundle of crates on board the brig."

"You can hardly blame me for that."

"And I lost all of my belongings."

She pursed her lips and looked away, her face reddening.

"Then the hurricane."

"Now storms are also my fault?" Her bottom lip quivered. "Next you'll be blaming me for droughts and famines and wars."

"You haven't been to Spain lately, have you?" He grinned, picturing the havoc she might have wreaked amidst Spain's recent attempt to conquer Italy.

"How dare. . .of course not!"

"And let us not forget that Major Paine nearly sliced me in two." He raised a brow.

She hugged herself and thrust out her chin. "I didn't ask you to defend me."

Moments passed as Nathaniel studied her. The laughter of splashing water and the warble of happy birds did naught to ease the tension between them. She stared at the pond, her eyes misting, and Nathaniel swallowed his rising guilt. He'd wanted her to know what he'd suffered at her expense, but found the sorrow lining her face brought him no pleasure. He opened his mouth to apologize when she shot eyes that now sparked in anger his way.

"Since you find my company so dangerous, I shall relieve you of it." She clutched her skirt and swung about, stomping toward the edge of the trees.

"Wait. You shouldn't go alone," Nathaniel yelled after her, but the wall of green swallowed her whole.

"I am not your concern." Her sharp voice warbled from the thicket.

Grabbing the bucket and his shirt, Nathaniel trudged after her, wishing with all his heart that her words were true.

CHAPTER 15

Hope blew out a sigh, annoyed at the constant prickling over her skin. She lifted the hem of her skirt to scratch the tiny red marks sprinkled over her legs—courtesy of unseen fleas that lived in the sand and feasted on human flesh. Just another amenity of this tropical paradise. Flipping down the filthy fabric, she drew her knees to her chest. Before her, the Caribbean Sea shimmered like a giant sapphire in the noonday sun. Wavelets formed intricate designs along the smooth shore, but despite her efforts to admire the scenery, her gaze kept wandering to the tall, bare-chested, sun-bronzed man with wavy hair the color of a dark walnut, who stood knee-deep in the surf with spear in hand. The muscles of his arms bulged as he tensed for the kill, reminding her of their time in the untamed forest four days ago when he'd doffed his shirt so suddenly. She hadn't expected to find such a firmly muscled chest and finely chiseled arms beneath his scraps of soiled linen. Nor had she expected the sudden heat that claimed her when his bare chest came into view. And he'd noticed her reaction, only adding to her mortification.

But from beneath the shade of this tall palm, she could admire Nathaniel discreetly. Certainly there was no harm in that.

"He presents quite a handsome figure, does he not?" Abigail's teasing tone jarred Hope and brought her gaze to the girl sitting beside her, weaving thin, pointed leaves into some sort of basket. Was there nothing Abigail couldn't do? She had been so quiet, her presence had slipped from Hope's mind.

Feeling her face heat, Hope started to deny she'd been gazing at Nathaniel, but why bother? Apparently Abigail had been doing the same. Hope dismissed the familiar jab of jealousy. How could she blame her friend? Especially when she was a far more suitable match for Nathaniel than Hope would ever be.

"Yes, I suppose he does," Hope finally admitted.

"And resourceful, too."

Hope shot a glance over her shoulder at the shelter Nathaniel had built for them that first day. It had taken him three hours to latch together a wooden frame with vines and cover it with fig leaves and palm fronds, and another hour to make a raised floor laden with soft leaves and moss for them to sleep upon. Watertight and warm, it afforded her and Abigail the privacy they needed among so many men. Several yards away, he and Mr. Keese had slapped together another, bigger shelter for themselves and Kreggs and Hanson, the two crew-men who had joined them. The other three sailors had opted to join Major Paine's party, although Hope could not understand why.

"Would ye like some mango, Miss Hope, Miss Sheldon?"

Kreggs grinned down at her, his teeth stained brown and his arms bursting with red and yellow fruit. Though he stood no taller than Hope, his arms were as thick as her thighs. Short gray hair stuck out in all directions around his leathery face.

"No, thank you, Mr. Kreggs, but save one for me, will you?" Hope smiled. Although the fruit appeared ripe and juicy, the sight of it made her stomach curl.

"Sure thing, miss."

"I'll take one. Thank you, Mr. Kreggs." Abigail held out her hands, and he tossed the mango into them before he lumbered over to the fire and dropped the remainder into a barrel. Plucking a knife from his belt, he sat on a log and whittled away at a piece of wood.

"Are you ill?" Abigail touched Hope's arm, her brow furrowed. "You're pale, and you haven't eaten all day."

A sudden chill gripped Hope, and she rubbed her arms. Truth be told, her stomach had been doing flip-flops like a fish all morning. "Nay, I'm just tired."

"Yes, 'twas a fierce storm last night."

"But the shelter Mr. Mason built for us held up well." Hope shuddered, remembering the torrential downpour pounding on the thick ceiling of leaves and the claps of thunder that shook the frame of their tiny hut. Yet only a few drops of rain trickled down to where Hope and Abigail crouched together waiting for the storm to end.

Abigail bit into the fruit, dabbing at the juice dribbling down her chin with her handkerchief, and gazed back out at Nathaniel. He thrust his spear into the water then yanked it back. A fish thrashed on its tip. Adding it to a pouch slung over his shoulder, he sloshed through the water a few paces and regained his stance. Admiration burned in Abigail's eyes, and Hope let out a ragged breath. She had a long road to travel before she could be respectable enough to catch the eye of an honorable man like Nathaniel. And she was beginning to fear that particular road would be all uphill.

Besides, after Hope had stomped away from Nathaniel by the pond, he'd not uttered a single word to her. Clearly his interests lay elsewhere.

A loud curse drew her attention to the motley band under the direction and guidance of Major Paine. Three sailors, all bare-chested and drenched in sweat, hacked away at logs while Major Paine and Mr. Hendrick sat on a rock in the shade, periodically shouting orders to the workers. Off in the distance, Mrs. Hendrick and Elise sat beneath a huge calabash tree. Elise played with something in her lap while poor Mrs. Hendrick leaned back against the trunk, fanning herself with an oversized leaf. Hope longed to go visit them and see how they fared, especially Elise. But Nathaniel had forbidden her and Abigail to go near Major Paine without an escort.

Hope shivered and drew her knees to her chest, wondering why the weather had suddenly turned cold, yet finding no cause for it. The sun hung high in the sky. No breeze fluttered the leaves of the trees. And waves of heat rippled up from the sizzling sand. Belying the chill on her skin, beads of perspiration rose on her forehead, and she batted them away. Perhaps she was just tired, after all—tired of being filthy and hungry. What she wouldn't give for a bath and a change of clothes. But she was complaining again, and as she gazed at Abigail, humming a tune as she took the last bite of mango, Hope realized she had a far way to go before she could claim such a sweet spirit as the girl beside her.

Leaves rustled, footsteps thudded, and the charming Mr. Keese appeared, hoisting two buckets splashing with water. Setting them down, he placed his hands on his hips and gave her a saucy wink. "May I offer you a drink, Miss Hope?" He gave Abigail a cursory glance. "Miss Sheldon?"

Hope couldn't help but smile at the tall, robust man who, although but a few years younger than she, seemed boyish in many ways. His straight sandy hair grazed his shoulders, contrasting his dark eyebrows that seemed to be in a perpetual sarcastic arch. That, coupled with his mischievous grin, made him look both dangerous and inviting.

"That would be nice, Mr. Keese, thank you."

"Freshly drawn just for you." He plunged a large shell into the liquid and carried it to her, cupping the bottom. Kneeling beside her, he tipped it as Hope sipped the cool liquid. "Thank you." She pushed the shell away. Mr. Keese leaned to hand the shell to Abigail, and his thigh rubbed against Hope's. The grin on his face said he'd noticed the contact as well. Hope scooted back. She could not deny his attentions eased the ache in her heart, especially in light of Nathaniel's blatant disregard, but she must resist the urge to keep returning to her old ways.

After Abigail drank her fill and returned the shell, Mr. Keese dunked it in the bucket again and poured water over his head, then shook his hair like a dog, raining droplets all over them.

"That be one way to stay cool, says I." Kreggs chuckled.

But Hope didn't need any assistance in that regard—not today. Brushing the water from her gown, she fought off a shiver, all the while admiring Mr. Keese's strong jaw and his playful mannerisms, and wondered why her heart wasn't drawn to him. They were kindred spirits, after all—carefree, wild, unbeholden to any God—and he certainly kept his interest in her no secret. But then again, Hope had never had any difficulty attracting men of his ilk.

Everyone resumed their tasks, and Hope mounded sand around her feet. "I feel so useless. Mr. Keese, you collect water and wood. Kreggs and Hanson pick fruit. Abigail weaves baskets." She smirked toward her friend. "Next she'll be making clothes for us all, no doubt. And Mr. Mason catches fish. I can't even crack open a coconut." She grabbed a handful of sand and let it sift through her fingers.

Mr. Keese plopped beside her. A whiff of sweat and the musky scent of the island wafted over her. Taking her hand in his, he kissed it. "Why distress yourself, miss? Why not enjoy the fortune of having so many to care for you. Like a princess among her admirers."

"A condition Miss Hope should be quite familiar with." Nathaniel's brown eyes locked upon her, disapproval tightening the lines of his face.

He held a spear in one hand, a sack of fish in the other, and he towered over them like a god of the sea emerging from its depths to punish his subjects. He chucked the spear into a tree and ran a hand through his tousled, wet hair.

"On the contrary, I wish to help." Hope struggled to rise, but the scenery began to spin around her. She shook her head. Tiny sparks flitted across her vision as Mr. Keese assisted her to her feet. She forced her eyes to focus on Nathaniel. At least he had finally spoken to her. "I know I can't do much, but I'm not beyond attempting any task you give me, Mr. Mason."

Nathaniel snorted and tossed the sack of fish to Hanson, who had just sauntered into the clearing. "Skin those, if you please, Hanson."

"Aye, sir." The lanky sailor sank down by the fire and went to work.

"How did you learn to fish like that?" Mr. Keese asked. "And to build these shelters? Sink me, such skill. It's incredible."

Nathaniel shrugged off the compliment. He rubbed his left side, where a long purple scar etched his otherwise perfectly tanned skin, and Hope wondered where he'd received such a wound. On his arm, the cut from Major Paine's sword still healed. He glanced over his shoulder toward the other camp. "I spent time on the shores of Barbados fending for myself."

"We owe you a great debt, Mr. Mason." Abigail laid down her basket and rose to her feet.

"Indeed." Mr. Keese clapped him on the back. "We have all benefited from such an adventurous childhood."

"Adventurous?" Nathaniel snickered. "I would not call it such." He frowned.

Hope wondered how Lord Falkland would handle himself in such a savage environment. Always adorned in the latest London fashions without spot or wrinkle, Arthur was not a man to be found half naked, thrusting a spear into the crashing surf. Hope giggled at the vision.

The smell of fish curled beneath her nose as Nathaniel's gaze found hers again and seemed to bore right through her. Hope pursed her lips. "I may not be able to contribute very much, but I believe I shall take some food over to Mrs. Hendrick and her daughter. They don't look well, and I doubt they're being fed as well as we are." She skirted around Mr. Keese, grabbed some mangos and plantains from the barrel, and dropped them into an empty bucket.

"Why not leave a platter out for them tonight?" Mr. Keese's tone stung with sarcasm. "They've been stealing our food after we retire anyway."

"They have?" Abigail's voice lifted.

Grabbing the full bucket, Hope swerved around, then wished she hadn't moved so fast. She took a deep breath and waited for the trees to stop spinning around her.

"Aye." Hanson's knife halted over the fish he was skinning. "I've heard 'em more than once. Thought they was rats at first. Then when I peeked out o' the hut, I realized they were—big rats." Mirth skipped across brown eyes that were far too big for his narrow face.

Hope had heard rustling around her hut at night, but the thought it might be some dangerous animal had kept her inside. "There's plenty of fruit on the island. Why can't they eat that?" She wiped the perspiration dotting her neck.

"Naw, miss." Kreggs pointed his knife toward the trees. "We've scavenged most o' the food near the shore. Ye have t' go deep in the forest, an' it be slim pickin's even there."

Nathaniel closed his eyes a moment as if frustrated with the topic. "I'm well aware of the situation."

"And it doesn't prick your ire?" Mr. Keese snorted.

"I says we post a guard." Kreggs dug his knife into the chunk of wood in his hand.

"They are welcome to whatever fish we have to spare." Nathaniel squatted by the fire and poked a stick into the simmering embers. "We can't very well let them starve."

Abigail sauntered over to stand beside Nathaniel. "Of course not. What's ours is theirs."

Setting down the bucket, Hope looked out toward the incoming rollers, anywhere but at Nathaniel and Abigail united in cause, united in temperament, united in beliefs, united in. . .

She sighed. The crystalline waters beckoned her.

"But they ain't worked for it." Hanson swatted at a fly hovering over his fish.

"And don't forget the major drew a sword on you," Mr. Keese added.

Nathaniel stood and rubbed beneath his chin where the major had aimed his blade. "I can hardly forget that."

"Then explain to me why we should supply them with food when they threatened to tie us to trees?" Mr. Keese plucked a papaya from Hope's bucket.

"Because they are fellow human beings, and we are called to forgive," Nathaniel replied.

Abigail and Nathaniel exchanged a smile. Despite her jealousy, Hope could not help but admire a man who would share food with his enemies.

Hope rubbed her forehead against another wave of dizziness. "Mrs. Hendrick is in a family way, and Miss Elise is but a child. They have not a choice in the matter."

Tossing her chin in the air, she started toward the other camp when a wave of nausea gripped her and stole her breath. Icicles pricked her skin. The bucket became an anchor in her hand. It slipped from her grasp. Horrified, she stared at the fruit as it tumbled onto the sand. Could she not even do this one thing right? The yellow, red, and orange colors blurred into a jumbled rainbow. She raised a hand to her head. The trees, the hut, the people, the sea spun around her—a landscape of hazy browns, blues, and greens.

"Miss Hope. Miss Hope?" Nathaniel's voice sounded hollow and distant. Strong hands clutched her arm. "Blast it all!" She recognized his angry tone.

Hope tried to walk, but her feet turned to jelly and she collapsed, much to her relief, into the safety of welcoming arms.

A cool hand touched her forehead. Abigail's sweet voice eased over her.

"Heaven help us, she's burning up with fever."

CHAPTER 16

Red flames leapt all around Hope. Crackling, sizzling, blazing. She bolted to her feet. Fiery talons snapped at her, nipped at her gown, fingered her hair. Sweat slid into her eyes. She blinked and ran the sleeve of her gown across her forehead, then spun around. The flames blurred in a flickering circle of red and orange.

The hut was on fire.

Her mouth was parched, as dry as sand. Her heart crashed against her ribs. Where was Abigail?

"Abigail!" Hope screamed. "Abigail, Mr. Mason!" Searing pain spiraled through her, starting at her feet, then cinching around her stomach and storming into her head. She tossed her hands to her ears to drown out the hammering ferocity of it.

Beyond the fire, the gray silhouette of a man shifted in the darkness. "Mr. Mason?"

The shape took form: eyes, nose, lips, hair, and clothing dropped onto the figure as he approached. The man stepped through the flames and halted before her. He stared at her—yet through her.

"Arthur." Hope's breath caught in her throat at the sight of the man she'd once thought she loved with all her heart.

The fire disappeared and the bulkheads of a ship's cabin formed around them.

"I tell you, Captain, I don't know the woman." Lord Falkland's handsome lips flattened, and he turned to face another man who materialized from the darkness.

Captain Brenham doffed his plumed tricorn and tossed it onto his desk. "Then perhaps ye can explain t'me why she insists ye are her betrothed?"

"Preposterous!" A woman's voice screeched from a dark corner. She emerged to stand beside Lord Falkland, annoyance marring her comely features. "My Arthur cannot be engaged when he already has a wife." She waved a silk fan over her elegant coiffure, sending tiny curls dancing about her neck. "Why, look at her. She is no doubt a fortune-hunting strumpet." She eyed Hope with disdain and tossed her nose in the air.

"How dare you!" Hope charged toward her, but Lord Falkland held up his cane, barring her passage. Halting, she faced him. Fear and desperation coalesced in a burning lump in her throat. "Arthur, why are you doing this? Tell them who I am. Who is this woman?" Placing her hand on his gold-trimmed coat, she searched his eyes for a hint of affection, a hint of the love she'd grown to expect, the love she'd risked everything to possess.

He would not meet her gaze. He thudded his cane onto the deck and yanked his arm from beneath her touch.

"As I have told you, Captain. I've never seen this delusional woman before." He patted the other woman's hand and placed a kiss upon it as he used to kiss Hope's.

Blinking, Hope reeled back. Memories danced through her mind like jesters, taunting her—memories of the tender love she and Arthur had shared, of sweet promises whispered in the middle of the night, memories of being loved, cherished, cared for.

"What d'ye intend I do wit' her?" The captain cocked his head and studied Hope as if she were a chest of gold.

Lord Falkland shrugged. "Why should I care?"

"Because you love me! You promised to marry me!" Throwing all propriety aside, Hope clung to him with both hands. The lavender scent he doused himself with snaked around her, making her dizzy. "What are you doing?" Her heart thumped wildly. Her knees shook. Tears poured down her cheeks.

"Madam, control yourself." Arthur attempted to tug his sleeves from her grasp.

"Release my husband at once." The woman clawed at Hope's hand, prying it from Arthur's arm, then shoved her back. "Captain, I protest. Must we continue to endure this humiliation?" Panting, she pointed her fan in Hope's direction. "The woman is deranged."

Hope fell to the deck, splinters piercing her skin. Heat surged through her, and the floor began to spin.

Captain Brenham clamped his massive fingers onto Hope's arm and jerked her to her feet. Stabs of pain shot into her shoulder. "Me apologies, Lady Falkland. By all means, take yer leave. I'll be more 'n happy to deal wit' her."

"Very well, then." Casting one last repugnant look toward Hope, Lady Falkland turned and pulled Arthur along behind her.

Lord Falkland glanced over his shoulder, and for the first time, his gaze met Hope's. Through her tear-blurred vision, Hope thought she glimpsed a flicker of remorse cross his features. Then he was gone.

Along with all of Hope's dreams.

Greed glinted in the captain's eyes. "Aye, I know jest what t' do wit' ye."

Flames shot up around her again, suffocating her and consuming all her remaining strength.

Something touched her forehead. Soft and cool. "She's dreaming," a muffled voice said.

"Seems more like a nightmare." A deep male tone responded. *Nathaniel's voice.*

Had he come to save her? Hope tried to pry her eyes open, but someone seemed to have sewn them shut. She lifted a hand to her face, groping for the cause, and found naught but moist, simmering skin. Thrusting out her arms, she probed for the source of those wonderful voices.

A large, calloused hand gripped hers and held it tight. "'Tis us, Miss Hope. We are here." She clung to it with what little strength she could muster, drawing comfort from the caring touch of another human being.

Thrashing her head, she tried to make sense out of her jumbled thoughts. "He left me. He lied to me."

"Shhh... Hope, you have a fever." Abigail's soft voice caressed her like the cool cloth brushing over her forehead. A spark of joy assuaged her grief. Her friends had not perished in the flames.

"The hut is on fire." The words squeaked from Hope's dry throat.

"No, you are safe. Nothing is on fire," Nathaniel said. Was he caressing her hand? And what was that infernal pounding in her head?

She rubbed her eyes and managed to pry them open, but only blurry mirages met her gaze. "Where am I?"

"You are in our hut." Abigail's hazy figure leaned over her and dabbed a cloth on her neck.

Hope shifted her gaze to Nathaniel. The slight wave of his brown hair came into focus, then his dark eyes that reminded Hope of the coffee her sister Faith liked to drink. He shifted his jaw, dusted with black stubble. But it was the look in his eyes that drew her attention. Concern, fear, and something else. Such a different look from the one she had just seen in Arthur's eyes.

"Lord Falkland was here." She shook her head, trying to jar loose the tangled web in her mind.

"It was only a dream."

"Only a dream," she repeated. An unrelenting heaviness pressed upon her eyes, and no longer able to fight it, she closed them and faded into darkness.

❧

Nathaniel released Hope's hand with a sigh and rubbed his aching eyes. The hint of dawn glowed through the leaves of the hut as the crickets hushed to silence. After Hope had collapsed in his arms on the beach, he and Abigail had attended her through the remainder of the day and all through the night. But despite their continual ministrations, she had remained unconscious, save for the brief moment when she'd just awoken. Regardless, her fever still soared, and Nathaniel feared the worst. "At least she awakened."

Abigail smiled as she dabbed the wet cloth over Hope's face, pink with fever. "'Tis a good sign." But her unsteady voice stole conviction from her statement. "Who is Lord Falkland?"

"The man who abandoned her in St. Kitts." Nathaniel flexed his jaw, but pity soon eased his taut muscles. From the few intelligible words Hope had uttered, he gleaned her memory of Lord Falkland's betrayal had been quite traumatic—and quite painful.

"Ah, no wonder she has nightmares about him." Abigail sank back, folding her legs beneath her, and dropped the cloth into the bucket. "Her fever is far too high."

Nathaniel grimaced and sat on a barrel on the other side of Hope. "Do you know the cause?"

Abigail swallowed, her hazel eyes stricken. "I fear it is marsh fever. I saw much of it on Antigua when I worked with my parents."

Marsh fever. Nathaniel's stomach coiled in a knot. "But isn't that. . ." He didn't want to say the word *fatal* aloud, couldn't bear to think it, let alone hear it.

"Yes. It can be." Abigail's eyes swam, and she stood, wiping sand and leaves from her skirt. "I'm going in search of Indian fever bark. I believe I saw some in the woods." She headed for the flap of sailcloth that served as a door. "I can make some tea from it. It's all I know to do."

"Ask Kreggs to accompany you. I heard him up earlier."

She nodded, pushed aside the cloth, and left the hut.

Several hours later, Nathaniel shielded his eyes from the sun as he emerged from the tiny shack. He stretched his cramped legs and stared at the breakers glistening in white, foamy bands across the blue sea. Their beauty held no allure for him today. Gavin stood knee deep among the incoming waves, spear in hand, and battled to keep from falling. When he saw Nathaniel, he plowed through the water and onto the shore.

Hanson entered the camp, his arms full of firewood, as Gavin rushed toward Nathaniel.

"How is she? What news?"

Nathaniel shook his head. "Abigail. . .Miss Sheldon and I gave her some tea, but I don't know how much she swallowed. She's resting now."

Hanson dropped the load of wood onto the sand and scratched his chest, eyeing the hut nervously.

Panic sparked across Gavin's boyish face. "And the fever?"

"It hasn't broken." Truth be told, the fever had only worsened. Nathaniel's gut hardened into a ball of lead.

"I must see her." Gavin tossed down the spear and started for the hut.

Nathaniel held up a hand. "I'm told it is contagious. Miss Sheldon and I have already been exposed. No sense in putting yourself in danger."

Hanson's eyes widened. "I'll jest go find some fruit." He darted from the clearing.

"But if there's something I can do," Gavin said. "Some comfort I can give her." Nathaniel had seen evidence of Gavin's affection for Hope, but the stark clarity of the desperation on the man's face hit him like a punch in the stomach.

Shrugging off the uncomfortable feeling, he released a heavy sigh. "She's not conscious. We can do nothing now but pray."

"Pray?" Gavin snickered. "A desperate measure for weak men."

"Or a powerful measure for courageous men," Nathaniel responded with authority, even as he wondered where the words had come from. For he felt weak and desperate as Gavin had said. But perchance the answer had come through his own lips—from God's heart. He needed to pray—and pray hard.

Gavin gave him a look of derision, then shook his head.

Hoping to alleviate the tension, Nathaniel pointed to a flounder lying on a bed of leaves near Gavin's spear. "I see you've caught a fish."

"Only one in two hours." Gavin's boyish smile returned. "And a tiny one, as you can see. I'm afraid I don't possess your skills." He raised his brows in an invitation. "We could use some fish for supper."

"I need some rest first." Nathaniel hated spending even a few hours away from his vigil, but if he didn't, he wouldn't be much use for anything.

He headed toward his hut, but a red and white figure storming toward him caught the corner of his eye. Major Paine. Nathaniel groaned.

Drawing up to his full height, the major gripped the hilt of his sword. "What has happened to Miss Hope?"

"She is sick with fever, Major." Nathaniel rubbed his eyes, willing the man to disappear.

"Fever? Egad, I knew you couldn't take care of her." He brushed past Nathaniel, leaving the stench of sweat and moldy clothes in his wake. "I shall take her back to our camp where she can be tended to properly."

Nathaniel turned "Be my guest, Major. Perhaps you have discovered a cure for marsh fever?"

The major stopped in mid-stride. "Marsh fever, you say?" He faced Nathaniel, his ruddy face faded to white. He adjusted the torn black cravat at his throat. "Miss Sheldon attends to her?"

Nathaniel nodded.

"Then 'tis best not to disturb her." He stretched his neck. "But be advised, Mr. Mason, I shall return to check on her soon."

"I cannot wait." Nathaniel bowed, an unavoidable grin on his lips.

With a snort, the major sauntered off to where the sailors still hammered away on a raft that was beginning to take shape.

But Nathaniel had neither the time nor the inclination to worry about that now. The totality of his thoughts and his heart focused on the lady burning up with fever not five yards away. As he plodded toward his hut, memories twisted through his mind, setting off a blaze of panic. His mother had been deathly ill, eaten alive by some unnamed disease. Her vocation and poverty kept all doctors at bay, and even the priests would not set foot in her house. Nathaniel had been only eleven years old, but he had done the only thing he could think to do. He prayed. But his prayers had fallen lifeless before God's throne, leaving him an orphan.

Staggering into his hut, he fell to his knees and clutched a fistful of palm fronds and squeezed until the sharp edges stung his skin. "God, if You answer just one of my prayers, please let it be this one."

CHAPTER 17

Two days had passed. Exhaustion crushed Nathaniel like an anchor. Sitting beside Hope in the stifling hut, he dabbed her burning face and neck with a wet cloth, easing the moist strands of hair from her forehead so that her golden curls formed a halo in the lantern light around her head. Like an angel. Night had fallen as black as ebony outside the hut. Although he and Abigail took turns attending Hope, continuing to douse her with cool water, her fever remained high. Now, with her breathing shallow and labored, he feared the end was near.

Dark lashes fluttered over her inflamed cheeks as she moaned and writhed on the leafy bed. Oh, how he longed to see those clear sapphire eyes staring back at him again—even when they shot sparks of biting sarcasm his way—instead of the dull hazy blue that had fixated on him of late.

He bowed his head. "O Lord, don't take her. Please let her live."

For the life of him, he could not understand the dread that consumed him at the thought of losing her. He'd seen many people die—friends, shipmates, even his mother. But as grievous as their passings had been, he could not shake the feeling that if Hope died, he would lose a part of himself forever.

Rubbing his eyes, he wondered at his sanity. The woman had brought him nothing but trouble. Yet she had been his obsession since the first time he'd laid eyes on her in Charles Towne. A burning rose in his side, and he rubbed his old wound and released a sigh of frustration. He could only attribute this pernicious enchantment to a flaw in his character—something passed down from his mother and perhaps from her parents before her.

Which was precisely why he must continue to resist it—later after

Hope had recovered, of course.

Hope gasped and tossed her head back and forth. Sweat beaded on her neck and chest and streamed down onto the bed of leaves. Her petticoat clung to her moist body, and he eased the sailcloth a bit higher, forbidding his gaze to wander into danger.

Drawing his knees to his chest, he dropped his head onto his arms and allowed his tired eyes to close, if only for a moment.

"Nathaniel?"

He pried his heavy lids open and stared at the fronds by his bare feet. How long had he been asleep?

"Nathaniel?" The voice sounded weak and muffled.

Rubbing his eyes, he lifted his head and smiled when he saw Hope staring up at him. She reached a trembling hand toward him, and he took it in his own. Searing heat scorched his skin and radiated up his arm, but he did not allow the stab of fear to weaken his smile. "You spoke my Christian name."

"Surely," her faint voice cracked, "formalities can be tossed out the window when one is dying."

"Dying. . . You're not dying."

A smile. "You're too honorable a man to be a good liar. You forget I've had much experience with liars."

Nathaniel swallowed. "The tea Miss Sheldon has been giving you may yet perform its magic."

"I fear I shall need more than simple magic." She struggled for a breath and glanced around the hut, then out the door. "What of Mrs. Hendrick and Elise? Did you take them food?"

Nathaniel flinched. "You concern yourself with them when you are. . . in such a state?" By the board, this lady constantly surprised him. Her gaze remained locked upon him, and one determined brow arched, awaiting an answer.

"Yes, never fear, I took them enough food to last several days."

"Thank you." She squeezed his hand, the minuscule effort visible in the lines on her face.

"Nathaniel." She coughed and gazed up at him, her blue eyes dull and cloudy. "I must tell you something."

"You need your rest." Nathaniel patted her face with the cool cloth.

The normal pearly glow of her skin had faded to a gray sheen, broken by red blotches where the fever consumed her. Dark half circles hung beneath her once luminous eyes. His heart ached.

Hope's chest heaved. "Nay. I must. I know I've told you this before, but it weighs heavy on my heart." She swallowed. "I am so sorry about your ship."

"Fire and thunder." He dropped the cloth into the bucket with a *splash* and raked a hand through his hair. "You think that matters to me now?"

"Now? Why wouldn't it?" Her forehead wrinkled. "Nothing has changed for you, save you have been struck with a multitude of disasters." She gasped. "As you have said, I brought you bad fortune."

A chill etched down Nathaniel's back, followed by the eerie sense *something* was in the hut with them. Running a sleeve over his sweaty forehead, he scanned the palm fronds that formed the walls and roof. The dark shadows cast by the lantern light hovered like beasts about to pounce.

"See. You do not deny it." Hope choked out a laugh.

Shaking the prick of unease from his shoulders, he dropped his attention back to her. "I will not deny misfortune has followed me lately, but as to the cause, I cannot say."

"Cannot, or will not?" She brushed her fingers over his hand in a familiar way that shocked and delighted him. "You are too kind, Nathaniel, but then, that is your nature, is it not?" She flung a trembling hand to her head.

Releasing her other hand, Nathaniel wrung out the cloth and brushed it over her cheeks and forehead.

Hope blinked and drew a deep breath. "Please tell my sisters how sorry I am to worry them so. I've not been a good sister." A smile faltered on her lips. "And tell my father he owes you a ship."

"Shhh now. You can tell him yourself."

"Nay." She chuckled, then broke into a cough. "He won't listen to me. He has never had much use for me, I'm afraid."

Sorrow constricted Nathaniel's throat. He'd always assumed Hope had grown up in a good home, sharing her life with an adoring father and loving sisters.

"Surely your father loves you."

"He's oft gone, and when he's home, he does not hide his disappointment in me."

"I don't see how he could be disappointed." Though shocked by the bold admiration in his words, Nathaniel realized he meant every one of them. Before him lay a sweet, humble, repentant girl, not at all like the libertine woman her prior actions had revealed.

"Now I know I'm dying." Her lips curved in a sly grin. "You're being far too kind."

Nathaniel eased a finger over her cheek. She closed her eyes. He'd not seen such bravery in the face of death, even from hardened sailors.

He would not relinquish her to the grave. He could not. *Lord?*

"Death need not be the end, Hope. God has offered a way to eternal life." Nathaniel detested the fear muffling his voice. He hated talking about death. Just saying the word gave the consuming entity more power. But he had to ensure Hope's eternal destiny—just in case.

She groaned. "For some, I suppose. For people like you. But not for me."

He dropped the cloth and took both her hands in his. "For all. You have only to accept His gift."

"Nay. Don't waste your efforts on the likes of me. I fear in my case, your God has withdrawn His offer."

Nathaniel opened his mouth to respond, but she squeezed his hands and shook her head. He let out a ragged sigh.

The stench of decay and hopelessness crept around him, and his skin prickled despite the heat. Crickets harped their shrill cries into the night, vying with the thunderous crash of the surf. The wind fluttered the leaves of the hut as if trying to gain entrance.

"Please don't laugh when I tell you this," Hope whispered, her eyes closing again. "I always dreamed I would open an orphanage—take in every unwanted child I could find and raise them with more love than they would ever need."

Nathaniel stared at her agape. Children? Hope? Somehow he'd always pictured her marrying a wealthy landowner, surrounding herself with opulence, and being waited on by a bevy of servants. Yet he could not deny the ease with which she had befriended Miss Elise and the way the child adored her.

But children? Nathaniel had abandoned his desire to sire offspring long ago, for he did not trust himself to raise children. No doubt he'd corrupt them with whatever depravity slithered through his veins. No. He could not take the risk nor even entertain the thought.

Hope moaned and began wheezing. Thrusting his arm behind her shoulders, he lifted her and grabbed the shell beside the bucket. Fiery heat radiated from her frail body. He dipped the shell into the water and raised it to her mouth, water sloshing. "Drink." Although she parted her lips and took in a few sips of the fluid, she folded into his arms with a wretched sigh and faded again into unconsciousness.

Nathaniel laid her down, forcing back the sobs clambering to escape his lips.

"How is she?" Abigail's soft voice jarred him from sinking deeper into grief.

He shook his head as she plopped to the ground on the other side of Hope. Sighing, she rubbed her arms as if chilled. Hadn't he felt a cold draft only moments ago?

"Sounds like a storm is coming." He took Hope's hand in his again. Though hot, the life flowing through it brought him comfort.

"Yes. The wind has picked up, but I—"

Nathaniel looked up. Abigail's wide hazel eyes shifted across the shadows, then locked it upon his. Terror and urgency flashed across her face.

"What is it?"

She nodded toward Hope. "How fares her soul?"

Guilt churned in Nathaniel's gut. "If you mean, did I speak to her of her eternal destination, I tried, but her heart remains locked."

Abigail's face paled. She took Hope's other hand. "Something dark pulls her. I feel it."

Nathaniel studied Abigail, remembering their time in the hold of the merchantman with the dying sailor. "You have a sense of these things, a spiritual sense."

Truth be told, he believed he did as well. How many times had he sensed the same malevolent force in his mother's chamber when he was a boy?

"Perhaps." She shrugged. "My parents told me I saw things as a child that were not there. Beautiful beings." She huffed. "But as I've grown, the things I perceive are not so beautiful." She took the cloth and wiped Hope's neck. Then she stiffened. "Perhaps this is no sickness at all. Perhaps this is a battle."

"A battle?" But Nathaniel knew what she meant. The enemy wanted Hope, wanted to kill her and drag her down to hell. What did Paul say in Ephesians? *"For we wrestle not against flesh and blood, but against principalities, against powers, against the rulers of the darkness of this world, against spiritual wickedness in high places."*

Righteous anger welled up inside him. "What can we do?"

"We must pray."

"I have been." He shot to his feet and fisted his hands.

"Pray like they did in the Bible." Abigail rose and gripped his arm. "James, the brother of our Lord, said that if anyone was sick among us, we should have the elders pray over him and anoint him with oil in the name of the Lord."

The wind began to howl outside, flapping the loose leaves of the hut.

"I have no oil, and I am no elder."

"You have water, which I'm sure God would bless, and I'm not so convinced about the other." Abigail released him and brushed the hair from her forehead.

Nathaniel snorted.

"What harm could it do?" Her voice held a challenge.

Nathaniel glanced at Hope. Her lips had turned a bluish gray, her chest pitched as she struggled for each breath. Sweat glistened on her skin. His palms grew sweaty, and a metallic taste spilled into his mouth. He was afraid. Afraid to pray for the healing of another woman. Afraid he would fail again.

A burning sensation ignited in his hand. A warm tingling. He shook it, trying to stir his blood, but it grew in intensity.

His throat went dry.

Abigail stared at him expectantly.

Nathaniel closed his eyes. *Lord, is this Your will?*

No answer, save a soft whisper floating on the breeze. *"Believe."*

Dropping to his knees, Nathaniel dipped his finger into the bucket and traced a cross on Hope's forehead. "In the name of Jesus, I command you, Sickness, to leave this woman!"

His shout echoed against the green walls, pounding through the moist air like the sound of a judge's gavel.

Hope didn't move. The wind ceased howling outside, and silence descended over the hut like a shroud. The lantern flickered. The crickets silenced, and Nathaniel gaped at Abigail. Instantly, the heavy presence fled the hut. The bristling over his skin eased. His muscles relaxed, and the stink of death dissipated, leaving the smell of moist earth and leaves in its wake. The insects resumed their chorus outside as the wind danced once again through the leaves covering the hut.

Wide-eyed, Abigail scanned the enclosure, then smiled. "Thank God!" She clapped her hands.

Nathaniel laid the back of his hand on Hope's forehead. Searing hot. He nudged her, but she did not awaken. "She's still sick."

"Did you not sense it? Something powerful happened here." Abigail's voice rang with excitement.

Truth be told, Nathaniel had felt something, not in the physical sense, but somewhere deep inside of him. Perhaps it had just been wishful thinking.

"Call me if she wakes up." He rose, pushed the flap aside, and stormed from the hut.

His prayers had failed once again. And once again, a woman he cared for would die.

CHAPTER 18

Clank, cling, chime, clank. The jarring sounds jolted Hope from a deep, peaceful place. She peeled open her eyes. Glittering patches of sunlight danced across a dome of green like dancers flitting across a stage. A light breeze, laden with salt and the sweet nectar of flowers, feathered over her. She breathed deeply, allowing the air to fill her lungs, then ease back out. The breath of life. She was alive.

Pressing her hands onto the leaves on either side of her, she struggled to rise but leaned back on her shaky arms as a wave of dizziness threatened to plunge her back onto her bed.

Clank, clink, clank. Male laughter blared above the pounding of waves.

To her right, a damp cloth sitting beside a bucket of water brought visions to her mind of angels holding vigil throughout the long hours of the night. A plate of half-eaten mango near the leafy wall evoked memories of Abigail tenderly coaxing the sweet fruit into Hope's mouth.

Raising a hand to her chest, Hope dropped her eyes to her ragged petticoat, whose worn fabric did not leave much to the imagination, and then to her gown draped over a branch strung across the ceiling of the hut. Heat blossomed up her neck and onto her face. How much of her state of undress had Nathaniel seen as he had ministered to her?

Cling. Clank.

With great effort and after several attempts, Hope rose to her wobbly legs and managed to slip into what remained of the once attractive green muslin dress she'd borrowed in St. Kitts.

St. Kitts. Just thinking of that nefarious port sent a shiver through her. Yet for some reason, the harrowing day she'd spent there seemed an eon ago.

Clank, clink, clank. If not for the accompanying laughter, she would think they were under attack. Pushing aside the flap of sailcloth, Hope stood in the doorway and leaned on the bamboo pole forming the front brace of the hut. The trill of myriad birds announced her entrance even as sunlight caressed her face with warmth. The glint of flashing steel drew her gaze to Nathaniel and Mr. Keese hard at swordplay upon the shore. Sweat glistened on their bronzed chests in the morning sun. Beyond them, the glittering turquoise sea billowed toward the island as if it hadn't a care in the world. Nathaniel twirled the tip of his sword over Gavin's midsection and offered some taunt Hope could not make out. Gavin chuckled as he dove to the left, spun around, and met Nathaniel's blade with a *clank*. Back and forth they parried, their feet spitting up sand as they shuffled across the beach. Nathaniel moved with the confidence and ease of a man who had been weaned on the sword. The muscles in his arms bulged as he dispatched Gavin's latest attack and offered him another mocking challenge. Hope's breath quickened. A sudden lightheadedness struck her, and she raised a hand to her brow.

"Hope!" Abigail entered the camp, carrying a bucket of water. Her bright smile reached her eyes with a sparkle. "You should have called me to assist you." She set down the bucket and clutched Hope's arm, bearing her weight and helping her to sit on a fallen log at the center of camp.

Returning her smile, Hope struggled to catch her breath. "You've done far too much for me already."

"How are you feeling?" Abigail placed a hand on her cheek. "The fever is gone. Thank God."

"I feel a bit feeble." Hope dug her toes into the sand. "How long have I been sick?"

"A week."

A week? The past few days jumbled together in a blur that seemed at times only minutes and at others as long as months.

"Let me get you something to eat." Abigail started to rise, but Hope placed a hand on her arm. "How can I ever thank you, Abigail? I don't remember much, but I do remember you—your soothing voice, your gentle touch. You seemed always to be at my side."

Abigail's eyes moistened, and she patted Hope's hand. "'Twas my pleasure. But I wasn't the only one who tended you."

Laughter and another *clank* drew Hope's attention back out to the beach, where Nathaniel sprang to the left just as Gavin thrust his sword into the vacated spot.

Abigail followed her gaze and smiled. "I've not seen Mr. Mason so distraught. He barely slept during your illness and refused to leave your side for more than a few minutes at a time."

Shock tightened Hope's jaw. Fleeting memories flickered across her mind—Nathaniel's firm grip on her hands, his scent of wood and tar drawing her from her sleep, his whispers of encouragement tantalizing her ears. Were the memories real? Or had she conjured them from her feverish dreams? "I should think he'd be pleased to be rid of me." She let out a tiny chuckle that belied the statement's stab in her heart.

Abigail's eyes sparkled with playfulness. "Rid of you? Why, he was struck with grief at the thought of losing you." She leaned toward Hope. "I do believe the man fancies you."

Hope flinched, even while trying to ignore the sudden thrill surging through her. Abigail's tone carried naught but elation, not the jealous sting Hope would expect from a woman who had set her affections upon the same man. Hope studied her friend. The more she became acquainted with Abigail, the more Hope realized how virtuous she was. And what a high standard she set. And how unattainable that standard was becoming for Hope.

"Preposterous." Hope chuckled. "The man is a saint. He cares for everyone." *And he deserves someone like you. Someone who won't tarnish his reputation and break his heart.*

"Hmm." Abigail grinned as if she withheld a grand secret.

Kreggs scampered into the clearing and scratched his mop of gray hair. "Well, I'll be a two-legged swine. Look at ye. Up and well after we all thought ye were knockin' on the gates of Hades."

Hanson followed on his heels and tossed an armload of coconuts onto a growing pile. His wary gaze wandered over her, and he turned to Abigail. "There be no more fever?"

"Nay. God has healed her."

God? Hope could not fathom that possibility. Fresh water, salty air, bark tea, the love and care of others, perhaps. But God? Save *her?* She couldn't imagine Him wasting His time or His power on someone like her.

The clanking stopped. Nathaniel held the tip of his sword at Gavin's neck. Mr. Keese dropped his blade to the sand and shrugged his surrender. Laughing, Nathaniel lowered his sword and faced camp. His gaze locked upon Hope, and a slow smile curved his lips as he trotted toward her, Gavin following quick on his heels.

Hope's heart lurched in her chest. She brushed aside the tangled curls from her face and straightened the drab lace at the bodice of her gown as he entered the camp. Thrusting his sword into the sand near a cassia tree, he stared at her as if she were a lone spring of water in the middle of a desert.

Gavin plopped down beside her. The smell of musky sweat met her nose. "Miss Hope. 'Tis wonderful to see you up and looking so well."

She couldn't help but smile at the playful gleam in his blue eyes and the upturn of his lips. "Thank you, Mr. Keese."

"Gavin. If you please. I believe being stranded together on an island calls for the tossing aside of formalities, don't you, Nathaniel?"

Nathaniel shoved a wayward strand of hair behind his ear. "Indeed."

Something intense burned in the brown depths of his eyes, forcing Hope to once again tear her gaze from his. Unfortunately, it landed on his thickly corded chest still flexing from exertion, then it drifted to his breeches clinging to his narrow hips. Fingering the lace at the edge of her sleeve, she shifted on the log and focused her attention on the white foam atop the incoming waves. She chided herself for the direction of her thoughts. Not the behavior of a true lady.

"I owe you my heartfelt thanks, Mr. Mason," she said without looking at him. "I understand from Abigail that you spent many hours caring for me."

"It pleases me to see you well again." At the sound of his deep voice, scattered memories flashed through her mind, bits and pieces of intimacies she shared during her feverish trance—intimacies about her sisters, her father, her dreams. Horrified, she scanned the shoreline, wondering what other things the fever had loosened from her tongue. A flush settled over her face as if she'd been doused in hot water. The sensation intensified when she caught sight of Major Paine striding in their direction. Gavin shifted an apprehensive glance between her and Nathaniel.

"Allow me to get you something to eat, Hope." He hopped from his seat and plucked a shiny green guava from a pile of assorted fruit, then tore off a piece of dried fish hanging over the fire.

Hanson broke a stick on his knee and tossed it into the flames. "What baffles me is how she sits here to tell the tale. I ne'er seen anyone with marsh fever rise from their bed again."

Marsh fever. Fear bristled the back of Hope's neck.

"God is more powerful than marsh fever, Mr. Hanson." Abigail straightened her skirts and folded her hands upon them. "Nathaniel simply did what God's Word instructs. He anointed Hope and prayed the prayer of faith over her." Her dauntless tone attempted to cast all doubt away. Yet a frown marred Gavin's brow, echoing the niggling questions burrowed deep in Hope's heart.

For if what Abigail said was true, if God was real, and if He loved Hope enough to heal her, it would change everything.

"Two hours later, the fever left her." Abigail sent an admiring glance toward Nathaniel as if he were Moses parting the Red Sea, and a nod of intimate understanding passed between them.

Gavin snorted as he sat beside Hope and offered her the guava. "Perchance this smacks of some divine touch, perhaps not. I care only for the outcome, and that is to see this beautiful lady restored to full health." He winked at her, his flirtatious ways temporarily soothing her pangs of jealousy. Accepting the fruit, Hope took a bite. The sweet pulp burst in her mouth and slid down her throat like a soothing balm. "Thank you, Gavin." She admired the sharp cut of his jaw and his hawklike nose, but against her will, her attention drifted back to Nathaniel.

Kreggs's forehead puckered. "Ye healed her? Ye aren't some kind o' witch, are ye?" He took a step back.

Nathaniel raised a palm. "Nay. You speak of the wrong source of power. And I didn't heal her. God did. I was only His instrument. Though I'm ashamed to admit I didn't truly believe God would perform the miracle."

"Well, I can't deny me own eyes." Hanson rubbed them and squinted toward Hope once more as if making sure of what he was seeing.

"Some do recover from marsh fever." Gavin bit a piece of fruit and dragged his bare arm over his mouth, wiping away a trickle of juice.

"Beggin' yer pardon, sir, but none this quick. And 'tis a rare thing." Kreggs rubbed his chin.

Abigail smiled at the aged sailor as Hope took another bite of the delicious fruit, then plopped a piece of fish into her mouth. Her stomach began to complain at the onslaught of food.

Hanson sank onto a boulder and stretched his lanky frame. "It do make me wonder about God. Whether what I heard about Him is true."

Nathaniel glanced over his shoulder at Major Paine, who shouted a greeting, and the lines on his face tightened. "If you've heard He is a good, loving, and almighty God"—he faced Hanson with a flash of his brown eyes—"then you've heard correctly."

Setting her half-eaten fruit aside, Hope tugged upon a lock of her hair, unable to deny both the lingering effects of the deadly fever on her body and the erratic memories her mind had formed as she approached death's door. She closed her eyes against an eerie sensation. Death's door, indeed. Yet in the depths of her unconsciousness, she had sensed an evil beyond the barrier. A hungry, malevolent force, greedily waiting for her to pass beyond this world.

"I daresay, Miss Hope, so good to see you well again." Major Paine's nasal tone snapped Hope from her dismal musings. He stood at the outskirts of their camp, one hand at his waist and an insincere leer upon his lips. "Mr. and Mrs. Hendrick and I were most concerned."

Nathaniel cleared his throat, and Gavin coughed into his hand.

"Why, thank you, Major, I am touched by your kind regard." Hope nodded but did not return his smile. A breeze tossed the coils of his hair about one shoulder of his tattered red coat, where a gold epaulet once sat. The missing ornament seemed to set the major off balance as he leaned slightly toward his other side.

"Very good. Very good, then." The major perused Nathaniel with disdain. "I perceive you and your friend here"—he wagged a cursory finger toward Gavin—"were partaking in a bit of swordplay."

"Your perception is exceptional, Major." Nathaniel smirked. "'Tis best to keep one's skills sharp. A man never knows when a sword might be drawn on him."

Hanson chuckled.

Tossing the pit of his fruit into the foliage, Gavin rose to his feet. "What do you want, Major? More food?"

The major stretched his neck and gripped the white baldric that crossed his red coat. "I have come to inform you we plan to set off the day after tomorrow. Our raft is complete, and we are confident we shall be able to sail safely to Puerto Rico." He shot Nathaniel a haughty glance.

"I bid you bon voyage, then." Gavin waved him off, eliciting chuckles from Kreggs and Hanson.

Nathaniel grunted and rubbed the back of his neck. "Did you use bamboo instead of pine as I suggested?"

"By the time we received your *wise opinion*, it was too late, I'm afraid." Major Paine shifted his stance and swatted away a bug. "Never fear. We have tested her, and she floats quite well."

"In these shallow waters. But out at sea is a different matter." Nathaniel pointed toward the ocean and huffed out his frustration. "Even if you make it to Puerto Rico, how do you hope to procure passage to Jamaica from those loyal to Spain? I beg you one last time, Major, to wait for a ship to arrive."

Hope blinked at Nathaniel's kindness. Even after all the major's insidious affronts, Nathaniel still cared for the man's fate.

The major snorted. "We shall be delivered from the sea by one of the many merchant ships that sail the route to Jamaica. But if we do land on Puerto Rico, I am not without my resources, I assure you." He gave Nathaniel a supercilious grin. "I'm a man of action, Mr. Mason. That is what separates you and me. You choose to wait. I choose to act."

"Let him go, Nathaniel." Gavin spat. "We'll be better off without him."

"What of Elise and Mrs. Hendrick?" Hope asked. The mother and child lay nestled in the shade of a tree. "Surely you aren't planning on taking them along on such an arduous journey?"

"Mr. Hendrick will not part with his family." The major shrugged. "Besides, we have every confidence in the sturdiness of our craft."

She bit her lip. Poor Elise. She had been frightened on the merchant brig. How much more terrified would she be on a tiny raft? And Mrs. Hendrick would certainly fare no better with her nausea upon waves that would seem much larger by comparison. But it was the look of concern on Nathaniel's face that sent a wave of dread washing through Hope.

Abigail laid her hand firmly upon Hope's. "Major, I implore you. There is no sense in risking your lives. I am confident we shall be rescued soon."

"Dear lady, I have not achieved second in command under the captain general of the Leeward Islands by following the instructions of a common sailor." The major raised a haughty brow and brushed a leaf from his coat as easily as he brushed off Abigail's concern. "But I do wish that you, Miss Hope, would consider joining us."

Hope cringed, too weak to disguise her disgust. "I thank you for the offer, Major, but I would prefer to stay here."

"With these"—he wrinkled his nose—"men?" He spoke the word as if it hurt his lips.

Hope nodded. "Indeed." She gave him a labored grin and turned to Abigail. "I would prefer the company of savages to you," she whispered.

Major Paine huffed. "Very well."

The muscles in Nathaniel's arms twitched. "I will pray for you, Major, for all of you." Frustration edged his tone.

"Pray if you will." Major Paine waved a hand through the air. "But when we sail into Kingstown Harbor, it will be by my wise ability." He fingered his mustache, paused to study Hope, then spun around and strutted away.

Hope stared across the beach toward Mrs. Hendrick and Elise, fear clawing at her unsettled stomach.

Grunting, Nathaniel watched Major Paine leave. "The fool. He's leading them all to their death."

CHAPTER 19

A h, the water is most refreshing." Abigail dove beneath the surface of the pond, sending circular ripples across the clear aquamarine water. Chuckling, Hope shook her head. No sooner had they arrived at the pool than Abigail had stripped down to her chemise and splashed into the water, seemingly unconcerned with the utter lack of privacy.

When she broke the surface, it was with a smile and a burst of laughter. "Come in, Hope. It will do you good and improve your humor, which I daresay still wallows in the mud after Major Paine's visit." Water dripped off her chin and cheeks and glittered in pools on her lashes, making her look all the more like the angel Hope suspected she truly was.

Hope dug her bare feet into the silt lining the shore and allowed the cool mud to steal away the last remnants of both her fever and her frustration. "He is an odious bore."

Abigail splashed water on her arms. "You mustn't say such things, you know. We never know what causes a man to behave a certain way."

In the major's case, Hope assumed it was an overblown sense of his own importance coupled with a mind as shallow as a basin, but she doubted she would find agreement with the saint splashing in the water.

Hope loosened her final bindings and stood, watching as Abigail dipped below the surface again and swooped back up, water streaming down her face. "Is there no one who meets with your disapproval?"

Abigail drew her long chestnut hair in a bunch over her shoulder and squeezed out the water. "There are some, to be sure." She gave Hope a sly look. "But I try not to voice those opinions. They serve no purpose other than to invoke pain."

Expounding on the faults of others had always improved Hope's humors, but perhaps Abigail was right. To malign someone's character, no matter how true her observations were, was not the mark of a proper lady. As difficult as it would be to practice such restraint with someone like the major, Hope must try to follow the same rule.

Putting all thoughts of the offending man aside, Hope took in the abundance and variety of plants surrounding the pond, reflecting their beauty in the tranquil waters. The cheerful melody of a multitude of colorful birds flitting from branch to branch coupled with the soothing rush of the waterfall loosened the tightness in her back and chest. She had been here once before with Nathaniel to wash his wound. Their playful banter brought a smile to her lips, but she brushed the memory away. That meeting had not ended well.

The clear water of the pond beckoned, reminding Hope she had not had a proper bath in weeks. Even as her nose wrinkled at the malodorous scent emanating from her, the location gave her pause. She shot a wary gaze at the surrounding trees, not altogether sure they were alone. Yet they had told only Nathaniel of their intended destination, and Hope knew he would not intrude upon their privacy. Major Paine, Mr. Keese, and the sailors were another sort of animal altogether. But the major had stormed off in a huff. Gavin and Nathaniel had gone fishing upon the reefs, and when Hope and Abigail had left the camp, Hanson and Kreggs had been fast asleep in the sand.

Abigail dunked beneath the waters again, then rose with arms spread over the green liquid and twirled around and around. "Come in, dear Hope."

Hope slipped from her gown, eyeing the foliage, then stuck a toe into the water. The cool liquid sent a rush of refreshment up her leg, and unable to resist it any longer, she plunged in the pond after her friend. Careful not to go beyond where she could feel the soil beneath her toes, she took a breath and sank into the water, allowing it to envelop her and draw away all the tension. She rose for a breath of air. "Oh, sweet mercy, I forgot how good it feels to bathe!" A spray of water showered over her, and she turned to see Abigail, a mischievous twinkle in her eyes.

"Of all the. . ." Hope giggled and splashed her friend in return, and soon they were frolicking like schoolgirls on a summer day without a care in the world.

Except Hope did have a care in the world. She had many cares. Not the least of which was getting back to Charles Towne safely. But that was not the concern consuming her thoughts day and night. It was how to erase her shameful past and become a lady—a lady like Abigail.

Abigail flung water into the air, then closed her eyes as the droplets sprayed over her. Joy and peace flowed from her like the water pouring over the cliff into the pond. It sprinkled on everyone around her and brought as much refreshment as the cool water surrounding Hope. A flower petal floated by, and Abigail picked it up, her face and eyes aglow with delight as she examined it. She seemed to live her life as if every moment was a precious gift, yet she had neither love, family, nor fortune.

Hope could make no sense of it. Diving into the water, she scrubbed her chemise, her skin, and her hair, washing away all the filth, the sickness, the despair of the past months.

After their swim, Hope perched on a boulder by the edge of the pond to allow her undergarments to dry, while Abigail stretched out in a sunny spot on the sand beside her. Shaking the water from her hair, Abigail leaned back on her arms and gazed over the pond. Her sodden chemise clung to her tall, thin body—a body that did not lack feminine curves in the appropriate places. Long chestnut hair, glinting with gold and red in the sunlight, danced down her back in the light breeze. With those striking hazel eyes and noble cheekbones, the lady could make a fine match back in the new colonies, where title or fortune did not matter as much as in England. Yet she chose to deny herself the basic comforts of life and follow a God who had allowed her parents to be butchered.

Lifting her face to the sun streaming in through the branches, Hope drew a deep breath of the fresh air perfumed with musky earth and tropical flowers.

"How are you feeling?" Abigail asked.

"Much better. The fish and guava Gavin gave me seem to have given me a burst of energy, though I'm still a bit lightheaded."

"'Tis to be expected. You shall regain your strength in full soon. I've no doubt." Abigail cocked her head and smiled. "You are the perfect example of one of God's miracles, you know."

Hope snorted. "Most who know me would not agree."

"It matters not what most would say, does it? It was God who valued you enough to save your life. His opinion is all that matters." Abigail inched her feet into the water licking the shore.

Hope swallowed. She was not fully convinced God had healed her. If she admitted to that, then she'd be forced to ponder why. "You wouldn't believe that if you knew me, and knew what I'd done."

Abigail reached over and took Hope's hand in hers. "You could have killed a hundred men and been the town harlot, for all I care. God values everyone."

"Well, I haven't been that bad." Hope chuckled, an odd wave of comfort flowing through her as she thought how different this girl was from her sister Grace and from all the haughty, captious women in Charles Towne.

"Well, there you have it." Abigail grinned and released her hand.

A light breeze rustled the leaves of a nearby fern and brushed a lock of Hope's hair from her face as if God Himself had reached down to caress her. A warmth that came not from the sun blossomed within her.

"Do you believe someone who has been. . .compromised"—Hope gauged her friend's reaction, but Abigail stared out over the water unmoving—"who has been sullied, can be restored?"

Drawing her knees to her chest, Abigail clutched her hands together. "God is a God of fresh beginnings. He makes all things new." A hint of sorrow rang in her tone, yet she said the words with assurance.

"But surely He cannot restore one's purity?" Could Hope dare to believe she could start over?

"He cannot erase things that happened in our pasts, but He can erase the stain of them."

Hope sighed. "But aren't they the same thing?"

"Not at all. If you allow your past to dictate who you are now, then it still holds you in chains, does it not?" A wounded look filled her eyes, giving Hope pause.

Scooting off the boulder, she took a seat beside Abigail. "Did something happen to you?"

Abigail stared down at the ground. She twirled a finger through the sand and released a heavy sigh. Hope placed a hand on her shoulder. A slight shudder passed through her. Abigail's face, flooded with anguish, lifted to Hope's.

"What happened, Abigail?"

Abigail shook her head.

Hope took her hand in hers. "You can trust me."

"On Antigua, two years ago." Abigail studied Hope as if deciding whether she should proceed. Finally she took a deep breath and continued. "I wasn't feeling well, and my parents left me home while they ventured to deliver some food to a nearby village. A wealthy landowner who had just purchased a nearby sugar plantation sent his son to call on my father. Apparently, there was some disagreement between his father and mine regarding treatment of slaves. When the son found me alone in the house. . ." Abigail squeezed her eyes shut, and Hope grabbed her hand and swallowed against a burning in her throat. She didn't want to hear the rest, didn't want to know what her heart was already telling her, but she waited in silence for her friend to continue.

Abigail faced Hope, a tear slid down her cheek, and she wiped it away. "He assaulted me."

Hope drew Abigail close, and she leaned her head on Hope's shoulder and released a shuddering sigh.

How could anyone hurt this precious lady? Toiling with a strand of her hair, Hope tried to quell the fury rising within her. "What did your father do?"

"I never told him."

Hope nudged her from her shoulder. "Why not?"

Abigail brushed the tears from her face as if the casual motion could as easily erase the awful memory. "It would have killed him. Besides, the damage was done, and the young man sailed back to England within a fortnight."

Hope wondered if she should share her own harrowing story, but her mind refused to budge beyond the shock of what she had just heard. "I don't understand."

"What?" Abigail drew her shoulders back and smiled as if the telling of the tale had released some burden.

"One would never know such a travesty happened to you. You are so kind and sweet, so humble and willing to serve others. And this God of yours. This God who did nothing to protect you." Anger raged through Hope, anger at the spoiled landowner's son, anger at her own attacker, but mostly anger at God. He had not protected Abigail, and He had not protected Hope.

"Why should I blame God for the actions of men?" Abigail picked up a stick and twirled it in the sand. "If I did that, I'd be perpetually angry at Him."

"But He could have prevented it."

"Of course. But He didn't. For what reason, I may never know." She smiled at Hope. "Perhaps for the very reason of this exact moment when I have shared it with you."

Horrified, Hope shrank back. "I could not bear it if that were so."

Abigail patted her hand. "Let us let God be God, shall we?"

Shame trampled over Hope. While her heart had grown bitter and angry and she'd allowed her dreadful incident to define who she was—who she'd become—Abigail had risen above it and had allowed it to make her a better person, a stronger person.

Abigail rose to her feet and stretched her arms above her. "Let's not talk of such things. 'Tis too fine a day to be in a bad humor. We have food, safety, your good health restored, and I'm sure we soon shall be rescued."

Hope laughed at her friend's exuberance. "You have a far more hopeful point of view than I, for we have no promise of rescue or even that our food will hold out. And no one knows where we are."

Abigail flashed a knowing grin. "God knows."

Hope studied her friend and lowered her gaze. "I wish I could be more like you. I wish I could erase my past and start over."

"But you can." Abigail kneeled and took Hope's hands in hers. "If you allow God to help you."

As Hope forced a smile, a flash of red over Abigail's shoulder caught her eye.

"What is it?"

"I thought I saw something in the bush."

"We should be going anyway." Abigail rose and grabbed her dress from a nearby bush. "It grows late, and I'm sure Nathaniel will begin to worry."

At the sound of Nathaniel's name from Abigail's lips, Hope cringed. She ran her fingers through the tangles of her hair, wondering whether she'd ever be pure enough, good enough to attract someone like him.

Hope donned her dress, trying to shake off the feeling of foreboding that rose to sour one of the most glorious days she'd had in a long time.

But as the stale scent of her dirty gown covered her clean body, it seemed to foretell bad things.

"Let's be gone. The sun is beginning to set."

Pushing aside the thick leaves, Hope followed Abigail down the narrow path pounded out from their many trips for water. Although Abigail kept a slow pace, Hope had difficulty keeping up with her. The leaves and fronds spun around her, and she clutched her forehead to still the whirling when her foot hit something hard. Sharp pain spiked up her leg, and her toes refused to budge. She toppled to the ground.

"Oh my!" Abigail dashed to her side. "Let me help you up. I'm so sorry. I should have realized you still required my assistance."

"'Tis not your fault. I'll be fine." Leaning on Abigail, Hope clambered to her feet, but burning pain seared her ankle. She tested it and moaned. "My ankle. I don't think I can walk."

Abigail led her to a small clearing, where she eased her down upon the fallen trunk of a tree. "Wait here. I shall run and get Nathaniel."

"No, don't bother him. I shall be fine in a moment."

Abigail gave her a patronizing look and squeezed her arm. "You stay here. I will return before you know it."

Abigail disappeared into the foliage, casting a reassuring smile over her shoulder. But no sooner had she left than dread surrounded Hope like a dense fog. The warble of the birds became an eerie chant. The leaves and branches rustling in the breeze seemed to claw at her. Leaning over, she rubbed her ankle, willing herself to remain calm.

The swish of foliage jerked her attention upward in anticipation of seeing Nathaniel. But it was not Mr. Mason who entered the clearing.

CHAPTER 20

Major Paine smirked at her as a ravenous wolf might regard an injured lamb.

"What do you want, Major?" Hope took a deep breath in an effort to stifle her rising terror.

"Well, well. I went in search of fruit, and it appears I have found a luscious morsel." After a quick glance around, he stepped toward her and raised his brows.

"I asked you what you wanted." Hope heard the tremor in her voice.

"What do I want?" He laughed. "Now you wish to know what I want. Earlier today you did not give me the impression you cared what I wanted. In fact"—he laid a finger on his chin—"I remember something about preferring savages to my company."

"That is not *precisely* what I said."

"Then you do not prefer savages to my company?"

Placing one hand on the trunk of a nearby tree and all her weight on her good foot, Hope struggled to rise, all the while keeping a steadfast eye upon the major. "At the moment, I am not so sure."

The major spluttered. "Yet I have treated you with naught but civility." He licked his lips. "Certainly more than your situation deserves."

Fury replaced her fear. "And what situation is that?"

Shrugging off his red coat, he tossed it onto the log Hope had vacated and loosened his cravat. "Stifling hot in these tropics. Almost makes one wish we could abandon the need for clothing." His gaze scoured her, lingering.

"You!" Hope shouted. "'Twas you I saw lurking by the pond."

He stroked the greasy strands of his hair. "I must protest, miss." He lifted his lips in a smug grin. "I never lurk."

Hoped peered about, seeking an escape, seeking an ally. Her gaze locked upon the fan of leaves into which Abigail had disappeared. "Mr. Mason will be here any moment, sir. So I suggest you state your business and leave."

"Egad, you think that mere carpenter—mere sailor—frightens me?" He flicked one tip of his cravat through the air. "Why, last I saw him, he and that degenerate companion of his were fishing several miles down the shore. Nay, I don't believe he'll arrive anytime soon."

Hope's chest tightened.

Major Paine took another step toward her. She could smell the mildew of his clothes and the staleness of his breath. She tried to step to the side, but a sharp pain stabbed her ankle. Moaning, she leaned back against the tree and met his bold gaze with a defiant one.

"Ah, the little dove's wings have been clipped." He clicked his tongue. "And she cannot fly away."

"I asked you what you wanted." Hope pressed a hand to her roiling stomach. "Or do you enjoy bullying young ladies?"

"Zooks, bullying? Nay, I had quite the opposite in mind." He once again took liberties with his gaze, sending a shiver of disgust through Hope.

"But I fear I am getting ahead of myself." He retreated, clasped his hands behind his back, and took on the air of a gentleman at court. "I came to offer you one more chance to accept my invitation to voyage with us day after next."

Hope furrowed her brow. "Why do you press the matter?" The man had not shown much interest in her before, save an occasional salacious glance.

"As a man in the service of His Majesty"—he took on a condescending tone—"I represent the nobility of my office. I cannot in good conscience allow a lady to stay in the company of men whose reputations are, shall we say, less than refined."

Hope grimaced. Nathaniel's actions had more than proven his reputation, whilst this man's character remained dubious. Major Paine fingered the gold buttons of his waistcoat and waited as though expecting an outpouring of praise for his kindness and nobility. She narrowed her eyes. If even a bit of what he said was true, then his concern should also include Abigail. "But what of Miss Sheldon? Is she not worth your protection as well?"

The major flattened his lips and shrugged. "By the manner of her vocation, Miss Sheldon chooses to associate with. . .shall we say. . . questionable sorts."

"She is a missionary, sir, bringing God's Word to those in need. The manner of her vocation, as you call it, exalts her situation high above the rest of us here on this island. And it would seem to me that fact alone would necessitate your protection."

The lines of his face grew taut. "If she is as exalted as you say, then let her God protect her. She matters not to me." He looked down at the dirt and ground his teeth together. "I will not, *cannot* bear to see a man of Mr. Mason's station enjoy a beauty as yourself."

"Enjoy? How dare you!" Hope drew back her hand to slap his face, but her ankle gave way, and she bent over in pain. "He does not enjoy me at all," she panted, realizing the grim truth of her own words.

"Come now. Let us put pretense aside, madam. I am a worldly man, and I understand the way of things." The major took her elbow to assist her, but she jerked from his grasp.

"You understand nothing." Hope hobbled backward. "This has naught to do with your sense of honor, nor your concern for me. 'Tis merely a matter of your wounded pride."

He glanced off as if pondering the question for the first time. "Perhaps." He tugged his loosened cravat from his neck. "You could call it that, I suppose." He stepped closer. "But if you're worried about my affections, I'm sure they will come in time." He slid a finger over her cheek and down her neck. Hope slapped his hand away before he could go farther. She turned to run, willing herself to endure the pain in her ankle, but he clamped his hand around her arm and swung her around. Wincing, she faced him. Nausea churned in her belly.

Visions of another man and a time long ago slithered through her mind, awakening terror. A man much like the major. A man who crept into her bedchamber at night. Blood pounded in her ears. Her chest heaved. *Not again, Lord. Not again.*

"Will you come with me or not?" the major fumed.

Hope lengthened her stance and grabbed a lock of her hair.

"No, I will not."

"Foolish girl," he spat, his face reddening. "I will have you one way or another." His gaze crawled to her mouth.

Hope's ankle throbbed. Her heart constricted, and her knees began to buckle. But rather than shrink back in fear, rather than accept her fate as she had done the last time, she narrowed a scathing look upon him. "If you try to kiss me, I warn you, I shall take a bite out of those despicable, slimy lips."

~

"If you try to kiss her, Major, you'll feel the bite of my sword as well." Nathaniel shoved the last branch aside and burst into the clearing.

Releasing Hope, the major swung around, his hand flying to the hilt of his sword.

Nathaniel stepped toward him and leveled the tip of his blade at the major's chest. He clenched his jaw, trying to quell the fury storming through every muscle.

"Swounds, calm yourself, man." The major cocked one brow. "The lady and I were merely getting better acquainted."

"I don't believe the lady was enjoying the experience."

The major's hand twitched over his blade, and Nathaniel gave a slight shake of his head.

"I would not consider that, Major. I suggest you take your leave before my temper gets the best of me and I run you through."

Major Paine stretched out his neck as if trying to untie a knot in his throat. "Very well." A low growl of anger simmered beneath the quiver in his voice. He snatched his coat and cravat from the log and fumbled with them.

Relieved, Nathaniel sheathed his blade and dared a glance at Hope. When he'd first caught sight of the major's body hovering over her, terror and fury had charged through him. But aside from the slight quiver of her bottom lip and the moist sheen covering her eyes, she appeared unharmed.

The major stomped toward Nathaniel, directing a look of reproach at Hope, then spread his coat over his arm. A supercilious grin played upon his lips.

A bright flash caught Nathaniel's eye. Before he could react, the major swung his blade out from beneath his coat and jabbed its tip upon Nathaniel's throat.

Hope gasped and Nathaniel chided himself for not watching the man more carefully.

"You may have her." The major twirled the tip of his sword across Nathaniel's chest and flung his coat over his other arm. "What would I want with a mere strumpet anyway?"

Nathaniel would have laughed at the man's pompous display if not for the vulgar name he'd just called Miss Hope. He swerved to his left and snatched the major's coat from his arm. Casting it around the offending sword, he snapped the blade from the major's hand and hurled it into the air. With a *swoosh*, it whipped through the clearing, flashing where the sunlight caught the steel, before a large clump of foliage swallowed it up.

The major stared incredulously as if he had not yet digested what had happened. He opened his mouth to speak, but Nathaniel slammed his fist across his face. The major's head jerked to the left, and he stumbled back, arms flailing, and collapsed in the middle of a bush. His dirty, bare feet poked out from the shrubbery, twitching. A low growl filled the air.

Pulling out his blade, Nathaniel stormed toward him, parted the leaves with his sword, and leveled it upon the major's chest. "Begone, before I finish the job."

The major scrambled to his feet, rubbing his jaw, his eyes wide with fury and fear. Then he turned and scurried into the undergrowth like a rat caught in the sunlight.

Hope sank back onto the tree and stared at Nathaniel. Her golden hair danced across her waist in the light breeze. Her chest rose and fell, and her moist sapphire eyes brimmed with such admiration and desperation, Nathaniel swallowed against the thrill they evoked in him. Sheathing his sword, he dashed to her and allowed his eyes to search for any injuries. He thanked God when he found none.

Tears streamed down her cheeks. Nathaniel reached up, hesitated against a rush of confusion, then brushed them away with his thumbs. She closed her eyes beneath his touch.

"Are you hurt?" he asked.

Hope shook her head. Her eyes opened and searched his as if seeking an invitation. Although he tried to force all desire, concern, and affection from his face, she fell into his embrace anyway. As she pressed against him, his body went rigid, unsure, ill at ease with her so close. Then slowly he wrapped his arms around her and held her head against his shoulder. She needed him. How could he deny her? Sobs racked her body, and she squeezed him tighter. "Thank you, Nathaniel."

She smelled like sunshine and clean water, and he drew in a deep breath of her, berating himself for not arriving sooner. When Abigail had come to him, and in an urgent voice told him Hope needed assistance, he'd been reluctant to rush to her aid. The last week of caring for her had taxed his emotions beyond the point of breaking, and he'd hoped to put some distance between them now that she was well. So, after he insisted Abigail remain behind due to the rapid approach of darkness, he'd ambled across the island like a spoiled boy sent on an errand.

"Shhh. You are safe now, Hope."

As she leaned against his chest, a pleasurable, dangerous shard of heat went through him, and he eased her back.

"Ouch," she murmured, and only then did he remember her ankle.

Daring to touch her again, he circled an arm around her waist and lowered her to a fallen log. "Forgive me." He knelt beside her.

"'Tis nothing. I told Abigail not to bother you." She sniffed and raised a hand to her nose. "But as it turns out, I'm glad she did."

"May I?" He gestured toward her foot, and when she nodded, he eased the hem of her gown back, wondering all along at his sanity in doing so. He could have Abigail check her foot back at camp. Nathaniel examined the puffy skin around the ankle and turned it ever so slightly.

She groaned.

"My apologies." He lowered her foot to the ground. "I believe 'tis only a sprain, but you should stay off of it for a few days."

A tear slid down her face, and her bottom lip quivered again. He swallowed, searching for the anger, the disdain he'd once felt for this woman, but the feelings had fled him like traitorous cowards when he needed them most. "The major is a swaggering cur. But we shall be rid of him soon."

"One can only hope."

Against his better judgment, Nathaniel took her hand in his and held it as he had through the long hours of the night while her fever had raged. He reached up to wipe another tear from her face, but his thumb landed on her lips and he eased it over them, longing to take away her pain.

She closed her eyes and parted her lips beneath his touch. Instinctively, he leaned forward and placed his mouth on hers. A light kiss, meant only to comfort her, to erase the memory of Major Paine, but its effect set Nathaniel aflame. He backed away, unable to calm the violent beating of his heart.

Her eyes met his. Innocent, questioning. "What was that for?"

"To comfort you." His voice came out raspy and deep, and he hoped she didn't notice the desire burning within it.

She smiled. "I believe it worked." She brushed her fingers over his stubbled jaw and studied his face. Admiration and a spark of apprehension flickered in her eyes, creating a tumult of conflicting emotions within Nathaniel.

He brushed his thumb over her moist lips again. When she didn't turn away, all resolve left, and he claimed her mouth, kissing her hungrily. Wrapping one arm around her back, he pressed her closer and lost himself in her touch, in her need for his comfort and protection.

A bird squawked overhead and a gust of wind blew over him, jolting him, and he jerked away from her.

Shock and joy mingled in her sapphire eyes. Her chest rose and fell as heavily as his. Her sweet breath swirled over him, luring him back into her mesmerizing spell.

Nathaniel tore his gaze from her. "Forgive me."

"I don't believe I will." She smiled and gave him a playful look. "But just to be clear, this time, you kissed me first."

"Aye, I'll admit to that." Nathaniel rubbed the back of his neck, an unavoidable smirk lifting his lips. "I wanted to ease your fears."

"You have succeeded."

And he would love nothing more than to continue the treatment. Why did he so easily succumb to her charms? *Lord, where is the strength You promised? And Your promise not to allow me to be tempted beyond what I can resist?* Yet the truth of that verse meant he could have resisted her. He should have resisted her.

Perhaps the truth was that he didn't want to.

Shame deflated his desire, and he released her.

Her wounded look pierced him. "You want so badly to be angry at me, to disdain me."

Nathaniel shot to his feet. He must distance himself from her—put the temptation out of his sight. "I cannot associate with you, Hope. We must stay away from one another." He turned his back to her.

"'Tis Abigail, isn't it?" Her voice quivered with pain.

"Abigail?" He shook his head but still did not face her. "What has she to do with this?"

A green and yellow bird dove into the clearing, swooped by Nathaniel's head, and landed on a branch, then began twittering as if scolding Nathaniel for his behavior.

"What frightens you?" Hope asked.

He raked a hand through his hair and took up a pace across the sandy soil. "I'm not good for you, and you're not good for me." He could no longer deny his growing affections for Hope, but simply because they existed did not mean they were in God's will. Men were drawn to many things—greed for wealth, liquor, illicit affairs—that in the end caused their destruction. If Nathaniel was to rise above his past, he could not do it with a woman like Hope. He faced her.

"What you mean is I'm not good enough for you." She lowered her gaze and fingered the lace spilling from her sleeves. "Good enough to kiss, but not good enough to love." Spite rang in her voice, along with despondency.

"That was not my meaning." A pain sliced his heart, and he headed toward her.

She held up a hand. "Keep your distance, Mr. Mason, or you may be tempted to accost me again. Apparently I have that effect on men."

"Accost you? Fire and thunder." Nathaniel halted and rubbed an old ache burning on his side. He clenched his fists. "You have that effect on men because you freely toss your affections at every man who looks your way."

"How dare you?" Fire shot from her eyes. She tried to get up but winced and shrank back onto the log, releasing a sigh of defeat. "Maybe I have done so in the past, but I've not behaved in such a way lately."

"Really, and what of Gavin?"

"What *of* Mr. Keese?"

"Can you deny you have affection for him? That you constantly flatter him and play the coquette in his presence?"

"I do no such thing!" Hope tugged on a lock of hair and tossed out her chin. "Jealous?"

"Ha!" He snorted, more from the guilt assailing him at the truth of her statement than in defiance of it. Regardless, he must make her see her part in these dangerous dalliances. "'Tis why men take liberties with you." He pointed in the direction Major Paine had gone. Yet even as he said the words, he chided himself for being unfair and softened his tone. "Hope, why do you cast your virtue, your very self—something so precious—to the dogs?"

Her cheeks burned red. She opened her mouth to speak but snapped it shut and raised her seething gaze to his.

Her obstinacy rekindled his fury. "Fire and thunder, woman, I will not forfeit my last ship to rescue you from another wanton affair."

Struggling to rise, she let out a gasp of pain but managed to stand, leaning her weight on one foot. "Never fear, Mr. Mason, I would never allow you to do so again."

She stared at him stonefaced, her twitching jaw indicating her inner turmoil. Sniffing, she raised a hand to her nose again as grief pooled in her eyes. Despite every effort, Nathaniel's anger fled him once more, and he opened his mouth to apologize. She spoke first.

"How wonderful to be so perfect, so indispensable. You supply our food, build our shelters, preach God's Word, and even heal us, all the while looking down your imperious nose at us sinners." She waved a hand through the air. "You are correct, sir. I beg you, do not associate with me further, for I have no doubt the filth of my past, of my very character will soon tarnish you. And we can't have that. Not while you're building your merchant fleet and making a name for yourself."

Nathaniel grimaced, her words boring deep into the truth in his soul. Regardless, they bolstered his decision to keep his distance from her. A decision once made and firmly resolved to keep should have brought him relief, strength, but all he felt was anguish, pain, and regret. He steeled himself to approach her. "I'll carry you back to camp."

"I'd rather crawl." She raised her nose and looked away from him, but not before he saw the moisture in her eyes.

"You will do no such thing. I'll not leave you out here to be attacked again."

"Relieve yourself of the burden, Mr. Mason. I shan't expect your rescue in the future."

Back to Mr. Mason, is it? Sorrow tugged at him. He held out his hands. "Nevertheless." Without awaiting further protest, he hoisted her into his arms. She stiffened at his touch but did not struggle, nor reach her arms around his neck, nor even look at him. And the loss he felt threatened to outweigh any prior loss—even that of his ship.

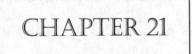

CHAPTER 21

Hope lay on a bed of fresh leaves and listened to the sweet chorus of birds beckoning her awake. Slowly, she opened her eyes to see their oblong shadows drifting over the sunlit palm branches that formed the roof of her tiny hut. She smiled at the happy way they flitted about, singing their carefree melody. The island boasted a multitude of birds, each one adorned in the most crisp bright shades of green, yellow, red, even purple and blue, that Hope had ever seen—more beautiful than the most elegant and plush gowns on London's finest ladies. These exquisite creatures didn't possess wealth or title, yet they flew about happily as kings and queens of the air, all the while gazing down on the pathetic human race bound to sand and dirt.

The birds' melodies heightened and joined in perfect unison as if they were inviting Hope to join them. How she wished she could shed her human stains, her ugliness, and transform into one of those more lofty creatures and fly away, away from her earthbound existence, away from her past, away from the pain of rejection.

A scripture verse popped into her mind from a long time ago, something about birds not sowing or reaping or worrying about tomorrow, yet their Father in heaven feeds them and cares for them. Hope sighed, forcing down her longing to be loved—to be cared for in such a way.

True to his promise, Mr. Mason had not spoken a word to her nor graced her with one glance of his handsome brown eyes for three days. In fact, wherever she happened to be, whether sitting on the beach or lolling about the camp, he made every effort to position himself elsewhere.

The stab of his rejection surprised her. Hadn't she always known he deserved a far more chaste and pious lady than she? Someone like Abigail. The more Hope had tried to prove herself a lady to this virtuous man, the less he seemed to believe it—even though she had not behaved to the contrary.

Except she had welcomed his kiss.

She rose to her elbows as a bath of heat drenched her at the memory. And what a kiss it was! The gentleness, the yearning she felt in his every movement. A fiery heat had flooded her entire body, stealing her ability to think, to breathe. Not at all like the manner in which he had kissed her on board the merchantman. Passion had driven that kiss, but this one. . . A pleasant shiver ran through her even now. It was as if Nathaniel were truly kissing her—Hope Westcott—not who she appeared to be on the outside. She'd experienced none like it before. And certainly never would again.

A jab of guilt struck her. What of Abigail? Obviously, she harbored affections for Nathaniel. In light of that, Hope should have rejected Nathaniel's advance, should have pushed him away. Could she not resist one man's attentions for the sake of a friend? Hope's heart grew heavy even as the bird's morning ensemble drifted away. The beautiful creatures had no doubt given up on her joining them and flown away in search of a better prospect.

She tested her weight on her ankle and found only a light twinge remained. Running her fingers through her hair, she squared her shoulders and emerged from the hut to a blast of hot, salty air and the tiresome smell of fish.

Gavin lay in the sand at the center of camp, his hands pillowing his head. Turning, he gave her a sultry grin and sprang to his feet. "Allow me, milady." He took her elbow to assist her.

Hope smiled at his gallantry. "Thank you, kind sir, but I believe my ankle is much better today. I may even venture out for a walk. . .or perhaps a hobble." She warmed to his look of compassion.

"If you would permit me, I'd be honored to escort you on your stroll." He led her to a chair Nathaniel had fashioned from pinewood and twine and knelt beside her. Taking her hand in his, Gavin brushed his thumb over her skin, and Hope shifted in her seat, uncomfortable with his familiarity. His blue eyes, a shade darker than her own, held a brighter glow than their normal playfulness. Truth be told, after Nathaniel's rejection, Gavin's kindness had broken down the wall of her resolve to resist his flirtations. His regard dulled the incessant lance in her heart and made the long days upon this island pass much quicker. And what did it matter? She'd failed to win Nathaniel's admiration, and since he had already accused her of playing the coquette with Gavin, what harm would it do to fulfill his expectations?

Hope sighed and gazed out upon the calm morning sea, a plate of turquoise glass stretching to the horizon. Her thoughts drifted from Gavin, to Nathaniel, and ended with Lord Falkland. Did he ever think of her? Had he inquired who had purchased her at that heinous auction? A lump of sorrow and remorse lodged in her throat. Perhaps her obsession with Nathaniel was only a symptom of her still-broken heart.

Lifting her hand, Gavin placed a kiss upon her bare fingers, drawing Hope's attention back to him.

Bang. Clunk. The sound of wood dropping jolted Hope. Tugging her hand from Gavin's grasp, she peered around him in time to see Nathaniel wiping his hands—as if he were wiping them of her—and storming from the camp onto the beach, never once looking her way.

"A bit of a grouch this morning, eh?" Gavin watched Nathaniel leave.

Hope let out a ragged breath. "I fear 'tis my presence that dampens his humor."

"But why let him dampen ours?" Gavin grabbed a lock of Hope's hair and fingered it, a mischievous grin on his lips.

A pinprick of unease filtered over Hope. "Where is Abigail?" She scanned the beach then the leafy wall beyond the sand.

"She went to get water with Kreggs. And Hanson is gathering fruit on the other side of the island." Gavin lifted one brow in her direction. "We are very much alone."

The taunting glint in his eyes put Hope's fears to rest. "Should I be frightened, Mr. Keese?" She gave him a coy smile.

"Do you want to be?"

Her heart skipped, longing to continue this harmless dalliance, but a vision of Major Paine filled her mind, and the smile she intended to give Gavin faded to a frown.

He scratched the whiskers on his jawline. "Forgive me, Hope. I had forgotten about the major."

"You know?"

"Aye, Nathaniel made mention of it."

Hope nodded, wondering why Nathaniel would bring up such a sordid story, especially when the major and his party had been gone now for two days.

She watched Nathaniel walking down the shore, his focus intent upon the sand, perhaps hunting for crab.

Gavin released her hair and stood. "The cad. If I had been there—"

"No harm came of it. Nathaniel arrived in time." Hope remembered the way Nathaniel had looked when he burst into the clearing, She'd never seen such fury on his face. His sword thrust before him, his eyes narrowed like daggers. And the way he'd dispatched the major so quickly and sent him scurrying off like a frightened rabbit. She would have laughed if she hadn't been so terrified.

And so in awe of Nathaniel.

She shook her head, trying to dislodge the nagging memory, especially the memory of his kiss.

"You are safe with me." Gavin winked, and Hope longed to reach out and take his hand again, if only to aid in ridding herself of the remembrance of Nathaniel's touch. But she resisted. A breeze flapped his cotton shirt and fingered through his light hair.

"Thank you, Mr. Keese."

"Gavin, please."

"Gavin." She nodded.

Wiping sand from his breeches, he gestured toward a bucket of fruit. "Some fruit for milady?"

"You may cease with the pretensions. I am no lady." Hope huffed.

"You are to me." The sincerity in his eyes stunned her. Turning, he plucked a roasted plantain from the pile and handed it to her.

She gave him a puzzled look. Was he flirting with her? Telling her what she longed to hear in order to have his way, like so many men before him? Yet nothing devious slithered in his gaze. Just a boyish innocence that belied the worldly man she knew dwelt inside. Perhaps he was simply playing a part, playing a game. Then why did moisture fill her eyes at his kind remark?

She shifted her gaze and thoughts back out to sea and wondered at the fate of Elise and Mrs. Hendrick and the others. Had they made it to

Puerto Rico, and if so, had they avoided the Spanish? Even if they did somehow make it to Jamaica, would they bother to send back a ship? If Hope thought God would listen to her prayers, she'd pray for their safety, especially Elise's. But since she had already heard Abigail petitioning on their behalf each night, Hope supposed that was good enough, for if God would listen to anyone, He would listen to Abigail.

An enormous blast thundered through the air. Hope jumped, threw a hand to her chest, and rose from her seat. Gavin dashed to her side and together they peered toward the beach. Nathaniel halted and stared at something offshore. His calm stance indicated no alarm. Hope's heart leapt. Perhaps a ship had come to their rescue after all.

"Stay here." Grabbing two swords and a pistol, Gavin raced toward Nathaniel. Though she tried, Hope could not remain still. Taking a tentative step on her sore ankle, she followed after him, limping across the sand. As she passed an outcropping of palms, she followed the gazes of the men to see a ship, a puff of dissipating smoke lingering in the air above its larboard hull.

A ship!

They were to be rescued at last.

Yet as she approached Nathaniel and Gavin, they did not seem to share her glee.

"Blast it all, my fortune for a telescope." Nathaniel planted his fists on his waist. "Can you make her out, Gavin?"

"Nay, but it appears she raises her colors." Gavin handed Nathaniel his sword, which he grabbed with a nod. "Let us wait and see."

"Do you think they mean us harm?" Hope asked.

Both men swerved to face her. "I told you to stay put." Gavin gave her a scolding look. Nathaniel barely allowed his eyes to land on her before he uttered a "harrumph" and turned away.

The anchor splashed into the sea, and cockboats were lowered. Thoughts of home made her spirits soar. A merchantman perhaps, or a ship sent back by Major Paine. In either case, soon she would be on her way home to her sisters and away from Nathaniel and the disturbing effect he had upon her.

A flag was hoisted upon the mainmast. Beads of sweat formed on Nathaniel's brow as he squinted his eyes against the rising sun.

Suddenly his grip upon the hilt of his sword tightened.

Gavin groaned. "Well, sink me, of all the luck."

"What is it?" Hope peered at the ship. A black flag flapped in the breeze atop her foremast.

The muscles in Nathaniel's jaw tensed, and he leveled his dark eyes upon her.

"Pirates."

CHAPTER 22

Nathaniel grimaced as the anticipation on Hope's face paled into bristling fear.

"Pirates?" she squeaked. Her gaze flashed back to the ship and her hand went to her throat.

Dread sank like an anchor into Nathaniel's stomach as he once again studied the flag flapping in the light morning breeze, hoping, praying he'd made a mistake. But the white skull and crisscross of swords stark against the black background gave no room for error. Of all the ships to land on this island, why did it have to be a pirate ship? He eyed Hope again. Her breathing had sped to a rapid pace. As had his own. How was he to protect her and Abigail from these salacious brigands?

Oars splashed into the water, and the cockboats, overflowing with men, surged toward shore, jeering insults flying upon the wind, announcing their arrival.

O Lord, I need Your help. Give their captain some shred of decency toward us.

Gavin shot Nathaniel a wary glance, his jaw flexing. "Should I get Kreggs and Hanson?"

"Nay, 'tis best they remain hidden. They've seen only us so far."

Gavin nodded and planted his bare feet firmly upon the sand. "Any suggestions?"

"Stand our ground." Nathaniel rubbed the rising ache on his side. "And pray."

Gavin snorted and instead primed and cocked his pistol then shoved it down his breeches.

Hope gripped Nathaniel's arm. Not Gavin's arm, but his. He glanced down at her. "Go back to the hut."

"Please. Let me stay with you." She dug her fingers into his skin. "I don't want to be alone." Her brow wrinkled and she lifted pleading eyes to his. "Besides, they know I'm here."

"Get behind me, then." He took her hand from his arm and eased her back. Though he felt a quiver run through her, she didn't whimper or swoon like most women would under similar circumstances. "I'll do everything in my power to keep you safe." His tone failed to carry the reassurance he hoped it would.

"As will I," Gavin added.

Terror ripped holes in Nathaniel's gut. He could not stand the thought of Hope or Abigail being hurt, not in this way, not by these men. Nevertheless, he lengthened his stance, planted the tip of his sword into the sand, and awaited his guests. He'd dealt with pirates before. They fed on fear, and he vowed to not give them their meal for the day.

One cockboat struck sand with a crunching thud, jolting the boisterous passengers from their seats and sending one man overboard. After the pirates recovered from their laughter and the one had risen from the shallows, looking more like a sea snake than a man, they spilled out of the boat like ants over an anthill and sloshed through the water toward shore. Greed dripped from their twisted lips as they scanned the island, searching for anything to satisfy their appetites. Their gazes swept over Nathaniel and Gavin in complete disregard and latched upon Hope as if they could see her right through him. Clutching Nathaniel's arm again, she shrank farther behind him. He felt her tremble.

Though he did not raise it, Gavin gripped his sword and frowned at the crew of men, some of whom lined up before them, arms across their chests, while a few others wandered over the sand, surveying their new conquest. The men ranged in age, girth, and stature, but all wore the same scowl and the same devilish look on their sun-battered faces. Their colorful attire, though mismatched and filthy, bore the elements of nobility in the gold and silver embroidery, the silk lace, and the metallic threaded brocade and damask coats—all no doubt stolen. Armed with a cutlass and a brace of pistols across his chest, each man wore the imperious facade of invincibility. They were masters of the sea, and they well knew it.

Though he could not squelch the fear racing through him, Nathaniel saw behind their masks of insolence. These were lost men wandering the seas in search not only of treasure but also of purpose, of meaning, of true life. No different from most men's quest, save the method they chose to go about it.

The second boat hit shore, and more men leapt over her gunwales and splashed through the waves, some remaining in the water, while others lumbered onto the sand.

From their midst, a tall dark man sporting a blue plumed tricorn and black velvet waistcoat trimmed in silver marched toward Nathaniel, a jeering grin on his lips.

Doffing his hat, he bowed to the knee. The sun glinted off a gold earring in his ear. "Captain Poole of the pirate ship *Enchantress* at yer service." He slapped the tricorn back atop his head. "And ye are?" he asked Nathaniel, but his gaze angled around him to where Hope huddled. His eyebrows rose.

"I am Mr. Nathaniel Mason, and this is Mr. Gavin Keese."

Gavin slid his fingers over the silver handle of his pistol and inched closer to Nathaniel. Together they formed a wall in front of Hope. With a quick shake of his head, Nathaniel hoped to dissuade his impetuous companion from attempting anything foolish.

"Pleased to make yer acquaintance." Cocking his head, Captain Poole studied them; then he glanced over his shoulder and lifted his lace-covered hand.

Splashing sounded, and the mob of pirates in the water parted. Major Paine, Mr. and Mrs. Hendrick, and Elise emerged in the grip of four men, who dragged them toward their captain. Salt encrusted their filthy clothing, and their faces bore the marks of an arduous journey.

Hope gasped and rushed forward, but Nathaniel reached out and forced her back.

"Do these wretched creatures belong to ye?"

Laughter broke out among the pirates.

Nathaniel shifted his stance. His yes and Gavin's no echoed at the same time above the lapping waves, causing further hilarity among the ribald crew.

"Well, since they told us where to find ye, I'll expect yer the one tellin' the truth." Captain Poole pointed to Nathaniel, then surveyed Gavin. "And ye the liar." His eyes landed on Gavin's pistol, and he snorted as if it were naught but a stick.

"Unhand me." The major's sullen command drew Nathaniel's attention his way. Stripped down to his white shirt and breeches, his hair hanging in saturated strands about his face, the major looked more like an uprooted kelp than a man wielding the king's authority. Nevertheless, he tossed his chin in the air, as was the habit of all men bred to power, regardless of whether they still held it.

Mr. Hendrick fared no better. His sopping red beard clung to his chin like a sea urchin, and both shock and dread swam in his eyes. White faced, his wife and child huddled by his side.

"We found 'em floatin' in the sea, hangin' on for dear life to shreds of wood." Captain Poole chortled, waving a hand in their direction. "We wanted to have some sport with 'em, but since we found ourselves in need of fresh water and fruit, and they swore they knew of a place close by laden with such amenities, we decided not to kill 'em."

"Very kind of you." Nathaniel bowed.

"Aye, we pirates are not without mercy, are we, men?"

Ayes and curses filled the air.

"But since we are here now. . ." A malicious look burned in the captain's dark gaze as he eyed the captives.

The pirates shoved the major and Mr. Hendrick to the sand and released Mrs. Hendrick and Elise. The little girl gripped her mother's skirts like a lifeline, her eyes big as portholes, but not a sound escaped her lips. Her mother, however, sobbed, clutching her stomach, and fell into a heap.

Shoving Nathaniel aside, Hope squeezed between him and Gavin and dashed toward Mrs. Hendrick before Nathaniel could stop her. She brushed past the pirates, unaware of the multitude of eyes following her. When she reached Mrs. Hendrick, she knelt and put her arm around her shoulders. Elise fell into Hope's embrace, and she squeezed the girl and planted a kiss on her head. Nathaniel didn't know whether to be amazed at her bravery or appalled at her foolishness.

Captain Poole's eyes lit up. "I see you have other delicacies on the island as well."

"Some delicacies you are welcome to." Nathaniel forced a commanding tone into his voice. "Others you are not."

The captain belched. "Indeed?" He cocked his head at Nathaniel as if he were studying a specimen under a quizzing glass. He snapped his fingers in the air. "Spread out and search for others," he ordered. As some of his men dispersed, he swaggered up to Nathaniel. "Rather bold for a man with only one sword."

"Two swords and a pistol." Gavin cast a look of challenge his way.

"Ah, I stand corrected. Did ye hear that, men? Two swords and a pistol." The crew chuckled as Captain Poole shoved his face into Gavin's, but the man did not blink. "Against thirty blades and twice as many pistols, not to mention me guns aboard the ship. Are ye that cocky or jest plain stupid?"

Nathaniel clenched his fists and prayed Gavin would hold his tongue, but the young man returned the captain's glare with equal intensity and a spark of playfulness. "Perhaps a bit of both."

Captain Poole's hard features softened into a grin, and a deep chuckle bellowed from within his gut. "Aye, that be a true word ye spoke. But I'll have to ask ye to hand over yer weapons, in any case."

Nathaniel handed his sword, hilt first, to a pirate who came forward to retrieve it. He prayed Gavin would do the same. Though a groan emanated from his lips, his young second mate followed suit. Relieved, the captain seemed to possess a sense of humor and, for the moment, was disinclined to do them harm. Nathaniel wondered how long that intent would last.

Hope continued comforting Mrs. Hendrick and Elise. The major struggled to his feet and attempted to brush the sand from his breeches. A jagged wound marred Mr. Hendrick's left cheek as he stared at the proceedings, mouth agape and a look of horror on his face.

"There were others, Captain," Nathaniel said, remembering the other men who'd left with the major. "Four sailors, I believe."

"Aye." Captain Poole stuck his thumbs into his breeches. He nodded toward his ship. "They guard me ship with the rest o' me men."

Nathaniel nodded. When given the choice of turning pirate or dying, most seamen chose the former. But Nathaniel would never consider such an option. He must find another way to convince this man not only to let them live but also to rescue them from this island. "Our ship went down in the storm, and we've been stranded on this island for weeks."

Captain Poole doffed his hat and ran a hand through his coal black hair. "And what d'ye want me to do about it?"

"Since you are merciful pirates, give us safe passage to Kingstown."

Captain Poole grinned, revealing an unusually full set of teeth, then kicked sand up with his boot. "And what will ye give me in return?" His gaze locked upon Hope. "We've been out t' sea for quite some time, if ye know what I mean."

"Our undying gratitude, Captain." Nathaniel bowed, hoping to draw the man's gaze off of Hope.

"Strike me down." The captain snickered, but his eyes never left her. "But I was thinkin' of something a tad more warm and soft."

Mrs. Hendrick's sobs shot up in volume. Nathaniel ground his foot into the sand, eyeing her protruding belly. Surely these cretins were not cruel enough to harm a woman in her delicate condition.

"Haven't you had enough rapine?" Gavin voiced Nathaniel's concern with more disgust than Nathaniel would have liked.

Captain Poole seemed unaffected by his tone. Instead his face scrunched, and his eyes moved from Hope to Mrs. Hendrick. "Her? Nay. A bit of a shrew, if ye ask me, but I make it a habit never to steal another man's wife. Was done to me once by a motherless Judas, and I'll not stand for it."

Nathaniel shook his head at the pirate's odd sense of decency.

Without warning, Captain Poole grabbed Hope by the arm and hauled her to her feet. "I'll grant ye safe passage for the woman." He flung an arm around her waist and pressed her against him. Her face paled, and her frenzied gaze met Nathaniel's. The pirate sniffed her hair, recoiled, then fingered it. "Doesn't smell like a lady, but she feels like one."

Blood drained from Nathaniel's head. His chest tightened, and his mind reeled, searching for a way to save her. "You cannot have her."

Captain Poole flinched and his eyes narrowed. "And why not?"

"She's my wife." The thought had barely passed through his mind before it formed on his tongue and left his lips.

Hope's jaw dropped.

"Yer wife, you say?" Captain Poole eyed him suspiciously, then examined Hope again.

Major Paine snorted, and for a moment Nathaniel thought he would reveal the ruse. But one stern glance silenced him, and he turned away.

"Very well. Take yer wife." He shoved Hope toward Nathaniel, and she barreled into him. Grabbing her, he eased her behind him again.

"I'm beginnin' to hate that code o' mine." Captain Poole spat onto the sand, then crossed his arms over his chest. "But now ye have naught to bargain with, sir."

Hoots and hollers blared from behind Nathaniel, where Captain Poole's men broke through the line of trees, Hanson, Kreggs, and Abigail struggling in their grasps. At the sight of Abigail, Captain Poole's eyes once again glinted with delight.

"What have we here?" He sauntered up the beach to meet his men and halted before Abigail. Her chestnut hair flowed in ringlets over her shoulders, and she met the pirate's gaze with brazen confidence. Nathaniel's throat went dry.

"And who might you be?"

"Abigail Sheldon." She raised her chin toward him as the pirates released her arms.

Captain Poole eased a finger toward her cheek, but she flinched and backed away, making him cock his head in interest. "And are ye married as well, Miss Sheldon?"

Nathaniel nodded a frenzied yes in her direction, hoping she'd see him over the pirate's shoulder. When she didn't, he faced Gavin, using his eyes to urge the man to claim her. Gavin furrowed his brow, then nodded and opened his mouth, but Abigail's voice rang across the beach.

"Nay, I am not married, sir," she replied, her chest heaving. "What is that to you?"

Captain Poole threw back his head as a deep chuckle rose from his belly. Scanning his crew, he snapped his fingers, and the pirates released Kreggs and Hanson. "Is that all o' them?"

"Aye, Cap'n."

"Very good." He grabbed Abigail's arm and turned to Nathaniel. "This girl will suffice for your fare."

Nathaniel's heart cramped. He started toward the captain when Hope wove around him and darted to Abigail and Captain Poole, all the while shouting, "Release her at once! She is not for sale."

The captain and his crew froze in mid-stride and gaped at this slip of a woman who dared defy a band of pirates.

Clenching his fists, Nathaniel stormed after Hope. *Lord, I need Your help.*

Hope grabbed Abigail's other arm, attempting to pull her from the pirate's grasp.

"You should control your wife, sir." The captain huffed, a look of shock still on his face.

"Believe me, I have tried." Nathaniel took a stand beside her. "Nevertheless, she is correct. We will not use a human being as barter."

Gavin came alongside him, his face red with fury.

"Then I'll take her for free." The captain jerked Abigail from Hope's grasp and turned toward the seclusion of the forest.

"Captain, please do not." Hope cornered him and threw herself in his path. "Take me instead."

"No, Hope." Nathaniel barreled after her.

Abigail shook her head, her eyes moistening. "Do not do this."

Captain Poole's lips twisted as his malevolent gaze flickered over Hope. "As I've told ye, I'll not be touchin' another man's wife." Pushing Hope aside, he stormed forward.

"But she is on her way to Kingstown to be a missionary." Hope grabbed his arm, stopping him once again. "I am nobody, but she will do great things for God."

"God, you say?" The pirate's face contorted, and his head jerked back as if someone had punched him. "A missionary?" He dropped Abigail's arm and slowly retreated from her. She fell into Hope's embrace, and Nathaniel threw himself between the ladies and Poole, not caring at the moment by what odd turn of events they had been delivered.

"'Tis a godly woman!" Captain Poole bellowed to his crew crowding around them.

Groans of disappointment and gasps of trepidation filled the air as if the captain had just informed the band of men they were outgunned. Nathaniel shook his head at the madness but offered a silent prayer of thanks just the same.

Doffing his hat, Poole wiped the sweat from his brow. "No one touches 'er, or the other one neither, or ye'll answer t' me!"

A mixture of fear and respect alighted upon the pirate captain's face. "I'll not be riskin' the anger o' the Almighty," he mumbled to himself, his gaze locked upon Abigail. "Well, no matter." He shrugged and faced Nathaniel. "Give us food and water. We shall partake of yer hospitality for a few days and then be on our way. An' if ye do not give us trouble, we may permit ye to live."

Gavin started toward him, his mouth a firm line of protest, but Nathaniel held up a hand to stop him.

The captain huffed out his disgust, then directed a probing gaze at Nathaniel. "I see the same anger burns in yer eyes as in yer friend's, yet ye keep it under hatches. The sign of strength." He slapped Nathaniel on the back. "I like ye, Mr. Mason. I may yet let ye live." With that, he sauntered toward the camp, his crew ambling after him.

Nathaniel released a heavy sigh. At least the women were safe, though he had no idea how long this pirate's moral code would stand up against his lewd desires. Nor did he know how to convince him to take them to Kingstown. With the fruit on the island nearly gone and the fishing uncertain, they would not last much longer. And if they were delayed another week or two, Nathaniel's ship, the *Illusive Hope*, that was to meet him in Kingstown, might leave without him. Then he would have no way to get back to Charles Towne.

Hope released Abigail and raised her eyes to Nathaniel, appreciation beaming from their blue depths.

A hideous scream filled the air, jolting him and drawing their attention to the shore.

Nathaniel charged across the sand, Gavin, Hope, and Abigail on his heels.

Mrs. Hendrick lay folded on the ground, her arms clutching her belly. Mr. Hendrick had his hand on her back and a look of fright on his face. Little Elise sat beside her mother, tears streaming down her face.

Hope and Abigail dropped to Mrs. Hendrick's side and whispered to her. She uttered a loud, sickly moan that sent shivers down Nathaniel's back.

"What is the matter? Is she ill?" Mr. Hendrick asked.

Hope glanced at him and then over to Nathaniel. "Nay, I fear the baby comes."

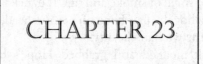

CHAPTER 23

Hope gathered a mound of soft plantain leaves, then squeezed her arm beneath Mrs. Hendrick's shoulders and gently lifted her, easing the makeshift pillow beneath her head. Mrs. Hendrick groaned and pried her eyes open. Hope turned away, swiped the tears from her cheeks, and avoided her gaze—avoided the question she knew would rise to Mrs. Hendrick's lips and the answer Hope knew she must give.

On the other side of Mrs. Hendrick, Abigail gathered bloody cloths, a quiet sob escaping her lips. Her eyes met Hope's, and she laid a gentle hand upon her arm.

"There was naught we could do."

"I know." Hope swallowed, not allowing her eyes to wander toward the tiny bundle in the corner of the hut. The tiny bundle who would never have a chance to live, the tiny bundle who would never grow to be a man.

Mrs. Hendrick's agonized screams continued to blare through Hope's ears, drilling holes in the calm exterior she'd managed to maintain during the ordeal. Each torturous wail had brought Hope back to Portsmouth, sitting in the hallway outside her mother's chamber, trembling in anguish and fright. Only this time, Hope had been forced to watch as Mrs. Hendrick writhed in agony, watch the pain etch lines of misery on her comely face, watch as she expelled the lifeless child from her body. And Hope saw her mother in each dreadful trial. The physicians could do naught to ease her mother's pain, just as Abigail and Hope could do naught to ease Mrs. Hendrick's.

Hope lifted the bloodstained sailcloth covering Mrs. Hendrick and peeked beneath it. A shudder ran through her. "She's bleeding again."

"I'll go get some more bedding and fresh cloths." Abigail stood, her arms full of stained rags. "And some water."

A warm night breeze wafted in through the open flap as Abigail left, bringing with it the smell of smoke and salt. It danced through a strand of Mrs. Hendrick's mahogany hair lying on her forehead, and Hope brushed it aside, admiring the woman's beauty.

Mrs. Hendrick moaned and grabbed Hope's hand, startling her. Another breeze swept in, sending the two lanterns perched on either side of the hut flickering their light like sparkling jewels across Mrs. Hendrick's eyes.

"Boy or girl?" she rasped.

"Boy." A tear slid down Hope's cheek, and batting it away, she grabbed a cloth and wiped the perspiration from Mrs. Hendrick's forehead. "You must rest now."

Her breathing grew ragged, and she eased her other hand over her flat belly. "A boy. William, like his father," she whispered, then squeezed her eyes shut. A tear slid from the corner of her eye and trickled down into her hair. "I know he didn't survive."

Hope caressed her hand. "I'm sorry."

Mrs. Hendrick's eyes popped open, and she studied Hope. Her chest rose and fell rapidly. "Mr. Hendrick will be angry."

Hope flinched. "Nay, how could he blame you for what happened?"

"I never do anything right." Mrs. Hendrick struggled to rise.

Hope gently pressed her shoulders down. "That's rubbish, and you know it." Fury raged through Hope. Fury at Mr. Hendrick's stubborn pride. He should not have taken his wife and child on a raft upon the open sea. If the child's death was anyone's fault, it was his and his alone.

"Elise." Mrs. Hendrick gripped Hope's arm, her eyes wide.

"She is well." Hope patted her hand. "She is with her father. They are both worried about you."

The lines on Mrs. Hendrick's face folded, and gasping, she threw both hands to her stomach. "You've been so kind to me, and I've been naught but. . ." She wailed then slumped onto the bed, panting.

A spark of fear shot through Hope. The pains of birth should be over now. "It matters not, Mrs. Hendrick. Just rest. Abigail has gone for some more bedding and some tea so you can regain your strength."

"Please call me Eleanor."

"Eleanor."

Laughter coupled with profane curses rumbled in the distance like thunder, reminding Hope they were no longer alone on the island. At least Captain Poole had allowed her and Abigail to attend to Mrs. Hendrick during her lying-in. And he had provided the cloths and lanterns they requested. Perhaps the pirate captain possessed some measure of compassion despite the vile behavior he demonstrated when they had first come ashore.

"He loved me once." The soft, scratchy sound of Mrs. Hendrick's voice brought Hope's attention back to her. Her eyes glazed over as she stared at the roof of the hut, and a slight smile teased her lips.

"I am sure he loves you still." Hope ran her fingers through the damp hair around Eleanor's face, wondering all the while where her *adoring* husband had gotten himself off to.

"He was so agreeable, so attentive and caring. A real gentleman. All the women adored him. But he had eyes for only me." She winced and pressed a hand to her belly, then caught her breath, and her smile returned. "He had everything a woman could want: wealth, looks, wit, and charm. I must admit, I was quite captivated."

Eleanor's description brought another man to Hope's mind, a man much like Mr. Hendrick—Lord Falkland. Shaking the vision away, Hope mused over Eleanor's words. Mr. Hendrick. Attentive? Caring? He seemed anything but those things—especially with his beautiful wife. "He is a fine man, I'm sure."

Eleanor laughed. "He is a cad, and you know it." She closed her eyes. "Elise is the only good thing that came from him."

Hope raised a brow at the woman's honesty, then peered beneath the sailcloth once again. She glanced over her shoulder, trying to keep the fear from her face. Where was Abigail? The bleeding had grown worse.

Mrs. Hendrick's moist eyes flickered with sorrow. "Can I tell you something?"

Hope nodded.

"Elise was conceived before we were married." Eleanor searched Hope's face tentatively, and then she released a sigh. "I knew you would not judge me. Perhaps that is why I loathed you so much when we first met. I saw myself in you and hated you for it."

Shock held Hope's tongue. She never would have thought this fine lady would have behaved with such impropriety as to give herself to a man before wedlock, nor divulged such an indiscretion to anyone—especially Hope. That Mrs. Hendrick hated Hope she had not kept secret, but Hope never could have imagined her true reason.

"He married me, of course." She waved a hand through the air, then dropped it as if the effort exhausted her. "But soon after the wedding, he changed. He stopped spending time with me. He rarely paid me a compliment. He spent hours and hours away from home. He drank heavily, and I oft smelled perfume on his clothes. Nothing I did was good enough for him. He criticized the way I managed the household, the way I dressed, my conversation, even the way I laughed." Tears poured from her eyes and dripped onto the leaves beside her head. "And of course I disappointed him with Elise. He wanted a son."

"I'm so sorry, Eleanor." Hope could not imagine the despair of such rejection. Would Lord Falkland have done the same thing had they been married? Yet as thoughts of his recent betrayal burned in her memory, she already knew the answer. Even amidst the torment of the past month, even amidst the despair of the present moment, a bud of relief sprang up within Hope. Though she and Eleanor had traveled down the same road, Hope had thus far been spared the same tragic fate. Why? She certainly did not deserve a reprieve.

"I fear he's never warmed to Elise." Agony cracked Eleanor's voice.

Hope pressed her hand over a tangible pain in her heart—a pain for both Eleanor and Elise, but especially for Elise, for Hope knew what it felt like to grow up without a father's love.

"I gave myself to him wholly, thinking I could win his love." Eleanor struggled to catch her breath. "But in the end, all I won was his hate."

"Shhh, now. You must rest." Hope took her hand, shocked by how cold and limp it suddenly felt.

Eleanor shifted her misty eyes to Hope. "I used to be beautiful like you."

"You are still comely, Eleanor." Hope brushed her fingers across Eleanor's cheek. "I was most jealous of you when I first saw you."

She smiled and looked away. "William says I have lost my youthful glow."

"William has gone blind." Hope no longer tried to hide the disdain in her voice.

A breeze blasted over them, sending the lanterns flickering and shadows crouching across the ceiling of leaves. Abigail entered, her arms full of tattered cloths.

Kneeling beside Eleanor, Abigail lifted the sailcloth and peeked beneath her bloodstained petticoat. Her face went white, and she raised a tremulous gaze to Hope.

Terror curdled in Hope's belly, and once again she was in Portsmouth, this time beside her mother's bed, holding her mother's hand as she now held Eleanor's.

Eleanor groaned. "I feel so weak." She let out a ragged breath and turned to Abigail. "Thank you, Miss Sheldon. You both have been beyond kind. I wish I hadn't been so reserved and had gotten to know you better." She smiled. "Perhaps we could have been friends."

"I am sure we shall be. There will be plenty of time for that." Abigail cupped her cheek in her hand.

"You know what the worst part is?" Eleanor faced Hope. She swallowed, and a foggy sheen covered her eyes. "I still love him."

Tears burned in Hope's eyes, and she squeezed them shut, releasing streams down her cheeks. She understood that kind of love just as she understood the heartache of giving it to someone who did not, or perhaps could not, return it.

Eleanor coughed and struggled for a breath. She gasped. Hope drew nearer, gripping her hand. "Eleanor!"

Mrs. Hendrick's eyes focused on the leafy roof, then went blank. Her chest fell, and one final breath escaped her lips.

Abigail dropped her head into her hands and sobbed.

"No!" Hope grabbed Eleanor's shoulders and shook them. "No!" Not again. "Mother. No!" Falling onto Eleanor, Hope embraced her. "Don't leave me."

"Hope." Abigail pulled her from Eleanor and drew her close, wrapping her arms around her. "Shh, shh."

Leaning on Abigail's shoulder, Hope opened the floodgate of years of sorrow and loss and allowed her tears to flow unrestrained for Eleanor, for her baby, for a brother Hope would never know, and for a mother she never had. "It isn't fair. It isn't fair."

Abigail planted a gentle kiss upon her head. "Life isn't fair."

&

Numb, Hope trudged from the hut, the tiny, cold bundle cradled in her hands. The sultry night air struck her like a wall, thick with sorrow. She barely felt it. She barely felt anything save the agony wrenching at her heart. Crushing her toes into the sand, she peered into the darkness. In the distance, flames danced high into the night, circled by a raucous band of pirates flinging chortles and curses and lewd ballads through the air. Enjoying themselves as if two precious lives had not been snuffed from this earth.

Her gaze moved to five shadowy figures sitting on a log outside the mob of pirates. One pirate, armed with pistols, stood guard over them, yet his attention and his body drifted toward his companions.

Pressing the bundle against her chest, she started toward the men. Over the sea, a full moon flung sparkling diamonds upon the liquid ebony. The crash of the waves offered a soothing alternative to the boisterous revelry of the pirates, but she didn't want to be soothed right now. She wanted justice. She wanted revenge. As she approached the log, Nathaniel's gaze shot to hers, as did Gavin's. The major lay upon the sand, snoring, and Kreggs and Hanson seemed oblivious to anything save the pirate's unrestrained festivities.

She halted before Mr. Hendrick, glancing only briefly at Elise, curled up in a ball at his feet.

His drowsy eyes widened, and he rose. "'Tis the babe?" He held his arms open to receive the wee bundle.

"I'm sorry, Mr. Hendrick. Your son did not survive." Hope took no care to soften the blow with a sentimental tone. Her only thought was to whisper the ill tidings so as not to disturb Elise.

"What's this? What are you saying? My son?" He took the bundle in one hand and peered beneath the cloth. For a moment his expression registered grief and sorrow and perhaps a bit of remorse, and Hope felt a spark of sympathy for him. But then his eyes flashed dark with anger. He shoved the dead child back into Hope's arms and stormed toward the hut.

Nathaniel shot to his feet as Hope turned and marched after Mr. Hendrick. Though he couldn't make out what she'd said to him, from Mr. Hendrick's reaction, Nathaniel assumed the child had been stillborn. He deduced from the fury on Hope's face that a barrel of trouble would soon explode.

Grabbing Mr. Hendrick's arm, Hope jerked him around to face her. Her words were muffled, but their effect boomed louder than a broadside. "Gone! Of all the—gone where?"

Nathaniel reached her side as Gavin circled around Mr. Hendrick, taking a stand behind him.

"The childbirth was too much for her. She is dead." Hope's tone was laced with anger, giving Nathaniel pause.

Mr. Hendrick took a step back, his mouth contorting into an O, yet his face devoid of any emotion. "Dead." He glanced at the hut and then at the bundle in Hope's arms.

Nathaniel's throat constricted. *Mrs. Hendrick dead.* Her ear-piercing screams had trumpeted through the camp all day and half the night, but he assumed they were a result of the normal birthing pains. Hope's expression was drawn, her shoulders sagging—with exhaustion or sorrow? Perhaps both. What she and Abigail must have endured.

Anger tightened Mr. Hendrick's otherwise placid expression. His jaw twitched. "Stupid woman! She couldn't do even this right without killing herself and my son."

As if in protest to his scornful affront, a roller crashed on the shore, reaching its foamy fingers toward them.

Gavin shook his head. "Sink me, man, but you are a heartless beast." He voiced the sentiment that rang through Nathaniel's dazed mind.

"What would you know of matters of the heart?" Mr. Hendrick dismissed him with a wave.

Hope shoved her face into his. "You dare call your wife stupid when it was your choice to take her upon the open seas!"

"The woman insisted on traveling with me." Mr. Hendrick shifted his shoulders. "She insisted on constantly hovering around me."

"How can you say such a thing?" Nathaniel could not hide the disgust in his voice. "'Tis obvious you did not honor her in her life. But fire and thunder, man, at least honor her in her death."

Mr. Hendrick lowered his chin as if pondering Nathaniel's words. He kicked the sand with his foot and sighed.

Hope held the bundle closer to her chest and lowered her gaze. "She loved you, Mr. Hendrick." When she lifted her face, grief pooled in her eyes. "Though I cannot imagine why."

The riotous sounds of the pirates' merriment faded, and the hairs bristled on the back of Nathaniel's neck as the sound of their boots sifting through the sand took its place. He had hoped they would have been too far gone in their drink to notice the commotion.

Mr. Hendrick snorted. "You can't imagine why, you say?" The hint of moisture in his eyes dried into a hard sheen. "Many fine ladies set their cap for me—some in possession of quite a fortune, I might add—before I was forced to take Eleanor as wife." He raised his dark brows. "How unfortunate for you that you were not as successful as she with your last beau. Perhaps then he wouldn't have abandoned you to the auction block."

The smell of unwashed bodies and rum wafted over Nathaniel as shadowy figures circled around them.

Hope's chest heaved. She pursed her lips and took a step toward Mr. Hendrick. Nathaniel got the impression she would have struck him on the face if not for the bundle in her arms.

Taking her elbow, Nathaniel eased her back, hoping to quell her rage and her tongue before she sparked Mr. Hendrick's temper further. The man was grieving, and no matter how heartless he seemed, he deserved to be left alone.

Turning toward him, Nathaniel stifled his own anger and put on his most sympathetic expression. "I realize this must be a shock, but you have no cause to insult Miss Hope. Your wife's death was no one's fault. It was simply her time."

"But it is his fault!" Hope pushed her way toward Mr. Hendrick. His eyes bulged with rage. Bypassing Hope, he directed their fury toward Nathaniel.

"You could have healed her. You healed this strumpet." He nodded toward Hope. "But you wouldn't heal my wife." His face darkened. "And now she is dead!"

The words rang ominous between a lull in the waves, and Nathaniel opened his mouth to explain he couldn't heal anyone without the power of God. But grunts and groans filtered through the mob of pirates, followed by the crunch of sand beneath heavy boots. Captain Poole appeared beside Nathaniel, his hands planted firmly on his waist.

"Mr. Mason, the man has just insulted yer wife beyond what any man should tolerate. And yet ye stand here and do nothing?"

"He's got the heart of a yellow dog, says I," one pirate bellowed.

"Yellow blood runs in 'is veins," another chortled, and the pirates broke into a chorus of insults.

The captain snapped his fingers to silence his men. "Unless, of course"—his voice took on a sinister tone—"she is not yer wife and indeed a trollop, as the man claims." Even in the shadows, Nathaniel could see the lust dripping from the captain's eyes as he gazed at Hope.

Nathaniel ground his teeth together and glared her way. Would this woman's unanchored emotions never cease to cause him trouble?

The apologetic look in her eyes did naught to appease his rising anxiety. He lengthened his stance, knowing he could not appear weak in front of these pirates. Their lives—all of their lives—depended on it.

"Mr. Hendrick." He addressed the man in as calm a tone as possible.

Mr. Hendrick crossed his arms over his chest and eyed Nathaniel, a haughty smirk upon his lips.

"You will apologize at once to my wife, and to me."

Mr. Hendrick's eyes flickered between Hope and Captain Poole, igniting a flash of terror in Nathaniel. Would he give them away? Surely the man had enough decency not to put Hope in such a precarious position. If he would simply apologize and walk away, the whole matter could be put to rest. But instead he snorted. "I will not."

Nathaniel's heart fell to his feet. "Then you shall meet me at dawn."

"It will be my pleasure." Mr. Hendrick fingered his beard and nodded.

The pirates cheered, shoving muskets into the air, one of them firing into the night.

"Since you are the one being challenged, Hendrick, you may choose the weapons," Captain Poole stated as if he often presided over duels.

"I choose pistols," Mr. Hendrick said smugly.

Nathaniel's blood froze. He stood a fair chance with swords, but pistols? He had little experience with them and had never been a good shot.

"Pistols it is!" Captain Poole shouted, then turned to survey his crew. "We have ourselves a duel, men."

The pirates cheered. "To the death," they chanted. "To the death!"

CHAPTER 24

The riotous celebration of the duel sent Elise into a frenzy of tears, and the next hours occupied Hope with trying to comfort the little girl. Finally slipping her arms from beneath Elise, Hope sat up and stretched her tired shoulders. Abigail's deep breathing filled the hut like a soothing chant. Hope glanced down at Elise, relieved to see she had also succumbed to exhaustion. At least for the moment, she was in a better world, a world where her mother was not dead and at dawn her father would not engage in a fight to the death.

When Abigail and Hope had first broken the sad news to Elise, shock had kept her silent for quite some time. Then, like a sudden storm at sea, anger raged through her, and she searched the camp, demanding to see her mother. Thankfully, Abigail had already wrapped Eleanor's body in sailcloth and, with the assistance of Kreggs and Hanson, had placed her in the cleft of some rocks down the shore, in preparation for burial on the morrow. With the bloody leaves and cloths removed from the hut and fresh ones strewn in their place, it was as if the dear woman had never existed.

Save for the little girl lying beside Hope. Elise had her mother's blue eyes and the creamy color of her skin.

Hope swallowed against the burning in her throat at the memories of her own mother's passing seven years ago. Hope had been fifteen, surely more equipped to handle such a tragedy than Elise at only six. Yet the pain of her mother's death remained as fresh as if it had occurred yesterday. Afterward, her father withdrew into his own shell of agony, withdrew from his friends, withdrew from society, and withdrew from his daughters—especially Hope.

She brushed a finger over Elise's soft face, noting even in the shadows

515

how much she favored her mother. Was it Hope's resemblance to her own mother that had caused her father so much grief, or was it, as he so often said, that she disappointed him?

Though she tried to shrug off the sorrow, Hope's heart weighed heavy in her chest.

A hint of red peeked through the leaves forming the walls of the hut. Dawn approached, and with it, the terror of what Hope had done. Nathaniel would soon risk his life for her honor. *Honor.* She snorted at the irony and cursed herself for putting him in this position—yet again. No wonder he wished to keep his distance from her. If only she could have controlled her anger. If only she could have kept her mouth shut, Mr. Hendrick would not have insulted her.

Rising, she brushed the leaves from her gown and emerged from the hut. A light breeze wafted in from the sea, stirring the coals in the fire until they glowed red. Despite the heat, a chill overtook Hope, and she wrapped her arms around her chest. Her eyes ached—from exhaustion, from sorrow, from spending all her energy comforting Elise, and all her worrying on Nathaniel's fate.

Where was he now, and what thoughts raced through his mind? Surely he wasn't sleeping. Snores filtered through the air from the men's hut and from down the shore where the pirates had given in to their drink and exhaustion and fallen where they'd stood.

A sliver of yellow floated atop the pink on the horizon, drawing her outside into dawn's first light. The sound of a male voice drifted to her on the breeze. Turning, she headed toward it, brushing aside tangled foliage as she went. When she emerged onto another part of the beach, the dark shape of a man sitting atop a boulder took form against the pre-dawn glow.

Hesitating, Hope bent her ear toward him, trying to distinguish the voice amid the roaring surf. It took only seconds for her heart to skip at Nathaniel's deep, resonating tone.

She crept toward him, wondering to whom he spoke and more than curious as to what he said. But as she approached, words like *God* and *Father* spilled from his lips, and she realized he was praying. Ashamed to be eavesdropping, she stepped back. He turned in her direction.

"Hope?"

"Yes."

He ran a hand through his hair. "What do you want?" Annoyance rang in his tone.

Swallowing, she approached him. His dark brown eyes scoured her as if he were trying to see her in the shadows, but giving up, he turned away.

"You were praying," she said.

He nodded. "I thought it wise, since today I may meet my Maker." Humor tinged his voice.

Hope found nothing humorous about the situation. "I'm afraid I have brought misfortune upon you once again."

Planting one bare foot on the rock, Nathaniel leaned his arm atop his bent knee and gazed at the sea. "The man was in shock and grieving. He did not need your carping wit."

His reprimand stabbed Hope, but she threw back her shoulders. "That he harbors no affection for his wife or for his daughter, you cannot deny." She spoke more adamantly as anger flared within her. "But that he shrugged off Eleanor's death so easily was more than I could bear."

"'Tis possible he has other things on his mind." Nathaniel's jaw twitched. He rubbed his eyes as the wind flapped his linen shirt.

"Why do you defend him?"

"I'll grant you he's an ill-tempered mongrel, and perhaps his behavior is deserving of our scorn." He faced her, his eyes glinting with apprehension as well as reproof. "But might I suggest that you would do well not to allow everything that passes through your mind to slip off your tongue without censure."

Hope bunched her fists and looked away, but guilt soon smothered her anger. He was right of course. And once again, she'd failed to behave as a lady.

"How is the girl?" Nathaniel's expression softened.

"She cried half the night but sleeps now." The first twitter of birds drew Hope's gaze to the vegetation around them.

"You are good with her," Nathaniel said.

A compliment. Hope's heart skipped, and she gazed up at him. But he turned his face back to the sea, depriving her of his expression.

"She is a sweet child, undeserving of this tragedy." Hope shifted her bare feet across the sand. "I also lost my mother in childbirth." Why she told him that, she did not know.

Nathaniel shifted on the rock. "I'm sorry." He sighed. "I am sure that made yesterday's task all the more odious."

Hope blinked at his compassion.

"Were you close to her?" he asked.

"Nay. We often fought." Hope tugged on a lock of hair. "'Tis the way with mothers and daughters, I'm told."

"They say we were too much alike—like two stones grinding away at one another." Hope smiled, remembering how often her sisters would tease her with such sayings.

Nathaniel looked at her now, and she caught a whiff of his woodsy scent, a scent she'd come to associate with protection and warmth, a scent she would never tire of. "I am sure your mother only wanted what was best for you."

Hope wanted to believe that was true. Yet more often than not, she wondered if her mother had ever loved her. Or did she see too much of her own follies in Hope to care for her at all? "I wish I could go back and erase all our silly squabbles. I wish I had time to get to know her better."

"We never appreciate someone when that person is with us." Nathaniel lowered his foot back to the sand and rubbed the stubble on his jaw.

Hope wondered if he thought of his own mother. She didn't know much about her save she had died when he was young. That they shared the same loss endeared him to her all the more. A memory sparked in her mind—one only the past day of bitter travail could have hidden from her.

"You claimed me as your wife," she said with incredulity as she took a bold step toward him. Even as the words flew off her lips, the elation, the thrill of that moment came crashing back upon her. Could it be he harbored some small measure of affection for her, after all?

He snorted. "Surely you do not think me so callous as to feed you to the sharks. Not when it was within my power to save you."

Hope lowered her gaze, her heart shriveling. He'd done for her no more than he would do for any woman. No doubt if Abigail had been there, she would be the one honored with the title. And Hope could tell from the look of aversion burning in his eyes he would have preferred that outcome. "Nevertheless, I owe you my life once again."

He shifted his shoulders.

Hope inched toward him, longing to memorize every line of his face, every muscle, every inflection, just in case he would be taken from her. "I don't want you to die."

He chuckled. "We are of the same mind in that."

"I'm sorry for putting you in this position. It was not my intent."

The curve of the sun peered over the horizon, spilling gold and orange ribbons upon the sea. A breeze laden with salt and rain fingered the waves of his hair and flapped his shirt again, revealing his strong chest beneath. He faced her, regarding her intently. As she watched him, she knew. She no longer yearned only for his admiration, his approval. She yearned for his love.

Hope took a step back, her gut wrenching at the realization she would never claim the depth of his affection. And for the first time in her life, her beauty, her charm, and her feminine wiles were not enough to purchase the man she longed to possess.

He rose and rubbed the back of his neck, then let out a deep sigh.

An extreme urge to run into his arms overcame Hope. To feel his strong embrace, to inhale a deep breath of his scent. She took a step closer to him. Her eyes burned, but she would not let them fill with tears. "Nathaniel, I cannot bear to lose you."

He swallowed, and for a moment the hardness in his eyes softened. For a moment, she thought he might open his arms to receive her. But instead, he grunted and swerved around her. "Dawn has arrived. I have an appointment to keep."

⌘

Nathaniel stood, hands fisted at his sides, as Gavin primed and loaded his pistol. The major did the same for Mr. Hendrick, who stood beside him, inspecting his progress. A horde of pirates circled them, including Captain Poole, who had leapt upon a boulder to survey the proceedings like a prince watching a cricket match. Hope, along with Kreggs and Hanson, stood amongst the pirates to his right. He assumed Abigail was with Elise and thanked God the little girl would not have to witness her father engaged in a duel to the death.

The sun hovered over the horizon, flinging its cruel rays upon them, only accentuating the sweat now dripping down Nathaniel's back. He ran a sleeve over his moist forehead as the pirates' incessant grumblings transformed into wagers and calculations of odds. He tried to drown them out, not wanting to know how much coin hinged on his demise.

The major, looking impotent without his red coat and white baldric, handed the pistol to Mr. Hendrick and sauntered over to Nathaniel. "I fear you have met your match, Mr. Mason." He snickered. "Mr. Hendrick informs me he is an expert marksman. Finally there will be an end to your insolent meddling in the affairs of competent gentlemen." His eyes glided over Hope, and he leaned closer to Nathaniel. "Let me put your fears to rest regarding Miss Hope's safety. I shall be happy to assume the role of husband in your stead."

Nathaniel's blood boiled. The intolerable man would never lay a hand on Hope. Not as long as Nathaniel lived. But that was his point, wasn't it? "How did your raft fare upon the seas, Major? Competent craftsmanship of a gentleman?"

The major narrowed his eyes and spun around.

Mr. Hendrick, who had settled into a pompous stance reflecting the cocky assurance of his success, chuckled. "Ready to die, Mr. Mason?"

"If God wills it, then yes, I am." Nathaniel lifted his shoulders and eyed his opponent. "It is your eternal destiny, however, which concerns me."

Mr. Hendrick snorted and laughed again. This time his laughter carried a twinge of fear.

"Enough chatter. Let's be on with it," Captain Poole bellowed, and a cacophony of cheers saturated the air.

"Very well." Gavin handed the pistol to Nathaniel with a wink of assurance, bolstering Nathaniel's weakening confidence. "Mr. Hendrick, Mr. Mason, back to back, if you please."

Turning, Nathaniel stared past the horde of pirates onto the green maze of trees lining the beach. He heard Mr. Hendrick shuffle in the sand and felt the heat from his body compress between their backs.

"On the count of six, gentlemen," Gavin continued.

Nathaniel dared one last glance at Hope. Fear bristled in her eyes, along with the same yearning and admiration he'd seen on the beach earlier. The yearning that had nearly broken down his resolve to keep her at a distance. Did she care for him, or was it another alluring tactic she had perfected over the years? It mattered not. He tore his eyes from her and focused on the task at hand and the sound of Gavin's thundering shout. "One!"

Nathaniel took a step. He should be angry at Hope for the precarious situation in which he now found himself. Nevertheless, how could he blame her for her outburst? Mr. Hendrick's cold disregard toward his family and his insufferable arrogance were not to be borne.

"Two!"

Nathaniel took another step. The muscles in his fingers twitched over the gun's trigger.

"Three!"

The pirates cheered and thrust their weapons into the air. "Thar be some blood spilt today, says I," one man shouted with glee.

"Put a ball betwixt 'is eyes," another chortled.

"Four!"

The grumbling mob parted as Nathaniel continued. Sweat slid over his palms, and he tightened the grip on the handle of his pistol. Being raised by a reverend had not afforded him the opportunity to master pistols. Swords, yes, for Reverend Halloway enjoyed swordplay as sport, but the man abhorred guns. *Oh, why did he have to hate guns, Lord?* Nathaniel clenched his teeth, wondering what a bullet would feel like penetrating his flesh. *Nevertheless, Lord, have Your will in this today. Protect me. But if I should die, please protect the ladies.*

"Five!" Gavin yelled.

Nathaniel's heart took on a frenzied beat. The cock of a pistol snapped behind him. He gripped his own weapon with both hands.

A white egret flew overhead, squawking a protest.

"Six!" Gavin shouted.

Hope gasped.

"Fire at will!" Gavin and the major roared together.

Nathaniel spun around, pressed his finger over the trigger, and aimed at Mr. Hendrick's leg. But before he could fire, the crack of Mr. Hendrick's gun reverberated through the air.

Nathaniel waited for the pain to start. He glanced down at his shirt, his breeches, but no red spot appeared.

"I shot him. I know I shot him!" Mr. Hendrick's face twisted in unbelief as he pointed his pistol toward Nathaniel. He glanced across the crowd. "You saw me. I shot him!"

The major stared agape at Nathaniel as if he were a ghost and shook his head. "Egad, the man's luck."

A huge smile spread upon Gavin's lips. "Your shot, Mr. Mason."

"Finish him off!" Captain Poole gave a wave of permission to Nathaniel and then glanced aloft as if he were bored.

"Kill 'im, kill 'im, kill 'im," the pirates chanted.

An expression of terror contorted Mr. Hendrick's features. He tossed his gun to the sand. "I demand we begin again. There's something amiss with my pistol."

"You missed him, Mr. Hendrick." Captain Poole hopped down from the rock, and the crowd parted to allow him passage. Planting both boots firmly in the sand, he fisted his hands upon his waist. "Now take your stand like a man."

Mr. Hendrick's gaze skittered past the captain over the crowd, as if looking for a miraculous escape. His chest heaved. Sweat dripped down his forehead. Then he turned and bolted to his left. A snap of Captain Poole's fingers brought the tips of ten swords leveled upon his chest. Sniveling, Mr. Hendrick faced Nathaniel. "I beg you, sir. By all that is decent and holy."

Disgust soured in Nathaniel's belly. This man had wealth, a successful merchant business, a good name—all the things Nathaniel had worked so hard to attain. Yet beyond all the achievements, beyond the respect he received, he possessed not only the heart of a blackguard, but the heart of a coward.

Still, Nathaniel could not kill him. Would not kill him. He glanced at Captain Poole, who stood urging him with a lift of his brow to complete the task. How to end this without appearing a coward to these pirates?

Nathaniel raised his pistol again, closed one eye, and aimed it upon the trembling Mr. Hendrick.

He pressed the trigger.

CHAPTER 25

rack!

C A plume of smoke rose from the barrel of Nathaniel's pistol, and he coughed at the acrid cloud that blew back in his face.

Mr. Hendrick shrieked, patted his chest for wounds, then allowed his gaze to follow the direction in which Nathaniel's pistol was pointed. "You fired into the air." His incredulous tone was edged with relief.

Nathaniel shrugged and tossed the vile weapon to the sand. "You're not worth having a man's death on my conscience."

Grunts and curses flooded over him. Captain Poole belched and shook his head, glaring at Nathaniel.

But Nathaniel cared not. No one had been killed, especially not him. *Thank You, Lord.* The pirates were not so pleased. They cursed and spat onto the sand, then shot glances at Nathaniel as if he had deprived them of their only entertainment for a month.

"Aw, what kind o' duel be that? No one be dead!"

"I say we make 'em do it over," another pirate with a silver ring in one ear and one eye sewn shut shouted toward Nathaniel.

"Be gone with ye!" Captain Poole waved the crowd aside as he marched into the center. "Nothing more to see here." His men dispersed and ambled away, calling in bets and exchanging coins with clanks and chinks as they went, one of them grumbling, "Perish and plague me, I knew he wouldn't kill 'im."

Major Paine took a wide swath around the pirate captain, casting him a dubious look, and stood beside his still-trembling friend.

Gavin gave Nathaniel a disapproving glance. "Sink me, man. Why didn't you kill him?" He scratched his whiskers. "He would not have hesitated to kill you if he'd possessed a better aim."

"There is no need to take the man's life." Nathaniel released a heavy sigh and rubbed the back of his neck.

Gavin stared at Nathaniel as if he had just walked on water. "Of course there is. Especially when the man is a blubbering, pompous toad."

Captain Poole chuckled. "A truer word as e'er were spoke."

"The pistol was faulty," Mr. Hendrick whined.

Nathaniel's gaze locked upon Hope, a few yards behind him. Elise stood at her side, clutching her skirts. Even from a distance, he could see the relief and joy beaming from Hope's expression.

Gavin thrust his face toward Mr. Hendrick. "Instead of complaining, sir, you should thank Mr. Mason for his charity. I daresay you would not have received such grace from me."

"Nor from me," Captain Poole added with a grunt. He picked up Mr. Hendrick's pistol from the sand and studied it for a moment. "Ye were beat fair, Hendrick. And as I sees it, ye owe this man yer life."

Mr. Hendrick winced, but the firm line of his jaw and the hard glint to his eyes spoke of his obstinate dissent.

Dismissing him with a wave, Captain Poole took a turn about Nathaniel, examining his back and chest. "Split me sides, but I saw the man's aim. 'Twas dead on. At six paces an' even wit' the unsure accuracy of these metallic beasts, he should o' clipped ye at least." Turning, he glared at the major. "Ye there. Give me some powder and shot."

"What is your intent, Captain?" The major's eyes flitted across the group, and he took a step back.

"None of yer business, ye half-masted cockerel. Now give them to me, or I'll put a shot betwixt yer ears."

The major's sunburned face blanched. He fished in his pocket, pulled out the powder container and a ball, and hurried over to hand them to the pirate.

After loading and priming the pistol, Captain Poole took a few steps away from the group, cast a glance over his shoulder toward where Hope, Elise, and Abigail stood, then cocked and aimed the weapon at a palm tree a few feet down shore. "See them coconuts?" Without awaiting a response, he closed one eye and pulled the trigger. A resounding *crack* whipped through the air, and a coconut thudded to the sand. He eyed the weapon, batting away the smoke. "Nothing wrong with this pistol,

Hendrick." He stuffed it into his breeches. "Either you are a horrible shot and a worse liar, or this man should have a hole in him."

"'Twas God's doing." Abigail's voice shot over them. Captain Poole spun on his heels, his face lighting up as he watched the lady approach.

Abigail reached Nathaniel's side, then shifted her eyes to Captain Poole. Nathaniel tensed, praying she knew what she was doing. Behind her, Hope and Elise inched their way toward the group.

"God, you say?" Captain Poole cocked his head and studied Abigail with interest.

"You have proven, Captain, that the pistol is not faulty," she began, her tone a paragon of confident tranquility. "We have Mr. Hendrick's testimony that he is an expert marksman, and why would he lie under these circumstances? And we have Mr. Mason here without a mark on him. What other explanation would you give?"

Captain Poole circled Abigail, fingering the stubble on his chin. A sly grin slithered over his lips. Abigail stood tall, her chestnut hair dancing idly down her back in the breeze. She brushed a few strands from her forehead with the back of her hand and commanded his gaze.

"A wise conclusion, miss," Captain Poole said. "I've forgotten yer name."

"Sheldon. Abigail Sheldon."

"Ah, Miss Sheldon. I should like to discuss this further with ye, if ye don't mind." He proffered his arm as though he would escort her to a ball.

Abigail froze; her jaw quivered. Nathaniel took her arm and eased her away from the pirate.

"Have ye two wives now, Mr. Mason?" Captain Poole snapped. He dropped his arm to his side. "I wish only to speak with the lady. Ye shall be rid of me soon enough. We set sail on the morrow and shall be no more of your concern."

Gavin moved to stand beside Hope in a protective gesture that grated over Nathaniel. Ignoring it, he fixed his gaze upon the captain, both pleased and alarmed at the man's declaration to leave. "So soon?"

"Ye'll miss me, eh?" Captain Poole eyes sparkled with mischief. "Seems ye've picked this island clean of fruit. And we've loaded up all the water we need. There be naught left for us here."

"Will you take us to Kingstown, then?" Nathaniel crossed his arms over his chest and risked pricking the capricious pirate's ire. He had no choice. He had no idea when another ship would arrive.

The captain inhaled a deep breath as if he were trying to calm his temper, then nodded toward his ship. "Does that look like a passenger ship to ye, Mr. Mason?" He ground the words out through his teeth, but then he gazed at his ship, and his face softened with pride. "Nay, that be the *Enchantress*—named for me last wife. And with that beauty, me and me crew have taken three merchantmen, two East Indiamen, one Spanish argosy, a Dutch *fluyt*, and a German barque." He seemed to grow taller with the mention of each conquest, then leaned toward Nathaniel and raised one brow. "Now if ye and yer friend here and those two"—he motioned toward Hanson and Kreggs—"wish to join me crew, then we have somethin' to discuss."

"I can't speak for these others, but I am no pirate, Captain Poole," Nathaniel said without hesitation.

"Too good for the trade, eh?"

"Mr. Mason is a godly man, Captain." Abigail raised her chin a notch. "Pirating would go against everything he believes in."

"Saints' blood." Captain Poole waved his hands through the air, the lace at his cuffs fluttering in the breeze. "This island's crawlin' with godly people. Where have I landed, Christ's Church, London?"

Gavin chuckled and then coughed into his hand beneath Abigail's stern glance.

"What of ye, sir?" Captain Poole directed his gaze at Gavin. "Be there pirate blood in ye?"

"I have yet to discover that, Captain." Gavin winked. "But one never knows."

"I thought so. I can see the fire of the brethren in yer eyes." The captain clapped him on the back, the compliment molding over Gavin like the perfect fit of a garment.

"And ye two." The captain swung about and faced Kreggs and Hanson. Fear skittered across Hanson's face, but Kreggs shifted his stance and furrowed his brow. "We stick with Mr. Mason. He's not led us astray thus far."

Captain Poole turned a curious eye to Nathaniel. "Your men revere you. Such loyalty be hard to come by." He studied Nathaniel as if searching for the reason, then shrugged. "Well, so be it. Ye can all stay on this bloomin' island for all I care."

"We are both able seamen." Nathaniel gestured toward Gavin. "We will work your ship to pay for our passage as long as you don't engage in any pillaging along the way."

Captain Poole's wicked, menacing laugh bristled the hair on Nathaniel's arms. Instantly, his face turned to stone. "I don't bargain with the likes of you." He spat. But when he glanced at Abigail, the tight lines on his face softened. "I tell ye what. Allow me a moment with Miss Sheldon, and I'll think on yer offer."

"No." Hope stepped forward. "Leave her be." Abigail sent an appreciative glance toward her friend, and Hope gripped her hand.

"All I wish is to speak with her, an' I'll do it with or without yer permission or that o' yer husband's. Only if ye do give me yer blessin', it may soften me mood when I consider yer offer."

Over the pirate's shoulder, Nathaniel saw Abigail nod her consent, though fear sparked in her wide eyes.

"Very well, Captain," Nathaniel reluctantly agreed.

"There be some sense to ye." Captain Poole proffered his arm again, and this time, Abigail released Hope and slipped her hand through it.

Nathaniel could do naught but clench his fists and say a prayer as he watched the two saunter away.

⤚

Abigail drew a breath, trying to quell the quaver in her voice and the tremble in her legs. "If you mean to assault me, Captain, I must warn you, I *will* put up a fight."

"Promise?" Captain Poole gave a mischievous chuckle but then patted her hand, still hooked in the crook of his arm. "Ye've naught to fear from me." She caught his gaze from the corner of her eyes—as dark and brooding as any she'd seen. "At least for the time being." His lips curved slightly as he continued to lead her along the shore.

"What would you like to speak to me about, Captain?" His salacious dalliance unnerved her. She wouldn't have agreed to this time alone with him, not even to stifle his temper and soften him to the idea of taking them to Kingstown, save for the fitful yearning she'd seen in his eyes. A questioning, a hopeless pleading that nipped at her heart.

A breeze picked up, bringing with it the scent of the sea and a whiff of rum and sweat from the man walking beside her. His boots crunched over the sand as he swerved away from the waves that crept toward them in arcs of restless foam.

After casting a glance over his shoulder, the captain led her to a boulder beneath a shady palm and gestured for her to sit. Abigail spotted Nathaniel standing on shore and was thankful for his careful watch. Not that there would be much he could do to stop this pirate from taking whatever he wanted, especially with his savage crew so close at hand.

The rising sun shot its blazing rays upon the island, and Abigail ran a hand over her moist neck, thankful for the shade and wondering how the pirate tolerated his velvet coat and breeches. Though seemingly undaunted by the heat, his expression bore evidence of a battle raging within his thoughts.

A breeze quivered the fronds of the palm above her until they sounded like the laughter of angels, reminding her that she was never alone. Silently, she thanked the Lord for the good outcome of the duel and for their safety thus far, and prayed for the right words to appease this volatile man beside her.

Captain Poole doffed his plumed hat and tossed it to the sand. His black hair fluttered in the wind over the golden ring in his ear, and she swallowed at the intense look in his dark, flashing eyes. Tall and broad shouldered, he would be a handsome man if not for the lines of cruelty that often marred his face.

Lowering her gaze beneath his perusal, she waited for him to begin.

He shifted his boots. "Yer a missionary."

Abigail nodded.

"Ye speak of God as if ye know Him." His tone was not accusatory, nor caustic, but carried a curiosity that both shocked and delighted Abigail.

"He *can* be known, Captain. He longs to be known."

He scratched his chin and stared out at the sea. Abigail eyed the pistols stuffed in his baldric and breeches, the cutlass that hung at his side, and she knew this man had killed many men in his life. Never before had she been in the presence of such evil, yet at this moment, she felt no fear.

"I'm wonderin' if ye would enlighten me with what ye know of Him," he said without looking at her.

Abigail blinked. "You want to know about God?"

He cast a glance over his shoulder at Nathaniel, then thrust his face into hers. "Aye, as ye heard me say."

A spark of unease shot through Abigail, but she stiffened her jaw. "What do you wish to know?"

He crossed his arms over his chest, his coat flapping in the breeze behind him, and dug his boots in the sand as if preparing himself for a long discourse. "Start at the beginning."

CHAPTER 26

Tears burned Hope's eyes. Perhaps it was Eleanor's death, perhaps the terror of the duel, or perhaps it was. . .one glance toward the beach told her Nathaniel remained at watch like a fierce sentinel over Abigail conversing with Captain Poole nigh twenty yards down the shore. During the past hour, he had not budged from his post, not even when the blazing heat of the sun scorched the sand, not even after everyone else had abandoned him. From time to time, he would pace ferociously as he was prone to do when he was distraught. But now he stood still, his fists planted firmly at his waist.

Hope had longed to join him, but his aversion to her company had kept her standing at a distance for as long as her ankle and the glaring sun allowed. She, too, was most concerned for Abigail's safety, but from all observations, it did indeed appear the captain only wished to speak with her, though regarding what subject Hope could only imagine.

She entered the clearing and sank onto the chair. Bending down, she rubbed her ankle and then leaned back, trying to enjoy the respite from the heat. Wrapping her empty arms around herself, she released a sigh. She missed Elise. Mr. Hendrick had taken his daughter into his hut with the major, and Hope wondered how she fared. The poor girl feared her father, but he *was* her father, after all. Perhaps now that his wife was gone, Mr. Hendrick would become a better parent. Deep down, Hope doubted it.

Leaning forward, she picked up a shell and fingered it. She flipped it over and examined the symmetrical ridges—so patterned, so perfect, so unlike real life. Had God intended His children to be this perfect? Did He intend their lives to follow a specified pattern? If so, perhaps one day they would all end up as beautiful and flawless as this shell.

Gavin bounded into the clearing, his bare chest glistening with sweat. Though his expression was somber, the usual playful spark glimmered in his eyes. "Kreggs and Hanson are digging the grave." He glanced at Nathaniel out on the beach. "As soon as Abigail is free, we'll bury Mrs. Hendrick."

Hope nodded, even as her gut shriveled. She hated funerals. She hated death.

Taking a shell-full of water from the bucket, Gavin poured the liquid over his head, and Hope averted her eyes from his muscled chest. The man presented a constant barrier in her efforts to become a lady. Grabbing his discarded shirt, he dabbed at the moisture on his torso, then thrust his arms into the garment and tossed it over his head.

"Nathaniel must harbor deep affections for Miss Sheldon, wouldn't you say?" He took a seat on the log beside her chair.

Hope shifted against the uncomfortable twinge of jealousy. "Perhaps he is concerned for her safety." She longed to believe her own words but deep down doubted they carried any truth.

"We all are concerned, to be sure, but you don't see any of us standing guard like a sentry. Sink me, he's ready to slap the captain's hand should he make a single untoward gesture toward the lady. Nay, seems like the actions of a man quite besotted." He laughed, and his gaiety stung Hope's heart.

Shoving her pain behind a wall of rejection, Hope diverted her attention to the man beside her. His easy smile and flirtatious ways swept over her like salve on a wound. "How would you know the actions of a besotted man?" She smiled.

He took her hand in his and planted a kiss upon it. "Allow me to demonstrate."

An hour later, Nathaniel and Abigail entered the camp, interrupting Hope and Gavin's playful conversation. Anxious to hear what had occurred between Abigail and the pirate captain, Hope rose. Gavin assisted her, keeping his hand possessively upon her arm.

Nathaniel grunted and shot Hope a look of reproach. "Did we interrupt something?"

"Nay." Hope tugged her arm from Gavin's grasp and inched away from him.

Shaking his head, Nathaniel turned toward Abigail.

Abigail clasped her hands together, her eyes dancing with joy. "The captain has agreed to provide safe passage to Kingstown."

"Indeed?" Hope could hardly believe her ears. From the pirate's fluctuating moods and volatile mannerisms, she'd feared their best hope might be that he would simply leave them on the island. "But how?"

"Well, sink me." Gavin eyed Abigail curiously, a slight grin rising on his lips. "What did you offer the man to make him so agreeable?"

Nathaniel took a firm step toward his friend. "What are you implying?" The sudden flame in his eyes jarred Hope and confirmed her suspicions of his deep affections for Abigail.

Gavin held up his hands. "No disrespect intended. Just wondering."

Nathaniel gave him a glance of warning, then crossed his arms over his chest and looked at Abigail with pride.

"I cannot say for sure." Abigail sauntered to the bucket of water and knelt to draw herself a drink. "We spoke about God."

Hope sank back down to her chair, battling a plethora of emotions, shock and jealousy among them.

"God? You spoke of God? With the pirate?" Gavin scratched his whiskers and chuckled.

Hope glanced toward the pirate camp and spotted the captain waving his cutlass in the air and spouting a slur of curses. "Difficult to believe, indeed."

"I can hardly believe it myself." Abigail stood and brought her long hair over her shoulder in a tumble of silken chestnut. Her hazel eyes swept toward Nathaniel. "I will tell you more later, Nathaniel." She smiled, their gazes locking in understanding.

Hope picked up the shell again, wishing her life would flow along the same perfect pattern. But it wasn't the same shell. This one was chipped and one of the ridges had gone askew. Just like her. Smiling, she slipped it into her pocket.

"But he wishes to hear more about God," Abigail continued, "so I convinced him to take our party to Kingstown with the promise of further discussions." She clapped her hands together as if to seal the deal.

Gavin shook his head, his expression a mask of confusion. "Do you suppose 'tis a trick, a pretense for his otherwise lecherous intentions?"

Abigail shrugged. "The thought occurred to me as well." Her brow furrowed. "But I think not. I saw sincerity in his eyes. He seems to have a genuine awe for God and a fear to harm anyone who knows Him."

"Whatever it takes, I suppose." Gavin snorted. "But I would not have guessed such an interest to be found in our Captain Poole if you'd paid me a chest full of gold."

Nathaniel chuckled. "A miracle of God."

"A miracle, indeed," Abigail said, and they exchanged another intimate glance.

Shaking off the rueful weight that had settled on her shoulders, Hope stood again. "Well, I, for one, shall be glad to finally get off this island." Her sharp gaze unavoidably landed on Nathaniel. "And be on my way home." He did not glance her way. Instead, he stood with the regal authority of a prince, his hair fluttering in the breeze, his eyes flitting about the camp, toward the hut, Gavin, Abigail, anywhere but on Hope.

"We must prepare," Abigail said. "The captain wishes to set sail at midnight."

"Why not wait until morning?" Hope's nerves tensed as she thought about boarding a pirate ship.

"We sail with the high tide, no doubt," Gavin said.

Hope lowered her chin. "But we must bury Mrs. Hendrick."

Abigail approached her and took her hand. "And so we shall."

After the dismal funeral, Hope and Abigail convinced Mr. Hendrick to allow them to take Elise back to their hut. They lay down with her, longing to console the devastated child and perhaps allow her some rest before their journey at midnight.

⤜⤙

"What an incredible turn of events. I am beyond astonishment." Nathaniel scratched his head and stared out upon the ebony waves.

Abigail chuckled. "I can't imagine what my face must have looked like when he first asked me. I'm surprised I didn't scare him off."

Her eyes sparkled in the moonlight, and Nathaniel thanked God for providing him someone with whom he could discuss spiritual matters. Since he'd left Charles Towne, he'd missed his nightly chats with Reverend Halloway. "And after all you told him, he still wishes to hear more?"

"Yes. Apparently he has a Bible on board but has been hesitant to even touch it." Abigail stretched her legs out and crossed them at the ankle. "I suspect some miracle happened to him, or perhaps he saw something that convinced him of God's mighty power."

"God does work in mysterious ways." Nathaniel rubbed the back of his neck. "For He has sent us a pirate who fears Him." He laughed but then sobered when he saw a shiver run through Abigail.

"I have to admit, I was rather frightened of him at first." She swallowed. "Something in his eyes—a look I have seen once before."

Fear tightened her expression, giving Nathaniel pause. Through all their terrifying circumstances, Abigail had always been the epitome of courage. He longed to inquire what type of look she referred to and where she'd seen it before, but he dared not pry. "I have noticed the way he looks at you. He fancies you." Nathaniel rubbed his burning side and stared at the dark horizon, lit up by occasional sparks of lightning.

Abigail sniffed and raised a hand to her nose. When her eyes met his, they glistened with tears.

"What is it? Have I upset you?"

"Nay. I fear the pirate's attentions have resurrected a bad memory, 'tis all." She gave a little smile and brushed the hair from her face.

Nathaniel eased an arm around her shoulders and drew her close. "May I?"

She nodded and leaned her head against him. "Forgive me, Nathaniel. 'Tis been quite a difficult day."

"I am concerned for your safety," he said. "You play a dangerous game with a dangerous man."

"There is no other way. Besides, how could I deny a man's true interest in God?"

"I will do all I can to protect you." Nathaniel squeezed her, knowing she wouldn't misread it as anything other than brotherly comfort.

"And Hope. You will protect Hope?"

He nodded, but he did not wish to think of Hope right now. Mainly because he'd done naught but think of her the entire day, wondering what to do about his rising affections for her, wondering if God were not keeping them kindled for a reason.

Hope shot up from her bed of leaves and tossed a hand to her chest, where the wild beat of her heart pounded against her palm. A dream. It was only a dream. As she searched her mind for the remembrance of it, it escaped her like a mist before the sun. As her eyes grew accustomed to the pitch-black night, she glanced down and saw Elise curled up beside her, her puffs of deep sleep echoing throughout the hut. A dark void loomed on her other side, where Abigail had retired. Where had she gone? Hope had not heard her leave.

Thud, thud, thud sounded outside the hut, no doubt what had woken her so suddenly. Her heart squeezed. Some animal? Or worse, a pirate, besotted with rum, seeking a companion. And she had no idea where Nathaniel or Gavin were. Slowly rising so as not to make a noise, she inched toward the flap and peered behind it.

A dark form sitting by the fire came into view. Gavin. Easing the cloth aside, she emerged from the hut. He turned to face her, a grin alighting upon his lips. "Forgive me, Hope. I didn't mean to wake you." He held a thick stick in his hand.

"What are you doing?" A breeze swirled around her, and Hope wrapped her arms across her chest.

"I couldn't sleep." He sighed. "I didn't realize I was making noise." He dropped the stick, an eager look in his eyes, and Hope grew worried that, once again, she found herself alone with this man who made her feel beautiful and cherished and desired. But was it really love he felt for her? Or just a shadow of the real thing—an imposter drawn by her beauty and not by who she truly was on the inside? For no matter how wonderful that type of attention felt, Hope knew it would not be enough for her anymore. Not after Nathaniel.

"Did you see where Abigail went?"

He cocked his head toward the beach. "About an hour ago."

"Alone? With all these pirates on the island?" Hope bit her lip.

"She seems to handle herself well enough with the mongrels." Gavin shrugged, his voice nonchalant.

"What do you have against her?"

"Abigail? Nothing. I have naught in common with the woman, 'tis all, and besides, she is married to her God."

Hope sighed. As was Nathaniel. Why couldn't she accept that fact as easily as Gavin had?

Clutching her skirts, she stepped over a log, then headed out of the camp. Regardless of Gavin's lack of concern, Hope must ensure Abigail's safety. Thunder rumbled in the distance, and a brisk wind laden with rain ruffled her long hair.

"I'll go with you." Gavin gave a frustrated huff and hurried to join her.

Cool sand eased between her toes as the gentle crash of waves washed over her agitation. But it quickly returned when her thoughts drifted to the funeral. A most dreary affair, especially for Miss Elise. The poor child had stood beside her father in abject despondency, and not once had he offered her an ounce of comfort. Her swollen red eyes had kept shifting from her mother's wrapped body laid gently in the earth, to Hope, as if somehow Hope could raise her mother from the dead. Hope would have given anything at that moment to possess that kind of power—the kind of power of which Nathaniel's God boasted. But where had He been when Eleanor had cried out in pain? When Eleanor had died?

Nathaniel had spoken over Eleanor's grave, sweet words that gave her life and her death meaning and that spoke of a resurrection to glory someday. But Hope had a hard time swallowing any of the placating soliloquy, though a part of her longed to believe it more than anything.

"This way." Gavin tugged on her arm as though he knew exactly where Abigail had gone. Through a cluster of sea grape trees and out onto a small bank of sand. Lightning flashed across the sky, drawing Hope's gaze to the shadow of someone sitting on the sand. No, two people huddled together. Two people embracing each other. She froze, Gavin halting at her side. Nathaniel's and Abigail's voices drifted to her on the capricious wind.

"Why did you bring me out here?" Hope tromped back through the patch of sea grapes, weaving around their trunks.

"I didn't bring you," Gavin huffed. "You wanted to find Abigail."

"But you didn't tell me Nathaniel was with her."

"How was I to know?" He grabbed her arm, spinning her around. "What ails you? Surely you haven't been blind to their affections for one another?"

Hope swallowed down the clump of pain in her throat. Of course she'd noticed the attachment between Nathaniel and Abigail. "Forgive me, Gavin. I'm behaving foolishly. My concern was for Abigail, and now that I've found her safe and sound, all is well." She continued on her way, chiding herself for her infantile display.

"You love him." Gavin's words took flight on the brisk wind, taunting her with their truth.

"Don't be absurd." Hope stomped into camp, trying to contain the conflicting passions within her. One of the signs of a true lady, she had learned, was to control one's emotions. Surely she could do that one small thing. Forcing the anguish from her eyes, she faced Gavin. A frown replaced his roguish grin. She'd hurt him with her callous display.

"Forgive me, Gavin. I've distressed you, and that was not my intention." She stepped toward him. "You've been kind to me."

His smile returned. "I'd like to be so much more." He brushed the back of his hand over her cheek. Hope closed her eyes to his gentle touch, but her thoughts drifted to Nathaniel, and then to Falkland, and the pain returned. Why did no one truly love her? Tears spilled from her lashes, and Gavin whisked them away. He eased his fingers through her hair, then laid his hand on her shoulder, pulling her toward him. Hope could resist him no longer and fell into his embrace. Gavin's arms surrounded her. Easing her back, he lifted her chin and lowered his lips to hers.

⌐☙

Nathaniel walked back to camp in silence, Abigail at his side. A light rain misted over them. He glanced out at the pirate ship drifting nigh thirty yards off shore, and fear stabbed his gut at what lay in store for them all upon it. But Abigail's tale had given him hope that God indeed was with them and would see them through. And then he could take Miss Hope home to Charles Towne. Thunder cracked with warnings of a storm, and he remembered the tears streaming down her face at the funeral and the tender, loving glances she'd bestowed upon Elise. How could such a vixen possess such a caring heart? Yet despite his efforts otherwise, despite his urgent prayers for deliverance, he found himself drawn to her more. Perhaps Hope could change. Perhaps with God's help, she could become a moral, respectable lady. Perhaps God was using Nathaniel's infatuation with Hope for her good and God's glory.

Happy with the thought, he tramped through the last grove of trees. Against his first inclination to leave Mr. Hendrick and Major Paine on the island, he must wake them for the journey ahead. And of course Gavin—and Hope. But as he approached the camp, the green glimmer of Hope's gown caught his eye. She was awake already. Another step and Gavin's tan breeches came into view. Nathaniel continued onward, peering into the camp. He halted.

Gavin's arms circled Hope, pressing her against him, and his lips were on hers.

Swerving around, Nathaniel marched toward the incoming waves. *Infuriating woman!* This morning declaring her affections for him, her ardent concern for his safety, and then tonight allowing another man to take liberties with her. How could he have fallen for her wiles?

"Nathaniel." Abigail followed him. "I'm sorry." She laid a hand on his arm. "I know you care for her."

He dragged a hand through his hair. "Against my every inclination. But no more. Fire and thunder, no more."

❧

Panic shoved its way through Hope's desire, dousing the flame as it went. She pushed away from Gavin. "Forgive me." Disgust simmered in her belly. "I cannot."

Gavin flinched then grabbed her arms. "Why?"

"It is wrong." She tore from his grasp and turned around, wiping her lips.

"What could be wrong between two people who care for one another and find comfort in each other's arms?"

"Because we are not betrothed. We are not married. And we do not love one another."

"The first two can be remedied, and the last one"—his feet shuffled over the sandy soil, and she felt his warm breath on her shoulder—"I would not discount so soon."

"I believe you mistake desire for love." Hope grabbed a lock of her hair.

"Are you so sure?"

She swung about. His blue eyes were etched with pain and a spark of expectancy.

"I'm sorry." Hope dashed away from him, stumbled into the hut, and fell into a heap on the leaves.

Why, oh why, couldn't she behave like a real lady?

CHAPTER 27

The tiny ship's cabin looked like an animal pen in the shifting shadows, and Hope's heart beat wildly against her chest as if she were indeed a beast about to be caged.

"I will not—"

Nathaniel's firm hand over her mouth smothered her protest to a mumble. He removed it as Captain Poole swung about, lantern in hand.

"You will not what, Mrs. Mason?" One dark brow rose on Captain Poole's face as his eyes flashed with amusement.

Mrs. Mason. Good gracious. The sound of it spoken aloud both terrified and elated her. "I will not. . .be needing anything else." Hope forced a smile. "This is perfect." Clutching her wet skirts, she sloshed past him and examined the small enclosure, more to hide the look of horror on her face than to inspect her new home—a twelve-by-eight-foot space she was to share with Nathaniel. *As husband and wife.*

"I'm happy yer pleased." The captain's tone tingled with sarcasm.

"Yes, thank you, Captain." Nathaniel had yet to place a foot inside the door. "I'll come assist you in setting sail."

"No need, Mason. 'Tis been awhile since ye've been alone with yer wife, eh?" Captain Poole winked at Nathaniel. "I'll jest be leavin' ye alone. Oh, and"—his gaze dropped to Hope's dripping gown—"I'll send some fresh clothes fer ye both to wear."

Captain Poole handed Nathaniel the lantern. "So I'd be doffin' yer wet breeches if I was ye." He nudged Nathaniel inside and closed the door with a thud, his laughter fading down the narrow hall as he left.

Thunder roared, sealing Hope's fate. The *pitter-patter* of rain striking the deck above reminded her of the sound of little feet, and she thought of the orphanage she'd never have. Anything to keep her mind off the

540

man standing just inside the door, apparently too repulsed to be in the same room alone with her. She plopped down on one of two wooden beds attached to the bulkhead and grabbed a lock of her saturated hair.

Nathaniel's deep breathing filled the room, along with the drip-drop of rain spilling from his breeches and shirt. She did not want to look at him. She didn't want to see him standing there tall and handsome. Most of all, she didn't want to see the disgust simmering in his eyes.

He'd not spared her one glance all night. Not when they'd gathered to board the cockboat, not during the trip out to the ship, and not when Hope had crawled onto the deck from the rope ladder. Not when myriad eyes swarmed over her and Abigail from the dark figures that spread across the deck. And not even when she shuddered as the realization struck her: She was indeed aboard a pirate ship.

Nathaniel cleared his throat and set the lantern down atop a wooden table. Water dripped off his hair onto his collar. He rubbed his side and inched to the farthest corner of the tiny room. "Unfortunately, we must play along with this foolery."

Hope swallowed. "You look as though you'd rather be locked up in the hold with Major Paine." She regretted the words as soon as they left her mouth, but the pain of his rejection was too much to bear along with everything else.

"The fool." Nathaniel spat. "'Twas the only thing I could do to save his life." He looked at her now, but he immediately shifted his gaze away as if the vision sickened him.

"But knock him unconscious?" Hope couldn't help a giggle as she envisioned the major's staunch refusal to board a pirate vessel, then Captain Poole's obliging response in the form of a pistol leveled at the major's temple. And just when Hope had thought she would be forced to witness a murder, Nathaniel had grabbed a piece of driftwood and slammed it over the major's head.

"The captain would have shot him with no more thought than he gives a belch," Nathaniel said.

Hope brushed her dripping hair from her face.

"But I wouldn't rather be with the major." His brown eyes stared into hers and remained there, the golden flecks within them shimmering with a depth of feeling that baffled Hope.

Shifting in her seat, she glanced down, shaking the vision of him and Abigail together on the beach from her mind. "At least you find my company slightly more favorable than the rat-infested hold."

The ship creaked beneath a wave, and Captain Poole's voice bellowed above deck, issuing orders to weigh anchor and hoist the sails. The pounding of footsteps added to the patter of rain, and Hope pushed back a sudden sorrow at leaving the island. It had been home to her for nearly three weeks, a place made bearable, even pleasurable at times, by the man standing before her now.

"I am sure you would prefer Abigail to be here in my stead." There went her mouth again. Hadn't Nathaniel warned her to test her thoughts before letting them fly from her lips?

He flinched. "Abigail?" His tone sounded incredulous.

Hope stood, wondering at his reaction. Was he so kindhearted that he attempted to spare her feelings? She sighed. "What does it matter? You're right. We must make the best of this situation." Though as she gazed around the cramped cabin, the thought of spending three days *and nights* in this space with Nathaniel completely unnerved her. "You sacrificed your freedom to protect me. I thank you for it, and I promise to do my best to make this journey comfortable for you."

Nathaniel gave a derisive snort.

Pound, pound, pound. Nathaniel released a jagged sigh and opened the door to a spindly pirate with a pointed chin. "Cap'n says to give ye these." He handed him a pile of what looked like a gown, chemise, bodice, and stomacher, in addition to a pair of breeches and a shirt. The pirate sent a leering grin over Hope before he sauntered away.

Closing the door, Nathaniel eyed her. The tight grimace that had taken residence on his face since they entered the cabin relaxed. "This must be quite daunting for you. Being aboard this ship."

"A bit, yes. There are so many pirates. And the looks they give me."

"I will do my best to keep you and Abigail safe."

Hope smiled. Always the honorable gentleman.

"This appears to be for you." His face reddened as he handed the intimate garments to Hope. "Perhaps not clean, but dry nonetheless."

Closing the two steps between them, she took them and bundled them in her arms. The scent of wood and tar and Nathaniel mixed with the musky aroma of rain and swirled around her, sending her senses reeling.

He cleared his throat and tried to weave around her, but they bumped together in the small space. His closeness jarred Hope, and she leapt to the side, trying to escape the overwhelming sensations. He dashed in the other direction but tripped on her foot and thudded headlong against the bulkhead.

He moaned, and Hope peered at him. "Are you hurt?"

"Fire and thunder, woman. You will be the death of me yet."

She retreated as his spiteful tone tore through her, gripping the dry garments to her chest, not caring that they got wet. "Perhaps you should call on Abigail to tend your wound."

"Abigail?" He swung around, rubbing his forehead, where a red bump rose upon his skin. "What is all this with Abigail?" He tossed his dry clothing onto one of the beds.

"I saw you two on the beach." There, she'd said it. But the shame of revealing her jealousy stole any satisfaction from the declaration.

His face scrunched, and he shook his head. "You saw us. . . ." He ran a hand through his wet hair. "Blast it all, I saw *you* kissing Gavin."

Hope's breath caught in her throat, and she raised a hand to her lips. "I was not kissing him." She stomped her foot and felt a splinter jab her toe. "He was kissing me." Before the words left her lips, she realized how ludicrous they sounded.

"Of all the. . .you cannot expect me to. . ." He took up a pace in the tiny cabin, which only amounted to two steps in either direction. Halting, he glared at her. "You gave me every indication yesterday morning that you felt something for me—" He began pacing again, and confusion kept Hope speechless. Why would her feelings matter to him?

"And then you turn around and kiss another man. What am I to believe?"

Tears swam in her eyes. She wanted to give him the explanation he sought. She wanted to tell him she had pushed Gavin away, that his kiss meant nothing to her, that she was trying so hard to be good. She wanted to tell Nathaniel that she loved him. But he wouldn't believe her. He would always think of her as wanton. "Believe what you want. It matters not to me."

His mouth opened as if he wanted to say something. His brown eyes turned hard. He grabbed the door latch.

"Where are you going?" Her voice squeaked.

"Anywhere but here." He opened it and slammed it behind him.

~

Nathaniel emerged onto the deck to a blast of wind and rain that did naught to cool his humors. Sails rumbled and snapped like thunder above him as the ship veered to starboard. He marched to the railing and peered through the darkness toward the island, now a black smudge on the horizon. He bowed his head.

Lord, rid me of this obsession. I long to do Your will.

A hard slap on the back jarred him from his prayer, and Nathaniel looked up to see Gavin slide beside him. Shaking the rain from his hair, he gave Nathaniel a sly look. "Fight with the wife already?" He gestured toward Nathaniel's forehead. "Looks like she got the best of you."

Nathaniel growled and gripped the railing, trying to shake the vision of Gavin's arms circling Hope and his lips upon hers. Better to change the subject than to succumb to the overwhelming urge to grab the man by his collar and toss him into the sea.

Nathaniel shook his head, ashamed the thought had even entered his mind. *Forgive me, Lord. The woman has clearly driven me mad.* Whatever had happened, it wasn't Gavin's fault. Hope's charms could not be resisted without difficulty—especially for a man devoid of the power of God. Which made Nathaniel's own weakness seem all the more inexcusable.

Hope was an enchantress, just like the name of this pirate ship. An enchantress with blue eyes the color of the sea—eyes a man could dive into and never find his way out of again.

"Where is Abigail?" he asked Gavin, attempting to divert his thoughts toward anything but Hope.

Gavin frowned then shrugged. "The captain has seen fit to house her in one of the best cabins—even tossed out his first mate to accommodate her."

Rain stung his face and Nathaniel grimaced as fear for Abigail's safety bristled through him.

"Never fear." Gavin eyed him. "I don't think he means her any harm.

Truth be told, he seems quite besotted with her." He chuckled as if the idea were preposterous.

"Why wouldn't he be? She's comely, in possession of a good mind, and is a proper, kindhearted lady."

"Pious and boring, if you ask me."

Nathaniel winced at his friend's poor judgment. He longed to tell Gavin that a pious lady is to be preferred, but he feared it would sound insincere on his lips in light of his infatuation with Hope. "Obviously the pirate finds Abigail interesting enough."

"Baffling, to be sure." Gavin wiped the rain from his face and glanced across the ebony waters. "Ah, 'tis good to be out at sea again."

Nathaniel could not agree more. The ship swooped over a roller, spraying them with a salty mist that, joining with the rain, cooled his already wet clothes, along with his temper and the heat that always swept over him in Hope's presence. The first eleven years of his life, Nathaniel had spent most of his days cooped up in a room with his mother. He supposed that's why he loved the freedom of the sea so much. "And where are Mr. Hendrick and Elise?"

"Sharing quarters with me." Gavin leaned onto the railing and shot Nathaniel a disparaging look. "And that imbecile, Major Paine, is locked below where he belongs. You should have let Poole kill him."

A cascade of curses swept over them, and Nathaniel glanced over his shoulder at a huddle of pirates up on the quarterdeck, playing cards. It had been a long time since he'd been among such vile men. Shaking off their blasphemies, he gazed at Gavin, so young and adventurous. He prayed for his young friend not to follow in their footsteps. "Have you no value for human life?" Nathaniel asked, hoping to find some mercy within his friend's heart.

"For some, yes. My own, for example." Gavin straightened his stance and laughed, and Nathaniel gave him a disapproving look, then joined him.

The rain ceased, leaving behind a refreshing sting in the air. Thunder growled its retreat in the distance, and Nathaniel thanked God the storm had been light. One hurricane was enough to endure. All he wanted now was to meet with his last remaining ship and sail to Charles Towne as soon as possible. He rubbed his forehead, wincing as his fingers grazed the knot where he'd slammed into the bulkhead. Because Hope had tripped him. Yes, the sooner he relieved himself of Miss Hope, the safer he would be. In more ways than one.

A tall man, whom Nathaniel assumed to be the first mate, barked an order to ease off the foresheet and clear the braces, sending the pirates scampering across deck. He had heard pirate ships were havens of disorder and drunken brawling, but the seacraft he'd seen displayed since he boarded spoke otherwise.

A group of men emerged from the shadows on Nathaniel's left, and in the dim lantern light, he made out Kreggs, Hanson, and two pirates. One of them, a man Kreggs introduced as Boone, stood at least a foot taller than Nathaniel. His shoulders stretched as wide as a ship's yard, and he had a head like a cannonball. Jones, the other pirate, seemed but a twig beside Boone, but a jagged rope scar around his neck drew Nathaniel's gaze.

"We've been telling these men about how you healed Miss Hope," Kreggs said. "They want to hear more."

Elated to discuss the things of God, especially with these pirates, and also to have something to do—anything to do—besides retire below with Hope, Nathaniel felt his exhaustion flee. "I didn't heal her. God did. But I'd love nothing more than to honor you with the tale."

"That's my cue to retire." Gavin grinned and disappeared into the darkness, his footsteps fading over the deck. Sorrow overcame Nathaniel at his friend's lack of interest in God, but turning toward the men whose wide eyes were trained upon him, he began the story of Miss Hope's healing; then he spoke of other miracles he'd witnessed.

At least an hour passed in which the pirates listened with rapt attention to everything Nathaniel said, even periodically asking questions. Amazed at their interest in God and heaven and eternity, Nathaniel spoke with conviction and compassion. The more he spoke, the more empowered he felt. He knew God was with him, putting the right words in his mouth and drawing these men to the Truth.

But one by one, Hanson, Kreggs, and the pirates excused themselves to go below and get some sleep before dawn, leaving Nathaniel with no reason to avoid his bed any longer. He assumed it was past two in the morning, and he needed at least a few hours of sleep in order to stay alert on the morrow.

Heading down the companionway, he trudged toward his and Hope's quarters, praying she was asleep. Praying she wouldn't hear him enter, that he wouldn't bump into her in the darkness, and that he wouldn't be forced to listen to her soft, deep breaths throughout the night, knowing that if he did, he wouldn't find a second's rest.

CHAPTER 28

The door clicked shut. Ever so quietly. Not the hollow thud of a ship's cabin door, but the deep clunk of oak—the door of Hope's chamber. She slid her hands over her bed, her fingers gliding over the coverlet of silk she'd not felt since she lived in Portsmouth. Footsteps sounded on the wooden floor. Her breathing halted. Her heart thumped so loudly in her chest it drowned out all other sounds. She opened her eyes, not daring to move, and shifted her gaze across the dark room. Gauzy, cream-colored curtains flung wildly at the open window. Lit by moonlight, they danced ghostlike in the breeze. Across the room, eerie shadows danced along with them.

One of the shadows moved.

Hesitant, it stepped toward her bed.

"Faith? Is that you?" Hope whispered and started to sit up. Who else would be in her chamber at this hour?

The dark figure darted toward her. Before she could move, a firm hand slammed over her mouth. Another pushed her down onto the bed. The man clutched a fistful of her hair and yanked her head. Pain shot from her neck down her back. She tried to scream, but only a garbled muffle proceeded from her mouth.

"Not Faith, my dear." The slick voice spilled brandy-drenched breath over her. A voice that made her blood grow cold. A voice that sent shivers of terror over her. The voice of Lord Villemont.

❧

"No! No! Let me go! No, please!"

Nathaniel shot up in bed. His heart slammed in his chest. He scanned the darkness, trying to remember where he was. *The pirate ship.*

Movement beside him. "No! I beg you. Do not!"

Hope. Someone assaulted Hope! In one leap, Nathaniel was at her side, ready to throttle her attacker, but only empty air surrounded her.

"No!" She thrashed over the bed and began to sob.

"Hope." Nathaniel gripped her arms and shook her gently. "Hope, wake up."

Her ragged breathing filled the room. She struggled against his grip and tossed her head back and forth.

"You're dreaming, Hope. Wake up." Nathaniel grabbed her face with both hands to quiet her.

She jerked, gasped, then placed her hands atop his, feeling his fingers.

"'Tis me. Nathaniel."

She flew into his arms and clutched the back of his shirt as if he were her only lifeline. He engulfed her in his embrace, feeling her heart crashing against his chest.

"Nathaniel." She uttered a breathless appeal.

"Yes, 'tis me. You are safe."

Laying her head on his shoulder, she wept.

"Shhh." He stroked her hair and pressed her closer against him. Sobs racked her body. Whatever she had dreamed must have been terrifying.

Nathaniel kept a firm hold on her, hoping he could make her feel safe from whatever had frightened her so. She cried for several minutes until finally her whimpers softened, and she released a deep breath. She fingered the sleeve of his shirt. "I thought I was back there again."

Nathaniel eased a hand down her back, grateful she was fully clothed. "Where?"

"Portsmouth."

Releasing her, he nudged her back and started to rise.

She gripped his arm and held on tight.

He gave her a reassuring look. "I'm going to light the lantern. I'll be right back."

She loosened her grip and slid her hand down his arm as he left, tightening her fingers around his for a moment before he stepped away.

Swallowing a lump of conflicting emotions, Nathaniel groped through the darkness, finding steel and flint and tinder to light the lantern. Rubbing the back of his neck, he turned to face her. She sat on the bed, her hair a wild cluster of golden curls. Wounded, desperate eyes stared back at him. His heart shrank in his chest.

Something terrible had happened to this woman.

He approached, kneeling beside her, and took her hand in his.

Hope ran her fingers over his calluses. "I'm sorry to have disturbed your sleep. I rarely have nightmares anymore." She looked away and tightened her lips.

"I'm glad I was here." The ship creaked, the lap of waves against the hull soothed over him, and he released a deep breath. "What happened in Portsmouth?"

Her eyes filled with tears, and she lowered her chin. Her hands trembled. "I cannot tell you."

Nathaniel brushed a lock of hair from her face. She flinched. "Someone hurt you."

Tears spilled down her cheeks, and she squeezed his hand. A shudder ran through her. "My sister's husband." Hope's lips quivered.

Nathaniel clenched his free fist and felt the muscles in his face tighten. What had this man done to her to cause such agony? Not sure he wanted to know, he remained quiet, nonetheless, allowing her the opportunity to tell him if she needed to.

"He grabbed my hair." She released his hand and seized a handful of her hair as if to demonstrate. Anger and terror screamed from her eyes. "I couldn't move. I couldn't do anything." She dropped her hands to her lap and bowed her head.

Rage tore through Nathaniel, ripping his gut apart. The man had ravished her.

He wanted to punch something, someone. He wanted to yell. He wanted to pound the bulkhead. Instead, he slid to his knees and took her in his arms.

"I was seventeen." She laid her head on his shoulder again and sobbed.

"I'm so sorry, Hope." Fury set his muscles on edge. How could this man—and a relation at that—hurt such a precious creature? An innocent girl who trusted him? No wonder she harbored anger toward God. No wonder she behaved the way she did. Another emotion shoved its way to the forefront. Shame. Nathaniel had judged Hope severely, without any knowledge of her past.

He buried his face into her hair, breathing in her sweet scent. Her sobs quieted. One final emotion rose to the surface of Nathaniel's heart, drowning out all the others.

Love.

He loved Hope. He could not help himself. And the thought terrified him.

Nudging her back, he ran his thumb over her tears. Her crystal blue eyes met his, brimming with pain, desperation, and something else. . . . Could it be she returned his affections? Or was it just her need for love, her need for attention that he saw in her gaze?

As if reading his confusion, she looked away, and the loss startled him.

"I shouldn't have told you," she said.

"Why not?" He eased her chin forward.

She batted the tears from her cheeks, then brushed her hair back as if suddenly worried about her appearance. "I must look a fright."

Cupping her chin, he caressed her moist face. She stopped fussing. "You're the most beautiful thing I've ever seen." And he meant it. Despite her red-rimmed, bloodshot eyes; her puffy, swollen face; and hair that looked like Medusa's, she beamed with a beauty that had naught to do with her appearance.

She laughed, sniffed, and gave him a tiny smile that sent a wave of warmth through him. He didn't know whether to kiss her and declare his love for her or dash from the cabin and throw himself into the sea, risking the swim to land, rather than face the feelings surging through him.

O Lord, please tell me what to do.

⌘

Later that day, when Hope awoke to find Nathaniel gone, memories of the intimate moments they'd spent in the early morning hours came back to haunt her. As well as the memory of what she had shared with him. Shame had kept her below for hours until she could no longer stand the stifling cabin.

Lifting her skirts, she grabbed the rope and climbed up the

companionway ladder. Emerging into the brilliant sun reflecting from the open sea around the ship, she planted her bare feet firmly on the hot deck. A wave of whistles and catcalls assailed her, as well as a few lewd suggestions that almost made her duck back down below. Instead, she raised her chin and made her way to the starboard railing, not daring to glance at the pirates whose eyes she felt boring into her from all directions.

"Good day to ye, Mrs. Mason." Captain Poole hailed her from the quarterdeck, where he stood regally by the wheel.

Nodding in his direction and ignoring the sardonic gleam in his eyes, she continued on her way, bracing herself over the teetering deck as she tried to regain her sea legs. She had searched for Abigail below and smiled as she now saw the young lady making her way toward her from the foredeck, where she had been talking with Gavin. The young sailor winked at Hope before turning to finish tying down a halyard. No doubt Nathaniel was on deck as well, working the ship, but she couldn't face him—not yet.

"Good morning, Hope." Abigail reached her side, a wide smile upon her lips as if she were on a pleasure voyage instead of a pirate ship. She held a tiny brown book against her chest.

"Good morning." Hope returned her smile, trying not to picture her in Nathaniel's embrace on the beach. "How have you fared aboard this ship thus far?" Hope gave a sideways glance and nodded toward the pirates littering the deck.

"Other than a few untoward comments, they haven't bothered me." Abigail gestured toward the quarterdeck, and Hope turned to see Captain Poole's brooding eyes leveled upon them. "He protects us for some reason."

"Hmm. 'Tis *you* he protects, but let us pray he does not change his mind." Hope didn't want to alarm her friend, but Abigail's false sense of safety frightened Hope. With her nightmare so fresh in her mind, Hope realized if a lady wasn't safe in her chamber at home, then surely she wasn't safe aboard a pirate ship—no matter the apparent favor of the captain.

"Pray? What a grand idea." Abigail smiled and adjusted the lace bounding from her sleeves. She'd pinned up her chestnut hair into a loose bun, several curls of which dangled over her collar. She opened her Bible. "Captain Poole wishes to speak to me today about God, and I thought to read him this verse. Would you care to listen to it?"

Although the thought of listening to scripture unnerved her, Hope nodded in agreement as she gazed over the sea. The sun, now high in the sky, ignited the turquoise waves in silver flames that made the scene so beautiful it seemed like a dream.

"This is the parable of the sower, where Jesus explains how the farmer scatters the seeds along the ground. The seeds represent God's Word, and the soil represents people. But although they receive God's Word, not every type of soil produces a crop. The first seed falls on rocky soil, but troubles and trials fall upon the hearer, and the seed never takes root. Now, here's the type of soil I think most represents Captain Poole." Abigail's voice heightened with excitement as she pressed open the Bible and held down the pages against the wind.

"'He also that received seed among the thorns is he that heareth the word; and the care of this world, and the deceitfulness of riches, choke the word, and he becometh unfruitful.'"

She slammed the book shut and looked at Hope with expectation. "Don't you see? Captain Poole has heard the Word of God, yet the riches of this world have pulled him away."

The words set Hope's mind whirling. She felt a tingling in her toes and shifted her feet across the deck. "Can other things pull someone away?" She tugged a lock of her hair and gave Abigail a questioning look. "Like other desires. . .for love, for affection, for attention?"

"Of course. Riches can be anything someone craves besides God."

A gust of wind laden with the smell of fish and sunshine wafted over Hope. She glanced down to watch the waves licking the hull with tongues of bubbling foam. She had heard the gospel at a young age, but nothing had come of it in her life. She hadn't changed; rather, she had gotten worse. Perhaps she would never become like Abigail.

"You will make a good missionary."

"Really?" Abigail smiled. "I wonder."

"You have opened my eyes to many things." Hope hugged herself against a sudden chill. "My sister Grace is as zealous in her faith as you are." Hope sighed. "Yet she is so judgmental, always pointing out others' faults."

Abigail smiled. "I'm sure she means well."

"I know she loves me. You would like her. She spends much of her time traveling into dangerous places to feed the poor and Indians."

"Very noble, indeed." Abigail nodded her approval.

"Yet she takes no care for her safety. I fear for her life." Hope thought of the countless times Grace had gone missing for hours, returning muddied and exhausted from some long mission of mercy.

"You must pray for her." Abigail squeezed her arm, and Hope gazed out to sea, not wanting to inform Abigail that God often ignored her prayers.

The ship bucked over a roller, and Hope gripped the railing as a spray of seawater showered over them. They both laughed and brushed droplets from their gowns.

Hope pointed toward Abigail's dress, a lovely shade of green trimmed in creamy lace. "'Tis beautiful."

"Thank you." Abigail nodded. "And yours as well. That shade of blue matches your eyes."

"Truth be told, it feels wonderful to be in fresh clothes devoid of scratching sand and biting fleas." Hope risked a glance at the pirate captain, but he had disappeared from the quarterdeck. She patted her sleeve, where she'd tucked the chipped seashell she'd found on the island. Somehow she couldn't seem to part with it. "I wonder where Captain Poole got these gowns."

"I don't want to know." Abigail shook her head, then leaned toward Hope. "How did you manage last night"—a tiny smile lifted one corner of her mouth—"with Nathaniel?"

Hope studied her friend. Shouldn't she be envious of Hope for being forced to share lodging with Nathaniel? Yet not a flicker of jealousy marred her comely face. Of course not. Not Abigail.

"We managed well enough." Hope had no intention of sharing the intimacy that had occurred between them because of her nightmare, especially not with Abigail. But what did it matter? For despite his care for her last night, Nathaniel no doubt still found her unworthy. Most likely even more so now that he knew the truth of her past. He might even believe she had encouraged Lord Villemont's assault, as most people had accused her of doing.

He probably wanted nothing more to do with her.

Which was why he had left the cabin so early. Which was also why he hadn't greeted her thus far this morning. "You need not fear, Abigail. There is naught between us."

"Fear? My heavens. I fear only that there *is* naught between you." She chuckled, drawing Hope's confused gaze.

"But you. . .but you and Nathaniel." Hope studied her friend. "I saw you on the beach in his embrace."

Abigail's eyebrows rose, and a gleam of understanding flittered across her eyes. "Oh my, you thought—" She laughed. "You thought—oh my, nay, he was only consoling me."

Hope could not help the quick jaunt her heart took in her chest. "Then you don't have affections for him?"

Abigail shook her head. "Not in the manner you mean, nay. I think of him as a brother, and I am sure he feels the same way about me." She laid a hand on Hope's arm. "You poor dear. All this time under such a misconception." She patted her hand. "I assure you, Nathaniel Mason, whether he admits it or not, is quite besotted with you. Although," she added, "I can't say he was all too happy when he spied you kissing Gavin."

Hope huffed and gazed down at the churning water. "It was a mistake."

"I've never seen Nathaniel so distraught."

Shame taunted her again even as Nathaniel's deep voice soothed over her from behind. She glanced over her shoulder, and he came into view, talking with a pirate at the larboard quarter. Wearing a white cotton shirt and clean brown breeches that fit him too perfectly, he made her heart leap at the sight of him.

Hope swerved back around. "He could never love me." Hot wind blasted over her, loosening her curls. No matter how hard she had tried to pin them up this morning, no matter how hard she always tried to pin them up and make herself presentable, something always came along to tear them down. Just like her efforts to become a lady. "I cannot behave like a proper lady, no matter how hard I try. My flighty emotions get the best of me, and I cannot seem to control them."

Abigail laughed. "There's your difficulty, then."

Hope raised her brows. "What do you mean?"

"You cannot change in your own strength. The power to change comes only from God."

An odd rumble of thunder roared in the distance, and Hope scanned the clear horizon for the source. A crisp line of blue met her gaze. "Why would God help me?"

Abigail laid a hand on Hope's arm. "Because He loves you."

Loves me? Hope shook her head. Why would He love her when not even her own father did?

"He will not only change your heart," Abigail said, "but He will also cleanse it from all the filth of your past."

Hope's breath halted in her throat. "As if I were pure?"

"Not *as if,* but He *will* make you pure." Abigail grinned and then raised her face to the sky as if adoring this God of hers.

A gust of chilly air struck them, and Abigail shivered. Her brow furrowed as she glanced across the sea, but all Hope could think about was the girl's last statement. "Pure? How?"

"You have only to repent of your past and ask God to cleanse you, to change you, and then make Him your Lord."

Hope swallowed. "Seems too easy."

"It is a free gift."

The warm rays of the sun dissipated, and Hope looked up to see a massive black cloud slide over the shining orb.

Abigail snorted. "Odd. The skies were clear a moment ago."

"I hope a storm is not on the way."

Abigail stared at her. Concern clouded her eyes. "I fear one is brewing indeed."

CHAPTER 29

Nathaniel teetered on the topgallant yard, trying to keep his mind on his work and not on the lovely vision of Miss Hope standing below on the deck. But his eyes kept roving her way. And when they did, his palms grew sweaty, his head grew light, and his concentration went flying off with the hot, humid wind that blasted over him. Why did she have to look so beautiful? With her hair combed and pinned atop her head in a bouquet of glittering gold and that blue gown flowing in delicate folds about her feet, every man on the ship stared agape at her.

Salacious wretches.

After he had rocked her to sleep, he'd lain back on his bed and tried to quiet his rapid breathing and thumping heart and relax his taut muscles, but when dawn peeked in through the porthole, slumber still had not found him. Rather than staring at Hope sleeping like an angel, he had slipped from the cabin and done the only thing he could think to do to quiet the tormenting emotions within him.

He had worked. And he had worked hard.

Now after hours of the sun beating down on him and the sweat streaming off him, he still felt the press of her curves against him and smelled her feminine scent. His muscles ached and exhaustion weighed heavy on his eyelids, but the tumult inside him had not weakened. It had only grown stronger.

For all his efforts, he could not shake her sad tale from his mind. Her purity had been stolen when she was a mere child. By a trusted relation. And from what Nathaniel knew of her father, she had received no comfort or support from him. 'Tis no wonder she harbored such a low opinion of herself—an opinion that drove her to seek love and acceptance in the arms of whoever offered it. And he had judged her for it.

"Loose topgallants. Clear away the jib!" The command was bellowed from below, and Nathaniel worked to loosen the topgallant sail alongside the other men, while his thoughts drifted to his past. Had his mother suffered a similar tragedy in her youth? If so, she had never shared it with him. And he had judged her as well.

Some man of God he was.

Yet the sting of his past, the stain of his mother's profession would not leave him. Indeed, they fueled his resentment toward Hope. Regardless of the reason for her actions, Nathaniel would not pursue his feelings for her. For surely a match between them would only bring them both pain.

"Let go topgallant chewlines, lee braces. Let fall!" The men dropped the topgallant sail, and it began flapping in the wind. Easing across the yard, Nathaniel followed the others down into the shrouds and then climbed onto the ratlines and jumped, thudding to the deck below.

The sail caught the wind with a jaunty snap, and Nathaniel dared a glance toward Hope. With head bowed, she stared at the water, immersed in an intense conversation with Abigail. Captain Poole's gaze locked upon Abigail.

Turning, Nathaniel leaned upon the railing, taking in a deep breath of sea air. No matter what he felt, he would not give his heart to a woman who could not help but stomp on it as soon as the next man paid her any attention. He must be strong. He rubbed the sweat from the back of his neck. Surely this was a test from God—one he intended to pass.

"Nathaniel." Gavin's worried tone jarred him as the man clapped him on the back. "You've been working too hard."

"It keeps my mind occupied."

"And off of what? Or should I say whom?" Gavin grinned and glanced toward Hope. "I've seen the way you look at her. Although I daresay she does look rather fetching in that gown."

Nathaniel grimaced and wondered if he should give his friend his blessing to pursue Hope, but a twisting in his gut forestalled the words.

Gavin smirked. "How, pray tell, did you fare playing the part of her husband last night?"

Thunder rumbled, drawing Nathaniel's gaze out to sea where no evidence of a storm revealed itself. "She was asleep when I retired."

"Ah, 'tis the way of those long married, I'm told." Gavin chuckled, then grew serious. "If you have no interest in her, I should like to pursue her myself, that is, if you don't mind."

Nathaniel shrugged. "You are free to do as you wish. And so is Miss Hope." His insides twisted into a knot so tight he doubted it would ever come undone.

"Splendid." Facing the main deck, Gavin leaned his elbows back upon the railing. "Sink me, but Captain Poole seems an odd excuse for a pirate."

"Hmm." Nathaniel wished his cheerful friend would depart. He was in no mood for idle chatter at the moment. Not when his insides felt like a grenade about to explode.

"Not only is he quite taken with Miss Sheldon," Gavin continued, "a missionary, no less, but he refused my offer to join his crew."

Nathaniel blinked and stared at him. "You wish to become a pirate?"

"Why not?" He crossed one foot over the other and grinned, his eyes alight with mischief. "A life of adventure, freedom, and riches."

"Then I do mind if you court Miss Hope." Nathaniel's tone was more caustic than he intended.

Gavin cocked his head and gave him a curious look. "Why?"

"I do not wish to see her associate with pirates."

"Then you do care for her?"

"No more than any other woman." Nathaniel winced beneath his lie but then gazed at his friend, worried for the dangerous path he so casually pursued. "There is more to life than riches, Gavin. And even so, 'tis the way in which these men gain their wealth. Governor Rogers of New Providence has vowed to rid the Caribbean of all pirates who refuse the king's pardon. Do you want to lose your life at the end of a noose? Do you want to be labeled a thief, a brigand?"

"I do not mind dying, if I have truly lived." The sails rumbled overhead as the ship veered to larboard, and Gavin drew in a breath of sea air. "Besides, I care not for the opinions of others."

Nathaniel rubbed his eyes against the pull of exhaustion even as a heavy weight hung upon his heart for his friend. But one thing rang true: Gavin did not concern himself with the judgment of men. A good quality, to be sure, and one that grated over Nathaniel's conscience for his lack of it. Why did he care so much about what society and men of good breeding thought of him? "You have not truly lived, my friend, until you have known God."

Gavin grunted.

The sun's rays disappeared, giving Nathaniel a welcome relief from the heat. But when he glanced up, a dark cloud hovered over the ship.

Gavin followed his gaze. "I hope we are not in for another tempest."

Nathaniel scanned the horizon. Clear and bright. "No, this is something different." Something worse, he feared. He glanced toward Abigail, and her gaze locked upon his in understanding. Hope remained by her side. But what of the others? "Are Mr. Hendrick and his daughter still below?"

"Aye, I believe so." Gavin turned around and faced the sea. "The man wasn't feeling well. And when I offered to escort Miss Elise to see Hope or Abigail, he wouldn't allow it."

Nathaniel stepped away from the railing. "I shall see to them. And bring the major some food. I doubt Captain Poole will give a care to provide for the man."

The features of Gavin's face pinched. "I cannot fathom it."

"Fathom what?"

"That you would concern yourself with the major's welfare after all he's done. He would have killed you if he'd had the chance. Yet you saved his life and now bring him food."

"God tells us to love our enemies." Nathaniel headed toward the companionway.

Gavin snorted behind him. "Pure rubbish."

⌁

Hope paced across the tiny cabin. When she realized she'd picked the habit up from Nathaniel, she smiled. Where was he? Halting, she stood on tiptoe and peered out the oval window. After her discussion with Abigail, thick black clouds had consumed the entire sky, casting a shroud of darkness on the sea and the ship. Yet not a drop of rain had fallen. Even Captain Poole proclaimed he'd seen naught like it in all his days. An odd sense of foreboding had driven Hope below deck to the safety of the cabin she shared with Nathaniel, although she was beginning to wonder if he hadn't taken residence elsewhere. She couldn't blame him—not after she'd kept him up half the night with her nightmare.

Abigail had come by, and they had shared a light supper of hard biscuit and plantains. Then she had dashed off to meet with Captain Poole and answer his questions about God. Hope feared for her safety, but Abigail would not be persuaded to stay.

Hope wiped mist from the window. Night had fallen, and the sky matched the inky water. Not a speck of starlight or a wisp of moonlight broke through the thick blanket of clouds. The ship floated through a dark void, which had engulfed the world and was now trying to engulf her.

Dread gripped her heart, and she gazed at the door, longing to go above and find Nathaniel, but not wanting to risk wandering the darkened deck on a ship full of pirates. Why was she suddenly so frightened? The lantern flickered, though not a breath of air stirred in the cabin, and Hope flopped onto her bed and dropped her head into her hands.

Abigail's assurances would not let her mind rest. God could make her pure. Wasn't that what she'd been seeking all this time, to be made pure again? To be a real lady? She had tried so hard to achieve it on her own, but all her attempts had ended in failure.

She may have lost any chance of gaining Nathaniel's admiration, but if God could truly make her pure and help her to behave with propriety, perhaps she could still gain the respect of her community and open an orphanage when she returned to Charles Towne.

Should she dare speak to the Almighty? Fear struck her. Thunder roared outside, shaking the ship and sending a shudder through her. Surely she was not worthy. Surely He would either ignore her, laugh at her, or strike her dead.

"I love you, beloved."

Hope wiped the tears from her eyes and glanced around the cabin. She had heard the words as clearly as if someone had spoken them—yet she hadn't heard them at all.

"You are precious to me."

Precious to God? Then she remembered the fever and how Nathaniel and Abigail told her God had healed her. *God had healed her.* Perhaps He did love her, after all.

Falling to her knees beside the bed, Hope sobbed. "O God, help me."

❧

A silent yet imperative voice made Nathaniel wince. He clutched the railing and turned to Abigail, who'd come to see him for counsel before she met with Captain Poole. "Did you say something?"

She shook her head, but her eyes widened, and she gazed across the deck as if she, too, had heard a voice.

Pirates clustered in groups drinking rum and playing cards. A crowd on the foredeck joined in a ribald ballad. The sails hung limp and lifeless upon the yards. Though black clouds churned above them, not a wisp of a breeze stirred the air or ruffled the dark sea.

The ship floated, lifeless, as if it had drifted into a dark cave.

"What did you hear?" Abigail laid her hand on his arm.

"Pray." Nathaniel swallowed. "I heard 'pray,' and then my thoughts swept to Hope."

Abigail nodded. "Then we should." She squeezed his arm and bowed her head, and Nathaniel followed suit. Several minutes passed as they made their appeals to God for Hope and for the safety of the ship. When Nathaniel lifted his gaze to Abigail's, alarm sped through him. "I should go see her."

"Nay." Abigail shook her head, her wide hazel eyes flickering in the light of the lantern hanging from the mast. "Leave her be. She's in God's hands now."

❧

A frigid wall of air enveloped Hope, and she hugged herself and rose, dabbing at her moist cheeks. "Is someone there?" She peered into the shadows beyond the lantern, sensing a presence. Yet the door remained closed, and she had heard no one enter.

Thunder roared through the ship, shaking the hull, and Hope sank to her knees onto the hard deck. "God, if You're there, I'm sorry. I'm so sorry for the things I've done." She lowered her head, ashamed, waiting for the lightning to strike her, but an eerie silence ensued. Only the creak of the ship sounded, accompanied by her own rapid breathing.

A blast of cold air circled her, stealing the breath from her throat. Her heart thumped wildly.

No one loves you. You're not worthy of God's love.

Hideous laughter cackled in her ears, and tears filled her eyes anew, dropping to her gown in blotches.

Clunk. Clank. Crash!

The noise sent Hope bolting to her feet. The lantern had fallen to the deck. Dashing toward it, she snatched it up before the flame could set anything afire. Instead it flickered out. Darkness swallowed her.

Groping her way to the table, she set down the lantern, her breath catching in her throat. The ship had not moved, and no wind strong enough to make the lantern fall had swept through the cabin.

"Who's here?" Terror squeezed her heart. She gripped her throat.

No sound save the tiny creak of the ship.

As she backed away, Hope struck the bedpost and whimpered in pain, then crumpled to the deck. "If You're angry with me, God, I don't blame You." She could barely squeeze the words from her constricted throat. "But please, if You find it in Your heart to forgive me, like Abigail says You will"—the invisible hand loomed near her windpipe, threatening to tighten its grip, but she forced her words out in a mad rush—"to forgive me and help me change, to be better, then I beg You, please make me Yours."

Instantly, warmth covered her. A weight fell off her as if an anchor she'd been holding had been cast into the sea. She began to shake. Tears streamed down her face. A tiny ray of light pierced the darkness of the cabin. Hope dashed toward the window and peered out. The black clouds drifted away, revealing myriad stars sparkling against the night sky. A half moon splashed its silver light onto the sea in glimmering ribbons.

Hope smiled as she gazed across the stunning scene. God loved her. *He loved her.* When no one else truly had: not her father, or her mother, or even Lord Falkland. She knew in that instant that God had always loved her—even when she had gone astray. A tingling swept through her like a brush scrubbing away the filth, the impurity, the stains of her past. Like a baby dove nestled beneath her father's wings, she felt cherished and safe and clean for the first time in her life.

CHAPTER 30

Tap, tap, tap. Abigail rapped on the door to Captain Poole's cabin and tried to quiet her hurried breathing as well as the thunderous beat of her heart. Rustling sounded from within, and she almost turned and dashed down the narrow hallway. But his "Enter" blared over her, keeping her from fleeing. Clicking the latch, she took a deep breath and pushed the door ajar.

"Ah, Miss Sheldon, how good o' ye to come." Captain Poole rose from his chair, straightened his black velvet waistcoat, and wove around his desk to greet her.

"Come in. Come in. I won't bite ye." He chuckled and, taking her by the elbow, led her to a stuffed leather chair.

He closed the door with an ominous *thud*, and Abigail swallowed, once again wondering about the sanity of agreeing to meet with this pirate alone in his quarters. She sensed his gaze upon her and met it, and she shivered beneath his sensuous perusal that ran over her as if she were a treasure chest filled with gold.

As if reading her mind, he smiled. "Ye've naught to fear from me, miss." But his voracious expression spoke otherwise.

Tearing her thoughts from their dangerous bent, she set her Bible on her lap and scanned the cabin, twice as large as the one she stayed in. A large desk stood guard before windows that stretched the width of the stern. Charts, quill pens, and a quadrant littered the top, as well as a half-full bottle of rum, a cutlass, and two pistols.

Two high-backed leather chairs flanked the desk, one of which she occupied. And those, along with the desk and its chair, made up the only furniture in the room, save the bed built into the bulwarks on the starboard side. Before the bed, a cannon—at least an eighteen pounder—stood with its muzzle pointed toward a closed gun port, reminding Abigail what type of man she found herself alone with. His gaze remained fixed upon her. She drew a breath to stifle the shudder that ran down her back and looked anywhere but back into those dark, probing eyes.

A glint drew her attention to a row of swords lining the larboard bulkhead like trophies, glimmering in the lantern light: a French rapier, a Spanish broadsword, a saber, and an English long sword—all no doubt seized from the hands of conquered victims she could only hope were still among the living.

Despite a sudden chill that overtook her, her palms began to sweat.

He ambled toward his desk, swerved around, and leaned back on it, his riotous black hair flinging about his shoulders. Crossing his arms over his chest, he cocked a brow in her direction as if he enjoyed watching her squirm.

Abigail forced a disapproving glance his way. "I suppose you've had many women in this cabin, Captain." She hoped to disarm his superior demeanor, but instead he laughed—heartily and shamelessly.

"That I have, Miss Sheldon. That I have. Does it distress ye?"

"Only if I am to be another of your victims." She straightened her back and pursed her lips.

"Victims? Upon me life, all came willingly and left happier than when they arrived, if I do say so." He stomped his thick leather boot over the deck, and his lips curved in a taunting grin.

Deciding it best to leave before the pirate assumed she had also come willingly, Abigail stood and made a move toward the door, but Captain Poole dashed toward it, blocking her way. "Me apologies, miss. I meant no disrespect." The gold earring in his ear sparkled in the lantern light as if to affirm the validity of his statement—or perhaps to warn her to take flight while she could.

"What is it you wish, Captain?" She raised her chin.

He searched her eyes as if he could see straight into her soul. She fidgeted but did not lower her gaze. The scent of rum wafted over her, stinging her nose.

"A brave one, ye are. I admire that." He backed away and gestured toward the chair. "If you please."

"I'll stand, thank you." Abigail gripped her Bible closer to her chest.

Captain Poole huffed and gazed out the windows. "'Tis an odd darkness that overcomes us, eh? Thunder, but no lightning. Clouds but no rain or wind."

Abigail nodded and glanced out the stern windows. The same dark shroud that she'd seen while up on deck still hovered over the ship.

"I've seen other things—even more odd." He swung around, and the arrogant facade had faded. He scratched the dark stubble on his chin as if pondering what to say.

"Odd?" Abigail prompted him to continue.

"Can I tell ye a tale?" He sat back on his desk.

"Of course."

"Nigh on a year ago, me crew and I came across a Spanish merchant ship hauling pearls from Porto Bello. We boarded her with ease." He waved a hand through the air, fluttering the lace at the cuff of his sleeve. "Relieved her of her goods, and set her adrift without benefit o' her sails or rudder." He chuckled as if remembering the jollity of the event, but then his gleeful expression faded to a frown. "We rescued an Englishman imprisoned in her hold. A preacher. Said he was the grandson of the famous pirate Captain Edmund Merrick." Captain Poole shook his head. "There was something 'bout him."

Abigail brushed the hair from her forehead. Her heart settled to a normal beat. "What do you mean?"

The captain gripped the edge of his desk. "There was a peace, yet a power about him that set me nerves to spinnin'." He gazed up at her. "Much like what I see in yer eyes and Mr. Mason's."

Abigail's heart sped again, but this time from pure joy.

"We encountered a wicked storm like none I e'er saw. Fierce winds and angry waves that would have sunk us to the depths for sure, save. . ." He released a sigh.

"Save what, Captain?"

"When we thought all was lost, this preacher Merrick comes up on deck as calm as if he was walkin' down Bond Street. He speaks to the storm as if it were alive and commands it to cease in the name of his God—this Jesus."

Abigail took a step toward him, excitement twirling within her. "And?"

The captain snapped his fingers. "The storm died off, just like he told it to. The waves settled, the winds died, and the clouds sped away quicker than a trollop from a penniless vagrant." His eyes grew big as he remembered it, and Abigail thought she saw him tremble.

Jumping from the desk, he turned his back on her and stormed to the window. "What do ye make o' that?"

Abigail said a silent prayer for the right words to say. "I think you already know."

He grunted.

"'Tis what we discussed on the island." A renewed strength that could only come from above emboldened her. "God exists. He is the God of the Bible, and He is all powerful, all knowing, and all loving."

As if confirming her words, the dark clouds dissipated, revealing a sky that sparkled like diamonds, and the chill Abigail had felt earlier fled her as well. Raising the Bible to her lips, she placed a kiss upon it. She didn't know what had just occurred, but she knew God had preformed a miraculous feat.

⌒

"Nathaniel, wake up." A rough hand shook him, and Nathaniel opened one weary eye. Gavin's cheerful face filled his vision.

"What do you want?" Nathaniel asked, groggy with sleep.

"Sink me, 'tis near midday, and you're still asleep on the deck."

Nathaniel struggled to sit, every muscle in his back and neck screaming in rebellion. He rubbed his eyes and surveyed the ship bustling with activity as the pirates scampered across deck tending to their various tasks. Shielding his eyes, he glanced above. White sails, gorged with wind, snapped at every yard.

"Did Hope toss you out of the cabin?" Gavin chuckled.

Nathaniel tried to shake the fog from his mind. "Nay, I was up late and didn't wish to disturb her." Truth be told, he'd waited half the night for Abigail to finish conversing with Captain Poole. Unable to sleep without ensuring her safety, he had loitered outside the captain's cabin for hours. Abigail had finally emerged on the pirate's arm. Nathaniel slunk into the shadows and watched as the captain escorted her to her cabin as if they were nobility returning from a concert at Dillon's Inn in Charles Towne.

"Not disturb her?" Gavin cackled. "So you spend a restless night on the hard deck?"

Nathaniel suppressed a laugh, for it would have been a far more restless night's sleep in a cabin with Hope so near. Besides, the captain had been too occupied last night to notice Nathaniel's absence from his "wife's" bed. So he had curled up beside the foredeck, hoping to catch a few hours of sleep before the sun rose. But he'd slept half the day away.

Assisting Nathaniel to his feet, Gavin gazed across the azure sea. "We should arrive in Kingstown in two days. It will be good to be in a civilized port again."

"Kingstown is anything but civilized, I'm told." Nathaniel stretched.

"As long as it boasts a soft bed, a hearty meal, strong drink, and plenty of women, it could be in the middle of a desert for all I care."

Nathaniel chuckled and ran a hand through his unruly hair. "Your definition of civilization leaves much to be desired."

"Speaking of women, where, pray tell, is your wife?"

Nathaniel cringed, but still his heart leapt at the title bestowed upon Hope. Ignoring both reactions, he scanned the deck. "I have no idea."

"Good morning, Nathaniel." Abigail approached with a swish of her green skirts and a beaming smile upon her face.

"Good morning."

"Spent some time with the captain, did you?" Gavin asked, his tone sarcastic.

"That I did. We had a rousing discussion."

"What could you two possibly have in common to discuss?"

Abigail pressed the folds of her gown and gave him a placating smile. "As I have told you, he wished to discuss the things of God."

Gavin snorted, then directed a curious gaze toward the captain.

Tall, brawny, and fully armed, Poole appeared to be exactly what he claimed to be—a ruthless pirate. Not a man given to religion.

"I shall leave you to discuss these matters with Nathaniel." Gavin stomped away.

Abigail giggled. "You look a sight, Nathaniel."

"How gracious of you." He bowed. "I fear I haven't been sleeping well since we boarded this ship."

A flash of blue caught his eye as Hope emerged from the

companionway, hand in hand with Elise.

Abigail followed his gaze. "Yes, I see."

He ignored her taunting grin. "What did the captain want?"

Clutching her skirts, she sauntered to the railing. "He speaks of a miracle he saw aboard his ship. It seems to have both frightened and intrigued him." She sighed. "He asked many questions about our Lord, and I answered him the best I could."

"I'm sure you did well." Nathaniel eased beside her, allowing the sun to warm his face. "An odd turn of events. Do you suppose it was the cause of the black clouds yesterday, the oppression we both felt?"

"Perhaps, but Captain Poole thus far wishes only to satisfy his curiosity. Nay, I think something else occurred last night." She glanced at Hope again.

"Miss Hope?" Nathaniel blinked.

"You should speak with her."

Nathaniel shook his head. "Nay. 'Tis better I keep my distance."

Yet after Abigail went below to rest, Nathaniel could do anything but keep his distance from the enchanting woman. With Gavin engaged in a game of cards and the rest of the crew napping, drinking, or tending the sails, Nathaniel had nothing to do but saunter about the deck. And every time he looked up, he found himself nearer to Hope. Finally, he could hear her conversing with Miss Elise.

Hope embraced the girl, and Elise's little arms wrapped around Hope's neck.

"Then I will go to heaven to be with Mother?"

"Yes, my dear." Hope kissed her cheek, and Nathaniel nearly leapt at her declaration of belief. "And your mother isn't frightened or sad there. Heaven is a beautiful place with no sorrow and no fear. A place where only love and joy and hope exist."

"Like your name!" Elise smiled.

Hope nodded and brushed the girl's hair from her face. "Only you must love God with all your heart and all your strength for all your days."

Nathaniel's heart leapt into his throat.

"What of Father? He told me there is no heaven." The little girl's lips drew into a pout.

Nathaniel glanced at Mr. Hendrick standing across the deck, staring out onto the sea as if in a daze.

"Your father is sad and angry right now," Hope answered. "We must pray for him."

Shock froze Nathaniel. He gasped for a breath that seemed to escape him. Pray? Could it be true? Could Miss Hope have given her life to God?

"Elise, come here." Mr. Hendrick bellowed from across the deck.

The little girl turned wide eyes to Hope. "Must I go?"

"He is your father. Be good and love him." Hope rose. "And remember to pray for him. I won't be far away."

Elise started off, then turned around. "I wish you could be my new mother, Miss Hope." She wrapped her arms around Hope in a fierce embrace, and Nathaniel forced back the moisture that threatened to fill his eyes.

Hope eased a finger over the girl's cheek. "I do, too, precious one." Her voice cracked.

Elise dragged her feet across the deck to where her father received her and drew her close beside him, but not before sending a disdainful glance Hope's way.

Hope turned to face the sea, and Nathaniel slipped beneath the foredeck ladder, watching her, not wanting her to know he had eavesdropped on her conversation. Was it possible a woman like Hope could change? Yesterday she had not believed in God, or at least in a loving God, and today she spoke of Him as if she knew Him.

"For with God, nothing shall be impossible."

Nathaniel's heart swelled, and heat stormed through him. If Hope had given her life to God, perhaps with His strength she could indeed change—she could become a virtuous lady, moral and good. The kind of lady he longed to share his life with. He must speak to her, find out what happened, confirm what every inch of his heart yearned to be true.

He took a step toward her, but Gavin sped past him and took Hope's elbow. "Miss Hope, would you care for a turn about the deck?"

Startled, she turned, then slid her hand through his proffered arm. "Why, thank you, Mr. Keese." Only then did she notice Nathaniel. She offered a smile of resignation and headed off with Gavin, who winked at Nathaniel over his shoulder.

Clenching his fists, Nathaniel resolved to speak with Hope tonight, for he could no longer deny his feelings. He must tell her he loved her.

CHAPTER 31

Later that day, Hope finished praying, raised her head, and opened her eyes to the most glorious sight: violet, crimson, peach, and saffron ribbons glittered across the horizon as the last traces of the sun dipped below the dark blue line of the sea. She thanked God for the beauty of His creation—something she had never appreciated before. Truth be told, since she'd given her life over to the Lord, everything seemed more beautiful, more filled with life. She gripped the railing and braced her feet against the foredeck as the ship rose and plunged over a swell. She felt alive and free for the first time. No matter what happened, no matter where life took her, she knew she had a Father in heaven who loved her, who found her worthy, and who would never leave her.

Remorse nipped at the edges of her joy like the wind that now clipped over her curls, trying to loosen them from her pins. So many wasted years spent searching for love to fill the void deep within her—a void she now realized only the love of God could fill. She shook her head. The stupid choices she'd made, the pain she had caused. And the loss. Of her reputation, her purity. . .of Nathaniel.

She loved him. She would always love him. But her poor choices had erected a sturdy wall between them that even the strongest love could not breach. She deserved his rejection and much worse. But the ache of loss remained.

A warm evening breeze swirled around her, teasing her nose with the scent of the sea, with the sweet fragrance of the coming evening, and with life, and she inhaled a deep breath. When she returned to Charles Towne, despite the financial difficulties she would face, despite the impossibility of restoring her reputation with the citizens of the burgeoning port city, she intended to open an orphanage. In her recent conversations with

God, He had made His will plain, further bolstering both her confidence and her faith. At last she could offer lost and unwanted children a safe home, a home where they would be loved and would learn about God's love. Then they wouldn't have to make the same mistakes she had and suffer for their bad choices.

In addition, she must beg her sister Grace's forgiveness for snubbing all of Grace's efforts to tell her about God. Though perhaps she had gone about it the wrong way, Grace's heart had been concerned only with Hope's happiness and eternal destination. Hope smiled at the possibility she and Grace could now become close as sisters should be.

A sail snapped overhead as if sealing her deal with God, and the ship bucked over a wave, anointing her with a refreshing spray. She smiled and gripped the railing as the last bright traces of the day sank beneath the sea, leaving a faint glow on the horizon. But despite the encroaching shadows, the day had not disappeared. It was only hidden for a time, for the darkness could never hide the sun's bright light for long. It would rise again, forcing back the gloom as it announced a new day.

Digging beneath the sleeve of her gown, Hope pulled out the chipped shell she had found on the island. Holding it up, she smiled at the way it glistened in the fading sunlight. She turned it over, searching for the broken part she had seen before. But it was not there. Perfect in form, symmetrical and beautiful, the shell appeared to have been plucked from the ocean, fresh, clean—pristine.

Had she picked up the wrong shell? Confusion twisted through her, followed by a surge of certainty. No, she had not. Humbled and awed at the love of God, Hope bowed her head and gave Him thanks.

Wiping tears of joy from her face, she turned around and scanned the ship. Two pirates lit lanterns hanging upon the mainmast and foredeck railing. The rest gathered in huddles, drinking and boasting and playing cards. Better she got below before their revelry got underway and they forgot she was a guest of Captain Poole. She crept down the foredeck ladder and tiptoed across the deck, keeping her eyes straight ahead and not acknowledging the lewd remarks tossed her way. She had not seen Nathaniel since earlier in the day and had no idea where he was. That he avoided her was obvious. That his disdain caused her great pain was something she resolved to endure.

Making her way down the companionway and then the dimly lit hall-way, she saw a thin strip of light shining beneath her cabin door. Had she left a lantern lit? Horrified, she pushed open the door and rushed inside.

Nathaniel stood beside a washbowl, water dripping down his chest glimmering in the lantern light.

Hope averted her eyes. "Forgive me." She turned to leave.

"No, please stay." His voice held a pleading tone that halted her steps.

Leaving the door open, Hope skirted an empty basket on the floor and inched toward her bed, keeping her eyes on the floor. She had seen his bare chest ofttimes on the island, but in this tiny cabin, it seemed inappropriate, and she didn't like the way her heart leapt.

Grabbing a cloth, he rubbed at the moisture on his chest and closed the door with an ominous thud.

"You wish to speak to me?" She backed into the hard bulkhead.

He approached. His shadow blocked out the lantern light. Stopping before her, he released a heavy sigh, and his warm breath and woodsy scent flowed over her. He placed a finger beneath her chin and lifted her gaze to his.

Moist brown hair, pressed back from his face, eased down his neck and dangled in wet strands across his broad shoulders. His face filled with curiosity, concern, and. . .she couldn't be sure what she saw, for her head began to spin. Her pulse raced, and her breathing quickened.

He smiled. Did he notice her discomfort? She tried to look down, but his finger held her head in place.

He brushed his thumb over her cheek, and Hope closed her eyes. Then he released her, and she heard him take a step back. She thanked God because her knees had begun to shake, and she wasn't sure she could remain standing much longer with Nathaniel so near. Placing her hands behind her, she braced against the bulkhead and dared to gaze up at him.

Just in time to see his lips lowering to hers.

Gasping, Hope flattened her back against the wood, but there was no escape. *Lord, help me*, her plea for strength screamed through her mind. She turned her face away. "We shouldn't."

He blinked, and one eyebrow rose in an incredulous arch. Stepping back, he scrubbed the cloth over his damp hair. "And why shouldn't we?" His tone carried no anger, only curiosity.

Despite the yearning storming through her body, Hope gathered her resolve. "Because we are not courting. Or ever will be courting. You have made that quite plain. And I wish to save my affections for the man I plan to marry." There, she had said it, albeit too fast and perhaps a bit too sharply. But at least she had said the right thing—had done the right thing—and not leapt into his arms and received his kisses like every ounce of her body longed to do.

A grin lifted one corner of his lips. "'Tis a new philosophy of yours?"

"And one which I intend to live my life by. God has shown me a better way." And it had to be God who was giving her the strength to resist Nathaniel at the moment, for her attraction to him seemed only to have grown.

"He has?" Nathaniel laughed. "Indeed, I am pleased to hear it."

He turned away from her and tossed the cloth to the table, sending his muscles rippling across his back like swells over a stormy sea. When he faced her again, the respect, the love she had craved to see beaming from his eyes poured over her like warm sunshine. Hope swallowed and threw a hand to her heart to steady its chaotic beat. "You are pleased?" Her voice squeaked.

He smiled, that mischievous, sultry half grin that set her body aflame. Flustered, she dropped her gaze to the fading wound on his arm and then to the bluish scar marring his left side. She must divert the conversation to a safer topic, away from the possibility she saw in his eyes—the possibility that caused her hopes to soar, the possibility that would leave her devastated once again if she entertained its promise. He had made it clear how he felt about her. Nothing had changed. And she mustn't think otherwise. "What happened to you?"

He followed her gaze to his scar and rubbed it. "I was stabbed."

"Stabbed? Oh my." Hope took a step toward him.

"When I was young." His jaw stiffened. "I was protecting my mother."

Hope nearly stumbled at the pain burning in his eyes. "Your mother. From whom?"

"A man she displeased," he spat out, then stared out the porthole. "She was a harlot."

A harlot? How could such an honorable man have such a wayward mother? The ship creaked over a wave, and Hope gripped the bulkhead, but Nathaniel kept his balance without effort. The muscles in his face twitched, and his mouth flattened into a thin line, his anger keeping him firmly planted to the deck.

"And your father?"

"I never knew him." He snorted. "My mother thought he was a mason by trade, so she named me Nathaniel Mason." His laughter shook with suppressed fury.

Hope's heart collapsed. "I'm sorry." At least Hope had known her father, though he'd been anything but loving. At least she had a legitimate name, a heritage she could be proud of.

Nathaniel ran a hand through his hair and faced her.

Hope took another step toward him. "What happened to her?" She longed to ease his pain, to smooth the tight lines of sorrow from his face.

He leaned back on the table and gripped the edges, then stared at the dirty floorboards. "We lived in Barbados. When I was eight, my mother grew sick. We had no money. So I moved her down by the beach on the east side of the island." He crossed his arms over his chest. "'Tis where I learned how to fish and build a hut. Those were good times." He smiled, but then grief consumed the momentary joy lighting his face. "Mother got well again, and with the money she made, we traveled to Charles Towne. She had heard the ratio of men to women was four to one. Good odds for someone in her trade." He snickered. "We lived in a room above a tavern. Plenty of men had enough coin to pay, but some were vicious, even cruel to my mother. They beat her."

"You stayed in the room with her?" Hope's eyes burned with tears as she stepped closer to Nathaniel.

"When I was little, yes. But later I would wander the town for hours while she worked. One night, I returned to find a man holding a knife to my mother's neck. When I attacked him, he stabbed me and ran off."

Hope reached out and eased her fingers over the scar as tears spilled from her eyes. "How horrible."

He grabbed her hand and held it. "Odd, it still pains me at times."

Hope nodded, remembering how often he'd rubbed it on the island. "Whenever you feel threatened."

Nathaniel's eyes widened, and he ran his fingers through the loose strands of her hair, brushing them back from her face. "You tug your hair for the same reason. I hate it that Lord Villemont hurt you."

Hope shifted away from his discerning gaze. "'Tis done with." She sighed. "But you never told me what happened to your mother."

"Mother grew sick again after that. We had no money for a physician." Releasing her hand, he stared off, his eyes glazed. "I could not help her. I watched her die."

Hope swallowed. "So much pain for such a young boy." She eased beside him. "How did you survive?"

"I wandered the streets for a year before Reverend Halloway found me and took me in." The haggard lines on his face softened. "You know the rest."

Hope leaned against his chest, and he wrapped his arms around her. "I had no idea," she muttered. No wonder he had been repulsed by her licentiousness. No wonder he feared entangling himself with a woman like her. Heat from his skin warmed her cheek, and she could no longer hold back her tears.

"Don't cry for me, Hope. God gave me a good home, and Reverend Halloway loved me as a father." He pressed her against him and leaned his chin atop her head.

Hope pushed away from him, swiping the tears from her face. "That's precisely why I wish to open an orphanage when I return home. Think of it, Nathaniel. A place for children like you to grow up and receive all the care they need and be taught about God's love and grace."

He flinched, and a spark of fear dashed across his face. "'Tis a noble venture for you, and I lo—admire—you greatly for it."

Hope's throat constricted. Though he had not said it, his cutting tone spoke volumes. He had no interest in her plans. Which meant he did not see her in his future. Which meant he did not love her—at least not in the way she loved him. A heavy weight landed on her chest. "Your admiration is all I ever wanted, Nathaniel." She forced a smile. "And much more than I deserve."

"Is it *all* you ever wanted?" He cocked his head and grinned.

She studied him, her heart performing a traitorous leap. "Nay. But it is all I dare to expect. You have made your feelings clear."

Nathaniel shook his head. "I have fought them, to be sure." He caressed her cheek with the palm of his hand. "But the only thing clear to me now is that I love you, Hope."

Hope's heart thundered. "You love me?"

"Is it so inconceivable?" He chuckled.

Hope stared into his eyes, waiting for him to recall his words, deny their veracity, waiting for the jest to play out before she dared to believe it true. A nervous giggle spilled from her lips.

Nathaniel raised a brow. "Am I to be left standing here with no answer but your laughter?"

"No, of course not. I love you, too, Nathaniel." She leapt toward him, inadvertently kicking the empty basket across the deck just as he took a step in her direction. He tripped on the basket and stumbled across the cabin. Hope threw a hand to her mouth, praying she would not injure him again. He regained his balance, lengthened his stance, and faced her. "Still trying to kill me, eh?" He grinned.

Placing one hand on her waist, Hope gave him a coy grin. "I am a determined lady." She approached him and gently touched the bump on his forehead, where she'd caused him to slam into the bulkhead, then ran her fingers down the scar on his arm, the one from the sword fight with the major. "Truly, I don't know what comes over me when you are around."

"I hope that whatever it is, it will diminish, for I plan to be around you as much as possible."

"But I am a danger to you." She pouted.

"That you are." He swung her around, eased her against the bulkhead, and flung a hand upon the hard wood by her head. "Extremely dangerous."

His gaze wandered to her lips.

Hope smiled. "Why do I feel as though I'm the one in danger now?"

He chuckled, and she felt his warm breath on her face. Then his lips were on hers, caressing, loving her. And the cabin around Hope faded into a dream world—a world where she was safe, secure, and loved.

⁓

With Hope's sweet kiss still warm on his lips, Nathaniel leapt upon the deck, lighter and more vigorous than he'd been in days, despite his lack of sleep. He made his way up to the bow of the ship, hoping the night breeze would cool his heated skin. It took every scrap of strength within him to leave Miss Hope for the night. He had the perfect excuse to stay, after all, with the captain prowling about, but if he stayed with her after declaring his love, he doubted he could keep from holding her close throughout the entire night. And that would not be wise—for either of them.

Gripping the railing, he bowed his head and thanked God for saving Hope, for changing her heart, and for her love. He still found it hard to believe she returned his affections, especially in light of her obvious attachment to Gavin. But Nathaniel could not deny that her heart belonged to him—he'd seen love burning in her eyes and felt her impassioned response to his kisses. Heat scorched through him at the remembrance.

He had loved Hope from the first moment he'd seen her in Charles Towne, despite the way she snubbed him, despite the salacious rumors spreading throughout the city about her that he had prayed were not true. But now after giving up his prize ship to save her and after all the harrowing events of their journey, as well as his own misgivings about her character, they had finally declared their love for one another. And he vowed to spend the rest of his life giving her all the love she had missed as a child and protecting her from every danger and heartache.

The moon hung high in the sky, smiling down upon him and flinging its sparkling light onto the rolling dark waves. The soothing purl of water as the bow sliced through the sea washed over Nathaniel, releasing from his shoulders a burden of tension he'd been carrying for weeks. Swerving around, he found a level place near the foremast beside a huge barrel and lay down on the hard deck. Putting one hand behind his head, he gazed up at the sails fluttering in the moonlight and drifted to sleep.

Hours later, thumping noises jolted him awake, and he rubbed his eyes and sprang to his feet, ready to defend against some unknown attack. A flash of blue caught his eye, and he glanced to the main deck below, where he saw Hope standing near the railing, her blond hair a beacon in the darkness. A dark shadow loomed beside her.

Alarm stiffened Nathaniel. Was someone accosting her? He dashed to the foredeck ladder, intending to pounce upon the villain, when the figure took Hope in a full embrace—and she did not resist. Slinking into the shadows, Nathaniel rubbed his eyes and peered toward the couple, his heart crumbling in his chest. Perhaps it wasn't Hope after all? Yet after several seconds, in which the lovers remained entwined, the woman broke away, stepped into the lantern light, offered the man a tender smile, and descended down the companionway. *Hope*. Nathaniel's legs betrayed him, and he stumbled.

The man leaned over the railing, and Nathaniel allowed his anger to surge, overcoming his grief. "Who goes there?" he shouted. Whoever it was, he would pound him to the timbers for touching Hope.

The figure turned, allowing the light of a lantern swinging at the foremast to spill over him. Gavin's sharp eyes met his. "Ah, Nathaniel. There you are. Enduring another sleepless night, I see."

Shaking the shock from his face, Nathaniel leapt down the foredeck ladder. "Was that Hope I just saw?" He needed to hear it from the man's lips.

Gavin studied him for a moment, then clapped his back and winked. "Aye. We had quite an evening."

"Evening?" Nathaniel fisted his hands.

"Aye. You told me I could court her, did you not?" Gavin stretched his arms out like a man quite content with life.

Nathaniel stared at his friend. His tongue had gone numb, along with the rest of him.

"Well, I daresay, the woman moves quick." Gavin chuckled.

Nathaniel moaned.

"Are you ill, my friend?" Gavin grabbed his arm. "Do you need some water?"

"Are you saying that you and Miss Hope, you. . ."

Gavin grinned like a cat who had just been fed a satisfying meal after a long fast. He glanced across the deck, then leaned toward Nathaniel. "And she was far better than I expected."

CHAPTER 32

"Hoist the Union Jack, if you please, Mr. Drury," Captain Poole bellowed as Hope climbed onto the main deck. A burst of moist wind swirled around her, taunting her with the scent of flowers and musky earth. Making her way to the railing, she shielded her eyes from the sun and peered into the distance where a mound floated upon the horizon like a tortoise shell upon liquid turquoise. *Jamaica.* They had made it.

Swerving about, she surveyed the ship and spotted Nathaniel upon the quarterdeck, speaking to Abigail. No jealous twinge gripped her at the sight of them together, for she finally knew where his true feelings lay. When his gaze met hers, she waved, but instead of returning her smile and dashing to join her, he frowned and turned his back. Her chest tightened. Perhaps he hadn't seen her.

Clutching her skirts and ignoring the pirates' salacious stares, she started for the quarterdeck ladder when Gavin jumped in front of her, blocking her way.

"You look lovely this morning, Hope." He winked and gave her one of his saucy smiles.

"Thank you, Gavin, but if you please." Hope tried to nudge him aside, but it was like attempting to push an aged tree trunk from its deep roots. "I need to speak with Nathaniel."

"Indeed?" Gavin scratched his whiskers and gave her a puzzled look. "Can it not wait? Miss Elise is asking for you."

Hope tensed. "She is? Is she well?"

"Yes, quite, but Mr. Hendrick requests your help in dressing her for the trip ashore." His blue eyes would not meet her gaze.

"I doubt it, Gavin." Hope huffed. "Mr. Hendrick's hatred for me is no secret. He has not required my assistance since we boarded this ship. Why

581

would he require it now?"

Gavin shrugged. "I'm just relaying his message."

Hope studied her friend and pursed her lips. "Is this another one of your tricks, Mr. Keese?"

"You wound me, milady." He placed a hand over his heart. "Are we reduced to Mr. Keese again?"

Hope forced back a smile. "You know what I am referring to. Last night?" She raised a questioning brow.

"I did hear Miss Elise crying and would swear upon my mother's grave I saw her up here on deck." A spark of mischief flashed across his eyes. "I hope you'll forgive me for waking you so late, but since you have such a good rapport with the girl, I didn't know who else to turn to. She wouldn't come when I called to her. Out of fright, I suspect, and her father was nowhere to be found."

"Yet she was not on deck, after all, but sound asleep in her cabin." Hope glared at him. "With her father, I might add."

"They were not there when I went to wake you." A blast of wind wafted over them, and Gavin shook his hair from his face, then leaned toward her, a pleading frown playing upon his lips. "Oh, do say you'll forgive me."

Hope huffed then cast a quick glance toward Nathaniel, still busy with Abigail. If Elise really did need her, Hope wanted to be of assistance. Especially since she'd not seen much of the girl since they'd boarded the ship. "Very well. Lead me to her."

With a smile, he held out his arm, and taking it, Hope followed him below.

⁓

Turning his back on Hope, Nathaniel tried to quell the anguish ripping through his belly and listen to what Abigail was saying. But though her lips fluttered rapidly, naught but garbled tones met his ears.

"Are you listening to me?" She peered into his eyes.

"Forgive me. I was distracted." Nathaniel ran a hand over the back of his neck where a nagging ache refused to abate. An ache not caused from sleeping on the hard deck, but one that had spread upward from his wounded heart.

Abigail glanced over his shoulder. "Hope waved at you."

Nathaniel stiffened his jaw and shifted his gaze to Captain Poole standing by the helm. A group of pirates crowded around him in deep discussion.

Abigail persisted. "I thought you two had come to an understanding."

"So did I." Nathaniel released a pained sigh, then followed Abigail's gaze over his shoulder. He regretted it instantly as he watched Gavin and Hope descend the companionway, arm in arm. He faced forward again. His gut wrenched, and he thought he might lose the hard biscuit he'd forced down that morning. After no sleep. Yet again.

"I'm sorry, Nathaniel." Abigail's brow wrinkled. "She doesn't mean to hurt you."

Nathaniel grimaced and studied the gouges and bloodstains marring the deck by his feet and wondered how many battles this ship had seen and how many men had died upon these oak planks. Anything to divert his thoughts from Hope and the questions that had tortured his mind throughout the dark hours of the night. He knew he must speak to her, must give her a chance to explain, but he wasn't ready to hear her answer.

The ship lurched, and he steadied Abigail. "What of you? You must be excited to start your adventure in Kingstown."

But fear, not excitement, flickered in her eyes.

Four pirates swarmed around them, Kreggs and Hanson among them. The other two he recognized as the men he'd spoken to about God a few nights prior.

"Mr. Mason." Kreggs spat to the side and scratched his stained shirt. "Jones and Boone got somethin' ye should hear fer yerself."

Nathaniel turned to the other men, noting an unusual glow in their expressions even beneath the hard crust of sunburn and months of unwashed dirt. The stench of unwashed bodies stung his nose, but clear eyes, devoid of red streaks and the usual rum-induced haze, met his.

Jones shifted his feet over the deck and rubbed the scar around his neck. "What ye said the other night about God made sense t' us."

Nathaniel's heart leapt. "I'm pleased to hear it."

Abigail gripped his arm. He could feel excitement rippling through her.

Jones crossed his arms over his chest. "We gave our lives o'er to yer God. And we is determined t' change our ways an' become good men."

Abigail clasped her hands. "Praise God!"

Nathaniel blinked, allowing the shocking revelation to make its way into his reason. *Gave their lives to God? These pirates?* "All of you?"

"Aye." Kreggs and Hanson nodded. "Us, too."

Nathaniel took Hanson by the shoulders and shook him then clutched the other men in turn. "This is wonderful news!"

Jones's face reddened. Boone's eyes grew wide, and he stiffened beneath Nathaniel's touch. Kreggs and Hanson chuckled nervously. They each took a step away from Nathaniel as if he'd gone mad. *Mad indeed. The best kind of mad.* The seeds God had given him that night had landed on good soil, hearts willing to believe and to humbly submit to God. "Fire and thunder, I am most pleased!" He scratched his head and chuckled so loudly, it drew the attention of the other pirates hard at work.

"We want t' thank ye for openin' our eyes." Hanson scanned his fellow converts, receiving their affirming nods. "We felt the presence of yer God when we asked 'im to show Hisself."

"Not my God. Our God," Nathaniel said, then smiled at Abigail, whose eyes sparkled with delight. "Everyone's God. The only God."

"Aye," they shouted in unison.

An urgency swept through Nathaniel, and he silently prayed for wisdom. "You must read God's Word and speak with Him daily. Promise me you'll do that."

"Aye." Jones glanced at the others. "We will."

Nathaniel cast a quick look toward Captain Poole standing by the helm. "But what of your pirating?"

"We just told Cap'n Poole we be leavin' the ship in Kingstown." Boone gripped his baldric with both hands and grinned, an expression devoid of most of his teeth, but the most wonderful smile Nathaniel had seen.

As if on cue, the captain barreled toward them, a scowl on his face. Nathaniel braced himself for the rash man's temper, but instead of lashing them with his tongue, he halted in their midst and raised a supercilious brow toward Nathaniel.

"And I'll be thankin' ye to be gettin' off the ship, too, Mr. Mason, before ye convert me whole crew an' I'm left wit' nothin' but a ship full of pious ninnies." Though his tone was harsh, the twinkle in his eye spoke otherwise. "That won't bode well for pillagin' and plunderin'." He let out a coarse chuckle, and his gaze landed on Abigail and softened.

"I'll be happy to leave your ship, Captain," Nathaniel said. "Unless, of course, you would like to partake of the treasure these men have found?"

"Treasure! D'ye take me for a fool? Nay, I'm seekin' me own kind of treasure." His hard gaze scoured the men. "But yer still me pirates until we weigh anchor. Get back to work, ye maggots!" he barked, sending the men scampering off. His dark eyes took in Abigail before he sauntered back to his spot by the foredeck railing.

Beaming, Abigail clutched Nathaniel's arm. "Nathaniel, did I not tell you that you have the gift of evangelism? See the impact you have had on these men—hardened sailors and pirates all?"

Truth be told, he had been exhilarated that night when he had spoken to the pirates about God. As if his heart and tongue had been on fire.

"Do not deny the calling of God," she added.

"Perhaps He has blessed me not with a gift, but a calling." Nathaniel shook his head. "You do not know from whence I came."

"But I can see where you should be going." Abigail gave him a sideways glance and patted his arm. "Follow your heart, Nathaniel." She released him and turned toward Captain Poole standing at the foredeck railing, staring out upon the fast-approaching island.

A flash of blue drew Nathaniel's eyes to the main deck where Hope had reemerged from the companionway. *Without Gavin.* Nathaniel's elation of moments ago sank back into despair, and he turned around and leapt up into the ratlines before she could spot him. Although he wanted with all his heart to believe otherwise, he could not deny what he'd seen or what Gavin had confirmed. For why would his friend lie? There was no other explanation but that Hope had not changed after all.

Although Nathaniel intended to confront her, he could not face her, not yet. The pain of her betrayal was too raw, too fresh. Had all her talk of God and doing His will been naught but a ruse? A lie? But for what purpose? Nathaniel hoisted himself into the shrouds and made his way up to the mizzen yard. How quickly she had fallen back into her old ways. And only hours after she had kissed him—and so passionately. He rubbed his lips, trying to rid himself of the memory, but instead heat swept through him.

Angered at his reaction, he inched his way across the yard, battling both the fierce wind blasting over him and the anguish storming within him. A creamy, bubbling wake gushed from the ship's stern, reminding Nathaniel of the joy he'd felt last night with Hope in his arms, but the swirling foam soon faded into the sea. The ship plunged over a roller, and he gripped the mizzen stay to keep his balance, still finding it difficult to believe he sailed aboard a pirate ship. The pirate ship *Enchantress*—appropriately named for the cargo she carried.

For that was what Hope was and always would be—an enchantress.

⤝

Abigail eased toward Captain Poole. In between shouting orders to his men, he seemed to settle into a trance—deep in thought and heavy laden with sorrow. Though they had conversed often since their time in his cabin, the captain had not questioned her further on God, and whenever she had broached the subject, he abruptly ended the conversation.

She followed his gaze to the growing mound of land and knew she hadn't much more time with this daring pirate. "Captain Poole, I hope you have given some thought to our discussion night before last." Abigail studied him. His stubbled jaw flinched, and he rubbed a rough hand over his chin. Planting his fists upon his waist, he braced himself against a gust of wind that fluttered the blue plume atop his tricorn.

"I have thought on it, aye," he said with finality.

"That pleases me." Abigail laid a hand on his arm. His brooding eyes met hers, and she smiled.

The roughened skin of his face softened. "That I have pleased ye warms me down to me soul, miss."

The snap of the Union Jack sounded from above, a disguise of the true nature of the ship. "Do you fear sailing into Kingstown?"

"Fear?" He jerked his head back and chuckled. "Fear never enters a pirate's head, nor his heart, or he'll be lost forever. Nay, I don't fear it."

"Then what has you so vexed?"

His brows rose, and amazement swept across his face. "How can ye know me so well when we have jest met?" He huffed. "Kingstown, 'tis yer final destination?"

"Yes, I am to join a missionary there. A friend of my father's." Even as Abigail spoke the words, dread pinched her chest, and she bit her lip.

"Man the yards!" the captain shouted, sending pirates leaping into the shrouds. Abigail gripped the railing as the ship bucked over a wave. Spread out before her glistened a pool of azure blue. Right in the middle sat the island of Jamaica. Menacing. Waiting to devour her.

"Now I must ask ye, what has *ye* so vexed?" Captain Poole covered her hand on the railing, and although propriety and the dozens of eyes around them demanded she remove hers, his touch brought her more comfort than she cared to admit.

"Is it so obvious?" She brushed her hair from her forehead. "My parents were brutally murdered on Antigua—by the very people they were there to help." Abigail swallowed. "I found them butchered in their bed."

A twinge of sympathy rose in Captain Poole's eyes, and he squeezed her hand. "'Tis a cruel world, miss."

"Every time I think of it, fear consumes me—fear I will end up with the same fate."

"Humph." Captain Poole doffed his hat, and the wind whipped his dark hair. "Did you not say that this God o' yers loves ye beyond measure and will protect ye?"

Abigail released a startled gasp. "You were listening."

"To every word that comes forth from that pretty mouth." His dark eyes swept over her lips before he faced the sea again. "And if ye do meet yer death, d'ye not believe to be goin' to a far better place?"

Abigail nodded, stunned at his words.

"Then what's t' fear?" He plopped his hat back atop his head and shrugged as if that settled the matter.

Guilt and joy battled within Abigail. Guilt for her lack of faith and joy that this wicked man understood everything she had told him about God.

She smiled. "You have put me to shame with your faith, Captain."

"Faith? Perish and plague me. 'Tis yer faith we speak of, not mine. My faith is in me ship, me men, and me skill as a gentleman o' fortune."

"Flighty things to lay your hat upon, to be sure."

He narrowed his eyes upon her, and for a moment, she thought she had angered him. "'Tis enough fer me." His black hair fluttered against his coat as he shifted his shoulders.

Abigail stared at the powerful hand still covering hers. "I hope someday you will find it lacking."

"D'ye now?" He grinned, his earring mirroring his mirth. "And if I do, do I have yer permission to seek ye out?"

A rush of warmth sped up Abigail's neck, and she shifted her gaze to the glittering blue waves. He brushed his thumb over her hand.

"Perhaps I misspoke." He removed his hand from hers and stared out to sea.

"Nay." Abigail took back his hand, her heart convulsing. Against everything she knew to be right, against all her inclinations, she had formed an undeniable attachment to this man—this pirate. "I would be most pleased to see you again."

Captain Poole's handsome lips curved upward, and he placed a kiss upon her hand. "Then I think 'tis fair to warn ye to be on the lookout, miss. For ye'll never know when Captain Poole may drop anchor in Kingstown again."

⤏

As the island of Jamaica loomed larger, dread loomed in Hope's heart. Nathaniel had been avoiding her all day, just as he had done so many times before, just as if they had not declared their love for one another, just as if they had not embraced so passionately in their cabin below.

After discovering Mr. Hendrick had not summoned her and chastising Gavin for his deception, Hope had returned on deck to seek out Nathaniel, only to find him sixty feet above her, clinging to the mizzen royal yard.

But he would have to come down sometime, and then she would discover the cause of his odd behavior. Perhaps the uneasiness bubbling in her stomach was only a result of her own insecurities. She had done naught to anger him. Then why did a sense of dread clench her heart? Perhaps he had come to his senses and changed his mind about her during the long night. She couldn't blame him. Why would he want to associate with a woman whose past indicated a propensity to become just like his mother?

She squared her shoulders into the wind and tried to prepare her heart for his rejection, but for now she would enjoy the sight of land:

the way the white sandy beaches swooped up to meet lush aquamarine mountains rising toward the blue sky, and the circle of emerald trees that now began to take shape as the ship soared over the waves toward them.

"Lay aloft and furl the topsail!" Captain Poole shouted as the wind caught the sails in a keen snap. Soon they rounded a corner of the island, and a long, narrow headland came into view, forming a natural fortress in front of Kingstown Harbor. Beyond it, ships rocked at anchor in the bay. Was Nathaniel's ship there? She hoped so, for then they could return to Charles Towne, and home, as soon as possible. Haphazard buildings dotted the lower hills of the bustling port town while people as small as ants scrambled to and fro. *Civilization.*

The thud of feet upon the deck alerted her, and she spun around to see the top of Nathaniel's head disappearing down the main hatch. Within minutes, he emerged with Major Paine, dragging the pale man over to the railing. Squinting in the sun, the major's eyes shot to hers, but a hollow glaze had replaced the impudent spark within them. He drew a deep breath, exhaling it in ragged gasps, and gripped the railing before his thin frame folded over it beneath the next plunge of the ship.

Nathaniel gave him a look of warning and, without a glance at Hope, turned to leave.

Before Hope could call to him, Elise barreled into her. "Miss Hope. Miss Hope," she squealed.

Kneeling, Hope took the little girl in her arms and relished the exuberance of her embrace, the swishy sound of her gown, and the sweet smell of her innocence. "Hello, Elise, how have you been?"

"I've missed you, Miss Hope. 'Tis been so dull sitting with Father all day."

Brushing dust from his silk waistcoat as if it weren't a tattered and torn remnant of its former glory, Mr. Hendrick scowled in her direction. His once-handsome face fared no better than his waistcoat, its normal ruddiness faded to a gaunt ashen shade, further marred by the jagged wound across his cheek. No wonder Hope had seen so little of him on the voyage. The seasickness he'd sworn only women succumbed to apparently had dealt him a humbling blow.

Hope smiled at Elise. "No doubt your father needed your care."

The little girl nodded, sending her red curls bobbing. "I took good care of him."

"I'm sure you did." Hope kissed her forehead and stood, pressing the girl protectively to her side.

A glance across the ship told her Nathaniel was nowhere in sight. Abigail stood beside Captain Poole, both of them deep in conversation. Hope shook her head. If she didn't know Abigail better, it would appear the pious woman had become fond of the crusty pirate. Behind them, Gavin hovered with a group of pirates, laughing and partaking of their rum as if he'd been a part of the crew all his life. Hope wanted to be angry at him for his recent deceptions. Their purpose made no sense to her, other than playful antics. But how could she harbor anger toward a man she would most likely never see again after they reached Kingstown? In many ways, they were alike; in other ways, completely different, especially now that she'd given her life to Christ. But Gavin's interest in her, mischievous as it was, had soothed her pain through difficult times as well as endeared him to her heart. She would miss him.

Hope patted Elise's head as the girl stared toward Jamaica. "We shall soon be on land again. Won't that be nice?"

Elise's blue eyes shone with her unspoken answer.

"Come here, Elise," her father barked, and the little girl's expression faded. With one last glance at Hope, she shuffled to where her father stood by the capstan.

Turning, Hope leaned on the railing and watched the steady rush of water against the hull. The gurgle played a soothing tone in her ears, helping to allay her fears for the young girl. *Oh Lord. Please be with Elise. Don't let her grow up unloved like I was. Protect her. Let her know early on how much You love her.*

"Ease away the sheet. Haul up to leeward!" Captain Poole's commands echoed across the ship, and the thunder of flapping sails being lowered brought Hope's gaze to the marshy headland barricading Kingstown Harbor. The noon sun set the bay sparkling like ripples of diamonds as a dozen tall ships drifted majestically among the turquoise waters. Beads of perspiration formed on the back of Hope's neck and began sliding beneath her gown. How she longed for a bath and a fresh change of clothes.

Movement caught the corner of her eye. Nathaniel approached the foredeck railing. Taking a deep breath, she climbed the ladder, her heart clamoring in her chest.

"Good day, Nathaniel." Her palms dampened as she slipped beside him.

He did not so much as glance her way. Dread consumed her.

"Are you ill?"

"Nay, I feel quite well." He crossed his arms over his chest. A breeze swirled around him, fluttering his wavy hair across the top of his shirt.

Hope raised a hand to her throat to still her throbbing pulse. "What is the matter?"

"I said I am quite well." The tone of his voice sliced through her heart.

"Nay, I mean. . ." She took a breath and forced back the burning behind her eyes. "I mean, why are you behaving this way?"

"And what way is that, Miss Hope?" He finally looked at her, and the anger searing in his gaze sent her reeling back a step.

She looked down. "I thought. . . I thought we had. . ." The words caught in her throat. She grabbed a lock of her hair. "In our cabin."

"Indeed, so did I."

"What has changed?"

"You tell me." He stared down at her as if he were a magistrate and she on trial for murder.

Hope shook her head. "Tell you what? I don't understand."

"Last night?" Nathaniel raised his brow. "I saw you on deck." He looked away as if the sight of her made him ill. "With Gavin. In quite a compromising position, I might add."

Hope recoiled, anger throbbing through her veins. "Oh, you did, did you? And you assumed what? That he and I were engaged in a tryst? That I proclaimed my love for you, kissed you in our cabin, then dashed straightaway into Gavin's arms?"

"I didn't need to assume. I was told." Nathaniel gripped the railing and thrust his face into the wind.

Told? The ship lurched, and Hope stared at a belaying pin near the railing, searching her mind for an explanation. A dull, empty ache began to gnaw at her soul. Everything blurred beneath the tears filling her eyes.

"Besides, I saw it with my own eyes, Hope." He glared at her, hard as stone. "Can you deny it?"

How could he think so little of her? How could she convince him otherwise when he had already made up his mind? She swung her hand to slap his face, but he caught it in midair.

She ripped her hand from his grasp.

"Hard to starboard!" The thumping of feet sounded like war drums across the deck.

Nathaniel drew a deep breath but kept his lips stiff as taut ropes. "I wish you the best, Miss Hope, and I shall pray for you."

"I do not want your prayers," she spat as anger crowded out her pain.

"You are a difficult woman."

"And you are a judgmental, merciless clod."

The golden flecks in his eyes simmered. He pushed himself from the railing and tipped his head in her direction. "Then I shall bid you good day." Turning his back to her once again, he stomped away.

Facing the sea, Hope batted away the tears spilling down her cheeks. Her heart plummeted to the dark depths below the ship. What a fool she'd been to entertain the hope of gaining such a noble man's love. Not someone like her.

Never someone like her.

She clung to the railing as the ship rounded the tip of the headland and sailed into the bay.

"Ready the gun!"

The Lord had forgiven her of her past, of all her sins. Not only that, He had completely forgotten them.

"Ready, fire!" The thunderous boom of a cannon roared across the sky, announcing their arrival and sending a quiver through Hope.

The Lord had forgotten her past. But Nathaniel never would.

CHAPTER 33

Nathaniel thrust his oar into the swirling water and pushed with all his strength, sending the jolly boat gliding across the bay. Hanson, Kreggs, Gavin, and two of Captain Poole's pirates rowed along with him, three on each side of the narrow craft. Water gurgled along the hull and splashed cool drops onto his feet and breeches. He shook the hair from his face and tried to avoid looking at Miss Hope, perched like a delicate flower on the bow thwarts, her loose curls glittering like gold, her chin raised, her arms around Miss Elise, who snuggled in her lap.

Nathaniel's gut churned as he remembered the pain on her face when he had dismissed her affections so ardently, the tears spilling down her cheeks, the life fading from her eyes. It had been almost too much to bear. Almost, for he had nearly taken her in his arms, nearly showered her with kisses of forgiveness. But then he pictured her in Gavin's embrace, receiving Gavin's kisses. And the blood froze in his veins.

Shaking the vision from his mind, he shifted his eyes to Abigail sitting beside Hope. The young woman's rueful eyes had been locked upon the receding pirate ship ever since they had shoved off from its hull. But one glance behind him had told Nathaniel it was not the ship but her captain who had Abigail so captivated, for Captain Poole stood at the main deck railing, returning her gaze with equal fervor.

One of the pirates plunged his oar into the water, sending a spray over the major.

"Be careful, you bumbling fool," Major Paine brayed and swatted at his damp, bedraggled shirt.

"Back to your old self so quickly, Major?" Gavin remarked, drawing a snarl from the man.

Mr. Hendrick moaned and gripped his midsection, his eyes upon the steady shore and what he must consider the only salvation from his riotous stomach.

Gavin and Nathaniel exchanged a knowing smile, both happy to be rid of the portentous merchantman and the obnoxious major.

Nathaniel dipped his oar in the water again as a swift breeze blew over him, bringing with it the smells of the port: stale fish, roasted pork, and horse manure. The scents brought him comfort, reminding him of Charles Towne. His ship, the *Illusive Hope,* floated in the bay, and his excitement soared at the sight of her dark hull and sharp lines. His last remaining ship—named after the woman who had not only stolen his other ship, but his heart as well. The sooner he set sail for Charles Towne, the sooner he could be rid of Miss Hope.

Once the jolly boat reached shore and disgorged its passengers, Captain Poole's pirates returned to the ship. Hanson, Boone, and Jones approached Nathaniel, their gap-toothed smiles reflecting their appreciation.

"We thank ye again, Mr. Mason, fer openin' our eyes to the truth," Hanson said.

"'Twas my pleasure, gentlemen." Nathaniel shook their hands in turn and bade them farewell as they scampered down the dock and onto the main street to their new life. Only Kreggs remained behind.

Nathaniel led them down the pier to Harbor Street and glanced across the bustling town. After the earthquake had destroyed Port Royal in 1692, the survivors had moved here to begin again. Since then, the city had grown into a major trade center. Rows of brick and wood buildings lined the dirt street; drapers, bakers, taverns, blacksmith, warehouses. People scurried across the busy street, weaving among carriages, horses, wagons, and slaves. A bell rang in the distance, the *clip-clop* of horses hooves, the grating of wagon wheels, myriad voices, and the far-off music of a fiddle combined in a cacophony of sounds that made Nathaniel long for the peace of their tiny island.

A groan from behind drew him around to see Mr. Hendrick gripping his belly.

"Elise." He gestured for the little girl to come to him.

She peered out at her father from within the blue folds of Hope's skirts and lifted a pleading gaze to her.

Hope gave the man a venomous look. "Where will you take her, Mr. Hendrick?"

"She is none of your concern." He attempted to stand straight and winced. "I have business here in town and a ship that awaits us."

Hope knelt by the little girl. "Go with your father now." She brushed the curls from the child's face. "But always remember God loves you. He loves you very much. And so do I." A tear slid down Hope's cheek, and Nathaniel tore his gaze away, determined not to allow her kind gesture to soften his anger.

The little girl shuffled over to her father, who took her hand and dashed off, dragging her behind him. Hope rose, wiped her face, and stared after her.

Major Paine cleared his throat. Stripped of every insignia, regalia, and frippery save his white breeches and shirt—neither of which could be called white any longer—and with his brown hair spiraling out in all directions like a sea anemone, he looked more like a pirate than a major in His Majesty's service. "I know we've had our differences, Mr. Mason, but I hope we can part with civility."

"If I were you, Major," Gavin hissed, "I'd be kissing Nathaniel's bare feet for not only saving your life but for bringing you necessities aboard the pirate ship." He scratched his whiskers and chuckled. "'Twas more than any of us would have done."

"Humph." The major glanced over the town as if anxious to leave.

"Where will you go, Major?" Abigail asked.

"I am to report to the fort to procure passage to England. No doubt they anxiously await my arrival." His gaze sped to the bay. "And first on my list of duties will be to inform them of the presence of a certain pirate. I am sure the authorities here in Kingstown will take proper care of Captain Poole."

Hope took a step toward him. "How can you? He saved your life."

Major Paine's gaze took her in from head to toe, causing Nathaniel's blood to boil. "'Tis my duty, miss, and what separates me from men devoid of honor." He waved a hand in Gavin's direction.

Gavin's eyes narrowed. "Then you had better attend to your invidious task, Major, for I believe the *Enchantress* sets sail." He nodded toward the harbor and grinned.

White sails rose like handkerchiefs waving farewell on the ship's masts, and foam caressed her hull as she picked up speed near the mouth of the bay.

Nathaniel gave a mock bow. "The best to you, Major."

With a lift of his nose, the major turned on his heel. He stumbled on a rock as he sauntered away, a curse blowing on the wind in his wake.

"He will escape, will he not?" Abigail bit her lip as she stared at the *Enchantress*.

"Never fear." Nathaniel gave her a curious look. "Captain Poole shall be long gone before the major makes his grand entrance into the fort."

Abigail smiled, but her expression suddenly sank. "I must part ways with you here as well."

Dashing to her side, Hope gripped her hands. "Can't you come with us to Charles Towne? Oh, say that you will!"

"Nay, my dear friend." Abigail's eyes glistened. "My place is here." She looked at Nathaniel. "I know it now."

Assurance and conviction shone from Abigail's eyes, and Nathaniel gave her a nod of understanding. "So you are no longer afraid?"

She glanced toward the ship, almost clearing the headland. "A certain pirate convicted me of my fears and reminded me to keep my eyes on God."

Gavin snorted.

Abigail turned back toward Hope and squeezed her hands. "We shall always be friends."

"Always." Hope sobbed. "You have been my only friend. You spoke the truth to me when I refused to hear it. You sat by my side when I was sick. Your words of God changed my heart."

Abigail cast a quick glance at Nathaniel. "So I have been told. I am most pleased to hear it. Please say you'll visit sometime."

"I shall make every attempt." Hope swallowed, agony brimming in her eyes.

Nathaniel shifted his gaze away. Why did the blasted woman always cause his heart to wrench? "Do you need an escort to the reverend's house?" he asked Abigail. "It isn't safe to walk these streets alone."

"I'll be happy t' take her," Kreggs said.

Nathaniel gave him a questioning look.

"I wouldn't mind talkin' to a reverend. Mebbe even workin' fer him if he'll have me."

Nathaniel scratched his head, still amazed at the sailor's transformation. "Very well. Miss Sheldon, would you mind?"

"Of course not." Abigail smiled at Kreggs then turned to Gavin. "Mr. Keese, 'tis been a pleasure."

Gavin took her hand and laid a kiss upon it.

Abigail swept a loving gaze over Hope and Nathaniel as tears filled her eyes. "I shall see you all again." Turning, she took Kreggs's outstretched arm, and together they made their way down the dusty street.

Gavin shifted his bare feet over the sand and balled his hands into fists. His eyes flittered about the town, giving Nathaniel pause. He'd never seen the man so agitated.

"Are we to go to your ship now?" Hope's shaky voice pricked his guilt. "That is, if you still wish to escort me home." Though she had suffered the loss of a good friend, the loss of Elise, and Nathaniel's rejection, Hope carried herself with a humble strength that only increased his ardor for her.

"I am a man of my word, Miss Hope." He stiffened the lines of his face so as not to express the emotions battling within him and turned to Gavin. "And what are your plans?"

"At the moment, I have none." Gavin's customary joviality returned.

"Then join us." Nathaniel hoped he would, for he could not bear to be alone with Hope. "I am to meet my first mate at the Stuffed Boar."

"A tavern?" Gavin rubbed his hands together. "I do believe I will."

Nathaniel started to offer Hope his arm, but instead he pulled away from her and marched toward the tavern, leaving her in Gavin's company. Each thud of his feet over the hot sand reminded him of the time not too long ago when he'd barreled toward another tavern in another port town, Miss Hope in tow, having sold half his fleet to save her life. At least this time he hadn't lost a ship on her behalf.

Entering the dim tavern saturated with the stench of rum and sweat, Nathaniel wiped his forehead on his arm. His bare feet landed in a sticky pool on the floor. Making his way through the maze of tables, he peered into the shadows, searching for his first mate and friend, Richard Ackon.

Hope gasped. No doubt she had stepped into the same slimy

puddle that he had. He heard Gavin hastening to her aid, his indulgent ministrations causing Nathaniel's stomach to fold.

A boardinghouse as well as a tavern, the Stuffed Boar was accustomed to having feminine clientele, yet that did not prevent the lewd calls and whistles sent Hope's way from the men scattered about the room. Nathaniel longed to grab Hope and draw her near to keep her safe, but that was no longer his job. 'Twas Gavin's for the time being, and after him, the next man who took his place. Besides, Nathaniel had heard she frequented these types of places in Charles Towne and no doubt knew how to handle herself.

After determining that Richard was nowhere in sight, Nathaniel chose a table in the back, kicked out a chair, and sat down. The man would show up sooner or later, and Nathaniel could use a drink. Gavin took a seat across from him and led Hope to a chair between them; then he went to purchase their drinks.

An awkward silence fell upon them as if they'd been plunged underwater, even muting the boisterousness of the men around them. A lantern in the middle of the table flickered its light over Hope's face, and Nathaniel dared a glance into those deep blue eyes. Though laden with sorrow, they returned his gaze with the same passion, the same affection, the same yearning he felt inside. He shifted away as he heard her gasp.

He looked at her again. Her eyes wide, her mouth open, she stared at someone who had just entered the tavern. She began to tremble. She raised a hand to her throat and seemed to be having trouble breathing.

Nathaniel laid his hand upon her arm. "Hope, what is it?" He followed her gaze to the doorway, where a man of medium build stood, plumed hat in one hand, cane hanging on his other arm. Jewels decorating his fingers sparkled in the lantern light from beneath heavy lace at his cuffs. His satin waistcoat and breeches bespoke either great wealth or ostentatious pride, and he perused the room with haughty disdain as if he owned the place.

Hope panted out a ragged breath. "Lord Falkland."

CHAPTER 34

Hope stared at the man standing before her, hardly daring to believe her eyes.

When Lord Falkland insisted upon speaking to her in private, she nodded her assent. A spark of apprehension filled Nathaniel's eyes before he frowned and dashed across the gloomy room as if he couldn't get away from her fast enough. Gavin, on the other hand, barely looked her way. Instead, he and Falkland exchanged a glance that caused Hope's nerves to tighten even further before he joined Nathaniel.

As the shock of seeing him faded into a raging fury, she regretted agreeing to speak with him.

Feeling returned to her legs, and Hope slowly rose. With one hand perched on his hip, Falkland slid his fingers over the gold trim of his waistcoat and studied her. His dark hair was pulled back and tied with one of his gaudy bows—this one a bright purple that matched the satin of his waistcoat. He tugged at his white cravat.

"My dear, I must say I expected a more amorous greeting." His stern jaw flexed as his green eyes scoured her, claiming his possession.

Hope cast a quick glance at Nathaniel and Gavin leaning against the far tavern wall, their eyes peeled in her direction. "The last time I saw you, Arthur, you were walking away from me as I was being auctioned off into slavery. What are you doing here?"

"I came for you." He grinned and took a step toward her, holding out his hand.

Hope backed away. "I urge you to keep your distance, sir, or my friends will be upon you." Moist heat suffocated her, stinging her nose with the putrid smells of the tavern.

Lord Falkland cast a dismissive glance at Gavin and Nathaniel and chuckled. "Harmless rodents, by all appearances." He pouted. "And when did you begin to call me sir again, my sweet one?"

Hope cringed at the sound of Falkland's pet name for her. "I don't know what your true purpose is for being here, nor do I care. But if you think to make amends for what you did, you are sorely mistaken." Belying her outward composure, she grabbed a loose curl at her neck and tugged upon it. *Lord, help me. Why are You doing this to me?* She had at one time hoped with all her heart that she would see this man once more. Now that he stood before her, she couldn't be sure of anything.

His eyes narrowed, and he cocked his head. "You have changed. You are stronger. More defiant." He raised one brow and leaned toward her. "I find it quite alluring."

Hope's stomach knotted. "Did you expect me to run into your arms?"

"You are beautiful." He brushed a knuckle against her cheek, but she jerked out of his reach. He frowned. "Will you at least hear my explanation?"

"Pray, get on with it."

"I did not abandon you to the fate you assume." He laid his cane atop the table with a *clank* and straightened the cuffs of his sleeves. "Do you remember Mr. Garrison?"

A vision of the stocky, puffy-faced man at the auction block came to Hope's mind, renewing her revulsion and fear. "The merchant who nearly purchased me? How did you. . . ?"

Arthur smiled.

Hope blinked. "He was your man?"

"Yes. And I paid him quite handsomely to purchase you. All money lost, of course." He sighed and patted his money pouch like an old friend.

The jangle of coins grated over Hope. Her mind reeled, and she gulped for a breath of fresh air, not the stagnant muck that infiltrated the tavern. "For what purpose?"

"To keep you safe, of course. Captain Grainer had his heart set on selling you. Though I tried desperately to dissuade him, I could not." He shrugged. "My only other option was to purchase you myself. And my plan would have worked, too, if that poor excuse for a hero"—he pointed toward Nathaniel—"hadn't swept in to the rescue."

Hope's anger cooled. So Arthur hadn't abandoned her, after all. He gave her a conciliatory smile, and Hope waited for her heart to leap as it always did at the sight of him. But then a vision of Lady Falkland—Arthur's *wife*—lifting her pert little nose in the air blasted through Hope's mind, and Hope's anger returned, deflating her heart. "And what would you have done if your plan had worked?"

"Why, send you home safely on one of my ships, of course." He furrowed his brow in concern. "Do you think I would ever do anything to harm you? I love you, sweet one. I always have."

Hope's knees turned to pudding, and she sank into her chair. *He loves me still.* "What of your wife?"

Lord Falkland knelt beside her and reached for her hands, but she snatched them away. "I meant to tell you about her, I truly did." He sighed and looked down. "But there was never a proper time."

"A proper time?" Hope shouted, drawing the gaze of Falkland's two men sitting at the next table. "You promised to marry me," she whispered, seething.

"And I still intend to, my dear. All in good time." He placed a hand on her leg, and Hope shot to her feet, knocking her chair over behind her. Not long ago, his touch would have sent waves of heated pleasure through her, but now his hands felt as cold as ice.

A look of genuine pain sparked in his eyes. "My wife is quite ill. The doctors do not expect her to live much longer."

"She looked quite well to me," Hope snapped.

"'Tis an insidious disease that does not manifest itself in obvious ways." He flattened his lips and sent her a look of appeal. "I cannot tell you how taxing it has been."

Hope rubbed her brow, unsure whether to believe a word this man said. "Taxing? How taxing can it be when your wife lies near death and you are bedding another woman?"

"Can I help that I fell madly in love with you?" He stepped toward her again "It was not my intention."

Hope eyed him, searching her heart for any scrap of affection, any spark of tenderness remaining for this man. His expression beamed with a charming appeal that normally sent her heart fluttering, but now all she felt was confusion and doubt.

"So you see," he continued, "I have been ardently searching for you for months, until I discovered Mr. Mason had a ship berthed in Kingstown and came straightaway."

"And as I have already inquired, for what purpose? You have a wife."

"Nothing has changed between us, my sweet. Nothing. We are still betrothed. I still intend to marry you." He inched toward her, sweeping his gaze over her hair, her lips. "I have a ship. I can take you back to Charles Towne post haste, and we can carry on as if none of this nightmare had ever occurred." He waved a hand through the air as if to dismiss the agony she had suffered over the past months.

He still loved her. He still wanted to marry her. Wasn't that what she had longed for? Wasn't that what she had endlessly cried for after he'd abandoned her? Hope's heart wrenched. She glanced at Nathaniel and back at Arthur. That Nathaniel had rejected her proved no honorable man would ever want her. If she didn't accept Arthur's proposal, she would most likely spend the rest of her days alone and unloved.

Never alone and always loved. The soft voice filtered through Hope, soothing her and lifting her spirits.

Falkland's scent of lavender crept over her, but instead of setting her senses aflame as it used to, nausea brewed within her belly. How could she ever go back to this man? Not only was he married, but his love paled in comparison to the love of God. Hope gazed into his green eyes. And she knew. She knew she no longer loved him, no longer needed him. She wondered why she ever had.

Thank You, Lord.

Hope clasped her hands before her and thrust out her chin. "But this nightmare did occur, your lordship, and you are right, I have changed. I find I no longer have a shred of affection for you. Indeed"—she could feel Nathaniel's piercing eyes upon her from across the gloomy room—"my affections lie with God, and with another."

"God, bah." Lord Falkland glared at Nathaniel. His brow crinkled. "I see." He faced her. "But what would I have expected from a woman who so freely offers her wares to any man with interest."

"How dare you!" Hope slapped his face, and his head snapped to the side. Fingering his jaw, he grinned. "I have learned much about Mr. Nathaniel Mason over this past month. I would hate to see the young merchantman's business ruined before it has begun."

Fear spiked through Hope, and she stepped back. Her bare foot landed in something almost as cool and slimy as the man before her. "What are you saying?"

"Shall I spell it out for you, my sweet one? Either you come with me willingly and remain my mistress, or I will ruin your lover. Mark my words, I will ruin his business, I will ruin his reputation, and Mr. Nathaniel Mason will end up a beggar on the streets."

Nathaniel took up another pace across the sticky floor. He crossed his arms over his chest, scratched the back of his neck, then crossed his arms again. Why did Hope give that pig Falkland an audience after what he had done to her? And the odd look on her face when she first saw Falkland. Shock. . .anger. . .love? The chaotic spin of his own emotions made it impossible to tell.

Hope had committed her life to Jesus, yet since then, she had betrayed Nathaniel's trust, thrown herself at Gavin, and now appeared to be falling back into the trap of that charlatan, Lord Falkland. And after Nathaniel had rescued her from near slavery, had given up his ship, had endured over a month of starvation, discomfort, and danger. He didn't know whether to be angry at his losses, at her betrayal, or be sorry for her quick slip away from the Lord back into her old ways.

Regardless of the pain she'd caused him, Nathaniel longed for her to remain true to her faith. *O Lord, please help her to do the right thing.*

Gavin's whistling began to chafe over Nathaniel. The man had not said a word or even looked at Nathaniel. Instead, he spent his time kicking a piece of stale bread across the floor.

Across the tavern, Lord Falkland advanced toward Hope. She backed away, and it took all of Nathaniel's resolve to stop himself from charging toward them and pummeling the man to the floor. Nathaniel peered through the shadows and craned his neck, but he could not make out Hope's expression or hear her words. Two things were sure. Lord Falkland made a heartfelt appeal, perhaps even begging for her forgiveness. And Hope was listening. Though she seemed to resist at first, now her shoulders slumped, and she sank back into her chair.

Falkland snapped his fingers, and his two men leapt to their feet and flanked Hope. Nathaniel started toward them, wondering how he and Gavin were going to take on three armed men. Turning, he gestured for Gavin to follow, but the man's attention remained riveted on the floor. "Take heed, Gavin." But still his friend ignored him. When Nathaniel faced forward, it was to an advancing Lord Falkland. Hope shuffled at his heels.

Falkland held up his hand. "Calm yourself, Mr. Mason. Your lady is unharmed. Or should I say, *my* lady." He chuckled.

Nathaniel's heated blood stormed through him.

The pompous fop halted and tapped his cane on the wooden floor, the sound as hollow as Nathaniel's heart. Behind Falkland, Hope's head remained bowed.

"What's the meaning of this?" Nathaniel asked.

"I'll make it simple for you, Mason, since you are a simple man." Falkland gave him a malicious grin. "Miss Hope and I have reconciled our differences, and she has agreed to set sail with me this evening for Charles Towne."

Nathaniel's throat went dry. His heart seemed to collapse in on itself. It couldn't be true. Not after all they'd been through. Not after her encounter with God. "Hope?" He peered around Falkland. He must hear it from her lips. "Is this true?"

Hope lifted her head, then quickly looked down again. Her eyes pooled with tears. For him? For Falkland? For her shame? Fire and thunder, he was weary of trying to figure her out.

Falkland cleared his throat and looked at her.

"'Tis true," she muttered.

Falkland brushed invisible dirt from his satin coat. "But I do wish to thank you, Mason, for keeping her safe thus far." He turned toward Gavin. "And I believe I owe you five pounds, Mr. Keese."

Gavin shuffled forward, and confusion rattled through Nathaniel.

Plucking out his money pouch, Falkland counted the amount into Gavin's outstretched hand.

"Gavin?" Nathaniel's voice came out like sludge from the bilge.

"I'm sorry, Nathaniel." Gavin pocketed the coins, their clank piercing Nathaniel like arrows.

Hope gasped, and a sob escaped her lips.

Falkland's brows shot up. "Oh, of course—you didn't know. Mr. Keese is the first mate aboard my ship. After you purchased Miss Hope, I offered him five pounds to follow her, both to ensure her safety and keep her from, shall we say, any liaisons." He shot a quick glance at Hope, then leaned toward Nathaniel with a grin. "I know how enchanting she can be, and I wouldn't want her sullied before she was returned to me."

Hope's shoulders fell beneath Falkland's insinuations.

Nathaniel shook his head, the fangs of yet another betrayal sinking deep into his gut. "You work for him?"

Gavin gave a half smile. "You know me, Nathaniel. I love an adventure, especially one that pays. How could I resist?" He lowered his gaze, but not before Nathaniel thought he saw a spark of remorse.

"Enough of this frivolity." Falkland tapped his cane as if that put an end to things. "I shall bid you adieu, Mr. Mason." He nodded toward Nathaniel, then faced Gavin. "Are you coming?"

In a flourish of satin and lace, Falkland swerved about, grabbed Hope's arm, and escorted her from the tavern, his men and Gavin following on their heels.

Nathaniel stumbled backward into his chair. Hope did not spare him a backward glance.

CHAPTER 35

The rising sun cast glittering lights of gold and white onto the sleepy waves of Kingstown Bay, caressing them to life around Nathaniel's ship. He wished it were so easy to breathe life back into his own body. For he felt as dead as if a cannonball had blasted through his chest. All that remained was to toss his carcass into a watery grave.

Ships of all shapes and sizes rocked in the bay. Beyond their bare masts, the mountains of Jamaica rose in a glistening mound of green that normally inspired Nathaniel with the beauty of God's creation. But this day, he found no pleasure in the sight.

Activity in the port drew his gaze to the slaves and dock workers scrambling across Harbor Street, crates and barrels hoisted on their heads and shoulders as the rising heat of the day shoved aside the shroud of slumber—that sweet repose of the night that had eluded Nathaniel yet again.

Lord, what is wrong with me? He should be happy to be rid of Miss Hope. She had brought him naught but hardship and heartache. He had been spared not only the trouble of escorting her to Charles Towne, but also the vexation of her company. Then why did the vision of her walking out of the tavern and out of his life make his heart feel as though it had been ripped from his chest?

He paced across the floor, his boots thumping over the wooden planks. At least he had connected with his first mate and was once again aboard his ship, the *Illusive Hope*. He gave a sorrowful chuckle. He had named the ship after Miss Hope, a condition he intended to rectify as soon as he returned to Charles Towne. For once again, she had proved to be as illusive as ever, not only to him, but to God as well. Perhaps she'd had no real encounter with the Almighty, after all. Perhaps it had all been an act to win Nathaniel's affections. But why then did she run into Gavin's arms after she had procured it? Nathaniel would never understand women. Especially those like Miss Hope—those like his mother.

He sank into the chair behind his desk. *Lord, take this pain from me. I fear I cannot bear it.*

Taking in a deep breath, he allowed the familiar smells of his ship—tar, wood, and oakum—to ease through him. He glanced over his desk: charts, books, a quill pen, his hourglass, logbook, and quadrant spread haphazardly across the wooden slab. He let out a final sigh, expelling his sorrow, and stood. He had one ship left and one being built in the dockyard at Charles Towne. He had pocketed some coin from the cargo his first mate had sold in Kingstown. Now he would put Miss Hope and the past few months out of his mind and continue with his plans to build a merchant fleet, a fortune, and a name.

"I want you to preach. I want you to lead others to Me." The gentle words pierced his heart.

Nathaniel bowed his head. *I cannot, Lord.*

Yes, Nathaniel's preaching may have influenced a few pirates. But not the most important person. *I failed You. She is back with the enemy. Do not ask this of me.*

A knock on the door jolted Nathaniel from his thoughts. "Enter."

Mr. Timmons, his steward, appeared in the doorway, his face twisted in confusion. "A note for you, sir." He approached and held out a piece of paper. "And a child arrived with it."

"A child?" Nathaniel grabbed the note and tore off the wax seal:

Mr. Mason,

I deeply regret the course of my present actions, but I find I have no other recourse. As you must imagine, I am a man of enormous responsibilities and cannot possibly care properly for a child. I am rarely home and would be constantly afflicted by guilt should I assign Elise to the care of a governess who would possess no real affection for the girl. Hence, I am handing her over to Miss Hope.

Having seen the attachment formed between Miss Hope and Elise, and Miss Hope's reluctance to bid farewell to my daughter, I believe this is the right course of action. I trust Miss Hope will be pleased with the arrangements and both she and Elise will be better off for it. It is the kindness of my heart which prompts me to this action.

Truth be told, I am unsure whether I am the girl's father.

Your humble servant,

Mr. William Hendrick

Humble indeed. Nathaniel dropped the letter, allowing it to flutter to his desk, and stormed from the room, shoving past Timmons. "Is he still here?"

"Who, sir?" Timmons's footsteps pounded after him.

"The man who left this note."

"Nay, sir. He handed me the letter and the girl and shoved off before I could speak a word."

Nathaniel leapt onto the deck, spotted Elise trembling beside Haines, one of his sailors, then dashed to the railing and scanned the bay. A small boat manned by two rowers made its way toward the dock. A third man sat in the midst of her, but even at a distance, Nathaniel could tell it was not Mr. Hendrick.

Timmons halted beside Nathaniel. "He did say to tell ye Mr. Hendrick had already left the island. Last night, he said."

"Fire and thunder!" Nathaniel swerved about. Elise's wide blue eyes stared up at him, her tiny face contorted in fright. "Where is your wife, Mr. Timmons?"

"In the galley, Cap'n."

"Please ask her to come on deck." Nathaniel raked a hand through his hair and knelt beside Elise. He dismissed Haines and took a deep breath, trying to calm his fury. "You remember me, Miss Elise?"

She nodded, sending her red curls shimmering like rubies in the rising sun. Her bottom lip quivered. Nathaniel clenched his fists. What sort of man abandoned his daughter? And in the pretense of being kind—of doing the right thing.

"Where is Miss Hope?" she squeaked.

He took her hand in his. "She is not here."

Her blue eyes swam with tears that spilled through her dark fringe of lashes, and Nathaniel's gut coiled into a knot. He knew how she felt. Pushing aside his anguish, he forced a smile.

"But I am here. And I'm going to take good care of you."

"Where is my father?" Elise whimpered, the quiver in her lip radiating throughout her body.

"Your father had to go on a trip. But you'll be safe here with me."

"Father always goes away." Her face took on a haunted look.

Nathaniel gripped her shoulders, not knowing what to say to bring her comfort.

Mrs. Timmons emerged from below deck, a portly woman in her forties. She huffed from the exertion of climbing the companionway stairs, but when her eyes landed on Miss Elise, she rushed to her side. "What 'ave we 'ere?" She stooped and gave Elise such a huge smile that the fear from only a moment ago faded from the little girl's face.

Nathaniel stood. "Mrs. Timmons. It seems we have a special guest on board, Miss Elise Hendrick. Would you be so kind as to escort her to your chambers and look after her? Make her as comfortable as a princess."

Elise's eyes swept to his, sparkling even amidst the tears.

"I would at that." Mrs. Timmons opened her arms, and without hesitation, Elise flew into them. "Oh, you poor dear. Nothin' to be afraid of." She patted her back and looked up at Nathaniel. "What o' me duties, Cap'n?"

"I'll have Mills take over the galley."

Grumbles flung his way from all around, no doubt due to Mills's lack of culinary skills.

"A boat approaches, Cap'n." A shout from the foredeck brought Nathaniel's attention to the harbor, where a small craft manned by one person made its way toward them. Now what? He faced Mrs. Timmons and Elise.

"Thank you, Mrs. Timmons."

With effort, the woman rose. Elise's arms clung to her neck like barnacles to a ship's keel. "Come now, little one." She headed toward the ladder, and Elise waved at Nathaniel over her shoulder. He smiled. What in heaven's name was he going to do with a little girl? He couldn't give her to Hope, who most likely was already cavorting about the Caribbean with Falkland.

Nathaniel faced the incoming vessel. "Mr. Ackon, spyglass, if you please."

Richard Ackon leapt down the foredeck ladder and thrust the telescope into Nathaniel's hand. Raising it, he surveyed the approaching craft. Fury knotted in his back when Gavin Keese came into view. "Man the swivel!"

Ackon looked dazed. "Cap'n?"

"You heard me. The swivel gun." Nathaniel lowered the glass and slapped it across his palm.

"Are we to shoot an unarmed man?" His first mate's voice heightened.

Nathaniel would like nothing better. "You are mistaken, Ackon. This man comes with all guns loaded. Trouble is, he hides his weapons well." Nathaniel had been so distraught over Hope, he hadn't taken time to ponder Gavin's betrayal. Naught but one of Falkland's minions. Memories surged into eruptions of rage as he remembered all the times Gavin had indeed come between Hope and Nathaniel. And all the while, pretending to be Nathaniel's friend.

"Gregson, Matten, load the swivel," Ackon bellowed.

"Aye, sir." Two men scrambled to the gun mounted amidships on the railing and began loading it as Gavin continued to row toward them.

"Ready, Cap'n," Matten announced.

"Fire on my command." Nathaniel squeezed his eyes shut for a moment. "But do not hit him."

"Do *not* hit him, Cap'n?" Gregson scratched his head, and a wave of disappointment soured his features.

"That's what I said." Nathaniel glanced back at Gavin. "Fire!"

The men lit the fuse, and the swivel exploded in a thunderous boom. The ball splashed inches from Gavin's boat, dousing him with a spray of seawater. An obscenity drifted to them on the wind, but he continued rowing, more energetically than ever.

Nathaniel coughed and batted away the acrid smoke. "Load another shot." The men worked furiously to remove the breech, swab the barrel, and load another round, but before too long, Gavin had brought his craft within earshot of the ship and too close to be fired upon.

"Sink me, Nathaniel, what are you trying to do?" Gavin's indignant voice rose from the small boat.

Nathaniel leaned over the railing. "Precisely," he shouted. "Now take your leave, or I *will* sink you, Mr. Keese."

"I must speak to you." Gavin sent up a look of humble appeal.

"I've heard all I care to hear from you." Nathaniel growled. "Now be gone with you."

The boat thudded against the hull. "Permission to board, Captain?"

"Nay." Nathaniel turned toward Ackon, whose brows wrinkled. "Shoot him if he tries to board," Nathaniel shouted, ensuring Gavin was duly warned.

"Egad, man, I have information you must know."

Nathaniel rubbed his left side and paced before the bulwark. Perhaps he should hear the man out. Perhaps he had news of Hope. Perhaps she was hurt. He leaned over the side, battling the rage churning inside him at the sight of the charlatan whom he had once called friend. A twinge of guilt pricked his soul. He was supposed to love his enemies, not hate them.

"Come up," he shouted, then stood back as Gavin climbed the ropes and leapt with ease over the railing, the usual cavalier smirk missing from his boyish face. Freshly shaven and clad in a white shirt and dark breeches, leather boots, and a black cravat, he no longer looked the part of the madcap he so often played.

Nathaniel planted his fists on his waist. "Out with it."

"In private." Gavin raised his brows and glanced around at Nathaniel's crew, who closed in on the newcomer, no doubt expecting an altercation.

Nathaniel gestured to the foredeck, and then he followed Gavin up the ladder and to the bow, dismissing the few sailors who loitered about.

Eyeing his one-time friend, Nathaniel tried to quell the fury gripping every muscle, the urge to pummel the man into dust. He would hear him out first.

Gavin shifted his boots over the deck, then met Nathaniel's gaze. "Nice ship. You built it?"

Nathaniel nodded.

"Nathaniel. I deceived you. I don't blame you for trying to blast me out of the water." He chuckled, but the smile slipped from his face beneath Nathaniel's glare.

"I trusted you. I called you my friend." Nathaniel grimaced.

Gavin swallowed. "I didn't know you. I didn't know Hope when I agreed to do the deed." He shrugged. "It sounded like an amusing diversion. I meant you no harm."

"What is it you want, Gavin? I'm a busy man."

"I gave Falkland his money back. I'm no longer his first mate."

"Why did you do that?"

"It wasn't right. What I did." Gavin ran a hand over the back of his neck and gazed out upon the bay. "You changed me."

"Me?" Nathaniel narrowed his eyes. What was the man up to now? Was this another trick of Falkland's?

"Aye. You are so honorable, so good—even to those who do you harm. You always do the right thing." Gavin huffed as if he found the qualities frustrating.

"Not always." Nathaniel thought of his obsession with Hope. It had never been the right thing to pursue her.

Seagulls flapped overhead, squawking.

"Despite every effort to the contrary, I found my respect growing for you daily." Gavin jerked his hair behind him and leveled a sincere gaze upon Nathaniel. "My friendship was real."

"Friends don't lie to each other." Nathaniel looked away. The sound of water purling against the hull did naught to ease the acid fermenting in his stomach.

"I know." Gavin gripped a halyard and shook his head. "Then the miracle of Hope's healing. All this talk of God, and Captain Poole." Gavin's laughter came out a bitter chord. "Do you know I always wanted to be a pirate?" He grinned. "And then this notorious pirate advises me against it. Not only that, he pours his affections upon Abigail. Sink me, a woman of God?" Gavin snorted. "I could not understand it. You represent everything I loathed: rules, integrity, honor, religion, piety. Everything I avoided my whole life. But I found I admired them. Egad, I actually admired them."

Nathaniel studied Gavin, searching for a breach in his guileless soliloquy, wondering what purpose this confession would serve.

"I now know these things make a man strong, make him good. They give a man a higher purpose than serving himself. And after Falkland gave me the money and I went back to his ship, I realized I no longer want to live without them."

Nathaniel looked up, half expecting a storm cloud to form and lightning to strike Gavin for such blatant lies. Only the crisp blue sky stared back at him, dotted with the usual billowing clouds.

Gavin scratched the whiskers lining his jaw. "I don't expect you to believe me. But after I came to know you. . .and Miss Hope, I—"

"You did your job well coming between us." Nathaniel rubbed sweat from his forehead and marched toward the railing. "Of course, Miss Hope gives her affections so freely, the task could not have been too difficult or unpleasant."

Gavin approached Nathaniel. "That is another matter I have come to clear up. I lied to you regarding Miss Hope."

"What is one lie among so many?"

"Nay, you misunderstand. She never gave herself to me."

"What are you saying?" Nathaniel's gaze snapped to his. Despite his suspicion of everything Gavin said, a spark of hope lit within him.

"I lured her on deck under the pretense Miss Elise was in need of her. I knew you would see us." Gavin stared at the deck by his boots.

"So you didn't?" Nathaniel clutched his arm. "She didn't?"

"Nay." Gavin shook his head and grinned. "Not that I didn't try. Truth be told, in all my pretending, and despite my promise to Falkland, I became quite enamored with her. But when I declared my love and tried to seduce her, she spurned me. Gave me some balderdash about loving you and never giving herself to a man who wasn't her husband."

Releasing Gavin, Nathaniel gripped the railing and glanced over the bay, though he saw naught but a blur of blues, greens, and browns. He faced Gavin. "So you never?"

"Sink me, man, are you daft? That is what I'm trying to tell you. Her affections have always been for you and you alone."

Hope hadn't betrayed Nathaniel. Agony tumbled through him. He'd treated her so horribly on the ship, rejected her so cruelly. His throat burned, and he clamped his fingers on the wood until they ached. But she had betrayed God. "What does it matter? She chose Falkland."

"Is that what you think?" Gavin chuckled. "Then you are not only daft but mad as well." He gave Nathaniel an accusatory look. "I don't know what spell Falkland may have cast on Hope, but from the way she was behaving on his ship, I don't think she was at all pleased to be there."

Nathaniel's mind spun, trying to grasp Gavin's words. He stepped back. "In what manner was she behaving?"

"Miserable, heartsick, more like a prisoner than a lover."

Miserable? But why? Nathaniel could think of no explanation other than that Hope had gone with Falkland unwillingly. But why would she do such a thing?

"Did you hear me?" Gavin asked.

"Aye, and I cannot believe it."

"You are quite a pair." Gavin chuckled. "Neither one of you believes the other's love when it's plain as a white sail against a dark sky to the rest of us."

"Which one is Falkland's ship?" Nathaniel stormed across the deck.

"He set sail last night."

Nathaniel spun on his heels. "For where?"

"Charles Towne."

"Lay aloft, yardman. Lay out and loose the sails!" Nathaniel barked to his crew. "I must speak to her," he shot over his shoulder toward Gavin.

Gavin's boots pounded behind him. "His ship is well armed. Twelve guns, not counting his swivels. You have only two." He caught Nathaniel's shoulder. "I doubt Falkland will grant you an audience with her. He will fight you. And you will lose."

Nathaniel faced Gavin. "I cannot let her go without knowing her reason." He scanned the bay. "Where can I get a well-armed ship?"

"Why not the *Enchantress?*" Gavin grinned.

"Captain Poole sailed yesterday. I watched him leave."

"Aye, but I have it on good authority he's anchored around the bend in a hidden cove." Gavin lifted a brow.

Even if they found Poole, Nathaniel wondered if he'd be able to convince the self-serving pirate to help him find Hope. But what choice did he have?

"Then let's pay him a visit, shall we?"

CHAPTER 36

"Ah, and to what do I owe the pleasure of yer company this fine evening?" Captain Poole failed to rise from his seat behind a desk that looked more like driftwood than a piece of furniture. Leaning back in his chair, he crossed his booted feet atop the wooden slab that was home to sundry charts and maps, a set of brass flintlock pistols, a near-empty bottle of rum, two flickering candles, and, oddly, a fiddle.

The pirate who had escorted Gavin and Nathaniel below waved them inside, showering them with the rancid odor of his unwashed body.

"Miss me so soon, Mr. Mason?" Captain Poole took a bite out of an apple.

"We have a business proposition, Captain." Nathaniel glanced over the cabin, a room he'd not been permitted to enter on his last voyage aboard the *Enchantress*. Besides the desk and the chair on which Captain Poole sat, two high-backed leather chairs littered the center of the room. An open chest filled with weapons gleamed as brightly as the row of trophy swords lining the wall, and a cannon stood guard at the foot of a bed on the starboard side.

Captain Poole grunted. "Well, I hope 'tis a better proposition than the last one. What did I get for me trouble escortin' ye to Kingstown? Naught but one of His Majesty's ships sharp on me tail."

"Major Paine," Gavin uttered beneath his breath and plopped down into one of the chairs.

"Yet I see you have managed to evade them," Nathaniel said.

"Would ye expect any less?" The pirate grinned. "I'm Captain Poole, after all." He took another bite of his apple and tossed it across the room. It landed in a barrel with a precision that defied the rum-induced glaze across his eyes. "But how did *ye* find me?"

Nathaniel crossed his arms over his chest and replied in a waggish tone, "I'm Captain Mason, after all."

A faint smirk took residence on the captain's mouth, followed by a deep chuckle. Slamming his boots down onto the deck, he stood, grabbed the bottle of rum, and took a swig.

"Well, out with it. What be yer business?"

"I need your ship."

A shower of rum sprayed from the captain's lips, and Nathaniel jumped back to avoid getting wet. The pungent scent of alcohol stung his nose.

"And how d'ye propose to take it from me?" A sharp challenge skipped across Poole's dark eyes.

"I don't propose to take it at all, Captain." Nathaniel rubbed his chin, praying the rum would put the captain in a fair mood instead of a more belligerent one, as it did most men. "I am no pirate. I simply wish to borrow it, along with you and your crew."

"Borrow, ye say." Captain Poole cocked his head. "And what be yer purpose?"

"To find Miss Hope." Nathaniel clenched his jaw. *Lord, please soften this pirate's heart. Please make him agree.*

"Miss Hope?" Captain Poole circled the desk. "The fair mistress with the hair of gold? Yer wife?"

Nathaniel swallowed. Amidst all the stress, he'd forgotten their ruse. "I must beg your forgiveness. She is not my wife."

"A truer word ain't ne'er been spoke." Captain Poole chortled. "D'ye take me fer a fool, Mr. Mason? I knew it all along." He fingered the pistol on his desk, and Nathaniel wondered if he intended to shoot him for his deception. But then Captain Poole's gaze drifted to the thick darkness outside the stern window, and for a moment, he seemed to get lost in it. "And why does yer fair lass need findin'?"

"She may have been taken against her will." The sound of the words ignited an urgency within Nathaniel.

"By Lord Falkland," Gavin said. "They are headed for Charles Towne."

"A lord, eh?" Captain Poole spit to the side, his dark eyes shifting between them. "But ye've got a ship, don't ye, Mason?"

Gavin stood. "Lord Falkland's ship is heavily armed."

Captain Poole eyed Nathaniel. "And yers isn't, I take it."

Nathaniel shook his head.

"Heavily armed, ye say." The pirate scratched the stubble on his chin. "Which means he's got somethin' worth stealin' aboard."

"That he does," Gavin said. "A belly full of goods he intends to sell at Charles Towne."

At the mention of the wealth, Poole's face lit up.

Nathaniel shifted his stance and fisted his hands at his sides. "Don't start salivating over the treasure. If you agree to our plan, you cannot plunder his ship."

Captain Poole jerked back as if Nathaniel had hit him. "Of course I can. I've done it many a time before."

"I have no doubt." Nathaniel sighed. "What I meant to say was that I cannot allow you to steal anything nor to take the ship as prize." Though Nathaniel would do almost anything to speak with Hope, he would not break God's law.

"Cannot allow?" Captain Poole's brow furrowed into a jumble of lines as if no one ever dared tell him such a thing. "Are ye tired of yer life? If ye dare to hire a pirate, ye cannot expect him *not* to pirate."

Nathaniel glanced at Gavin, who shrugged his agreement with Poole. Untying the pouch at his side, Nathaniel tossed it to the captain, who caught it in midair. "Here is your pay for the deed, Captain. But I cannot in good conscience be a part of thievery."

"Ah, there's yer problem." Captain Poole gave a mischievous grin. "Ye must rid yerself of that good conscience."

"By God's good grace, that will never happen."

"Hummph." The captain eyed Nathaniel with disdain then opened the pouch and poured the coins onto his desk. Clinks and clanks echoed through the cabin as the glittering pile grew into a gold and silver mound. "So allow me to get a clear understandin'." Tossing the empty pouch down, Poole clasped his hands behind his back, the silver trim on his velvet coat glimmering in the candlelight. "Ye want me to attack this Lord Falkland's ship, but I can't sink 'er, can't pillage 'er, can't steal 'er, and all I'll be gettin' is this measly bag of coin?"

"That is the way of it, yes, Captain." Nathaniel tried to keep his voice calm and his tone commanding, all the while praying for God's grace to change this pirate's heart.

Grabbing the rum bottle, Captain Poole took another gulp and wiped his mouth on his sleeve. "I've got to hand it to ye, Mason. Ye've got pluck." He chuckled. "The pluck o' a pirate, to be sure."

"The money is all I have, Captain. But it's yours if you'll help me."

"Not all ye have." His dark eyes glinted greed.

Nathaniel shook his head. Had the rum gone to the man's head? What else could he mean?

Captain Poole's brows lifted. "I believe ye own a ship?"

⋯

Hope paced across the captain's cabin, wringing her hands. Soon Falkland would join her, as he always did this time of the evening. So far, he'd been a gentleman, but behind his docile facade, impatience simmered in his eyes. He was not a man accustomed to rejection, and she'd seen him unleash his cruel temper many a time on those who dared to cross him.

Three miserable days had passed. Although she'd been treated like nobility, given the run of the ship, and fed like a queen, Hope much preferred to be locked in the hold than to face Lord Falkland's constant advances. Her thoughts drifted to Nathaniel, as they always did, and she wondered how he fared. Was he on his way back to Charles Towne? Did he think of her, and if he did, were his thoughts consumed with only his poor opinion of her character? But how could she blame him? He believed she'd betrayed him with Gavin, and now he must believe she had rushed back to her old ways. No doubt he was glad to be rid of her.

Shoving memories of Nathaniel aside, Hope approached the bulkhead and swerved to cross the cabin again, tripping on the plush Turkish carpet at its center. Lord Falkland liked to surround himself with beauty, even in his ship's cabin, from the intricately carved mahogany desk, to the velvet upholstered Queen Anne chairs, to the twinkling brass lanterns and the tapestries depicting scenes from the English countryside that decorated the walls, to the imposing oak bed in the corner, complete with silk coverlet. Hope shivered at the sight of it. Perhaps she was just another one of his trophies—another thing of beauty to add to his collection.

And like all his precious possessions, he enjoyed putting her on display, all the while keeping her close and guarded.

But Hope didn't need Lord Falkland any longer. She didn't need his wealth. She didn't need his title, and she didn't need his attentions to make her feel valued and loved. That empty yearning within her had been filled to the full by the love of God.

The ship creaked as it rose over a swell, and Hope braced her feet on the deck and glanced out the stern windows. The sun dipped below the horizon, absconding with the light of day and pulling a dark blanket over the sky. She rubbed her arms against a sudden quiver. Everything seemed worse at night, more threatening, more frightening. As if God took all the light and all that was good in the world and retired with it to His chamber for the evening.

"*I am here, beloved.*"

Hope's eyes burned at the soft inner voice, and she glanced over the cabin. "Thank You, Father. For I fear I will need Your strength tonight." She doubted she could put off Lord Falkland one more night. What would he do when she rejected him again? Would he force himself on her? Would he lock her below? Cast her into the sea? Or perhaps sail to St. Kitts and complete the task of selling her to one of the island's grotesque planters.

But this time, who would be there to rescue her?

She tugged a lock of her hair and hurried her pace as fear stole her breath. *O God, please help me.*

The thick oak door creaked open, and in swaggered Lord Falkland as if he were entering a levee with the king. "Ah, my sweet one." He smiled, but beneath the smile, frustration stewed. He shut the door with an ominous thud. After laying his cane atop his desk, he doffed his tricorn and shrugged out of his coat, draping it over a chair. Then, straightening the lace at his cuffs, he approached her. Hope swallowed.

"You look lovely tonight." He perused her, his eyes burning with desire.

"You provided the gown, Arthur." Hope swished away before he saw the fear in her eyes. "Your wife's perhaps?" She faced him, willing to do anything to deter him, even anger him if necessary.

"Nay, love. My wife could never"—his licentious gaze swept over her again—"shall we say, fill a gown quite like you do."

Hope's stomach sickened under his salacious perusal. Why had she ever been attracted to this man?

He laid a finger on his chin and approached her. "But come, come, are you to be cross with me forever?"

She stepped back. "You have a wife, Arthur. It is no little thing."

"Hmm." He loosened his cravat and tugged it from his neck. "But it is, sweet one. Or she is, I should say."

Hope gasped in disgust. "How can you be so cruel?"

"There's naught I can do about her ailment." He shrugged. "And 'twas not a marriage based on love." He slid his fingers over his cravat and snapped it tight between his hands as if he intended to choke her with it. "But do not speak of her. It puts me in such a bad humor." He yanked her close and kissed her cheek. "I have missed you, Hope," he whispered into her ear.

The nauseating stench of lavender and tobacco swirled around her, and Hope tore from his grasp and walked away. *Lord, what do I do?* She had to stay with Falkland, or he would ruin Nathaniel. Yet even if the thought did not repulse her, she could not give herself to him and be true to God.

His boots thudded over the deck, and Hope spun around to see him opening his desk drawer. He pulled out a bottle of port and poured himself a glass. Taking a sip, he glared her way.

"Why did you marry her?" Hope thrust her nose into the air in a pretense of composure.

"For her wealth, what else?" His eyes glinted in the lantern light. "Not that it impressed the grand Earl of Wrexham." Arthur gulped down the rest of the port in his glass and poured himself another. He skirted the desk, bottle in hand.

"Who is the Earl of Wrexham?" Hope tried to divert the conversation to anything besides herself.

"My father." He took a sip and sank into one of the Queen Anne chairs.

By the sullen look on his face, Hope surmised this new subject would cause him to become either extremely morose or extremely angry. Either emotion might save her for one more night. "Did he not approve of the match?"

"Approve? Humph." Arthur grunted. "I doubt the man knows the meaning of the word, save when it came to my brother, Gifford."

"I didn't know you had a brother." Clutching her skirts, Hope moved to the chair farthest from Arthur and sat down.

"Yes, the grand Viscount of Buckley." He lifted his glass into the air in a feigned toast.

"So he is your older brother?" Hope gave him a skeptical look, for only the eldest son assumed a title, and Arthur called himself *lord*. No matter. If Hope could keep him talking—and drinking—perhaps he would eventually pass out.

"Older, and apparently much wiser." Arthur downed his glass and poured another. "Much better at every task he undertook, if you ask my father." He slouched back into the chair and seemed more like a little boy than a man.

"Was it my fault I was always sick as a child?" He tone grew caustic and threaded with pain. "How could I keep up with strong, robust Gifford—a head taller and a pound wiser? Whatever I did, it was never good enough." He stared off into the room, a dull haze covering his eyes, and snickered. "*I* was never good enough."

Hope eyed the man she'd once loved and suddenly felt sorry for him. Falling short of a father's approval was something with which she was quite familiar. "I'm sorry."

"I don't want your pity!" He sprang to his feet and thrust the half-empty bottle toward her.

Hope shrank back, her heart thumping wildly.

He slammed the bottle onto the desk and snapped his remaining drink to the back of his throat. "I need no one's pity. For I have made a success of myself without anyone's help. I possess more wealth and land than my brother ever will. That is why I give myself the title lord, due my brother only by birth." Setting down the glass, he turned and leaned back on the desk. "'For he that is least among you all, the same shall be great.'"

She cringed at his distortion of the scriptures.

Rising, he stumbled toward Hope, tearing at the buttons on his shirt. "Enough of this talk. You are mine, and I will have you. It will be just as sweet as before."

Hope slowly stood and sucked in her breath. Her fingers went numb. Retreating, she held her hand up. "It can never be that way again, Arthur."

"What do you mean? Of course it can." He pulled his shirt over his head and laid it on the chair.

He clutched her arms. Pain spiked into her shoulders. "I know you love me. Tell me you love me." He shook her. The smell of alcohol stung her nose.

"I did love you, Arthur. But I cannot give you that kind of love anymore." She gazed into his green eyes, rife with anger, confusion, and pain. He could still harm Nathaniel. He *would* still harm Nathaniel. "I cannot be yours until we are married." She blurted out her agreement to marry him, though it made her heart crumble to pieces. But it was the only way to keep Nathaniel safe.

Arthur nudged her toward the bed and shoved her down upon it. "Balderdash. You had no compunction about giving yourself to me before." He stood, hands on his waist, and studied her.

Hope's skin grew clammy, and her hands trembled. Surely he wouldn't force himself upon her. "You don't love me, Arthur. Don't you see? I'm simply a prize in your battle for supremacy over your brother. A trophy to display before your father."

Arthur's eyes glinted steel. "You *have* changed."

"Yes, I have." She was no longer the desperate, wanton girl who tossed her affections like garbage to ravenous dogs. She was a precious child of the King. Cleansed, purified, made holy. A burst of joy flooded her, despite her dire circumstances. For no one could take that away from her. Not even Lord Falkland.

She gave Arthur a determined look. "I have changed for the better."

"I shall be the judge of that." He snorted. Then he released a heavy sigh and brushed his fingers over her cheek.

Taking his hand, she pressed it between hers. "Arthur, I have found God. Or should I say, He found me. He exists. He loves me. He loves you. There is a better way to live." *O Lord, please help him to see.*

He snatched his hand from hers as if she'd stabbed it. His face contorted like a mass of tangled rope. "Scads, I knew I shouldn't have allowed you to spend time with Mr. Mason. A reverend's son, isn't he? He has poisoned you with that pious rubbish."

"'Tis not poison. 'Tis truth, and life."

Falkland took a step back, disgust simmering in his gaze. Then his eyes widened and his jaw drew into a taut line. "You gave yourself to that carpenter, Mason. He's sullied you." He wrinkled his nose.

"I did not." Hope's voice emerged in strangled tones, boiling with temper. She grew tired of being accused of things she had not done.

"And Mr. Keese, too, I am sure. That's what all this talk of God is about—a diversion, an excuse." He narrowed his eyes. "You forget, my sweet one, I know you too well. You, religious? Absurd! The truth of it is you no longer want me." A flicker of pain crossed his eyes, and he turned away, stumbled across the carpet, and grabbed the back of a chair.

"I assure you, I did not—"

"Mr. Keese gave me my money back." Grabbing his shirt, Arthur swerved around, tossing it over his head. "No doubt he'd already been well paid for his services." He gave a huff of disdain.

"How dare you." Hope jumped to her feet, resisting the urge to charge toward him and slap his face. It would do no good. In his condition, he'd probably slap her back.

He clicked his tongue. "I'll hear no more talk of God. Or of marriage. You've ruined my mood for tonight." He clutched his coat and flung it over his shoulder then faced her, a wicked grin twisting his lips. "But mark my words, you will be mine tomorrow. And if you resist, I promise you, I *will* ruin your precious Mr. Mason."

Hope dropped back onto the bed, her heart plummeting.

"You haven't changed." Arthur grabbed his cane and the bottle of port and marched toward the door. Opening it, he gave her a scorching look. "God or no God, you're a trollop, and you'll always be a trollop." Storming out, he slammed the door. The resounding finality of the *boom* shook the foundations of Hope's newfound faith.

CHAPTER 37

Boom! The blast jarred Hope awake, and she shot up in bed. Rubbing her eyes, she glanced across the room, the details of Falkland's cabin forming in her hazy vision. The pounding of boots sounded above her, adding to the wild thumping of her heart. Was it thunder she heard? Were they in the midst of a storm? Though the rays of sunshine filtering in through the stern window defied her assumption, she flung off the coverlet and dashed toward the salt-streaked panes. The bright orb of the sun hung above the horizon in the east. White, puffy clouds dotted an otherwise clear azure sky. No storm. At least not the natural kind.

Boot steps pounded louder, and Falkland's nasal shouts echoed across the ship. Though Hope couldn't make out what he said, she could tell from the urgency in his tone something frightening was upon them. She scanned the horizon, just catching the stern of a ship passing beyond the window on the right.

A ship!

Without concern whether it be friend or foe, Hope donned her gown, slipped on her shoes, and dashed into the dark hallway. Whoever it was, perhaps they offered a reprieve from the torment of Falkland's confinement. Weaving around sailors rushing past her, she grabbed one by the arm. "What is happening?"

"Pirates." His eyes bulged, his face twisting in fear. Yanking from her grasp, he darted away.

Hope's breath quickened as a chill coiled up her back. Pirates. *Lord, Your salvation does indeed come in odd forms.* Bumbling through the crowded companionway, she leapt up the ladder and emerged onto deck. A mad scene of fury and frenzy met her gaze as men dashed to and fro, some arming themselves, some climbing the ratlines, others tugging upon ropes

624

and halyards. The acrid scent of gunpowder, sweat, and fear assailed her.

"Run out the guns. Man the swivels." Falkland's shrill voice, rippling with terror, crashed over her as he jumped onto the main deck from the quarterdeck. His harried gaze locked onto something off their larboard side, and Hope slunk against the rise of the quarterdeck and glanced aloft.

Her heart stopped. She tossed a hand to her throat to loosen the lump that had formed there.

The *Enchantress*, her creamy sails bursting with wind, foam bubbling against her hull and crashing over her bow, and the black flag of Captain Poole flapping from the mainmast. Hope squinted, trying to make out the men who stood atop her foredeck, but only Captain Poole came into focus, his black velvet coat clapping in the wind, his dark hair flailing about his face in abandon. Had he come for her? But she'd made no connection with the capricious pirate. Perhaps this was simply a routine raid, an event of happenstance, and she another of his unfortunate victims. Nevertheless, she could not help the joy that surged through her, for she would take salvation in whatever form it came.

Oh Lord, make his attack swift and sure and allow no deaths this day.

"Hope, go below!" She turned to see Falkland's eyes glinting with anger and his face mottled red. "Go below. I cannot be bothered with you now." Before she could respond, he spun around and bellowed further orders to his crew.

"She's coming around again, Captain," a sailor cried from the crosstrees.

"Blast!" Falkland loosed a string of curses that stung Hope's ears. Sinking into the shadows beneath the quarterdeck, she prayed he would take no more note of her, for she had no intention of leaving. Whether she lived or died was in God's hands, and if her future held naught but the company of Falkland, then she preferred the latter.

The *Enchantress* veered to larboard, showing her rudder, and opened fire with the stern chasers. Hope ducked beneath the pelting shots as the air quivered with the roar of guns. Profanities marred the silence that followed. Hope rose and gazed upward to the slivered remains of the *Victory*'s main and mizzen topsails.

Cursing, Falkland stormed across the deck, pounding his cane against the hard oak as he went. He studied the pirates, his chest heaving beneath his satin waistcoat. The *Enchantress* swung fully about and shouldered the sea high and wide as she brought her starboard guns to bear.

"Fire on my command!" Falkland, stripped to his waistcoat, barked, his voice a dissonance of fear and rage. His white shirt edged with lace dangled atop his breeches. Strands of tawny hair had loosened from his tie and tumbled over his face and shoulders. Rage flashed in his eyes and poured from his mouth in nonsensical mutterings.

The *Enchantress* bore down upon them, lowering sail as she went.

"Fire!" Falkland shouted, and Hope plugged her ears as thunderous booms exploded one after the other, causing the ship to tremble and sending Hope's heart into her chest. Black plumes shot into the air, then dissipated over them. Hope threw a hand to her nose. Coughing, eyes stinging, she batted the vapors away and squinted toward the *Enchantress*, slowing on her tack and sailing by them with no apparent damage.

"Did we hit her?" Falkland leapt onto the bulwarks, his voice spiked with urgency.

"Nay, Captain." A tall man beside Falkland spat with disgust. "Not a scratch. She's out of our range."

Falkland swore, gripped the hilt of his sword, then faced the foredeck. "Back astern and bring our other broadside to bear, Mr. Deems. Lay me athwart her stern. Load the starboard guns!" he bellowed, then lowered his hardened gaze to the deck. "We'll come in closer," he said to no one in particular. "Closer, yes. Then I'll blast her from the sea."

But before the crew could respond, an ominous *boom* split the air. Hope snapped her gaze to the *Enchantress*. A spike of gray smoke darted from the hull.

"Hit the deck!" Falkland commanded as a metallic *zing* and *zip* rang through the air above them. An earsplitting *boom* thundered. A shudder ran through the ship. Eerie silence ensued. Hope opened her eyes to see the crew slowing rising from the deck.

Crack. Snap. The sound of splitting wood grated over her ears, followed by the shouts and screams of the men. "The mainmast! Clear away!"

Falkland stumbled back, falling to the deck, his eyes as wide as doubloons. Hope backed against the bulkhead and winced. The giant mast toppled, showering a web of lines, spars, and billowing sails upon the men. The ship staggered under the blow that smashed her bulwarks at the waist, then she canted to starboard beneath the strain. Hope clung to the quarterdeck to keep from falling.

Cheers and hollers blared from the *Enchantress*.

Biting her lip, Hope peered through the tangled mass of ropes and spars, praying no one had been injured. Soon every sailor who'd fallen to the deck lumbered to his feet and made his way from beneath the wreckage. Including Falkland, who wobbled with each tentative step he took.

"What do we do, Captain?" one of the sailors asked him, but Falkland only stared at the shattered mast as if he could resurrect it by sheer will. His numb gaze swept to the *Enchantress*, her decks littered with pirates thrusting weapons and curses into the air.

"Captain?"

"Set the white flag aloft," he finally said, his voice heavy with defeat. His eyes shifted toward Hope, and she thought he would order her below again, but his glance breezed past her as if he didn't see her.

The *Enchantress* swept around again, lowered sails, and came even on the *Victory's* keel.

Hope's throat grew dry. Her chest heaved. Without Nathaniel, without Abigail, who would restrain the licentious urges of Captain Poole? Had she been delivered from one monster's hands into another's?

The pirates, many of whom she recognized, lined the railing of the *Enchantress*, their grins dripping with wicked intent, their weapons glinting in the sunlight. They flung ribald insults toward their victims.

"Out, grappling hooks! Prepare to board," Captain Poole howled, though Hope could not yet see him through the crowd.

Falkland brushed the dirt from his waistcoat, tucked in his shirt, and adjusted the tie in his hair, then took a stance upon the deck as if he were greeting royalty. Some of his crew amassed behind him; others draped themselves over the railings above, their sweaty faces streaked with black lines of defeat and fear. Being overtaken by a pirate was a death sentence. If the sailors weren't killed, they would be marooned at sea or on an island. Often their only choice was to join the pirate crew. Hope's heart went out to them despite her fear for her own safety.

Grapnels clanked into the deck. The snap of splintered wood filled the air. Poole's pirates tugged on the ropes, and the two ships thumped together, sending a tremble through the timbers. Captain Poole leapt to the bulwarks, cutlass in hand, a brace of pistols slung over his chest. "Board 'em, ye swabs!"

He leapt onto the *Victory*, his boots sounding an ominous thud on the deck.

Hope's gaze shifted to the pirates behind him, and she threw a hand to her mouth and shrieked.

CHAPTER 38

Nathaniel scanned Falkland's ship for any sign of Hope. A flash of golden silk caught his eye. She stood by the quarterdeck, trembling, wide-eyed, but from all appearances, unharmed. Her gaze met his, and he offered her a reassuring grin, but her face blanched and she jerked backward as if she saw a ghost.

Gavin appeared beside him, the thrill of excitement beaming on his boyish face. Nathaniel nodded at him, then thrust out his blade and charged onto the *Victory*. A horde of pirates followed in his wake, brandishing swords that were quickly leveled upon Falkland and his crew.

Falkland swallowed but did not move. His sailors stumbled back, their faces twisting in fear.

Captain Poole sauntered toward the defiant captain, the tip of his sword steady upon his chest. "I'll ask ye to lay down yer arms, Captain, if ye please."

Fury stormed across Falkland's face. His lip curled, and for a moment it seemed he would not comply. "Do as he says," he shot over his shoulder but made no move to deliver his own sword. His crew tossed their swords, knives, and pistols to the deck in a series of clanks and clunks, and a snap from Poole's fingers sent four of his men to gather the weapons.

Lifting his nose in disdain at the pirate, Falkland addressed Gavin. "And you, traitor. I suppose you led them to me. I should have known I couldn't trust you."

"Kindred spirits, you and I, Falkland." Gavin gave a mock bow.

Falkland flattened his lips. "Be about your business, pirate, and then leave us be."

"Me business?" Captain Poole chortled. "Well, I'm glad ye asked." He pointed his cutlass toward Hope. "We require an audience with the fair lady."

"An audience?" Falkland barked. "What business could you possibly have with her?"

"'Tis Mr. Mason who has the business, ye snivelin' toad." Poole gestured toward Nathaniel. "Not that it be any o' yers. An' he'll speak to the lady in private, if ye don't mind."

Silence invaded the ship. Falkland's face crinkled into a tangle that resembled the mass of cordage littering his deck. "Did I hear you correctly?"

"Aye, I believe ye did, unless yer hearing's gone by the board along wit' yer mast."

Hope crept out from her spot by the quarterdeck, nudging pirates aside as she went. Her gaze locked upon Nathaniel, and he tried to offer her a reassuring look, but it did naught to penetrate the dismay that claimed her features.

Falkland shifted his stance. "Do you mean to tell me that you destroyed my mainmast and disabled my ship for a mere parley with the likes of her?" he spat. "Why did you not signal me and send a boat?"

Poole shrugged. "Where'd be the fun in that?" He grinned.

Falkland moaned, then narrowed his eyes upon Poole. "And what else do you want while you're here?"

The captain's jaw twitched. He scanned the ship as if assessing its value. "Nothing." He seemed to force the words out with difficulty. "For now."

A collective sigh of relief emerged from Falkland's crew.

"Get on wit' it, Mr. Mason." Poole nodded toward Hope.

Nathaniel sheathed his sword and took Hope's arm, leading the dazed girl up the quarterdeck stairs to the stern of the ship. She stumbled along beside him but said not a word. When they reached the far railing, well out of hearing of the crew and pirates, he turned her to face him.

A glaze of disbelief covered her eyes. "What are you doing here?"

"'Tis precisely what I came to ask you."

"I don't understand. Why did Poole attack Falkland?"

"Answer *my* question first."

Hope swallowed and gripped the railing, swerving her face away from him. "Falkland still loves me. He asked me to go with him." Her tone wobbled as if saying the words pained her.

"Love? Is that what he says?" Nathaniel clenched his jaw. "I would have thought you could recognize real love by now." A wave lifted the stern, and he laid a hand upon the small of her back to steady her.

Her knuckles whitened on the railing, and she looked down at the foamy crash of the sea against the hull. A whiff of wind stirred the golden tendrils dancing down her back.

"Tell me you love him." Nathaniel grabbed her shoulders and turned her to face him. "Look me in the eye and tell me you still love him."

Hope struggled in his grasp, then halted and released a fearful sigh. "Nathaniel, I beg you, please leave. Make your apologies to Arthur, take Poole, and go." Urgency sparked in her eyes. "For your own good."

"I'm not so sure leaving you with Falkland would be for my good."

A flash of confusion crossed her face then she lowered her gaze. "Trust me, it will."

He lifted her chin. "Do you love him?"

She squeezed her eyes shut, the lines of her face etched with sorrow.

Nathaniel released her and stared across the restless sea, as unsettled and ambiguous as the lady before him. "You cannot admit that you love him, yet here you are, playing his mistress once again. After you gave your live to God? What ails you, woman?"

Hope opened her eyes and took a step back, hugging herself. "Falkland is powerful. You must get as far away from us as you can."

Nathaniel gazed into her moist eyes, searching for an explanation. Love and sorrow pooled there, along with a smoldering determination.

Then he understood.

The revelation crushed him to the core. "He threatened to hurt me, didn't he?"

Tears filled her eyes. She looked away and tugged on a strand of hair.

Nathaniel enfolded her hand with his and stilled its nervous toiling. "Didn't he?"

"He can ruin you, Nathaniel. Everything you've worked for." Tears trickled down her cheeks. "I can't let him do it."

He kissed her hand. She had sacrificed everything to save him even after he had believed the worst of her and treated her horribly. Shame weighed upon him. He had not believed she had changed, when in truth, it was he who hadn't changed. He was still the judgmental, merciless cad she had claimed he was.

He drew her close, and her initial resistance melted as she folded into him.

"I owe you an apology," he whispered in her ear.

Hope stepped back. "Whatever for?"

"For not believing you." He bowed his head. "I thought you and Gavin. . ."

"How can I blame you?" Hope lowered her gaze, a pink flush rising up her neck. "My reputation has not been. . .well, it has not been one to foster much faith in my conduct."

"I should have believed you."

"It doesn't matter now." She withdrew and wiped the moisture from her face. "I will not see your life destroyed. Not because of me. I could not bear it." She ran her fingers over his jaw. "Promise me you will leave now and never try to find me again."

Nathaniel shook his head. "I cannot. Don't you see? I don't care if he ruins me. The most profitable merchant business in the world will mean nothing without you."

Renewed tears filled her eyes, and she hurled herself into his arms.

Nathaniel led Hope down to the main deck where the pirates lumbered about, grumbling from boredom, and the sailors stood stiffly behind Falkland, awaiting their fate. Captain Poole perched on a crate, conversing with Gavin. Nathaniel approached Falkland. "Miss Hope agreed to accompany you under false pretenses, sir. She'll be coming with me now."

Lord Falkland's upper lip twitched, and he turned a cold eye onto Hope. "Is that so? You choose this carpenter, this nobody, over me?" His face darkened.

"Arthur." Hope stepped toward him. "I am changed now. God has changed me, and I realize my feelings for you were not love at all. Neither are yours for me."

Nathaniel grimaced at her close proximity to the beast while at the same time admiring her tender, forgiving heart toward a man who had caused her so much pain.

The agony on Falkland's face flashed to rage, and in one quick motion, he grabbed Hope, drew his sword, and pressed the edge of his blade against her throat.

Nathaniel's heart turned to stone. Gavin charged toward them, but Nathaniel held up a hand, halting him.

"All this talk of love. Quite touching." Falkland snorted, pain threading his voice. "But I am not ready to give her up. Mr. Mason, take this pirate and his crew of thieving vagabonds and leave."

"Gentlemen of fortune, if ye please." As Poole approached, he waved a jeweled hand through the air in unruffled disinterest. But the hard glint in his eyes told a different story.

Falkland snorted. "Begone with you. All of you! I'll see Hope dead before I let her go with the likes of you." Nathaniel knew he meant it.

Hope struggled in the man's grasp, wincing beneath the steel biting her neck. Terror sparked in her eyes.

Nathaniel stiffened. Blood rushed through every muscle, sending his fury into a boil. Sweat trickled down his back. He squeezed his fingers around the hilt of his sword, waiting for one perfect moment when Falkland's concentration would falter. The sounds of the ships thundered like warning knells in his ears: the rustle of waves over their hulls, the flap of sails hanging impotent on their yards, the threats and flourishes of pirates and sailors.

Falkland's blade gleamed in the sun, and Nathaniel squinted against the glare. Above it, Hope's eyes sparked with fear, yet she shook her head ever so slightly as if to dissuade him from making a move. A thin line of blood appeared on her pristine neck, and Nathaniel ground his teeth together until they ached. He had not come this far to lose her now.

The sun rained hot arrows down upon them, and Falkland shifted his stance.

Nathaniel curved his lips in his most unnerving grin. A cloud of uncertainty crossed Falkland's eyes. He loosened his grip on the sword.

Nathaniel charged toward Falkland and Hope, sending them tumbling backward. In the chaos, Falkland loosened his grip on Hope. Nathaniel grabbed her by the waist and tore her from his grasp, shoving her aside. Gavin caught her before she fell to the deck.

Falkland recovered his stance and looked about wildly. He raised his sword. His brow grew dark as his eyes smoldered with fury. "Then I shall kill you. No matter."

"You may try if you wish." Nathaniel chortled, wiping the sweat from his forehead with his sleeve and lifting his sword in answer.

Falkland's crew moaned, but a wave of excited laughter and yelps emanated from the pirates. "A duel. A duel." They began to chant.

Captain Poole sauntered forward. "A duel, indeed. Seems only fair t' me." He grinned, planting his fists at his waist. "An' the winner gets the girl."

Cheers erupted from the pirates.

Nathaniel cast him a look of protest. A duel had not been part of their bargain, but it was obvious from the gleam of anticipation in Poole's eyes and the prevailing furor of his men that it was not to be escaped.

"No, Falkland will kill him!" Hope's scream drew Nathaniel's gaze to her as she struggled in Gavin's grasp.

"I am overcome by your confidence." He smiled, trying to allay her fears, but she shook her head as her eyes glistened with tears.

A sinister grin fell upon Falkland's lips, as if he knew a grand secret. He pointed his sword at Nathaniel and raised a haughty brow. "I accept," he snapped.

He leapt toward Nathaniel.

Nathaniel met his blade with a ringing *clank*, amazed to find strength behind the fluff and pomp with which Falkland arrayed himself. Falkland swooped at him from the left. Nathaniel sidestepped his attack and spun to the right, striking a blow to Falkland's side.

Shock tightened the man's features. He rubbed his rent waistcoat and withdrew fingers painted red with blood. Then in a flurry of rage, he charged Nathaniel, slashing his blade back and forth. The glint of sun on steel blinded Nathaniel.

Meeting each forceful blow, Nathaniel retreated into the mob. The crowd shrank away from the dueling pair, all the while spitting encouragements as well as insults their way. Forcing Nathaniel against the starboard railing, Falkland pulled back, a smug look settling on his face like a robe on a king, the kind of look that spoke of a sudden awareness of his advantage in the match—and of his impending victory.

Wiping the sweat from his eyes, Nathaniel caught his breath. He could not lose. He would not lose. He swooped down upon Falkland. Their blades crossed, sending an ominous *clang* over the ship. Falkland stepped to the side, grinned, and twirled his sword in the air as if he were engaged in an afternoon contest.

Rage clamped every muscle, urging Nathaniel forward. He wanted to kill Falkland. He wanted to kill him for using Hope. He wanted to kill him for hurting her, but right now he wanted to kill him for being such an insolent dog. They circled each other. *Lord, forgive me. Give me the strength to win this battle and the courage to do this man no harm.*

Even as he breathed the words, Nathaniel feared he should have prayed for his own life. Falkland's attacks came swift and skilled, and it took all of Nathaniel's concentration to ward them off.

Then, as if Lord Falkland grew tired of the match, he turned on Nathaniel, his red face streaked with sweat and fury. With a fierce swipe, he sliced Nathaniel's breeches.

Pain etched up his leg.

Hope shrieked.

Nathaniel backed away, panting, gulping in the oppressive air.

"Had enough?" Falkland leaned upon the hilt of his sword and cocked his head.

Nathaniel longed to slash that supercilious smirk from his lips.

"Surely the trollop isn't worth dying for." Falkland eyed his fingernails.

"Perhaps you should ask yourself that, your lordship." Raising his blade, Nathaniel charged toward the man. Off guard, Lord Falkland still met his blow, their blades ringing over the ship. Their hilts locked and Nathaniel shoved him backward. The arrogance slipped from Falkland's face.

Snapping their swords apart, Nathaniel plunged the tip of his blade into Falkland's boot. The man uttered an indignant shriek and glanced down. Nathaniel took the hilt end of his weapon and pounded Falkland's hand, sending the man's blade clanking to the deck.

Lord Falkland's face mottled in a mixture of shock and agony as he clutched his hand. His breathing became ragged as the reality crashed over him; he'd been bested—by Nathaniel. He squared his shoulders and assumed a thin mask of superiority.

"You can have the wench. She's only good for one thing, anyway."

Nathaniel raised his fist and slammed it across Falkland's jaw, sending him reeling. "She is a lady. And daughter of the King. You'll pay her the respect she's due."

Falkland slumped to the deck and moaned. Glaring at Nathaniel, he rubbed his jaw. "Daughter of the king, indeed." He sneered. "What king is that?"

"The King of kings." Nathaniel's gaze swept to Hope. She clutched her skirts and dashed toward him. Dropping his sword, he wrapped his arms around her, breathing in her fresh scent. She lifted her eyes to his, tears streaming down her face, and he brushed them away and lowered his lips to hers.

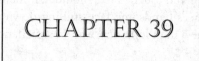

CHAPTER 39

Hope stood at the bow of the *Enchantress* and leaned back on the foremast. A gust of wind, sweetened by the Caribbean, eased over her as the ship rose and plunged over a turquoise swell. A spray of salty mist showered her face and neck, and she smiled and shifted her gaze to the setting sun in the west. A bouquet of purple, red, and orange spread over the horizon as flickers of bright gold sparkled over the waves.

She was finally going home.

Captain Poole had begrudgingly agreed to drop her and Nathaniel, Mr. and Mrs. Timmons, and Miss Elise as close to Charles Towne as "his good sense would allow him to go within range of the filthy, pirate-hanging town."

Elise.

Warmth spread through Hope as she remembered the little girl leaping into her arms when she had first boarded the *Enchantress* from Falkland's ship. Overcome with joy, Hope had been reluctant to release Elise, fearing she was only a dream conjured up by continual prayers for the little girl's safety. But the trembles coursing through Elise were real enough—no doubt due to the gun battle and being aboard a pirate ship— and after comforting her for hours, Hope had finally eased the little girl to sleep, nestled in her berth.

She closed her eyes, feeling the last rays of the sun kiss her face. *Thank You, Lord. Thank You for Elise, and thank You for sending Nathaniel to rescue me. Thank You for his love, a love I no more deserve than I do Yours.*

Unable to find Nathaniel, Hope had ascended the foredeck to pray and watch the sun set. Perhaps he would find her here. She hoped so, for she had many unanswered questions. What had changed his mind about her? And what was the strange ship that followed them off their larboard quarter?

A warm, strong hand touched her shoulder. Flinching, she opened her eyes to see Nathaniel's handsome face smiling down at her. His hungry gaze took her in like a man long deprived of sustenance. He ran his palm over her cheek.

"Oh, Nathaniel, how can I ever thank you for saving me?" Hope's throat burned, and she swallowed, afraid to embrace the love beaming from his eyes. She dropped her gaze to the bloodstained slash in Nathaniel's breeches. "Once more, you risked your life for me."

Nathaniel stretched out his leg. "Falkland wields quite a skilled sword."

Hope huffed, but then a giggle escaped her lips. "The look on his face as we sailed away, leaving him foundering in the water."

Nathaniel chuckled. "Indeed. Especially after Captain Poole threatened to come back and finish the job." He gazed across the darkening sea. "Have no fear. He'll make it to Charles Towne." He grinned. "Albeit a bit later than planned."

The ship bucked, and Hope gripped Nathaniel's arm. "His welfare is of no concern to me. I hope I never see him again." She took in a deep breath of salt-laden air, amazed at the truth of the words she'd just spoken.

Nathaniel cupped her chin and ran his thumb over her cheek. A warm tingle swirled within her, and she took a step back. Nathaniel affected her like no other man ever had. It frightened her, for she no longer wished to give in to every impulse storming through her.

She clutched her hands together and squinted toward the sun still sinking beneath the sea. Glittering feathers of gold and crimson spanned the choppy waves. A breeze tore a curl from her pins and fluttered it over her neck, but she no longer associated it with her inability to be pure, for God would give her all the strength she needed in that endeavor. "Falkland can still harm you."

"How? I've nothing left for him to destroy."

She faced him. "You still own a ship."

Nathaniel's gaze slipped to the two-masted vessel behind them. A sense of longing tugged at his features.

"Is that your ship?" Hope's voice squeaked in disbelief. "The one that sails behind us?"

The cloud of sorrow dissipated from his eyes, replaced by a glimmer of satisfaction. "Not anymore."

Hope furrowed her brow. Dread clutched her heart.

"I gave it to Captain Poole." He waved the ship away as if it were but a trifle.

The words sank like anchors in her belly. "Why?" But she already knew the answer.

"Do you think he aided in your rescue out of the goodness of his heart?" Nathaniel chuckled and ran a hand through his hair.

"What of your crew?"

"Most of them stayed in Kingstown to find work on other ships. Some joined the pirates. All save Mr. and Mrs. Timmons and, of course, Elise."

Hope shrank back. "You gave up your last ship to find me when you didn't know for certain whether I went with Falkland willingly?"

He shrugged and gave her a playful grin. "It worked out well."

Hope shook her head. "You've lost everything because of me. And"— she glanced at the wounds on his leg and arm and the bruise on his forehead—"I've nearly killed you—several times."

Her foolish actions had caused the man she loved unthinkable pain and loss. Turning her back to him, she stormed to the railing.

His boot steps thudded behind her. Strong hands grabbed her waist and pulled her back against him. His arms wrapped around her as his hot breath swept down the side of her neck. "Worth every timber, plank, sail, and wound."

Placing her hands atop his, Hope lowered her gaze to the restless sea below. Elation and fear tangled in her throat. His loving words soothed her doubts. As hard as it was to believe, Nathaniel must truly love her. Yet she couldn't stop entertaining one fear. Why would he attach himself to a woman with her sordid past?

"Remember ye not the former things, neither consider the things of old. Behold, I will do a new thing; now it shall spring forth." The words Hope had read in Isaiah that afternoon eased over her. She lifted her face to the sun.

Nathaniel turned her around to face him. Specks of gold gleamed within his dark eyes. "I love you, Hope. Why do you not believe me?"

She swallowed, breathing in the scent of wood that always clung to him. "Nobody has ever loved me before." Tears burned behind her eyes. "Not truly loved me."

He brushed a curl from her cheek. "Then allow me the privilege of being the first." His lips met hers.

Hope folded into his embrace, submitting to his kiss, and finally permitting herself to believe this honorable man loved her. He pressed her close, caressing her hair and kissing her with gentleness that soon rose to a hunger that matched her own. Heat exploded around her like a thousand cannons set ablaze. The ship, the sea, the sky melted away. Her knees weakened.

Withdrawing, he hovered close to her face. His warm, musky breath tingled over her skin. For the first time, Hope longed to give herself to a man completely, wholly, for no other reason than pure love.

But no.

Breathless, she spun away from him, searching for her traitorous wits amidst the passion that had set her insides aflame. "What will you do now? You have no ships left." She waved a hand over her face and neck, directing the breeze to cool her torrid skin and remove the flush before she faced him again.

❧

Nathaniel drew a deep breath and rubbed a hand over the back of his neck. The woman caused every sinew, every fiber, every particle within him to explode. And then she tore away from him, leaving him in a cold sweat. He gripped the mast, dragging his fingers over the rough wood. A splinter tore at his flesh. Good. The pain would jar him from her trance.

"Perhaps God is trying to tell me something," he finally said, cursing himself for the passion still thick in his voice. He cleared his throat. "Perhaps I should heed His call on my life to preach."

"Preach?" Hope twirled around.

"I seem to have a talent for it." Nathaniel shrugged, concerned by the anxious look on her face. Perchance she did not approve. Perchance she did not wish to marry a poor preacher. His stomach tightened. Regardless, he must follow the call of God on his life. The loss of his last ship had not left the gaping hole within him he'd assumed it would.

Instead, when he'd made up his mind to become a preacher, a peace like he'd never known had fallen on him. "I suppose I've been running from God for quite some time, hoping to make a name for myself through status and wealth, trying to remove the stain of my past."

"Only God can truly cleanse you." She gave him a sweet smile, her blue eyes beaming with an innocence that had not been there before.

"You learn quickly." He returned her smile. A gust of wind blasted over him, cooling his skin. He tossed the hair from his face as the sails snapped overhead. "But I've also learned that status and reputation do not make a man. Look at Hendrick, Paine, Falkland."

"You need say nothing more. Hendrick." Hope blew out a sigh. "I cannot fathom a man who abandons his own daughter."

"You read his note. Perhaps he truly believes she is not his child."

"No matter. He is the only father she has known. Poor Elise." The ship bucked, and Nathaniel reached out to steady Hope, keeping his hand upon her arm.

"But it is an answer to prayer in a way." She gazed up at him. "I shall raise her as my own daughter, give her all the love she needs, and teach her about the everlasting love of God."

Nathaniel forced a smile. What did he know about raising children? His only parent had been a prostitute. *Lord, if Hope is to be a part of my future, I will need Your help with this.*

If she was to be a part of his future.

"You will make a good mother."

"With God's help, I hope so." She glanced toward the sun. The frown of its arc cresting the horizon reflected the one now forming on her lips.

Nathaniel drew her close, longing for her smile to return. "What troubles you?"

"Elise needs a father, too." Her blue eyes searched his. Anticipation sparked in their depths.

Nathaniel looked away, unsure of the intent of her statement, unsure whether Hope would choose to live without the luxuries to which she'd grown accustomed.

When he looked at her once more, the gleam in her eyes had faded to disappointment, and she tipped her face down.

Lifting her chin, Nathaniel brushed his lips against hers. "I love you, Hope," he whispered.

"I love you, too, Nathaniel." Her words melted over him. "With all my heart."

He pulled back and studied her. "I have nothing to offer you."

"You offer me more than anyone else ever has."

Nathaniel took Hope's hands in his. His heart thumped against his chest.

"Then will you marry this poor preacher?"

Hope leapt into his arms, giggling, and showered him with kisses. "I thought you'd never ask."

Embracing her, Nathaniel stumbled back as the ship lurched over a wave. Unable to keep his balance—or his concentration—as Hope continued planting kisses on his face and snuggling her body next to his, Nathaniel bumbled and slammed into the railing. The ship canted again, and quickly releasing Hope, he clutched the railing just before he would have toppled over the side and plunged into the sea.

Hope braced her feet on the deck and threw a hand to her mouth, her eyes wide with horror.

He raised a patronizing brow her way, allowing a playful sparkle to fill his eyes. "Perhaps we should marry as soon as possible before you do indeed manage to kill me." He chuckled, and she fell into his arms, her laughter joining with his.

EPILOGUE

"A sail! A sail!" A man on the yards above Hope roared across the ship. She looked up from her spot sitting on a barrel beside Elise, reading her a copy of the *Tales of Mother Goose* that Mrs. Timmons had procured.

Captain Poole leapt upon the foredeck, grabbed the glass from Hawkins, and raised it to his eye.

Across the deck, Nathaniel instructed a group of pirates on the use of the quadrant. Glancing at her, he gave her a reassuring nod and gripped the hilt of the sword he wore constantly aboard the pirate vessel.

Gavin slid down the backstay and landed with a thud beside her. He tickled Elise beneath her chin, sending her into a flurry of giggles, and then winked at Hope. He'd taken the news of her and Nathaniel's engagement with more joy than Hope would have expected. Either he had never harbored any affection for Hope, or he hid his feelings well beneath his usual facade of charm. Yet he seemed somehow different these past few days.

He sauntered over and stood beside Nathaniel, who clapped him on the back. The two had formed a close bond, one that Hope prayed would drive Gavin to his knees before God.

A band of pirates gathered on the main deck, awaiting their captain's assessment of the intruder.

Within a day's journey of Charles Towne, Hope could hardly contain her excitement at seeing her sisters again. She'd been praying for Faith, whom she'd last seen in the Watch Tower Dungeon, awaiting trial for piracy. Even now, Hope found it difficult to believe she'd been so self-centered as to leave Faith in such a predicament with her fate unknown. But thanks be to God, Hope was a different person now.

Putting the book aside, she shielded her eyes and peered in the

643

direction of the men's gazes. They'd not come across another vessel in two days, and she had been praying for a safe and uneventful passage home. Hope didn't know if she could endure further excitement.

Lord, let this be a friend and not a foe.

~

"Scupper, sink, and burn me," Captain Poole exclaimed. "'Tis the *Red Siren.*"

"The *Red Siren.*" Hope snatched the glass from Poole's hand, as a foul curse spewed from his mouth.

Ignoring him, she held the telescope to her eye and twisted the ship into focus. The words *Red Siren* stood in bold red across the ship's bow. Excitement soared through her. "'Tis my sister."

"Yer sister?" Poole swung a startled gaze her way. "But the *Red Siren* be a pirate vessel."

"Her sister *is* a pirate." Nathaniel eased beside her, slipping a protective arm around her waist. "Or at least she was."

"Your sister is the notorious Red Siren?" Poole's eyes lit up, and he slapped his knee. "Well, upon me life."

Gavin gripped the railing and stared at the fast-approaching ship. "Why, pray tell, would anyone withhold such an intriguing fact? Quite astonishing!" He pushed from the railing, his blue eyes alight with interest. "Will she fire upon us?"

Poole spit to the side and thrust his hands upon his waist. "I'll introduce 'er to the sharks, if she does." He glanced at Hope. "Beggin' yer pardon, miss, sister or no, no one fires upon Captain Poole without a sharp reply."

"I would expect nothing less, Captain." Hope forced a smile that belied her inner turmoil. "But I assure you, if it is my sister, and she spots me on your ship, she'll not fire upon us." Bracing her shoes against the heaving deck, Hope raised the spyglass once again, scanning the oncoming vessel, squinting into focus the people on board. What if it wasn't Faith? She could have sold her ship, or it could have been stolen. Perhaps she had been sentenced to the gallows, after all. A sick brew welled in her stomach. *Oh Lord, don't let it be so.*

A shock of red hair swept across her vision, and Hope swung it back and twisted the handle.

"'Tis my sister, indeed! She's aboard." Hope leapt for joy.

"Are you sure?" Nathaniel asked.

"Yes, and there's a man beside her." Hope hesitated, peering through the glass. "Captain Waite. 'Tis Captain Waite, I'm sure of it. Ah, this is good fortune indeed."

"Who the blazes is Captain Waite?" Captain Poole tore the glass from her eye and pressed it against his own.

"A lieutenant in His Majesty's Royal Navy." Too late, Hope realized the implications of her words.

Poole lowered the glass. "Be ye out of yer head?" He swore, then stomped to the foredeck railing and stared at the mob of pirates clustered on the main deck. "Load the guns! Clear the deck! Run up our colors."

As the men scrambled to do their captain's bidding, Hope dashed to Poole's side, daring to touch the raging pirate's sleeve. "Nay, Captain. He is not in uniform. And he does not sail under British colors. I assure you he will not fire upon us." At least Hope prayed he would not.

Captain Poole's narrowed eyes sent a chill through her as he shifted his gaze between her and the ship.

Nathaniel approached, nudging Hope behind him. "They've no doubt seen us by now, Captain, and their gun ports are still closed. Lend us a boat and send us to their ship. If their intent is anything but friendly, you have my word, we will convince them otherwise. In either case, you shall be relieved of our company, as I am confident Miss Westcott and Captain Waite will be happy to escort us into Charles Towne harbor."

"I'll join you," Gavin shot over his shoulder from the railing.

"I thought you were turning pirate." Nathaniel faced him, a faint smirk on his lips. "Or have I managed to persuade you to change your course?"

"Perhaps." Gavin gave one of his boyish grins. He scratched his whiskers and gazed at the *Red Siren*. "But truth be told, I can't pass up the opportunity to meet a lady pirate."

"Belay me orders," Poole shouted below; then he grunted and crossed his arms over his chest. "So be it. But if she fires upon me, I'll hold to no bargain."

Nathaniel extended his hand. The pirate gripped it. "'Tis been quite an experience, Captain. I shall not forget you."

Captain Poole snapped his hand back and shifted uncomfortably.

"Be gone wit' ye now before I change me mind."

Hope had grown fond of the beastly pirate. "Where will you go now, Captain?"

He scratched his chin, the twinkle in his eyes matching the glitter of the ring piercing his ear. "I hear there be a pretty young missionary back in Kingstown. I have it in me mind to pay her a visit."

Moments later, Hope gripped Nathaniel's hand as he assisted her over the railing of the *Red Siren*, her heart lodged permanently in her throat. Before she placed both feet on the deck, a flash of red filled her vision, and Faith barreled into her, wrapped her arms around her, and squeezed the breath from Hope's lungs.

"Hope, Hope. I cannot believe 'tis you." She held her out for a moment and inspected her from head to toe, then pressed her close again, her voice a cacophony of sobs and laughter. "Where have you been? We've been searching for you!" Her joy snapped to anger in seconds—as only Faith could do—and she released Hope and took a step back, placing her hands on her hips. Curls of flaming red fluttered around her face in the ocean breeze—a face that now grew tight with anger. Her white cotton shirt flapped beneath a leather baldric. Brown breeches were stuffed into dark boots that tapped an ominous chant over the wooden deck.

Hope couldn't help but smile. "I'm glad to see you, too, even if you do look like a pirate." She swiped a tear slipping from her eye and placed a hand on her sister's arm. "Never fear. I am well."

Faith's gaze shot to Nathaniel, who assisted Mr. and Mrs. Timmons and Elise on board, then it swung to Gavin as he swept over the bulwarks after them, plopping to the deck with a smile. She cocked a curious brow at Hope, awaiting an explanation.

Mr. Waite's imposing figure stomped past them and gripped Nathaniel's shoulders. "Nathaniel. How did you. . . What are you doing here?"

Hope smiled. "You remember Mr. Nathaniel Mason, Faith, do you not?"

Nathaniel nodded at Faith. "Miss Westcott. We have much to tell you."

Faith slid her arm through Hope's. "As in, what you're doing with my sister? And who these people are?" She gestured toward Mr. and Mrs.

Timmons, Elise, and Gavin. "And isn't that a pirate ship? Captain Poole's, I believe?"

Hope glanced at the *Enchantress*. Poole's pirates scrambled to unfurl sail as soon as the cockboat returned. "Yes. But how did you know?"

"I've heard of him." A wind thick with moisture swirled around them and seemed to wash away the anger from Faith's face.

Elise inched her way to Hope, grabbed onto her skirt, and hid herself among the folds.

Faith eyed the little girl, then she knelt and smiled at her. "And who might this be?"

The little girl curtsied. "My name is Elise, and Hope is my new mother."

"Indeed?" Faith took her hand. "Pleased to meet you, Miss Elise." Faith stood and tossed her hair over her shoulder. "You *do* have much to tell me."

"And I will in good time." Hope sighed, then she clutched her sister's arm. "Did you receive the pardon from the governor? I was so frightened for you."

"I did." She glanced at Mr. Waite conversing with Nathaniel.

Gavin approached and gave a gentlemanly bow. "I am honored to finally meet the notorious Red Siren." His blue eyes took her in with interest.

Clearing his throat, Mr. Waite slipped beside Faith, laid a hand on her back, and glared at the young upstart.

Hope giggled. "Faith, Mr. Waite, may I present Mr. Gavin Keese. Mr. Keese, my sister, Miss Westcott, and Captain Dajon Waite."

Faith smiled. "Mr. Keese, my pleasure, but my sister errs. I am no longer Miss Westcott. I am Mrs. Waite." She smiled at Dajon.

"Married?" Hope flew into her sister's arms, laughter bubbling from her lips. "Oh, I knew it. I knew it! I'm so happy for you." Withdrawing from Faith, Hope took Mr. Waite's hands in hers. "For you both!"

"Thank you, Miss Hope." Mr. Waite gazed at his wife, his eyes warming with love—a love Hope had never dreamed she'd experience, not until Nathaniel.

"God has abundantly blessed us," he said.

"God has blessed us as well." Hope slipped her hand into Nathaniel's.

"Did I hear you say God?" Faith gave her a questioning look.

"You did."

"And does this blessing include Mr. Mason?" Mr. Waite asked.

Hope gazed up at Nathaniel and nodded. Warmth flooded her at the consuming look in his eyes.

"I am truly happy." Faith hugged her. "I cannot wait to hear all that has happened." The *Red Siren* careened over a wave, drenching them with salty spray. The joyful exuberance slipped from Faith's face. "But there is a matter of grave importance we must attend to first."

Hope's heart shrank.

Faith's jaw tensed. "It is the reason we have set sail."

"Pray tell, do not hold it from me." Hope clung to Nathaniel.

"'Tis our sister, Grace." Faith swallowed and glanced at Mr. Waite. Her face twisted in fear. "She's been kidnapped."

"Kidnapped?" Hope felt the blood rush from her head. "By whom? For what purpose?"

Faith swallowed and glanced at her husband. "We do not know. Her ladies' maid, Alice, was quite distraught when she returned home yesterday evening without her."

"Without her? Where was she?"

"On another one of her errands of mercy." Faith drew a shaky breath, then frowned.

Mr. Waite crossed his arms over his chest. "Alice said a band of ruffians came and carried her away."

The ship began to spin around Hope, and she grabbed Nathaniel's arm for support. He wrapped his other one around her back to steady her. "How do we know where. . . ?" Hope gasped for breath. "How can we find—"

"We know they set sail from Charles Towne and headed south." Mr. Waite glanced off the bow of the ship.

Elise snuggled against Hope, perhaps sensing the tension, and Hope rubbed her back to reassure her even as tears burned behind her own eyes. Squaring her shoulders, she held them at bay. "Then we must go after her right away."

Faith gave her a nod of encouragement. "We are, dear sister, we are. Never fear. We will find her."

"Are you up for another adventure, Mason?" Mr. Waite laughed and slapped Nathaniel on the back.

Hope glanced up at her betrothed, wondering if perhaps he'd had enough excitement for a time, wondering if he wouldn't prefer to just go home. But a playful spark flickered across his dark brown eyes. "I wouldn't miss it for the world." He planted a kiss on Hope's forehead, and she leaned against his chest, loving him now more than ever.

Faith swung about on her heels just as Mr. Waite glanced upward. "Away aloft!" they shouted simultaneously, then glanced at each other and chuckled. Finally, Faith dipped her head toward her husband in abeyance.

"Let fall the main and foretopsails!" Mr. Waite barked. Then he lowered his gaze to them and winked. "We have a lady to rescue."

DISCUSSION QUESTIONS

1. In *The Blue Enchantress*, Hope's greatest weakness was throwing herself at any man who would look her way. What three major things in her childhood caused her to seek value, self-worth, and love in the arms of men who didn't truly love her? Explain from your own experience or that of someone you know, how each of these three things can create an empty hole inside someone's heart.

2. What was the only quality Hope possessed that she believed was of any value? How did she use it to her advantage? Do you know any young girls today who believe the same way? And if so, what do you think caused it? Do you see this trend in our present day culture? What can we do, if anything, to prevent it in our own lives and the lives of our daughters?

3. What were some of the things the other characters did to try and fill the void in their own hearts? Major Paine? Mr. Hendrick? Mrs. Hendrick? Captain Poole? Gavin Keese? Lord Falkland? Do you know people who seek fulfillment in the same type of things today?

4. In what ways were Mrs. Hendrick and Hope alike? How did Mrs. Hendrick's choices and their consequences affect Hope? Did Abigail have an effect on Hope? In what way? Do you believe God sends people into your life to teach you things?

5. What did Hope come to realize was the only thing that could fill the void in her heart, cleanse her of her past, and give her self-worth? What seven events or influences led up to this awakening in her?

6. Nathaniel Mason felt the call of God on his life. What was that call? And why did he ignore it? Have you ever felt the specific call of God on your life to go in a certain direction? Explain what happened.

7. What happened in Nathaniel's childhood that left a gaping wound in his heart? How does he feel toward his mother at the beginning of the book? What did he value more than anything because of his past?

8. How did Nathaniel's past and his goals conflict with his attraction toward Hope? What did he learn by the end of the story about her past that helped him see things differently?

9. How did God get Nathaniel's attention and reinforce His plan that Nathaniel should become a preacher? What things did Nathaniel lose? What things was he able to accomplish through the power of God?

10. Even though Nathaniel was running from God's call, did God give up on him? Do you believe God can use circumstances and even great loss to guide you in the right direction? Do you have examples from your own life or someone you know?

11. What things did you like about Gavin Keese? What things did you not like? What was his effect on Nathaniel? On Hope? How did he change by the end of the book and why?

12. Though Abigail was willing to do God's will no matter what, what was her biggest fear? Who helped her overcome it? God sometimes uses the most unlikely people to accomplish his tasks. Can you think of an example in your own life?

13. What caused Captain Poole's fear of God? Does God still use miracles to get people's attention? Captain Poole had a reverence for God that seems lacking among many Christians today, and yet he was seeking the truth. What does the Bible say about those who seek God with all their heart?

the Raven
SAINT

Charles Towne Belles / Book 3

DEDICATION

To the bit of Pharisee in all of us.

ACKNOWLEDGMENTS

My deepest appreciation to all the wonderful people at Barbour Publishing, who not only believe in my writing, but treat me as if I were family.

To my agent, Greg Johnson, who works hard on my behalf, and who also lends a shoulder to cry on when I need one.

And what would I do without my incredibly talented critique partners: Laurie Alice Eakes, Louise M. Gouge, Ramona Cecil, and Paige Dooly, who are not only great authors, but good friends.

To my editor and partner through all my books, Susan Lohrer. You're the best!

And to Traci DePree for making me work harder than I ever have on a book, and for making it the best it can be. Thanks, Traci!

To all the writers at HisWriters Yahoo group, a plethora of historic knowledge and Christian kindness. Love you guys!

Special thanks to Angela Robinson for winning the contest on my blog to name the cat in this story Spyglass!

My fondest appreciation goes to Cathi Hassan for help with all the French phrases which I conveniently forgot from high school French class.

And last but not least, to my dearest husband and my children who put up with my long hours in front of the computer and that glazed look in my eye when I'm off in my story land somewhere.

Finally, all praise and glory to my Savior, my friend, and my King, Jesus Christ.

CHAPTER 1

Outside Charles Towne,
Carolina, October, 1718

Black, menacing clouds snarled a warning from the Carolina skies.
Clutching her skirts, Grace Westcott trudged down the muddy path. A shard of white light forked across the dark vault, and she glanced up as thunder rumbled in the distance.

"I hope the rain doesn't catch us, miss." Alice's shaky voice tumbled over Grace from behind.

"Never fear, Alice, we are almost there." Grace pushed aside a leafy branch that encroached upon the trail. As the wind picked up and raindrops began to rap on the leaves above them, the wall of greenery arching overhead provided a shelter that brought an odd comfort to Grace.

"Look, miss. This plant. Isn't it bloodroot?" Alice squeaked. "To heal afflictions of the skin?"

Grace huffed. Her legs ached from the mile-long journey from Charles Towne. She could hear the rush of the Ashley River in the distance. They were close to the Robertses' cabin, to poor little Thomas, sick with a fever and in desperate need of the medicines they brought.

Whirling around, Grace examined the leaf in her maid's hands. "Nay. 'Tis not bloodroot, as you well know." She searched Alice's eyes, but the maid kept her gaze lowered. "Whatever is the matter with you today?"

The maid cast a quick glance over her shoulder and shrugged. "I am only trying to help, miss."

"You can help by hurrying along. Thomas may be failing as we speak." Grabbing her skirts, Grace turned and forged ahead. A drop of rain splattered on her forehead, and she swiped it away.

"But the rain, miss. Shouldn't we return home and don some proper attire?"

"Mercy me, Alice. We are nearly there. A bit of rain will not harm us. We've been in far more dangerous situations." Grace hoisted the sack stuffed with herbs, fresh fruit, and rice farther up her aching shoulder. "Besides, we are going about God's work. He will take care of us."

Grace heard Alice's shoes *squish* in the mud. "Indeed, miss."

Her maid's voice quivered—a quiver that set Grace's nerves on edge, along with the dark tempest brewing above them. Something was bothering the woman, Grace couldn't guess what.

Another flash lit up the sky. Releasing her skirts to the sticky mud, Grace pushed aside a tangled vine that seemed to be joining forces with Alice in attempting to keep her from continuing. Musky air, heavy with moisture and laden with scents of earth and life, filled her nostrils. Thunder bellowed, closer this time, and raindrops tapped upon the canopy of leaves overhead. Plowing ahead, Grace ignored the twinge of guilt at her most recent expedition. One of many expeditions she'd been strictly forbidden to embark upon—both by her father, before he set sail for Spain, and more recently, her sister Faith and Faith's new husband, Dajon. But Grace could not allow anyone or anything to stop her from doing what God had commissioned her to do: feed the poor, tend to the sick, and spread the good news of His gospel.

She glanced up at the dark clouds swirling like some vile witch's brew. Perhaps she should have left a note informing Faith of her whereabouts. No matter. She would drop off the food and herbs, attend to Thomas, and be home before sunset.

Grace emerged from the green fortress into a clearing. Thunder bellowed, and she shivered as a chill struck her. In the distance, the wide Ashley River tumbled along its course. A cabin perched by the water's edge, smoke curling from its chimney. Squaring her shoulders, she took a deep breath and quickened her pace. "Here at last. And, as you can see, Alice, all is well."

A nervous giggle sounded from behind her.

Hoisting the sack higher up on her shoulders, Grace clutched her skirts and climbed the steps of the cabin, but before she could knock on the door, it swung open. Mr. Roberts, a burly red-faced man with unruly dark hair, stared curiously at her for a moment then cocked his head and smiled. "Miss Grace. A grand pleasure to see you." His glance took in Alice standing on the steps behind Grace. His forehead wrinkled. "What brings you this far from home on such a rainy day? Helen, Miss Grace has come for a visit," he yelled over his shoulder. The scent of smoke and some sort of meaty stew wafted over Grace.

"Why, we've come to help Thomas, of course." Lightning flashed, casting a momentary grayish shroud over Mr. Roberts's normally ruddy face.

"Thomas needs help?" He scratched his thick, dark mane.

Alice's boots thudded on the steps, and Grace turned to see her maid inching away from the cabin, her chin lowered.

Shaking her head, Grace faced Mr. Roberts. "Yes, you sent Alfred yesterday to inform us of Thomas's fever and ask for my help, did you not?" The man looked puzzled. Grace slid the sack from her shoulder and set it down on the planks of the porch. "I've brought elder root and dogwood bark for his fever and some fresh fruit and rice for you and your family."

Mrs. Roberts appeared in the doorway, her infant daughter cradled in her arms. "Grace, what a wonderful surprise. Henry, don't just stand there. Invite her in out of the rain."

"Thomas isn't sick." Mr. Roberts's nose wrinkled. "And Alfred was here with us all day yesterday."

Grace swerved about to question Alice, but the girl was nowhere in sight. Descending the stairs, she dashed into the clearing, her heart in her throat as she scanned the foliage for any sign of her maid.

A *swoosh* of leaves and *stomp* of boots reached her ears, then a band of five men materialized from the foliage. Armed with cutlasses and pistols, they stormed toward Grace. She tried to move her feet, but the thick mud clung to them like shackles. Mr. Roberts cursed and ushered his wife inside. The baby began to howl.

A tall, sinewy man halted before her. A burst of wind struck him, fluttering the green feather atop his cocked hat and the tips of the black hair grazing his shoulders. He shifted his jaw, peppered with black stubble, and gazed at her with eyes the color of the dark clouds churning above them. A slow smile crept across his lips, lifting his thin, rakish mustache. "*Mademoiselle* Grace Westcott, I presume." His thick French accent turned her blood to ice.

Grace met his gaze squarely. "I am, sir."

With a snap of his fingers, two of his men flanked her. "You will come with us."

"I will not." The men wrenched her arms behind her back. Pain shot across her shoulders.

The snap of a rifle sounded, drawing the man's attention to Mr. Roberts pointing his musket in their direction. "Leave her be."

A flicker of relief eased over Grace, quickly fading when she examined the man before her. Instead of fear, amusement sparked in his eyes. The men on either side of Grace chuckled as if Mr. Roberts had told a joke.

"*Quel homme galant,* but I fear I cannot do that, *monsieur.*" The leader crossed his arms over his gray waistcoat and scraped a finger along his lean chin. "With a bit of fortune and a good aim, you may shoot one of us. *Mais* that would leave you and your family completely at our mercy. *Comprenez-vous?*"

Mr. Roberts stared at him for a long moment, obviously measuring the man.

"Toss your weapon to the ground, monsieur, and go into your house. If you come out, we will shoot you. If you fire another weapon at us, we will kill your family."

A short, barrel-chested man beside the leader drew his pistol and leveled it at Mr. Roberts. The sneer on his face suggested he would love nothing more than to shoot the man where he stood.

The musket quivered in Mr. Roberts's hands as he perused the band of ruffians, but still he did not relent. Grace shook her head, sending her friend a silent appeal. She would not allow him to put his family in jeopardy for her.

Mr. Roberts swallowed, threw his weapon into the mud, and gave her an apologetic look before slipping inside the cabin and closing the door with an ominous thud that echoed Grace's fate.

She faced the leader. Thunder roared across the clearing. "What have you done with Alice?"

"Alice? Hmm." His eyes lit up. "*Votre servante?* I merely paid her well for leading you to us." He grinned.

The skies opened and released a torrent of rain upon Grace as if God Himself shed the tears that now burned behind her eyes. How could Alice have done such a thing? She had been Grace's personal maid for the past five years—had traveled with her in the crossing from Portsmouth to Charles Towne.

The rain bounced off the cocked hat and the broad shoulders of the man before her. Drops streamed down Grace's face, her neck, soaked into her gown, and befogged the scene before her. If only the fresh water from heaven could wash away these devilish creatures like holy water sprinkled upon evil.

The black-haired man turned and marched away as though her desperate wish had reached God's ears. But then his two minions wrenched her arms again and dragged her behind him. Panic seized her. This couldn't be happening! She dug her heels into the mud but her captors merely lifted her from the ground. Pain scorched across her arms and neck.

"Please, sir. Please. What do you want with me?"

But the only reply came from the rain pounding on the leaves and the thunder rumbling across the sky.

They plunged back into the thick forest. Grace struggled against the men's meaty grips. Even if she did manage to break free from them, tree trunks rose like prison bars on either side of her, holding her captive within the dense thicket. They trudged down the path for what seemed an eternity. Each step dug the knife of fear deeper into Grace's heart. Silently, she appealed to God for her salvation, begging to hear His comforting voice, but her petitions were met with the same silence her captors afforded her. Finally, they emerged onto a secluded shore, and the men shoved her onto the thwart of a small boat then launched the craft into the rushing river. In the distance Grace saw a two-masted brig swaying with the rolling tide.

Lord, where are You? She clasped her hands together and tried to catch her breath.

The black-haired man locked a smoldering gaze upon her. He did not look away as propriety demanded but perused her with alarming audacity. Rain streamed off his hat onto his black breeches, and a smirk creased one corner of his mouth. Averting her gaze to the agitated water, she considered leaping overboard. She couldn't swim. At least not well enough to fight the strong Ashley current. Besides, surely God would rescue her from these brigands. He was simply testing her faith by waiting until the last minute when things were at their worst. Lifting her chin, she cast a defiant look upon her captor, but it only caused his smirk to widen.

Within minutes, they reached the ship and thudded against its hull. Shouts pitched upon them from above as faces popped over the bulwarks to peer down at her. Grace glanced about for the rescuer God should have sent by now. The leader pulled her to her feet, and before she could make a move, he hoisted her over his shoulder like a sack of grain and climbed the rope ladder without effort.

Grace could no longer feel the fear or even the damp chill. Numbness gripped her, born of shock at her predicament. Blood rushed to her head, and she closed her eyes, breathing in the musky scent of the man's damp wool waistcoat and praying for the nightmare to end.

Once aboard, he carried her across deck as he issued a string of orders in French, sending his crew scrambling in every direction.

"Welcome back, Captain," a deep voice shouted, then a shock of brown hair appeared in Grace's vision. "I see you found her."

"*Oui, bien sûr.*" His tone carried the haughtiness that excluded any other possibility as he tapped her on the rump.

"How dare you!" Grace shouted and tried to kick her legs, but the captain's arm kept them pinned to his chest. The two men shared a chuckle.

"Weigh anchor, away aloft, and raise the main, Mr. Thorn. We set sail immediately."

Raindrops bounced over the wooden planks, pelting her from all directions. Her head bumped against his damp coat. His hard shoulder pressed into her aching stomach as he carried her down a ladder. She stretched her hand to grab the hilt of his rapier, but it taunted her from its sheath at his other side, out of her reach. She pounded her fists against his back. Muscle as unyielding as steel sent pain through her hands.

With a chuckle, he sauntered down a hallway and kicked open a door. Grace tensed, fearing the man would toss her to the floor. Instead, grasping her waist, he gently set her down inside the tiny cabin.

Gaining her balance, Grace wiped the matted strands of wet hair from her face and faced him. "Who are you and what do you want with me?" she said in a stalwart tone that surprised her.

He doffed his feathered hat and banged it against his knee, sending droplets over the floor. Tucking an errant strand of wet hair behind his ear, he bowed. "Captain Rafe Dubois at your service, mademoiselle. I welcome you aboard *Le Champion*. And regarding what I want with you"—he raised one brow and allowed his gaze to scour over her—"I am to deliver you to Don Miguel de Salazar in Colombia."

"Colombia?" Grace took a step back and gripped her throat.

"Oui, he has promised to pay quite handsomely for you."

"For me? But why? I don't even know the man." A shudder ran through her.

"Ah, but your father does apparently. The two men are not...how do you say? Agreeable? Don Miguel holds him responsible for the death of his son in a skirmish with a galleon. He thought you would be adequate payment for the transgression."

"Payment!" Grace's fear gave way to anger. "I am no one's payment. How can you take part in such a wicked scheme?"

The captain shrugged as if her words rolled off him. "Like I said, he's willing to pay handsomely." He offered her a devious grin then donned his hat and closed the door with a resounding thud.

CHAPTER 2

Rafe stormed up on deck, struck by both the rain in his face and the vision of the lovely Mademoiselle Westcott staring incredulously at him as he slammed the door of her cabin. He took the quarterdeck ladder in two vaults and positioned himself by the helm. Arms across his chest, he surveyed his crew as some of them climbed aloft to loosen sail, while others hauled in the cock boat. Monsieur Thorn stormed the planks, braying orders to keep the men at task. Soon fore- and mainsails were lowered and drawn taut, catching the wind in deafening claps.

"Take her out, Mr. Atton," Rafe shot over his shoulder at the helmsman.

"Oui, *Capitaine*," came the quick reply.

The ship bucked, and Rafe braced his feet against the deck and doffed his hat, allowing the rain to pound down upon him. Closing his eyes to the pellets, he hoped their crisp sting would douse the heat that had taken over his senses after his encounter with Mademoiselle Grace Westcott. He could not keep his eyes off her. No matter where he tried to focus them, they always landed back on her as if drawn by some invisible bowline. It was not so much her *beauté*, although she possessed a comeliness ranked above most women. There was an aura about her, a presence that reached out through those emerald green eyes and grabbed hold of his senses, his reason. He rubbed his belly. Perhaps it was the weevil-infested biscuit he'd eaten for breakfast that morning. Just a case of indigestion, *sans doute*. Oui, that must be it. Once out upon the open sea and in possession of an empty stomach, he'd be his normal dispassionate self again.

"Let fall," Mr. Thorn bellowed from the main deck. "Hoist storm staysails and main topsail!"

The ship picked up speed as the thunder of the sails accompanied the roar of the skies. The bow rose and plunged over a swell, sending foam upon its deck. Before long, they rounded the tip of the peninsula and Rafe spotted O'Sullivan's Island.

"Hard alee, Monsieur Atton," he ordered.

"Hard alee, Capitaine."

Once free of the Charles Towne harbor, Rafe had only to deliver the girl unscathed to Colombia. Although Don Miguel had never met Mademoiselle Grace, Rafe was confident he would be pleased with his purchase. The mademoiselle was well worth the five hundred pounds in gold the loathsome Spaniard had offered for her. *Peut-être*, Rafe could bargain for more doubloons for such a valuable prize.

His first mate appeared beside him and gripped the railing. Doffing his hat, he shook the water from it then plopped it back atop his head. The rain had lessened to a sprinkle. Releasing a sigh, Thorn grinned at Rafe. "Quite an alluring woman Grace Westcott turned out to be, eh?" he remarked as if reading Rafe's thoughts.

Rafe shrugged. "I take no notice. She is cargo to me."

"Cargo, eh?" Monsieur Thorn chuckled. "Much more appealing than those crates in the hold, I'd say."

A vision of the mademoiselle stretched across Rafe's mind. Rain dripping from her skirts, her black hair clinging in saturated strands to her face, her shoulders arched back in a regal stance of superiority. The way her bottom lip quivered, belying the imperious defiance burning in her eyes. She'd handled herself with more bravery than he would have expected from a lady born to comfort. An admiral's daughter. Perhaps she'd gotten her stout heart from her father. *Sacre mer*, why was he thinking of her again? He shook his head, sending droplets flying, then ran a hand through his wet hair.

"More appealing only in the gold she'll bring me."

Monsieur Thorn fingered the whiskers sprouting on his chin and gave Rafe a look of censure. "I trust this particular cargo is not to be handled? You may want to remind the crew—and yourself—of that. 'Tis been awhile since we anchored at port."

Rafe nodded and lifted his gaze to the angry clouds. "She will not be touched, *je t'assure*, but not due to any of your lofty principles, *mon ami*."

"You should try living by some of my lofty principles, Captain. You may find them agreeable." Instead of the expected lift of sarcasm in his first mate's voice, the clamor of disdain rang loud and clear. Thorn's jaw tightened and a look of spite flared across his eyes that set Rafe aback. Rafe returned the look with one of his own, hoping to remind the man that he rarely suffered impertinence, even among those close to him.

Thorn raised his hands in surrender and looked away. But the man had given Rafe an idea. It had been a long time since he'd felt the warmth of a woman beside him. Perhaps that was what ailed him, what caused his strong reaction in Miss Westcott's presence. Though he knew better than to allow his mind to wander in her direction again, not if he was to deliver her to the don unspoiled.

Mr. Atton navigated the shoals of the bay with expertise, and soon *Le Champion* plunged from the narrow Charles Towne harbor onto the open sea. The dark clouds lifted from the horizon, allowing the setting sun to spread its bright wings of crimson and gold across the western tree line. *C'est bon.* It would be a clear day tomorrow.

Thorn tugged his cocked hat further upon his head. "Where should I point her, Captain? Colombia?"

Rafe flattened his lips. "Perhaps a side trip to Port-de-Paix is in order, Monsieur Thorn. I need to offload the cargo in the hold, and the men could use some diversion."

"Aye, Captain." Thorn winked, touched his hat—a habit he picked up during his two years serving in His Majesty's Navy—and sped off, barking orders as he went.

Rafe smiled. Oui, a quick stop in Port-de-Paix would do everyone good. And he would welcome a chance to see his old friend Armonde again. Afterward, all he had to do was deliver the lady to the don in Rio de la Hacha, and his pockets would be lined with enough gold so that finally, after all these years, he could keep his promise to Abbé Villion—a promise that would save many lives. A promise that was worth the kidnapping of one insignificant lady. Rafe winced beneath a pang of guilt that was quickly assuaged when he brought to remembrance the lady's heritage. She was British and therefore his enemy.

He shoved his hat back onto his head and thrust his face into the wind. What could be so hard about delivering one small woman to Colombia?

⤐

Creak, creak, slosh, slosh. The sounds of strained wood and rushing water crept uninvited into Grace's consciousness. She pushed them back, preferring the ignorant repose she'd fallen into during the night. A chill ran across her back. Her legs trembled. Where was her goose-feather coverlet? Had she kicked it off in the night?

"Oh, mercy me." She reached down, groping for the warm covering but found only a stiff counterpane beneath her hand instead of her feather bed. She rolled on her side. A splinter stabbed her arm. Grace bolted up and she opened her eyes, her heart crashing into her ribs. The room that met her gaze was not her bedchamber at home but a ship's tiny cabin. A bowl, mug, and lantern perched upon a small table that was bolted to the wall. Beside it, a green gown draped over a stuffed leather chair. A large ornamented chest guarded one corner while an empty armoire with open doors filled the other.

Throwing a hand to her throat, Grace squeezed her eyes shut as memories of yesterday flooded her wakening mind. *Lord, make it go away.* But when she opened her eyes, the same sordid scene filled her vision.

Don Miguel de Salazar. The name slunk around the cabin. Her throat tightened. She could not go to Colombia. Her life was in Charles Towne. Her work was in Charles Towne. People depended on her for food, for clothing, for medicine. God depended on her to share His love and truth with those who would listen.

She sprang from the bed. Rays of sun spiked through a tiny porthole like daggers. Trembling, she hugged her gown, still damp from yesterday's storm, then eyed the dry one strewn over the chair. Sometime in the night, an old man had ambled in with a bowl of stew, a mug of rum-infused lemon juice, and a gown he tossed over the chair. He'd stared at her for a minute, grunted, and then stormed out. The meaty odor of the food still permeated the cabin, but her churning stomach could not accept the sustenance any more than her propriety could accept the unseemly gown. After the man had left, Grace had spent most of the night upon her knees, begging God to rescue her, begging Him to protect and save her, but the Almighty had been silent.

Finally, when her eyes had swelled from crying and her knees ached from the hard wood floor, she had dropped onto the narrow cot attached to the bulkhead and was finally lulled to sleep by some ribald ballad slinking through the planks from below.

Grace covered her mouth with her hands as tears burned behind her eyes. She thought of her sister Faith and her brother-in-law Dajon. They would be so worried about her, along with the household servants, Lucas, Molly, and Edwin. And what of her other sister, Hope? They still had no idea where she was after she'd run way with Lord Falkland. How could Grace honor the promise she made on her mother's deathbed to ensure the salvation and spiritual well-being of her sisters if she were lost to them forever? *Oh, what am I to do? Where are You, Lord?*

Boot steps thumped outside the door. The latch lifted. Grace swiped the tears from her cheeks and she took a step back. The thick oak slab crashed open against the bulkhead, and in stomped Captain Rafe Dubois with all the authority of a king and the swagger of a brigand. Behind him, the old man who'd brought her food the night before entered, followed by a gray cat, which bounded in and leapt upon the table.

Captain Dubois's presence filled the room, shrinking its size and draining it of air. Dressed in a loose-fitting white buccaneer shirt, with a gold and purple sash strung about the waist of his black breeches, and heavy jackboots, he approached her, the silver hilt of his rapier gleaming in a ray of sun.

He raised a brow. "Do you shiver from fear, mademoiselle, or is it because you prefer your wet attire?"

Grace drew a deep breath to steady her nerves. "A bit of both, I believe."

The captain cocked his head and studied her. "Honesty. *Comme c'est rafraichissant.* Do the garments Father Alers provided not meet with your satisfaction?"

"They dip far too low in the collar." Grace felt a blush rising on her cheeks. "Only a woman of questionable morals would wear them."

Captain Dubois' jaw tightened, and the mirth slipped from his gaze. "They belonged to my sister."

Grace gulped. The old man who'd entered behind the captain chuckled and took a seat in the chair.

"I thank you for the dry attire, Captain, but I cannot in good conscience wear that gown."

The captain snorted in disdain. "Of all the women to kidnap, I get a *prude pieuse.* Fortune has fled me once again."

Wincing beneath his insult, Grace lifted her chin. "I believe 'tis I whom fortune has deserted."

"Hmm," was the captain's only reply, but a glimmer of appreciation for her honesty shone from his eyes.

The sound of lapping drew his gaze to the gray cat, partaking of Grace's dinner. Raising her head, the feline licked her whiskers and stared at Grace with one eye. Naught but fur covered the spot where the other eye should have been, and Grace wondered what had happened to the poor creature.

Sails flapped above as the ship careened. Grace stumbled backward. Captain Dubois reached out for her, but she jumped out of his reach and laid a hand on the bulkhead to steady herself.

He frowned. "You will eat what is provided for you. Unlike *l'excès* you are accustomed to, we cannot afford the luxury of wasting food."

"I am not accustomed to excess, Captain." Grace's anger rose up. " 'Tis but my stomach which protests at the moment. Surely you can understand that?"

The captain's eyebrows arched, and he gave a quick snort of unbelief. "*C'est-ça.*" He gestured toward the old man still sitting in the chair. "Nonetheless. This is Father Alers. He will bring you food and whatever you need."

Grace blinked. A father? Or was it just some odd pirate name? Father Alers nodded, briefly meeting her gaze, as he pressed down a mass of gray hair coiling around his head like a silver spiderweb. Years of hard work lined his ruddy skin, but Grace found naught to fear from his amiable expression.

"He is the ship's cook. You can trust him," the captain said.

"Trust?" Grace snapped. "How can I trust anyone aboard this ship? Are you all not complicit in my abduction?"

He grinned and slid the back of his finger over her cheek before she could stop him.

She jerked away from him. "I am the daughter of Admiral Henry Westcott. And I assure you, sir, he will come looking for me."

"I know who you are, mademoiselle."

"If you do, then you know I speak the truth." Grace squared her shoulders even as her insides began to crumble beneath his haughty disregard. "And you are as good as dead for kidnapping me."

Not a speck of fear crossed the captain's features. Instead, he broke into a chuckle, soon joined by Father Alers. "We shall see, mademoiselle."

Anger dried the tears burning behind her eyes, anger at this beast before her, anger at his arrogance, his audacity. "I insist you release me at once!"

He cocked his head and studied her, and she thought she saw a flash of admiration cross in his gaze, but then the hard sheen returned. "But of course." He waved a hand toward the entranceway. "The door remains unlocked. You may wander freely through the brig, though I must warn you, avoid going below deck. My crew may not be as, shall we say, *courtois* as I."

"Courteous, faugh, I've been treated better by savages."

Father Alers coughed a laugh into his hand.

Captain Dubois gripped his baldric. "If it is savages you want, mademoiselle, there are plenty aboard." He smiled. "Regardless, I encourage you to stay above deck. The don will not accept soiled goods."

Soiled. The word sent a flood of horrifying visions into Grace's mind. She cringed.

Captain Dubois leaned toward Grace until she could smell the brandy on his breath and the sea in his hair. "I will not have you ill when you arrive in Colombia. You will take off your wet gown and put on this dry one by the time I return, or I will do it for you." A lewd flicker crossed his eyes, and she knew he meant it. He turned to leave, gesturing for Father Alers to follow him.

Anger seared through Grace, stealing the chill from her bones. "You're naught but a pirate."

He halted. The skin on his face grew taut. "You are mistaken, mademoiselle. I am a mercenary."

Grace's stomach tightened. A soldier for hire. "Which nation do you serve?"

"Whichever one pays the most." He grinned.

"Then you are a pirate, indeed."

His brooding eyes narrowed. "Take care, mademoiselle. *Gardez vos lèvres.* I give no quarter to the weaker sex."

Grace swallowed and raised a hand to her chest.

"Come, Spyglass." He swerved about and the gray cat leapt into his arms. "There is no way off this ship, mademoiselle. If you behave yourself, things will go pleasant for you. If not, well." He shrugged, a twinkle of deviant mirth in his expression. "The gentleman in me will not permit the utterance of such atrocities."

CHAPTER 3

The door to her cabin creaked open, and Grace turned her aching head to see who had entered. Father Alers offered her a smile from the entrance before he shut the door and set the tray he carried atop the table. "How are you feeling, mademoiselle?"

Grace rubbed her forehead and winced at pain that pounded beneath her fingers. "Not well, I'm afraid." Blurred images drifted through her feverish mind. Images floating on the shadows of night and the glare of day as they passed like specters through the cabin, images of Father Alers and the captain entering and leaving, their whispers lingering in the stale air. The last thing she remembered with any clarity was the captain's threats before he had stomped out, leaving her to face the night alone. She had cried herself to sleep that night and awoken to a body in complete rebellion, expressing its dissent at her predicament with a fever and a seething stomach. Why did she have to get sick at a time like this, when she needed all her strength to plan an escape? She forced back her hatred toward this unknown don and the scoundrel who had kidnapped her, knowing it was wrong. "How long have I been ill?"

"Five days, mademoiselle." Father Alers lifted a bowl from the tray and sat in the chair beside her cot. "You must eat something." The rank odor of some type of fish caused her nose to wrinkle and her stomach to convulse.

She pressed a hand to her mouth. "Forgive me, Father, I cannot," she mumbled. "But I thank you for the food. You have been most kind."

He returned the bowl to the tray with a huff then faced her, leaning back into the chair. "The fever has lessened, mademoiselle. You should feel better soon." A look of concern softened the lines at the corners of his eyes. He started to rise.

"Father." Grace held out her hand. "Please stay a moment. I feel as though I shall go mad all alone in this cabin." She moaned. "Especially not knowing what is to become of me."

He settled back into the chair but averted his eyes from hers.

The momentary glimpse of shame she saw in them emboldened her to ask the question that had been burning on her lips ever since she had discovered kindness in Father Alers. "Father, why do you sail with such a villain?"

Father Alers shifted in the seat and folded his hands over his belly. "*Le capitaine* has some villain in him, I admit, but he does much good *aussi*."

Grace's head pounded as she tried to make sense of his words. "I do not understand. He has kidnapped me. How is that good?"

Releasing a deep breath, he glanced toward the window but said nothing.

"Why do they call you Father?" Grace remembered praying for an ally aboard this ship, a friend, someone who would help her. Truth be told, she remembered praying for many things. None of which had been answered.

Father Alers grimaced. "I used to be of the Jesuit order."

"Used to be?"

"I am no longer a priest, mademoiselle." Anger pierced his tone.

"But surely you still have faith." Grace struggled to rise. How could anyone turn away from God? "My faith is all I have," she said. Although even as she said the words, she wondered at their truth.

He nodded. "You spoke of God often in your dreams these past few days."

Grace's cheeks heated at the intimacies this stranger must have heard her utter in her delirium. She was afraid to ask what she'd said, but he continued nonetheless.

"Oui, something about the Catawbas and Alice and a boy named Frederick and the Hendricks." Father Alers scratched his beard and smiled. "Ah, and always a praise to God. That is how I knew of your faith."

The sound of familiar names washed over Grace like a refreshing mist, bringing with them memories of a time when God walked with her daily. " 'Tis what I do back in Charles Towne. Alice"—pain sank into Grace's heart as she remembered the girl's betrayal—"my lady's maid and I often visit the Catawbas, a local Indian tribe, to bring them blankets and kettles and other cooking utensils, and to tell them about God. And little Frederick." Grace smiled as she remembered the ragged, starving orphan boy she had found on the streets of Charles Towne. "He's an orphan I placed with a couple who couldn't have children. And the Hendricks are a poor family who live on the edge of town. I take food and medicine to them when their children are sick." Relaying the stories out loud brought memories of God's faithfulness to the forefront of her mind, chipping away at the despondency she had built up over the past days.

Father Alers cocked his head and gave her a knowing grin. "And why would a young lady do these things when you could be attending *les soirées* and be courted by beaus?"

"To share God's love and truth with others and help those in need. Isn't that what we are supposed to do?" Unlike her sisters, parties and courtship had never appealed to Grace overmuch.

A beam of admiration glimmered in the father's golden-brown eyes. "A worthy goal, mademoiselle. Your faith is admirable, and the many prayers you offer during your *maladie* have, sans doute, risen straight to heaven."

Horrified that this man had also overheard her intimate conversations with God, Grace fought the tears that filled her eyes. "Yet He does not answer them. Can you explain to me why?"

Father Alers shook his head. "If I could, mademoiselle, than peut-être, I would still be a priest."

Grace swallowed against the anger and fear clogging her throat. "Why are you with Captain Dubois? You are nothing like him."

"Le capitaine and I. . .have a long *histoire* together."

"That still doesn't explain why a man of God would lower himself to partake of such iniquity."

Father Alers pressed down the coils of his silver hair and glanced out the window. He hesitated and seemed to drift to another place and time. "I had a nephew, Armonde." He shifted in his seat. "A bright boy, full of life and love. A bit of a rebel at times, like any boy his age." A slight smile alighted upon his lips but then disappeared. "He was a Huguenot."

The word struck a chord of sorrow within Grace, for she had heard that the Huguenots had undergone horrific persecution in France.

"When Louis XIV issued the Edict of Fountainebleau, Armonde was captured, tortured, and put to death." Father Alers's jaw tightened and he glanced down at the deck.

Grace reached out, but he made no move to accept her hand. "I am so sorry, Father."

He shrugged. "After that I gave up on all religion. It causes men to fight and kill each other. It causes death. I want no part of it. So, I sailed to Saint Dominique where I met Rafe, I mean Captain Dubois." He grinned and finally took her hand. "He reminds me of Armonde."

Her heart filled with compassion, and she placed her hand atop his knobby fingers. "Do not give up on God, Father." Yet her words seemed to drift away for lack of true conviction in her voice. For it appeared God had, indeed, given up on her as well.

The door burst open and in stomped Captain Dubois bringing with him a gust of wind, laden with the smell of salt and damp wood. His dark eyes latched upon her and then shifted to Father Alers, and then to their clasped hands. His jaw stiffened, and he gripped the hilt of his rapier.

~

Rafe grimaced at the stupidity of his friend and took a step forward. He had told the father not to get too close to the mademoiselle during her maladie. He knew the man's heart and how easy it would be for him to take pity on her.

But Rafe certainly did not expect to find their hands clasped together. *L'idiot.* Sans doute *la femme* attempted to charm Father Alers into helping her escape. "I see the mademoiselle is recovering. There is no further need for your ministrations, Father."

Father Alers lifted one defiant gray brow his way then gently placed the mademoiselle's hand back on the cot.

Grace flattened her lips. "Father Alers was just informing me why he sails with a man such as you." Though weak, her voice spiked with disdain.

"*Vraiment?*" Rafe shifted his stance and jerked his head toward the door in an attempt to get Father Alers to leave.

Rising, the father pressed a hand over his back. "Mademoiselle Grace was also informing me how she spends her time in Charles Towne helping to feed and clothe the poor and take care of the sick." He faced Rafe and gave him a taunting look. "Who does that sound like?"

Rafe huffed. The daughter of a British admiral feeding the poor. Not likely. "It sounds like la femme has poisoned your mind, *mon vieux.* Now, attend to your duties."

The mademoiselle shook her head and took a labored breath as Father Alers brushed by Rafe, gave him a grunt in passing, and headed out the door.

Coughing, Mademoiselle Grace lifted her emerald eyes to his. Gone was the glassy shield of courage and defiance he had seen five days ago.

In its stead, a pleading innocence stared at him and seeped through the cracks in his armor headed straight toward his heart. But he wouldn't allow it entrance. Not again. Was it true she cared for those less fortunate than her? Was it true she spent her life caring for others? *Non.* He would not believe it.

He could not believe it.

A drop of sweat slid down the back of his neck, and he wiped it away as he stared at the deck and conjured up a vision of what the British navy had done to his mother. It was the only way to combat the rising guilt those green eyes stirred within him.

He found the anger. He welcomed it and allowed it to burn away any tender spots on his heart, crusting them over until they were once again hard.

Mademoiselle Grace must have sensed his fury, for when he lifted his gaze to hers, she flinched and her face drained of color.

So she *was* afraid of him. When he had first brought her on board, he had expected either a swooning female, begging for her life, or a ferocious wildcat, clawing and hissing at him. What he had not expected was a woman with the courage of a soldier and the heart of an angel.

She struggled to get up on one arm, her chest rising and falling, either from the exertion or from her fear, he didn't know. "Why are you doing this?" she said. Her bottom lip trembled, and Rafe felt that tremble down to his soul.

He planted his fists upon his waist and tore his gaze from her. "As I have said, for the money."

"What will the don do with me?"

Rafe shook his head. His anger began to retreat again. He must get away from her before it left him defenseless. "You can ask him when you see him." Turning, Rafe stormed out the door and slammed it behind him.

CHAPTER 4

Rafe burst into his cabin. Grabbing the decanter of brandy from his desk, he poured himself a swig and snapped it toward the back of his throat. The sharp liquor burned a soothing trail down to his belly and radiated a numbing heat through his body. Just what he needed. He poured himself another and strode to the stern window, watching as the sun's orange glow slipped behind the horizon, tugging a curtain of black in its wake. He felt like kicking something—or someone—and what bothered him the most was that he didn't know why.

A *tap* sounded on his door and at his *entrez*, Father Alers ambled in with a tray. "I thought you would want to eat in your cabin tonight." The old man's eyes took in the empty glass in Rafe's hand.

"And why do you assume that?"

"The crew says you are in a foul mood, Capitaine."

Rafe emitted a sinister chuckle.

The man set the tray on Rafe's desk. "And they know you well enough to leave you alone." The plate of salt pork, beans, and a hard biscuit stared back at Rafe, taunting him with the scent of spice and molasses, though he could find no yearning for the food in his belly.

He huffed. "What, no drink to accompany this savory *mélange*?"

"What need? You have supplied your own." Father Alers glanced at the decanter of brandy and raised a haughty brow.

Rafe turned on his heel and stared into the growing darkness outside. The ship groaned beneath a swell and a bell rang above deck, announcing a new watch.

Father Alers grunted, and Rafe heard the shuffle of his shoes retreating over the wooden planks.

"*Asseyez-vous*, Father. I wish to speak to you." Turning, Rafe gestured toward one of the high-backed *fauteuils* in front of his desk and set his empty glass down.

The cook scratched his beard as if contemplating whether or not to obey, then he dropped into the chair. "What has soured your *humeur*, Capitaine? Seeing me holding hands with the mademoiselle?" He chuckled.

Ignoring him, Rafe opened a desk drawer and chose a French cheroot from within a lined case. Then lighting it from the lantern, he inhaled a draft, allowing the pungent smoke to fill his lungs and calm his fury. He would not give his friend the pleasure of seeing his inner turmoil. "She has no affect on me, mon vieux. I simply want her well." Rafe circled the desk.

Father Alers leaned back and clasped his hands together over his portly belly. "She will survive. Since that is all you care about, non?"

"Oui. I mean, non. I do not want her emaciated." Rafe crossed his arms over his chest. "Does she take in fluids?" He'd seen many a stout sailor die from fever and nausea aboard a ship, especially if they refused to drink.

"She will not partake of the lemon juice—it contains liquor, she says—so I have brought her the water we collected in the last rain storm."

"She *will not*?" Rafe gave a humorless snarl.

"Quite politely refuses." Father Alers crossed his buckled shoes at the ankles and smirked. "With sincere apologies. *En fait,* she treats me more as a friend than a captor."

"As I saw." Rafe puffed on his cheroot, masking the annoyance bristling his nerves.

Father Alers shook his head. "I admire the woman. Despite her malaise, she spends hours in prayer. A true testimony to her faith." He chuckled. "Be careful, Rafe, you may find that God answers her supplications."

Rafe snorted. "Strong words coming from a man who has spent the last four years hiding from God." He poured himself another swig of brandy.

"If I am hiding from Him, then you are surely running."

"You cannot run from someone who does not exist, Father. I run from no god and no man." He downed the liquor.

"Perhaps not. Yet you have proclaimed war upon both." Father Alers's golden eyes sparkled with playful humor. "And if you would, please abstain from addressing me as Father. I am no longer of the order."

"From Jesuit priest to ship's cook." Rafe smirked. "How far you have fallen."

"And you. From wealthy planter's son to abductor of virtuous ladies."

Rafe puffed upon his cheroot, more annoyed at his friend's continual approbation of Mademoiselle Westcott than the insult. "That you find the lady *agréable*, you have made quite clear."

"She has a humble, kind spirit and her mood is always pleasant—which is more than I can say of you."

"You live and die by my grace, mon vieux." Rafe waved a hand through the air. "Why should I be pleasant?"

Father Alers leaned forward in his chair and directed a patronizing gaze at Rafe. "Because it is in you to do so, Capitaine. You can call me *old man*, but I have known you since you were a boy, and the only reason I remain in your service is the charitable acts you perform." He sighed. "Now what of *la dame*? Surely you do not intend to deliver her to this don."

"Mais oui. That is my exact intention." Rafe poured another swig into his glass.

Father Alers shook his head, his chin sinking to his chest. "It is not like you. Never have you dealt in innocent human flesh. You've escorted prisoners, dealt in espionage, battled enemies in time of war, even thievery, but never this."

Guilt assailed Rafe's already bruised conscience, and he downed the brandy. That was the problem. He had grown soft over the years. "Innocent? A lady?" He snickered. "None in her gender can claim such a state."

"They are not all like Claire."

Rafe slammed his fist on the desk, unsettling its contents. "I told you never to speak her name."

Unmoved by Rafe's outburst, Father Alers held up a wrinkled hand in acquiescence.

Rafe ground his teeth together. "Besides, Grace is the daughter of Admiral Henry Westcott. Eye for an eye. Does it not say that in your Holy Book?"

Father Alers rose. Muffling a moan, he placed a hand on his back. "It is not *my* Holy Book, and what would you know of it anyway?"

"I know more than I care to." Rafe took another puff of his cheroot, hoping the tobacco would calm his temper. "But to appease your sense of righteous mercy, the price I get for her will save many lives."

Father Alers flapped his hand through the air as if arguing with Rafe was a waste of his time. "And put out that cheroot. You will light the ship aflame."

Rafe scowled. Why did he allow this old man to play the father to him? He only taunted him with his inadequacies. "I am the capitaine of this ship, and I'll do as I please!" he shouted in a tone that sent most men cowering.

Father Alers guffawed. "What has pricked your nerves tonight if not la dame Westcott?"

"*C'est absurde.*" Rafe sat back against his desk and rubbed his chin. "But I will not have her waste away and lower my profits. Force her to eat, if you must, and inform me when she fully recovers."

Father Alers turned and waved a hand through the air. "Force her yourself, Capitaine. You forbade me to attend to her further, did you not?" And with that, he hobbled out and closed the door.

Rafe put out the cheroot in the empty brandy glass and avoided the temptation to toss the glass across the cabin. They'd been at sea barely a week, and Mademoiselle Westcott was already proving to be more of a problem than he expected.

Grace climbed the companionway, her legs trembling with each step. Whether from weakness or fear, she didn't know, and she no longer cared. After doing naught but retch and pray for days—she'd lost count of how many—all she had to show for it were a pair of bruised and scraped knees. Not to mention her spinning head which continually induced her to lose the contents of said stomach—which of course was already empty, making the action all the more painful.

To make matters worse, nightmares from long ago attacked her feverish mind with ferocity. One nightmare in particular—a nightmare that had been so terrifying, she'd never spoken of it to anyone. A nightmare that had changed the course of her life forever. The night she had seen a vision of hell.

Even now she couldn't bring herself to think of it, but its memory always lingered at the edge of her thoughts, prompting her with greater and greater urgency to save those who were heading down a path that led to the horrifying place. Finally, pushing aside the hellish vision, she decided to venture on deck for some fresh air and to see if perhaps God could hear her pleas more clearly out in the open. Perchance this ship and its occupants were so evil that they blocked her prayers from rising to heaven. But now as she rose above hatches and slid her shaky foot across the deck, she questioned the wisdom of her actions. Instantly, a dozen pairs of eyes fastened upon her as tightly as the hooks on the bodice she'd been forced to squeeze into.

Her sister Faith had always told her never to cower before bullies, so she lifted her chin to meet their gazes. A cacophony of whistles flew her way.

"Shiver me soul, if it ain't the captain's piece," one portly sailor in a red shirt said.

"An' a handsome petticoat she be." The man next to him elbowed his friend and grinned.

A lanky man with a pointy chin licked his oversized lips. "Don't she look as tasty as a sweet berry pie."

"Come join us, mademoiselle," another sailor gestured toward her. "We haven't had our dessert yet." The men all joined in an ear-piercing chortle.

Grace lowered her chin, flung a hand to cover her bare neck, and made her way to the railing, hoping not to topple to the deck from weakness and humiliation. Perhaps this had not been a good idea, after all.

Trying to erase the vision of the ribald men behind her, she gripped the railing and gazed across the sparkling turquoise sea. She drew in a deep breath of the heavy salt-laden air, hoping it would chase from her lungs the moldy staleness that had taken residence there from her confinement below.

Movement caught her eye, and she turned to see three sailors peering at her from the bulwarks on her left. One of them, a tall man attired in a modish style that belied the crude look in his eyes, spoke passionately to the man beside him. His companion, a rotund fellow made all the more large by the third man's wiry frame beside him, chuckled and raised an inviting brow her way. His wide mouth stretched into a wet smile.

Grace's stomach lurched.

A deep voice she recognized as the captain's bellowed over the ship, immediately sending the men scampering and silencing the salacious onslaught. "Back to work, *crapaud stupides!*" The stout man did indeed look like a toad.

Grace glanced over her shoulder to see Captain Dubois standing by the companionway, fists on his waist. His unfettered black hair blew behind him in the hot ocean breeze, and his dark smoky eyes latched upon her, an inscrutable emotion brewing within them.

Grace faced forward and tugged upon the chain at her neck, pulling out the gold cross tucked within her bodice. Gripping it with both hands, she slid her fingers over the jewels. She wanted to pray, to plead with God for help, but she had no words left. Why wasn't God answering her? She had spent her life serving Him, and now when she needed Him the most, He seemed to have disappeared.

The thump of the captain's boots faded across the deck, and she released a deep sigh. At least for the time being, it appeared that he would leave her be and keep his men away from her as well. She had come up here to spend time with God, but as she gazed over the huge expanse of blue, she felt more alone than ever. The ship bucked, and she released the cross to grab the railing. The ornament struck the wood with a clank, and she stuffed it down her bodice again. A gift from Reverend Anthony at St. Philips for her exemplary charity work in and around Charles Towne. It was all she had left to remind her of God's love and faithfulness.

Closing her eyes, she gripped the ship's railing lest she collapse from the lightness of her head and weakness of her knees. She must regain her strength. She must plan her escape. If she could discover what this don planned to do with her, perhaps she could convince the captain to appease him in some other way. Her heart pounded slow and heavy in her chest as if it pushed through molasses, reminding Grace that she needed sustenance.

Something furry tickled her arm. Grace shrieked, jumping back, and opened her eyes to find the gray cat balancing on the railing. The feline stared at Grace curiously through one eye. Laughter tumbled over her from behind.

A man approached, retrieved the beast, and held it in one hand. "Now, Spyglass, don't go scaring the lady." He scratched the cat behind the ears. The feline's loud purrs could be heard even over the purl of the waves against the hull. The man bowed. "Justus Thorn, miss."

"You are British." Grace studied him. He could be no older than her own twenty years. Brown hair the color of almonds danced wildly in the wind and brushed the top of his pristine gray doublet. A swath of white lace bounding from his neck matched the lace at the cuffs of his white shirt. A bulbous nose and a thin red scar that ran from his left cheek to the middle of his neck were the only deterrents to an otherwise flawless countenance.

"Born in Wellingborough, Northamptonshire." Mr. Thorn set the cat onto the deck. "Have no fear. Spyglass may look fierce, but she is harmless."

" 'Tis not the cat that worries me, Mr. Thorn."

His gaze rose to Captain Dubois standing on the quarterdeck amidst a group of crewmen, and for a moment Grace thought she saw a spark of bitterness cross his hazel eyes. "Aye, 'tis a most perilous situation in which you find yourself." He said the words as if remarking about a rainy day or a pair of lost tickets to a play.

"Most perilous, sir, when you consider what my future holds." Grace reached up to clasp the buttons at the top of her gown, but her fingers met bare skin instead. She'd forgotten about the low-necked bodice and spread her hand across her naked flesh in horror. "But then, why do I complain to you? You are an accomplice in the captain's nefarious scheme."

"I am a member of his crew only."

"Then you disagree with his plans?"

He swerved his gaze to the sea and clenched his fingers around the railing. "Often."

The spite ringing in his tone ignited a spark of hope within Grace. Had she found an ally? Or like Father Alers, did this man hold some affection for the French captain? "Perhaps the captain reminds you of some fond relation?" She could not help the sarcasm in her voice.

Mr. Thorn's brows shot up and he gave a humorless laugh. "I have no affection for the captain, I assure you."

"Then why do you remain in his service?"

"It serves my purpose for the time being."

Grace shook her head, as confused with Mr. Thorn's excuses for wickedness as she was the father's. "A grand purpose it must be to implicate yourself with such atrocious deeds."

Mr. Thorn drew in a deep breath. He swallowed hard, and Grace sensed her accusation had struck a nerve of shame within him. The man appeared to possess some measure of honor. But could she trust him? "Do you not care that an innocent woman is being led to the slaughter?"

He faced her, and she detected a hint of moisture in his eyes. "I am not a man without a heart, miss."

Desperation tossed propriety to the wind, and Grace laid a hand on his arm. "Then save me, sir, by all that is good and holy."

"I cannot." He turned away. "There are bigger forces at work here than you realize, miss."

Grace's head began to spin, and she felt as though it would dislodge from her body and float into the cloudless sky. "Then you are equally duplicitous in this heinous act and will be punished accordingly." She regretted her harsh tone, but how could anyone choose to join the side of evil with such deliberation?

He chuckled, all traces of concern fleeing from his tone. "And who, might I ask, will execute the sentence?"

"God's justice will suffice." Grace rubbed the perspiration from the back of her neck.

"God's justice is too long delayed. Therefore I fear it not." Mr. Thorn stiffened his jaw, and he slid a finger over the scar lining his neck.

" 'Vengeance is mine; I will repay, saith the Lord.'" Grace quoted from Romans, hoping the word of God would soften this man's heart.

Mr. Thorn snorted. "Begging your pardon, but I have yet to see that promise fulfilled. Not in this life, anyway."

Dismayed by his lack of faith, Grace closed her eyes to a blast of hot wind. She was surrounded by miscreants and unbelievers. Yet as she allowed the muggy air to swirl around her, a glorious idea began to form in her mind. Perhaps she had been sent here by God to convert the poor souls on this ship? Perhaps the Almighty could find no other dedicated servant willing to do the task, so He had allowed Grace to be kidnapped in order to bring her on board.

The ship rose and plunged over a swell, showering Grace with a salty mist. Thankful for the momentary reprieve from the heat, she dared a glance over the deck and found most of the crew hard at their tasks. A menacing band of men, if ever she saw one. Composed of all ages and sizes, most wore faded checkered shirts and stained breeches, while others attempted—but fell woefully short of—a semblance of nobility with their gold-trimmed waistcoats and frayed satin neckerchiefs. All were armed with pistols slung about their chests as if they didn't trust the man beside them.

She felt Captain Dubois's gaze upon her from his position upon the quarterdeck. A shiver ran through her, and she turned around. Doubts assailed her, drifting atop her fears.

How, Lord, will I ever be able to reach such miscreants?

She grew dizzy, and her knees buckled. Mr. Thorn reached out for her, but she latched onto the railing instead.

"Are you ill, Miss Grace?" Mr. Thorn asked.

"Oui." The captain's heavy voice filled her ears as his massive frame filled her vision. "She has been indisposed below with a stomach ailment and has not eaten much in six days."

"Zooks. Six days? No wonder she's weak," Mr. Thorn exclaimed.

"I am feeling better today." Grace managed to sputter out the words as she caught her breath. But in truth, her nausea was returning.

"Get back to work," Captain Dubois ordered Mr. Thorn. The man bowed toward Grace, cast a look of scorn at his captain, and stomped away.

The wind whipped the captain's ebony hair about his shoulders, bringing with it the scent of brandy and tobacco. Cocking his head, he narrowed his gaze upon Grace. Her throat went dry. That the man invoked fear in those around him was evident. That he invoked it in her, she would not give him the satisfaction of knowing.

⤐

"You must eat something, mademoiselle, or you will never get well." Rafe crossed his arms over his chest to stop the urge burning in them to hold her, lest she fall.

Her brilliant green eyes stared at him from beneath a fan of dark lashes. An innocence beamed from them, a purity, coupled with a strength he had rarely seen in a woman.

"And why, pray tell, do you concern yourself with my health, Captain?" she asked.

He offered her a playful grin. "You know why."

"I know you are a thief, a kidnapper, and only God knows what else." A sail snapped above them as if sealing her words. Her raven hair glistened like onyx in the sunlight, though not a strand could escape the tight bun she had formed at the back of her head.

"The Bible says that neither thieves, nor the covetous, nor drunkards, nor revilers, nor extortioners will inherit the kingdom of God." Mademoiselle Grace lifted her chin; then her eyes softened. "But that does not have to be your fate, Captain."

"My fate is not your concern." Rafe flexed his jaw in irritation and leaned his elbow on the railing. "I may be a thief, mademoiselle, but I am also a man of my word, and I promised to deliver you to Rio de la Hacha, Colombia, in one piece." He said the words as much to remind himself of his task as to inform her of it.

"A man cannot be held to a promise of evil."

"I make no such distinctions."

"That much you have spoken in truth." She released a sigh of disap=pointment that jabbed his conscience. "But please be warned, Capitaine"— her attempt at the French pronunciation sent a shiver of delight through him—"evil begets evil."

"Is that so? Then you must have done something quite wicked to deserve such a fate as this"—he grinned and slid a finger over his mustache—"while I on the other hand must have done something admirable to have fallen into the fortune you will surely bring me."

Mademoiselle Grace's bottom lip began to quiver, and she looked away, but not before he saw tears fill her eyes. An unexpected pinch of remorse caused him to shift his stance and clear his throat.

"What does this don want with me?" she asked, still staring out to sea.

Rafe allowed his gaze to wander to the swell of her bosom above the lace of her bodice. "I suppose what all men want with beautiful women."

A noticeable shiver passed through her, and Rafe forced down another wave of regret. Sacre mer, what was wrong with him? She was merely a woman, a spoiled, wealthy woman encased in a pretense of saintly propriety and feminine beauty that would suck the life out of a man's soul if given the chance.

She splayed her fingers across the bare skin above her bodice as if she knew where his gaze wandered. "Men and their wars. What care have they for their innocent pawns?" she said to no one in particular as she gazed across the sea.

Disgust and hatred stole the sparkle from her eyes and left him cold. The ship pitched over a wave, and she staggered but quickly righted herself.

Another urge to place a hand on her back to steady her overcame Rafe, and he fisted his hands and folded them across his chest. The blood of a certain British admiral flowed in her veins. That alone had been enough to persuade him to accept the don's proposal. That and fulfilling a promise to Abbé Villion that would save hundreds of lives.

"How can you do something so cruel?" The look in her eyes cut into his heart.

Rafe stiffened his back. "For a greater cause, mademoiselle."

"Everyone has a choice, Captain."

"Not everyone, mademoiselle. Choices are often stolen from us. As, unfortunately, yours has been."

"I have no choice in my current situation, 'tis true, but I can choose the direction my heart takes, and I choose to continue to pray for God to deliver me. And I will pray for you, Captain. That you will repent of your evil ways and seek life in the arms of the Almighty."

Rafe ground his teeth together. Did these religious zealots follow him everywhere? "You have been praying for six days, mademoiselle. Perhaps God is too busy." Sarcasm filled his tone.

She glared at him below heavy lids. "Be on your guard, Captain Dubois. God is on my side."

Rafe opened his mouth to tell the exasperating woman that God was on no one's side, but her eyes fluttered shut, and she collapsed.

CHAPTER 5

Hot fluid seeped into her mouth. Spicy, bitter. It slid down her throat, stealing her breath. Grace jerked her head away. Her cheek brushed against something soft. The pungent scent of meat intermingled with the sting of brandy that bit her nose. Vague, nightmarish memories lurked like shadows in her mind, taunting her. Memories of her capture and a tall Frenchman with a heart of stone.

A hand gripped her chin and forced her face forward. Fingers that felt like rough rope and tasted of salt pried her lips apart. More hot liquid burned her tongue, poured down her throat, and she gagged. Raising a hand to her mouth, she sprang up, coughing. Dark eyes peered down at her, the spark of concern in them instantly hardening.

"Drink this, mademoiselle." Captain Dubois inched the bowl toward her mouth.

She pushed it away, shaking the fog from her head. "Can you not wait until I am conscious?"

"When you are conscious, you do not eat." A shadow of a smile played around his mouth. He rose from the bed and set the bowl atop a table.

Only then did Grace realize she lay upon a real bed. She scanned her surroundings. Two massive wooden chests ornamented in gold and bolted shut with iron locks guarded the wall opposite her. Upon the plush Persian rug at the room's center sat three colorfully upholstered armchairs. Beyond them, a cabinet housed a haphazard assortment of books, swords, pistols, and bottles. A large carved mahogany desk perched before a span of windows that stretched across the stern of the ship. Two guns, perched in their wheeled carriages, flanked either side, ready to be shoved through portholes should an enemy dare to approach from behind.

She was in the captain's cabin.

In the captain's bed.

With the captain looming over her, wearing that sardonic smirk upon his lips.

Her chest tightened. "Why am I in your bed? What day is it? How long have I been here? And why are you feeding me instead of Father Alers?" She glanced down at the loosened ties of her bodice, and a flush of horror heated her face. "How dare you?" She cowered away from him.

Captain Dubois raised his brows. "Which question would you like me to answer first, mademoiselle?"

"None." Grace swung her legs over the side of the bed. "I wish to leave this instant." But her body would not cooperate. Her breath caught in her throat. Her head spun like a waterspout upon the sea, and her legs quivered like pudding. She lifted a hand to her forehead.

A warm hand gripped her arm. "I suggest you lie back down, mademoiselle, and eat something. It has now been seven days since you have partaken of a full meal."

Grace shifted from beneath his touch and gazed out the windows where the rays of the morning sun angled across the captain's desk, setting the brass lantern aglitter. The glow lit the quadrant, backstaff, charts, and quill pen and beamed off a rapier, setting aglow the amber liquid in a half-empty bottle.

"Mercy me, I slept here all night?" She snapped her gaze to Captain Dubois. The possibility sped through her mind, seeking an alternative, any alternative besides the one that her purity could never consider.

He grinned, yet a spark of playfulness flitted across his dark eyes. Remembering the loose bindings of her bodice, Grace threw a hand to her chest. "What have you done?" Terror crowded in her throat.

He gave a derisive snort then shook his head and gripped the baldric strung over his white shirt. "Never fear, mademoiselle. I prefer *mes conquêtes* to be awake." He sauntered to his desk.

Conquests. Grace swallowed, praying he told the truth, praying she had not become one of his conquests during her unconscious stupor.

He picked up a chart, examined it, then tossed it back to the desk, sending dust particles floating within a ray of sunshine into a frenzy that reflected on his face. Danger hung on his broad shoulders like a well-fitted cloak, but there was a depth to this man that went beyond the baseness of a common brigand, a depth that lurked behind those dark, smoky eyes. He spoke of a greater cause—what had he meant by that?

"You should not treat women as property to be conquered or sold to the highest bidder," she finally said. Grace clasped her moist hands in her lap, trying to stop them from trembling. "Intimacies"—her voice squeaked and she cleared her throat—"between a man and a woman should remain within the sanctity of marriage."

He turned, crossed his arms over his chest, and chuckled as if she'd told a joke. "Do spare me your proverbs, *mon petit chou pieuse*."

"Did you just call me a shoe?"

A smile broke across his lips and widened. He chuckled. "Non. A little pious cabbage."

"A cabbage? Of all the..."

"It is a term of endearment." He waved a hand through the air, then settled his gaze upon her.

Endearment, indeed. More likely an insult to her intelligence. Fidgeting, she looked away beneath the warmth in his eyes. She'd never been alone in a room with a man other than her father. And Father Alers. What would Reverend Anthony say? Her reputation would be besmirched beyond repair. But what did it matter? Where she was going, she would not require a reputation.

He approached her. "You slept here because I feared your fever would return, and I loosened your bindings to allow you to breathe."

Graced fiddled with the ties. "Though I am appreciative of the clothes, Captain, the bodice is far too tight."

"Perhaps you are too fat." He grinned.

"Fat?" She jumped to her feet. The cabin spun around her. "You are no gentleman."

"And it took you only seven days to reach that conclusion?"

Grace sank back down to the bed, studying his cavalier attitude with curiosity. "You seem proud of your boorish behavior."

"I am proud of many things that would not engender your good opinion."

"Of that we are in agreement, Captain. But as I am sure you know, 'Pride goeth before destruction, and an haughty spirit before a fall.'"

He chuckled. "So, do you chastise me for being proud or being a boor?"

"Both."

"Yet you are the one who has fallen."

"I have not fallen," Grace snapped. "I am here for a reason."

"Oui, to line my pockets with gold." He smiled.

Grace's stomach knotted. She hated this man. She knew hatred was wrong. She knew it was as bad as murder, but at this moment, if she had a pistol, she would probably shoot him where he stood. "You are naught but a French rogue." She struggled to her feet. "I will leave now."

Captain Dubois blocked her exit. "This French rogue demands you eat something first, mademoiselle." He advanced toward her.

Grace sucked in her breath and retreated. Her foot struck the bed, and she collapsed back onto it.

Placing one hand on the edge of the mattress, he leaned toward her and laid the other upon her forehead. She flinched. "C'est bon. No fever." His warm breath wafted over her, bringing with it the smell of brandy. He righted himself. "Never fear, I have no interest in you, mademoiselle. My tastes lie in women *plus* agréables."

Grace tore her gaze from his and stared at the gold and purple sash tied around his waist and the leather baldric cutting across his chest. "I have no doubt in what direction your tastes lie."

"I have every doubt that you do, mademoiselle." He retrieved the bowl and handed it to her. "Now will you drink this, or shall I continue to pour it down your throat?"

"If I drink it, I fear it may end its journey upon your boots." Grace took the bowl and offered him a cautious smile.

The taut lines on his face faded. "I shall take that chance."

A tap on the door sounded, but the captain did not break the lock his gaze had upon her—an admiring, hungry gaze that set her nerves on edge.

The door creaked open and footsteps sounded. A man cleared his throat. "Capitaine, *s'il vous plaît*."

Captain Dubois's features instantly stiffened, and he turned to face the cook. "Father." He cleared his throat and stepped back from Grace. "See to it that the mademoiselle drinks all of the broth, then escort her back to her cabin."

The captain grabbed his rapier from the desk, slid it into his sheath with a metallic *chink*, and stormed out the door.

Father Alers shifted sympathetic eyes her way. A stained red shirt hung loosely over his corpulent frame, dangling below his waist where it met black breeches that spanned down to sturdy buckled shoes. He huffed out a sigh of impatience but finally took a seat and scratched his thick beard. "Come along, mademoiselle, finish your broth."

With the captain's exit, Grace's heart returned to a normal beat. She sipped the meaty soup. The warm broth slid down her throat like an elixir and plunged into her ravenous stomach.

"His methods may be a bit severe, mademoiselle," Father Alers said. "He only wishes you to keep your strength so you do not fall ill again."

Grace took the last sip and then tested her legs. Though still shaky, she felt her strength returning. "You have been too long at sea, Father, if you think there is an ounce of kindness in that man."

Father Alers chuckled and stood with a moan, then offered her his arm.

She placed her hand in the crook of his elbow. "He only wishes to fatten me up for the slaughter."

Father Alers's only reply was a grunt as he escorted her out the door and into the dimly lit companionway.

The ship canted, and Grace was thankful for Father Alers's support as they made their way down the hallway and around a corner to her cabin—especially when they were forced to squeeze past several crewmen who ogled Grace as if she were the evening meal.

"I will bring you some more food soon. *Pour maintenant,* you should rest." He turned to leave and Grace, feeling light-headed again, sank into the only chair in her small cabin.

Halting, Father Alers faced her, a pensive look on his aged face. "The capitaine is not as bad as he seems."

Grace blinked. "He is selling me as if I were cargo to an enemy who will subject me to a life of pain. How much more evil can he get?"

Father Alers rubbed the back of his thick neck. Compassion softened the lines on his face.

Struggling to her feet, Grace took a step toward him. "You are not like him. You don't agree with what he's doing. I can see it in your eyes. Will you help me, Father? Will you help me escape?"

Golden eyes snapped to hers, hesitant, sympathetic, but then they froze like two ponds beneath a winter's frost. "Non, I could never deceive him. He has seen too much betrayal in his life." His curt tone slammed a heavy door on her hope. He shrugged. "I am hoping he will figure this out on his own."

"You cling to a hope of the captain's redemption while my life is being destroyed." The blood rushed from Grace's head, and she crumpled into her seat. "'Tis a sin to know the right thing to do and not do it, Father."

"Peut-être, mademoiselle, but I've seen greater sins perpetrated every day in the Church." With a jerk of his head, he waddled out and closed the door.

Dropping to her knees, Grace leaned over the chair. "Why do You close all the doors to my rescue, Lord? If it is indeed my task to bring these nefarious men to redemption, please show me how. Give me the words to say. Please do not let me be handed over to this Don Miguel." Yet no answer came, no feeling of peace, no assurance of God's presence. Tears slid down her cheeks onto the chair just as droplets of her hope continued to seep from her heart with each passing day.

~~~

Rafe stood at the bow of *Le Champion* and closed his eyes against the hot, raging wind, allowing it to blast away the memory of Mademoiselle Grace: her scent that reminded him of the sweet pastries his mother used to bake, the silky feel of the mademoiselle's skin beneath his fingers, and those sharp green eyes that sliced right through his soul into his heart. Femme *exaspérante*!

He had barely slept two minutes all night. It wasn't the hard floor that kept him awake. He had slept on far worse in his day. It was the sound of her deep, restless breathing, her occasional quiet moans, and his concern that she would fade into a perilous fever and die during the night.

Finally, before dawn, he had risen, lit a lantern, and watched her as she slept. The way her lips twitched and her eyelids fluttered as if she were dreaming, the strands of raven hair curling across her cheek like feathers spanning a creamy river. Her delicate fingers coiled around her arms in a protective embrace. She appeared as fragile as a tender flower in the field, yet possessing enough tenacity to push above the others in her quest for the sun. Honesty coated her lips like honey. He doubted a lie would survive among its sweetness. And in a world where lies were commonplace, her candid jabs brought him more amusement than insult.

That she was innocent, he could tell from her reaction to him. That she possessed a gracious heart was evident from the errand in which he found her engaged when he'd captured her. That she nudged awake a long-dormant spirit of protectiveness within him caused his blood to boil.

He did not want to protect her. He did not want to admire her. He wanted to hand her to the don as planned and get his money. Why could she not have been pompous, churlish, and deceitful like the women to whom Rafe had grown accustomed among high society?

The ship rose and plunged over a wave, drenching him with salty spray. He opened his eyes and shook it from his face. Spyglass pressed against his boots. He picked her up and laid the damp cat across one shoulder. She purred her approval, and he ran his fingers through her fur.

Zut alors, why was the mademoiselle always in his thoughts? He flexed his muscles as if strengthening his defenses. He must. He must hand her over. The money she would bring would save hundreds of lives. What was the fate of one pretentious girl compared to that? And pretentious she was, full of the same religious banalities he had been beaten with all his life. She was more like his father than he realized. He must look beyond his reaction to her, beyond her admirable qualities, and remember that fact.

A slap on his back startled him from his thoughts. "What brings you here to the fo'c'sle, Captain?"

Rafe turned to see his friend, Monsieur Thorn, smiling at him. He had been a good friend, Rafe's only friend this past year. "Clearing my head."

"Ah, the lady is quite enchanting."

"My thoughts were not directed toward her." Rafe grimaced at his friend's discernment.

"Indeed?" A coy grin lifted the lad's thin lips. "Has she recovered from her illness?"

"Oui." Rafe laid a hand on Spyglass and braced his boots on the deck as the ship plunged over another swell.

"Captain." Thorn cleared his throat and adjusted his hat. "Has the lady's family laid some unpardonable insult upon you? For I've yet to see you barter in human flesh."

A spark of shame seared Rafe, but he drowned it under his rising ire. Had his whole crew gone soft? "She is a woman, and her father is an admiral in the British navy. Need I say more?"

"I was in His Majesty's service, Captain, as were several of your crew. And yet you do not despise us."

Spyglass ceased her purring, and Rafe began caressing her again, resurging her soothing tones. "You quit the navy, as did they, because your conscience could not bear their cruelty. How can I fault you for that? Instead, I applaud you."

Monsieur Thorn rubbed the scar on his neck and gazed across the choppy sea. "We should be coming alongside Inagua Island soon."

"*Bien.* Only a few more days to Port-de-Paix. I could use some time ashore." Where he could seek comfort in the arms of one of the town's many willing females. And distance himself from Mademoiselle Grace.

"What of the men? They haven't been paid since we sank the Dutch merchantman and delivered her crew and cargo to Monsieur Franco." Thorn fingered the feathery whiskers on his chin. "We wouldn't want a mutiny on our hands."

The sprinkle of glee in Thorn's tone bristled over Rafe's nerves, but he shrugged it off. They had all been on board this ship far too long. "The crew never complains about enjoying les *plaisirs* de Port-de-Paix. Besides, we will be there only a few days."

Dropping his hands to his sides, Thorn began clenching and unclenching his fists. He shifted his stance then gripped the railing.

Rafe frowned at his friend. Thorn was usually the essence of unruffled composure. "What has you so skittish, mon ami?"

His first mate's gaze darted over the horizon as if searching for something. He gripped the hilt of his sword, then scratched his chin before dropping his hands again. He shook his head and turned to Rafe. "What did you say?"

"You are jumpier than a cat on hot coals."

"Me? No. Just anxious to get to port." Thorn rubbed his hands together.

Rafe shook his head. As long as he had known Mr. Thorn, the man had never enjoyed the amenities of port, had often opted to stay on board when the rest of the crew went ashore. Especially in Port-de-Paix. No matter. Perhaps the man's long days at sea had changed his appetites.

Sunlight set the peaks of waves aglow in silvery strips that glittered as far as his eye could see. The smell of oakum, pitch, and salt filled his nostrils, and Rafe took a deep breath. He loved the sea. The ultimate playing field for those who craved danger, excitement, and freedom. They were the outcasts of society—those who did as they pleased and answered to no man.

A speck appeared on the horizon just as "A sail, a sail!" bellowed from the masthead. Setting Spyglass upon the deck, Rafe plucked the telescope from his belt and leveled it upon the intruder, wondering if perhaps the mademoiselle's family had pursued them. Thorn coughed beside him. Two red sails glutted with wind filled his vision, and from the white foam clawing the bow of the ship beneath them, she appeared to be rushing straight for them.

"Who is she?" Thorn asked as Rafe handed him the glass.

"Have a look."

Mr. Thorn peered toward the ship. "I can't make her out yet, Captain."

"Only one ship I know of has crimson sails."

"Captain Howell." The first mate lowered the glass. "Isn't he one of Roger Woodes's men? I wonder what he's doing out here."

"Oui, one of his *laquais*, and he searches for pirates is my guess. Those who did not accept the king's pardon or who have since broken the accord."

"Then we have nothing to fear from him." Thorn slammed the glass shut and handed it to Rafe, but not before Rafe heard the slight tremble in his voice.

"I trust no one." Rafe crammed the spyglass into his baldric. "Ready the guns, but do not run them out. And send the men aloft in case we need to unfurl topsail."

"Aye, Captain." The first mate touched his hat, spun on his heel, and marched away.

Within an hour, Rafe could easily make out the schooner *Avenger* crowding every stitch of her red canvas and housing a full tier of guns fore and aft. Captain George Howell stood regally at her helm.

Rafe's gut churned. What did Howell want with him? He glanced upward where the flag of France flapped regally from *Le Champion*'s foremast. There were no hostilities between France and Britain, unless some war had broken out of which he was unaware.

But he didn't have to wait long for an answer as the *Avenger* veered to larboard and ranged up alongside *Le Champion*. One by one gun ports popped open, and the charred muzzles of twelve guns bade him welcome.

A thunderous boom roared across the sky and shook the sea.

CHAPTER 6

Boom! Grace jerked awake. A colorful pattern blurred in her vision. She rubbed her eyes. The pattern came into focus, and she realized it was the upholstered back of the chair she knelt beside. The bulkhead quivered. The planks shook beneath her legs. Her heart seized. She sprang to her feet. Ignoring her dizziness, she bolted for the door. A gun had been fired. That meant an enemy was in sight. And that carried the possibility of her rescue. She darted down the companionway and up the ladder, praying that perhaps her sister Faith had somehow found her. *Oh, Lord, let it be so!*

Pushing aside her fear, she rushed across the deck, weaving among the sailors dashing here and there as they obeyed their captain's orders. Gripping the railing, she batted away the smoke and peered toward a two-masted ship bearing down upon them off their larboard bow. Red sails, stark against the blue sky, gorged with wind as they pushed the vessel onward. Her heart sank. 'Twas not her sister Faith's ship, the *Red Siren*. But perhaps the ship's captain might still be noble enough to save her from these villains. She coughed as the dissipating smoke stung her nose.

"Sacre mer, what are you doing? Get below, mademoiselle!" Captain Dubois clutched her arm and dragged her to the companionway hatch.

"Who are they?" Grace could not keep the hope from her voice.

"Ah, you think they are your *sauveteurs*, your champions, eh, mademoiselle?" He raised a brow then released her arm. "Je t'assure, they will not save you. Now get below. I have no time for this."

"The *Avenger* wishes a parley, Captain," Mr. Thorn shouted from the quarterdeck.

Swerving away from Grace, Captain Dubois darted to the bulwarks. His men ceased their frantic activities and formed an audience upon the main deck. Grace slunk into the shadows beneath the quarterdeck. She would not allow her fear to send her below when a possible rescue was at hand.

SAINT*the Raven*

The schooner ranged up alongside them keel to keel within twenty yards, and her captain, a brawny man with a full beard and plumed tricorne hailed them in a powerful voice. "I am Captain Howell of the *Avenger*."

Captain Dubois leapt upon the gunwale and grabbed a backstay for support. "I know who you are, monsieur." His deep tone full of cheerful insolence held not an ounce of fear. With his tricorne atop his head, his gray coat flapping in the breeze behind him, and the sun glinting off the long rapier at his side, he appeared every bit the pirate he claimed he was not.

"We come with the compliments of Captain Roger Woodes," the man bellowed, waving his plumed hat through the air, "who bids you to haul down your colors and surrender your ship."

Coarse chuckles bounded over the sailors, and Grace wondered what they found so amusing. She had heard of Roger Woodes, the ex-pirate turned governor of New Providence—a man who thought nothing of rounding up his one-time colleagues and stringing them upon the scaffold.

"For what reason, monsieur?" Captain Dubois asked.

"For the crime of piracy," boomed the captain of the *Avenger*, who replaced his hat atop his head and began fingering the hilt of his sword.

Snorts of derision replaced the laughter among the crew, and Mr. Thorn broke away from the agitated mob and retreated toward the starboard side of the ship as if frightened of the altercation. But when his eyes met Grace's, only malevolence brewed within them.

"With my compliments," Captain Dubois shouted, "you may tell Governor Woodes that I am no pirate and as such, am in no position to surrender anything." He turned and whispered something to a sailor behind him, sending the man scampering below.

"Most unfortunate, Captain, for I have been instructed to blast you from the sea should you resist." Howell's laughter bounced over the sapphire waves between them, silencing all within its hearing upon the deck of *Le Champion*.

All save Captain Dubois.

"By all means, I beg you to try, monsieur." Captain Dubois swept his hat out before him, hand on his heart.

Seeing that she only had a few moments before the battle began, Grace rushed to the railing, waving her hands through the air. "Captain Howell! Captain Howell!"

The man halted and squinted in her direction. She continued, "I am a prisoner aboard this ship. I am the daughter of Admiral Westcott. Please save me!"

Instead of the expected look of horror on the captain's face, followed by his quick action to save her from these scoundrels, the man chuckled, put his hands on his waist, and replied, "What is that to me, miss?"

The crews on both ships broke into coarse laughter as Grace's heart sank to the deck. One of the sailors fired a pistol into the air, initiating the battle, and Grace attempted to go below but found her feet would not move—no longer from curiosity, but from pure terror. Instead she uttered a prayer for the souls on both ships, herself included.

Captain Dubois, on the other hand, stormed the deck with all the confidence and courage of a man born to lead, his crew close on his heels awaiting his commands.

"Haul foresheets to the wind!" he bellowed, and seconds later the ship lurched and sped on its way.

A gust of hot air struck Grace, bringing with it the smell of salt and wood and the sweat of the crew as they readied for battle. Managing to pry her shoes loose from the deck, she crept toward the companionway just as the air reverberated with the thunder of guns. Streams of dark gray smoke spurted from the *Avenger*'s hull as the ship sped by their larboard quarter. Grace braced herself for the impact of their broadside. But instead of the jarring crunch of wood, the snap of coiled lines, and the screams of the injured, only hollow splashes met her ears.

"Bring her about, Mr. Thorn!" the captain shouted, planting his hands upon his waist and staring at the enemy as if they were naught but a temporary annoyance.

The ship yawed widely to starboard, and Grace flung herself against the mainmast to keep from tumbling across the deck. She gripped the rough wood. Splinters jabbed her tender skin. Above her, the sails clapped as loud as a cannon blast. Sailors darted around her, some jumping into the ratlines with muskets in hand, others hauling shot to the various guns positioned about the deck. Curses filled the air and took flight on the wind, burning her ears, but the men took no notice of her.

As *Le Champion* veered on her tack, the *Avenger* slipped from Grace's sight. She lifted a silent prayer that the ship had slunk away in cowardice. But no such luck. The threatening red sails appeared again on the horizon like bloated demons flying through the sky. In minutes, the ravenous schooner swooped down upon *Le Champion*'s lee quarter with her rigging full of men and white foam salivating over her bow.

"They hope to board us." Captain Rafe chuckled. Doffing his coat, he laid it over the capstan and rolled up his sleeves as if he were commencing a day's work. The sash strapped about his waist whipped upon the gleaming metal of his rapier, whose pommel he now gripped with a tight fist.

"Load the swivels," he shouted. "And arm yourselves with hand grenades, men."

A furious rumble filled the air, and Grace clapped her hands over her ears. Small shot from the *Avenger*'s swivel guns whistled through *Le Champion*'s shrouds, ripping holes in her canvas and sending the sailors into a frenzy.

Grace threw a hand to her throat to still her chaotic breathing then swept a gaze over the deck for injured men. But she saw none. *Thank You, Lord.*

"Strike their rigging only," the captain ordered.

Before her eyes could locate him, Mr. Thorn shouted, "Fire!" and the air was set aquiver with the roar of guns.

Sooty smoke blasted over Grace, stinging her eyes and nose. She gasped for air, then peered through the haze. The men aboard the *Avenger* staggered back beneath the onslaught and made haste for the stern of their ship. Their captain stood by the helm, spewing a string of unending commands.

The *Avenger* continued on its tack, cruising by *Le Champion*, its occupants scurrying back and forth across the deck like ants upon an upturned anthill.

Rafe nodded to Mr. Thorn, who in turn yelled to a man standing at the entrance to the companionway. "Fire the crossbar!" A second later, a gun exploded in a thunderous *boom* that shook *Le Champion* from truck to keelson. Grace squeezed her eyes shut, fearing the ship would be rent apart by the force.

A massive crunch filled the air, followed by the eerie snap of wood.

A shout of victory ensued, and Grace opened her eyes to see the rigging upon the main and top mizzen sails of the *Avenger* fold into a tangled mass of rope and spar. Without their mainsail, the *Avenger* groped listlessly through the sea. Their captain charged toward the stern as if he would jump the distance between the ships and pummel Captain Dubois to the deck. Instead, all he could do was raise his fist in the air and assault them with his foul mouth. Captain Dubois leapt upon the gunwale and gave a mock bow. "Another time, perhaps, Capitaine. *Mes compliments à* Woodes." Chuckling, Captain Dubois slipped down to the deck where he was engulfed with cheers from his men.

His white shirt flapped in the breeze. The tanned skin on his chest and neck glistened with sweat in the noonday sun. He ran a hand through his coal-black hair, and his eyes latched upon Grace—dark eyes, flashing from the heat of battle. A shiver ran through her, the cause of which she could not explain. Fear, perhaps? More likely disgust at how easily he resorted to violence.

Tearing her gaze from him, Grace released the mast, ignoring the pain in her hands, and took a tentative step with her trembling legs. Her stomach lurched, and she was thankful the broth had long since digested, or she feared she'd lose it upon the deck. She'd never been in a gun battle. Everything had happened so fast, she hadn't time to consider that she could have been torn to pieces by a twelve-pound ball of metal. But now as relief flooded through her, she began to shake uncontrollably. She made her way to the companionway, hoping to manage a quiet exit, when she saw a gray mound rising out of the sea off their larboard side.

"Sir," she called to one of the crewmen who was passing by—a young, lanky lad with a braid of brown hair hanging halfway down his back. He turned to her, surprise and delight brightening his sun-baked face.

"What land is that?" She pointed to the sight on the horizon.

" 'Tis the island they call Inagua, miss."

"It appears so close."

"A mile or two, aye." He started to leave.

Grace grabbed his shirt, but quickly released it, not wanting him to think her wanton.

"What is your name?" She attempted a coy smile as a sour taste filled her mouth. How did her sisters feign such coquettish mannerisms?

"Andrew Fletcher, miss."

Grace leaned closer to him. "Mr. Fletcher, may I ask where we are heading?"

Huzzahs and hurrahs blared from the crew. The young sailor glanced nervously across the deck as if seeking his captain's permission.

Grace wondered if he or any of the crew were aware of the reason she'd been brought on board. "I am a prisoner, Mr. Fletcher. What harm would it do to tell me?"

He faced her and nodded. "We should arrive at Port-de-Paix in two days' time, miss. I'm told we'll anchor there for only a short while before setting sail again."

"Thank you." Grace smiled.

He gave her a curious look before being whisked away by his companions who passed around bottles of some vile alcohol in celebration of their victory.

Port-de-Paix? That would mean they'd be anchored close to land. Close enough to swim—or float—to shore. A daring idea began to form in her head.

CHAPTER 7

Grace released Father Alers's arm and entered the captain's cabin. The desk and chairs had been pushed aside, the Persian rug rolled up, and in its place sat a long wooden table laden with steaming platters of food, mugs filled to the brim, decanters of wine, and brass candlesticks. Pewter plates shimmered in the flickering candlelight, and the spicy scent of pork and the pungent smell of cheese swirled about her. At the head of the table sat Captain Dubois and lining each side were members of his crew, some of whom Grace recognized, and all of whom jumped to their feet at her entrance. Including Captain Dubois, looking rather dashing in his black silver-embroidered coat and gold and purple sash tied about his waist. He had tamed his unruly mane into a slick style which he tied behind him, revealing a strong jaw which flexed beneath a sprinkle of black stubble. His white shirt, devoid of its normal stains and wrinkles, appeared oddly out of place upon his broad chest. And without his pistols and knives draped across it, he could almost pass for a gentleman attending a soirée.

Almost.

Behind him, through the stern windows, the sea and sky melded into a smoldering curtain as dark as the captain's gaze.

Father Alers gestured to an empty seat at the opposite end of the table. All eyes remained fixed upon Grace as if the men had never seen a woman before, and she began to regret accepting the captain's invitation to dine with him and his officers.

She stepped forward and raised her chin. "Have I been invited to partake of a meal, or am I to be the meal itself?"

Chuckles rumbled around the table. Mr. Thorn coughed, and one side of Captain Dubois's lips lifted in a sly grin that sent an uncomfortable quiver through her belly.

"Whichever you prefer, mademoiselle."

"I prefer that you turn this brig around and take me back to

Charles Towne at once."

"That is not one of your choices." He raised a brow.

"Then what exactly are my choices?"

"To dine with us or return to your cabin hungry." Cocking his head, he sent her a lazy grin.

Grace bit her lip and scanned the men. A chill pricked her skin. She'd never envisioned herself dining with such depraved characters without benefit of chaperone, without a proper escort—without protection. And though she'd love nothing more than to turn and make a mad dash down the companionway, if God had placed her aboard this ship to convert these men, she couldn't accomplish that task alone in her cabin. Which was why she'd accepted the captain's invitation. And why she must now stay.

"I will remain, but not because it pleases you." She didn't want to inflate the captain's already billowing pomposity. Nor did she want to hide her loathing for him, God forgive her.

Captain Dubois rubbed his chin and gave her a haughty look. "Mademoiselle, I find no pleasure in your company. En fait, it was Father Alers who suggested you join us."

Heat flushed up her neck at his insult. *Insolent cad!* She'd like to tell him that she found no pleasure in his company either, but she knew that wouldn't be a very prudent thing to say.

Nor a very Christian thing to say.

"Our food grows cold." He waved a hand as if brushing her away.

Father Alers gestured again toward her chair. "S'il vous plaît, mademoiselle?"

Gathering her courage along with her skirts, Grace slid onto the wooden seat. Without hesitation, the men sat down and began piling food onto their plates as if it were their last meal.

"Please, gentlemen. Shouldn't we ask God's blessing first?" Grace raised her voice over the clank and clatter of silverware and plates.

Groans filled the room. Hands halted in midair. Looks of derision shot her way as one by one, the men lowered themselves back in their chairs and dipped their chins.

Grace sought some measure of support from Father Alers but found only a hint of surprise mixed with curiosity lifting the lines on his face.

Captain Dubois, on the other hand, shifted his jaw in impatience and nodded for her to continue.

Grace bowed her head. "Father, we thank You for the bounty that You have provided this night. Please bless it, and may we always be thankful for Your goodness."

The clank of spoons resurged like a rising swell before a storm.

"And Lord," she shouted. "I ask You. . ." Huffs and moans rippled across the cabin, ending in silence. "To open the eyes of these men so that they may see You and know You. Amen." Grace lifted her face.

The men stared at her, their mouths agape as if she'd asked for lightning to strike them.

Ignoring them, she swallowed a lump of fear and nodded toward a steaming platter in the center of the table. "The pork, if you please, Mr. Alers."

He smiled and handed her the tray as the men resumed their feast, rudely grabbing platters and bowls without discretion and shoveling food onto overstuffed plates, reminding Grace of pigs before their slop.

She took a bite of the meat and though it was tough, the spicy, rich taste burst in her mouth and was welcomed gladly by her stomach. Having consumed three meals yesterday, she found her strength returning in full force. "Did you prepare this feast, Father?"

Captain Dubois chuckled and poured amber liquid into his glass from a flagon.

"Address me as Monsieur Alers, s'il vous plaît," Father Alers said. "Mais oui, mademoiselle. I did."

"It is quite good." Grace grabbed a biscuit from a platter in front of her. "Thank you for all your hard work."

Again the men stared her way, and Father Alers smiled. "Finally I receive some recognition for my hard work." He glanced across the table. "You could all learn manners from this lady."

The man to Grace's left belched in reply and poured himself another mug of what Grace assumed was ale. The bitter, grainy smell rose to join the fruity scent of wine, overpowering the savory aromas that filled the cabin. Grace lifted her own cup and found Mr. Alers had provided her with lemon-flavored water to drink.

Spyglass leapt onto the captain's lap, but instead of pushing her aside, Captain Dubois set down his glass and offered the feline a morsel of his food. His expression softened as he coddled the animal, and Grace found his affection for the cat curious. She scanned her other dinner companions, who were too busy scooping pork and peas into their mouths to converse with one another. Captain Dubois took a bite of a biscuit and leaned back in his chair.

Grace shifted in her seat. "Captain, would you introduce me to your men, please?"

He narrowed his eyes and lifted his lips in pretense of a smile that seemed to hurt his face. "Mais oui." He flung out his arm and beginning with the man seated to her left, he introduced each sailor in turn: the ship's bosun, the carpenter, Mr. Thorn, then to her right, the helmsman, the second mate, and finally Father Alers.

Grace nodded at each man, her stomach tightening when her gaze landed upon the second mate, Mr. Weylan. She recognized him as the foppish man she'd seen on deck with two other sailors—the ones who had gawked at her with such alarming bawdiness. Even now, in front of his captain, Mr. Weylan took such brazen liberties with his gaze that Grace felt soiled by proximity.

She looked to the captain for assistance, but he busied himself refilling his glass. Why should she assume the captain could control his men's passions any more than he could his own?

❧

Heat stormed through Rafe, and he poured himself another drink. Why was Mademoiselle Grace being so courteous? One would assume she was attending a soirée at a friend's estate rather than eating alongside dissolute, reckless sailors who held her captive. And now, those green eyes bored into him, condemning, slicing through him like emerald ice. He wouldn't have invited her at all, save to answer Father Alers's challenge that Rafe was somehow uneasy in the girl's presence. But in truth, his gut had been in a knot since she entered the room.

"Pleased to meet you, gentlemen." Mademoiselle Grace smiled, but the slight tremor in her bottom lip gave her unease away. She wasn't at all pleased to meet them. Then why ask for introductions?

She took a bite of cheese then washed it down with the lemon juice Father Alers had provided. Her rosy lips puckered, and Rafe had trouble keeping his eyes off them. Setting down her glass, she met his gaze briefly, then she gripped a chain that hung around her neck and glanced over the men. "May I inquire, gentlemen, what brings you into the captain's service?"

Monsieur Atton thought for a moment then raised a glass toward

Rafe. "The captain's a fair man, a good seaman, and he's lined me pockets wit' many coins."

Rafe returned his helmsman's salute.

"Yet I have seen none of those coins in quite a while," Monsieur Weylan grumbled beneath his breath, and exchanged a quick glance with Thorn.

Rafe eyed the two with suspicion, hearing only pieces of the exchange.

Monsieur Maddock halted his spoon, overloaded with potatoes, halfway to his mouth, "Aye, 'tis been some time, now that I think about it." He tossed the mound into his mouth, dropping some onto his lap.

Rafe continued petting Spyglass, but his insides tightened like a sail beneath a hard wind. "You were all paid handsomely for our last job. I heard no complaints." He eyed each of the men but none would meet his gaze. "And we stand to make a fortune on our current mis—" He froze and glanced at Mademoiselle Grace.

Her face blanched and she bit her bottom lip. "Mission, as in me." Simmering green eyes rose to meet his. "No need to mince words, Captain. Everyone at this table knows what heinous future awaits me so that all of you can—how did you say it, Mr. Atton—line your pockets?"

Spyglass leapt from Rafe's arms to the deck, sans doute to escape the hatred firing from her eyes. Brushing away the twinge of pain caused by her scorn, Rafe preferred to focus on her courage and forthrightness, qualities he had not expected in a British admiral's daughter.

"Regardless." She squared her shoulders and glanced over the men. "You all should be ashamed of yourselves. Surely there are far more worthy and honorable ways to make a living!"

Rafe chomped on his biscuit, knowing he should be angry at her insult, but instead found himself amused by her audacity. His crew was not in agreement.

Monsieur Maddock, the carpenter, choked on his food. "Honorable, lud." He set down his spoon with a clank. "Beggin' yer pardon, miss, but what does honor have to do wit' anything?"

She leaned forward, spreading her fingers over the bare skin above her bodice. "Honor, sir, is doing the right thing, living the right way. Obeying God and those He places in authority over you. Honor has to do with everything."

"Honor never did me no good." Monsieur Atton, the helmsman sitting to Rafe's left, spewed crumbs over his plate.

The bosun, Monsieur Legard, pointed his spoon at her. "Honor is for the weak minded."

Her face crumpled. "But what does a man have, what can he acquire that can truly satisfy? 'Tis only what he does in the name of goodness, what he does for God that counts in the end."

"I quite agree, Miss Grace." Monsieur Thorn dropped a slice of cheese into his mouth and gave her a nod that grated over Rafe. His friend's pious prattle had become quite bothersome lately. And now, with the encouragement of a like-minded zealot, no doubt it would become far worse.

"Then pray tell, Mr. Thorn." Mademoiselle Grace's reprimanding tone rang through the cabin. "Why do you partake of such wickedness?"

Monsieur Thorn faced his captain, a supercilious smirk on his face, and Rafe leaned his elbows on the table. "Do enlighten us, Monsieur Thorn. Why *do* you keep such nefarious company?"

Monsieur Thorn hesitated and his face paled, but then he winked at his captain. "Perhaps to shine as a beacon of sanity amidst this treacherous mob. Or"—he shrugged—"perhaps I was in need of a holiday from the rigidness of society."

Rafe settled back in his chair, relieved that the brandy began to spread its numbing fingers through his senses. "Then you and Father Alers have that in common. He, too, feels the need to take a *répit* from the shackles of religious obligations."

"They are not shackles, Captain." Mademoiselle Grace shifted a gaze to Father Alers as if seeking an ally, but the father's focus remained on his food. "In truth, the love of God will set you free."

"Yet you are not free now, mademoiselle. Neither physically nor, it appears, in any other way." Rafe moved his chair back from the table, his stomach disinterested in the food he'd heaped upon his plate. "You do nothing but point a finger of condemnation on everyone around you. If this is freedom, you may keep your religion, mademoiselle."

"You mock me, Captain." Mademoiselle Grace hung her head, one delicate strand of ebony hair feathering over her cheek. "God is but a joke to you."

"That there is a God who created this world of pain and injustice would indeed be a joke—a joke upon us," Rafe shot back. When Mademoiselle Grace lifted her head and he saw the moisture that filled her eyes, he instantly regretted his tone.

"Such strong faith is quite admirable, mademoiselle." Monsieur Weylan said, drawing her gaze to him. He steepled his fingers together.

"Ye don't believe in God, ye cockerel." Monsieur Maddock chortled. "Don't listen to Weylan, miss. He'd say anything to win a lady's affections."

Rafe studied Weylan and the way he ogled Mademoiselle Grace as if she were a morsel of food on his plate. The vain peacock had a reputation with the ladies. His good looks, fashionable dress, and cultured tone deceived them into believing he was a gentleman, when nothing could be further from the truth.

Yet, much to her credit, Mademoiselle Grace seemed undaunted by his flirtations; *en effet*, she seemed more repulsed than enamored.

Turning from him, she faced the men and spoke in a voice urgent with sincerity, "Mercy me, don't any of you believe in God?"

Monsieur Thorn finished the food in his mouth and took a sip of his wine. "I do."

"Mais oui," Monsieur Legard grunted.

"Haven't really taken much thought of it." Monsieur Atton shoveled a spoonful of peas into his mouth, sending one shooting across the table like a miniature cannonball.

Monsieur Maddock shrugged while Father Alers focused a convicting gaze upon Rafe.

"God is real." The pitch of her sweet voice rose. "He created this world, and He created you. He does not approve of such licentious living, wasting your talents on dissipation and thievery. There will come a judgment one day, gentlemen, and my hope, my desperate prayer, is that you will not be found wanting." Her eyes flamed with sincerity and true concern.

And Rafe knew she meant every word she said.

But he didn't have the heart to tell her she was a fool for putting her hopes in such nonsense.

Monsieur Legard took another swig of ale. A trickle ran down his bearded chin, and he wiped it with his sleeve. "You are fair to look at, mademoiselle, but you should pray the don is deaf. Your religious jabbering will drive a man *fou*—even a devout Spaniard."

Chuckles of agreement spanned over the table.

Rafe winced beneath Monsieur Legard's insult, and he opened his mouth to reprimand the man, but then he hesitated, his gaze shifting to Mademoiselle Grace, curious to see her response to the injurious affront.

Her cheeks reddened, and she glared at the man as if she would shoot him where he sat. But then her features softened like the settling of waves upon the sea, and she gave him a sweet smile. "I have been told I talk overmuch, Monsieur Legard. Please forgive me if I have offended you."

The man blinked then shook his head. "No offense, mademoiselle."

Rafe sipped his brandy, trying to quell the unease gripping his belly. Such charity in the face of insult and hostility. *Incroyable.*

Spyglass jumped into her lap, and she ran her fingers over the cat's fur. She met Rafe's gaze but quickly lowered her lashes. This evening could not be easy for her. Yet she'd accepted his invitation, and not only that, she had engaged the men in a discussion of what was important to her, no matter the cost to her dignity.

"D'ye think we'll see more of Captain Howell?" Monsieur Maddock shifted uncomfortably in his seat and faced Rafe.

"Non. I'd say he's been sufficiently humbled." Rafe chuckled, eager to follow the conversation on its new tack.

"He'll have to assemble a fleet next time to catch you, Captain." Monsieur Thorn lifted his mug in salute.

Monsieur Atton scratched his head. "I still can't figure out what sent 'im after us."

Monsieur Thorn coughed and poured himself more wine.

Rafe couldn't make sense of it either. He'd never committed piracy, and his reputation as a mercenary was well known throughout the West Indies. That Capitaine Howell sailed the Caribbean in search of him only made Rafe's job more difficult. As soon as possible, he would send a dispatch to Governor Woodes to inquire after the matter.

"How long will we anchor at Port-de-Paix, Capitaine?" Monsieur Legard scooped another helping of pork onto his plate.

"*Je ne sais pas.*" Rafe shook his head. Mademoiselle Grace continued to pet Spyglass, the cat's purrs filtering over the table. The woman had not eaten much of her food. Her shoulders slumped, and she seemed to have detached herself from the conversation. Rafe felt the loss immediately.

"Long enough for me to visit Mademoiselle Bertille?" Monsieur Legard asked, his eyes aglow.

"That trollop." Monsieur Weylan snickered.

"She's no more trollop than the women ye frequent."

Mademoiselle Grace cringed.

"Jealous?" Weylan grinned.

"*Assez!*" Rafe slammed down his mug. "Hardly proper conversation with a lady present."

"If you'll excuse me, gentlemen." Mademoiselle Grace rose from her chair, cuddling Spyglass in her arms. "My absence will surely allow you to continue your engaging discourse without censure." She offered the men a weak smile.

Father Alers pushed his seat back, its legs scraping over the wooden deck. "I will escort you back to your cabin."

"Non. Allow me." Rafe stood, feeling the brandy swirl in his head. Steadying himself, he wove around the table and held out his arm while Father Alers gave him a curious look and resumed his seat.

Fear dashed across Mademoiselle Grace's eyes. She hesitated then set Spyglass down, nodding her assent but refusing to take his arm.

"C'est-ça." Rafe hid his disappointment beneath a shrug.

With a swish of her skirts, she followed him out the door and into the dark companionway.

"My men have not had opportunities to polish their social graces. My apologies if they offended you."

"They did not offend, Captain. I merely wished them to see the peril of their souls so they can choose God's love rather than continue in a life of sin." They passed beneath a lantern hanging on the bulkhead. Rafe noticed how its light sought her out and showered over her as if she were the only thing worthy on board the vessel.

"I would leave the fate of their souls up to them, mademoiselle, if I were you. They do not take kindly to religious reprimands. En effet, most left their homes to avoid such castigation."

He rounded the corner, opened the door, and ushered her inside.

She turned to face him. "I fear for your soul as well, Captain. I urge you to flee from this sordid life you have chosen before it is too late." Yet no urgency or concern could be found in either her tone or in her expression.

Rafe cocked his head. "Before I sell you to the don, you mean?"

She looked down. "If that is my destiny, I accept it. But that is not why I warned you."

"I do not believe you care for my soul, mademoiselle. In fact, I think you despise me. Am I right?" Rafe laid a finger beneath her chin and tipped her head up to face him, longing to see a glimpse of emotion, a spark of feeling, anything that would prove him wrong.

But her eyes were as hard as glass. She stepped back, breaking their contact and sending a chill through him. "What do you expect?"

Rafe studied her. What *did* he expect? Nothing but the hatred he received. Why then, did he long for something else? Longing made him weak. And weakness was not to be tolerated. So, he attacked her where he knew it would hurt. "Are not Christians supposed to love everyone? Even your enemies?"

Sighing, she clasped her hands together and hung her head. "I love you as a fellow human being and a lost soul in need of God." She lifted narrow, spiteful eyes upon him. "But in truth, I loathe you and what you've done to me."

He tore his gaze from her hatred and feigned a chuckle. "Ah ha, mademoiselle has a crack in her holy armor. But at least you speak the truth and not lies."

She flattened her lips. "I am only human." Stuffing a loose strand of hair into her tight bun, she shifted her gaze to his, then away, then back again. "Why do you stare at me like that?" She retreated a step. "'Tis impertinent and rude."

"What do you expect from a French rogue? Is that not what you called me?" He leaned on the door frame and folded his arms over his chest. "I stare at you because you are beautiful." She was *la belle femme*, but in truth he did not stare at her for her comeliness. He stared at her because she hated him and he wanted to make her uncomfortable for it. He stared at her because a devilish idea began to hatch in his brandy-drenched brain.

"Outward beauty is fleeting, Captain."

"Perhaps. But while it is here, I will admire it if I please." He lifted his brows and tossed any propriety he still possessed to the wind. "Most women would offer themselves to me in the hope of buying their freedom."

The mademoiselle's face flushed to a deep shade of burgundy. Her chest rose and fell. She retreated even further and raised her chin. "I am not most women, Captain Dubois."

"But you do want to go home?"

"Of course." Her bottom lip trembled. "But not at the cost of compromising everything I hold dear."

Rafe studied her, desire and admiration warring within him. He nodded, conceding to admiration, then walked out and shut the door behind him before he gave in to the stronger emotion.

Suddenly five hundred pounds didn't seem a large enough sum for such an exquisite treasure. En fait, he wasn't sure any amount would be.

CHAPTER 8

Grace crept down the lower deck ladder, cringing with every creak of the wooden steps. She didn't know whether to hold her free hand to her nose to block the stench of rot, mold, and waste or to cover her mouth to stifle her nervous breathing that seemed as loud as the sea purling against the hull. She had hoped that perhaps her second trip to the hold wouldn't be as horrifying as the first, but as her heart cinched in her chest and her feet rebelled with each shuffle forward, she realized she'd probably never possess the courage of her sister Faith.

She took another step, and her shoes met the layer of muddy rocks covering the bottom of the ship. In the hold, heat seemed to take on its own persona and cling to whoever dared venture below as if in hope of escaping with them when they ascended. With the sleeve of her gown, she dabbed at the perspiration on her forehead, surprised at the damp chill seeping from the rocks through her shoes.

Lifting her lantern, she allowed its glowing circle to create a barricade of light around her. Perhaps a false barricade, for she knew not what crept beyond its borders, save for the rats she heard pattering away. But within its lighted walls sat an assortment of crates, barrels, and sacks broken from their bindings and scattered haphazardly wherever the sea had tossed them. She moved forward. More pattering caused her to shudder. At least the tiny beasts were afraid of the light. She'd have no such luck if she happened upon a sailor. Since it was well past midnight, most of them should be asleep, an assumption she confirmed by the barrage of snores that had assaulted her as she descended past the crew's berth.

All she needed was one more slab of wood to match the one she'd retrieved the night before. Just one piece of wood and she could return to her cabin.

She coughed and bent over, trying not to breathe too much of the foul air, focusing her thoughts on something else, anything else besides the stench suffocating her and the roast pork now roiling in her stomach.

After the captain had deposited her in her cabin, she'd waited for hours as the ship drifted into slumber, pondering the sanity of her plan. But the captain's mention of bartering her purity for freedom only increased the urgency of her escape.

Standing tall, she threw back her shoulders. *Be strong and of a good courage; be not afraid, neither be thou dismayed: for the Lord thy God is with thee withersoever thou goest,* she thought, quoting from Joshua. But the bold words sank to the deck beneath the dank, weighted air. Did she believe them anymore? Truth be told, she did not feel God's presence at all. Which is why she must take measures into her own hands. She took a step forward and scanned the cargo for the broken crate she'd stumbled upon—or stumbled over—the night before.

A gray streak flashed across her vision, and before she could swerve the lantern to see what it was, it sprang at her and landed on her chest. Sharp claws and soft fur scrambled over her skin. *A rat! A* large *rat!* She screamed. Stumbling backward, she tried to swat the beast away. The lantern slipped from her hand, struck a crate, and hit the deck with a clank. The flame flared, sputtered. . .then went out. Thick, inky darkness molded over her. The eerie creak and groan of the ship grew louder as if it were laughing at her misfortune. Her feet went numb.

The furry animal clinging to Grace's chest began to purr.

"Spyglass, is that you?" The cat nestled beneath her chin, her pleasing rumble soothing Grace's nerves. Releasing a sigh, she ran her fingers through the cat's fur and waited for the thumping of her own heart to slow and her feet to regain their feeling. "You frightened me, little one."

The ship pitched, and Grace braced her shoes on the uneven pebbles to keep from falling. She peered into the darkness. Not a speck of light. Not a glimmer. Nothing but charcoal black met her gaze. The hair bristled on her arms.

"Now look what you've done," she whispered to the cat. "Hold on, let me find the ladder, and I'll take you up to my cabin." Where she'd have to grab another lantern and come back down again.

A thump sounded. Her ears perked. Was that a boot step? Another thud. She turned toward the sound. A glimmer of light appeared from above, streaming down the ladder. Grace slunk backward, petting Spyglass, more to comfort herself than the cat. Her stomach tightened. *Lord, please help me.*

Spyglass continued to purr. "Shhh." Grace ceased stroking the cat, but the rebellious feline only rumbled her approval louder.

A man descended the ladder. Handsomely dressed in a laced waistcoat, gray sash, and trousers, with silver-plated pistols and a dagger in his belt, he raised his lantern above his head and squinted into the darkness.

Mr. Weylan.

A scrawny man in a checkered shirt and torn breeches slinked behind him, casting his gaze this way and that. A third man wobbled down the ladder after them, the wooden steps bowing to near breaking beneath his considerable weight.

The three men who had leered so blatantly at her on deck two days ago.

"We know yer down here, mademoiselle," Mr. Weylan said with a sneer.

Grace's knees quivered. How did they know where she was? She backed up and hit a stack of crates. One of them toppled to the deck with a bang. The men jerked their gazes her way, and all three grinned simultaneously. "There she be."

Mr. Weylan started toward her, his eyes gleaming with malice. He reminded her of her sister Hope's latest beau, Lord Falkland—the one she'd run away with. The same striking features, same debonair mannerisms, yet for those with discernment a facade covering the corruption within. The other two men came alongside her, the third one holding his lantern up to her face. Brown sweat streamed from the folds of his neck. Two yellow teeth perched along his bottom gums, like sentinels guarding an empty cave.

Spyglass leapt from Grace's embrace and darted up the ladder. *Traitor.* Grace swallowed and gathered her resolve. "What is it you want?"

Mr. Weylan chuckled and raised his brows at his friends. He reached out to touch her cheek. She jolted away.

He frowned. "We thought ye might want to accommodate us lonely sailors who've been out to sea far too long. We don't often come across *une femme si belle.*"

A sickening wave of terror washed over Grace. "I don't know what you mean by accommodate, sir." Her voice came out in a rasping squeak. "But I seem to have lost my lantern and would appreciate an escort back to my cabin." Perhaps if she appealed to their male instinct of chivalry, they'd rise to the occasion.

Again she seemed to have said something amusing.

"We'd love to escort you, mademoiselle, wouldn't we, *messieurs*? That is, after you do us a favor." Mr. Weylan fingered the lace atop her neckline then dropped his hand to the ties of her bodice.

Grace slapped the offending appendage. "Shame on you, sir." Anger burned hot, snuffing out her fear. She eyed each one in turn. "On all of you! To take advantage of an innocent lady. The Bible says, 'As ye would that men should do to you, do ye also to them likewise.' Would you like someone to accost you?"

Again their chuckles filled the room. The man who was beginning to look more like the huge barrel he stood beside leaned toward her and drew a deep breath of her hair. "I'd love to be accosted, miss, if ye'd oblige me."

Grace's mind reeled. She must get through to these men. Were they so depraved that no goodness could be found in them? "Look inside of you, gentlemen. You are better men than this." She gave them an affirming nod. "God has made you to be better men than this."

Mr. Weylan cocked his head and studied her while the other two snickered beside him. For a moment, Grace thought she had pierced the evil crust around his soul.

"God has nothin' to do with this," he scoffed.

Grace's hopes plummeted to the sharp pebbles beneath her feet. "On that I will agree." The metallic taste of horror filled her mouth. Her heart felt as though it would crash through her chest. "Do you wish to spend eternity in hell?"

"Hell don't scare me, miss. I'm livin' in it already." Setting down his lantern, Mr. Weylan approached her, devouring her with his gaze.

"I assure you, sir, you know nothing of hell." A chill bristled over her at the memory of her vision—a vision that if these men caught even a glimpse, they'd fall to their knees and repent right here. But at the moment, with their wicked intent toward her screaming from their eyes and dripping from their salivating lips, she wished them all the eternity they deserved.

Grace squeezed her eyes shut and screamed, but Mr. Weylan's hand smothered the sound. She tasted dirt and sweat and fish on his rough skin and braced herself for the assault. Seconds passed. The creaks and moans of the ship taunted her from all around. And something else. The thud of boot steps reached her ears, then gasps and curses. Weylan's hand left her mouth.

Slam. Thud. Crash.

The sounds of a brawl pounded in her ears, and she pried her eyes open to see Captain Dubois dragging Mr. Weylan through a pile of sacks. The captain slammed him against the hull then gripped the man's throat until his eyes bulged and his face purpled. The other men struggled to rise from the deck, where they'd obviously been tossed, and rushed to the aid of their friend.

Grace shrieked, and Captain Dubois released Mr. Weylan, swung about, kicked the scrawny man in the stomach, sending him crashing backward into a stack of barrels, while he drew his rapier and leveled the tip upon the other. Fury stormed from the captain's dark eyes. His hair hung in black strands about his face. "You dare attack your capitaine, Holt?"

Mr. Weylan groaned from his spot on the deck, gripping his throat and gasping for breath. "*Et vous,* Monsieur Weylan?" Rafe shot over his shoulder.

"We jest wanted some female companionship, Cap'n." The portly man that Dubois held at the tip of his rapier offered a conciliatory grin and shrugged. "We's lonely men."

"You'll be even lonelier when I toss you overboard." Captain Dubois pressed the blade upon Holt's chest, drawing a drop of blood that stained his brown shirt.

The lanky man emerged from the barrels, pressing a hand against his back.

Grace's fear resurged. Could the captain handle all three?

"Ye shared the last woman on board." Mr. Weylan rose to his feet, still clutching his neck.

"*You* shared the last trollop, not lady, and she came aboard willingly. I never touched her." The captain lowered his blade and wiped the sweat from his brow.

"What do it matter?" Holt jerked a thumb in Grace's direction. "This one's ending up a Spanish whore anyway."

Without hesitation, the captain slammed his fist across the man's jaw. Holt spun around beneath the blow and stumbled backward, crashing to the deck. Grace threw a hand to her mouth, both in shock at the violence she witnessed and the speed with which the captain came to her honor. But why would he? When he was the one leading her straight into dishonor?

The captain turned on Mr. Weylan, who fingered the handle of a knife stuffed in his belt.

"Make sure you know what you are doing, mon ami, before you draw that." Captain Dubois snapped his hair from his face. Behind his back, the skinny man shook his head at Weylan, his eyes wide.

Mr. Weylan released the handle with a huff. "This isn't a British warship, nor even a pirate ship, and we have signed no articles." His jaw tightened beneath eyes alight with fury. "Someday you'll regret this, Captain."

"I never regret," came the captain's sharp reply. "Now off with you. And if I see you so much as glancing at the lady, I'll string you up on the yardarm."

Amidst a cacophony of grunts and curses, the men eased by Captain Dubois, Mr. Weylan rubbing his neck, the skinny man his back, and Holt his jaw. They disappeared up the ladder.

Sheathing his rapier, Captain Dubois ran a hand through his hair and faced her. "*Allez-vous bien?* Are you all right?"

Grace tried to find her voice, but her heart still hung in her throat. The harsh lines on the captain's face softened, and she found herself mesmerized by the way the lantern light flickered across his dark eyes. It was the concern burning within them that set her aback. Could the man actually have some goodness in his heart? She rubbed her own eyes. Perhaps she was too tired or the light too dim. He had saved her for no other reason than the protection of his property. Hadn't he?

He took a step closer, so close she could smell the brandy on his breath. "Did they hurt you?" He eyed her from head to toe.

Grace lowered her gaze. "No. I am fine."

His countenance stiffened. "Sacre mer, what were you doing down here, mademoiselle?" He backed up and snorted. "If you wish to be ravaged, then by all means, let me know and next time I shall remain in my bed."

In his bed. Now that her mind no longer reeled in fear, she noticed he wore no boots and his shirt hung loose instead of being tucked into his breeches. Even the belt housing his blade hung haphazardly about his hips. "How did you know I was down here?"

"Answer my question first." He cocked his head.

"I was looking for something." Grace bit her lip, not wanting to lie.

"*Qu'est-ce que vous recherchez?*"

Grace squared her jaw. "*You* must answer *my* question now."

A hint of a smile lifted his lips. "Spyglass woke me. She clawed into my cabin and would not stop meowing. The last time she did that, a thief snuck on board and had captured one of my crew. So I thought I should *enquêter sur*"—he paused and flattened his lips—"how do you say, investigate."

Grace blinked and let out a tiny chuckle, amazed she found anything amusing amidst her subsiding terror.

Captain Dubois swept a hand toward the ladder. "May I escort you back to your cabin, mademoiselle, or do you prefer to spend the night in the hold?"

Grace allowed him to lead her up the two decks to her cabin, reluctantly taking his proffered arm lest she collapse beneath her still-trembling legs.

Sweeping open her door, he ushered her inside, and then he set down his lantern. Spyglass slipped in after them, perched upon the table, and began licking her paws then wiping them over her face as if pleased with a job well done.

The corner of the slab of wood Grace had retrieved the night before stuck out of the open armoire. She hastened to stand in front of it and whirled around, her stomach tightening. If the captain saw it, he'd no doubt remove it from her cabin, and with it, her last hope of escape.

～

Rafe studied the baffling woman. She possessed an intriguing mixture of courage, purity, and strength in the midst of delicacy he had not seen in any lady he had encountered. And he had encountered quite a few ladies in his day. Such pluck, such bravado in the face of certain assault. He could still hear the admonition she'd expounded to the trio of brigands as they were about to ravage her. He'd been barreling down the ladder, following Spyglass, when those words drifted up to him, halting him in his tracks, jarring him to his soul—that God had made them to be better men—that they *could* be better men. Even now, he couldn't shake the words from his mind. But then she had spewed her pious condemnations upon the men, jolting Rafe back to reality—people who professed to follow God sat in judgment on others.

Mademoiselle Grace splayed her fingers over the skin above her gown and looked away. "You are staring at me again."

Rafe's heart leapt at her innocence. "Next time you find yourself in such a precarious situation, mademoiselle, might I suggest you avoid the moral censure. Men who would accost a lady have no care for what the

Bible says. You will only infuriate them. Your God will not save you upon your insult to others."

"I was not insulting them. I was telling the truth. And God did save me. He brought me you." She swept her green eyes back to him—sharp, clear, convicting.

"I accept your gratitude." He bowed, longing to see some spark of appreciation for him on her face.

"You do not have it, Captain," she snapped. "Why should I thank you? You deliver me from the wolves only to feed me to a lion."

He winced inwardly, unable to deny that truth. Yet at the moment, deep down, he wished he had met this lady in a different time, in a different place, and that she was not the daughter of Admiral Henry Westcott. He ground his teeth together. What was wrong with him?

She seemed to sense his conflict, and the haughty veneer fell from her face. "Captain, return me to my home. I beg you." Her eyes moistened. "There are so many who depend on me. Not the least of whom are my sisters. Faith is so new to her beliefs, and Hope, my other sister." The mademoiselle sighed and wrung her hands together. "She ran away and we do not know where she is, but she will need me when she returns." She clasped the chain around her neck and stepped toward him. The vulnerability, the desperation, the appeal in her eyes softened the shield around his heart. "Surely you have family somewhere that you love?"

At the mention of family, Rafe's armor stiffened once again. "I have no family."

"But I heard Father Alers make mention of your father."

"My father is a beast." Rafe's back stiffened. "A man who beats innocent children and preys on young women. To me, he is dead." Why was he telling her this? he thought. What was it about her that made him want to tell her?

Her forehead wrinkled and she looked at him curiously. Heat stormed through him as he realized the irony of what he had just said. He clenched his fists. "Contrary to what you might think, mademoiselle, I am nothing like him." He turned to go, displeased with the course of the conversation and the way it made him feel.

She laid a hand on his arm, drawing him back by her touch. "Then behave differently, Captain. Take me home. I promised my mother, don't you see? I promised her I would keep my sisters close to God, that I would keep them on the straight path."

Rafe knew of promises. Promises that had been nothing but smoke and dust, here one day and then blown away with the trade winds the next. But something in her eyes made him want to believe that some promises could be kept, that some people could be trusted.

And that angered him all the more.

"Stay in your cabin, mademoiselle," he snapped, "or the next time I may allow the men their play."

She winced, but Rafe steeled himself against caring. He could not care. Would not care. "I will have Father Alers bolt a lock and chain to this door tomorrow, so that by the time we arrive at Port-de-Paix, you will be unable to cause any further trouble." He patted his chest, looking for the cheroot he usually kept in his waistcoat pocket, but he had not donned his waistcoat. He needed a smoke. A brandy. Anything. He needed to get away from this woman. "Come, Spyglass."

The cat shifted her one eye from Rafe to Mademoiselle Grace but did not move.

"Spyglass." He snapped at the rebellious feline, yet the cat remained. "Zut alors!" Rafe stomped out and slammed the door with a *bang* that echoed down the companionway. Even his cat was under her spell.

❧

Grace jumped as the door slammed. She sank into the chair. Spyglass leapt into her lap and began to purr. Petting the cat, Grace drew a deep breath and then released it, hoping to ease the tightness in her chest. Not just tight from the harrowing events below but from her time in the captain's presence. He befuddled her. She wanted to hate him. Did hate him. But then he had rescued her and the look in his eyes when she pleaded for her freedom. . .it was almost as if he cared. Regardless, she did not fear him as she did the men in the hold. Though he was as wild as the sea he sailed upon, she didn't believe he would hurt her. Sell her, but not hurt her himself. Instead she sensed an overwhelming sorrow in the captain, a hopelessness, and a passion so deep it seemed fathomless.

"I suppose I should thank you, little one, for saving me." She snuggled the purring feline against her chest. "A smart one, aren't you? Leading the captain to my rescue." She scratched beneath the feline's chin, and Spyglass nestled against Grace's cheek. "But I would go with the captain next time he summons, if I were you. From what I've seen, his temper is not to be trifled with."

A temper that flared at a moment's notice. Every time Grace saw a softening in his eyes, every time a hint of goodness crossed his face, he'd stiffen, as if being held at musket point. And he became hard as stone, unfeeling, uncaring, volatile—like a ship bracing for an enemy attack.

The chipped corner of the slab of wood peeked at her from the open armoire. She didn't dare risk another trip below tonight. Not with Mr. Weylan and his minions on the prowl.

She gulped at the fear clawing at her throat. "Lord, why have You thwarted my last hope for escape?" Releasing Spyglass, Grace rose and crossed to the tiny window. Darkness as black as coal blanketed the sky and sea so thick it seeped into her soul. But she couldn't let it. Grace must continue forward with her plan to escape—a plan made all the more pressing by the captain's threat to lock her in her cabin, and all the more harrowing if she couldn't procure another piece of wood. Regardless, she was willing to face anything in order to avoid the fate Captain Dubois had planned for her—even her own death.

CHAPTER 9

Rafe stood at the quarterdeck rail and watched as the island of Hispaniola blossomed on the horizon. *Home.* At least the only home he knew. Though a foreigner by descent, Rafe had been born on this island. His family had hailed from Bordeaux, France, but Rafe possessed no memory of the land of his heritage, and from what he'd heard of her atrocities, he was glad for it.

He gritted his teeth, still enraged at Mademoiselle Grace for putting herself in such a precarious position last night, and equally enraged at Weylan, Holt, and Fisk for daring to assault her, but most of all enraged at himself for allowing the woman to affect him so.

"You care for her." The words startled Rafe as Father Alers slipped beside him, two mugs in his hand. Rafe shook his head. The priest's uncanny ability to read Rafe's mind had, of late, become more of a nuisance than a wonder.

The smell of coffee rose and swirled beneath Rafe's nose. "C'est absurde. You've grown blind as well as deaf, old man. Is that for me?"

Father Alers handed him the cup. "Yet you knew exactly to whom I was referring."

"There is only one woman on board the ship." Rafe gave his friend a look of dismissal.

The priest huffed. "Drink it. It will dull the effects of the brandy you have been drowning yourself with."

Embracing the cup, Rafe allowed its warmth to penetrate his hands. "And why would I want to do that?"

"Because the liquor transforms your few redeeming qualities into demons. Because it hides what you truly feel inside."

The snap of canvas above Rafe muffled his chuckle. "I feel nothing inside but a desire to assist those who cannot provide for themselves."

"Ah." Father Alers sipped his coffee and stared across a rippling sea transformed into ribbons of diamonds by the rising sun. "The grand

Captain Dubois, champion of the poor and downtrodden."

Rafe gripped the baldric strapped over his chest, wondering why he tolerated his friend. "Be careful, mon vieux. Your taunting words may be the death of you."

Father Alers grinned, revealing a bottom row of crooked teeth.

Rafe shook his head and glanced aloft. "Furl topsails, Monsieur Thorn!" He bellowed over the deck, and his first mate echoed his command, sending sailors scampering. They should make port in a few hours, and Rafe found himself unusually anxious to get off the brig.

"But what of Mademoiselle Grace? Is she not one of the downtrodden aussi?" A gust of wind lifted the father's gray hair until it circled him like a halo.

Rafe clenched his jaw, no longer wishing to speak of the lady below deck. "She is Admiral Westcott's daughter."

"Guilty by birth?" the man raised an eyebrow.

"*Précisément.* You know what His Majesty's Navy did to my mother. Do you think I would have accepted this job if the mademoiselle were an innocent?"

"On the contrary, she seems to be more innocent than you expected. Besides"—Father Alers waved a bony hand through the air—"you cannot punish the entire British navy for the actions of one commander."

Rafe grunted. "And why not? How many innocent people have they slaughtered?"

"How many of theirs have we?" Luis shrugged. "It is the way of war."

"My mother was at war with no one."

"Many suffer who are not soldiers during war."

Rafe slid a finger over his mustache. The brig crested a wave and spray came sweeping over her bow. He drew in a deep breath of the salty wind, seeking the sweet scent of earth and hibiscus that reminded him of home. Anything to assuage the anger, the bitterness, the guilt warring within him.

"You care for Mademoiselle Grace." The priest repeated the words that sliced through the air like a sharp blade.

"So you have said." Rafe feigned a nonchalant response.

"Then deny it."

Rafe took a swig of coffee, its soothing elixir sliding down his throat and warming his belly. "Care? I hardly know her, but I will admit she is a surprise. She intrigues me." He snorted. "The sentiment will pass."

"What will you do?" Father Alers rubbed his back and turned toward him.

Rafe narrowed his eyes against the glitter of the sun that reflected off the turquoise sea, then he glanced over his shoulder at the helmsman. "Veer three points to starboard, Monsieur Atton. Keep your luff."

Ile de la Tortue rose off their larboard bow like a giant sea turtle as its name denoted. Across from the once famous pirate haven, distanced by the Canal de la Tortue, the lush green mountains and white sands of Saint Dominique came into focus.

Father Alers cleared his throat and raised a gray brow, reminding Rafe of his question, though he needed no reminding; it had haunted him ever since he had brought Mademoiselle Grace on board.

What *would* he do?

⤳

Grace pressed her face against the porthole glass and peered at the harbor. The commands to bring the brig about and shorten sail blaring from above alerted her that they had reached Port-de-Paix. That and the splash of the anchor as it plunged into the shallow bay and the thud of boots and the clamor of excitement as the crew amassed on deck for their journey to shore. Ships of all sizes and shapes rocked idly in the sapphire water of the harbor. Grace squinted against the glare of the sun as she made out merchant brigs, slavers, barques, schooners, an East Indiaman, and other vessels she didn't recognize. Beyond them, docks jutted into the water, peppered with dark-skinned slaves carrying the goods from ships to warehouses and shops. Blue-green mountains loomed in the distance while the leaves of a multitude of trees glinted myriad variations of green in the noonday sun.

Grace rubbed the blurry glass but could get no clearer view. A knot formed in her belly. She'd heard Port-de-Paix had once been a notorious pirate haven. And although most of the seafaring brigands had moved their home base across the narrow channel to Tortuga and then to Petit Goave, she wondered what remnant of debauchery had been left behind. Whatever villainous activities remained, Captain Dubois would no doubt be an avid participant. Though a small part of her doubted that assessment.

Early that morning, before they had sailed into the harbor, Mr. Maddock, the carpenter, had strung a chain through the latch on her door and clanked it shut with a padlock. True to his word, Captain Dubois had imprisoned her in this muggy fortress. For how long, she couldn't know. For as long as it took the crew to commit as many wicked acts on land as their depraved minds could conjure up, she supposed.

Stepping away from the porthole, she blew out a sigh. That was as close a look as she'd get at Port-de-Paix. Perhaps it was for the better. Even if she made it to the port floating on her broken crates without drowning—or worse, being picked up by some sailors—what would she do once she got there?

Hugging herself despite the heat, Grace began to pace across her tiny cabin. She reached the bulkhead in three steps and swerved about. A million fearful questions assailed her. Had Captain Dubois joined his men ashore? And who would keep his remaining crew at bay? Her heart took up a frenzied pace as the cabin closed in on her. She gasped for a breath in the stagnant air and perspiration streamed down her back.

"Oh, Lord." She sank onto the bed and dropped her head into her hands. "Please help me." Prayer was such a habit with her that she momentarily forgot God wasn't answering her pleas as of late.

"I will never leave thee, nor forsake thee."

Grace looked up and batted the tears from her face. It was the first time she'd heard the Lord's voice since her capture. "Where have You been, Lord?"

"I will never leave thee, nor forsake thee." The words repeated, and Grace bowed her head.

"I know Your Word says that, but I've had such a hard time believing it, Lord." Grace tucked a loose strand of hair back into her bun and gripped her stomach. Fleeting memories dashed through her thoughts—memories of the time when she brought medicine to the Jacobs family on the edge of the frontier and the Yamassee Indians attacked, memories of her father taken ill with smallpox, of her sister Faith in the Watch House dungeon about to be hanged for piracy. And all those times, God had answered her prayers and delivered her and those she loved.

"Forgive me, Lord, for doubting You. You have always been with me before. I just don't understand. Why is this happening to me? Why am I here? I have done no good. No one listens to me, especially the captain. They all continue in their wicked ways. They deserve their fate, but I have done nothing to deserve mine."

She glanced over the cabin. "Please help me understand." Her thoughts drifted to Hope, her sister who had run off with Lord Falkland over a month ago, much to their family's shame and disgrace. Too angry at her sister's foolish and licentious behavior, Grace had given up praying for her, for she had believed Hope also deserved whatever fate she received. Year after year, Grace had tried to instruct Hope in righteous living and turn her sister away from the path of sinfulness she'd so ardently chosen to follow. But to no avail. The silly girl would not listen. Yet, why was the vision of her sweet face ever before Grace? Haunting her, just as another vision haunted her. A vision of fire and a barren land and an unrelenting hot wind that brought no relief.

Shame pulled her to her knees beside the cot. She would use this time to pray. Not only for herself, but for Hope, for Faith and Dajon, for her other sister, Charity, and her father. And for Captain Dubois. Leaning her forehead against the scratchy counterpane, she poured her heart out to God.

Hours later, the chain upon her door clanked against the wood. Lifting her head, Grace tensed as the door opened, and Mr. Thorn entered with a tray of food.

He smiled. "It isn't much. Some dried beef and a hard biscuit. And the rum-sweetened lemon juice Father Alers insisted I give you." He set the food down onto the table as Spyglass pranced inside and darted to Grace. The scent of meat and butter jolted her stomach awake, and it began to growl.

"Looks like you've made a friend." Mr. Thorn nodded toward the cat and straightened his freshly pressed dark blue waistcoat, looking more like a gentleman about town than a sailor.

"Where is Father Alers?" Grace nestled Spyglass beneath her chin and slowly rose.

"He went ashore with the captain and most of the crew."

"And why have you not joined them, Mr. Thorn?" Spyglass nudged her chin, begging for more caresses.

He shifted his polished boots over the deck planks and shrugged. "I take no pleasure in the nefarious diversions the port has to offer."

She studied him, noting that the frequent smile he offered her rarely reached his eyes. "And yet you do not swear allegiance to God?" The ship creaked over a tiny roller, sending a splash of waves against the hull.

"I do not believe He requires it." Mr. Thorn stuffed a lock of his brown hair behind his ear and rubbed the scar on his neck with his thumb. "I fear, Miss Grace, He has left us to our own devices."

"I am sorry you believe so." Grace nuzzled her nose into the cat's furry neck.

"Your own situation is a testament to my belief, is it not?"

Grace set Spyglass down on her cot and crossed her arms over her waist, unable to find a suitable answer to the question she'd wrestled with for days. That God was with her, she now believed, but that He was not helping her as she wished was only too plain.

"Humph. I thought so." Mr. Thorn glanced over the cabin. His brows rose at the sight of her open armoire. "Ah, what is this?" He pulled out the piece of broken crate and a coil of rope and examined them.

Grace's heart clenched. "'Tis nothing."

He arched a brow and gave her a devious look. "Methinks the lady has a plan."

Grace huffed. What did it matter if she told Mr. Thorn of her foolish scheme? "I did, but it was ruined when the captain put a lock on my door."

"And what precisely were you planning on doing with this?" He set the crate down with a thump. "Hitting the captain over the head?" He chuckled.

"Nay." Grace stifled a laugh. "But I wish I had thought of that."

He smiled, revealing a set of unusually straight, white teeth, and fingered the whiskers on his chin. "Zooks, quite bewildering. I don't believe the captain expected to find such a wildcat in an admiral's daughter."

"I don't know what being an admiral's daughter has to do with anything."

Mr. Thorn lowered himself into the only chair in the room, adding to Grace's uneasiness. Did he intend to keep her company all day? She eyed the open door and wondered how many crewmen were on board.

He seemed to notice the direction of her gaze. "I have a better idea, Miss Grace."

"Than what, Mr. Thorn?"

"Than your swimming ashore. I doubt you'd have made it to land without being picked up by even more unsavory sorts than you'll find on this brig."

A flicker of playfulness sparked in his brown eyes, and Grace wondered if his proposal involved the same thing the captain had in mind last night. But no, there was no desire in his expression—at least not for her. "What are you proposing, Mr. Thorn?"

"I am proposing to grant you your freedom."

CHAPTER 10

Rafe leapt from the longboat onto the quay and ordered his men to shoulder the crates and follow him. He strode down the wobbling dock onto sturdy ground, bracing himself as he switched from sea legs to land legs. Doffing his hat, he wiped the sweat from his brow.

"Monsieur Dubois!" A familiar voice hailed him, and Rafe turned to see his old friend Armonde waving and heading his way. "We did not expect you so soon."

"*Bonjour*, mon ami. I did not expect to be here either." Rafe met his embrace. "But I needed some time ashore"—Mademoiselle Grace invaded his thoughts once again, but he shook them away—"and I have brought some goods for Abbé Villion. Have you seen him?"

"Oui, this morning at the church." Armonde dabbed at the sweat on his neck with his cravat. "How long will you stay? Let us have a drink together before you sail again?"

"*Absolument*. I'll speak with you later." Rafe watched his friend saunter away. Turning, he snapped at his crew to hurry behind him as the other longboat made dock, and Weylan led the men and the crates down the wharf.

Cheerful hails and greetings swarmed over Rafe as word spread of his arrival and people ran out to greet him. Smiling faces bobbed all around like waves lapping against a buoy, assailing him with their admiration and approval. Precisely what he needed to erase the memory of a pair of convicting emerald eyes and the shame that sliced through him in their wake. He was doing something good here, something worthwhile. His life had meaning, purpose, unlike so many who squandered their time, wealth, and energy on pleasing themselves.

His father, for one.

The thought of the man who'd sired him put a sour taste in Rafe's mouth. He hoped to avoid him during his stay at port. But then again, his father rarely tainted himself with the stench of poverty that lingered down by the docks.

"God bless you, Captain Dubois!" one old man yelled.

A haggard woman pushed through the crowd. "What have you brought for us this time, Monsieur Rafe?"

"Many good things." Rafe ordered his men to set down one of the chests. "Take the rest of the cargo to Abbé Villion, Monsieur Weylan, and tell him I'll be along shortly."

"Aye, Capitaine," Weylan snarled, obviously still angry over their altercation the night before. Turning, he barked orders to the men behind him who hoisted the remaining crates, chests, and barrels onto their backs and followed him down the muddy street.

⋘

Shoving the tip of the oar against the hull of *Le Champion*, Thorn pushed the tiny cockboat away from the ship. A roller struck the bow and splashed over him, and he glanced at Miss Grace sitting among the thwarts behind him. "Hold on."

The lady, appearing much smaller in her new attire, smiled at him from beneath the floppy hat that perched atop her head as she gripped the sides of the small boat.

Thorn faced forward and continued rowing toward shore. This would trouble the captain sorely. Losing his precious cargo and the fortune that went with her. No doubt the crew would be furious, perhaps even mutinous when they discovered they were not to be paid anytime soon. He grinned and shoved the paddle through the swirling turquoise water, urging the craft onward.

The sun beat down upon him, and sweat began to trickle beneath his waistcoat. But nothing could sour his humor today. Finally something was going his way. A seagull cawed overhead and then dove toward the water, spreading its wings across the surface to scan for a delectable morsel.

Bells rang and voices brayed from the port as they drew near. Making his way around an anchored schooner, Thorn plunged his oar on the other side and pushed the water back. His muscles ached from the strain.

After spending a year with Rafe, Thorn had concluded that the only thing the man cared about was his precious ship and his ability to make money for the poor. Thorn hoped the captain had developed affection for his prisoner. It would make his revenge all the sweeter. Though Thorn wondered if Captain Dubois was capable of caring for anyone.

It was better this way. Miss Grace did not deserve the fate which the captain planned for her. Now she could return home. Tugging his hat down further on his forehead against the bright rays, Thorn thrust the oar through the choppy water. The sounds of splashing and gurgling rose like the guilt bubbling in his stomach for leaving her alone in Port-de-Paix. Wasn't he using her as a pawn to further his own agenda just as the captain was? No. He would give her enough money to convey her safely home. And since Rafe would be spending his days and nights in town in his usual manner—saturating himself with alcohol and women—and Thorn had volunteered to attend to Miss Grace's needs himself, no one would be the wiser. Thorn felt the heavy pouch hanging from his belt and smiled. If Rafe only knew that he was the one funding the mademoiselle's journey, no doubt he would be even further enraged.

Hot wind blasted over Thorn, cooling the sweat on his neck and forehead, and taking his guilt with it. There was no other way. When Thorn took Rafe's ship from him, everything that was important to the captain would go with it. Having Rafe arrested for piracy would have proved simpler, but Woodes had sent that imbecile Howell to do the job. The only other option was mutiny, but most of the men were loyal to the captain. Even so, Thorn had heard mumblings of discontent recently that gave him hope. Without the mademoiselle to sell, Rafe's position would become precarious.

Quite precarious indeed.

≈

Grace braced her oversized boots against the thwart in the wobbling boat and stared at Mr. Thorn's outstretched hand. "'Tis best if I do not accept your assistance, Mr. Thorn." She gave him a playful glance. "If I am to pass myself off as a boy, I must behave accordingly."

"Indeed." He withdrew his hand, his face reddening, and busied himself tying the bowline onto a piling. Gripping the rough wood of the dock, Grace struggled to hoist herself upon it but instead tumbled back into the boat. On her second attempt, she managed to extract herself from the rocking vessel but paid for her clumsy efforts with splinters in her hands, adding to the collection already planted there when she'd clung to the mainmast.

Mr. Thorn flipped the dock master a coin and led the way toward the main street as Grace did her best to strut behind him. Yanking upon the waist of her baggy breeches, she hoisted them so the hems wouldn't drag through the dirt. But her cumbersome clothes, coupled with the muddy street that seemed to wobble up and down as if the whole island were afloat, sent Grace nearly tumbling to the ground. Which she would have done if not for Mr. Thorn's quick reach and firm grip.

"It takes a while to get used to solid land again, miss." He quickly let go of her.

"Thank you, Mr. Thorn." She stopped to catch her breath. Tugging the brim of her hat lower over her forehead both to shield her eyes from the blazing sun and to hide her gender, she surveyed the port town.

The scene that met her gaze made her stomach fold in on itself. Worse than anything she'd seen in Charles Towne or Portsmouth. On a platform to her right, Africans—including small children—were being auctioned off. The obnoxious voice of the auctioneer spouted their strength and breeding capability as if they were naught but animals, while a bevy of boisterous planters vied for their bids to be heard above the uproar. Open taverns lined the street, filled to the brim with men laughing and sloshing their drink and half-naked women sprawled over their laps.

In broad daylight!

A mob of people in tattered clothes swarmed around something in the center of town. Somewhere in the distance a musket fired, and a scream pierced the air. Yet no one seemed to notice. An African woman with a basket of fruit atop her head sauntered by. Pigs and chickens ran freely through the streets. Grace's nose stung with the fetor of animal dung, human sweat, and rotten fish.

She was struck by an overwhelming urge to dash back to the boat and return to the ship at once. But no. God had finally heard her prayers and had offered her a way of escape. She would not turn her back on His gift of freedom simply because of her fears.

Mr. Thorn gave her a sorrowful look. "Sorry, miss. I know these sights must shock you."

She pursed her lips and shifted her shoulders beneath the overcoat. Perspiration trickled down her back, but she dare not remove the heavy wrap lest the curves of her figure betray her gender. And from the looks of things, enduring discomfort would be preferable to being discovered as a lady alone in such a place as this. " 'Tis not your fault, Mr. Thorn."

"I'll take you as far as the port master, miss." He handed her a pouch that jingled in her hand. "This should be enough to procure passage back home on one of the merchant brigs." He ran a hand over the back of his neck and gazed nervously about the street.

"Why are you doing this, Mr. Thorn? I sense it is not purely out of kindness for me."

"I'll admit it serves more than one purpose, miss." Tiny green flecks burned in his brown eyes, and he brushed a speck of dirt from his otherwise clean coat as if somehow his kind deed was ridding him of something troublesome.

Grace didn't want to know what. "Regardless, I thank you. I know you risk the wrath of Captain Dubois."

They headed down the street, weaving among the crowd of sweaty humanity and repugnant farm animals. "I can handle his wrath, Miss Grace," Mr. Thorn said. "What I fear is being left in some port with no job and no prospects."

As if offering them a vision of such a future, a man appeared on their left, slouching beneath a huge calabash tree. Before Grace drew within three yards of him, his fetid smell nearly stole her breath away, and she covered her nose. His scraggly beard hung down to his belly, and the dirt smudging his face made it difficult to ascertain his age. She started toward him, intending to see if there was something she could do for him, but Mr. Thorn nudged her in the other direction. "What are you doing, miss?"

"Who is that man?" she whispered.

"Naught but a lazy beggar, a thief."

Grace glanced over her shoulder in disdain as Mr. Thorn ushered her past him.

"Nay, he's young and fit enough to work. He prefers to steal his food." Disgust stained Mr. Thorn's tone. "There are many like him in town."

They had no sooner made it to the fringe of shops and taverns edging the road when Mr. Thorn halted, then slipped behind a horse tethered to a post.

"What is it, Mr. Thorn?" Grace stared at him wide-eyed.

"'Tis Captain Dubois." He inclined his head toward the center of town where there was a crush of people.

Ducking behind the horse, she crept along its side then peered around its neck. The captain conversed with a woman and her child. He leaned over, retrieved articles of clothing from an open chest, and handed them to her. The woman kissed his hand and bowed to him as if he were royalty before grabbing her child and dashing away. Grace shook her head to jar the perplexing vision from her mind. An old man shuffled forward, and the captain dipped into the chest and pulled out two bags, which the man immediately received with a gap-toothed grin.

Grace slunk behind the horse. "What is he doing?"

"He gives gifts to his adoring masses." Mr. Thorn's tone hissed with disgust.

"What do you mean?"

Mr. Thorn huffed out a sigh of exasperation. "After the captain pays the crew their allotment, he distributes the rest of his plunder to the poor here at Port-de-Paix."

Grace lifted a hand to her brow to quell the shock reeling through her head. She peeked back at Captain Dubois as he embraced an older woman, then back at Mr. Thorn. "Are you telling me that he doesn't pocket the money he receives for his nefarious deeds?"

Mr. Thorn flattened his lips and nodded. "Odd, isn't it?"

"Then he is some sort of Robin Hood of the seas?" Grace could not believe it. Every word the captain had spoken, every threat, every evil glint in his dark eyes, all led to the conclusion that he was as greedy as he was heartless and wicked. But this. . .this changed everything.

"Sickening, isn't it?" Mr. Thorn rubbed his bulbous nose and snorted.

Grace flinched at the man's disdain. "Why do you find it so?"

"The act is kind. The motivation may not be, miss." Mr. Thorn took one last peek at his captain, then glanced toward the brig. "But I fear I must leave you before he sees me."

Grace's heart clenched. Alone? In this riotous bedlam?

He pointed past the grappling mob. "See that building by the docks?"

Grace nodded as her gaze found the clapboard shanty surrounded by sailors.

"You should have no trouble bartering there for passage on the next ship leaving port." He gave her a reassuring nod. "There are always ships heading to the colonies loaded with sugar and coffee. I'm sorry I cannot help you any further. The captain hates nothing worse than betrayal and surely would toss me from his ship should he discover I have done this much."

Grace bit her lip. Her palms began to sweat. "But I do not speak French."

"Most merchantmen know a pinch of English, miss. Never fear. You shall be well." He tipped his hat and abandoned her to her spot behind the horse.

The horse's tail whipped through the air and struck Grace in the face. Jumping back, she coughed and swiped at her cheeks as laughter tumbled over her from the storefront to her left. Three men and one lady, who'd just exited the store, enjoyed the moment at her expense. The man spewed a few sentences in French, which caused more laughter.

Face hot, Grace tugged her hat farther down on her head. Then skirting the horse, she made her way across the street. At least they had not seen past her disguise. All she had to do was procure passage on a ship, and if it didn't leave right away, purchase a room in a tavern and hide away until it did. How hard could that be? But with each step, her boots sank deeper into the mud—a sticky black ooze that made it as difficult to move forward as it did to have faith that all would be well, as Mr. Thorn had said. Her chest tightened, and she plucked one boot from the sludge and forged ahead.

Grace stepped away from the trail of shops and into a web of people and horseflesh darting this way and that as they went about their business. And like a fly caught in a web, she got the distinct impression she was about to be devoured by its occupants. She threaded her way through the crowd, bumping shoulders with a bare-chested sailor and barely missing being crushed beneath the wheel of a carriage. French words shot toward her from all directions, some tickling her ears with their beauty, while others jarred her with their harsh tones. She had no idea what the words meant and from the looks of their source, she preferred it that way.

The clank of chains drew her gaze to a black man clothed only in tattered breeches, bent beneath a huge barrel that balanced on a back striped with the punishing marks of his master. Iron shackles bound his feet together.

Grace swallowed the burning in her throat. *Lord, such misery.*

Music bounced over her from an open tavern to her left. The smell of roast pig and bitter alcohol mixed with human sweat saturated the air.

Careful to keep her head down, she edged past the center of town and peeked at Captain Dubois, who had concluded his charitable business and was instructing his men to pick up the chest and follow him. She shook her head at the dichotomy. A rogue, a villain by all inspection, yet possessing a heart for the poor? She could make no sense of it and found herself staring at him as if the answer would come by her perusal.

He glanced up and stretched his back, their eyes locking. Heart in her throat, Grace tugged her floppy hat down and darted to her left.

And barreled into the iron chest of a massive man.

"*Garçon stupide! Regardez où vous allez!*" He shoved Grace aside and she tumbled into the mud. The man spat on the ground beside her then snorted and swaggered off. Passersby wove around her, staring at her, but no one stopped to help. Placing one hand into the warm mud, she pushed herself to her knees and tried to collect her emotions. Fear threatened to crush her resolve to go on.

Then she saw him. Captain Dubois headed her way. His men proceeded along the street without him. She glanced over her shoulder to see what had captured his attention, but when she faced forward again, those smoky dark eyes were locked directly upon her. Did he know who she was, or was he only trying to help a boy? She didn't intend to stay and find out.

Leaping to her feet, she planted a hand atop her hat and dashed in the other direction, shoving her way through the crowd. Her breath strained in her lungs. Her legs burned. She bounded around the side of the tavern and into an alley littered with garbage and puddles of slop. Coughing from the stench, she splashed through the refuse, splattering it over the bottom of her breeches. She darted behind a stack of barrels and backed up against the wall of the tavern, listening for the sound of footsteps. Her breath heaved in her throat.

No thump of boots, no deep smooth voice. Just the clamor of the town. She peered around the barrels. The alley was empty. Leaning her head back onto the wall, she closed her eyes, caught her breath, and offered a prayer of thanks.

The click of a pistol cocking jarred her from her silent worship. She froze as every nerve within her tightened. The cold press of metal against her forehead forced her to open her eyes to the greedy sneers of two men. They spouted a string of French at her. Though she didn't understand the words, she knew what they wanted.

And she had no choice but to give it to them.

CHAPTER 11

Rafe strode up to the front of the stone church, shouldered aside the wooden door, and entered the dim vestibule. A haze of smoke lingered in the air from the candles burning in their sconces upon the walls. Wind slammed the door shut behind him, echoing through the room and enclosing him in its shadows. He doffed his plumed hat. The odor of beeswax, mold, and aged parchment tickled his nose as the air, kept cool by the stone walls, refreshed his heated skin. As his eyes grew accustomed to the shadows, stained glass windows appeared on either side of another massive door that separated him from the sanctuary. Taking a step toward the glass, he peered at the blurred shapes of several people sitting upon wooden pews or kneeling at the candlelit altar, praying to a nonexistent God.

A waste of time, to his way of thinking—sending appeals upward in the hope some powerful being would hear and answer them. En fait, it was a selfish act. Better to spend one's days helping the poor and needy as he did. He took a step back and gripped his baldric. If everyone would follow his example, the world would be a better place, and there would be no need for useless prayers.

The side door swung open and in walked Abbé Villion. The elderly priest's eyes lit up, and he opened his arms, the sleeves of his long gray robe swaying in the candlelight like apparitions. Taking Rafe in a hearty embrace, he smiled, his blue eyes sparkling. "Rafe, how good to see you! I did not expect you for another month."

Still unaccustomed to his displays of affection, Rafe stiffened beneath the man's enveloping grasp. "My crew needed some time ashore before our next stop. And I have brought you some more supplies." The door opened, and Father Alers peeked his gray head inside amidst a stream of sunlight.

"Come in, Father." Abbé Villion waved his hand. "Unless of course you will burn in hell for entering a haven of heretics." He grinned.

Father Alers chuckled and proceeded within. "I am no longer a Jesuit,

734

Révérend, and even so"—he glanced around the vestibule, taking in the wooden cross atop the sanctuary door and the open Bible on a table to his left—"I believe we worship the same God."

"Well said, Father." Abbé Villion folded his hands over his gray cowl. "I wish King Louis held the same belief." He shrugged. "But I suppose if his father had, I wouldn't have fled here. None of us Huguenots would have. And who then would help the poor on this island?"

Father Alers shifted his stance and looked away.

Rafe ground his teeth together. Would things have been different if his father had not also fled the persecution and brought his family to the West Indies? Non, sans doute, his father would have been the same hypocrite, the same monster, in France as he was here.

Abbé Villion grabbed Rafe's shoulders. "I am glad you have come, my boy. And you bring gifts just in time." He exhaled a sigh of exhaustion, reflected in the deep lines on his face. "There are so many needs."

"I will have my men take the crates around back. There are clothes, grain, corn, dried peas, as well as pearls, silver, and gold jewelry, which should bring you a good price."

"I won't ask how you came upon such wealth." The reverend's sharp blue eyes flashed a silent reprimand.

"It is best you do not." Rafe grinned.

Father Alers coughed and lifted a look of repentance upward.

"But regarding the other matter I promised you." Rafe scratched the stubble on his chin.

Abbé Villion's brows lifted. "The hospital?"

Guilt assaulted Rafe at his friend's exuberant look. Then anger burned in his gut—anger at Mademoiselle Grace and the spell she'd cast upon him. "Oui. There may be a delay."

Abbé Villion turned and stared out the front window to the swaying palms and beyond to a group of mulatto children playing in the sand. "We lose so many each day. Sometimes up to five."

Rafe clenched his jaw. "I promised I would build you a hospital, fill it with supplies, and bring a qualified apothecary from the Continent, and I will. Just not by the end of the year, as I had hoped."

"It is not your fault, son." The reverend's brows pulled into a frown. "I meant no dishonor. You have done so much for us. And all at great risk to yourself. My disappointment lies only in the thought of those who will die in the meantime." He forced a smile. "Only God knows how many lives you have already saved with your generosity."

Pride swelled within Rafe. In the three years he had known him, Abbé Villion had been more a father to Rafe than his own had been in six and twenty. "I wish I could do more." He had to do more. He could not let this kind, gentle man down. His thoughts drifted to Mademoiselle Grace—five hundred pounds' worth of sweet cargo sitting aboard his ship, all his for the taking. Then why couldn't he take her to the don and collect it? Every fiber within him longed to do so, to tell Abbé Villion he would have his hospital by year-end.

But he could not.

The reverend laid a hand on his arm. "God will indeed bless you."

Rafe winced as if God Himself had spoken to him—sealing His approval on Rafe's silent decision. A sense of peace, of acceptance, came over him so strong it felt as if someone else had entered the room. "I do not want His blessing. I wish only to help those in need, those whom the grand blancs have deemed unnecessary and unworthy."

"He will bless you anyway." Abbé Villion lifted one shoulder and smiled.

Father Alers snickered and reached for the door.

Suddenly Rafe was equally as anxious to leave the sacred place. "My men wait outside. Show me where you would like the goods stored, and I will be on my way."

"Oui, you are no doubt tired from your journey."

Rafe turned. "I promise I shall find a way to build the hospital."

"We need it, oui." Abbé Villion's eyes burned with concern. "But not at the cost of your life and not at the price of innocent blood."

Father Alers coughed, and Rafe squirmed beneath another wave of guilt but said nothing. Better to not add lying to his list of sins.

Especially not in a church.

⋙

Grace huddled beneath an old ripped tarpaulin she'd found discarded by the docks and crouched against the back wall of the warehouse to shield herself from the wind. *Pound pound pound.* Rain dropped like round shot on the cloth, begging entrance to her makeshift shelter. But when not granted it, the water slid down to seek an opening, quickly found among the tarpaulin's abundant rents. The rain dripped onto Grace, saturating her already damp breeches. She sneezed and held her stomach against another grinding roar of hunger.

Three days had passed. Three days since all her money had been stolen by the two thieves, three days since she'd lost all hope of getting off this evil island, and three days since she'd had a bite to eat. Now she must endure another long sleepless night, hiding from both the small rats, as they rummaged through the refuse piled up in the alley, and the big drunken, two-legged ones—far more dangerous.

At least the thieves had not seen through her disguise, or she would have lost more than the livres Mr. Thorn had given her. She supposed she should be thankful for that. Although, covered with bug bites, consumed by a fear that left her numb, and a stomach that rebelled at every scent of food that remained ever out of her reach, she found it difficult to offer any thanks to God at all.

Hugging her knees to her weak body, she leaned her head atop them and allowed her tears to fall. "Why, God? Why have You abandoned me? I've served You my entire life. I've done naught but try to please You." She waited, listening for the answer amidst the *pitter-plop* of the rain. Yet this appeal seemed to dissipate in the air above her.

She had contemplated sneaking aboard one of the ships, but she shuddered at the stories of what happened to stowaways. Out at sea, if she were caught, she'd be trapped with nowhere to run. She had even thought of signing on as a crewmember, but she couldn't speak French and had no idea how to work a ship. It wouldn't take long for the sailors to notice her incompetence. Not to mention what the crew would do with her should they discover she was a woman. She trembled at the thought. She had also searched for Mr. Thorn, but he must have remained on the ship, and she could find no one willing to row her back out to it for less than a livre. One tiny spark of hope ignited when she had convinced a young French sailor, who spoke a modicum of English, to take a post to her sister Faith in Charles Towne. Yet Grace was unsure of whether he understood her or even if the ship he sailed upon was actually going toward home.

She could, of course, try to find Captain Dubois, but she wondered if life as a slave to a Spanish don would not be worse than dying in the filthy alleys of Port-de-Paix. At least if she died here, she'd end up in a much better place.

A rat poked his twitching, whiskered nose beneath her covering, and Grace booted him away. "Find your own shelter."

A crack of thunder hammered through the night sky, and she jumped.

Puddles formed around her and began to soak through the bottom of her breeches. She hugged herself against the chill. "Lord, help me. Please help me. . . ." The petition faltered on her lips as she drifted into a nightmarish half sleep.

~

Grace dragged her boots through the mud, wincing as pain from the blisters covering her feet shot up her legs. The sun drooped in the western sky, sinking behind the mounds of green that bordered the nefarious port town. And nefarious it was. Worse than the worst parts of Charles Towne, worse than she ever imagined possible. The things she'd witnessed in broad daylight—brawls, drunkenness, lewdness, thievery—were nothing compared to the nighttime activities. If she hadn't had a clear vision of hell some years ago, she'd swear Port-de-Paix was indeed that place.

But she knew what hell was like. And the memory of her vision never ceased to send her heart racing and her skin crawling in terror. If only these people could witness it as well, if only for a second. Surely, they would fall on their knees and never commit another shameless act. Grace spent her days seeking either a friendly face among the crowd or a morsel of food—both of which rarely appeared. Even the scraps tossed from the taprooms and boardinghouses were quickly gobbled up by dogs roaming the street. Grace was beginning to feel like one of the hairy beasts and could soon envision herself on all fours, growling and fighting for a bone alongside the pack of mongrels.

Winding her way through the crowded street, she searched the passing faces for any sign of compassion, any flicker of kindness. Yet most of them looked beyond her as if she didn't exist. Some of the ladies pressed a handkerchief to their noses and glanced back over their shoulders in disgust. Grace dropped her chin and sniffed her clothing. Damp linen and an odd sour odor met her nose. Certainly not offensive enough to garner such a snobbish reaction. Yet perhaps Grace had simply grown accustomed to the smell.

Lifting her chin, she met the gaze of a haggard man sitting in the shade of a tree beside the road, and she recognized him as the beggar she and Mr. Thorn had seen when they first arrived in Port-de-Paix. But this time, she did not shift her gaze away as she had done then. This time, she did not cover her nose from the smell, nor send him a look of disdain. This time she knew exactly what he suffered day after day, and a sudden remorse for her judgmental attitude consumed her. She nodded her greeting and offered him an understanding smile as she passed, and he tipped his floppy hat at her in return.

The scent of fish swirled around her, taunting her and sending her belly into a ravenous growl. Pressing a hand against it, she allowed her nose to lead her down the street to a cart laden with fresh fish and mangos. The owner, a woman with spiny hair and a flat face that seemed in a perpetual frown, stood braying out the value and price of her wares. "*Poissons frais, mangues pour la vente, deux denier.*"

Grace ambled up to the cart and offered the woman all that she had—a kind smile.

"Qu'est-ce que vous *voulez?*" The lady ceased her calling and laid a knotted hand on her wide hip.

Pointing toward the mangos, Grace gave the woman a pleading look.

"Deux denier." The woman produced an open palm, but Grace shrugged and held out her own empty hands.

The woman's mouth puckered into a dark hole that reminded Grace of a cannon. "*Allez-vous-en!*"

Grace shrank back even as her stomach shriveled at this latest denial. Turning, she gazed out over the glittering bay, watching the ships swaying with the incoming waves. A blast of wind struck her, tearing away the putrid stench of the port and replacing it for a moment with the fresh smell of the sea—the vast, deep, magnificent sea, and all that stood between her and her home. She sighed. It might as well be a bottomless pit, for she had no way to cross it. Her gaze landed on *Le Champion*, and she was surprised to see Captain Dubois had not set sail. Had he discovered her missing? If he had, she'd seen no evidence that he had made any effort to find her.

Loud French words shot over her, and she swung around to find the cart lady in a heated argument with a man and his small son. The woman circled around her cart and with a pointed finger, spit a string of harsh words toward the man, who returned them with equal fervor. Numb and weak from hunger, Grace eyed the altercation as if in a dream. Her eyes finally latched upon the mound of mangos in the cart.

And not a soul around to guard them.

She glanced over the crowd and found everyone's eyes focused on the ensuing argument.

Just one mango. Would it matter if she took just one mango? She could almost taste the sweet, pulpy fruit. Her stomach lurched at the thought, and before she could ponder it another second, she dashed toward the cart, plucked a mango from the pile, slid it beneath her shirt, and sped away.

"*Voleur! Voleur! Ce garçon a volé mes mangues!*" came the condemning shout behind her. Followed by the thudding and squishing of shoes on the muddy ground. Grace clutched her treasure as if it were gold and wove through the startled crowd with more speed and agility than she'd have thought possible in her weakened condition. A whistle blew. Behind her, boot steps drummed a guilty sentence like the pounding of a judge's gavel. A man reached out to clutch her as she passed, but she pushed him aside and barreled forward.

Her eyes darted up and down the street as she went, seeking a hiding place. Heart pounding, she leapt up a span of stairs, barreled through an open door, and dashed across a dim room before she realized she'd entered a tavern. The stench of rum and moist wood assailed her as she sped past a group of men, tripped over a chair, and landed face-first in a sticky puddle on the floor. As if in final salute to her stupidity, her hat tumbled off and landed beside her head, spilling her matted hair into the slop.

"*Où est le garçon?*" A booming voice shouted behind her.

Grace's head began to spin. The putrid smell of whatever she'd fallen into saturated her hair and shirt, and she coughed, unable to rise, unable to even consider what the punishment was for thievery in this horrifying town.

Gentle hands gripped her arm and dragged her to her feet then wiped Grace's hair from her face. A lady with eyes the color of the sky and hair as light as honey stared at her with concern. Then gasping, she threw a hand to her mouth and bent over to retrieve Grace's hat from the floor. She shoved it atop Grace's head and tugged it down around her eyes and cheeks. "Keep your face hidden," she whispered. Boot steps thundered their way, and the lady whirled around to face the oncoming men, nudging Grace behind her.

"What's all this fuss over one young lad, gentlemen?" She placed her hands upon her hips.

"Step aside, Nicole. The boy stole a mango," the taller of the two men growled.

"A mango, is it? Sacre bleu, what a beastly crime." Sweet sarcasm chimed in her voice. "Why, most of the men in here have stolen far more than that, and you know it." She opened her palm behind her back, and Grace plucked the mango from within her shirt and gave it to her. All the while lifting a prayer of thanks heavenward for this unexpected protector.

The woman thrust the mango toward the men. "Here, take it and leave the poor lad alone." She sashayed toward the obvious leader, a man who looked more like a pirate than a magistrate. "Surely you have more important villains to catch, Pierre." She kissed him on the cheek, and a hint of a smile broke on his lips before he grunted and took a step back.

"*Très bien.* I suppose no harm was done," he muttered. "But only for you, Nicole." He winked at the lady, sent a harsh glare toward Grace, then turned and stomped out, the other man following him close behind.

As soon as the men left, the tense silence that had descended upon the place dissipated, and the patrons returned to their drink and cards with groans of disappointment. No doubt a hanging would have provided a pleasant diversion. Thankful she'd not become the afternoon's amusement, Grace took a deep breath as her heart settled to a steady beat.

The lady swerved around. Mounds of creamy skin burst from within a low-cut bodice that was far too tight for her voluptuous figure. Gaudy beads jangled from her ears and hung around her neck, but beneath the paint adorning her face beamed a caring smile. Taking Grace by the arm, she led her toward a stairway at the back of the tavern.

Tugging from her grasp, Grace halted, worried she'd escaped one danger only to find herself in another. "Where are we going?"

"Shhh. . .someplace safe." Lifting her skirts, she escorted Grace up a narrow set of creaking stairs, down a hall, and into a room not much bigger than Grace's cabin aboard *Le Champion.*

"I thank you for saving me from those men, mademoiselle." Grace shook the terror from her arms and neck where it stubbornly clung as if portending new dangers within this room. "But I. . .but I cannot impose upon your kindness, Miss, Miss—"

"Nicole. You may call me Nicole." She closed the door and bid Grace sit upon the bed at the room's center. "You are not imposing."

Though kindness sparked in the woman's gaze, Grace had learned these past four days to trust no one. Especially not someone with questionable morals. "I offer you my thanks, for I can offer you no more than that, but I shall take my leave now, if you please."

"Sit down, and I will bring you something to eat," Nicole commanded in a maternal tone, although from the looks of her she could not be much older than Grace.

Although Grace knew she should remove herself from this woman's presence as soon as possible, her stomach leapt at the mention of food, keeping her feet in place.

Approaching her, Nicole placed a finger beneath Grace's chin and lifted her face to examine it. "How long did you think this charade would last? You are *très belle* to be a boy."

Grace sighed and removed her hat, freeing her hair from its stale, matted confinement. The raven locks matted with dirt and slime fell to her shoulders like a rock, and she took a step back. "It has kept me unscathed until now."

Nicole ran a glance over her and chuckled, and Grace looked down at her torn, muddy breeches, her soiled, damp coat, and dirt-smudged hands and face.

"Unscathed? Perhaps. But you could use a bath." Nicole sniffed and raised the back of her hand to her nose. "What happened to you?"

Grace knew it was true, but the insult jarred her nonetheless. "I've been on the streets for four days," she said. "And how do you come to speak English so well?" Though the woman's French accent was strong, her words told of an education that defied her profession.

"I spent a few years in the acquaintance of a British sailor." She looked away for a moment, her expression drawn. But when she snapped her gaze back to Grace, her face pinked. Only for a second. "What is your name?"

"Grace Westcott."

"From where do you come, *ma chérie?*" Nicole batted the air. "Oh, never mind. Let me go get you some food." She swept a gaze through the room. "Madeline, *viens ici.*"

A shuffling sounded in the corner behind the dressing screen and out crept a little girl, no more than seven, with long, curly blond hair like Nicole's and large brown eyes. Grace smiled at such innocence amidst such wickedness, and the girl beamed at her in return.

"Keep our guest company until I return with your dinner," Nicole said.

Madeline nodded and trustingly took hold of Grace's hand while Nicole swept out the door, leaving Grace in a state of confusion, not only at the presence of the girl but at the ease with which Nicole entrusted her to Grace.

"Why are you dressed like a boy?" Madeline eyed Grace's clothing and wrinkled her nose.

"Because I don't want anyone to know I'm a girl." The shock at seeing such a small child in a tavern subsided, immediately replaced by fear for the little girl's safety.

"I like being a girl." Madeline plopped onto the bed.

"I usually do, too." Grace sat down beside her.

Grace glanced across the tiny room, which contained only the bed she sat upon, a wooden engraved chest, a dressing screen, and a small vanity upon which sat a bottle of perfume, a mirror, comb, hair pins, and jars of what Grace assumed to be face paint. A tiny open window—too high to peer out of—allowed a faint breeze to enter the room, not enough to cool the sultry air or to sweep away the putrid smells drifting in.

Madeline swung her legs back and forth over the side of the bed and began humming a tune, still holding onto Grace. Grace squeezed the girl's hand. She knew she should probably leave, should not remain in this woman's room, should not even be in this tavern, but the temptation of a meal was too much for her to resist.

Perhaps God had sent her here to help this little girl. "Is Miss Nicole your mother?"

The little girl nodded.

"And you live here? In this room?"

Releasing Grace's hand, Madeline lifted the coverlet on the bed and pulled out a straw doll. She held it to her chest. "Oui."

Grace cringed. "Do you stay here all alone?"

"Only when Mama works." Madeline's brown eyes lit up. "But when she does not work, she takes me outside to play, and to the market, and sometimes we walk along the shore."

Grace eased a wayward curl behind Madeline's ear as she remembered her own childhood and the many hours she had spent without her father and mother. But of course, there had always been a governess or a servant or her sisters around to look after her.

Nicole soon returned with two plates of fried fish, baked sugared plantains, and corn. After handing them to Grace and her daughter, she sat at her vanity for a moment to squeeze color onto her cheeks, pin up a loose strand of her hair, and dab perfume on her neck.

Then kneeling beside her daughter, she kissed her on the forehead. "Mother won't return until late. Be a good girl and keep Mademoiselle Grace company and go to sleep when you get tired."

"I will, Mama." The sweet obedience nipped at Grace's heart.

Nicole rose and gestured toward the bed. "You may stay here tonight if you wish."

Grace hadn't the strength to decline the invitation. "Thank you. . . *merci*. You've been so kind."

Nicole smiled then turned and flounced out the door.

Grace took to her meal with such desperation and lack of propriety, she nearly laughed at herself. Never had food tasted so good. Finishing her plate, she longed to lick it but resisted the urge, lest she appear rude.

Madeline also made good work of her dinner and afterward, Grace, stomach bursting, lay back on the bed and closed her eyes, unable to hold them open another minute. Sometime later, she jolted when Madeline crawled into bed and snuggled against her. Wrapping an arm around the little girl, Grace drew her close and faded back to sleep to a discordant French ballad meandering over them from below.

Sometime in the middle of the night, a lurid thought seeped into Grace's mind, jarring her consciousness. A picture of a ripe yellow mango danced through her mind. Lifting her hand to her throat, she gasped as tears of shame burned behind her eyes.

I am a thief.

CHAPTER 12

Rafe leaned back in the wooden chair and inhaled a deep breath, trying to still the spinning in his head. He immediately regretted doing so as a vile brew of malodorous fumes stung his nose and throat. Flanked at the table by Monsieur Atton and Monsieur Legard, Rafe cast his dizzy gaze around the tavern as curses, threats, and ribald laughter blended in a devil's chant that further goaded his ill humor. The throng of humanity twisted in odd shapes before him, even as it seemed to retreat to the long end of a tunnel.

Monsieur Legard grabbed a passing woman and pulled her onto his lap. Disgusted by the display and confused by his disgust—since he'd done the same thing a hundred times—Rafe grimaced and looked away.

He'd been in Port-de-Paix four days now, but it had not provided the diversion he hoped it would. Even Abbé Villion's deep appreciation for what he was doing for the hospital and the praises the people continually cast his way as Rafe strode through town had not provided him with the satisfaction and pleasure they normally did. Even spending every night in his favorite taverns, enjoying his brandy and an occasional game of faro, had not lifted the burden weighing upon his humors. En fait, his mood had grown fouler, and he found himself snapping at his men for no reason.

Mais, he knew the reason. The same reason that kept barging unbidden into his mind—and his heart. The lovely Mademoiselle Grace Westcott. The captive aboard his ship. Yet why did it seem as though he were the one being held captive? For no sooner did he begin to enjoy himself than a vision of those convicting green eyes appeared before him and stole all his pleasure like a schoolmaster with a ruler.

He poured himself a sip of brandy and tossed it to the back of his throat then drew a puff of his cheroot, allowing the spicy smoke to fill his lungs. He had no choice. He would return Mademoiselle Grace to her home. Admiral's daughter or not, he could not sacrifice such an innocent, kindhearted, brave lady to the wolves, or the lion, as she had put it. He smiled as he remembered how her bottom lip quivered when she was nervous and the way her raven hair made her skin look like porcelain.

But lives will be lost.

Rafe winced. He must find another way to procure the fortune he needed. He could not let Abbé Villion down. He could not allow more people to die when it was within his power to prevent it. Sacre mer, why couldn't the woman have been a shrew?

"What's wrong, Capitaine? You look as though someone died." Monsieur Atton leaned toward him, his wiry, spiky hair reminding Rafe of a sea urchin.

Rafe snorted. He felt as though someone had died—or something— some part of him that had the courage to do the sensible thing even if it meant doing the wrong thing.

The blurry shape of a man sauntering up to their table drew Rafe's gaze, and he ground his teeth together, hoping the haze of brandy deceived him. Unfortunately it hadn't.

Monsieur Gihon halted before the table like a king before his subjects. One hand pressed firmly upon the pommel of his rapier, he fingered his pointed, brown beard and shifted eyes as cold as steel onto Rafe.

"If it isn't Monsieur Dubois, the paladin of the poor. Come to receive the praises of your admirers?" He waved his hand through the air, the lace adorning his sleeve flapping in equal alacrity with his lips.

Monsieur Legard's wench abandoned his lap and melted into the crowd that settled into an unusual hush. Like pigs to slop, they no doubt smelled an altercation as their hungry eyes darted toward the men.

Rafe poured himself another drink, raised his glass in mock salute, then gulped the burning liquid. "Monsieur Gihon." The man had been a nuisance since Rafe's childhood. The bully who because of his unusually large size and position in society had hounded the other children. But he'd never been able to bring Rafe into subjection, for even before Rafe grew to his present size, he'd used his wits to defeat the half-masted brute.

Monsieur Gihon flung curled strands of his periwig over his shoulder. "Perhaps you should appoint yourself governor, or better yet, king, and set up a throne where you can receive a continual stream of your adoring masses."

"Thank you for the suggestion, monsieur. I may do that." Rafe grinned and took a puff of his cheroot.

Laughter rumbled across the mob.

Rafe leaned back in his chair. "What do you want?"

"You know, monsieur."

Messieurs Legard and Atton pushed their chairs back and stood, the smirks upon their lips evidence of their confidence in their capitaine. They backed away from the table to join the growing throng of bodies that undulated like waves upon the sea.

Frustration boiled within Rafe. He squeezed the bridge of his nose, trying to clear his head. "How many times must you come for retribution only to depart in humiliation?"

"I will have my revenge, monsieur." The ogre of a man narrowed his slit-like eyes upon Rafe.

"All you will have is a headache in the morning from your overindulgence in drink and a wound in your arm where my rapier will make its signature." Rafe batted him away. "Now, go and leave me be."

A fly landed on the rim of Rafe's glass and he swatted it, wishing he could rid himself of this man as easily. It was then that he noticed from whence the fly had come as the insect buzzed to join his companions in a swarm about Monsieur Gihon's wig.

Quelling a chuckle, Rafe downed his drink, resigned himself to trouncing this boor yet again, and studied his opponent: the way his beefy fingers twitched upon his sword's pommel, the apprehension flickering across his glassy eyes, the swagger of his massive frame caused by either an excess of alcohol or his overinflated pride.

Rafe yawned, patting his hand over his mouth, confident in the knowledge that his display of boredom would spark his longtime nemesis's capricious temper. As expected, Monsieur Gihon drew his rapier in one sweep and leveled its tip upon Rafe's gray waistcoat.

Cheers and howls surrounded them like a pack of hungry wolves while his own men stood to the side wearing expressions of abject tedium as if watching a play to which they knew the ending.

Rafe lowered his chin to examine the sharp point denting his fine cambric. "Tear this waistcoat and you shall pay, monsieur."

"It is you who shall pay. For ruining Mademoiselle Rachelle." The man's nostrils flared like those of a horse that had been run too hard.

"Mademoiselle Rachelle." Rafe scratched his chin thoughtfully. "Do remind me. Who is she again?"

The raucous mob brayed in laughter.

"The woman I was to marry, you scoundrel!" Monsieur Gihon's rapier point pressed deeper into Rafe's waistcoat.

"Ah, oui, I do recall her now." Rafe nodded and gazed off in pretense of remembering the lady. "Hair the color of mahogany and skin the color of fresh cream." He snapped his gaze back to Monsieur Gihon, whose face resembled an inflated pig skin. "Mais I also recall the betrothal of which you speak was only in your mind. The lady denied even knowing you."

Chortles sped through the rabble, and several women pushed their way through the crowd toward the front to watch the impending battle.

Monsieur Gihon's jaw expanded until Rafe thought it would explode. Something besides fury appeared in the man's eyes that set Rafe aback. Pain, real pain and sorrow. And the glimpse he caught of it sobered him instantly. The insolence that had taken over Rafe at the man's presence faded beneath a rising burst of sympathy. For Rafe understood well the agony of losing someone he loved.

He puffed upon his cheroot. "She came to me willingly, monsieur. How was I to know the depth of your interest in her?" When he had discovered Gihon's affections for the lady, Rafe had truly felt bad about the incident. He was not a man to meddle with another man's woman, not even Gihon's. "I offered you my sincerest apology at the time, non? And if I remember correctly, I returned her to you, mon ami."

"Soiled." Gihon spat and then slid his hand within the flap of his coat. "And I take no man's castoffs."

Rafe let out a ragged sigh. "Oui, neither do I." A pinch of pain stabbed his heart as a memory resurged from long ago—a memory of a lady he had hoped to marry who had been stolen by another. Shrugging it off, he faced his adversary, searching for the anger he knew he would need for a fight. "But can I help it if the ladies find me *irrésistible*?"

At this remark, one of the women batted her lashes and cooed at him, igniting more laughter from the mob.

"Will they find you so with my rapier through your heart?" Monsieur Gihon seethed.

Rafe cocked his head. "Even then I believe they would prefer me over you."

The man's hand trembled with rage. His face grew a deep shade of purple and he began sputtering nonsense. The tip of his rapier tore through Rafe's waistcoat, and Rafe heaved a sigh. He had no desire to fight Gihon. There was nothing to be done about the past—for either of them. But to back down in front of this crowd would be a death sentence. "Now you have angered me, monsieur." He stamped out his cheroot upon the wooden table.

A hush consumed the crowd.

Rafe inched his boot to the leg centering the table and gave Monsieur Gihon his most sardonic, confident stare—the one that had melted many men's resolve—hoping he would forsake this foolish squabble. Beads of sweat sprang upon the man's forehead, and he lunged at Rafe.

Rafe kicked the leg. The table slammed into Gihon. He stumbled backward, dropped his rapier, waved his arms through the air, then tumbled into the crowd. They caught him and threw him back toward Rafe. Booting the table aside, Rafe stormed toward the man, shaking the spin of brandy from his head and allowing all of his frustration and anger of the past weeks to flood into his clenched fists.

Monsieur Gihon recovered, eyed his rapier on the floor, and slid his hand into his waistcoat, no doubt in search of a pistol.

Rafe slammed his fist across the giant man's jaw, sending him reeling to the left. He didn't want to hurt him, just make him stop his foolish quest for revenge.

Turning, Rafe bent over to retrieve the man's blade. A punch to his back forced him to the floor. Burning pain seared across his shoulders. He gasped for breath.

"Get up, Monsieur Dubois," one man shouted.

"Can't let 'im beat ye," another chimed in.

"Rafe, Rafe." Female voices chanted his name.

Rising, Rafe whipped around to see a hairy fist fill his vision and flatten against his eye. He bolted backward. His anger boiled and his eye began to throb. The man's skill at fighting had improved.

While Monsieur Gihon lifted his arms to encourage the cheers of the crowd, Rafe charged toward him, barreling into his waist. Together they plunged into the agitated mob. The stench of sweat showered over Rafe as hurrahs filled his ears.

Grabbing the man's coat with both hands, Rafe lifted him off the floor then slammed him down. Before Gihon could recover, Rafe leveled a punch into his stomach followed by another across his jaw, snapping the man's head to the side and sending his periwig flying through the air. The giant toppled over like a felled tree and landed in a heap on the crusty floor. His moan echoed throughout the tavern.

Rafe plucked Gihon's rapier from the floor and tossed it at the man. It landed beside him with a *clank*.

The mob roared their approval, fists in the air, but Rafe felt no relief from the burden weighing upon him. He waved away the crowd, righted his chair, and dropped into it as his men picked up the table and snapped their fingers for more drink.

"Bravo, Capitaine!" Monsieur Atton slapped Rafe on the back. "Though ye had me scared for a moment."

Monsieur Legard took his seat and the trollop who had occupied his lap last slid back into place as if nothing had happened. "*Moi non*. I never seen the capitaine lose a fight."

Rafe touched the swollen tissue around his right eye. "He's a clod. I merely toyed with him."

A blond woman emerged from the throng and headed his way, carrying a bottle of brandy and a cloth. The brandy she set upon the table, the cloth she dabbed upon his eye. He brushed her hand aside. "Nicole. What are you doing here? I thought you worked at *Le Cochon Doux*."

"I missed you, too, Rafe." Perching on his lap, she continued her ministrations. "Quit behaving the imp and allow me to attend to you."

Though Rafe hated being coddled, he didn't mind the close view of her curvaceous figure nor the sweet smell of her lilac perfume that helped to drown the reek of the men beside him. "I heard you saved a boy today from the noose."

She flattened her lips. "He stole a mango. Poor thing was starving to death." She dipped some brandy onto the cloth, then continued dabbing around his eye.

Rafe winced as the alcohol stung his wound. "Quit wasting good brandy." He pushed her hand away. "You are a good woman to help the lad."

She dropped her hand into her lap. "Can I tell you a secret?" Before he could answer, she leaned toward his ear, her honey curls tickling his cheek. "The lad turned out to be a lady."

"Vraiment?" Rafe's brows shot up. Pain etched across his forehead.

Nicole put a finger to her lips. "You mustn't tell anyone."

"Dressed as a boy?"

"Oui, and she had not eaten for days, by the looks of her. I have her upstairs in my room now."

As long as Rafe had known Nicole, she was always taking in strays.

Once, she'd even forfeited some of her earnings to help Rafe feed a hungry family. "You amaze me, Nicole. Are you sure you are not an angel in disguise?"

Her blue eyes the color of the sky glistened beneath his praise, and he thought he detected a slight blush coloring her cheeks. She giggled. "Sacre bleu. An angel? Far from it, I am afraid." Despite her profession, Rafe had once considered pursuing something permanent between them. If not for one tiny obstacle.

"Has my father visited you lately?" His tone edged with more anger than he wanted.

She gave him a sideways glance. "Do you wish to know or are you just expressing your disapproval?"

"Neither." Rafe reached for the bottle of brandy. "Never mind."

She clicked her tongue. "So much anger, Rafe. You are just like one of your cannons about to explode."

"Yet you do not keep your distance, as wisdom would dictate."

"You would never do me harm." Nicole kissed his bruised eye then ran a finger over his stubbled jaw. "I can make it all feel better, Rafe." Her voice grew heavy with the sultry invitation.

Rafe grimaced. "You know I cannot." He gently nudged her from his lap, amazed her closeness evoked no reaction from him. In fact he had no appetite for any woman since he'd landed at port, much to the dismay of his usual flock of *jeunes femmes*.

Nicole huffed and planted her hands upon her waist. Her comely face lined in disappointment. "I have not seen your father in months."

"It matters not." Rafe tipped the bottle to his lips and allowed the spicy liquor to slide down his throat. Leaning the flagon atop his thigh, he raised his gaze to hers. "It only matters that you have been with him at all." A wounded look crossed her expression, and Rafe stood, set the bottle onto the table, took her hand in his, and kissed it. "I thank you for your care, mademoiselle."

Nicole smiled so sweetly, it seemed to wipe the stain of her profession from her face. Then turning with a swash of skirts, she sashayed away to the next customer.

Rafe faced his men. "Gather the crew. We set sail tonight."

"Mais, Capitaine," Legard complained, pulling back from the woman nibbling on his neck.

"One more night?" Monsieur Atton pleaded.

"I said tonight!" Rafe barked, and the men jumped to their feet. Monsieur Legard's woman nearly fell to the floor.

Rafe could no longer remain in this port. His life would never return to normal again until he returned Mademoiselle Grace safely to her home. Then he could get back to his mercenary work without her convicting presence dangling over him like a hangman's noose over a criminal's neck.

CHAPTER 13

A stream of light danced across Grace's eyelids and scattered into tiny diamonds. She stretched and savored the soft feel of a dry coverlet beneath her instead of cold, wet mud. Quiet, steady breathing filled the air, and the tiny warm body molding against Grace reminded her of the odd predicament in which she found herself.

On the bed of a trollop, snuggling beside the woman's illegitimate child.

Movement in the distance brought Grace to full attention. Slipping her arm from beneath Madeline, she rose on one elbow and glanced across the room, smoky in the dust-laden rays of the sun streaming through the window. In the far corner, with woolen shawl about her shoulders, lay Nicole, whose open eyes met Grace's.

She smiled. "How did you sleep?"

Grace blinked. "You slept on the floor? Why did you not come to bed?"

Nicole pushed herself to a sitting position and brushed the hair from her face. "I did not wish to disturb you. You and Madeline slept so soundly."

"When did you come in?" Grace swung her legs over the edge of the bed.

"Late," Nicole replied with a smile that seemed to carry a trace of shame. Then Grace lowered her gaze to Nicole's wrinkled gown, her disheveled coiffure, and the smeared paint on her face. A sudden embarrassment flooded Grace at the realization of what the woman had undoubtedly subjected herself to during the long night.

Grace clutched the top of her shirt and held it tight over her chest in fear that the condition might be contagious. She gazed down at the sleeping child, a beacon of innocence amidst this haven of debauchery. "Madeline is a lovely girl."

Nicole's eyes moistened, and she crawled over to sit beside the bed, gazing at her child. "She is my life." She took the sleeping girl's hand in hers, and from the look in her eyes, Grace knew she meant it.

Grace bit her lip, wanting to ask the woman why she subjected her daughter to this sordid existence, but feared to insult someone who'd been naught but kind to her.

Lifting her gaze to Grace, Nicole brushed a curl of her golden hair aside, and sighed, her blue eyes stinging with pain. "You look at me with such reproach."

Grace looked down, regretting that she wore her opinions so blatantly on her face. Or so her sisters had told her. "Forgive me. I mean no offense."

Rising, Nicole trudged to her vanity and sat down. "You forget, I am accustomed to the looks of disdain I receive from proper ladies. And even some men." She grabbed a cloth, dipped it in a basin of water, and attempted to wipe the paint from her cheeks. But after a few seconds, she faced Grace again, a grin forming on her lips. "But I didn't expect it from"—she chuckled—"a woman who dresses like a man and steals mangos."

Grace smiled at the ease with which this woman cast offense aside. Her sweet spirit transformed their conversation from one of strain to one of enjoyment as if they'd been friends for years. Which gave Grace the encouragement to ask the question that had burned on her tongue ever since she'd met Nicole. "Why do you. . .why do you—?"

"Sell myself for money?" Nicole raised her brows. "For her." She gestured toward the still-sleeping child. "To feed her. Keep her warm and off the street." She tugged the lace bounding from her bodice in an attempt to straighten it. "Otherwise we would both be wandering the alleys as you were yesterday and would probably die, hungry and alone."

"Surely there is another way." Grace thought of her sister Faith who had resorted to pirating to garner much-needed wealth. A shudder ran through her, and she thanked God that situation had turned out well in the end.

"What would you suggest?" Nicole snickered as she faced the mirror again.

"A trade of some sort, perhaps?"

"A woman in business on her own? Here in Port-de-Paix?" Her laughter bubbled through the room, and she waved away the thought. "Besides, I have no skills."

Grace clutched the chain around her neck. What did a woman do if she had no family, no husband, no money? In Charles Towne, some women had been permitted to run millinery shops as long as they were widowed or deeded the right to do so by their husbands. But apparently here in Saint Dominique that was not the case. "How did you come to this town? Where is your family?"

Nicole set down the cloth, shook her head at her appearance in the mirror, then swerved in her chair to face Grace. "I grew up an orphan on the streets of Creteil. At seventeen, I was rounded up by King Louis XIV's men and sent here to be a wife to one of the local planters." Her nonchalance gave no indication of the horror she must have endured. She chuckled. " 'Daughters of the King,' they called us. Simply a polite way to say *prostituées*."

Grace's heart sank. How atrocious. How could any woman have endured such a thing? She glanced at Madeline, and Nicole seemed to read her silent question.

"I was ravished by one of the sailors on the crossing, and when I arrived with my belly full of a child, no one wanted me for a wife." Nicole pressed a hand over her stomach as if remembering the incident; then she released a heavy sigh.

A sour taste filled Grace's mouth. "I am sorry."

"*C'est la vie.*" Nicole shrugged. "That sailor left me with two precious things: the ability to speak English and ma Madeline chérie. Besides, we have done well. Madeline lacks for nothing. And"—Nicole's blue eyes sparkled with hope—"I am saving money so that she and I can escape this place and sail for the British colonies in America. I hear they accept everyone, and there are opportunities for women that are not found here."

" 'Tis true. There are some." Swiping away a tear, Grace fingered the little girl's curls as shame sank into her chest. Grace had judged this woman—had spent a lifetime judging all women like her. And she'd never once considered the path that led them to such a life. She'd never considered the situations forced upon them by the world and its kings and its men, and the difficult choices they had to make. And as she stared at the little girl, she wondered for the first time if she wouldn't have chosen to do exactly the same thing Nicole had done. Anything to protect and provide for this precious child sleeping so peacefully. "Forgive me, Nicole, I have judged you unfairly."

Nicole tilted her head and smiled. "I may be a trollop, but you are a thief, remember?" She laughed and Grace joined her.

"Indeed."

When their laughter died down, Grace studied her new friend. This woman did what she had to in order to survive. Just as Grace had done when she had stolen the mango. It didn't make either action right. They were both sins. But for some reason, understanding the cause removed the guilt just a bit.

"I will go get us some breakfast." Nicole rose and patted down her wrinkled skirts. She opened the door then swung her gaze back to Grace. "And then you shall tell me all about how you came to Port-de-Paix and why a lady like yourself was running around town half starved and dressed like a boy." She gave Grace a look that said she wouldn't take no for an answer. "And I have a feeling it will be quite an interesting tale." She winked then stepped into the hallway and closed the door.

Interesting, indeed. Grace took a deep breath of the room's stale air as shouts and bells and the sound of horses' hooves drifted in through the open window. The port awoke to another day. Only this day, Grace would have a belly full of food and the strength of a good night's sleep.

Thank You, Lord.

Laying a hand upon Madeline's head, Grace said a prayer for the girl's life, her safety, her future, hoping that if God answered any of Grace's recent prayers, it would be this one.

Minutes later, as promised, Nicole returned bearing buttery biscuits and jam, along with hot steaming coffee and plantains. Grace's stomach leapt at the rich savory scents, and when Madeline awoke, the three of them gobbled up the food as if they were old friends sitting around a breakfast table.

Afterward, while Nicole brushed Madeline's hair, Grace stood over the washbowl and attempted to wipe the mud from her face and arms as she regaled them with the story of her capture, and her time aboard *Le Champion.*

"Did you say Capitaine Rafe Dubois?" Nicole's voice rose in surprise.

"Yes. Do you know him?"

Nicole laughed and nodded. "He was here in the tavern last night. Got into one of his scraps with Monsieur Gihon."

Grace halted her toilet and faced her, her blood racing. "You didn't tell him I was here?"

"I didn't know who you were." Nicole scrunched her nose as she battled a particularly stubborn knot in Madeline's hair.

"*Aïe, Maman.*" Madeline cried, her face twisted in a pout.

"*Je suis désolée,* ma chérie." Nicole kissed her daughter on the cheek and continued brushing. "I am almost done." She glanced at Grace. "And now that I know what he has done, I most certainly will keep your secret."

Grace released a sigh.

"I cannot believe Rafe, I mean Capitaine Dubois, would lower himself to commit such a vile task such as kidnapping an innocent lady. So unlike him."

Grace winced at Nicole's use of the captain's Christian name. No doubt they had done business together. Pushing the thought aside as well as the odd feeling of discomfort it caused, she set down the cloth and rolled down her sleeves. "On the contrary, I have spent enough time with him to know he is quite capable."

Nicole stared at her curiously, and Grace continued the story of how one of the crew brought her ashore, and then how all her money was stolen, and how she wandered around town until she was so hungry and desperate that she stole the mango. In a way, hearing the desperation in her own voice as she told the sordid tale aloud assuaged her guilt over the thievery. Almost.

"You poor thing." Nicole let Madeline slip from her lap. The girl grabbed her doll off the bed and approached Grace. "Do you like my doll? Her name is Joli."

Grace bent over and tapped the doll on the head. "Yes, I do very much. She is quite beautiful. Just like you."

Madeline beamed, then she jumped on the bed and began playing.

"What will you do now?" Nicole asked. "You could work here. I do detect a remarkable beauty beneath all that dirt."

Grace's face heated. "Mercy me. No. I could never do—" She caught herself and realized the haughty disdain in her voice had cast a sullen cloud over Nicole's expression. "Forgive me. Again I have offended you. But I have no child to provide for as you do."

Nicole attempted a smile and rose from her chair as someone below began pounding out a tune on the harpsichord.

"You have been so kind to feed me." Grace closed the gap between them and took Nicole's hands in hers. "You are an answer to prayer."

"I don't believe I've ever been anyone's answer to prayer." With the paint removed, Nicole's beauty beamed from her face, and Grace could almost see the innocent little girl she once was peering from behind her blue eyes.

"Well, now you have." Grace squeezed her hands. "And I shall pray for you. That God will deliver you from this life and grant you the money you need to sail to the colonies."

"I fear God will not listen to the prayers of a prostitute." Nicole released Grace's hands and strode to the window.

"I used to believe that, too," Grace said. "But I'm not so sure anymore."

Nicole flipped up the hem of her skirt and snapped open a hidden pocket. Pulling some coins from within it, she offered three to Grace. "Please take these. It won't buy you passage home, but it is a start."

Tears burned behind Grace's eyes and she turned around.

"What is the matter?" Nicole's skirts swished toward her.

"Your generosity overwhelms me." Grace swallowed. This woman, this trollop, had shown her more kindness and mercy than all of the so-called Christian ladies back in Charles Towne. She turned around to see Nicole still handing her the money, a questioning look on her face.

Grace pushed her hands away. "I could never accept that." She wiped a tear sliding down her cheek. "You need that for Madeline."

Nicole flattened her lips in disappointment and studied Grace for a moment before her eyes flashed. "I know what to do."

Grace shook her head.

"I know someone who will gladly help you."

At Grace's inquisitive look, Nicole continued, "A man, a prominent man here in Port-de-Paix."

"I told you I cannot—"

"Non, you misunderstand. A respectable, godly man." Nicole smiled and tapped a finger on her chin. "And someone who would love nothing more than to assist a victim of Captain Rafe Dubois."

CHAPTER 14

Grace leaned out the window of the landau and clasped Nicole's hand. "How can I ever repay your kindness? You saved me from certain death."

"Anyone would have done as much." Nicole squeezed her hand and then released it and bent down to pick up Madeline.

"Yet no one else did." Grace's eyes burned. She felt as though she were abandoning her only friend in the world.

"Be good for your mama, Madeline. She loves you very much." Grace slid a finger over the child's soft cheek.

Madeline giggled and leaned her head on Nicole's shoulder. "*Je l'aime aussi.*"

Thunder rumbled and Grace gazed up at the darkening sky, praying the incoming storm was not a portent of bad things to come. Black, swirling clouds swallowed up the afternoon sun, and Grace offered Nicole a weak smile. "I will pray for you. God is the only One who can truly deliver you from this life."

"You are kind to give me hope." Nicole smiled—a sad, desperate smile that bespoke a wounded heart too familiar with pain and disappointment.

A blast of wind blew in from the harbor where a bell tolled. The breeze danced among Nicole's golden curls, and Grace shook her head at the vision of this woman, this trollop, who was the epitome of humility and kindness.

"*Êtes-vous prête,* mademoiselle?" The footman snapped in disdain as he leaned over from his perch atop the carriage seat above her. His obvious disapproval of her filthy attire had been evident by his twisted features and the lift of his nose when he had opened the carriage door for her. Which only added to Grace's uneasiness about her destination. Would her benefactors be equally repulsed? But what did it matter? She had no other choice but to accept their hospitality.

"Oui," she replied with reluctance. And with a snap of reins, the carriage lurched and lumbered on its way. Grace waved out the window at Nicole and Madeline who were standing in front of the tavern until a curve in the road stole them from her sight.

As she sat back against the cushioned seats, loneliness fell upon her as thick and dark as the clouds overhead. Who was this Monsieur Henri, to whom Nicole referred? That he was an honorable man, Nicole had assured Grace. That he had sent his landau as soon as Nicole's note had arrived in his hands was indisputable, but it still did little to stop Grace's nerves from tightening into knots at the thought of going to an unknown man's home. Yet, this must be God's answer to her prayer for rescue. Mustn't it?

The carriage careened and jolted over the rocky path, twisting and turning around bend and over stream. Tall cedars, lush rosewoods, and the biggest ferns Grace had ever seen passed her window in a pageant of stunning greens and browns. Air fragrant with the sweet perfume of logwood flowers and pimento filled her nostrils. Normally, Grace would have enjoyed such natural beauty, but in her present state of mind, the shadows of the forest seemed like dark and nefarious creatures reaching out for her, trying to pull her into their wooded labyrinth to be lost forever.

"Oh, Lord, let this man be friend and not foe," she whispered as thunder growled in the distance.

Soon the greenery parted to reveal a vast parcel of cultivated land. Rows and rows of sugar cane extended as far as the eye could see. The heads of African slaves working the fields barely poked above the tall, spindly plants. Palm trees lined a gravel road that extended to a large house beyond the fields. Their fronds swayed in the heavy wind like foppish courtiers, gesturing Grace onward to the palace. And a palace it was. The massive structure perched upon a hill lording over its subjects below.

As the landau rumbled down the path, Grace couldn't keep her eyes off the house, or her heart from feeling a deep sense of dread that mounted with each turn of the carriage's wheels. Eight white columns guarded the front of the house, which boasted a full-length porch on both first and second floors before extending up to a steep hipped roof. French doors opened onto the upper porch where urns filled with orchids, lilies, and begonias bounded in a colorful display.

The carriage halted before a wide span of stairs leading to an ornately carved wooden door. Slipping from his seat, the footman snapped open the door and stood at attention but did not place a step down for her. Grace stumbled from the carriage and, avoiding his gaze, began inching her way up the stairs. She grabbed the chain around her neck, seeking its comfort and questioning the wisdom of putting her trust in Nicole. She halted, her throat closing. Hot wind tore at her muddy shirt and matted hair, bringing with it the sting of rain and the sweat of the oppressed. Perhaps she could convince the driver to return her to town. She started to turn around when the heavy door swung open and a man in a green waistcoat appeared in the doorway. "Mademoiselle Grace?"

Grace nodded, and he gestured for her to enter, but he kept his distance as if she had leprosy. Then with a *humph* he abandoned her to stand in a massive foyer that reminded Grace of Lord Somerset, Earl of Herrick's estate she'd visited once in London. An enormous chandelier hanging over Grace's head chimed in the rain-scented breeze that had forced its way in through the open door. Afraid to move lest she muddy the pristine marble floor, Grace glanced over the room, admiring the marble-topped salon table; butler bench, above which hung a gilt cameo mirror; the tall case clock; and console table flanked by two matching oil paintings of the same woman. A wide staircase led up to the second floor then split in two, ascending up either side of the house.

Shoes clipped on the marble, and Grace looked up to see an older gentleman, perhaps in his early fifties, heading her way. He marched with a pompous authority that grated over her, yet his initial look of repulsion quickly faded beneath the veneer of a smile. Stylishly dressed in a suit of black camlet with buttonholes richly bound in silver and his neck swathed in white silk, he halted before her and hesitated as if awaiting homage. His blue eyes glittered in the candlelight, but their lack of warmth caused Grace to shudder.

"Mademoiselle Grace Westcott." He bowed. "Nicole was not exaggerating about your appearance. Non?" He scanned her from head to toe and chuckled.

Grace drew a shaky breath and dipped the curtsy his comportment seemed to demand. "I thank you for your offer to help me, Monsieur. . ." Grace looked up into those cold eyes, not wanting to use his Christian name but knowing no other.

"Monsieur Dubois. Monsieur Henri Dubois."

❧

Rafe pressed the heels of his boots to the steed's flanks and leaned forward in the saddle, prodding the horse to as fast a canter as possible around the twists and turns leading to the Dubois plantation. Behind him, Monsieur Thorn's horse pounded an ominous cadence in the mud as the night wind laden with the spice of impending rain blasted over them. Rafe's hair loosened from its tie and whipped on his shoulders. Lightning sliced the dark sky, flinging a grayish hue upon the forest and granting Rafe his bearings. In his haste, he'd forgotten a lantern, but he knew this path—every bend and turn—as well as he knew the Caribbean currents. Like a long, spiraling fuse, the trail seemed harmless in its appearance and windings. That was until a man reached the end and found himself in the presence of a deadly explosive.

Thunder growled and it began to rain. Rafe urged more speed from his mount, every muscle within him drawn as tight as the halyard of a full sail. When he had returned to his brig the night before, he had taken to his bed, too exhausted and too inebriated to either set sail or deal with the mademoiselle. It wasn't until he finally woke the next morning, near midday, that he discovered her missing. What was the foolish girl thinking? Wandering the streets of one of the most dangerous port towns in the Caribbean, surpassed only by Tortuga and Petit Goave. And for five days! Zut alors, it was a miracle she had survived unscathed.

If he believed in miracles anymore.

Of course his men had claimed ignorance in her escape. All except Monsieur Thorn, who'd said he discovered her missing four days ago and for fear of invoking his captain's wrath had not told Rafe, but had instead been searching for her frantically on his own. *Les ruses, les déceptions.* Which was why Rafe insisted his first mate accompany him. If Rafe couldn't trust him, it would be best to keep him close.

As soon as he had left the ship, Rafe remembered Nicole's story of harboring a lady dressed as a boy, so he had made haste directly to the tavern, his fears temporarily subsiding—until he'd discovered where Nicole had sent her. Now they resurged all the more, for it would be better for Mademoiselle Grace to be on the streets than in the clutches of his father.

Nudging the horse onward, Rafe ignored the rain stinging his face. He swerved around another bend in a path that was fast becoming a muddy stream and emerged from the thicket onto the wide expanse of the Dubois estate, made all the more hideous by the gray shroud cast upon it from the storm. Pulling the horse to a stop, he wiped the rain from his eyes and stared at the eerie mansion he had called home for one and twenty years, a place he'd sworn he would never set eyes on again.

Monsieur Thorn reined in beside him and tugged his hat down on his forehead. The rain pounded over the trees, the sugar cane, the mud, its cadence sounding like the taunting laughter of a dissident mob.

Thunder rumbled a warning for the men to retreat while they could. Rafe's horse stomped in the mud and snorted, then it pranced sideways as if spooked by some unseen malevolent force. And though every ounce of Rafe longed to turn around and flee back to his ship, he steadied his mount, staring at the house in the distance, the white vision blurred by the constant stream of rain. Within the walls of that mausoleum, a treasure existed—a lady who had become Rafe's responsibility by his own foolish actions. And he could not abandon her to the fiendish devices of this plantation's master.

With a jab of his heels to the horse's flanks, Rafe brought the beast to a gallop over the muddy path, making quick work of the remaining distance. As he approached the front of the house, he shook off his apprehension, reined in the steed, and slid off the animal before it came to a halt. Taking the ostentatious stairs in two leaps, he gripped the pommel of his rapier and pounded on the door before he changed his mind.

~⌇~

Grace sipped the hot tea, savoring its sweet lemony flavor, and set the cup down with a clank that rang through the room. "Forgive me." She clasped her trembling hands together, still finding it hard to believe she sat in the same room with Rafe's father—the man Rafe had called a monster. "I can't seem to stop shaking."

"Understandable, Mademoiselle Grace." Monsieur Dubois smiled from the cream-colored Louis XIV settee centering the parlor. "You have been through more than a lady should endure." Lightly powdered chestnut curls streaked with silver hung well past his jaw. He shifted his broad shoulders and examined her with dark blue eyes that carried no trace of Rafe within them.

Lowering her gaze beneath his perusal, Grace pressed the folds of her gown—borrowed from Madame Dubois's wardrobe. "I am indebted to you for your kindness, monsieur."

Though shocked at meeting Rafe's father, Grace had found the man to be none of the vile things his son had indicated. He had accepted her into his home with open arms, provided a private bedchamber and a hot bath for her, and given her a lady's maid in attendance. Though she felt a bit uncomfortable sitting alone with him in his parlor, they were not entirely on their own as a footman stood at the door, awaiting his master's command. Besides, Monsieur Dubois had given her no indication his intentions were anything but pure.

So unlike his son.

"Ah, it is my pleasure to help a lady in need, especially one who has suffered beneath my son's bitter hand." He sipped his port. "I feel a sense of obligation to correct the ills which have come about by my offspring."

"That must keep you quite busy." The words flew from Grace's mouth before she realized the insult they contained. And although she meant the statement quite seriously, it drew a chuckle from the elder Dubois.

"I see you have become well acquainted with Rafe."

Grace blushed. "Only enough to observe that he holds to no moral code in his affairs, nor does he speak fondly of you, monsieur."

Monsieur Dubois stood, his imposing frame towering over her, and sauntered to the mantel, gazing up at a painting of a beautiful young woman. "Why would he? My son has abandoned the morality, the honor, the godliness with which I attempted to raise him."

Grace stared into the crackling flames of the fire as the rain tapped on the roof. She thought of her own mother's admonition on her deathbed, entrusting Grace with the responsibility of ensuring the salvation of her sisters. And what a task that had proved to be. She could well relate to Monsieur Dubois's anguish over his son's sinful behavior.

"Mais, let us not think on such things, mademoiselle." Monsieur Dubois sighed and straightened his black waistcoat. "Dinner shall be served shortly. I'm sure you're famished, and tomorrow I shall place you upon one of my merchant ships. I believe Captain Christoff will be traveling north up the coast with a hold full of sugar and coffee and can deliver you safely to Charles Towne."

Hope flooded Grace. She would finally be safe at home and could put the nightmare of Captain Rafe Dubois behind her. She shifted in her seat. Then why did she still feel so unnerved? "I don't know what to say, monsieur. You are too kind. I'm sure my father, Admiral Westcott, will reward you handsomely."

He waved a jeweled hand through the air and threw back his shoulders. "There is no need. Consider it a favor from one Christian to another."

Grace snapped her gaze to his, her heart leaping in her chest. "Then you follow the Savior, Jesus?"

"Oui." He clutched the lapels of his camlet waistcoat. "I and my family are Huguenots. We fled the persecution in France twenty-eight years ago."

Grace's heart soared. The Lord had brought her another Christian. "Did your tribulation not follow you here to the French colonies?"

"Non. Far from the mainland where many struggle simply to survive, not many care which faith one clings to." His mustached lip lifted in a smile devoid of warmth.

Pound. Pound. Pound. A loud banging filled the room from the foyer. *Pound. Pound. Pound.*

Monsieur Dubois's curious gaze shifted to the door. "Who could that be this time of night?"

Footsteps sounded. A door opened. Shouting in French that Grace couldn't understand. She didn't have to. She knew that voice.

Monsieur Dubois excused himself and exited the room. Unable to remain seated, Grace followed him out the door, down a short hallway, and into the vestibule.

She halted. There, just inside the open door, wind howling in protest around him and water dripping from his waistcoat and sash, stood Captain Dubois. He shook his head, spraying droplets over the marble floor, then ran a hand through his hair and met her gaze. Intense emotion flashed within his eyes before he shifted them to the elder Dubois.

"Bonjour, *Père*." One corner of his mouth lifted in a grin, but his voice carried the sting of spite.

CHAPTER 15

Bile rose in Rafe's throat at the sight of his father. The dried beef he had consumed on the ship rebelled in his gut.

"Je suis désolé, Monsieur Dubois." The butler's voice took on a fear-laced apologetic tone. "He forced his way inside."

Footsteps splashed behind him, and Rafe turned to see Monsieur Thorn stop just outside the door. Doffing his hat, the first mate shook the water from it before entering.

"Très bien, Francois." Monsieur Dubois dismissed the butler with a wave, and the man shut the door, raised his aquiline nose at Rafe and Monsieur Thorn, and left the room.

Rafe's father approached him, a carping smile on his lips and his arms extended. "Rafe. How good to see you. How long has it been? Years."

Rafe tightened the corners of his mouth. "Not long enough." He held up a hand to stop his father's advance. "Spare me the pleasantries, Père. I have come for the girl." The sight of Mademoiselle Grace in that exquisite jade gown, her raven hair pinned tightly atop her head, delighted him more than he wanted to admit. And helped soften the blow of seeing his father again.

"You mean Mademoiselle Westcott?" his father said innocently and gestured behind him at Grace. "I don't believe she wishes to accompany you." He turned toward Monsieur Thorn. "Forgive my son's ill manners, monsieur, I am Henri Dubois. Et vous?"

"Justus Thorn, monsieur." Thorn bowed slightly. "You son's first mate."

"Ah, you've brought your nefarious crew along." Rafe's father raised a graying brow.

"This is none of your affair." Rafe stroked the hilt of his rapier, his fingers itching to draw it.

"C'est mon *affaire* when I discover you have kidnapped an innocent lady from her home and intend to sell her to a Spanish don." Monsieur

Dubois shook his head and stroked his pointed beard. "To what depths have you sunk, mon *fils*? Do you try to break an old man's heart?"

Ignoring his father and the sharp barb twisting in his gut, Rafe marched to Mademoiselle Grace and took her by the arm. "I see you've already bribed her with fripperies, Père."

"She came to us wearing a torn, filthy shirt and breeches of all things—a product of your hospitality, I believe?" His voice sharpened in sarcasm.

Rafe pulled on her arm, but Grace yanked from his grasp and shot a fiery glare his way. "I will not go with you."

Rafe ground his teeth together. "Believe me when I say you are in far more danger here than with me."

His father laughed. "Yes, choose, mademoiselle. A warm home, clothing, hot food, and a chance to go home to the safety of your loved ones, or"—he gestured toward Rafe and shook his head in disgust—"back to the hold of my son's brig."

Rafe glared at Mademoiselle Grace. Her fresh scent swirled about him, setting aflame his senses and igniting an urgency within him to protect her—to keep her safe from men like his father. Little did she know that here in this house she was but an innocent lamb among the wolves. How could Rafe make her understand? "You will come with me now," he ordered her as if she were one of his crew. He grabbed her arm and tightened his grip, resorting to the only method he knew to ensure his will was accomplished. He felt a rush of heat to his head when instead of obeying she winced and widened her eyes in horror.

He loosened his grip and softened his tone, forcing his features into what he hoped was a pleading look—a look that sat most uncomfortably upon his face. "S'il vous plaît, mademoiselle. You are not safe here."

Confusion rumbled across her features. "And I am safe with you?" She backed away from him, clutching the chain around her neck as if terrified by his very presence. Rafe cringed beneath the sudden ache in his heart.

"I will not allow you to take her, Rafe." His father's sanctimonious voice stabbed him.

Fury gripped Rafe as he swerved about and stared at his father's arrogant stance: one jeweled hand on his hip, the other fingering his beard, his broad figure standing guard over the closest avenue of escape. And history replayed itself in Rafe's mind. Suddenly, he was a young man again, standing before his father—his hero—trying to come to grips with why his own flesh and blood had committed the ultimate betrayal against him.

But Rafe was older now, stronger, and he would not allow his father access to his heart, nor would he allow him to tarnish another innocent woman. Rafe squeezed the hilt of his rapier and took a step toward the man who had sired him.

Henri Dubois crossed his arms over his chest and smirked. "Will you draw a sword on your own father?"

Rafe would love nothing more. The man hadn't changed one bit in the past five years. The same pretension, the same arrogance, the same evil he remembered burned within his father's gaze. But he saw something else in those malicious blue eyes. Rafe saw his mother. And that one vision of her soft, loving face caused him to release his grip on the weapon. She wouldn't want him to harm his father.

"I didn't think so." His father gave him a condescending smile then he looked to Monsieur Thorn as if for approval, but Rafe's first mate maintained his stoic stance.

"I have an idea." A smile curved his father's lips. "Rafe, why not stay with us for a few days? Go upstairs. Your old chamber is still available. Change into some dry and"—he wrinkled his nose—"more appropriate attire, cool your temper, and we can discuss this over dinner. Your stepmother would love to see you again."

Stepmother. Rafe's gut curdled.

His father gloated in the victory of that one word, but Rafe only stared at him unflinching as he pondered his next course of action. He had three choices. Murder his own father—extremely tempting—abandon the foolish Mademoiselle Grace to the fate she had chosen, or accept the invitation to dine with them and await an opportunity to convince the lady to trust him.

Rafe clenched his fists. He could not allow another woman to be trapped in his father's web. Especially since she would not be here but for Rafe. "Très bien. I will stay." The words stung his lips as they flung from his mouth.

"I protest!" Mademoiselle Grace shouted from behind Rafe, and he turned to see her storming forward, her face flush. No doubt realizing the impropriety of her outburst, she halted and softened her tone. "Forgive me, Monsieur Dubois, but if the captain resides here, surely he will attempt to kidnap me again." The fear on her face sliced through Rafe's conscience, but how could he blame her?

"Never fear, mademoiselle." His father's voice boomed through the foyer as if he were giving a speech. "I shall hold myself personally responsible for your safety while you are under my roof." He hesitated and glanced over them all. "Well, that settles things." He rubbed his hands together as if he were anticipating a good meal. No doubt he hoped Rafe would be the main course.

❧

Grace stood at the window of her chamber and stared into the darkness. Raindrops splattered against the panes of glass and slid down in random paths, some twisting and turning, some going straight, others gliding alongside other drops and collecting in a pool at the bottom. Much like people wandering through life. She pondered the odd path her own life had taken of late and the other drops she'd been forced to slide beside. Drops she would have never associated with just a month ago. Drops like Father Alers, Monsieur Weylan, Nicole, Madeline, and of course, Captain Dubois. Yet she knew God had a plan for each person, each path, no matter how chaotic it all seemed. A plan to touch their lives for His glory. A plan of which Grace seemed lately to fall so short.

She sighed and rubbed the jeweled cross in her hand. "Am I bringing You glory, Lord? Have I led anyone to You since this whole horrid venture began? No one seems to listen to me. And now I find myself with an opportunity to go home, but what have I accomplished? What has all this misery produced?"

She thought of Captain Dubois, how his volatile presence had filled the foyer. He had come for her. But the burning flash in his eyes carried no wicked intent, no anger, no malice, but simply concern. She could make no sense of it, nor of the way her heart had leapt at the sight of him. Her cheeks burned in shame. The man was a rogue, a villain. Why did he affect her so? Up until this night, she had felt naught but repulsion, pity, and righteous anger toward him. Yet there was something behind those dark eyes, something that made her think there was much more to this man than his actions toward her intimated.

"Father, I'm sorry for this strange feeling that comes over me in his presence."

A firm hand covered her mouth. Grace's blood froze in terror.

A strong arm grabbed her waist. She struggled against the iron grip, but to no avail. The man forced her back against his muscled torso. "I hope it is a pleasurable feeling, mademoiselle." The deep voice flowed like warm silk over her ear.

Captain Dubois.

Heat stormed through Grace, the heat of embarrassment, the heat of anger. She tried to free her elbows to jab them into his stomach, but his strength forbade her.

"If you promise not to scream, I shall release you. I wish only to talk." His warm breath, edged with brandy and tobacco, tickled her neck.

Grace nodded and his hand fell away from her mouth. "How dare you sneak into my chamber and listen to my personal petitions." She jerked from his grasp, veered around, and raised her hand to slap the grin off his face.

He caught her arm in midair and his smile widened, reaching his eyes in a twinkle of playfulness.

Tugging away from him, Grace retreated into the shadows, praying the captain could not see the blossom of red creeping up her neck.

But by the mischievous look on his face, she knew he had. Not only seen, but he seemed to enjoy her discomfort. With his hair combed and slicked back, and wearing a black silver-embroidered velvet coat and breeches, he appeared more a French gentleman than a rogue. Almost. For a dark purple shadow circled one eye, no doubt from a recent brawl.

"This feeling you speak of, I hope you find it pleasing." He grinned.

"I was not speaking of you." Grace tucked the cross back into her gown and looked away, wincing at her lie.

"Of course not." The lilt in his voice spoke of his disbelief.

Grace stormed away, desperate to put enough distance between them to quell the odd stirring in her belly. "What do you want? To kidnap me again?"

He shrugged. "The idea has, how do you say, crossed my mind."

"I will scream."

"And my father will come to your rescue like the hero he is," he said nonchalantly as he circled the bed and made his way toward her, his boots thumping on the wooden floor. "But beware, mademoiselle, of wolves in sheep's clothing."

Thunder boomed overhead then drifted into a rumble, and Grace backed away from him, her chest tightening. "You are the only wolf

I see in this house."

He halted and raised a brow, but she saw no anger in his eyes, only hesitancy, as if he cared that he had frightened her.

"You should not be here alone in my chamber." Grace filled the uncomfortable silence. " 'Tis most improper."

At that he chuckled and stepped toward the fireplace. "I believe we are past such formalities, oui?" He laid a hand on the mantel, stomped his jackboot atop the footing, and stared at the burning embers. "I hear you spent five days on the streets of Port-de-Paix. Foolish."

Grace slid behind a settee, effectively using the sofa as a barrier between them. "What did you expect? For me to sit aboard your ship and await your return?"

He smiled. "Oui. Most women would not have the courage to leave." He stepped toward her and his brow furrowed. "Were you harmed?"

Grace swallowed, her stomach constricting at the look of concern in his expression. "I survived, as you can see. God took care of me."

"God?" He snickered. "It was a trollop, I believe, who rescued you."

"God can use whomever He wishes," Grace shot back, realizing Nicole had betrayed her confidence. "You didn't harm Nicole, did you?"

For a second, he seemed genuinely pained that she considered such a thing. "Non. I would never harm her. We are friends." Captain Dubois frowned then looked down at the silk Persian rug beneath his boots. He pressed a finger over his mustache as he took up a pace across the chamber. "Ah, the opulence of my father. What do you think of it?" He gestured toward the walnut bed frame, the pair of matching mahogany nightstands, the oak dressing table with three beveled mirrors, the French tapestries lining the wall.

Baffled by the captain's fluctuating moods, Grace eyed him curiously. "What do you have against him? He seems an honorable man to me."

The captain snorted. "You do not know him." He stopped his pacing and studied her, an odd mixture of frustration and hunger in his expression. "You must leave with me tonight."

Grace opened her mouth to protest, but he held up a hand to silence her. "I will take you back to Charles Towne."

Her breath caught in her throat. "Surely you don't expect me to believe you?"

"Non. I do not expect you to, but I would like you to." The hard sheen over his eyes softened.

"Why?" she stuttered and shook her head. "Why return me now after all this time? After all you have put me through? And what of the fortune you stand to make from my sale?"

"Things have changed."

"What has changed?" Grace dared to take a step toward him.

He swallowed and looked down, his jaw stiffening. "I was wrong to take you, mademoiselle. I thought you were someone you are not. I thought you deserved the fate I led you to."

Grace tried to make sense of his words, but they clattered around in her mind like pieces of broken china. "But you didn't know me. How could you know—"

"I know you, now." He lifted his gaze to hers.

The sincerity in his eyes sent a jolt through Grace, and she turned her back to him, not wanting to see this side of him, not wanting to believe the words he spoke. "You know nothing of me."

She heard his boots thud over the carpet toward her. "I know you are kind, generous, and courageous, that you stand true to your convictions, that you forgive those who insult you, that—"

"Stop." She held up a hand, unable to listen to the praises that slithered like lies around her ears. Was she any of those things? How could she claim such piety when she'd done naught but doubt God's love for her?

He placed his hand on her shoulder, and she spun around and stared into his dark eyes, longing to know what had caused this villain to drop his guard, to lower his devil-may-care facade. Yet all the while chastising herself for being enamored by what she saw behind them.

Rafe's hungry gaze swept over her, and Grace splayed her fingers over the bare skin beneath her neck. The maid had given her Madame Dubois's most modest gown, but still she felt exposed within its silken folds—especially when the captain's smoky eyes took her in so ardently.

As if sensing her discomfort, he took a step back. "My father has no intention of returning you to Charles Towne, mademoiselle."

"Mercy me. You expect me to take the word of a rake, a scoundrel, over that of an obvious gentleman, a man of rank and wealth."

His jaw stiffened and his right brow began to twitch. The glass wall dropped over his gaze again. Perhaps nothing had changed at all. Yet when she thought of his charitable acts in town, a spark of hope ignited. "There is good within you, Captain Dubois, I know it." Grace smiled and took another step toward him. "Your father is a Christian man. If you but follow

God as he does, you can have joy and peace in your life again."

Rafe narrowed his eyes and turned away. "You do not know what you are saying."

"I know he is kind and lives an honest, respectable life, and has the blessings of God that come with it."

The captain snapped stormy eyes her way. "How do you know that? When you have just met him?"

"I am a good discerner of people." Grace raised her chin.

Rafe snorted. "Do you know what I think, mademoiselle? I think you know nothing of people, except for the religious imposters who, in the name of God, flap their tongues in judgment on everyone around them, but cannot see the darkness of their own souls."

Grace's cheeks flamed. "I know that you are a French rogue."

"And you are a *prude pieuse*," he spat.

"What did you call me?"

"It means pious prude."

"I know what it means." Grace's eyes burned, and she hated herself for it.

The captain released a sigh. "You will come with me now." He closed the distance between them and grabbed her arm. Pain burned across her shoulder.

She whimpered. His face softened.

"Please, mademoiselle." He loosened his grip. "I do not wish to hurt you."

A knock on the door startled Grace. "Mademoiselle, *le dîner est prêt*."

"I must go." Grace tugged on her arm, but he did not release it, nor did he release the lock his eyes had upon hers. A strand of black hair grazed over his stiff, stubbled jaw. His dark eyes perused her face, drifting over her cheeks, lingering at her mouth, then meeting her gaze with such intensity it stunned her. Lowering her lashes, Grace watched the rise and fall of his chest beneath his coat and felt his hot breath on her skin even as her own breath took on a rapid pace. The scent of tobacco and leather swirled around her. Blood rushed to her head.

Tap tap tap. "Mademoiselle?"

Grace shook her head, trying to break free from the spell he had cast upon her. She jerked from his grasp. Throwing a hand to her chest, she looked away, her cheeks flaming. Had he noticed her reaction to him? *Oh Lord, forgive me. I do not know what is wrong with me.*

"*Une minute*, s'il vous plaît." Her voice emerged breathless.

He leaned toward her ear. "Your French improves, mademoiselle." He gave her a grin of defeat before retreating into the darkness behind the door.

A cold breeze swept over Grace as the shadows took him from her view.

"Mademoiselle?" The maid's voice rose in concern.

"Oui." Grace grabbed the door latch and turned to peer into the gloom behind the door, but she no longer saw his dark shape. He had left.

Thunder roared outside her window, echoing the silent roar inside her heart at the thought she might never see him again.

CHAPTER 16

Grace entered the dining hall, her shoes clicking on the Spanish tile. Oil paintings of ships at sea and the French countryside, along with wood-framed, hand-beveled mirrors, decorated the walls. A white marble fireplace spanned the wall to her right. The heat emanating from its smoldering red embers swirled around Grace even from across the room. Two candlelit chandeliers hung from the high ceiling, setting the long dining table aglitter in silver and gold. Swirls of steam rose from platters, spreading their aromas throughout the room. Grace's stomach leapt at the savory scents of cheese, fish, coriander, and cayenne.

In the center of the room Monsieur Dubois and a lady in a blue camlet gown conversed with none other than Mr. Thorn.

"Ah, Mademoiselle Grace." Monsieur Dubois broke away from the first mate and approached Grace, leading the lady on his arm. "May I introduce you to my wife, Madame Claire Dubois." Not much older than Grace, the petite woman with hair the color of candlelight and stark blue eyes dipped her head then rose to display a smile on her lips so tight, Grace feared it might crack her porcelain skin.

"A pleasure, mademoiselle." Her voice sang like the soft music of a harp.

"Thank you for having me in your home, Madame Dubois," Grace said. "Your husband has been most generous."

"That is Henri's way." Insincerity rang in her laughter, but Monsieur Dubois seemed to take no note of it. Behind them, Mr. Thorn nodded a greeting in Grace's direction.

"And you know Monsieur Thorn, I believe." Monsieur Dubois gestured toward the first mate, who looked quite dapper in his damask waistcoat.

"Yes." Relief swept over Grace at the sight of a friend. After her unsettling encounter with the captain in her chamber, coupled with her own forebodings of her future course, her nerves had snarled into tight knots. But surely, the presence of an honorable man such as Mr. Thorn spoke of Monsieur Dubois's sincerity to help her. Though she longed to cross the room and relay to the first mate all the escapades of the past five days and to thank him again for risking the captain's wrath to help her, propriety demanded she merely smile instead.

Madame Dubois stiffened, and Grace heard boots thumping on the floor behind her. She recognized the reaction in the lady, and knew Captain Dubois had entered the room.

"*Bonsoir.*" His voice, heavy with confidence, eased over Grace. "Père." A pause and then "Claire" spewed from his lips like venom.

Grace flinched at the curt tone he took with his stepmother, but the woman made no reply. Rafe slipped beside Grace and gave her a coy look as if they shared a secret. Her heart skipped a beat, and she clenched her fists, wondering why she felt relieved that he had not returned to his ship. *Why am I reacting like a common hussy, Lord? Please forgive me.*

Madame Dubois raised her thick lashes and gazed up at the captain as if he were a priceless statue. "Rafe." His Christian name floated from her pink lips, but the captain offered only a curt nod. He turned to acknowledge Mr. Thorn instead. Madame Dubois lowered her chin, and Grace thought she saw her shoulders quiver.

The hair on Grace's arms bristled at the odd relationship between stepmother and son as the tension stretched like a taut line between them.

"What happened to your face?" Monsieur Dubois pointed toward the purple, puffy skin circling the captain's right eye.

"It had an encounter with a man's fist, if you must know."

Monsieur Dubois snorted. "Brawling amongst the ignorant rabble again, Rafe? I thought you would have outgrown such childish behavior by now."

"What do you have to drink, Père?" Captain Dubois headed toward a teakwood *vaisselier* laden with bottles of all sizes and shapes.

"Same old Rafe, I see," his father mumbled.

"And you expected me to change?" The captain snorted and halted before the vaisselier. "Have *you* changed, Père?" His sarcastic tone lit the air like a fuse between them.

Monsieur Dubois frowned. "Your brandy is in its usual spot. But let us put aside our differences for one night, shall we? We have guests."

The captain smirked and poured himself a drink, and Grace felt like scolding him for being so flippant to his father when the man made every attempt to be kind.

"Shall we sit?" Monsieur Dubois led his wife to her place beside his at the head of the table.

The captain returned, a glass of brandy in his hand, and sank into a chair across from Grace but deliberately leaving an empty chair between himself and his stepmother. Madame Dubois frowned.

After they were all seated, and much to Grace's pleasant surprise, Monsieur Dubois inclined his head and led them in a prayer to bless the food. When Grace opened her eyes it was to the captain staring at her, drink already raised to his lips.

Averting her gaze, she stiffened her resolve to not allow his intimidating glances to ruin a much-needed meal or the generosity of his father.

Platters were passed and food dispensed in a much more orderly manner than on board Captain Dubois's brig. Blocks of cheddar cheese, sweet rolls, pea soup, red beans and rice, and some kind of fried shellfish passed beneath Grace's nose. She spooned a portion of each onto her plate.

"Mr. Thorn, how long have you served on my son's ship?" Monsieur Dubois asked.

"One year, monsieur."

"You are British, are you not?" Monsieur Dubois cocked his head, then at Mr. Thorn's hesitancy he added, "Ah, do not worry on my behalf. Madame Dubois has British blood in her. That is why Rafe and I are so proficient in your language."

Mr. Thorn nodded and tossed a bite of fish into his mouth, avoiding the older man's gaze. "Aye, sir. I am."

"And do you agree with my son's chosen profession?" The elder Dubois lifted a spoon of soup to his lips, which rose in a superior grin before he slurped the broth.

Mr. Thorn glanced at the captain, then back at Monsieur Dubois. "I need the work, monsieur, and your son is a good captain. I don't give much thought to how we acquire our profit."

"Profit, ha! A man can only claim a profit from honest, hard work." Monsieur Dubois tugged upon the foam of Mechlin around his neck. "And your lack of conscience in the matter only proves you have spent far too much time in the company of my son."

"As I have spent in yours, Père." The captain sipped his brandy through clenched teeth.

She gazed between father and son, expecting a fight to break out at any moment. A chunk of cheese lodged in Grace's throat before dropping into her stomach like a rock. Madame Dubois's eyes grew wide and her face paled. Setting down her spoon, she retrieved her crystal glass and took a large gulp of burgundy wine.

"And yet"—Monsieur Dubois pointed his spoon at his son—"when I brought you and your mother here from France, I had barely two livres in my pocket. Now I own one of the grandest sugar plantations on Saint Dominique as well as two merchant ships. All acquired by honesty and the sweat of my brow. Not thievery and murder." His blue eyes turned cold.

Captain Dubois's lips slanted. "Greed and malice hidden behind your so-called respectable business is still greed and malice, mon Père. Just like wickedness cloaked beneath a shroud of piety is still wickedness. What did your Jesus call your type, 'whited sepulchres'?"

Monsieur Dubois coughed, nearly choking on his food. "You go too far, Rafe." His voice rasped even as his face turned a bright shade of red.

Grace flinched and longed to kick the captain beneath the table the way she used to do with her sisters when they misbehaved. Instead, she gathered her wits and spoke in a calm voice. "He addressed the Pharisees as such, to be sure, Captain. But to call someone else that name is to say his faith is in vain, and certainly that is not the case with your father. Besides, he is not a religious leader."

The captain chuckled and raised a brow. "I believe he would question your assessment, mademoiselle."

"I try to be an example among the community." Monsieur Dubois, having regained his breath, toyed with the fish upon his plate.

"These beans and rice are delicious." Mr. Thorn made an obvious attempt to ease the rising hostility. "My compliments to the chef."

"The Africans introduced the dish, monsieur." Madame Dubois spoke her first words since they had sat down, and Grace hoped her soothing tone would cool the men's humors. But she ceased the explanation and instead poured herself more wine as her eyes gravitated to the captain like flowers toward the sun.

But Captain Dubois kept his gaze on the brandy swirling in his glass.

Monsieur Dubois stroked his beard. "It is my duty as a *grand blanc* and a Huguenot to ensure the truth of our Lord is held in high esteem in these savage lands."

Grace faced the elder Dubois and smiled, happy to hear his priorities were in line with scripture. "I agree, monsieur. It is important to use your position to glorify God. 'Tis what I have been attempting to do in Charles Towne."

"Before my rogue son tore you from your home." Monsieur Dubois snorted and plucked a sweet roll from the tray. And for a second, Grace thought he intended to toss it at the captain.

"What is a grand blanc?" Grace asked, hoping to allay that action.

"It means *big white* or *powerful white*," the captain's voice pitched in disdain, his jaw so stiff, Grace thought it would explode. "As opposed to *petits blancs*, the merchants and tradesmen, and then the *gens de couleur*, mulattos and freed slaves, and of course, the African slaves at the bottom. You know how the civilized have need to group people according to wealth and position in order to feed their pride." His dark eyes flashed toward the elder Dubois. "And my father finds himself on top, as usual." The captain took a swig of his brandy.

Grace shook her head at him, hoping he'd see her admonition at his overindulgence in drink.

But he took no notice of her warning. "How is business, mon Père?"

"Très bien. Très bien. I've expanded the plantation lands, acquired another twenty Africans, and should produce the largest sugar crop in Port-de-Paix this year." His face grew troubled. "The only problem I have is with the maroons."

"Maroons?" Grace took a bite of the rice and beans, savoring the unusual spicy, sharp flavors.

Mr. Thorn leaned toward her. "Runaway slaves, miss. Troublemakers and rebels."

"Oui," Monsieur Dubois added. "They raid my barns and steal my livestock and crops."

"No doubt they are hungry," the captain offered with a sneer.

"Then they shouldn't have left their masters," the elder Dubois retorted.

The captain's sharp eyes swerved to his father. "No man should have a master."

Grace gave the captain a venomous look, incredulous at his statement. "And yet you intended to enslave me."

Monsieur Dubois lifted his glass, a triumphant grin on his lips. "Touché, my dear, touché."

But Rafe ignored him and kept his gaze upon Grace.

"That was different." He scowled.

"I do not see how," she retorted, returning his stare with equal intensity.

A shadow of remorse passed over his gaze as seconds of tension ticked between them. All eyes shot to the captain, awaiting his response, but it was Mr. Thorn who broke the silence.

"If they were unhappy as slaves, I do not fault them for leaving." He sipped his wine and rubbed the scar on his neck. "We must do what we can in this world to provide our own justice."

"There are some ordained by God to rule, and some meant to be slaves." Monsieur Dubois wiped the crumbs from his cultured beard. "You both would understand that if you read your Bible."

"If it says that, I want no part of this God of yours," Captain Dubois shot back.

Grace's heart shriveled, both at the misunderstanding of God's Word and the captain's declaration. "I beg your pardon, Monsieur Dubois, but the Bible does not condone slavery. It merely mentions it as part of the culture at the time and suggests to those caught in its trap to rejoice that they are free in Christ."

"*Exactement.* These rebellious slaves should have rejoiced in their state and not abandoned it." The elder Dubois said this with such finality as to close the argument, and then offered Grace a spurious smile.

She took a bite of fish, deciding not to press the point, and noticing no one else enjoyed the food besides her and Mr. Thorn.

Madame Dubois passed the captain a platter of fried seafood. "Please eat, Rafe."

He pushed her hand away and held up his glass. "I am eating."

She cleared her throat and seemed to be having trouble speaking then laid a hand on his arm. "You look well. How are you faring in your life upon the sea?"

The captain stiffened. He moved his arm away and stared at his plate of uneaten food but offered her no reply.

"You are no better than a pirate, a brigand," his father muttered peevishly under his breath. "Just like that scoundrel, Jean du Casse."

The captain grimaced and leaned forward on the table. "Jean Baptiste du Casse was a hero. Governor of our island and an admiral in the French navy. If you compare me to him, I accept the compliment." He raised his glass.

Monsieur Dubois scowled. His brow grew dark. "He pillaged and plundered like any pirate, without a care for which nation he served." He snapped his drink to the back of his mouth then slammed the glass on the table. "Regardless, I do not approve of your life, boy, nor your part in it, Monsieur Thorn."

On that point, Grace found herself in agreement, yet she cringed at the harsh tone in the man's reprimand. Had she sounded equally as unforgiving when she chastised her sisters' sinful behavior? No wonder they paid her no mind.

As Mr. Thorn was doing now. With a shrug, he continued eating, obviously willing to endure insults in order to fill his belly.

The captain huffed out a sigh of impatience. "And I do not approve of your life, Père. So here we are."

"Ha! How can I expect you to approve of the honorable life I lead?" Monsieur Dubois plucked a silk handkerchief from his pocket and dabbed at the sweat on his brow. "Why is it so hot in here? Monsieur Ballin!" he barked at the servant standing at the door. "Douse those coals immediately." The man scurried to do his master's bidding while Monsieur Dubois turned steely eyes upon his son. "You were always rebellious. So much like *ta mère*."

Stunned by Monsieur Dubois's cruelty, Grace raised a hand to her mouth to stifle a gasp and then shifted her gaze to the captain, her heart aching for the pain he must feel.

But, instead of sorrow, his face reddened in anger. He slowly rose to his feet. "You may call me what you will, but you will not malign my mother's good name."

His father stood, his chair scraping over the tiles behind him. "Do you dare challenge me in my own home, boy? I should have silenced your impudence the last time we dueled."

"I was but sixteen, Père." That slow grin that so often graced the captain's lips now rose again. "I have learned much since then. And as I recall, it was I who would have bested you, if not for ma mère's intervention."

The food in Grace's stomach soured. She'd never witnessed such hatred in a family. A father and son dueling? Unheard of. She glanced at Madame Dubois, hoping to find a voice of reason, someone to step between these two, but the woman stared numbly down at her lap.

Mr. Thorn grabbed his glass and leaned back in his chair as if ready for the night's entertainment.

Gathering her courage, Grace stood. "Gentlemen, please."

Finally, Madame Dubois struggled to her feet as if weak from some disease and shifted pleading eyes to her husband. "Henri, s'il vous plaît. Do not."

He waved at her as if dismissing a servant. "Sit down and have some more wine. It is what you do best."

The food in Grace's stomach soured at the man's treatment of his wife.

Madame Dubois's shoulders slumped, and she collapsed into her chair in a shroud of despair.

Grace gripped the chain around her neck and said a silent prayer, shifting her gaze between the two men. Monsieur Dubois, her would-be rescuer—the man who only moments ago had proclaimed a devotion to spread the love of God—glared at his son, while the captain's dark eyes brewed with more anger and hatred than Grace had ever seen from a son toward his father.

Mr. Thorn finally spoke. "If I may, Monsieur Dubois, might we put the hostilities aside? Your son and I shall be gone soon enough."

"Back to the trade, eh?" Monsieur Dubois sneered, grabbed his glass, and took a swig.

The captain narrowed his eyes. "I have reasons for what I do. What are yours?"

"Ah, oui. The great Rafe Dubois, champion of those in need. I've heard enough of your praises throughout the city." Monsieur Dubois sank to his chair.

"Perhaps you should heed them and garner some praises of your own. There are many who would benefit from the riches you lavish upon yourself." The captain gestured toward their luxurious surroundings, and Grace heard naught but sincerity in his tone, and perhaps a speck of pleading, ever so slight, as if he truly cared for the poor and wished his father would do likewise.

His father guffawed. "I have no need of the praises of commoners. Besides, it is foolish to help people who by misfortune of birth, circumstance, and a propensity to slothfulness will not fend for themselves. It is the way of the world."

Madame Dubois groaned and took another drink.

Grace eyed the haughty disregard marring Monsieur Dubois's expression and could keep her tongue no longer. "But surely you understand that is not the way of God."

He gave her a cursory glance. "There is much about laziness and hard work in the Bible, mademoiselle."

"There is also much said about caring for those in need."

Monsieur Dubois's face soured, but he made no reply.

Grace could not comprehend how a man who professed faith in Jesus could be so callous. Her glance met Captain Dubois's, and he smiled at her. The smile of a friend.

She lowered her gaze, disturbed by the turn of events that had placed her on the same side as this villain.

"You will never reach my father's heart with your platitudes, mademoiselle." Captain Dubois sighed. "The man possesses no heart."

"Spoken by a man who, no doubt, has a heart." Grace said, hearing the sarcastic bite in her voice. "A heart that thinks nothing of kidnapping innocent women? Is that the type of heart my platitudes would reach, Captain?"

Without looking at her, the captain downed his brandy, rose, and headed for the vaisselier.

Monsieur Dubois grimaced and set down his fork with a clank, All emotion drained from his face as if a curtain had fallen upon it. "Mademoiselle Grace," he began in a tone of formality. "Forgive us for exposing our family contentions in front of you and Monsieur Thorn. I love my son, but as you can see, we do not agree on many things."

Madame Dubois leaned an elbow on the table. "Henri, I am not feeling very well."

The elder Dubois cast his wife a look of scorn and stood. "Pardon me, but my wife seems to have had too much to drink—yet again." He bowed to his guests then glanced at his son as Rafe returned to his seat with more brandy. "You and Monsieur Thorn may stay the night if you wish, but I want you both gone in the morning. Grielle!" He snapped his fingers, and a tall, dark man entered the room. "Escort the mademoiselle to her chamber." He inclined his head toward Grace. "For your own protection, mademoiselle. There are villains afoot." He swept a narrowed gaze over the captain and Mr. Thorn.

Then he assisted Madame Dubois from her chair and led her from the room. After their departure, a shadow fled from Captain Dubois's features. He sipped his brandy and eyed Grace as Grielle came and stood by her side.

She rose. "If I do not see you again, Captain, please know I shall be praying for you." She faced Mr. Thorn. "And you as well."

Mr. Thorn nodded. The captain stood but made no comment. Yet as Grace left the room, she felt his gaze searing her back. Resisting the urge to glance at him, she continued down the hall. She should be happy to be free of Captain Dubois, free from his plans to sell her as a slave, free to return home to Charles Towne. Then why, with each step away from him, did she feel as though she walked out of a prison only to step into a fiery furnace?

CHAPTER 17

Bong. Bong. The clock's chimes echoed through the dark halls of the Dubois home. Two in the morning. Rafe ran a hand over the back of his neck and took up his pace again over the silk-embroidered rug centering the library. Unable to sleep, he'd gone to the only room in the mansion that held more good memories than bad. A place where he and his mother had spent hours reading and playing her favorite game of *vingt-et-un*. His father detested this room. Said the flowery patterns on the chairs and walls made him squirm and softened his manliness. So it had become a ladies' parlor as well as the library, and as Rafe glanced over it now, even in the shadows, he could tell little had changed.

He ground his fists together, thinking that Claire must be using the room now for the same purpose his mother had. But he preferred to dwell on only the pleasant memories invading his mind. Breathing deeply, he could almost smell the *rose de mai* of his mother's *parfum*, which she imported from Grasse each year. Though he knew that would be impossible. She'd been dead these six years. But the pain was all too fresh.

He patted his coat pocket for a cheroot, took one out, and lit it from the embers in the fire then stood and took a puff. He glanced above the mantel where the massive emblem of the Dubois crest hung—two black lions battling against the backdrop of a red coat of arms. Rafe should have felt pride at the family insignia, yet only shame assaulted him.

His thoughts drifted to Mademoiselle Grace. When he had first seen her in his father's foyer, her raven hair wound in her usual tight bun, adorned in that satin gown that gave her an air to match her name, an unexpected thrill had sped through him. At that moment, he had been glad he had broken his vow never to return to this horrid place.

Then the meeting in her chamber. He grinned as he remembered the flush creeping up her face at his close perusal, and the petulant lift of her nose as she stood her ground against him. It had taken every ounce of his strength not to take her in his arms. He was, after all, alone with her in her chamber. But for once in Rafe's life, he cared more about not frightening a lady than he did for his own pleasure—an odd sensation that settled on him like an ill-fitting garment.

And he wasn't sure he liked it one bit.

Then after he'd restrained himself on her behalf, she had refused to listen to him; sacre mer, femme exaspérante! Rafe took another puff of his cheroot and tucked a lock of his hair behind his ear. He had given her another chance at dinner. A chance to see the true caractère of his father. And the man had not disappointed Rafe in his performance. Rafe shook his head. Where most women would have cowered before his father's commanding opinions, Mademoiselle Grace had expressed her own with polite bravado. The sanctimonious woman was no weakling. Yet despite the disgust Rafe had seen on her face at his father's boorish behavior, she still intended to accept his offer to return her home.

Rafe must convince her otherwise. She had no idea the danger she was in. Oui, his father may return her to Charles Towne, but it was in what condition that worried Rafe. For his father never met a person or object that he did not try to either possess or destroy.

"Rafe." His Christian name spoken in a desperate female tone swerved him about. Claire stood in the doorway in a white nightdress, her golden hair spiraling around her like a fallen halo. She floated toward him, a haunting apparition from his past.

He took a puff of his cheroot and looked away. "What do you want?"

"So sévère, so unfeeling. After all this time." Her voice was both melodious and melancholy like a sorrowful ballad. She halted beside him. Moonlight floating in from the tall French windows accentuated the sorrow etched upon her face.

Rafe let out a sarcastic chuckle. "Moi, sévère?" Drawing another puff, he slowly exhaled the pungent smoke, making no attempt to avoid her with the fumes.

She coughed and batted it away. "Since when do you smoke?"

"Many things have changed." He placed his boot on the fireplace.

"All things?" She stepped toward him.

Her scent of lavender swirled around him like an intoxicating elixir. "Oui." He pushed from the mantel and walked toward the window, his boots thumping his annoyance over the floor.

"I see you have recovered from your wine," he snorted.

"And you, your brandy." She paused. "It is difficult seeing you again,

Rafe. Having you so close. I thought perhaps it was difficult for you, also."

Her words knifed toward Rafe, trying to slice through his heart, but he threw up his shield—the hard crust he had built bit by bit over the past five years. He turned to face her. "Je suis désolé for causing you distress, madame, but you are mistaken. You made your choice."

She approached him, her blue eyes brimming with hopeful tears. "A decision I have regretted." The moonlight shimmered over her creamy skin. She eased beside him in that alluring, feminine way, like a cat snuggling up to its owner, trusting, begging to be coddled and loved.

Rafe swallowed, his body reacting to her closeness. He had missed her. He could not deny it. "We all live with regrets."

She laid a hand on his arm, and a spark shot through Rafe. "But must we live with this one?" Then planting a kiss on her finger, she dabbed it on his bruised eye.

Her touch, her scent, the sweet sound of her voice combined in a swirling pool of memories that played havoc with his senses. For a moment, he felt like a young man again, newly in love with the most beautiful woman in the world. Mais non. Too much had happened since that mystical time. He grabbed her hand and jerked it from him. "Sacre mer. You are my father's wife."

She lowered her gaze. "If that is what you call me."

"Oui, that is what I call you, madame. It is a truth that has invaded my worst nightmares these long years."

"Then you *do* still care?" Her voice cracked as she raised her chin.

Rafe clenched his jaw and averted his gaze from her pleading eyes. A battle brewed within him—a battle filled with desire, love, betrayal, and hatred, each emotion struggling for dominance.

"He is cruel to me, Rafe."

"You knew what he was like."

Rafe took a final puff of his cheroot, walked to the fireplace, and flicked it into the coals. He must leave before he gave in to every base impulse within him. "I suggest you return to your bed before my father wakes and finds you missing." He turned and stomped out.

⁓

Grace rose from the dining table and pushed back her chair. "Merci." She nodded her thanks to the servant manning the buffet laden with croissants, orange marmalade, and coffee. More exhausted than she realized, she had overslept and missed breaking her fast with Monsieur Dubois and his wife. An event she was not at all unhappy to have escaped.

She'd learned from the butler that Monsieur Dubois had business to attend to and Madame Dubois had taken to her chamber with a headache. Passing through the dining room out into the hallway, Grace couldn't shake the overwhelming cloud of despair that permeated the walls of the Dubois home. Rather than succumb to the weighty oppression, she headed out the front door for some fresh air. Making her way down the stairs, she squinted against the sun hovering above the eastern hills, not yet high enough to inflict its searing rays upon the inhabitants of the island.

Movement caught her eye, and she glanced to her right where Monsieur Dubois stood with his back to her, speaking with another man beneath a ficus tree. They huddled together as if exchanging a grand secret, only whispers of which drifted past her ears. She started off in the other direction, not wanting to intrude, when Monsieur Dubois chuckled. It was a maniacal chuckle that sent a shudder through her and drew her gaze back to the men. Monsieur Dubois slapped the other man on the back and stepped aside, giving Grace a view of his identity.

It was Mr. Thorn.

Slipping behind a hedgerow, she inched her way closer to the men.

"So everything is in order, then?" Monsieur Dubois said.

"Yes, I will meet you as planned."

The sound of hands slapping against each other filled the air. "Finally I will put Rafe in his place." Monsieur Dubois chuckled.

"And I will have my revenge," Thorn growled. "But what of Miss Grace?"

"What of her?" Monsieur Dubois's voice held a nonchalant lilt.

Grace couldn't help the gasp that escaped her lips. The men grew silent, and she could see through the leaves of the bush that their gazes had shot in her direction. Covering her mouth, she inched her way along the hedgerow away from them. Boot steps thudded toward her. In a frenzy, she plucked her handkerchief from the sleeve of her gown and tossed it to the ground just as Mr. Thorn and Monsieur Dubois cornered the bush.

Mr. Thorn's frown darkened. "What on earth are you doing, Miss Grace?" He studied her face, no doubt searching for evidence that she had heard their conversation.

"Mr. Thorn. Monsieur Dubois." Grace forced a smile to her lips and then lowered her gaze. "Oh, there it is." Bending down, she picked up her handkerchief. "This silly thing blew away from me in the breeze and I was just retrieving it."

Monsieur Dubois narrowed his eyes upon her. "I was on my way into town to arrange your passage back home, mademoiselle, when I ran into Monsieur Thorn. He has some amusing stories of his time in the British navy."

"No doubt he does." Grace smiled again. "Though I daresay I wasn't close enough to hear them." With her statement, both men's shoulders seemed to lower in relief. "I cannot thank you enough for procuring me a ship home, Monsieur," she added.

"My pleasure, mademoiselle." Monsieur Dubois nodded.

"Good day to you both." Grace excused herself and started on her way.

"Good day, mademoiselle."

It wasn't until she turned down a narrow pathway that Grace realized her heart was in her throat. What plans had the men been discussing? From the sounds of it, they were up to no good. Stuffing the handkerchief back into her sleeve, she hugged herself as a chill struck her. Her name had been mentioned and then batted away as if she were of no consequence. Did Monsieur Dubois still intend to escort her home?

Weaving around the corner of the house, Grace drew in a deep breath of air laden with moist earth, tropical flowers, a hint of the sea, and the sharp scent of sugar cane. She halted for a moment and watched as a group of slender white birds with long tail feathers and black markings on their heads flitted from tree to tree above her, their joyful warble helping to ease her tension. Perhaps she was making too much of a conversation she had heard only parts of. Careful to avoid the puddles formed from last night's storm, she silently gave thanks to God for bringing her to safety and for being faithful when her own faith had waned. She thought of Monsieur and Madame Dubois and sent up a petition for them as well, for it was obvious they were unhappy together. "They need You, Lord. They need Your forgiveness and love."

To her left, a vine of red and pink flowers spread over the side of the house as if trying to mask the misery within. How could she help this family? Monsieur Dubois had voiced his intent to serve God, although Grace had seen little to validate that claim. Perhaps all the man required was a bit of guidance on the scriptures, and in particular instruction on how to love his wife as the Bible commanded. Grace could certainly provide that.

Continuing on her way, she clutched her skirts to avoid another puddle and gazed out into the distant fields where the dark shapes of slaves tending the sugar cane bowed and rose in the rising sun. The crack of a whip sliced the air. She shuddered. She'd seen mistreated slaves back in Charles Towne, but the sight never failed to send a ripple of revulsion through her.

A path appeared through a patch of pine trees and Grace followed it, unable to shake the sorrow that had attached itself to her that morning before she'd even arisen from her bed. She was going home tomorrow. She should be happy. And though she tried to focus on her good fortune, her traitorous thoughts kept drifting to Captain Dubois. He had no doubt left the plantation at dawn and was at present preparing *Le Champion* to set sail.

She had been delivered!

But knowing she would never see the captain again left a gnawing ache in her soul. She didn't know why. *Please, forgive me Lord. Why am I obsessed with this miscreant who would no doubt sell his own sister for a profit?* Several minutes passed as shame hung heavy on her shoulders, weighing them down as she made her way along the muddy path.

And then she saw him.

The object of her thoughts, standing in an opening up ahead—a small graveyard—his cocked hat in hand, head bowed over a gravestone.

Her heart leapt, and she halted, wanting to call out to him. But not wishing to intrude, she turned to leave.

"Mademoiselle." That deep voice sounded through the clearing, easing over her like warm silk, turning her around.

"Forgive me, Captain. I did not know you were here."

"Of course not. How could you?" He attempted a smile.

She inched toward him, noting the moist sheen covering his dark eyes. "I thought you would be gone by now." He had replaced his gentlemanly attire with his buccaneer garb once again: purple and gold sash girding his waist, rapier hung at his hip, and his baldric strapped across his white shirt.

He dropped his gaze to the grave, and Grace read the markings on the stone:

MADAME ROCHELLE DUBOIS
NÉE LE CINQUIÈME OCTOBRE EN L'AN DE GRÂCE MILLE SIX CENT
SOIXANTE-TREIZE
QUITTÉE LE MONDE LE SEIZIÈME MAI EN L'AN DE GRÂCE MILLE SEPT
CENT DOUZE

"Your mother." She raised a hand to her throat. "Forgive me. I should leave."

He reached out and touched her arm. "Stay, s'il vous plaît." He glanced down again. "I have not visited her since they laid her in the ground."

"You haven't been home in six years?"

"Five, but the year after her death, I could not bring myself to see her—not like this." He shifted his stance and stomped his boot atop a rock as if trying to crush it. "She was a good woman. Kind, generous, a lady of great honor."

A sudden breeze blew in from the cane fields, stirring a pile of leaves beside the grave into a frenzy and loosening a coil of hair from Grace's bun. She hugged herself, unsure how to respond to this side of the captain that seemed so vulnerable, so troubled—a side that touched her heart in a way she had never thought possible. A villain, a thief, yet giving his wealth to the poor. Rebellious, disrespectful to his father, yet possessing such honor and love for his mother. His grief reopened an old wound in Grace's heart at the loss of her own mother some seven years ago.

"She was murdered," Rafe said, answering the question burning in Grace's mind.

"Mercy me." She clasped her chain, tears bidding entrance into her eyes.

"In a British raid."

Grace felt as if she'd swallowed a stone that now sank to the bottom of her stomach.

The captain gripped the pommel of his rapier. "In retaliation for Jean du Casse's raid upon Cartagena in ninety-seven, the British and Spanish raided Cap-Francais and Port-de-Paix, burning our homes, stealing our produce, slaves, and women. My father was away and I was"—he grimaced—"occupied in town. By the time I arrived home, she was dead."

"You found her?"

"Oui." His lips tightened. "She suffered greatly before she died."

The agony he'd endured made Grace long to reach out to him. But then something cold gripped her heart. "What year was it?"

"1712."

Tears blurred Grace's vision. Her father had been in command of a fleet in the Caribbean at that time. She remembered it clearly because her mother had been dead less than a year and she had been angry at her father for leaving her and her sisters alone so soon. Her head began to spin. Dare she ask? Did she want to know? She threw a hand to her throat to ease the fear and agony burning within it. "Was my father involved?" Agony garbled her voice.

The captain drew in a ragged breath, but he did not look at her.

"Tell me it isn't true?" Grace laid a hand on his arm, drawing his tortured gaze to hers.

"He was in command of the fleet." Rafe's brow darkened. "The captain who attacked Port-de-Paix reported to your father, but I do not know whether he followed your father's orders or not."

All the air escaped from Grace's lungs and she hung her head. Now she understood why Captain Dubois had no qualms about kidnapping her. She was the daughter of Admiral Henry Westcott. The blood of his worst enemies, the people who ravished and murdered his mother, flowed in Grace's veins. She longed to apologize but knew the words would fall meaningless into the mud at her feet.

"So that is why, then," she said as more of a statement than a question.

He shook his head and his shoulders sank. "It was the encouragement I needed to perform a task I normally would not have undertaken."

Her heart jumped. "So you don't normally kidnap innocent women?" She attempted a weak smile and was rewarded with the slight lift of his lips in return.

"The money would have provided a hospital for the poor." He shrugged, then his eyes grew serious. "There are many sick on this island. Many die each day." He swept his pained gaze toward the sugar fields. "I made a promise to a good man."

Grace's mind swirled in confusion. "One good deed is not enough to negate a wicked act."

"Perhaps." He gripped the pommel of his rapier. "But at the time I did not consider selling you to the don to be wicked, only recompense for the actions of your father."

"And now?" Grace's breath quickened.

He looked at her. "As I have said. Things have changed. You are not what I expected."

His words sang sweetly in her ears. She had misjudged him. He was not the rogue he often pretended to be.

Bending over, the captain plucked a small purple flower from a bush and laid it gently on his mother's grave. "*Reposez-vous en paix,* Maman."

A tear slid down Grace's cheek. Captain Dubois faced her, his stormy gaze filled with pain, not the anger she expected. His brow wrinkled, and he raised a hand to wipe her tear away then allowed his thumb to caress her cheek. "Do not cry for me."

Grace closed her eyes beneath his touch. Her breath lodged in her throat. She heard him move closer, and she stepped back.

He dropped his hand, the features of his face hardening. "You must come to the brig with me."

Only then did Grace realize her precarious position. With no servants around and Monsieur Dubois away from the house, the captain could easily capture her again.

"Your father has promised to deliver me to Charles Towne," she muttered a bit too fast.

"The price will be too high."

"He charges me nothing, Captain."

He huffed and ran a hand through his hair. "Not yet." He rubbed the purple and black bruise around his eye, and a strange desire overcame her to plant a tender kiss upon it. Pushing the thought away, she turned aside.

"I can see that there is bad blood between you. It saddens me to see a father and son fight so viciously." The shrill voice of a taskmaster and the snap of a whip in the distance only accentuated her statement. "Regardless of what your father has done to you, Captain, you have a Father in heaven. He is the Father of all—especially those whose earthly fathers have disappointed them." But the scowl on his face told Grace that her words bounced off his hard heart and disappeared into the air. "Perhaps I can help you reconcile your differences."

Captain Dubois gazed over the cane fields. "There is no reconciliation, mademoiselle, with or without God's love."

Grace swallowed at the finality of his tone. Yet by his father's words and actions the night before, she believed the elder Dubois suffered from the same hopelessness. "I must admit I feel a sense of unease in your father's presence." Truth be told, Monsieur Dubois's behavior toward his wife, his son, and his general attitudes about position and wealth did not indicate a changed heart within. "And I did not care for his behavior last night."

"Then come back to *Le Champion* with me."

His urgent tone startled Grace. She wanted to believe him—to believe he wasn't a villain, a scoundrel. But perhaps he was only toying with her.

He grabbed her arm. "If you come with me now, I promise to take you home."

Grace searched his dark eyes for some shred of truth. He had kidnapped her, insulted her, held her captive, and intended to sell her as a slave, yet naught but sincerity burned in his gaze now. "What is the promise of a rogue worth?"

"At the moment?" He raised a brow and grinned. "Everything."

"What of your hospital?"

He shrugged. "I will find another way."

Grace studied him. The wind whipped a strand of his dark hair across his jaw, yet the firm press of his fingers on her arm offered her more comfort than threat. *Lord, what do I do?*

He reached up and fingered the curl that had loosened from her bun. "Why do you hide this *beaux cheveux* in such a tight knot?"

Grace's breath escaped her. "To keep myself from vanity," she managed to mutter.

He leaned and whispered in her ear, "I doubt you could ever be vain, mademoiselle." His warm breath sent a shiver down her back. "But why deprive others of your beauty?"

Tugging from his grip, Grace threw a hand to her throat and stepped back. Her thoughts and emotions spun in a whirlpool of confusion that left her numb.

The captain gripped his baldric. "I know you have no reason to trust me. But I am begging you to believe what I say."

Gathering her wits, Grace snapped her eyes to his. "What concern is it of yours what your father does with me?"

"Because you have fallen into his hands on my account."

Grace frowned. Was Monsieur Dubois truly that dangerous? Or was the captain only playing a game? She gazed at him, enjoying the way the soft lines of concern had replaced the hard arrogance on his face. If he was lying to her, he was a master at deception, for Grace had always been good at discerning the intentions of others. Rafe made no pretensions about his lifestyle and seemed to exhibit shame at his mistakes. But Monsieur Dubois's actions defied his proclamation of Christian love. Not to mention the odd exchange she had heard between him and Mr. Thorn. Perhaps he did intend to do Grace harm. She closed her eyes for a second to drown out the sights around her—especially Rafe—and decide what to do. Neither man invoked her trust, but if she had to choose based on the leaning of her heart, she would choose the captain.

Perhaps it was Captain Dubois she was supposed to help after all. During their journey home, Grace would have time to recite scripture and expound to him the goodness of God. Yes, surely that was her mission. Elation surged through her at the thought of bringing this man to redemption.

"Very well. I will go with you." She gave him a weak smile as her stomach folded in on itself. Why was she putting herself back into this rogue's hands? Had she gone mad?

"I have your word, then?" He took a step toward her and looked down at her with more intensity than she had ever seen in his eyes. "Your promise. A promise that will not be broken."

"You have my word." She nodded. "I am not one to break a vow, Captain."

"Non. I would not expect so." He smiled.

"But please allow me to express my gratitude to your father and stepmother for their kindness and bid them farewell."

Disapproval shadowed his face. He scratched the stubble on his jaw. "Not a good idea."

"It is the right thing to do, Captain."

He grinned. "You realize I could kidnap you right here if I so desired."

"It has crossed my mind, Captain, and the fact that you haven't has convinced me of your sincerity."

He grunted in disappointment. "Très bien. But I will not set foot in that house again."

"I will meet you here, in this same spot, at seven tonight." A bead of perspiration slid down her back.

He cocked his head and examined her. "I will be here, mademoiselle." Then he bowed, donned his plumed hat, and strode away.

Grace's legs would not move. Her skin tingled where the captain's fingers had touched her arms. Glancing down at Madame Dubois's grave, she longed to ask the woman about her son. Could he be trusted? Should Grace go with him?

But it was too late for that. The woman was not here, and Grace had already given her word. She had willingly submitted herself back into the hands of a man who had given her no reason to trust him. Either this was truly God's will or she had gone completely mad.

CHAPTER 18

Grace swept a final gaze over her chamber and wondered why. She had no belongings to take with her, save the gown on her back. And even that didn't belong to her. Though a trifle low in the neckline, it was a far more beautiful gown than any of her own back in Charles Towne. And somehow the shimmering green satin embroidered with silver braided ribbons that laced across her ruffled bodice made her feel beautiful. Besides, she liked the way it sounded when she strolled across the room. Mercy me, what was wrong with her? She'd never cared about such fripperies before. Regardless, she'd promised to return the gown as soon as she arrived home.

If she arrived home.

Her discussion with Monsieur Dubois and his wife had gone better than expected. Though the captain's father could not understand Grace's decision to trust his son and not accept his free offer of transport to Charles Towne, he finally acquiesced to her wishes. But only after pleading with her most adamantly to change her mind.

Which she nearly had.

Especially when Monsieur Dubois kept referring to his son as a liar and a blackguard.

Yet after thanking the couple for their kindness, Grace had withdrawn to her chamber to await the appointed time she had agreed to meet the captain. Now, as the hands on the clock sitting atop the mantel inched toward seven, her heart cinched. Her stomach soured, and she found herself regretting her decision.

Lord, am I doing the right thing?

No answer came. No noise, save the swaying of the wind outside the window and soft footfalls outside her door. The oak panel creaked on its hinges, and Madame Dubois peered around the edge. Tearstains marred her pink face. "Bien, you are still here. May I speak with you a moment, Mademoiselle Grace?"

797

"Of course." Grace gestured her inside.

After slipping through the opening, Madame Dubois closed the door then leaned her ear against it as if listening to see if she had been followed.

"Whatever is the matter, Madame Dubois?" Unease rumbled over Grace's already agitated nerves.

The elegant woman lifted a finger to her lips, waited a moment, then released a deep sigh. Crossing the room, she eased onto the bed and dropped her head into her hands. Her golden curls bobbed as a sob racked through her.

Grace sat beside her, her heart breaking as it always did in light of someone else's anguish. "Is there something I can do?"

Lifting her head, Madame Dubois raised a handkerchief to her nose as tears rolled one after the other down her cheeks. "I cannot bear it another minute."

"Bear what, madame?" Grace longed to grasp her hand but didn't dare.

"My husband." She sobbed. "He is a cruel man. *Certainement,* you can see that."

Grace stiffened at the woman's confession. Did all French women speak with such alarming honesty—especially to a stranger? Yet Grace could not deny what she had witnessed. "He possesses a quick temper. I have noticed as much."

"It is far worse than that." Madame Dubois hesitated then squeezed her eyes shut against another wave of tears. "He beats me. He has many mistresses, many of whom he parades daily before my face."

The announcement struck Grace like a cold slap in the face. This man who declared that his purpose on the island was to glorify God. Could it be true? But why would Madame Dubois lie? Despite Grace's attempt to think well of her benefactor, she had witnessed his callous behavior firsthand.

"I'm so sorry, madame." Against propriety, Grace took the woman's delicate, soft hand and gave it a squeeze. Minutes passed as they sat in silence, and Grace wondered what to say to comfort the lady. "I have a sister, Charity, who married a beast of a man," she finally said. "She lives in agony every day of her life. But I cannot help her. I can only pray for her. As you must do, madame." Grace knelt before the woman and peered up into her swollen face. "Pray for God to change your husband's heart, to convict him of his sin. If he would but repent and turn back to God, his heart would change."

A look of disbelief crossed Madame Dubois's delicate features. Outrage followed it. "I have prayed, Mademoiselle Grace. For many years. And I believe God has answered by sending you to me."

"Me? What can I do but pray for you?"

"You can help me leave him." Madame Dubois leaned forward and enfolded Grace's hands with her own. "If you go to him and tell him you've changed your mind and wish to take him up on his offer, I will convince him that we should accompany you to Charles Towne."

"Accompany me?" Grace blinked. "But why would he agree?"

"He has been meaning to see to some business dealings he has in New France." Madame Dubois's blue eyes sparkled like the sea in bright sunlight. "Then when we reach Charles Towne, I will get off the ship with you."

Grace's head swam beneath the woman's suggestion—a suggestion that if Grace followed would change everything.

"I would not dare escape on my own," she continued. "For I have nowhere to go, no money. But perhaps your family could grant me lodging until I contact my mother's brother in Virginia."

The desperation flaming in Madame Dubois's eyes burned through Grace's resolve. She could not reject this poor woman's plea for help. Hadn't Grace prayed for someone to come alongside Charity should her sister ever decide to leave her husband? Someone who would help her get away to safety? How could she do any less for this pitiable lady?

But she'd given her word to Captain Dubois.

Madame Dubois awaited her answer, her eyes pooling with pleading tears that tore at Grace's heart.

"But I promised Captain Du—"

"Of what value is a promise made to a liar and a thief?" she snapped.

"A promise is a promise, madame." Grace lowered her chin, wondering at the woman's sudden disdain for her stepson when she seemed quite enamored with him last evening.

Madame Dubois patted Grace's hand as one would a little child. "Do you think he intends to honor his promise to take you to Charles Towne? Silly girl."

Grace stood. "Yes, I do." She surprised herself with the confidence of her tone.

Madame Dubois began sobbing again. "Then I am lost." She dropped her head into her hands. "Monsieur Thorn told me you were a kind woman."

"Mr. Thorn? What has he to do with this?"

"It was his idea that I come to you." She lifted her swollen, puffy face to Grace. "For both our well-beings, he said."

"But I am to meet the captain soon." Grace glanced at the clock. Ten minutes past seven. No doubt he was already waiting for her. She bit her lip. "Why do you not come with us?"

"With Rafe?" Madame Dubois's eyes widened as if Grace had asked her to jump out the window. "Even if he plans on taking you to Charles Towne, he would never allow me on his ship. He hates me."

"I doubt that, madame." Although as Grace recalled, the captain had been less than cordial to his stepmother.

Madame Dubois gripped Grace's hand again. "Please do not abandon me, mademoiselle. You are my only hope." The despair in her voice sent a shiver through Grace and drew her down beside the woman, where she wrapped an arm around her shoulder. Rafe had said his father was not to be trusted. This woman's tale only further endorsed that report, so how could Grace leave her in the hands of a monster? "What happened between Rafe and his father?" She could not help the question for she had to know the truth.

Madame Dubois glanced toward the window. "There has always been competition between them. From when Rafe was very little. Henri challenged him constantly. Everything was a contest. Then he would lash and humiliate Rafe afterward—especially if he won. Vraiment, I do not believe he loves his son. He treats him as if Rafe were not his own flesh and blood." She dabbed at her tears. "At least that is what Rafe has told me, and I have not seen evidence to the contrary."

A sudden pain gripped Grace's stomach, and she pressed a hand upon it. The sorrow of such a childhood was beyond her comprehension. But even more confusing was Madame Dubois's actions. "If you knew this, why did you marry Monsieur Dubois?"

"I was a foolish young girl who thought wealth would solve all my problems." She waved her handkerchief through the air, then turned anxious eyes to Grace. "Please do not leave me with him."

Grace felt as if a war raged within her members. Break a vow or save a life. Which was more important? Which one would God have her choose?

She squeezed the madame's hand. "I will not abandon you, madame."

"Merci. Merci," the woman sobbed. "You are too kind."

Maybe, Lord, this is the reason You have brought me all this way. To save this poor girl from the horrors of her marriage.

"I must tell the captain of my change of plans." Grace rose and turned toward the door.

"Non. Mademoiselle." Madame Dubois grabbed her arm. "If you go to him now, he will kidnap you again. You do not know him as I do." She gave Grace a look that intimated she too had affections for Rafe, and the sight of it took Grace aback.

"Monsieur Thorn said he would inform him if you agreed," she continued and dabbed the handkerchief beneath her puffy eyes. "And Captain Dubois must never know why you changed your mind."

"Why not?"

Madame Dubois's blue eyes turned to ice. "Because if he knew what his father had done to me he would kill him."

❧

Every step Rafe took over the muddy street sent a thunderous ache through his head. Doffing his cocked hat, he wiped the sweat from his brow and trudged forward. Irksome noises assailed him from all directions. Bells chiming, people screaming, horses clomping, the grating crank of carriage wheels, the lap of waves, and the incessant chatter of the mob, all increased in a cacophony of clatter in his pounding head.

Greetings and hails shot his way, but he dismissed them, in no mood for talking today. The fetor of manure, stale fish, and rotten fruit curled beneath his nose, causing his stomach to heave and nearly spew its contents—if there had been any.

Last night was a dismal, nightmarish blur. But beside his aching head and a knife wound on his arm, Rafe suffered no permanent damage. When Monsieur Thorn had met him at the graveyard and informed him that Mademoiselle Grace had changed her mind and would be leaving with his father on the morrow, Rafe had ordered him to make ready the ship, then he leapt upon his horse and galloped to his favorite tavern at the edge of town. After he had downed the first several drinks, the rest of the evening transformed into broken memories floating in his mind, none of which fit into any sensible pattern.

Femme exaspérante. Non. Liar, deceiver, *traître*. Just like all women.

Why had he been foolish enough to expect this one to keep her promise? Why had he not known she would run into his father's arms just as Claire had done? Rafe clenched his fists as he sidestepped a passing horse and rider. He heard his name called from a shop to his left, followed by another shout, but he ignored them.

Such intimacies he had shared about his mother with the mademoiselle at the graveyard; his face heated. And the way she had cried for him. A ploy? Another feminine trick to soften a man's heart into mush? He spit onto the ground and shoved his way through a mob of fishermen, ignoring their protests. Like her father, like all British, she wore a cloak of honor and kindness that did not exist once circumstances tore it from her.

Rafe had been duped again.

After he had vowed never to allow another woman access to his heart. The lovely raven-haired mademoiselle had pretended to care about Rafe only so he wouldn't kidnap her on the spot. Rafe kicked a rock across the road. *Je suis un imbécile!*

But it wasn't too late. If the mademoiselle could toss her vows so quickly to the wind, why couldn't he?

His father had won again. He had stolen another woman from Rafe. The thought sent waves of searing fury through him. He needed to leave this place as soon as possible. He must bid *adieu* to Abbé Villion, wipe the mud of Port-de-Paix from his boots, and head out to sea where he belonged—away from devious women and his depraved father.

Edging around the stone church, Rafe headed toward an oblong brick building. He shoved open the heavy door; its slam against the stones echoed through the building. Rafe stomped inside, squinting as his eyes grew accustomed to the dim light.

Then it hit him. A blast of hot, fetid air that smelled of human waste and mold.

And death.

His anger fell from him like an overused cloak.

Boxes, barrels, and crates flanked him, lit by four small windows, two on each side of the oblong structure. He recognized some of the goods he had recently delivered and began weaving his way down a narrow path between them toward a lighted area at the far end. Moans of pain slinked their way toward him as Abbé Villion appeared from amidst the clutter.

Despite the bloody rag in his hand, the abbé smiled. "Rafe. How are you?"

"Très bien," he lied, scanning the area behind the abbé where the sick lay on cots lined against the wall. An African woman dabbed a cloth on a young mulatto's forehead. "I have come to bid you *au revoir*. I set sail today."

"I am sorry to hear it, my friend." Abbé Villion's eyebrows pulled into a frown. "When will you return?"

A rat scrambled across the dirt floor by Rafe's boots while another moan sounded from the cots, drawing his gaze back to the sick child. "Who is that?"

Abbé Villion's face seemed to sag. He sighed and turned around, gesturing toward the cot where the woman tended the young boy. "Young Corbin, an orphan. He has the ague, I believe."

Rafe glanced from the boy to the other patients, noting how young they were, all except one giant African man curled up in a ball like a baby. "And the others?"

"Different ailments." Abbé Villion shrugged. "I am no physician."

"This is no place for the ill, in this squalor." Rafe's heart shrank, even as his frustration rose.

"At least here they are safe from the rain."

Brushing past the abbé, Rafe gazed at the sick, his already ailing stomach curdling within him.

From one of the cots, the dark brown eyes of a boy who looked to be no more than six years old stared blankly up at Rafe. In the child's vacant eyes, he saw a hopelessness so intense it made him shiver.

And in that instant, no matter the cost, Rafe felt a renewed sense of urgency. He could not delay his promise to the abbé any longer.

CHAPTER 19

Yellow and orange flames thrust their bony fingers toward the black sky, lunging, leaping, as if trying to escape their dark prison. Grace's heart seized and she whirled about. More flames shot up around her like blasts from a cannon. The heat scorched her gown, her skin, her hair. Pain seared through her. Pain that never ended. Pain that was never satisfied.

Because nothing ever burned.

She peered beyond the circle of flames. More fires flared, illuminating the massive jagged rocks strewn across the barren landscape. Balls of burning pitch and ear-piercing wails shot from black craters. Grace darted in the direction of one of them and peered over the side. Naught but molten blazing rock met her gaze. Yet the screams continued. Nothing had changed.

Always hearing, but never seeing anyone.

No, Lord, not again. Grace collapsed to the sharp rocks that made up the floor of the hideous place and she dropped her head into her hands. A soft voice slid over her. Wiping the tears from her face, she looked up. Not five paces from where she sat stood her sister Hope, her honey blond hair tossing this way and that in the hot blasts coming from the crater. Hope reached out her hand toward Grace and smiled.

Jumping to her feet, Grace darted toward her. "Hope! Hope!" But just as their fingertips grazed, Hope disappeared. "No! Come back! Hope!"

Grace's chest heaved, and she opened her eyes. Darkness everywhere. No flames, no moans, no screams. In place of the heat, a chill swept over her. She rubbed her eyes and saw the curtains fluttering at the window of her chamber.

Her chamber at Monsieur Dubois's house.

She released a deep breath. Another nightmare. Shivering, she hugged herself, dabbed at the perspiration on her forehead, then swung her legs over the side of the bed. Had she left the window open?

A form emerged from the shadows. A man's form. Grace tried to scream, but he grabbed her arm, twisted her around, and flattened his palm over her mouth.

The smell of tobacco and leather swirled beneath her nose. *Captain Dubois.* She struggled, but this time he didn't release her, didn't remove his hand, didn't allow her to speak. And though he didn't hurt her, his touch was firm, determined.

He turned her so she could see him in the mirror and motioned for her silence. His hand fell away. Grace opened her mouth to ask him what he was doing but before she could utter a sound, he shoved a handkerchief into it and tied it behind her head.

Terror consumed her. Why was he so angry? Mr. Thorn had told her that the captain had accepted her decision and had ordered him to prepare the ship to sail. He had reassured her all was well as he bade her farewell.

Grace groaned as loudly as the cloth in her mouth allowed and reached up to loosen it. But the captain grabbed her hands and tied her wrists behind her. Then hoisting her over his shoulder, he sat on the window ledge, grasped a rope he must have tied to her bedpost during her dream, and flung them both out the window.

"Stay still." His voice was stern, emotionless. Grace's head dangled against his back. The ground loomed in the shadows some thirty feet below her. He released his grip about her legs. Her heart froze as she realized she could fall if she moved the wrong way.

Bracing his boots against the side of the house, he grasped the rope with both hands and inched his way down. Grace squeezed her eyes shut, trying to keep her balance over his shoulder. The muscles in his shoulders and back flexed and strained as he ambled down the siding. Then he clutched her legs again and jumped to the ground with a thud that slapped her cheek against his back.

Grace's head gorged with blood, blurring her vision and making her upside-down world seem more like a dream than reality. Or rather, a reoccurring nightmare as the musky smell of his waistcoat brought back memories of the first time this man had stolen her from her home.

Taking her by the waist, he lifted her up to sit sideways on a horse then leapt behind her. Tugging the reins, he nudged the beast, and they dashed into the darkness.

Wind, heavy with moisture and the scents of forest and flowers, swept over her, flinging the loose wisps of her hair back over the captain. The heat from his body and the touch of his arms as he manipulated the reins alarmed her to the realization that she wore only a thin nightdress. An ache tugged at her throat. Her mouth parched until she could hardly breathe as once again all her hopes were obliterated beneath this brigand's volatile moods. And what would happen to Madame Dubois? Who would come to her rescue now?

The next hour passed in such stunning familiarity that if not for the gag in her mouth, Grace would have thought she only dreamed about the journey to Port-de-Paix, her frightening time alone in town, and finding freedom with Monsieur Dubois.

At the docks, Captain Dubois led her into a small boat, manned by two of his men, and in minutes Grace found herself once again staring at the dark hull of *Le Champion*. The captain pulled her to her feet. Grace tried to meet his gaze, desperate to discover his intent, desperate to find some shred of the concern she'd grown accustomed to seeing in his eyes of late. But he kept his face averted, refusing her a glimpse of his thoughts.

Up the rope ladder and down the companionway he carried her. Then, lowering her to the deck, he shoved her into her cabin. Grace's eyes filled with tears as he untied the gag and tore it from her mouth then freed her hands.

Slowly she turned to face him. His dark eyes blazed like the fires she'd witnessed in her nightmare. She swallowed. A tear escaped her lashes and slid down her cheek.

His chest heaved beneath his white buccaneer shirt, whether from exertion or anger, she couldn't tell. Strands of his ebony hair had loosened from their tie and wandered over his cheek as if seeking an anchor in this madness.

Grace shivered beneath his perusal and wrapped her arms over her nightdress.

His breathing slowed, and he shifted his jaw. "Who is Hope?"

"Why have you taken me again? Let me go!" She stormed toward him and tried to squeeze past him out the door, but his body might as well have been one of the ship's masts as strong and sturdy as it was. Sobbing, she retreated.

"Who is Hope?" he asked again.

"My sister." Her voice came out as if her mouth were stuffed with cotton. "I had a nightmare about her. She was in hell."

He stared at her, his eyes a glass wall, the twitch in his eyelid the only indication of any emotion.

The captain's bold gaze refused to leave her. Grace's face heated. "Now I'm wondering if I am not there as well," she added, trying to cover more of her nightdress.

The captain shrugged off his gray coat and handed it to her. As she reached out for it, a flicker of concern softened his eyes, giving Grace a moment of hope.

But then it was gone.

She held his coat up to cover her chest. "Why?"

He grabbed his baldric. "I thought you were something you are not."

"What am I, then?"

"You are the price of a hospital." Then he stepped out and slammed the door, leaving Grace alone in the darkness.

❧

Rafe bunched his arms over his chest and gazed across the indigo sea. A half-moon sitting a handbreadth over the horizon flung bands of glittering silver upon the waves, lending a dreamlike appearance to the scene. He inhaled a deep breath of the salty air, the smell of fish and life and freedom. Beneath him, milky foam bubbled off the stern of the ship before vanishing into the dark waters beyond—like everything beautiful, everything good. Anything worthwhile in this life turned out to be but a dream, a vapor; if one dared try to grab hold of it, it simply vanished.

The ship pitched over a swell, and Rafe braced his boots against the deck. He plucked a flask from his pocket and took a gulp of brandy before replacing the cork and slipping the container back into his coat. The liquor took a warm stroll down his throat as the sound of a fiddle and the voices of men playing cards blared from behind him. His crew seemed happy to be at sea once again and on their way to procure a fortune.

Rafe wished he could share their mirth.

But the vision of Mademoiselle Grace shivering in her cabin would not obey his order to vacate his thoughts: the braids of her long raven hair swinging over her white nightdress like liquid obsidian on cream; her emerald eyes moist with tears; her bottom lip trembling. And all he had wanted to do was take her in his arms and comfort her. Sacre mer, what spell had la femme cast upon him? Even after her betrayal, even after a day out at sea, he still couldn't get her out of his mind. He shook his head, scattering his thoughts of her. This time he must not allow himself to become attached to her. This time he would keep his distance.

Shoes scuffed over the deck behind him, and Rafe flattened his lips. He craved no company on this dark night, preferring to torment himself with the shame and guilt that had become his friends since he had stolen Mademoiselle Grace from his father's house.

"Mon ami." Father Alers eased beside him and folded his hands over his prominent belly. "You have been hiding from me."

"Apparently not well enough."

Father Alers chuckled. "The crew told me you were in a foul humor. And no wonder after what you have done."

"And what is that, mon vieux?"

His friend gave Rafe a reprimanding look but said nothing, only gazed over the dark waters.

"I had no choice."

"We all have a choice."

"She chose my father over me. She broke her vow."

"Vraiment?"

"I would have returned her home." Rafe fingered his mustache.

"And for one lie, you send her to her death instead?"

"Not her death."

"Ah, but a fate worse than death." Father Alers's tone carried the convicting ring of truth.

"She betrayed me. She intended to go with my father to Charles Towne."

"Oui, I heard votre père was involved. That explains much." Father Alers scratched his wiry gray beard.

"What do you mean?" Rafe reached for his flask, uncorked it, and took another sip.

"Only that I fear you are more angry at your father than at the mademoiselle."

"Absurde. I know what to expect from my father. But the mademoiselle. . .I thought she was different."

"I see nothing changed in her." Father Alers shrugged.

"She deceives you with her saintly behavior, but inside she is a snake like my father, like Claire." The thunderous clap of a sail sounded above him, and Rafe took another swig of brandy. "Not to be trusted."

"Hmm."

"Lives will be spared from the doubloons she will bring me." Rafe bristled as the words sounded more like an excuse than a reason. "Besides, the men haven't been paid in over a month and they start to complain."

"Is that how you justify your actions?" Father Alers coughed his disapproval and glanced into the dark sky above them. "The sacrifice of one for the many?"

Rafe scowled. "What do you want, mon vieux?" he barked. "Does the mademoiselle require something?"

"Non. She is well." Father Alers fixed Rafe with a withering stare. "More kind and accommodating than one would expect in her situation."

Rafe corked his flask and returned it to his coat. "Then excuse me." Turning on his heel, he marched across the quarterdeck, bunching his fists together—angry at Father Alers, angry at himself, angry at the world.

Not even the brandy seemed to numb his fury this night as he leapt down the companionway. Nor as he stormed down the narrow hall to his cabin and blasted through the door. He slammed it and stomped to his desk. Striking flint to steel, he lit a lantern and rummaged through the closet for another bottle of the brandy.

A soft scraping sound met his ears. Rafe froze. Slowly tugging his pistol from his baldric, he cocked it, then he spun around, pointing it toward the source. Out of the shadows drifted a lady in an azure gown.

"It is me, Rafe." Her soothing voice penetrated the haze that covered his mind.

She took another step, and the lantern light shifted across her face. Rafe lowered his pistol and rubbed his eyes as her form swirled in his vision. *It could not be. I have had too much brandy.* He opened his eyes expecting the apparition to have vanished. But she remained. A sweet smile lifted her lips, and she reached out for him.

Claire.

CHAPTER 20

"Claire, *sacre mer*, what are you doing here?" Rafe tucked his pistol back into its brace and narrowed his eyes upon the last person he expected to see aboard his ship.

She sashayed toward him, the swish of her blue gown setting his nerves on edge. Lifting her thick lashes, she gazed at him with all the love and adoration he remembered. "Are you not happy to see me?" She placed a hand on his arm.

Rafe jerked from her touch, turned around, and grabbed the bottle of brandy he'd been searching for. "I asked you a question." A question to which his alcohol-hazed mind could not fathom any rational answer.

"I could stand it no longer."

Rafe circled her, opened the bottle, and searched for a glass, not wanting to look into those crisp blue eyes. Spyglass leapt from the window ledge and landed on a chart stretched across his desk. Where had *le chat* come from? Ignoring the feline's nudge on his arm, Rafe found a glass, poured himself a drink, and faced Claire.

"What could you not stand, Madame Dubois?"

She drew her lips together in a pout. "I liked it better when you called me Claire."

He cocked a brow. "That was a mistake. Like many things between us."

"Oh, Rafe, must it always be so?" She fingered the lace atop her bodice. Her golden curls bounced around her neck with her every movement.

"What are you doing here?" He tipped back the brandy; if he drank enough, it would render him unconscious and put an end to this miserable night.

Inching toward him, she grabbed the edge of his desk, her delicate fingers kneading the rough wood as they had oft rubbed the stiff muscles in his neck. He swallowed.

"I ran away from your father."

Rafe jerked. Though her presence here had precluded any doubt of that fact, hearing the words aloud caused his blood to boil.

She reached out to him. When Rafe lurched away, she clasped her hands together and looked down. "He is a monster, Rafe. I could tolerate his abuses no longer."

"What business is that of mine?" Rafe slammed the liquor to the back of his throat.

Her eyes glistened. "I thought you might still care."

Spyglass rubbed against Rafe's back, vying for his attention.

He snorted. "How did you get on board?"

"I hired a man to row me out to your ship." She shrugged, sending her gold jeweled earrings shimmering in the lantern light. "I have no one else to turn to."

"I am the last person to whom you should run, madame." He clanked the glass atop his desk as his muscles tensed in anger. "Your presence here is unwelcome. Do you know what I do with stowaways?"

She eased beside him. Her lavender scent rose to tantalize his nose. "Help me, Rafe. I beg you. Help me escape him."

Rafe stepped back, his stomach knotting. "I toss them overboard."

"You would never harm me, Rafe." Tears pooled in her thick lashes and a shudder swept through her.

"And yet you had no qualms about harming me."

"I was young and foolish."

"And you are so much wiser now, I see."

"Let us forget the past." She toyed with a curl dangling about her cheek and pouted her lips. "Can I please stay? I will be no trouble. I've brought my lady's maid to attend to me."

Rafe's throat went suddenly dry and he cleared it. "I see you have planned well. I seem to have no choice. For now."

She gave him one of those sweet, seductive smiles that in times past melted his resolve. Rafe fought against the haze in his mind that prompted him to take what she so freely offered.

He licked his lips.

Spyglass batted Rafe's glass off the desk. The shrill crash jarred him from the woman's trance, and he glanced down at the glittering shards strewn across the deck. Spyglass pressed her head against his arm and he hoisted the cat onto his shoulder, thankful for the interruption.

A knock sounded on the door.

"Entrez-vous."

Rafe's helmsman entered, his eyes alighting upon Claire and widening in admiration.

"What is it, Monsieur Atton?" Rafe ground his teeth together. What fools men became in the presence of a beautiful woman.

The helmsman jerked from his trance. "Capitaine, Monsieur Thorn wishes to inform ye that the brig is sailing trim, the horizon is clear, and he's putting Weylan on watch."

"Très bien." Rafe nodded. "Tell Monsieur Thorn to come to my cabin before he retires."

Claire flinched at the mention of his first mate's name, and Rafe looked at her curiously. "You do not approve of Monsieur Thorn?"

She looked away. "I hardly know him."

Monsieur Atton turned to leave.

"Leave the door open, monsieur," Rafe ordered. Better not to be alone with this vixen.

"Aye, Capitaine." Atton's boot steps faded down the companionway.

Rafe patted his pocket for a cheroot. "You have placed me in a precarious situation, Madame Dubois."

She frowned.

"Sans doute, my father will come looking for you. And he will believe I stole you away."

"I wish that you had." Her voice was laden with sorrow, but instead of invoking Rafe's sympathies, it had the opposite effect. He picked up the lantern, lit his cheroot in its flame, then inhaled the pungent smoke, allowing it to filter into his lungs.

Turning, he glared at her, searching her eyes for a hint of the real reason for her sneaking aboard his ship. Whatever it was, she was up to no good. And now, on top of everything else, he must deal with this spoiled, self-centered woman.

She swallowed and flitted her gaze about nervously. "Why call Monsieur Thorn?"

"To escort you to your quarters." Rafe swung about and stared out the stern windows at the star-studded sky bobbing up and down beyond the panes.

"But I thought. . .I thought I could stay in here with you." The swish of her gown followed him.

She eased beside him. Feigned innocence beamed from her blue eyes as her lips once again drew together into that pleading pout. Rafe's blood heated at her salacious offer as memories swirled in his mind—pleasurable memories of their past together.

Spyglass leapt back on the window ledge, and Claire jumped, wrinkling her nose in disgust.

"You wished to see me, Captain?" Monsieur Thorn's voice rescued Rafe from his thoughts.

Claire stiffened beside him and looked down.

"Oui, Madame Dubois will tell you where her lady's maid is hiding. Then please escort them both to Mademoiselle Grace's cabin."

Monsieur Thorn nodded but oddly withheld his glance from Claire.

"Mademoiselle Grace?" Claire's normally soft tone ascended to a screech. Her eyes widened and her nostrils flared.

"*Quel est le problème?*" Rafe asked.

Claire planted her hands upon her hips. "What is *she* doing here? I thought she was leaving on Henri's ship tomorrow."

"There has been a change of plans." Rafe eyed Claire curiously, wondering what difference the mademoiselle's presence made to her.

Madame Dubois stared at Monsieur Thorn as if he had the answer, but he shifted nervously and gazed into the dark sky beyond the window.

She swept seething eyes to Rafe. "I will not share a cabin with that woman."

⌒

Grace rose from kneeling beside her bed and rubbed her aching knees. The brig creaked and moaned as it navigated another wave—sounds that had become her constant companions since Captain Dubois had kidnapped her the night before. With the exception of brief visits by Father Alers, she'd not spoken to a soul, especially not the captain, though she'd heard him storming through the companionway outside her door often enough. She knew it was him because his thick jackboots made a distinctive angry *th-ump* when he marched about.

Grace moved to the porthole. Stars winked at her from their posts positioned across the dark shroud covering the earth. Perhaps they guarded more than the night sky. Perhaps they were God's army of angels watching over her. It brought her comfort to think so.

She wove around her cot and glanced over the cabin. The lone lantern perched upon the table cast eerie shadows across the bulkhead, shadows that hovered over her heart and brought her to her knees in prayer. All day she'd been asking God why—when she had been so close to rescue—He had brought her back into captivity. When she received no answer, she prayed for Hope instead. The vision of her sister in hell had jarred Grace to her very soul and reminded her of the brevity of life here on earth and the urgency of bringing others to Christ.

Grace lowered her chin, ashamed that her anger and judgment at Hope's willful rebellion had caused her to cease praying for her sister. But from now on, she promised to pray for Hope every day. She'd also said a prayer for Madame Dubois—that God would heal her heart and her marriage, and only as a last resort, provide an escape from the brutality of her husband. And for her sister Charity and her marriage as well.

Yet heaven remained silent.

Grace sank to her bed and removed her shoes, then she began loosening the ties of her bodice on yet another borrowed gown that Father Alers had provided for her. Where he procured all these gowns, she didn't want to know. She did want to know, however, why she was here on this brig. Every time she thought she knew what God's plan was for her, every time she thought she knew who she'd been sent to help, everything changed.

The door crashed open, slamming against the bulkhead with a jarring crunch. Grace splayed her fingers over her loosened ties and slowly rose as none other than Madame Dubois entered the cabin. A mulatto woman, her face lowered, followed on her heels, and Monsieur Thorn completed the entourage, a trunk hoisted over his shoulder.

"Madame Dubois." Grace darted toward her, thinking that the captain must have kidnapped her as well.

But the woman ignored her to swing about and face Mr. Thorn. "This is all your fault," she snapped.

Mr. Thorn chuckled. "Zooks, madame. I do not see how." He lowered the trunk to the floor then shot a quick smile Grace's way. "Have a pleasant evening." Then looking as if he couldn't escape quickly enough, he left and closed the door.

A chill filtered through the stifling hot room, lifting the hairs on Grace's neck and arms.

Madame Dubois faced her. Gone were the soft tranquil lines of innocence and humility Grace had witnessed in Port-de-Paix, and in their place marched an army of defiance, petulance, and perturbation.

Grace blinked at the drastic transformation. Perhaps the woman was angry that Grace had failed to keep her promise to help her. "Madame Dubois. I was quite worried about you." Grace stepped toward her. "I fully intended to help you, but as you can see Captain Dubois stole me against my will."

"Of course I can see that." She waved toward the mulatto woman. "Annette, stop cowering in the corner, unpack my things, and hang them up." Then shifting her glance over the cabin, she thrust out her chin. "How are we all to fit in here? *C'est impossible.*" Her eyes landed on Grace's cot. "And there is only one bed." Her face drained of all color.

"Madame Dubois, sit down. You don't look well." Grace led her to the chair, and she flounced into it with a huff.

"Would you like some lemon juice?" Grace poured some of the sour liquid from her pitcher into a mug and handed it to Madame Dubois, but she batted it away.

Taking no offense, Grace set the glass down and gazed at the mulatto opening Madame Dubois's trunk. Tall, slender, with ebony hair and skin the color of bronze, her dark exotic eyes shifted toward Grace before she snapped them away.

Grace smiled. "I am Grace Westcott. And you are?"

"She is nobody," Madame Dubois barked from her chair.

The mulatto woman backed away from Grace. She glanced at Madame Dubois. "I am Annette."

"Pleased to make your acquaintance, Annette." Grace shivered beneath another chill, still baffled at its source, as a heaviness settled on her.

Madame Dubois turned in her chair to look at them. "Annette is my husband's child."

Grace blinked. "Your daughter?" She studied Annette, whose gaze had lowered once again to the deck. The young lady looked nothing like Madame Dubois.

"Non, *vous imbécile*. My husband's and one of our slave's," Madame Dubois shot back, her voice firing with spite.

Grace gulped. The more she discovered about Monsieur Dubois, the more his claim to be a man of God shriveled.

Madame Dubois clicked her tongue. "My husband, along with many of the grand blancs on Saint Dominique, is attempting to create a race of exotic beautiful woman by breeding with the African slaves." She gestured toward Annette. "They are called *les Sirènes*."

Grace clutched her throat, abhorring what she heard. "I cannot believe it."

"It is an acceptable practice among the grand blancs, mademoiselle, one which I despise."

"But why is she your slave? And what of her mother?"

"Annette is free, but at her father's request, she serves me. As for her mother"—Madame Dubois looked down—"Monsieur Dubois maintains a relationship with her." A vacant glaze covered her blue eyes then sharpened when she looked at Grace. "Now do you see why I must leave him?"

Grace's heart melted. She had heard of such practices in Charles Towne but had hoped they were rumors. How could any woman endure such infidelity? She rushed to Madame Dubois's side and knelt before her. "Of course. I understand. But how did you come to this ship?"

Madame Dubois took a deep breath but did not take Grace's outstretched hand. "I climbed aboard. How else?"

"But I understood you to say that Rafe hated you and would never allow you aboard."

"He had no say in it." Madame Dubois's tone sank.

Annette began unfolding her mistress's skirts, bodices, and petticoats and hanging them on knobs in the open armoire.

Grace rose and sat on her bed. "I don't understand."

"No, I suppose you wouldn't." Madame Dubois straightened the lace at her sleeves. "When I found you missing, I had no other option but to appeal to my stepson for help."

Grace thought back to the events of the prior night. "But how could you know I was missing when I was taken in the middle of the night?"

Madame Dubois's face flushed, and she stood, waving a hand through the air. "I could not sleep and went to your chamber to speak with you and found you gone."

"But we set sail as soon as the captain came on board. There would have been no time." Grace furrowed her brow and wondered why Madame Dubois would not meet her gaze.

The mulatto continued her work, but Grace did not miss the furtive glance she cast her way.

"Oh, what does it matter?" Madame Dubois's voice sharpened and she huffed out a sigh. "I am here now."

Grace grasped her chain. "Then you should be happy, madame. You are free from your husband."

"Except Rafe is angry and refuses to listen to me." Madame Dubois began to pace, the swish of her gown slicing through the cabin.

"We have that in common, madame."

Madame Dubois halted and raised a curious eye to Grace. "Why did he kidnap you again?"

"I betrayed him. I didn't keep my promise to return. You should have allowed me to speak to him about our plans."

Madame Dubois cocked her head, sending her golden curls bobbing. "What does he intend to do with you?"

"I don't know." Grace's stomach tightened. "Perhaps sell me to the don as he originally planned."

A hint of a smile appeared on Madame Dubois's lips as if the information pleased her.

Grace could make no sense of the woman. She seemed as volatile and unsettled as the captain. Perhaps the abuse she had endured at the hand of her husband made her that way. Could she be the one Grace had been sent to help? "Perchance if we explain to Captain Dubois our plans, he will understand your desperation to come aboard since he kidnapped your only means of escape. Surely then he would forfeit his anger against you."

The woman stormed toward Grace as if she'd asked her to jump overboard. She grabbed Grace's hands and shook them. "Non. You must promise never to tell Rafe of our prior plans. Remember what I said?"

Grace remembered. Madame Dubois said he would kill his father. Perhaps he would. Perhaps he wouldn't. Nevertheless, she had made a vow once to this woman, and she intended to keep it. "I promise."

CHAPTER 21

Rafe marched toward the door, intending to storm into the cabin, give his instructions, and leave as soon as possible. And he would have done just that, save for Father Alers's staying hand on his arm and the look of reprimand the former priest shot his way. "A gentleman does not enter a lady's chamber without knocking, Rafe."

"I am no gentleman. And this is a cabin aboard *my* ship, not a lady's boudoir." Rafe jerked from his grasp, but the old man forced himself in front of Rafe and tapped on the oak door. "Mademoiselle Grace, Madame Dubois, *pouvons-nous entrer?*"

Rafe folded his arms over his chest and shook his head while Father Alers waited for a reply.

"Une minute, s'il vous plaît," came a soft response.

Rafe stomped his boot and huffed in impatience as Spyglass scurried down the hallway and began scratching the door for entrance. "Le chat does not wait for permission." He smirked.

The door opened, and Claire's gaze passed over Father Alers and landed upon Rafe. She smiled and gestured them inside.

Stepping around the father, Rafe brushed past Claire, trying to avoid any contact with the woman, but she laid a hand on his arm in passing. Instead of his normal heated response to her touch, he felt nothing.

Putting distance between them, he glanced across the cabin. Claire's maid, Annette, stood, head lowered in the corner. On the other side of the room beneath the porthole, Mademoiselle Grace clung to a bundle of blankets as if she had just picked them off the floor. Her eyes met his, convicting green eyes tinted with anger and fear that bristled over his conscience.

Spyglass scampered inside and leapt onto the table beside a lantern set aglow by rays of morning sun beaming in through the porthole. The cat nibbled upon the few crumbs strewn over the plates that had held the ladies' breakfast.

Claire leapt back in disgust. "Take that filthy beast away!" She waved her hand toward Spyglass as if she could brush the cat from the scene.

"She is my pet, madame, and as such, you will not address her as a filthy beast."

Mademoiselle Grace giggled, drawing Rafe's gaze to her, to her wrinkled gown and disheveled hair. "Did you sleep on the floor, mademoiselle?" He inclined his head toward the blankets bundled in her arms.

She scrunched them closer to her chest then curled a stray lock of her hair behind her ear. "Madame Dubois was quite distraught last night."

"So you abandoned your bed to her?" Rafe did not like the odd sensation that welled within him at the revelation.

"Why shouldn't she?" Claire snapped. "She is your prisoner while I am your guest."

Rafe faced the woman, radiant as always in the morning light, her golden curls spiraling like gentle waves over her neck, lace abounding from her tight silk bodice that flowed down to an azure skirt. No doubt Annette had already spent hours fussing over her mistress. "You are many things, madame, but my guest is not one of them."

Claire drew her lips into a pout as Spyglass jumped into the chair beside her, giving her a start. The lines of her face folded in repugnance.

"I have brought two hammocks." Rafe retrieved the brown bundles from Father Alers, who remained in the doorway, and handed them to Claire.

She held them out from her body as if they were covered with mud then shoved them back at him. "You cannot be serious. This cabin is far too small for all of us." She threw a hand in the air. "It is stifling in here and it smells as if something has died. And I ache from that infernal thing you call a bed." She pressed her delicate fingers on her back.

A lump of disdain balled in Rafe's throat. "The other ladies slept on the deck, and yet, I do not hear them complaining."

"Humph," she snorted. "No doubt they are used to such conditions, while I am not." Claire laid the back of her hand to her forehead. "I am feeling faint." She attempted to bat Spyglass from the chair, but the cat hissed at her, sending her reeling backward.

A giggle escaped Mademoiselle's lips again, as one did Annette's. Claire glared at her maid. Tossing a hand to her throat, she threw back her shoulders. "Please, Rafe." She sidled up to him and fingered the lace atop her bodice, drawing his attention to the low neckline. "Surely you can find more suitable accommodations for me."

And by the seductive lilt to her voice, Rafe knew exactly to which accommodations she referred.

"Why, there is not enough room for my trousseau." Claire glanced at the armoire from which a multitude of colorful gowns overflowed.

"In fact, I can barely move in these cramped quarters." She continued her performance, and Rafe released a heavy sigh. Like a bad play, her theatrics became irksome.

He cocked a brow, wondering if Claire had always been this peevish, or had she been polluted by spending too many hours with his father? "And yet this is the only cabin I have to offer you."

"Not all." She gave him a pleading look that fell short of its intended mark on his heart.

Father Alers coughed.

"I am famished." She pressed a hand over her stomach. "Do you intend to starve me as well?"

"Father Alers brought you food this morning." Rafe gestured toward the empty tray atop the table.

Claire turned up her nose. "You cannot expect me to eat such slop."

Father Alers coughed again and shuffled his boots over the deck.

Rafe turned to his friend. "Would you show Madame Dubois and her maid to the galley? Perhaps she can find something more to her liking there." Although he knew she would not, knew that nothing aboard this ship would be to her liking, he longed to relieve himself of her company and speak with Mademoiselle Grace in private.

Father Alers gave him a look that said he'd rather be boiled in oil, but he nodded and gestured for Claire to follow him.

"Very well." She gathered her skirts and sauntered past him, brushing against his arm, and leaving her scent of lavender behind—a scent that used to delight him, but now turned stale in his nostrils. En fait, with her exit, fresh air filled the cabin, and a heaviness lifted from his heart.

He exhaled a ragged breath, set the hammocks on the chair, and turned toward Mademoiselle Grace. "You should not be so kind to her," he said, pointing to the blankets still in her arms. "She will not return the favor."

"I seek no reward." She placed the blankets on the bed and pressed the wrinkles out of a gown she had obviously slept in. Yet regardless of the creases in her skirts, regardless of the strands of raven hair that had escaped her pins and the shadows beneath her eyes, she was the most beautiful thing he had ever seen.

She splayed her fingers in modesty over the skin above her gown, so different from Claire who so blatantly tried to attract him by her physical charms. "Do you intend to sell me to the Spanish don, Captain?" Her bottom lip quivered as she leaned toward Spyglass. The cat willingly leapt into her arms, and Mademoiselle Grace stroked the gray fur atop her head.

Rafe clenched his jaw and rubbed the stubble upon it. Everything within him screamed non. He could never do such a thing. But then he remembered her lies, her betrayal, and the faces of the sick children in Port-de-Paix that constantly haunted his nightmares. "You betrayed me."

"How?" A delicate line formed between her brows—a tiny wrinkle in her otherwise lustrous skin.

"You did not meet me. You broke your vow." Rafe must always remember that, especially now when she looked at him with such sorrow and naïveté.

"But I sent Mr. Thorn—"

"Sacre mer. I heard what he had to say." Rafe held a hand up to stop her. He remembered it all too clearly. *The mademoiselle sends her apologies,* Thorn had said with a bit of scorn in his tone, *but she prefers the comforts which your father can offer her on the journey home rather than the inhospitality of your brig.* Rafe clenched his jaw. "Can you deny that you lied to me—that you dishonored your oath?"

She bowed her head, and Spyglass nuzzled beneath her chin. "I had good reason."

Rafe thumped his boot on the hard deck. "What reason?" If she would but give him an explanation, any explanation that made sense, any explanation that would appease the throbbing wound that had reopened in his heart. If she would do that, he might forgive her, he might take her in his arms as he longed to do, he might return her home safely, or take her anywhere she wanted to go.

If she would but speak the right words.

"I am not at liberty to say." She swallowed, and her hands began to tremble.

Rafe bunched his fists. "Not at liberty, or do not wish to admit that you received a better offer?" Just as Claire had done to him so many years ago.

Mademoiselle Grace lifted her chin, her eyes filling. "I am sorry." And in those eyes he saw no reason to believe otherwise.

"It is not enough." He grabbed the pommel of his rapier, rubbing his thumb over the silver until it ached.

"For now, it is all I can give you," she said softly.

"Then I fear it is all I can give you as well. I am sorry, mademoiselle, but oui, I must sell you to the don as planned."

"I break one vow and my sentence is to be a lifetime of slavery?"

Rafe ground his teeth together. "It is more than a broken promise, mademoiselle. All my life, not one person has kept their word to me. Not ma mère, not mon père, and not Claire."

Her eyes widened at the mention of Claire, but he continued, "Does a person's word mean nothing anymore?" He stormed toward her and she flinched at his anger. But he could not stop. "I will tell you what a broken promise means. It means there is no honor within, no decency. It indicates a heart filled with selfishness and deceit." He gripped the pommel of his rapier and tried to collect his emotions as her eyes grew moist. "You had me fooled, mademoiselle, with your pious act. But no more." He shook his head. "No more. And I, too, will keep my word—the vow I spoke to Abbé Villion."

Tears spilled from her lashes down her cheeks as she continued scratching Spyglass. Rafe knew he had better leave before he changed his mind.

"I bid you adieu." He nodded, stomped out, and slammed the door behind him. Then leaning back against the oak slab, he slammed his fists against it, trying to collect his raging emotions. Even in her betrayal, the woman still bewitched him.

❦

Grace clung to the railing amidships and gazed over the rippling turquoise sea. The afternoon sun cast bands of glittering diamonds atop the waves as they frolicked on their course without a care in the world. She envied them. White billowing clouds cluttered the horizon but rarely passed over the broiling orb to offer the ship's inhabitants any respite from the heat. Perspiration trickled down her neck and back and beaded on her forehead, relieved only by the continual salt-laden breeze wafting in off the sea.

Grace closed her eyes as the brig rose and plunged over another swell.

A burst of wind clawed at her hair, freeing a strand from her tight coiffure as she listened to the swish of the foamy waters against the hull and the thunderous flap of sails above her. Not to mention the ever-present creak and groan of the planks and the shouts of the crew as they went about their tasks. All familiar sounds to her now, replacing the pleasant music of home: the chirp of birds outside her window, the laughter of her sisters, Molly singing hymns as she prepared supper, the swish of the angel oak leaves dancing in the breeze in front of their home. Every place created its own unique music, and though the music aboard this ship carried a pleasant tune, the place to which it carried her would not be so pleasant.

Opening her eyes, she stared at the foam purling off the ship, and her thoughts drifted to Madame Dubois and her spiteful, curt behavior. Not at all like the charming hostess who had befriended Grace at the Dubois estate. The change in her demeanor had completely baffled Grace—that was until Captain Dubois entered the cabin and the lady transformed into an amorous coquette before Grace's eyes.

Mercy me. The captain was her stepson. Grace rubbed her eyes and dabbed at the perspiration on her neck. Apparently Madame Dubois was much more than his stepmother. Or had been at one time. Now Grace understood the hatred spilling from Madame Dubois's eyes. Jealousy. She was jealous of Grace. Though Grace could not imagine why. The captain intended to sell her to the don and be done with her. He had reassured her of that fact in the cabin that morning.

Yet right before he had declared her doom so vehemently, she had glimpsed a softening in his otherwise hard gaze, as if he wished their journey could take another course. And she longed to tell him the truth, the real reason she had broken her vow to him, if only to erase the anguish from his eyes. But she couldn't. If only she could go back in time and do things differently. But it was too late for that. She had wanted so much to help him—to help everyone, but instead, she had made a mess of things.

"Good day to you, Miss Grace." Mr. Thorn slipped beside her and tipped his hat.

Grace forced a smile despite her dismal thoughts. "Good day, Mr. Thorn." With his pristine blue waistcoat, white breeches, boots, and tricorne, the young first mate reminded Grace of a painting of a young British seaman hanging in her father's study—quite in contrast to the rest of the bawdy crew.

"I've been meaning to thank you again, Mr. Thorn, for helping me escape at Port-de-Paix."

He flattened his lips. "A lot of good it did, eh?"

Grace drew a deep breath. "It would seem God wishes me to remain on this ship for some reason."

He snorted. "I believe that is the captain's wish, not God's, Miss Grace."

A heaviness settled on her at the man's lack of faith. But how to reach him? Mr. Thorn behaved every bit the godly man: honorable, moral, kind. Yet without faith, where could it lead? "I suffered greatly while in town. I lost the money you so generously gave me, and I nearly starved to death. If not for God's help, I would have surely died."

"And yet, it would appear that He saved you only to imprison you again." Mr. Thorn brushed dirt from his waistcoat.

"We do not always understand the ways of God."

"I would say we never can and never will." He gripped the railing as the brig canted over another wave.

Two sailors passed behind them, laughing and cursing as they leapt up the foredeck ladder. Grace recognized them as Mr. Legard, the bosun, and Mr. Weylan, the man who had accosted her below deck. She shuddered, but could not miss the knowing glance they exchanged with Mr. Thorn. When she looked at the first mate in confusion, his face mottled. "Forgive their blasphemy, miss. I grow so tired of the crass language aboard." He glared after them as they continued across the foredeck. "Scoundrels, profligates all."

Grace examined him, curious at his extreme censure of his fellow sailors—men he must work and live with in such close quarters.

"And the captain is no better," he added. "You are fortunate he curbs his tongue in front of the ladies."

Grace raised her brows, surprised that Captain Dubois possessed the manners to restrain himself at all. "Aren't you and the captain friends?"

"Friends? I work for him, 'tis all."

"And yet he speaks much more fondly of you than you do of him."

"Can you blame him?" He chuckled.

Shielding her eyes from the sun, Grace studied the baffling man and wondered where his true loyalties lay. If not with the captain, and not his own countrymen, then where? "Do you have family somewhere, Mr. Thorn?"

"Yes, on Nassau. A mother, father, and younger sister." He clenched the railing.

"A sister? How nice." Grace had always wanted an older brother—someone to stand up for and protect her and her sisters when their father was out to sea, as he so often was.

Mr. Thorn took a deep breath and gazed out over the glistening water. "Yes. Her name is Elizabeth." The tone of his voice carried fervent love along with deep sorrow, giving Grace pause.

She laid a hand on his arm. "Is she well?"

He shifted his brown eyes to her, and the anguish she saw in them took her aback.

"As well as can be expected," he said. His gaze hardened into stone, and he swept it over the deck as if in search of some remedy.

Grace didn't know what to make of it. No doubt something horrible had happened to his sister. "What does she suffer from?"

Withdrawing his arm from beneath her hand, Mr. Thorn threw back his shoulders as if tossing aside some cumbrous memory. "Forgive me, miss. I misspoke." Then, he directed his gaze at a sailor sitting atop a barrel. "Bear a hand aloft, Mr. Fletcher!" he bellowed and watched as the man grunted then flung himself into the ratlines. Plucking a handkerchief from his pocket, Mr. Thorn dabbed the perspiration on the back of his neck. "Abominable heat. What brings you on deck, miss?"

Truth be told, when Madame Dubois and Annette returned, Grace found she couldn't escape their company fast enough. Between Madame Dubois's barbed looks of disdain and Annette's skittish demeanor, the atmosphere had become intolerable. Grace liked the mulatto woman, but could not shake the unease that slid over her in the maid's presence. Just that morning, Grace could have sworn she heard the woman chanting something in her dark corner before sunrise. "My cabin has become quite crowded as of late."

"Ah yes, the resplendent Madame Claire Dubois." He swirled his hand in the air like a courtier's bow.

Grace found his reaction odd. "You do not approve of her?"

"Do you? Vainglorious peacock, ill-tempered shrew," he spat in contempt. "She and her husband are suitably matched. Yet here she is seeking the affections of the captain."

"So my assumption is correct." Grace shook her head even as the man's words grated over her. Was she so quick to label others in such cruel terms? Though the accusations may be true, and she could not deny thinking them herself, hearing the acrid criticisms on another person's lips sliced deep into Grace's conscience.

Mr. Thorn leaned toward her as if he shared a juicy secret. "Aye, apparently they have quite a past."

The brig lurched, sending a cool spray over Grace, jarring her from participating in the man's gossip, though she longed to know the story. "But didn't you befriend her at the Dubois estate? Were you not involved in convincing her to elicit my help to escape to Charles Towne?" Though Grace had promised Claire she would not tell Rafe of their plans to escape to Charles Towne, surely it was safe to discuss the matter with Mr. Thorn since he was involved in the scheme. Besides, Grace wished to gain an understanding of the connection between Madame Dubois and Mr. Thorn.

His face reddened, and he drew out his handkerchief again and dabbed the sweat on his brow. "She sought my help, to be sure. Like you, she had me fooled into believing she truly wished your assistance to get to Charles Towne." He shrugged and gazed off to his right. "Apparently she had other plans."

Grace eyed him, sensing he knew much more than he was saying. She remembered the conversation she'd overheard between Mr. Thorn and Monsieur Dubois—something about revenge. "Mr. Thorn, may I ask you a personal question?"

He nodded, though hesitancy shadowed his expression.

"I still do not understand why you sail with Captain Dubois. You don't approve nor associate with the crew. And you have not hid your disdain for the captain, at least not from me."

He laughed. "Can you blame me? Sailing with such miscreants? I am indeed as out of place as a nobleman in a brothel."

His chuckle faded as his eyes focused on something behind Grace. Silence invaded the ship. Grace turned to see Madame Dubois emerge from the companionway, Annette on her heels. Shielding her eyes from the sun, the woman gave Grace a cursory glance before heading toward the other side of the ship, barking at Annette to follow her. The crew quit their ogling and returned to their duties.

"She is quite beautiful," Grace admitted.

"Yes, she is." Mr. Thorn's eyes remained locked upon the ladies as they took up their spot on the larboard railing. Then he jerked. "Oh, you mean Madame Dubois?" He snorted. "She is tolerable, I suppose."

Grace blinked. "Do you speak of Annette, then?"

"She is exquisite." His tone sang with admiration as his eyes never left the young mulatto.

Grace bit her lip, not wanting to disclose that Annette was Rafe's half sister. "Yes, she is."

Annette opened a parasol and held it over her mistress to shield her skin from the searing rays of the sun. Grace touched her own cheek and felt the heat emanating from it. In no time she'd be as tan as these sailors. Most unappealing. But then again, when had she cared for her appearance? Movement caught her eye and she swept her gaze to the companionway where Captain Dubois emerged. Their eyes met and he halted, his white buccaneer shirt flapping in the wind beneath his gray coat. Unsettled by his perusal, she faced the sea again.

Boots thumped toward her. "Monsieur Thorn, do you not have something better to do?" His deep voice tumbled over them.

"Nay. Not at the moment." Mr. Thorn raised an eyebrow that did not have the intended effect as Captain Dubois's expression remained as hard as stone.

Grace gazed between the two men. Captain Dubois fingered the hilt of his rapier, yet said nothing.

"Very well, then." Mr. Thorn ran a thumb along the scar on his neck. "I am sure I can find some of the crew to order about." He touched the tip of his hat and nodded to Grace. "Good day to you, miss." Then he left.

Silence spread between them.

"Why must you be such a bully?" The words came out of her mouth before she considered their content.

Instead of anger, his lips curved into a grin. "A bully? Moi? I am so much more than that."

"Yes you are. Kidnapper, rogue, and scoundrel are a few other titles that come to mind."

He chuckled. "The pious prude has acquired some pluck. But we have already discovered a few flaws hidden behind your proper facade, have we not, thief?"

Horrified, Grace turned away from him as a blast of wind raked over her hair, her gown, as if trying to peel back her saintly layers in order to reveal the darkness of her heart.

A scream from across the deck brought their gazes to Madame Dubois, who was swatting at Spyglass with her parasol. "Infernal beast!" she shouted, but the cat was far too swift, darting across the bulwarks back and forth as if taunting the lady.

Captain Dubois chuckled and leaned his elbows on the railing.

"Aren't you going to rescue your pet?" Grace asked as laughter erupted from the crew.

"Non. Spyglass does quite well on her own." His eyes met hers, playful mirth dancing across them, and again Grace thought she saw a hint of kindness lurking behind the hard shield. He took one last look at Claire and his features stiffened.

He faced Grace, studying her with that intensity that seemed to peer into her soul. He fingered a lock of her wayward hair.

She slapped his hand away. "You may be selling me as if I were cargo, but I do not belong to you, Captain."

"Do you not?" He gave her a rakish grin.

Grace attempted to stuff the loose curls back into her bun, but the traitorous strands refused to be pinned. She knew he could play with her hair if he wanted. Truth be told, he could do whatever he wanted with her.

Thunder bellowed in the distance, drawing the captain's gaze to the horizon.

"A storm approaches, mademoiselle."

She eyed him. "Yes, Captain, I fear it does."

CHAPTER 22

The brig rolled. Grace stumbled and raised her hand to the bulkhead to keep from falling. Rain pounded on the deck above her, sounding more like grapeshot than drops of water. Clutching the chain around her neck, she withdrew her cross and wobbled toward the porthole. Through the glass, lightning wove a smoky trail across the darkened sky. "Just a tiny squall," Father Alers had reassured her. "Nothing to worry about. This brig has been through much worse." Grace rubbed her fingers over the cross. Thunder growled. "Protect us, Lord," she whispered. A moan sounded from the other side of the cabin, reminding her she was not alone.

Turning around, Grace held her arms out in an effort to keep her balance over the teetering deck and ambled toward the mulatto woman who sat on the floor in the corner by the armoire—where she had been for the past two hours. Grabbing the table, Grace sank into the chair beside her.

Annette smiled but continued her work. In the light of a lantern she had tied to the armoire, Annette arranged a series of articles across a multicolored flag: an amulet, a string of beads, a rattle, and various polished stones.

The hairs on Grace's arm bristled. "May I ask what you are doing?"

The lady frowned but said nothing, as she had every time Grace had attempted conversation with her during the long night.

"There is no need to be frightened of me," Grace assured.

Annette's dark eyes lifted to hers as if searching the validity of her statement.

Grace forced a smile to her lips and wondered why the lady, who must be near her own age, held such a timid manner toward her. The brig pitched over a swell and Grace gripped the arms of the chair. Thunder hammered overhead, drowning out the sound of her nervous breathing, but only increasing the weight of heaviness that had fallen on her since the storm began.

"Living aboard this brig is quite a change from living at the Dubois estate." Grace once again attempted a light tête-à-tête with the woman. So often maligned by Madame Dubois and ignored by everyone else, Annette appeared lonely, withdrawn, in need of love and encouragement. And to think she was Captain Dubois's half sister. Did the captain know of the relation? If he did, he certainly made no attempt to acknowledge Annette.

The lady nodded and completed her arrangement. Black hair the color of coal tumbled over her left shoulder onto her plain cotton gown. With full lips, an aquiline French nose, and dark, mysterious eyes, the woman's beauty was unquestionable. The fact that she had been bred for that very quality made Grace's stomach sour. Yet, she reminded herself, regardless of the nefarious purposes for which man chose to bring life into the world, God had His own glorious plan for each precious soul. And this woman was as much a child of His as anyone else.

The sea roared against the hull. The deck rose and plunged, and Annette laid her hands over her trinkets, keeping them in place. Then staring at her display, she muttered words in a language Grace could not understand.

Words that sent a chill coursing through her.

Grace hugged herself as another blast of thunder rumbled through the planks of the brig.

"I cause the storm to cease," Annette said.

Grace eyed the lady, waiting for the smile, the laugh that would accompany such an astonishing statement, but with her lips in a firm line and her eyes staunch with sincerity, Annette remained unmoved.

"What do you mean?" Grace finally said. "How can you stop the storm?"

"With these charms." Annette waved a hand over her treasures. "And my prayers to the spirits of my ancestors."

Grace's stomach shriveled. The lady engaged in some kind of primitive religious ritual. No wonder Grace had felt a darkness, an oppression whenever she'd been in her presence, for she had learned from Reverend Anthony, her pastor in Charles Towne, that many of these ancient religions were mere covers for the worship of demons. An urge to rise and dash from the cabin surged within her, but she willed her breathing to steady and her face to remain placid.

Lightning flickered a deathly pale over the scene. Perhaps this was why the Lord brought Grace all this way—to deliver this girl from spiritual bondage. Grace's heart thumped wildly in her chest.

"Annette, I serve a God more powerful than the spirits of our ancestors."

The woman stared blankly at Grace. "I know. I felt His power when I met you."

Grace flinched even as a thrill went through her. "You did?"

"Why do you not pray and sacrifice to Him to stop the storm?"

Grace fingered her cross, appealing to God for the right words to say to this girl. "I have been praying. But there is no longer a need to offer sacrifices to God, because He offered His own Son as a final sacrifice for all people everywhere."

"He sacrifice His Son?" She shook her head, her brow pinching. "Why would He do that? C'est fou."

"He did it because He loves us all so much." Grace reached out her hand to Annette. "He loves you, Annette."

Refusing Grace's hand, Annette lowered her gaze. "No one loves me. I am a possession: one of Monsieur Dubois's prize mares. I am caught between two worlds, the ones of my ancestors and the world of the whites."

She said the last word with such hatred, it made Grace jump. "God loves you, Annette. Of that I am sure. He wants you to become part of His family. And if you do, you'll never feel lost again."

Annette tossed her long hair over her shoulder and sighed as if considering Grace's words. She lifted her chin, and her eyes glistened with tears.

The door crashed open and in flounced Madame Dubois. Turning, she slammed the oak slab in the face of whoever had escorted her to the cabin and then flung herself onto the bed.

Grace slouched in her chair at the woman's poor timing. A few more minutes and she may have been able to lead Annette down the path to a new life.

Instead, Annette's eyes widened as she shoved her trinkets into a burlap sack and jumped to her feet, no doubt in expectation of her mistress's command.

Which came within seconds. "Annette, come here. Help me undress. These bindings are squeezing the breath from me."

Grace cringed at the fear on the mulatto's face. "How was your dinner?" She turned to face Madame Dubois, who stood and clung to the bulkhead while Annette began untying the laces of her bodice. "Horrible. Simply horrible," she sobbed. "Rafe was in such a foul humor, and he barely spoke to me at all." Annette removed the ties from Madame Dubois's skirt and began unlacing the stomacher as the woman continued her groaning, only exacerbated by the rise and swoop of the brig that nearly sent her tumbling to the plank floor.

After regaining her stance, Madame Dubois shot a fiery gaze at Grace. "It was as if he blamed me for your not attending."

Grace laughed. "I am his prisoner. What does he expect?"

"That is exactly what I told him." Madame Dubois batted Annette away and sank onto the bed. "He barely touched his food—which was the same vicious sludge they serve us here, je vous assure—and his crew was quite *désagréable*."

Grace could well attest to that. "At least you are free from your husband's brutality, madame. Isn't that what you wished?"

She dabbed at her tears. "Oui."

Thunder roared from a distance, and the rain faded to a light tapping. Grace leaned toward Madame Dubois, trying to squelch her anger at the woman's selfishness. "Captain Dubois will not allow you to go back to such suffering, I am sure of it."

Madame Dubois nodded, her curls bobbing. "He intends to put me on a ship to Virginia when he makes anchor at Kingston."

"That is good news, is it not? Then you can live safely with your relatives."

"Non!" she shouted, causing Annette to jump. "I do not want to live with them." Her blue eyes turned to icy daggers. She waved Grace away. "Zut alors, what do you know?"

Grace closed her eyes beneath the woman's scorn as the depth of her deception became all too clear. "Then your plan was never to go to Charles Towne with me." She muttered the words without question.

In reply, Madame Dubois lay back upon her bed and resumed her sobbing.

Forcing down her rising fury, Grace stood, grabbed her blankets, and began arranging them into a makeshift bed on the floor beneath the porthole. Though she had tried to sleep in the hammocks the captain had provided, she'd been unable to get comfortable, preferring the hard deck to the swaying confinement of the tight bands of cloth. Finally she lay down, ignoring her stiff back, and soon drifted to sleep to the rumbling sound of receding thunder, the pitter-patter of rain, and Madame Dubois's incessant whimpering.

Hours later, Grace stirred, alerted by whispers across the room. Recognizing the voices as those of Madame Dubois and Annette, Grace's heart settled to a normal beat, and she attempted to fall back asleep, but the content of those words kept her awake.

"Do you promise me this will work?" Madame Dubois asked.

"Oui, madame. It works for many generations."

Silence for a minute. "Uhh, it tastes terrible."

"Oui, what is that compare to love?" Annette said.

"How long before it begins to take effect?"

"It work right away, but you must also give this to the captain."

A sigh. "I do not see how, but I will find a way."

Shuffling, swishing of a nightdress, and Grace heard the creak of Madame Dubois's bed as she crawled beneath her coverlet. Within minutes the sound of her deep breaths filled the room. Grace had just begun to ponder the meaning of what she had heard when footsteps tapped over the deck. The door creaked open and then thumped closed. Annette had left.

Grace sat up and braced her back against the bulkhead, gathering her blankets to her chest. Fear gripped her for the woman's safety. Perhaps Annette had never been on a ship before. Perhaps she didn't realize the dangers lurking among the less-than-scrupulous crew. Grace prayed for her. Minutes passed, and she stood and began to pace. But when Annette didn't return after an hour, Grace donned her bodice and skirts, checked to ensure Madame Dubois slept peacefully, and slipped into the companionway.

Though the storm had long since passed, the lanterns in the hallway had not been relit, and Grace chided herself for not bringing one of her own. Groping her way along the bulkhead toward Captain Dubois's cabin, she drew a shaky breath of the stale air. The scents of moist wood, tar, and a hint of tobacco filled her nose. Thunder growled in the distance, and Grace halted and hugged herself. A thick blackness crowded around her. Up ahead, a blade of light sliced the darkness beneath the captain's cabin door. He was awake. A knot formed in her throat. She knew it was not only improper but dangerous to go to his cabin alone late at night, but she didn't dare search the ship on her own, and she feared something terrible had befallen Annette.

CHAPTER 23

Rafe propped his boot on the ledge of the stern windows and stared at the retreating storm, barely visible in the predawn gloom. Yet as each cloud rolled from the sky, one by one the stars appeared, clear and sparkling against the ebony backdrop. He wished for the same clarity in his thoughts. Yet they remained as cloudy and turbulent as the storm that had just passed.

He took a swig from his bottle, the taste of brandy souring in his mouth. He set it down and pressed a palm against his forehead, trying to stop the incessant droning in his head. Too much liquor again. When Mademoiselle Grace had not appeared at dinner, his mood had grown peevish. He could not explain it. Perhaps it was because her absence had left him at the mercy of Claire's attentions. Attentions that had only further soured his mood. Attentions that had become nauseating to him. Six months ago—non, even two months ago—he would have sold all he had to win back Claire's love. Now, he was not so sure. He was not sure about anything.

Rafe began to pace. Yet Claire's obvious pursuit of him presented him with the perfect opportunity—an opportunity for *la vengeance*. He could steal Claire back from his father and cause the man as much suffering as he had caused Rafe. The impending victory—so close he could taste it—turned to ash in his mouth when he thought of Mademoiselle Grace.

Next to her, Claire was a spoiled schoolgirl with her vain mannerisms and constant bickering. Had she always been that way? Or perhaps Mademoiselle Grace made Claire seem abhorrent by comparison. Everyone paled in comparison to the mademoiselle.

But she betrayed you. The icy voice chanted in Rafe's head, stabbing his heart.

Oui, she did. Just like Claire. Rafe rubbed his temples. Maybe she was no different after all.

Then why did Mademoiselle Grace's actions and her words lead him to the opposite conclusion? The conclusion that she was an angel—a pure, kindhearted angel sent by God.

Wolves appear in sheep's clothing.

Rafe plucked a cheroot from his pocket and lit it in the lantern. He took a puff and plopped down on the ledge. But he was no imbecile. And he would not allow himself to be fooled by her charms.

Spyglass jumped onto the ledge and swung her one eye upon him—a reprimanding eye, a condemning eye. Rafe winced beneath a stab of unfamiliar conviction, and he waved the cat away. "She has you fooled, le chat stupide."

The cat yawned and licked her paws, unmoved by his accusations. Then, slinking by his leg, she crawled into his lap. With his free hand, Rafe caressed her. "So you wish to make friends again, non?" The fresh scent of the mademoiselle filled his nostrils, sealing the cat's betrayal even as the smell brought visions of her flooding into his mind.

"You have been with her!" He pushed the cat away. "Traître."

Spyglass gave him a cursory glance then leapt onto his desk and turned the other way.

But too late; Rafe could not force the mademoiselle from his mind. He took a draught of his cheroot and stared out the window, wondering what it would be like to be loved by such a woman.

Tap tap tap.

Rafe groaned, not wishing to leave his dream world just yet. "Entrez-vous."

The door squeaked open and light footsteps sounded, but Rafe continued staring out the window, hoping whoever it was would see he was occupied and go away. When no voice beckoned him, he swung around, ready to spew a string of blasphemies at the sailor who dared disturb him.

It was no filthy sailor who met his blurry gaze, no unkempt man, but a lady dressed in shimmering silk with skin the color of pearls and hair the color of the night—a glowing vision of the woman who hounded his dreams.

She jerked back at what must have been a look of desire on his face.

"Mademoiselle Grace." The words slid like silk off his brandy-drenched lips. He rose from the ledge and stamped his cheroot onto a tray.

"Captain." She clasped her hands together and took a step toward him.

Her shapely form spiraled in his gaze like smoke from a fire, and he inhaled a deep breath, hoping her scent would find its way to his nose. But all he could smell was the sting of his own tobacco and brandy.

"I came to. . .". Her bottom lip quivered. "I mean to say. . ." Fear skittered across her green eyes. "Forgive me. I shouldn't have come." She whirled about.

"Non. Please do not leave." He took no care to remove the pleading from his voice.

She slowly turned to face him. "You have been drinking."

Rafe wove around his desk, approaching her slowly so as not to frighten her off. "When am I not drinking?" He grinned.

She frowned as Spyglass jumped from the desk and began slinking around the lacy hem of her skirts.

Rafe continued toward the apparition, wondering if his brandy-hazed mind had only conjured up the focus of his recent thoughts. Where was his anger when he needed it? She had lied to him, betrayed him, and with the worst possible person—his father. But right now he could think of nothing else but that he must touch her. He must discover if she was real. And if she was, what other reason could she have for coming to his cabin at this hour of night besides the one that heated his blood?

He halted before her. She lowered her chin, and he allowed his gaze to soak her in from head to toe.

She cleared her throat and shifted nervously, then started to take a step away from him. Rafe touched her arm. The warmth of her soft flesh rose from beneath her sleeve to his fingertips.

Oui. She was real.

In that moment, he would forgive her betrayal, would forgive her deception, if only. . .if only she would love him. If only she would take away the emptiness in his soul.

Rafe ran his thumb over her cheek. Breath escaped her parted lips, but she did not retreat. Lifting her thick black lashes, she gazed at him with those emerald eyes, searching his face for something—if he knew what it was, he would gladly give it to her.

"Please do not sell me to the don, Captain," she whispered in a pleading tone, perhaps sensing his weakened condition.

Rafe ground his teeth together to keep from proclaiming what his heart longed to shout—that he would never do anything to harm her.

She lowered her gaze. "Is there naught I can do to persuade you to change your course?"

"Perhaps." He grinned, allowing his thoughts the freedom to roam into dangerous seas. Had she come to offer herself to him? Though every ounce of his flesh yearned for it to be true, a part of him would die of disappointment if it were. He took a deep breath, trying to clear his swirling head, and cursed himself for drinking so much brandy. Her womanly scent tickled his nose, and his body warmed at her closeness. He reached toward her. She flinched but did not back away. He fingered a lock of her raven hair, relishing the silky feel.

"You wear your hair loose for me, non?"

"No." She started to retreat, but Rafe touched her arm again, halting her.

He swept the back of his fingers over her neck, her jaw, her chin, lifting it. The look in her eyes nearly sent him reeling backward. Where was the hatred that had burned within them the last time they were on this brig? He would have expected it to have returned in full force after he kidnapped her again. But all he saw in its place was concern, admiration, and dare he hope, a shred of ardor.

"You have not answered my question," she said.

"En fait, I have had my doubts as to my present course." It was true enough, although he had not changed his mind about selling her. His fury had continued to fuel his resolve to do so, but at the moment he felt both weakening.

She placed a hand on his arm but immediately lowered it. "Perhaps God is convicting you of your wrongdoing."

Spyglass meowed as if in agreement.

"Oui." Rafe continued caressing her chin, wondering why she allowed him such liberties. Peut-être he had been wrong about her innocence. As he had been wrong about Claire's. "Or perhaps I can be persuaded to choose the right course." He swallowed against a burst of desire.

She regarded him with cynicism and a flicker of hope. "How so?"

He brushed a curl from her face. "Stay with me tonight."

A tiny line formed between Mademoiselle Grace's brows. It deepened. Her chest heaved, and she took a step back. Anger flashed across her eyes.

"How dare you suggest such a thing?" She raised her hand and slapped him across his cheek.

Rafe could have stopped her, but somewhere deep down inside, he knew he deserved her scorn. The sting radiated across his jaw and over his face, but it did nothing to ease his roaring conscience. He rubbed his cheek and grinned. If she had been any other woman, he would have dismissed her immediately, angry that his passions had been aroused for no reason. But not this woman. Delight surged within him at her rejection, for he would not have expected any other reaction.

Rafe stomped to his desk and took a swig from an open bottle. "Do you find me so repulsive that you would rather become a slave than spend an evening with me?" The thin gray line of dawn spread across the horizon. Wiping his mouth with his sleeve, he turned to face her. "I thought I saw some attraction, even longing in your eyes, non?"

"No." She snapped. "'Tis the drink that clouds your mind." She hugged herself. "You are naught but a French rogue. And you will not add me to your list of conquests."

He shrugged. "You may regret that decision someday."

"You flatter yourself, Captain."

"There are many women who would count themselves fortunate to receive my affections."

"Then they may have you."

"And yet you came crawling to my cabin late at night. What am I to think?"

Spyglass meowed, and Mademoiselle Grace scooped her up and held her against her chest.

Rafe leaned back onto his desk. "Sacre mer, you give more affection to my cat than to me."

"Spyglass isn't going to sell me to a don."

"Peut-être, if you give me the same attention, I will not either."

"'Tis not the same affection you seek."

"Oui, mais a much more enjoyable one." Rafe grinned at the way his words made her squirm.

She stiffened her jaw and met his gaze. "The affections of which you speak are sacred and meant only for marriage, not as a bargaining tool." She set Spyglass onto the floor. "I have never even kissed a man and do not intend to do so until I am betrothed."

Never kissed a man. Sacre mer. Her innocence stunned Rafe. "How difficult it must be to keep such strong passions contained."

"Strong?" She huffed. "You fool yourself, Captain. And it is not difficult to do the will of God."

"For la prude pieuse as you are, perhaps, mon petit chou."

She stiffened her lips. "So now I am a pious prude and a cabbage?"

He grinned and stroked his mustache.

"You are a brute when you drink." She swept her sharp eyes to his.

A twinge grated over Rafe's conscience.

"It does not become you, or any man, to benumb himself with alcohol. How can you behave like a gentleman when your senses, your very soul is thus bewitched?" The haughty reprimand faded from her gaze, replaced by one of appeal.

Grabbing the half-empty bottle of brandy, Rafe studied the amber liquid. It had always brought him relief from the pains of life. It had always been his friend when no one else cared. Yet at that moment he would gladly abandon it to see the approval swim back into Mademoiselle Grace's green eyes.

He made his way toward his bed and poured the contents of the bottle into his chamber pot. "Anything for you, mademoiselle."

She blinked and clutched the chain around her neck.

He started toward her, but she held up a hand. "Enough of this. Captain, I have forgotten myself. I came to tell you that Annette has disappeared."

Rafe halted. "Annette? Claire's lady's maid?"

Mademoiselle Grace nodded. "She left the cabin more than an hour ago and has not returned. I thought you should know."

Rafe sighed. This lady cared for everyone, regardless of status. "You were right to tell me." He grabbed his rapier, slung it into his sheath, and then added his pistols. "I will escort you back to your cabin." Rafe held out his arm, hoping she'd take it, but not expecting her to after his performance.

She hesitated, then started to raise her hand, giving him a flicker of hope.

Monsieur Thorn barreled into the room. His wild gaze shifted curiously between them before he inclined his head toward Rafe.

Mademoiselle Grace lowered her hand.

Rafe ground his teeth together. "Sacre mer. What is it, Monsieur Thorn?"

"A ship, Captain, a mile astern and bearing down upon us fast. And from the looks of her, 'tis Captain Howell again."

Rafe shook his head and ran a hand through his hair, trying to shake away the alcoholic daze. "How did he find me again so soon?"

"Bad luck, perhaps, Captain?" Monsieur Thorn's grin sent a sliver of unease through Rafe that he had no time to question. While in Port-de-Paix, Rafe had sent a post to Governor Woodes in New Providence, demanding an explanation for the misunderstanding, but of course he wouldn't have received it yet.

In the meantime, Rafe would have to deal with this imbecile Howell or any other captain, who dared try and sink him for piracy.

CHAPTER 24

Slowly closing the door so as not to awaken Madame Dubois, Grace crept across the squeaky deck toward her bedding. The faint glow of dawn filtered in through the tiny window and alighted upon Annette, who was sitting on the edge of Madame Dubois's cot.

Grace jumped, not expecting to find anyone stirring at this hour, least of all Annette, who she supposed was still wandering about the brig. Taking a breath to still the rapid thumping of her heart, Grace opened her mouth to question the mulatto, but Madame Dubois's shrill voice from the bed interrupted her.

"There you are. Where have you been?" Her tone lacked the usual sharpness, almost as if the energy required to speak the words stole her breath away.

Ignoring her, Grace moved to the chair and took a seat. "Annette, you are safe! I was so worried."

"Worried? About me?" Annette circled her fingers around a small vial in her hand.

"I heard you leave last night." Grace tried to rub the heaviness from her eyes. "And when you didn't return, I went to beg the captain's assistance to find you." Grace gestured toward the door where she'd parted ways with Captain Dubois, the warmth of his touch still lingering on her fingertips.

"You were with Rafe?" Madame Dubois struggled to rise, but sank back onto her pillows with a moan.

Shouts blared from above, followed by the booming snap of sails catching the wind. The brig canted, and Grace clasped the arms of the chair.

"I was not *with* the captain." Grace's harsh tone surprised her as did the unusual guilt grinding over her conscience. She had done nothing wrong. Except be alone with the captain in his cabin. Except allow him to caress her cheek and glide his fingers through her hair.

Annette stared aghast at Grace as the same oppressive heaviness that always surrounded the mulatto woman filled the cabin and clung to Grace like a dense fog. She hugged herself and ran a wary gaze over the shadowy bulkheads, expecting to find the source of the eerie feeling in the form of a hovering specter.

Madame Dubois laid a hand on her forehead and moaned. "Why worry about Annette? I am the one who needs *l'assistance*."

Grace sank to her knees beside the cot, chiding herself for not noticing the woman's distress. "Are you ill?" She lifted her hand to lay it upon Madame Dubois's cheek, but the woman swatted it away.

"Non, je suis *affligée*."

"Madame suffers from a broken heart," Annette offered, shoving the vial into the sleeve of her cotton gown.

A broken heart? The captain's history with Madame Dubois became all the more obvious as time went on. Grace's stomach curled at the thought of what must have occurred between them, before or after her marriage to his father. She didn't want to know. She bit her lip, shifting her thoughts back to the present and the suspicious vial stashed in Annette's sleeve.

She looked at Annette. "And you have the cure?"

The woman made no reply. She gazed at her mistress, then grabbed a damp cloth from the table and dabbed it on Madame Dubois's forehead.

Grace rose from her chair and went to gather her bedding. The ship pitched, and she threw a hand against the bulkhead to keep from falling. The mad gurgle of the Caribbean dashing past the hull filled the room, unsettling her nerves. Setting her blankets atop the chair, Grace faced Annette. "Where were you last night?"

The mulatto raised her dark eyes to Grace's, then lowered them again, but not before Grace caught a flicker of fear crossing them. "I stopped the storm."

The hairs on Grace's arm bristled. Indeed the storm had ceased, but whether it had anything to do with Annette's prayers, Grace could not say—did not want to even consider. Though she knew the forces of darkness were powerful, she shuddered to think they could be acting within such close range.

Madame Dubois groaned. "Oh, who cares about Annette! Go get Rafe. I need to see him." She waved a hand toward her maid. "Help me up, Annette. I want to look *présentable*."

BOOM! Cannon shot rumbled through the brig, shaking the timbers and echoing like the voice of God off the bulkheads.

Grace dashed to the window. Black smoke curled past the salt-streaked panes.

"Zut alors!" Madame Dubois shot up in bed. "Are we under attack?"

"Stay here," Grace ordered, rushing out the door and slamming it behind her without awaiting a response. Clutching her skirts, she bolted up the ladder and sprang onto the deck. If they were to be involved in another battle, she intended to face it head-on and not risk being blown to bits below deck without a moment's warning.

Sailors scrambled across the brig, some carrying cannonballs and others muskets, pistols, and axes. Men hauled ropes or flung themselves aloft—all of them mumbling curses as they went. Scanning the raucous mob, Grace's eyes found Captain Dubois. He stood with boots planted firmly apart on the quarterdeck, flanked by Mr. Thorn and Father Alers. His gray waistcoat and purple sash flapped in the breeze behind him. Beneath his hat, black hair streamed like liquid coal. With a spyglass pressed to his eye, he surveyed something off their stern as he bellowed orders to his first mate.

The brig crested a wave, and Grace stumbled but managed to make her way to the larboard railing. Wind too hot for so early in the morning struck her like the opening of an oven. The acrid scent of gunpowder stung her nose. The sun peeked over the horizon, transforming the crest of each wave into sparkling silver. Squinting against the brightness, Grace leaned over and glanced astern. In the distance, the curve of two red sails flamed in the rising sun. White foam swept over the oncoming ship's bow as she closed the distance between them.

Captain Howell's ship, the *Avenger*.

Grace rubbed her eyes as the sun glinted off a slight movement beyond the pursuing ship. Suddenly a pyramid of brimming white sails slipped into view.

"Two sails! Two sails!" A man yelled from aloft.

Grace swallowed, wondering if the other ship could be her sister's. But she knew her hope was in vain. Even if the sailor had kept his word to deliver her post to Charles Towne, Faith would not have had time to catch up with them yet. She gazed at the two ships swooping through the azure waters, fast on *Le Champion*'s stern. *Oh Lord, please be with us.* The brig rose and plunged over a wave, showering her with a spray of seawater and sending foamy water onto the deck, soaking her shoes.

The captain leaned toward Mr. Thorn and said something that sent the first mate leaping down the quarterdeck ladder, Father Alers on his heels. Surprise widened the first mate's eyes as he passed Grace, but he tipped his hat and continued on his way, dropping below deck. Father Alers halted beside her.

"You should go below, mademoiselle." He grabbed her arm, but Grace resisted and shook her head. "Did we fire a cannon?"

"Oui. A warning shot only. Maintenant." He gestured toward the companionway.

"Please let me stay, Father." Grace gave him a pleading look. "I promise I won't cause any trouble."

His shoulders slumped and he quirked a brow. "Only if you stop calling me Father."

Grace smiled. "Forgive me, but the title sits so well upon you."

He snorted and folded his hands over his prominent belly. A hint of a smile slanted his lips. "Très bien. Mais, I will stay with you. Non?"

"Didn't the captain give you some task to do?"

"Oui." He smiled. "To watch over you." The older man took a position beside her.

Mr. Thorn soon returned with a rolled-up chart in hand and rejoined his captain. Together, they spread it atop the binnacle, held it down against the buffeting wind, and examined it for several minutes. Finally, the captain rolled it up and handed it to Mr. Thorn with a nod. He glanced across the main deck, and his gaze found hers.

Delight brightened his eyes for a moment but quickly faded into annoyance. He gripped the hilt of his rapier and turned to face Mr. Atton at the helm. "Set a course west by south, Monsieur Atton." Then shifting to Mr. Thorn, "All hands aloft, Monsieur Thorn!" he bellowed. "Let fall the topsails and gallants!" Mr. Thorn repeated the commands, sending sailors leaping into the ratlines.

With straining cordage and creaking blocks, the ship swung slowly to starboard, and Grace clutched the railing to keep from falling. Above her, men who looked more like monkeys balanced on ropes no thicker than her wrists as they unfurled the white canvas to catch the swift Caribbean breeze. Sails flapped and thundered hungrily but soon found their satisfaction when an influx of wind filled their white bellies. Grace lowered her gaze to Captain Dubois. With Mr. Thorn beside him, he pointed to something off their starboard bow. She glanced in that direction and saw naught but an eternity of turquoise waves.

When she turned back around, the captain stood before her. She let out a gasp and clutched her throat as his dark gaze drank her in. She lowered her chin. Placing a finger beneath it, he raised her face until she was forced to look at him.

"I found Annette. She is safe." Grace winced at the stutter in her voice.

"I am happy to hear it."

His touch brought back memories of their time in his cabin, and shame struck her. Shame she had allowed him such intimacies, shame she had enjoyed the way his touch made her feel. And now as he stood so close to her, strands of his black hair grazing his stubbled jaw, all those feelings came flooding back.

What was happening to her? She should not be feeling such wanton sensations. Sensations that clouded her judgment and befogged her mind so that she did not remember why she'd gone to the captain's cabin in the first place. Not until she had slapped the captain and he'd stepped away from her.

Yet regardless of her inner turmoil, she had not deserved his salacious invitation. She called her anger forward, hoping the force of it would dissolve her shame and confusion.

He released her chin. "Go below, mademoiselle."

"Please, Captain, I do not wish to die in that tiny cabin."

"No one dies today. There will be no battle."

Father Alers shifted his amber eyes between them curiously then scratched his thick beard. "No battle? I have never seen you run, Rafe."

Captain Dubois huffed out a sigh and gazed at the ships bearing down on them. "I have already bested this buffoon in a challenge once. But we are no match for two ships. I know of an island to the southwest with many shallow inlets where we will be able to hide."

Grace followed his gaze to where the ships, though not advancing, had certainly not slackened in their pursuit. "But won't they see where we have gone?"

"*Le Champion* is shallow on the draft, mademoiselle. She can sail places other ships cannot." He doffed his hat and ran a hand through his hair. "Besides"—one side of his mouth lifted in that grin of his that sent her heart racing—"I have precious cargo aboard that I do not wish harmed."

"Yes, we wouldn't want your valuable *cargo* destroyed," she retorted.

"Non. We would not." He lifted a brow and replaced his hat.

"Captain, a moment, please." Mr. Thorn hailed him from the quarterdeck and after inclining his head toward her, Captain Dubois joined his first mate.

Thankful he seemed to have forgotten he'd ordered her below, Grace whirled around, gripped the railing, and closed her eyes. The hot wind, tainted with brine and fish and wood, whipped over her, loosening her hair from its pins. But she no longer cared, having grown long since weary of the battle to keep it properly pinned in place. Besides, she could not deny how free she felt as the wind spread its whispery fingers through her curls. *Mercy me, how I have changed.* But was it for the best?

Father Alers cleared his throat. "Le capitaine *est bien épris avec vous,* mademoiselle."

Grace snapped her eyes open and stared at him aghast, amazed at both his statement and that she had understood it. "He is taken with any female, Fa. . .Mr. Alers."

He smiled, revealing a row of crooked teeth. "Oui, that is true. But not in the same way, je vous assure."

Grace shook her head. "He intends to sell me. Forgive me if I do not believe any interest he has in me goes beyond his own needs or those of his precious hospital." Her words swirled around her, taunting her with their duplicity, and she attempted to bat them away into the rising breeze. But she could not deny the goodness, the deep affection she had seen in Rafe's eyes—beyond all the anger, beyond the pain. Nor could she deny her own growing feelings for him, conflicted as they were.

Father Alers brushed gray spikes of hair from his face and gave her a knowing look. "It is a sin to tell a fib, mademoiselle."

Angry that the man read her thoughts so easily, Grace folded her arms over her chest. "He kidnapped me—twice. What more is there to say?" Yet truth be told, his capture of her this time seemed to spring from some deep pain within him rather than any desire to harm her.

Father Alers raised a sardonic brow. Ignoring him, Grace pursed her lips and glanced behind at the two ships that were fast on their heels. A sudden fear clamped her heart. From what she'd seen of Governor Woodes's men, they were no better than pirates. Glad for a chance to change the subject, she faced Father Alers. "Will they catch us?"

"Non." He laid his hand upon hers on the railing. His warm fingers scratched her skin like rough rope. But she found it oddly soothing. "Rafe is the best capitaine I have seen," he added.

Grace chuckled. "I do not know whether that should make me happy or sad."

Father Alers's golden eyes twinkled in the rising sun as the light cast shadows over the crevices in his face. Yet nothing but warmth beamed from his expression.

"Land ho!" a booming voice echoed from the crosstrees. Grace scanned the horizon, and minutes later a gray mound rose from the azure water like the back of a crocodile. The captain barked a series of orders, sending his men scurrying across deck. Off their stern, the two ships maintained a fast pursuit, and Grace could not imagine how the captain expected to hide from them.

Flying through the water with every inch of canvas set to the breeze, *Le Champion* sped toward the burgeoning mass of land.

"Watch your luff, Monsieur Atton!" Captain Dubois barked, stomping across the deck. Though Grace tried to avoid looking at him, she found her gaze drawn to the captain as if a spell had been cast upon her that only the sight of him could appease. Never once did his voice wobble in fear, never once did he seem confused, unsure, or hesitant. He commanded his men with naught but confidence and authority. Grace faced the sea again, chiding herself for admiring anything about the rogue.

Within minutes, the small island loomed large before them, and Captain Dubois brayed a string of orders that brought the brig on a sharp tack around the western peninsula.

"Trice up, men," the captain bellowed. "Shorten sail!"

Shielding her eyes from the sun high in the sky, Grace watched as the men, dangling in the shrouds, hauled in the canvas on fore- and mainmasts. With only her topsails fluttering in the light breeze, the brig slowed, and without hesitation, the captain sailed her into the entrance of an oblong harbor riddled with sandbars and reefs.

Grace followed the captain's gaze off their stern, but the pursuing ships were nowhere in sight.

"She's shoaling fast, Captain," Mr. Thorn shouted, examining the lead and line that one of the crewmen had just pulled up from the water.

"Keep me informed." Captain Dubois jumped onto the quarterdeck and relieved Mr. Atton of his duty at the helm.

The captain stood at the wheel while his men hung over the bow, directing him which way to steer the brig. Another man tossed the lead and line repeatedly over the side, shouting out the dwindling depths of the sea. Grace leaned over the railing. She could make out the dim bottom of the sandy bay beneath the brig. Sharp, jagged reefs rose from the depths like sharp talons searching for a victim. One slip and their hull would be penetrated and all would be lost.

She raised her gaze to the pristine white shores of the island that framed the small harbor. Sand, sparkling like white jewels in the sunlight, fanned up to a lush web of greens and browns, making up the forest. The scent of tropical flowers and fruit wafted over Grace and she drew a deep breath. The smell of land—land where she was not to be sold. Not yet.

Hushed whistles alerted Grace to another female on deck, and she turned to see Annette dashing toward her. Fear flashed from her brown eyes.

"What is it, Annette?" Grace grabbed her hands.

"Madame Dubois. She is ill. You must come at once."

❧

After Mademoiselle Grace disappeared below, the deck of *Le Champion* groaned as if lamenting her absence. As did Rafe—an internal, silent groan. He had allowed her to remain above for the sole purpose of enjoying the occasional glances he stole of her when she was not looking. Her presence had a calming influence on him that he could not explain.

"Weigh anchor!" Mr. Thorn shouted, and the massive iron hook struck the water with a resounding splash. Within seconds the thick rope snapped taut and the brig jerked to a stop. Captain Dubois jumped down to the main deck, peering over both sides to ensure their safe distance from the reefs. Then raising the spyglass, he studied the wide mouth of the harbor.

"Any sign of them, Captain?" Monsieur Thorn asked.

"Non." He lowered the glass. "If luck is with us, they did not see which inlet we slipped into."

Mr. Weylan approached, a group of sailors following him like a foaming wake. "Capitaine, what is your plan?" The second mate adjusted his feathered hat and put his hands upon his waist. "We cannot stay here forever."

Ayes and grunts tumbled from behind him.

Rafe flattened his lips, feeling his ire rise at this new provocation.

"We will wait for an opportunity to slip by them." He forced confidence into his voice then studied his crew. The men's loyalties shifted like waves tossed in a storm, the respect he usually found in their eyes in short supply.

"What if they trap us?" Monsieur Legard asked, peering from behind Weylan.

"They cannot see us from the entrance to the harbor." Rafe pressed a finger over his mustache. "We will leave under cover of darkness."

The lines on Monsieur Weylan's face folded, and he scratched his matted hair.

"What else, Monsieur?" Rafe sighed in frustration.

"The men are unhappy, Capitaine. We have not been paid in over two months."

Rafe gripped the hilt of his rapier, his muscles tensing for a fight. He felt Monsieur Thorn stiffen beside him, but when Rafe glanced his way, a slight smile sat smugly upon his first mate's lips.

"And now we are delayed again," another sailor shouted. "When do we sell the woman?"

Rafe ground his teeth together. "I am to meet the don in seven days." Yet the thought of making that appointment ate away at Rafe's gut.

He eyed his men in turn. "With me as your capitaine, have you not lined your pockets with more coins than you could spend? *Où est votre confiance?*" Rafe frowned. How could he blame them? He was not sure he trusted himself anymore. But to let them see his hesitation, his doubt, would be certain death.

"I am still the capitaine of this brig. Unless one of you wishes to challenge me?" Rafe leveled a stern gaze at each man and then glanced over the sailors on the quarter and foredecks who'd gathered at the first sign of an altercation. "*Personne?*"

Some of his men stared blankly back at him; others shook their heads.

"Non. Of course not, Capitaine." Weylan smiled, but in that slick smile Rafe saw the makings of a mutiny.

Rafe narrowed a gaze upon him then glanced over the men. "Get back to work or I'll slice all of you through myself!" he barked, and the men scattered like flies before the whip of a horse's tail.

Then fisting his hands, Rafe spun around and stomped toward the companionway. In seven days' time he must either hand Mademoiselle Grace over to the Spanish don or face a mutiny—a mutiny he was sure would result in his death.

CHAPTER 25

Grace dabbed the moist cloth over Madame Dubois's forehead and cheeks. Heat radiated from the woman's skin as if it were a searing griddle. A lump formed in Grace's throat. She harbored no deep affection for the woman but certainly did not wish her any harm.

A soft moan slipped from Madame Dubois's lips, and she tossed her head across the pillow. Red blotches marred Claire's normally creamy skin, and dark circles hung beneath crystal blue eyes that were glazed with fever. Grace swallowed against her rising fear, laid the cloth down, and stood. Across the cabin, Annette rested on her bedding as if she hadn't a care in the world.

Making her way to the window, Grace peered out at the black sky, dusted with a myriad of twinkling stars. Her eyes ached from lack of sleep. She rubbed them and whispered a prayer. *Lord, please help me. Please help Madame Dubois.* As usual, God's voice was silent. *Where are You, Lord?* She scanned the endless expanse of night sky, remembering a time when her prayers were filled with faith. Now she couldn't affirm that God even heard her pleas, though certainly He had kept her alive to this point. But for what purpose?

Gentle waves licked the brig's hull. Somewhere up on deck, a fiddle moaned a sad tune, even as laughter bubbled up from the sailors' berth at the forecastle. Everything seemed so peaceful. Yet it was a delusory peace. For not far away lurked two fully armed ships ready to pound *Le Champion* into splinters and sink her into the sea. And within this tiny cabin one woman fought for her life, another lived as a slave, while the third would soon become one.

"Annette." The desperation in Madame Dubois's voice tugged at Grace's heart.

Annette glanced at her mistress, then closed her eyes, feigning sleep.

Grace moved to the cot. "'Tis me, Grace, madame." Retrieving the cloth, she patted it over her forehead. "How do you feel?"

Madame Dubois's lashes fluttered open. Blue eyes, sparkling in the lantern light, alighted upon Grace. "Where is Annette?"

"She is sleeping. But I am here, madame." Grace took the woman's hand in hers, wincing at the heat emanating from her skin, and surprised when the woman received her embrace without recoiling.

Madame Dubois's chest rose and fell, and she lifted a hand to her head. "What is wrong with me? Am I dying?"

"No, of course not." Grace attempted a comforting smile.

Rustling sounds rose from the corner, and Annette appeared beside them. Spyglass ceased her purring. Grace gave the mulatto a cursory glance before returning her gaze to Madame Dubois. "Can you eat something, madame?" The poor woman had not partaken of any food since last night.

"Je ne sais pas." Madame Dubois breathed out words barely above a whisper. "Perhaps."

"Annette," Grace said. "Would you please tell Father Alers to bring up some broth for Madame."

Annette blinked and gazed at her mistress as if she were an apparition before darting out the door.

Spyglass stretched on the table where she lay and began purring.

"My head hurts." Madame Dubois pressed her temples and turned toward Grace. "Where are we? Where is Rafe?"

"We are safe." Grace didn't want to add to the woman's stress by informing her of the two ships following them. "And Rafe, I mean Captain Dubois, is no doubt up on deck." Though Grace had not seen him for several hours.

Madame Dubois stared at Grace as if seeing her for the first time. The haughty sheen had dissipated from her eyes, along with the animosity that always fired from within them. "Why are you being so kind to me?"

Grace squeezed her hand. "Because you are ill. Surely you would do the same for me should I become waylaid by some malady."

Madame Dubois shook her head, a slight smirk upon her lips. "I do not think so."

Grace chuckled, knowing that in her delirium, the woman had spoken the truth. She released her hand and dipped the cloth back into a basin of water. Then wringing it out, she laid it over Madame Dubois's forehead. "It does not matter. I will care for you anyway."

"I do not deserve it," she muttered, her confession shocking Grace.

"None of us deserve anything good, madame." Grace flinched at her own words, wondering where they had come from. Yet tears filled her eyes as she realized how true they were. *For all have sinned, and come short of the glory of God. There is none righteous, no not one.*

The door creaked, and Annette entered, followed by Father Alers, a tray in hand. He ambled in and set it down on the table then eyed Madame Dubois with concern. The scent of lemons and beef broth swirled about the cabin. Annette closed the door and slunk into the shadows against the bulkhead.

Spyglass sat up, her ears perked.

"How is she?" Father Alers sank into the chair.

Grace shook her head. "I cannot cool her fever."

The old priest leaned forward in the chair and scratched his beard as if trying to conjure up a solution.

Grace stood. "It came upon her so suddenly. I've never seen such a thing."

A gasp came from the shadows, and Grace snapped her gaze toward Annette's dark form, wondering at the woman's odd behavior and then remembering the potion she had given Madame Dubois. "Do you know what happened to your mistress, Annette?" Her voice carried more accusation then she intended, and Annette cowered further into the shadows—so far Grace could not see her eyes.

"Non, mademoiselle," came her sheepish voice.

Father Alers gestured toward the tray. "Perhaps the broth will strengthen her."

"Do you have any herbs aboard, any feverfew, peppermint, or elderflower?" Grace clasped her hands together.

"Non."

"No one with medical knowledge?"

"Non." Father Alers shook his head.

A groan sounded from the cot. "Mademoiselle." Madame Dubois reached out her hand, and Grace fell to her knees and took it in her own.

"Yes, I am here, madame." She laid the back of her hand on Madame Dubois's cheek, then flinched at the heat radiating off her skin.

"I am dying." Her voice wobbled, and her chest rose and fell rapidly.

Visions of Grace's mother on her deathbed crept out from hiding and dashed tauntingly across Grace's mind. Madame Dubois looked so much like her: same blond hair, same striking blue eyes, and now the same feverish skin, same raspy voice, same delirium. Grace would not watch another woman die. "No, you will not die."

Father Alers handed Grace the bowl. "Help her drink this."

Gently placing her arm beneath Madame Dubois, Grace tried to lift her. "Madame, please drink this broth."

"Non. Non." She waved it away. "I cannot."

With a huff of defeat, Grace handed the bowl back to Father Alers, her heart sinking lower in her chest.

"Mademoiselle," the woman panted. "I must tell you something."

"You should rest, madame. Regain your strength." Grace wiped a saturated curl from her face.

"Non, s´il vous plaît. I must." She stopped to catch her breath. She peered at Grace below heavy lids and shook her head. "What you must think of me."

"It does not matter."

"I was not always like I am now." Madame Dubois swallowed and tried to gather her breath. "I grew up in France, in the small port town of La Havre. Mon père worked on the docks and ma mère washed clothes to make extra money. She was British like you."

"Shhh." Grace dabbed the cloth on her head, wondering why the woman cared to disclose her childhood now of all times.

"Mon père died in an accident. Ma mère died of the sickness two months later," she rasped.

Grace halted her ministrations. She had lost only one parent. She could not imagine the horror of losing both.

"I exist on the streets for many years." Madame Dubois coughed, and her face pinched in pain. "Then at sixteen I accept the King's offer to come to Saint Dominique to become wife to a planter."

Grace thought of Nicole. It would seem many of the women at Port-de-Paix shared the same past.

Madame Dubois squeezed her hand. "I never had enough *nourriture*. I never had *des belles robes*. I never had someone to love me. Comprenez-vous?" She lifted sincere eyes to Grace, and in that look, Grace no longer saw a vain, pretentious woman. She no longer saw a jealous shrew. She saw a frightened, innocent little girl.

Drawing Claire's hand to her lips, Grace kissed it and smiled. Her eyes moistened at the thought of what this woman had endured. "I cannot say that I completely understand, but I do empathize with your pain, for I too, have suffered loss." Grace wiped a tear pooling at the corner of Madame Dubois's eye. "Now you must rest and get well." Though by the rising heat on the woman's cheeks, Grace began to doubt that would happen.

Madame Dubois's breathing grew ragged and her lids closed. She turned her head and fell asleep. When Grace tried to wake her there was no response, not even a whimper. Leaning her head on the cot, Grace allowed her tears to fall. "Please, Lord, heal this woman. Please."

"She will not live." Annette's words pierced the air like a rapier.

Grace snapped her gaze toward the mulatto. "How can you say such a thing?"

Annette stepped out of the gloom into the lantern light. Malevolence, but also a spark of dread, burned in her brown eyes as she gazed at her mistress. Grace shivered.

Father Alers stood, the legs of his chair scraping over the planks of the deck.

"What have you done?" Grace asked as she rose and took a step toward her. Spyglass darted to the edge of the table, and shifted her one eye onto Annette.

The mulatto swallowed, her wide eyes sparking in the lantern light. "I gave her what she want, what she beg for."

Father Alers glanced over the cabin as if he, too, felt the darkening presence within, then he narrowed his eyes upon Annette. "And what did she ask for?"

"*Un philtre d'amour.*" She laughed. "To make her irrésistible to Captain Dubois."

Grace grabbed her arm. "A love potion? What was in it?"

"Nothing that would do any harm." Annette trembled, her gaze skittering to her mistress. "Except to one who has no heart."

If Annette had poisoned Madame Dubois, what hope did they have to save her? She thought to insist the mulatto give her an antidote, but from the look in her eyes, Grace didn't dare allow the woman to administer any further potions to her mistress. Blood surged to Grace's head even as her stomach knotted. "If Madame Dubois dies, her death is on your hands."

Tears swarmed into Annette's eyes, and she drew a ragged breath. "I gave her what she asked for," she repeated, her voice raised in fear. "It is the gods who decide if she deserves to live." She shuddered, tore her arm from Grace's hand, and dashed from the cabin, sobbing.

Grace started after her, but Father Alers held her in place. "Let her go. Our concern must be for Madame Dubois."

Spyglass curled into a ball again on the table.

Grace eyed the cat curiously then clutched the chain around her neck. "Yes. We must get her to port. We must find an apothecary."

"We cannot. Le Capitaine spotted one of Woodes's ships just outside the harbor entrance. Until they are gone or we have a moonless night, we are trapped in this cove." Father Alers pressed down the coils of his gray hair, but they sprang back into their chaotic web as soon as he withdrew his hand.

"So there is naught we can do for her." Grace glanced at Madame Dubois.

Father Alers crossed himself. "Nothing but pray."

❧

Thorn rubbed the back of his neck and took another turn across the foredeck. Unable to sleep, he'd dismissed the sailor on watch and took his place. He squeezed the muscles in his arms and stretched his back. Why was he so tense? Everything was going according to plan.

He slid his thumb over the scar stretching down his cheek and neck, a constant reminder to stay the course—to forge ahead until the vengeance that gnawed hungrily in his gut was satisfied. Glancing over the ebony waters of the bay, her shallow waves christened in silver moonlight, he smiled at the fortunate turn of events. Movement on the deck below caught his eye. A dark form ducked within the shadows by the starboard railing. One of the crew? No, the shape was far too small. Muffled sobs filled the air.

Thorn made his way down the foredeck ladder then crept across the main deck, trying not to alert whoever it was. But as he grew near, her sobs grew louder—for he could now tell it was a woman—a woman with hair the color of the night tumbling down her back. His heart leapt.

Annette.

He took another step toward her. His boot thumped. She whirled around to face him and let out a gasp, backing away.

He lifted a hand. "Don't be afraid. I heard you crying."

She glanced toward the companionway hatch then back at him, swiping the moisture from her cheeks.

"May I?" Thorn motioned to the spot beside her, hoping she would accept his company.

She said nothing. He slipped next to her and grabbed the railing. Trying to appear nonchalant, he glanced over the dark waters. "Beautiful night."

She sniffed and faced the harbor. "Oui."

Thorn took a deep breath, trying to still the thumping of his heart. He'd wanted nothing more than to speak to this dark beauty ever since she had boarded the brig, but her position and color created societal obstacles that had prevented him. Now, as she stood beside him, smelling of citrus and cedar, his senses inflamed. And all he wanted to do was discover the cause of her distress and stop her from crying. "Are you ill, mademoiselle?" He dared a glance at her. Her dark, thick lashes lowered to her cheeks that looked more like creamy *café* in the moonlight.

She shook her head. "My mistress is ill."

He nodded and leaned his elbow on the railing, trying to make out more of her exquisite features in the shadows. "I am sorry."

"Pas moi. I am not." Her French accent sharpened.

Thorn chuckled. She clicked her tongue and started to leave, but he grabbed her arm. "Please forgive me. I was not laughing at you. It is just that, well. . ." He released her, thankful when she stayed even though her suspicious gaze signaled she could bolt at any minute. "Your mistress is not a person to evoke much sympathy, non?" He mimicked her French, hoping it would please her and was rewarded with a tiny smile that set his heart soaring.

"Why do you, a white man, speak to me?" she asked, her sweet voice barely audible over the creaking of the ship.

Realizing he must look a fright, Thorn adjusted his coat and brushed dirt from his sleeve. "I have wanted to speak to you ever since you came aboard."

Her delicate brow folded. "*Pourquoi?*" She took a step back as if suddenly afraid of him.

He lifted a hand in an effort to assuage her fear but it only sent her farther away. "You misunderstand, mademoiselle. I have no untoward intentions. I only wish to get to know you."

"To know me?" She shook her head as if he'd said the moon were made of flour and milk.

"Yes. That is all." Thorn opened his palms in a gesture of innocence.

She faced the bay, the breeze dancing through her hair that reminded him of black silk. He longed to sift his fingers through it. "You are very beautiful."

She huffed in disgust. "Oui. It is what I was made for."

"Not all you were created for." Thorn laid a hand on her arm, but she snapped from his touch and shot fiery eyes his way. A cloud strayed over the moon, stealing Annette from his sight.

"Non? Mon père treats me as a slave. Ma mère is his mistress. And Madame Dubois despises me. I am half black, half white. The blancs shun me. The Africans are repulsed by the white blood in my veins. I live *suspendue* between two worlds, and I belong to none. I am nothing without my beauty. And if that is all you want from me, you must speak to Monsieur Dubois. I am sure you and he can make a good deal." Turning, she started to walk away, but Thorn jumped in her path, blocking her. He hoped she couldn't see the grin on his lips at her spirited oration. The woman was not only beautiful but full of pluck as well.

She tried to weave around him, but he grabbed her arm.

"Do not leave, Annette." His throat constricted beneath a sudden sorrow. Sorrow at a life so enshrouded with misery and rejection. "I assure you, I want nothing from you but your friendship." He peered in the darkness, longing to see her face. "I, too, find myself between two worlds. I am an Englishman on a French brig. I am a man of education and honor among a bevy of crude, ill-mannered sailors." He leaned toward her. The cloud abandoned its post, allowing the moon to bathe her in milky light. "We have much in common, mademoiselle."

She lifted her moist brown eyes to his. And in them he saw a spark of hope.

But then she looked away. "I must go," she said.

Thorn released her, and she dashed to the companionway ladder. Then casting one last glance his way, she disappeared below.

Thorn smiled and gazed up at the half-moon. If God listened to prayers, Thorn would thank Him for the moon tonight that kept them imprisoned within this cove. For if the white orb had not made an appearance, they would have attempted an escape in the darkness, and he may not have had the chance to become better acquainted with the alluring Annette.

In fact, each day they remained in this cove provided an opportunity for their refuge to be discovered.

Which could only bode well for Mr. Thorn.

And very badly for Rafe.

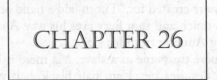

CHAPTER 26

At Father Alers's gruff "entrez-vous," Rafe entered the small cabin, Spyglass bounding in on his heels. The putrid stench of *infirmité* assaulted him and drew his eyes to the lithe, ghostly form lying on the cot amidst a tangle of blankets and golden hair. Thunder clapped outside, sending the brig aquiver with a sense of impending doom. Although storm clouds covered the tiny island, a few resolute rays of sunlight pierced the porthole into the tiny cabin.

Father Alers gazed at Rafe with those intense golden eyes, now filled with concern.

"*Comment va-t-elle?*" Rafe asked. When he had heard of Claire's illness, he assumed it was just another one of her tricks to get his attention.

Claire moaned and shifted on her coverlet.

Apparently, this time, Rafe had been wrong. He glanced across the cabin. Spyglass lapped broth from a bowl on the table. A jumble of blankets lay stuffed in one corner by the armoire alongside a candle, a necklace, and some stones.

"Where is Mademoiselle Grace?"

Father Alers stretched his legs out before him and folded his hands over his belly. "The mademoiselle went above for some air."

"Grace went above? *Sous la pluie?*" Rafe glanced at the porthole, where streaks of rain flattened beneath the prevailing wind.

Father Alers shrugged. "It stopped raining, and the poor mademoiselle has been attending Madame Claire throughout the night."

"*Vraiment?*" Though Rafe knew of the mademoiselle's charitable heart, he felt a twinge of shock that she would care for a woman who had done nothing but reproach her.

"*Oui*, the mademoiselle has been most *aimable* to Madame Dubois." Father Alers shook his head. "She returns each of Madame's insults with kindness."

Rafe scratched his jaw as his muscles stiffened in defiance of Grace's forgiving heart. Yet for as long as Rafe had known Father Alers, the man had dispensed his approbation of others as sparsely as he did the prize claret hidden in his trunk.

Claire moaned, and he stared at the red blotches marring her sweat-laden face. She had always been so beautiful. Even now, consumed with sickness, she still displayed the feminine charm he had once been unable to resist. Yet lately her beauty seemed more akin to a lovely gown of silk and lace—a garment one put on and took off and that faded and stained and wrinkled over time.

Rafe shifted his stance and spotted a cockroach scampering away. He smashed it with his boot, hoping to alleviate his aggravation.

"Where is Annette? She should be attending her mistress."

Father Alers's eyes took on a haunted look. "She ran out after Mademoiselle accused her of poisoning her mistress."

"Poisoning?" The word rebounded through Rafe's mind like round shot but found no place to land.

"Oui, un philtre d'amour." Father Alers snorted. "A potion to win your heart."

Claire moaned again and clamped her lips together. Spyglass finished lapping up the broth and begin licking her paws and washing her face.

A deep sorrow fell upon Rafe like the weight of an anchor, even as his anger burned. Why now? Why did Claire want so desperately to win back his heart now? When he no longer felt anything but pity for the woman. When his thoughts were constantly on another.

"Do you think Annette poisoned her?"

"*Qui sait?*" Father Alers quirked a brow. "For now, we must get Madame Dubois to an apothecary."

Claire's lashes fluttered, and she groaned. Father Alers wrung out a cloth and laid it atop her forehead.

Rafe stomped to the porthole. "We cannot. Woodes's ships cruise outside the harbor waiting to strike us as soon as we set sail."

Claire's eyes opened to tiny slits, and Father Alers removed the cloth. "We are trapped?"

"Non, I will think of something." Rafe flattened his lips and made his way to the cot.

"Rafe." Claire lifted a shaky hand toward him, and he knelt beside her, taking it in his. Whatever animosity he harbored against this woman, however much she had ripped out his heart and trampled upon it, he did not wish her dead.

Father Alers stood and pressed a hand on Rafe's back, then he stepped toward the door. "Can you sit with her for a minute? I need to make sure Yanez is attending his duties in the galley in my absence."

Rafe shook his head. What did he know about tending the sick?

But Father Alers waved him off. "I'll return straightaway." And then he was gone.

Rafe released Claire's hand, removed his rapier, and laid it on the table. Taking the chair Father Alers had vacated, he grabbed his baldric and began toying with the rough leather at its edge. Sweat beaded on the back of his neck as he glanced over the cabin, careful to avoid looking at the sick woman on the cot—the woman he had once loved, the woman he had intended to make his wife. Thunder rumbled outside, emulating the storm that raged within him. Fear, love, desire, hatred—all churned in a massive dark cloud hovering over his heart. A cloud that threatened to unleash a torrent on him at any moment.

Spyglass jumped into his lap, and he caressed her fur, thankful the cat had not completely abandoned her affections for him as everyone else seemed to have done.

"Rafe." Claire breathed his name on a sigh and turned her eyes upon him, once so clear, but now covered with a feverish haze. "You came to see me."

Rafe nodded and leaned forward, placing his elbows on his knees and forcing Spyglass from his lap.

Her breathing took on a rapid pace. "I fear I am dying."

Still Rafe said nothing, for he hated offering people vain hope only to ease their discomfort. And honestly, from the heat he'd felt sizzling from her skin, he could not deny that she spoke the truth.

"Do not look so pleased." She tried to laugh but coughed instead.

Thunder growled, and Spyglass meowed in reply then leapt to the foot of the cot and sprawled across the coverlet.

Rafe looked down at the tiny divots marring the deck. The brig rolled over a wave, its planks creaking and groaning. "I do not wish you to die, Claire."

"Then why can you not look at me?"

Rafe raised his gaze to hers only to see her eyes pool with tears. Sweat glistened on her forehead and neck, and the silky hair he had once adored lay matted in sweaty tangles around her face.

"I wanted you to love me." She swallowed.

Rafe closed his eyes. "I did."

"Did." She said the word with the finality of a judge's mallet.

"What do you expect?" Rafe snorted and sat back in his chair.

She licked her chapped lips. "Something to drink, s'il vous plaît?"

Rafe grabbed a mug from the table, lifted her shoulders, and raised it to her mouth. She took a sip then collapsed back onto the cot.

"Merci." The word escaped her lips as if the effort exhausted her.

Thunder bellowed, echoing through the ship like a mighty gong.

He returned the mug to the table but before he could get away, she grabbed his arm with more strength than he would have assumed remained within her.

"I did this all for you, Rafe."

"Did what?" He knelt on one knee, wanting to tear from her grasp, but the desperation in her eyes stayed him. Raindrops tapped on the windowpane.

"Came aboard your ship. Left your father."

"I did not ask you to come."

"I thought I could change your mind. I thought you may still love me." She gasped, unable to catch her breath.

Rafe shook his head, rummaging through the dunnage in his heart for any remaining feelings for this woman who had betrayed him so mercilessly.

Claire's brow furrowed. "It is Mademoiselle Grace, is it not? You love her."

Rafe plucked the cloth from the bucket and squeezed the water from it as if he were trying to squeeze the truth from Claire's words. "She has nothing to do with this."

Claire raised her hand to her forehead. "I tried to send her home."

"What do you mean?"

"I told her I needed her help to escape from your father's abuse. I begged her"—she drew a shallow breath—"to accept his offer to go to Charles Towne. . .where I would secretly get off the ship with her."

"You what?" Rafe dropped the cloth into the bucket and stood.

"Please don't be angry with me, Rafe." Claire coughed, her eyes flashing with fear. "I saw the way you looked at her. But I knew with her gone, you could still love me."

Rafe grabbed his baldric and paced before the cot. So that was the reason Mademoiselle Grace had not met him that night. It wasn't his father who had persuaded her to go with him, who had lured her away with his riches. It was Claire. And instead of riches, Claire had lured the mademoiselle with the only thing irresistible to her—the prospect of helping someone in need.

"But you stole her back." Claire laughed then clutched her throat. "I did not expect that."

Rafe hung his head and halted before the cot. Shame tugged upon him. He had believed the worst of Mademoiselle Grace and had stolen her from her bedchamber without giving her a chance to explain.

"Rafe." Claire held out her hand. "Please do not be angry with me."

Kneeling, Rafe took her hand in his. Staring into her blue eyes, he felt no love, no remorse, nor even anger—only pity.

"I am not angry." Rafe sighed and squeezed her hand. "Maintenant, you must get some rest."

And as if his hint of regard was all she needed to usher her into a moment's repose, she closed her eyes and drifted off to sleep.

The door creaked open, and Mademoiselle Grace stepped in, her raven hair hanging in damp tendrils about her face. Her emerald eyes alighted upon him and widened in surprise. She gazed at his hand holding Claire's. "Forgive me." She started to leave.

"Non." Rafe shot to his feet. "Do not go, s'il vous plaît."

She faced him, then swept the cabin with her gaze, carefully avoiding his eyes. Spyglass aroused from her nap and began to stretch. "Where is Father Alers?" she asked.

"In the galley."

"I did not mean to intrude."

"There is nothing to intrude upon."

"It is none of my business if there is." She swallowed and glanced at Claire with concern.

"She just fell back asleep. Will you sit, mademoiselle?"

Grace glared at him as if he were the devil himself. He winced beneath the pain it caused him. "I do not bite, mademoiselle." He attempted a grin.

She cocked a brow. "I am not so sure."

That he frightened her was obvious. That he disgusted her made his heart sink like a lead line. That he should leave her alone and offer her some peace, he knew was the right thing to do. He gestured toward the chair. "I will not torture you with my presence, mademoiselle."

With a hesitant swoosh of her damp skirts, she moved to the chair and sat down. No sooner had she alighted upon it than Spyglass leapt from the cot and jumped into her lap.

Rafe could not help but smile. "You have made a friend, I see."

"Yes, one friend aboard this ship, it would seem." Her voice was laden with sorrow as she caressed the cat's fur, and Rafe swallowed.

Retrieving his rapier, he sheathed it with a metallic *chink* and started toward the door. He gripped the handle, stopped and rubbed his thumb over the cool silver. He could not leave Grace, not with the judgment, the disdain for him, pouring from her eyes.

He swung about.

She swallowed but did not look at him. "I thought you were leaving."

"So did I."

"Claire needs medical assistance, Captain."

Raindrops pounded on the deck above like bullets assailing his guilt. "I am doing all that I can."

He gripped his baldric and cleared his throat. He wanted to tell her about Claire, wanted Mademoiselle Grace to understand why her betrayal had struck him so hard. "Did you know that Claire and I were betrothed?"

She twitched and her chest rose and fell, but she did not look at him. "It is none of my business, Captain."

"Perhaps not. But I want you to know."

She looked at him. "There is no need."

Rafe shifted his boots and glanced at Claire. "We had such great plans. She shared my dreams of helping the poor. We cared about the same things. Or so I thought." He walked to the porthole. Rain dashed and splattered against the panes just like the dreams he and Claire shared so long ago. "When I found her on the street, she was poor and in rags. We were young and innocent and full of hopes and ambitions." He turned around. Mademoiselle sat quietly petting Spyglass. Only her rapid breathing gave away her emotions.

"Turns out all she wanted was my money." Rafe chuckled. "And when she discovered my father had disowned me and I had forfeited my inheritance, she left me a week before our wedding. And ran straight into my father's bed."

Mademoiselle Grace flinched and pushed a damp curl behind her ear.

When she raised her eyes, they glistened with tears.

A wave of heat stormed up Rafe's neck and onto his face, and he felt instantly ashamed. Why had he shared such intimacies with her? He adjusted his coat and strode toward the door.

"Wait." Mademoiselle Grace set Spyglass on the deck and stood. She bit her lip and faced him. "I am sorry."

"I do not want your pity."

"Then what do you want?" she snapped.

Rafe approached her. He didn't know what he wanted anymore. He wanted to tell her he knew why she had betrayed him. He wanted to tell her he understood how convincing Claire could be. He wanted her to not look at him with such condemnation. But right now, all he wanted to do was kiss her.

He raised a hand to caress her cheek and grabbed a lock of her wet hair instead. "I like your hair unbound." He played with the soft, moist tendril.

She swung around, jerking it from between his fingers. "You should leave."

Perhaps he should. Perhaps he should walk out that door and never allow himself to be alone with this precious creature again. Laying a hand on her shoulder, he slowly turned her around. "It is my brig, mademoiselle."

"And I am your property." The sharp tone faded from her voice.

"You are so much more than that." His gaze took in her lips, her flushed cheeks, and those emerald eyes shimmering with tears—and something else. An invitation? He leaned closer until their lips were but an inch apart. The sweet smell of rain mixed with her feminine scent and swirled about his nose. She did not back away, did not slap him.

Instead she breathlessly awaited his kiss.

CHAPTER 27

Grace closed her eyes. Her heart thumped. She could feel the captain's warm breath wafting over her face. His lips hovered over hers.

The door crashed open. Grace opened her eyes and jumped backward, her heart in her throat. Father Alers strode into the room, his curious gaze shifting between her and Rafe. The captain huffed and shook his head.

Clutching her skirts with one hand and covering her mouth with the other, Grace dashed up the companionway ladder and bolted onto the deck. Slipping across the slick planks, she rushed to her favorite spot beside the foredeck where the bulkhead offered some protection from the buffeting winds. The rain had ceased again, but its spicy scent still stung in the breeze that now cooled the tears flowing down her cheeks.

What had she done?

She'd nearly kissed the captain.

She *would* have kissed the captain if Father Alers had not interrupted them.

She touched her lips where she could still feel Rafe's warm breath, could still smell his scent of tobacco and leather. What had come over her? Not only had she nearly allowed his kiss, she'd *wanted* him to kiss her. Horrified, she quickly bowed her head and gripped the railing. *Lord, please forgive me.*

Never in her life had she felt such an overwhelming attraction. Mercy me, she had never even kissed a man before. And there she was like a common hussy, accepting this rogue's advances. And with him on his way to sell her into slavery. Had all reason, all piety fled her mind and her soul when she needed them the most?

She lifted her face to the breeze and gazed at the island. The leaves of palms and banyans whipped this way and that in the wind as if waving to her, beckoning her to come and join them on land. And oh how she wanted to. If only to get away from the captain and the spell he had cast upon her. Perhaps Annette had slipped some of her love potion into Grace's food. She laughed at the thought but could find no other explanation for her unchaste behavior.

Black clouds hung like vultures overhead, making the afternoon look more like night. How long would they be cornered in this bay? How long would she be trapped with the captain, unable to escape? She drew a deep breath and tried to calm her nerves. She must not think of herself. She must think of Claire. The woman needed medical attention. Without it, she would most likely die.

Perhaps that was the reason Grace had been sent on this journey—to help Madame Dubois get well, to befriend the woman, to help her know God's love.

Grace bit her lip, remembering the look on the captain's face when he had shared what had happened between him and Claire. Despair had dragged his features down, dissolving the arrogant shield he sometimes wore until he looked more like a lost little boy instead of a vicious mercenary. Grace hugged herself as the wind whipped over her rain-dampened gown. She trembled beneath the chill. From what she could gather, Rafe had spent his entire childhood beneath the thumb of an unloving and cruel father. Then when he had finally found someone with whom to share his life and dreams, she had betrayed him.

And in the worst possible way.

How did one ever recover from such heartache—when everyone they had ever loved and trusted turned against them?

Grace's heart shriveled. No wonder the captain had reacted so violently to her betrayal. No wonder he had been so angry when he stole her from his father's house. He had assumed she was no better than Claire and his father. Gripping the railing, she closed her eyes, trying to make sense of it all.

Then what had changed the captain's mind? What had calmed his fury? For in that tiny cabin, his dark eyes had burned with such ardor, such warmth, it frightened Grace. Not the kind of fear she had for her life, but a different kind of fear—a fear of the desires that lay hidden in her own heart.

~≈~

Spotting Grace by the railing beneath the foredeck, Rafe headed toward her. He needed to speak with her. He needed to talk about their near kiss. And why she was so distraught when she rushed from the cabin. Was it possible she held some affection for him? He dared not hope.

He approached slowly so as not to frighten her, but she did not turn around. Her eyes were closed and she seemed in deep thought—or prayer. Not wanting to disturb her, he climbed up the foredeck ladder and found a spot nearby to wait until she finished. A few minutes passed and Rafe was about to peer over the side to check on her when Monsieur Thorn's voice blared up from the spot where Grace stood. Easing toward the edge of the foredeck railing, Rafe listened as he kept himself from their view.

⁓

"Miss Grace?" Mr. Thorn's voice startled her, and she flung a hand to her chest as she tucked her private thoughts regarding the captain behind a closed door in her mind. Too late. Her cheeks heated beneath a blush.

"Good day, Mr. Thorn." Her voice sounded husky.

Mr. Thorn slipped beside her and glanced over the choppy waters of the bay. "So you decided to brave the storm as well, I see."

Grace thought of the devilish look on the captain's face when she had leapt out of his arms. " 'Tis too hot below." She flustered at the insinuation of her statement. "I mean, 'tis crowded." Any room was crowded with the captain in it. "I mean—" She sighed in resignation of her befuddling verbiage. "Yes, I am braving the storm."

Mr. Thorn gazed at her curiously. "Are you well, Miss Grace?"

She gave him a flat smile. "As well as I can be, Mr. Thorn."

He leaned on the railing and glanced at the island, battered by the gusty wind, but still beautiful in the ashen light. "How is Madame Dubois?" His tone held no concern.

Grace shook her head. "Not well."

"Hmm." He doffed his hat. Shaking the dampness from it onto his knee, he ran a hand through his hair then snapped the tricorne back atop his head. "It must be quite daunting to be so close to land, miss, and have no way to escape."

The lift of his cultured brow and the hint of playfulness in his brown eyes sent a spark of hope through Grace. She narrowed her eyes. "Whatever do you mean, Mr. Thorn?"

He smiled and fingered his chin then glanced at the island. "I believe I recognize this island. Yes. I know I have anchored here before. Careened our ship here once, I believe. Plenty of fruit and water for the taking to last someone several months, or at least until another ship arrived—or say someone *sent* another ship." He gave her a sly wink.

Grace eyed him with suspicion. That Mr. Thorn's last attempt to help her escape had not worked out well was no reflection on him or his kindness. But something about the man set her nerves on edge. Though he appeared a just man, his critical attitude toward others gave her pause. And then there was the odd conversation she'd overheard between him and Monsieur Dubois. The two of them had been up to something, but what? Grace grabbed the chain around her neck and pulled out her cross, rubbing it between her fingers. "You would attempt helping me again?"

"Why not?"

"Why risk invoking the anger of your captain should he discover your treachery?"

"For the same reason I aided you before, mademoiselle. I do not wish to see an innocent woman sold into slavery."

☕

Fury clawed up Rafe's spine, stiffening it and sending a flash of heat to his chest. Liar, traître. He had trusted Thorn—had called him friend. Rafe gripped the hilt of his rapier, holding back his urge to call the man to swords right then and there, but wanting first to hear the mademoiselle's answer.

☕

Grace gazed across the deck toward the larboard railing where a group of sailors huddled beside the quarterdeck, rolling dice. "But with so many men on board, how could we escape their detection?"

"Leave that up to me." Mr. Thorn tugged upon his coat.

Grace rubbed her cross and gazed at the inviting shores. To remain on board would leave her at the mercy of the captain, not to mention her own unexpected passions. To leave would at least provide her a chance to live, to be free once again. Didn't the Bible say to flee temptation and wickedness? She gazed up at Mr. Thorn, unable to discern whether the warmth in his eyes sprang from sincerity or cunning—eyes that carried none of the innocence of his twenty years. Regardless, what choice did she have?

"When?"

"Tonight."

~

Later, back in his cabin, Rafe ground his fists together and stomped with the ebb and tide of a restless pace across the Persian rug centering the floor. Finding the silken threads sufficiently humbled, he stormed toward the stern windows and crossed his arms over his chest. Nothing but a black wall met his gaze, mirroring his mood. Well past midnight, the thick clouds had captured all traces of the moon, casting the earth's inhabitants in complete darkness—or at least his corner of the earth. Dark and barren—like Rafe's heart.

Thorn's betrayal blazed through Rafe like lightning. Was there no one in his life who would not stab him in the back? Rafe plucked a cheroot from his desk drawer and lit it from a candle. Drawing a puff of the pungent smoke, he hoped the tobacco would loosen his stiff nerves and numb the pain in his heart.

Grace was gone. He knew it. Nothing would have prevented her escape. The night was dark. Most of the crew remained below deck sheltered from the rain. No one would have stood in their way. Not even Rafe. For as much as he wanted to keep her with him and lock up his traitorous first mate, Rafe had realized their plan would serve his own purposes quite well. Thorn wasn't the only one betraying Rafe. He had been *trompé* by his own feelings. For the more time he spent with the mademoiselle, the more conflicted he became. He doubted he could sell her to the don or to anyone for that matter. This way, at least he would not have to face a mutiny when his crew discovered their pockets would not be lined with gold anytime soon.

Oui, Grace was gone, and the brig seemed nothing more than a hollow shell without her.

Rafe drew in another drag of sweet tobacco then blew out a cloud of smoke above him. It dissipated into the darkness as the mademoiselle had. He should be thankful to be rid of her.

Then why did his heart crumble within him? He grabbed a bottle of brandy from the shelf, opened it, and took a long draught. A rank of numbing fire marched down his throat. Mademoiselle Grace had told him the liquor turned him into a brute. Did it? The taste of it soured in his mouth, and he slammed the bottle down and wiped his lips.

Rap rap rap.

"Entrez-vous," Rafe barked; then he turned to see Monsieur Thorn stride in, wearing a confident grin of a snake.

"The sails have all been painted black, Captain."

"Très bien." Rafe's stomach clenched. He wanted to inquire whether Thorn had delivered Mademoiselle Grace safely to the island, but now was not the time. He would find out soon enough, and then as soon as they were free of Woodes's ships, Rafe would deal with this betrayer. In the meantime, Grace would be quite safe and well fed on the island until he could send a ship to rescue her and deliver her safely home. "Douse all lights, weigh anchor, and hoist away topgallants and jib."

"A very good plan, Captain, if I do say so." Thorn's eyes held an admiration that Rafe no longer believed existed in the man. "Under these clouds, 'twould be a miracle if we were spotted."

Rafe grunted in response, and Monsieur Thorn touched his hat and backed out the door.

After taking one last puff of his cheroot, Rafe extinguished it on a tray. He blew out the candle, sheathed his rapier, shoved his pistols into his baldric, and followed his first mate up on deck. The night would bring many challenges, not the least of which would be navigating the ship through the reefs of the harbor in the dark. For that he needed a sharp mind and quick reflexes. So he shoved all thoughts of Mademoiselle Grace from his mind—and his heart.

Two hours later, guided by four lanterns hanging over the sides of the ship, two at the bow and two amidships over larboard and starboard rails, Rafe had maneuvered the brig to the mouth of the harbor. "Hoist up and douse the lanterns. Lay aloft and loose topsails," he whispered to Thorn, who then marched across deck to deliver his orders to the men. Voices traveled far at night, especially in the oppressive dank air beneath the cloud-covered sky.

A thunderous *snap* sounded from above, and Rafe glanced up and peered into the darkness but could not make out the black sails that had just been raised to the wind. Planting his boots on the deck, he folded his arms across his chest and allowed the breeze to whip through his hair and bring with it the scent of brine and freedom. He shot one last glance over his shoulder at the bulky shadow of the island, and his chest grew heavy.

Mademoiselle Grace was there somewhere. Was she afraid? Was she lonely? Or was she glad to be rid of him? That she suffered under any one of those emotions saddened him. Turning back around, he thrust his face into the wind, trying to shake her from his thoughts. He must focus on their escape. Up ahead, lanterns blinked from the two ships that guarded the harbor, one to the north and one to the south. *Le Champion* would have to slip through the half-mile gap between them—barely enough breathing room. Was he le fou to attempt such a feat? One shift of the clouds, one beam of errant moonlight, one slip of a word from his crew, and all would be lost.

The mademoiselle's scent tickled his nose. Sacre mer, did her fragrance remain to taunt him?

"Do we have a chance, Captain?" Her soft voice floated on the wind.

Rafe jumped and snapped his gaze toward the source. Grace's outline shadowed beside him. He rubbed his eyes.

She released a sigh. "Your silence speaks volumes, Captain."

"You are here," was all he could think to say as his heart swelled.

"Where else would I be?"

"On the island."

He saw her flinch.

"I overheard Monsieur Thorn's offer," he admitted.

She said nothing.

Rafe scratched the stubble on his jaw. "Why did you not go? Why did you not escape when you had the chance?"

She was silent for a moment. "I could not leave Madame Claire so ill. No one else, besides Father Alers, seems to care about her, and she is in need of a woman to attend her."

Rafe gazed over the inky expanse, unable to discern sea from sky— just as he was unable to comprehend her words. "You refused a chance at freedom for *her*?"

"I may be a pious prude as you say, but I am not cruel, Captain." Her voice stung with offense, but also with a strength that pleased him.

Prude pieuse. Had he called her that? More than once, if he remembered correctly. Sans doute, she could behave like one, but at the moment all he saw was her heart of gold.

Thorn's tall figure emerged from the darkness. "Captain? The men await your orders."

Rafe turned to Grace, unsure what to say. He started to leave, then touched her arm. "A prayer to that God of yours for our success could not hurt."

"Of course." He felt her smile, though he could not see it.

❧

Grace inched her way to the starboard bow and gripped the railing. She'd never been in such oppressive darkness. Behind her, she heard the captain whisper orders to Monsieur Atton. Only the soft flap of sails and purl of water against the hull graced her ears as the ship slipped through the sea. Up ahead, their two pursuers guarded the harbor like sentinels. One lantern hung from the foremast of each ship, illuminating the pathway to freedom between them—much like the narrow gate to salvation. Grace bowed her head. *Lord, grant us safe passage through our enemies. Make us invisible to them and to all forces of evil.*

Raising her head, she nearly chuckled at the irony of her prayer. The shuffling of feet sounded behind her as the crew attended to their captain's orders. Invisible black sails filled with wind overhead. Ingenious. Her admiration of the captain's skills rose along with her conflicting sensations whenever he was near. Why would he have allowed her escape? It made no sense. Could he be having second thoughts about selling her into slavery? Or was he just testing Monsieur Thorn's loyalty? Betrayal was something she had learned did not sit well with the captain.

"You should go below." His deep voice startled her.

"I am praying as instructed." She noted the humor in her own voice.

"Très bien." He leaned on the rail beside her and brushed a strand of hair from her face. "It will not matter should they detect us. A broadside from both sides would sink us within minutes."

Grace swallowed. Sink? A lump formed in her throat as *Le Champion* glided between her pursuers. Silence consumed the ship as if the angel of death floated across the decks, quieting everything with a touch of his scythe: the tongues of the sailors, the creaks and groans of the planks, and the flap of sails. Only the ripple of water against the hull gave any evidence of their passage.

As if sensing her fear, the captain placed a hand on her arm. She jolted but dared not move. The lanterns of the pursuing ships winked at her from her right and her left. They were so close, she heard voices from their decks: laughter, song, and a heated argument.

Minutes passed like hours until finally the lanterns and voices were behind her. Facing the wind, she released a tiny breath.

Rafe tiptoed toward the helm, where Mr. Thorn stood beside Mr.

Atton. Whispers echoed back and forth, and several sailors leapt into the ratlines and scrambled above, their dark shadows like evil specters attempting to creep into heaven.

In the distance, the lanterns of the ships faded. They were safe!

A yellow burst of light lit the sea off their stern. Grace stared at it curiously, unsure of its source.

"All hands down!" Captain Dubois yelled and leapt on top of her, forcing her to the deck.

A thunderous boom racked the sea and air.

CHAPTER 28

The captain flung one arm around Grace's waist as he shoved her to the deck before covering her body with his own. The ominous whoosh of the shot heading their way filled Grace's ears, and she squeezed her eyes shut. The crunch and snap of severed wood crackled in the air, followed by a massive splash. Grace gasped to fill her lungs with air. A tingling sensation whirled through her. Rafe lifted his head, but inches from her own, and gazed at her as if he too experienced the odd feeling. Curses and shouts saturated the air.

"Capitaine?" someone shouted.

"Oui." He leapt off her and helped her to her feet. "Are you all right?" His voice rang with concern.

"Yes, thank you."

He shifted his attention to the ship that had fired upon them and instantly stiffened. "Monsieur Legard, take the mademoiselle below." Then he turned and began braying orders to his crew.

Weaving amongst the frantic sailors that scampered across the deck, Mr. Legard escorted Grace below and ushered her into her cabin, closing the door with a thud.

Dropping to her knees beside the cot, Grace held Claire's feverish hand in hers and closed her eyes. Deafening blasts exploded all around her, sending a tremble through the brig that matched the tremble already coursing through her body. Boot steps hammered overhead, accompanied by shouts and curses—all in French. Yet amidst the clamor, Grace could still make out the captain's deep timbre as he ordered his crew about.

The sting of gunpowder seeped through the planks of the cabin to join the fetor of death and disease within. Claire groaned, and Grace peered through the darkness where the woman lay. "Lord, please save us," she prayed as another cannon thundered. Her heart stopped. The blast came from *Le Champion*'s guns as the captain no doubt attempted to stave off their pursuers.

Weaving around Claire on the cot, Spyglass snuggled up to Grace, nudging her hand for a pet. Grace obliged the cat, then pressed her fingers over her right cheek and winced where a bruise formed from her tumble onto the deck. She might have been able to protect her face from the splinters if she'd known the captain intended to pounce on her. She hadn't felt any pain at the time. She hadn't felt anything but Captain Dubois's warm body atop hers and the tingles that rippled through her at such close intimacy.

Sobs filled the air, reminding Grace she was not alone. She scanned the dark cabin but couldn't make out Annette's slight form. "Annette, all will be well." Grace shoved aside her anger at the mulatto. "Come here." Shuffling sounded and Annette emerged from the shadows and knelt beside Grace. Grace put an arm around her, noting her sweet citrus scent and the quiver that sped through her. "I am frightened as well, but Captain Dubois is a skilled captain." She offered the lady a smile that was no doubt lost in the darkness even as she wondered where her confidence in Rafe came from.

Boom! A loud roar threatened to split the timbers of the brig.

Shouts and curses filled the air above them.

The *crack* of wood. Then a crunch. A snap. More shouting shot down from above, "*Prenez garde en bas!*"

Bam! The ship canted to larboard. Flakes of dirt showered on them from above.

Grace glanced aloft. Coughing, she batted away the dust. Silence consumed the brig. Only the mad dash of water against the hull reassured Grace that they still lived. But what of everyone else? Had they all died?

Annette whimpered and Grace drew her closer, embracing her. "Shhh. It will be all right." But would it? She had no idea. Truth be told, she wasn't sure she knew much of anything anymore.

They huddled together in the dark for what seemed an eternity. Madame Dubois's breathing grew ragged, and Grace took her hand again then released Annette and groped around for the bucket. Upon finding it, she wrung out the cloth and laid it atop the dying woman's forehead. How long could she survive? How long would any of them survive with two ships in fast pursuit and hard intent on sinking them to the depths of the sea?

Yet, Grace had not heard a gun fire for quite a while. In fact, she'd not heard anything.

A thin line of light appeared beneath the door and Grace took Annette's hand. A thousand terrifying thoughts rampaged through her mind. Had they been boarded by the enemy? Had the captain been killed?

The latch clicked and the door creaked open to reveal Mr. Thorn, his features distorted in the glow of the lantern he held. His eyes landed upon Annette and remained there for longer than seemed proper before he shifted them to Grace. "The captain wishes me to inform you that we are safe now." He placed the lantern atop the table.

"So he is well?" Grace pressed a hand over her pounding heart.

"Quite," Mr. Thorn replied. His answer sent an awkward rush of joy through Grace.

Annette stood, fidgeted with the trim on the neckline of her gown, and slunk out of the light.

Thorn's gaze followed her. "Are you ladies unharmed?"

"We are fine." Grace rose and brushed the dust from her skirts. "I heard a loud crash. What happened?"

Tearing his eyes from the mulatto, Mr. Thorn straightened his coat. "Our main-topmast was damaged."

Grace clutched her throat. "Isn't that bad?"

"It can be, but no one was injured."

"What of the two ships?"

"We lost them in the darkness." He gave a half smile.

Claire groaned, and Grace dropped to her knees beside the woman. Now doused in light, Claire's sunken cheeks bore the color of sunbaked sand and were just as hot to the touch. Her gray lips smacked in agony, and beads of sweat marched across her face and neck. Grabbing the cloth, Grace dabbed it over the woman's skin. She sighed. "Mr. Thorn, can you please summon Father Alers?"

"Will she die?" His voice was emotionless.

"Please get the father." Grace's exhausted tone bespoke her internal agony. Claire was dying. Grace was all too familiar with the merciless fiend called death—an ugly beast who delighted in torturing his victims, leaving behind a trail of hopelessness and pain. During her mother's tumultuous death, Grace had felt the monster's breath upon her neck, his laughter beating like demon wings against her skin.

She shuddered, and all hope drained from her. The only thing left to do was to ensure the woman's salvation. If Claire regained consciousness

Grace hoped she'd at least be willing to speak to the former priest.

With Mr. Thorn's departure, the room chilled. Grace hugged herself and lifted her gaze to Annette who stood beneath the porthole. The mulatto immediately lowered her chin. "Annette, did you poison your mistress?"

Her eyes filled with tears and she lifted a hand to her nose. "It was not only un philtre d'amour."

"What, then?"

The woman squeezed her eyes shut as tears sped down her cheeks. Spyglass ambled to the foot of the cot and directed her one eye upon the maid.

Grace rubbed her forehead. "Then at least tell me if there is some way to save her."

"There is nothing you can do." Annette met her eyes then, and the fear and hopelessness that burned within them frightened Grace. "What will become of me?" she asked.

"I do not know. You have done a terrible thing, Annette."

Claire's troubled cough brought Grace's attention back to her. A heaviness fell upon the cabin as if one of the storm clouds had infiltrated the tiny space. Grace gasped for a breath. Spyglass hissed—at what, Grace couldn't see.

Boot steps thundered in the companionway, and in marched Captain Dubois. His dark hair fell in disarray across the gray coat that spanned his broad shoulders. Black soot smudged his face. His buccaneer shirt was torn at the collar. But other than that, he seemed in one piece. Relief eased over Grace at the sight.

He glanced at Annette before focusing on Grace and narrowed his eyes as if sensing her discomfiture. "How is Claire?"

"Worse, I'm afraid."

He glanced over the cabin as if he, too, felt the dark presence. Father Alers and Mr. Thorn entered behind him.

The priest dashed toward the cot while Mr. Thorn took up a position beside his captain.

"Will she die?" The emotion in Captain Dubois's voice surprised her. Was it possible he still harbored some sentiment for Claire?

Father Alers stooped and laid a hand on Claire's cheek. He swallowed and in his golden eyes, Grace saw that he had reached the same conclusion she had.

She dabbed the cloth over Claire's moist neck. So young, so full of life. Too young. It felt wrong for her to die. An unconscionable betrayal.

"No." Grace spoke the word that was screaming within her. She would not watch another woman die.

Father Alers pressed down his coiled gray hair and shook his head. "Je suis désolé."

"No," Grace moaned and leaned on the cot. Spyglass pressed against her head, her soft purrs rumbling in her ears. *Lord, what do I do? Tell me what to do!*

For we wrestle not against flesh and blood. The verse from Ephesians drifted through her mind. For a moment, she did not know why. But then. . .

She sat up. "This is no sickness."

The wrinkles on Father Alers's face folded.

"At least not a natural one." She glanced over at the captain and then Mr. Thorn—who returned her stare with one of bewilderment. And finally Annette. The guilt pouring from the mulatto's face confirmed Grace's suspicions.

Claire coughed and began to heave as if frantically searching for air. There wasn't much time.

Laying a hand over Claire's forehead, Grace drew in a deep breath. "Father, in Your Son's precious name, the name of Jesus, I bind and cast out from this woman and from this cabin and from this ship, the evil forces that have made Claire ill." The words that slipped from Grace's lips sounded so weak, so human, so powerless. She studied Claire, but the woman groaned and her breathing grew even more ragged. Perhaps Grace should have yelled the words. Maybe she didn't have enough faith. She searched her heart for that mustard seed of faith God said was all that was needed to do anything in His name.

Claire's hand hung limp and cold in Grace's. Grace's stomach soured and she bowed her head.

"Do you believe I am who I say I am?"

The words flowed over her like a gushing waterfall. *Yes, I do, Lord.* Tears burned in Grace's eyes. She stiffened her jaw as anger now welled within her—anger at the wickedness trying to steal this woman's life. She lifted her chin. "Be gone, in the name of Jesus."

Mr. Thorn chuckled, and the captain shifted his boots over the deck. Father Alers met Grace's gaze with one of pity. He laid a hand on her shoulder as if to say, "A noble attempt."

Grace bowed her head and allowed her tears to fall. She had failed. Or maybe it wasn't God's will at all that Claire live. Lifting Claire's hand to her mouth, Grace laid a kiss upon it.

And the woman's fingers squeezed hers in return.

Grace popped open her eyes and stared aghast at Claire. Her breathing had calmed. Her eyelids fluttered.

Annette gasped, and Grace heard the tap of her slippers as she approached the cot.

"Claire?" Grace pushed damp hair from the woman's cheek.

Claire moaned and pried her eyes open.

Grace giggled between sobs of joy. It was only then that she realized the heaviness in the room had left.

Father Alers stumbled backward and plopped into the chair.

A faint smile lifted Claire's lips where a hint of pink peeked from behind the gray. "Grace," she whispered.

Annette backed against the bulkhead, her mouth hanging slack.

"Zooks," Mr. Thorn declared. "I cannot believe it."

Grace gazed at the men over her shoulder. The captain's dark eyes widened and he shook his head.

She smiled. "Thanks be to God, she will live."

CHAPTER 29

Standing at the stern of the brig, Grace drew in a deep breath of the night air, laden with salt and fish and a hint of flowers—the latter of which she must only be imagining. For they had not seen land since they left the island two days prior—in a frenzied dash to escape their pursuers. And she had not seen the captain, save in passing, since God had delivered Claire of the evil forces causing her illness. Grace longed to know what he thought about the incident. Had it convinced him of God's existence? Or did he merely think it coincidental, a bizarre accident, an act of black magic as she'd heard some of the crew declare. Perhaps witnessing the power of God had frightened Captain Dubois. But no, that didn't seem like him at all. Then why did he avoid her?

Due to the southern course the ship maintained, she assumed they were still heading toward Colombia. Yet the captain had known about Thorn's plans to help her escape and he had made no moves to stop them. Why? It didn't make any sense.

The ship bucked over a wave, then creaked and groaned in complaint. But Grace wasn't complaining anymore. She was convinced the purpose of her entire harrowing escapade had been for God to deliver Claire from the forces of death. She had stayed on board for that very reason. And now with that task completed, surely the Lord would rescue Grace. She must only wait and believe.

For two days Grace had stayed by Claire's side, and with Father Alers, had nursed some strength back into the woman, though she still had not risen from her bed. Father Alers was overwrought about the miracle, saying that in all his time as a Jesuit priest, he'd not seen the likes of it. He had told Grace that he'd begun to read the Holy Scriptures again. Grace smiled at the thought. Finally she had done some good.

She gazed out over the ebony sea, lit in glittering ribbons of silver by the light of a half-moon, and released a contented sigh. Nights upon the Caribbean held a mysterious beauty all their own. During the day Grace must not only endure extreme temperatures but also the incessant hammering of the crew as they repaired the mainmast. So she had waited until nightfall to emerge from below, no longer fearing the crew. Aside from a few ribald comments tossed her way—which unfortunately she'd grown accustomed to—they left her alone.

The ship pitched over a wave, and Grace gripped the railing as a spray of seawater showered over her. She shook it off and smiled as the curls that had loosened from her pins tickled her neck. She liked the way they felt. In fact, she relished the absence of the continual headache caused by her tight coiffure.

Annette appeared beside Grace. "Bonsoir, mademoiselle."

Grace caught her breath at the woman's sudden presence. "Bonsoir, Annette." She had hardly seen the mulatto during the past few days. The maid had darted in and out of the cabin, bringing stew and lemon water for her mistress, but never staying long enough to talk. Her actions and attitude seemed to indicate that she felt remorse for what she had done, but Grace needed to ensure that Annette had no intention of harming Claire again. "Where have you been?"

Annette shrugged. The moonlight transformed her skin into dark cream. "Are you angry with me, mademoiselle?"

Grace bit her lip. She had been angry. But she could not find her fury anymore. It had softened into pity and fear—fear for the girl's eternity. "No. I am not angry, Annette. I have been praying for you."

"Praying?" Annette fidgeted with the lace at the cuff of her gown. "My mistress recovers."

"Yes." Grace eyed the lady. "Does that make you sad?"

A moment passed as Annette scanned the dark horizon. "Oui."

As Grace suspected. At least the girl had not lied. "Thank you for being honest, Annette." Grace bit her lip, wondering how to ask her next question, but knowing she must regardless of how audacious it sounded. "Do you plan to hurt her again?"

The mulatto flashed her dark eyes at Grace. "Non. Though she deserves it."

Grace pushed a strand of hair behind her ear and sighed. "I know Madame Dubois is not often kind to you."

Annette gave her a sideways glance.

Grace squeezed the railing, the damp wood still warm from the sun.

She longed to know what Annette had done to Claire, to know exactly what Grace had been dealing with. "May I inquire. . .may I ask what you did to cause Madame Dubois's illness?"

"I cast *un maléfice* on her, a hex."

Grace's breath held tight in her throat.

"A curse from my ancestors," Annette continued in a matter-of-fact tone that sent a chill through Grace.

"Is that who you pray to? Your ancestors?"

"Oui." Annette wrapped her arms around her tiny waist. "My ancestors were strong warriors before my people were stolen from our land."

Grace flattened her lips. An urgency rose within her to help Annette see the dangerous path she was on. But how could she help this girl without offending her? "Your ancestors are dead, Annette. 'And as it is appointed unto men once to die, but after this the judgment,'" Grace quoted from Hebrews. "You are not praying to them, but to demons, to the evil forces that rule this world."

Annette's chest rose and fell rapidly as she stared out upon the sea. Her jaw stiffened, but she said nothing.

A blast of wind whipped over them, and Grace leaned toward Annette. "You cannot deny what you saw."

"Oui. I been thinking of that. Your ancestors are more powerful than mine."

"No, Annette. That power came from God—the one and only God. He is nobody's ancestor. He's the Creator of all. He's *your* Creator."

"If He is the only God, and my Creator, why does He allow my people to be *les esclaves*?" Her words came out in strangled tones.

Grace laid a hand on her arm. "I do not know. But I do know that this world is ruled by God's enemy. Much of the evil we experience is his doing. If you want to blame someone, blame him."

Guttural laugher bellowed from the main deck as if in derision of her statement.

From Annette's expression, Grace gathered she agreed with the sentiment. "I blame the blancs," she snapped. "They have caused my people to suffer. People like Monsieur Dubois and my mistress. They must pay."

"But you are half white, are you not?"

"Monsieur Dubois sired me, but he is not my father." She whipped her hair behind her, giving Grace a venomous look.

Grace's heart shrank beneath the girl's misery. Slavery was a wretched enough institution without enduring the stigma of being bred for beauty and strength like a prize horse. "If you are unhappy, why not run away?"

Annette snorted. "Where do I go? I drift in empty space between my two peoples. Neither wants me."

"God wants you."

Annette snatched her arm from beneath Grace's hand and she backed away, her chest heaving. "He is the God of the whites."

Grace reached out her hand, wanting so badly to help this poor woman. "No. He is the God of all and shows no partiality toward one race or another."

"I do not wish to hear it!" Annette's dark eyes simmered as she swatted tears from her cheeks. "Leave me be!" Then hoisting her shirts, she darted across the deck.

Grace lowered her gaze, her heart sinking. *Lord, where did I go astray? Why wouldn't she listen to me?*

Lifting her face to the humid breeze, she allowed the wind to dry her tears. Then whirling around, she scanned the deck for Annette. Perhaps Grace had been too bold, too forceful in her efforts to turn the woman to God. Determined to comfort her and offer an apology, Grace headed across the quarterdeck to find the mulatto. Passing by the helm, she nodded at Mr. Atton, then carefully made her way down the ladder. She scanned the shadowy deck, lit only by the circle of light coming from the lantern hanging at the mainmast, and spotted a cluster of sailors by the starboard rail passing a bottle. She wanted to ask them where Annette had gone but thought better of it. Averting her gaze, she felt their eyes follow her across deck. Then clutching her skirts, she climbed the foredeck ladder. Perhaps the girl had gone to the bow. She was rewarded when she saw a dark figure standing by the cathead.

⁓

Rafe took a sip of brandy then closed the flask. Why did he no longer find pleasure in the pungent liquor? Why did it sour upon his lips when he needed the numbing elixir so badly?

It was the mademoiselle.

Sacre mer, her disapproval of it had tainted it for him. As she had tainted all the pleasures he used to enjoy: his sanity, his reason, his indulgence in other women. Zut alors, even his food had become tasteless. Reaching back, he tossed the flask into the raging sea and watched it sink in the black waters—along with all the passing pleasures that had provided diversions from the futility of his life.

He had avoided Grace, hoping some of those old plaisirs would return. Hoping he wouldn't have to face the evidence of what he had seen in the cabin below. The miracle, as Father Alers kept proclaiming; the battle between good and evil; the way Grace's words, empowered by the name of Jesus, had snatched Claire from death's door. There must be another explanation. And until Rafe could figure out just what it was, he preferred not to speak to Mademoiselle Grace. It was bad enough he had to listen to Father Alers's incessant babbling about God and His power and His presence. Rafe's heart and mind chafed beneath the onslaught of their religious nonsense.

And to compound his angst, Rafe still had to deal with a possible mutiny when his crew discovered that he no longer intended to sell Mademoiselle Grace to the don. Oui, he had finally decided what his heart had known long ago—that he could never harm such a precious angel. Besides, after he had discovered the reason for her betrayal, his anger had swept away like seawater through scuppers. He would find another way to procure the money he needed for the hospital—even if he had to resort to piracy.

Rafe gripped the railing. He remained on course for Rio de la Hacha to keep the crew's suspicions at bay and to give him time to formulate a plan that would assuage their anger and appease their greedy hearts. Yet no brilliant scheme had forged in his mind.

Which was why he desperately needed to drown himself with brandy. His sudden distaste for it only further exacerbated the suffering in which he found himself.

Femme exaspérante!

Shuffling sounded behind him. Rafe's mood soured further at the prospect of company. He wanted no more of Father Alers's religious lectures, nor Monsieur Thorn's placating grins. "Allez-vous-en! Go away!" Rafe bellowed.

"Very well," the soft voice replied.

Rafe swerved about. Mademoiselle Grace's slight figure retreated. "Non. I did not know it was you."

She slowly turned around. "My mistake, Captain. I was looking for Annette." The moonlight sent shimmering waves of silver upon her, transforming her raven curls into glistening onyx.

Rafe swallowed.

She cocked her head. "Have you seen her?"

Gathering his wits, Rafe shook his head.

She nodded and started to leave.

"Do not go."

"Do you wish something, Captain?" A question as loaded as one of his twelve-pounders below. He smiled.

She looked down as if his perusal frightened her. "I have no time for your games, Captain."

"I fear I am done playing games, mademoiselle." He started to reach for her but gripped his baldric instead.

She turned to leave again, but Rafe closed the gap between them in one step and grabbed her arm. Her eyes shot to his as if he'd stabbed her. She jerked from his grasp.

"If there are no more games, then I must assume you still intend to sell me." She took a breath and gazed over the turbulent dark sea. "I cannot say I know much about navigation, but I can tell in which direction you have set your sails."

Rafe could not deny her words, nor could he for some reason find his voice. Her sweet scent swirled beneath his nose as his gaze was drawn to the silken curls of raven dancing over her graceful neck. He could no more hurt this woman than he could pluck out his own eyes. He hesitated.

"Have you been drinking?" She arched one beautiful eyebrow.

"Unfortunately, non." He grinned.

"Then why not answer my question?" A discordant fiddle chimed a sailor's ballad from the main deck, drawing her gaze over her shoulder.

Then facing forward, she released a sigh. "If you'll excuse me." She started to turn.

Rafe grabbed her arm again, rewarded by those emerald eyes shifting to his, searching his face for the answer to her question.

Rafe softened his grip. "I could never sell you, mademoiselle."

She wrinkled her nose. "What did you say?"

He released her and took a deep breath, then dug his thumbs inside the sash strapped at his waist—if only to keep his hands off her. "You heard me."

"I don't believe I did."

"I am not going to sell you." Rafe had expected a bit more appreciation. *"Est-ce que je me fais compris?"*

"I understand your words." She clasped her hands together and stepped toward the railing as if searching for the answer upon the seas. The ship pitched, and Rafe placed a hand on the small of her back to steady her. A spray showered over them, crystallizing into tiny diamonds on her cheeks and neck. She looked at him. Disbelief and a glimmer of hope battled in her eyes.

"What has changed your mind?"

"Do you need to ask?" Raising his hand, he cupped her chin and rubbed his thumb over her cheek, pressing lightly over the red abrasion. She winced.

"Je suis désolé. I did not mean to hurt you."

She swallowed. Fear dashed across her eyes. She lowered her chin. Rafe gently raised it and allowed his gaze to wander over her face: those sparkling emerald eyes, the tiny ringlets dancing over her forehead, and those moist lips. Her breathing grew rapid, and Rafe could stand it no longer. He lowered his mouth to hers.

Ah such sweetness, so soft, so willing. She received his kiss and returned it with a passion he would not have suspected existed within her. Never before had a simple kiss consumed so much of him, making him long to protect and cherish this woman forever.

He withdrew and leaned his forehead against hers. Her warm breath intermingled with his and filled the air between them for one treasured moment.

Before she pushed away from him and dashed across the deck, disappearing into the darkness.

CHAPTER 30

Grace halted before her cabin, wiped her tears, and slowly opened the door. Darkness spilled over her. Stepping inside, she clicked the latch shut and waited until her eyes could make out the contents of the tiny space. Deep, steady breathing coming from the direction of the cot reassured her that Claire was still asleep. Annette, however, was nowhere to be seen.

Assured of her privacy, Grace flung a hand to her mouth and sank to the deck in a flutter of billowing skirts. Tears poured from her eyes so fast she could not wipe them away before they slid from her jaw onto her lap. How could she have allowed such a thing to happen? With trembling fingers, she touched her mouth where the press of the captain's lips still lingered, where she still tingled from the passion in his kiss.

Where she had welcomed his advance without inhibition! Even worse, she had enjoyed it—every second of it.

What was wrong with her?

And her suspicion that the captain's promise not to sell her was only a trick to solicit her kiss only increased her guilt. She was smarter than that.

Plucking a handkerchief from the sleeve of her gown, Grace dabbed her cheeks and blew her nose. She hung her head.

I am a trollop. I am a woman of the lowest of morals.

Scenes from her recent past rose like specters to haunt her conscience. The lies she had told in Port-de-Paix, the mango she had stolen, the vow she had broken, the hatred in her own heart for Rafe and the members of his crew who had attacked her, her continual doubts and wavering faith, and now, her immorality. When she had always prided herself on following all of God's laws so faithfully, these infractions had begun to dissolve the very essence of who she believed herself to be. Now she wasn't sure who she truly was anymore.

Grace's tears wove a crooked path down her cheeks. Something furry brushed against her, and she jumped. "Spyglass, how did you get in here?" She lifted the cat into her lap and scratched her head.

"I am a liar, a thief, a murderer, and a trollop, Spyglass," she wailed upon a whisper. "I am undone."

The cat only purred in return.

The darkness of the room closed in on Grace. Claire's rhythmic breathing drummed out the sentence of her guilt. The creak and groans of the brig rose to scold Grace for her fallen state. And the snap of the sails pounded like the judge's mallet, condemning her.

Please forgive me, Lord. Please do not abandon me.

Drawing her knees up to her chest, Grace leaned her head on Spyglass and wept into her fur.

"Though your sins be as scarlet, they shall be as white as snow."

Grace peered into the shadowy room. "I do not deserve it, Lord."

"As far as the east is from the west, so far hath I removed your transgressions from you."

Grace took a deep breath to quiet the sobs still rippling through her. Setting the cat onto the deck, she gathered her skirts, struggled to her feet, and made her way to the window. As the moon washed its milky light over her, she prayed it would wash away her guilt as well, prayed she could accept the mercy so freely offered. *Lord, I do not understand why all this is happening, but I am still Yours if You will have me.*

The door creaked open and a footstep sounded, not the light step of Annette, but the hollow thud of a boot. Grace's chest tightened, and she turned to see Mr. Thorn's dark outline framed by the doorway. Spyglass leapt onto the chair between them.

"Forgive me, Miss Grace, I mean. . ." he stuttered as he glanced over the cabin. "I thought I heard crying. . .I thought perhaps, well, never mind. It was most improper of me to enter without permission."

Yet he didn't leave.

Grace dabbed at her tears and drew herself up. " 'Tis quite all right, Mr. Thorn. 'Twas me you heard."

He withdrew his hat and took a step toward her. "Are you hurt?"

Grace put a finger to her lips and glanced at the cot. "Madame Dubois sleeps."

And when he still remained, she added, "I am fine, Mr. Thorn," hoping he would leave her to her misery.

"I see you are distraught, miss," he whispered.

"It is nothing."

"Has Captain Dubois harmed you?"

Grace touched her lips as renewed tears burned behind her eyes. Quite the contrary. "No more than I have allowed him."

The brig canted, and a beam of moonlight sliced across Mr. Thorn, accentuating the warm sparkle in his brown eyes and the red scar angling down his face and neck.

"You should have escaped to the island." He fingered his chin.

"Then Madame Dubois would not have survived."

"Humph." He gazed at the sleeping woman.

"You do not believe, Mr. Thorn?" Of all the people, besides Father Alers, Grace would have thought the scrupulous first mate would be the first to embrace the miraculous intervention of God.

He shifted his stance. "I heard your prayer. I saw the woman recover, but I cannot connect the two without reservation."

"But you *do* believe in God?" Grace's heart skipped a beat.

"Most certainly, miss. I simply do not believe He takes much care of the happenings on earth." Mr. Thorn fumbled with his hat.

"Yet when presented with proof that He is very much aware and involved, you refuse to believe." Grace instantly regretted her churlish tone, but she was tired, emotionally spent, and suddenly unsure of her ability to do any further good for God.

Mr. Thorn leaned on the door frame. "If what you say is true, why would He waste time on...on someone like Madame Dubois, an insolent mean-spirited shrew?" His voice hardened like steel.

Grace winced at his harsh censure of Claire. "None of us are without fault, Mr. Thorn." The truth spilled from her lips before she realized they were meant as much for her as for the first mate.

"Some are far better than others," he replied.

Grace flattened her lips. If Mr. Thorn would give no credence to her opinions, perhaps he would believe the testimony of a priest. "Father Alers confirms the event as an act of God."

Mr. Thorn snorted. "Begging your pardon, miss, but Father Alers is a silly old fool who turned his back on his true faith and now seeks a sign to confirm what he once believed. He is what your Bible describes as a wave of the sea being driven and tossed to and fro."

Grace grabbed her chain, appalled at the man's assessment. "Is there no one on board who meets with your approval, Mr. Thorn?"

"You may call me Justus, miss. And yes. I find you to be above reproach, which is why I have done all in my power to aid in your escape."

Justus. Grace stifled a chuckle. And like a judge, he wielded his sword of justice on everyone he met.

Like me.

The words stabbed her conscience. Was she like Mr. Thorn? Did she pass such quick and merciless judgments on all those around her?

Thorn glanced over his shoulder. "And Annette, despite her circumstances, appears to be principled and virtuous."

Grace shook her head. Annette, principled? Had the man gone daft?

"Do you happen to know where she is?"

"No. I saw her above earlier." The last thing Grace had seen of Annette was the flash of blue cotton as she ran away after their conversation—a conversation that mimicked the failings of the present one. "What is your business with her?"

"Merely concerned for her safety. Nothing unscrupulous, I assure you." Then bowing, he donned his hat. "I beg leave of you, miss."

"Good evening to you, Mr. Thorn. . .I mean Justus."

After he left, Grace turned to gaze out the window, where the stars began to fade beneath the approach of dawn. Though she hadn't slept, she was thankful for the close of this peculiar night. It was as if the air had been tainted with some maddening elixir, or perhaps they sailed through an aberrant patch of sea where reality became warped.

For the world no longer made any sense.

❧

Annette gripped the backstay and stepped onto the gunwale. Her bare feet slipped on the polished brass, and she clutched the rope tighter until the rough threads burned her tender skin. A gust of wind raked over her, trying to tear her from her perch, but she would not let it.

Not yet.

The fresh scent of dawn approaching filled her nostrils, and she dared a glance some twenty feet below where black waters churned like a malevolent brew. Their foamy fingers clawed at the hull as if trying to grab her. Swallowing, she closed her eyes and prayed for her ancestors to receive her into their arms.

At last she would finally be home. With the people to whom she belonged. Finally she would be at peace. Finally she would be at rest.

All she had lived for these past years, her only purpose, had been to rid herself of Madame Dubois, to send the woman into the underworld and appease the revenge that gnawed daily at Annette's soul. Rochelle Dubois, the master's last wife, whom Annette had served one year prior to her death, had been nothing like Claire. Though the lady had known Annette was the result of her husband's philandering, Madame Rochelle had treated her with kindness. Annette had truly grieved her passing, but no more than when she'd been introduced to her new mistress. Since then, Madame Claire's spiteful insults, self-centered demands, and malicious reprimands had eaten away at Annette until she could stand it no longer.

She had attempted once to run away and join the maroons, a group of Africans who had escaped their masters and lived free and wild in the forests of Saint Dominique. But they would not have her. They treated her no better than they treated the grand blancs, even making the abhorrent assumption that she was one of them because of the white blood flowing in her veins. Beaten, bruised, and heartbroken, she had dragged herself home.

Because she had nowhere else to go.

That was when she dove into the religion of her ancestors, seeking answers. And the answer she kept hearing over and over again was that the woman must die. It was the only way to be free.

But Mademoiselle Grace's God had ruined Annette's plans. A loving God would not do such a thing. A loving God would have allowed Madame Dubois to die as she deserved. A loving God would have granted Annette her freedom. She wanted nothing to do with this cruel God of the blancs. Now all that faced Annette was a future of abuse and hatred—a future of slavery. And she could not bear the thought.

A ribbon of gray settled on the horizon, pushing back the shroud of night. She didn't have much time before the crew arose and the helmsman and night watchman spotted her.

"Receive my spirit, oh great *Loa*. I am coming home." Annette released the rope. Her heart crashed in her chest. Her sweat-laden feet began to slip on the gunwale. The ship pitched and plunged over a wave, and Annette released herself from all fetters of this world.

She fell through the air. Free at last.

Until rough hands grabbed her waist.

She crashed against a warm, hard body, then landed on the deck with a thud. Pain shot up her back. She opened her eyes. A man's dark face filled her spinning vision. "Are you all right, mademoiselle?" Monsieur Thorn's voice.

Annette raised a hand to rub her aching forehead. "What have you done?"

"I have saved you," he said, sitting beside her and taking her hand. "Can you sit up?"

Annette shook off her dizziness and welcomed the anger brewing in her belly. "What have you done?" she repeated and swatted his hand away. Scrambling to her feet—a bit too fast—she wobbled on the shifting deck. "Imbécile."

The gray ribbon expanded over the horizon, taking on a ruddy hue—the same hue that now blossomed upon Mr. Thorn's face. "I save your life and you call me a fool?" He retrieved his tricorne from the deck.

"I did not wish to be saved."

His head jerked as if she'd slapped him. The angry flush faded from his features, replaced by concern. "You did not slip?"

Annette twirled around, not willing to face him, not wanting to see the care burning in his gaze, not wanting to believe it existed. She felt him move behind her. Placing his hands upon her shoulders, he turned her around. "Why?"

The tears she'd successfully kept at bay filled her eyes. "Because my mistress lives to torture me. My father ignores me. My people despise me, and the whites use me. I belong nowhere but with my ancestors in the afterworld."

Monsieur Thorn's jaw stiffened, and the green flecks in his brown eyes brightened. The look within them startled her. A look of admiration, of concern. A look she had never seen directed toward her. He drew her against his chest and wrapped his arms around her. Strong arms that locked her in a cocoon of warmth and protection.

No one had ever hugged her before.

⇌

Thorn held his breath. He didn't want to frighten away the woman who stood stiff as a bowline in his arms. But at least she had allowed him to embrace her. Slowly, her body softened, and she snuggled into him and released a shuddering sigh. The fear that had surged within him at her mention of jumping overboard now subsided to a tiny squall. Why would such a precious creature wish to deny the world her presence? And why did he feel like he'd died and gone to heaven with her in his arms?

"No matter what, there is always hope, mademoiselle," he whispered in her ear. "Do not give up."

The sun shot golden arrows over the indigo sea and across Thorn's face, announcing the new day. He squinted and tightened his embrace on Annette, not wanting these precious moments to end.

But like all good things in his life, it did end, as she pushed away from him and took a step back. Wiping her damp face, she looked down as if embarrassed. "You must think me *une sotte.*"

Thorn shook his head.

She lifted her gaze to his, her dark eyes hardened with bitterness. "Before, I want Madame Dubois dead. I want my revenge. But when it is stolen from me, I believe I have no choice but to die."

Thorn studied her. So she *had* been responsible for Madame's illness. But who could blame her? The woman made Annette's life unbearable. It was justice. It was merited. But not until that moment did Thorn realize how quickly the thirst for revenge could turn on the ones wielding it and end up destroying them instead. He stiffened beneath the revelation but shrugged it away before he was forced to ponder its application to himself.

"There is always a choice. Choose to live, Annette." He gripped her shoulders. "Promise me you won't try to take your life again."

She looked down. "You do not know what you ask, monsieur. You do not know the life I face. No one cares about me."

"I care." He smiled.

She gazed at him, her eyes a mélange of disbelief and hope. But then she rewarded him with a flutter of lashes and the semblance of a smile upon her lips.

Something caught Thorn's gaze over her shoulder, and he stiffened.

White sails floated like puffs of cotton on the horizon. Annette saw them too and gave him a curious look. Thorn looked aloft at the watchman in the crosstrees. He had not seen the ship yet. Good.

The more time that passed without detection, the faster they would be caught.

CHAPTER 31

Grace pried her eyes open, still heavy with slumber. The creaking and groaning of the brig she'd grown accustomed to tried to lull her back to sleep, but the dusty ray of sunshine streaming through the porthole told her it was well past dawn.

And she needed to speak with Rafe.

After Mr. Thorn's visit, Grace had gathered her blankets and curled up on deck, hoping to get much-needed sleep and make some sense of the discord bristling through her. But slumber had dashed about the cabin most of the night like a child playing tag, outwitting and outmaneuvering her. Finally, some time before dawn she must have drifted into unconsciousness out of sheer exhaustion.

Spyglass leapt from the chair and sauntered toward Grace. Plopping down on her stomach, the cat began kneading Grace's nightdress and saturating the air with the rumble of purrs. "You never seem overwrought, my friend. Would that I could be like you." Grace scratched Spyglass beneath the chin, and the cat stretched her neck toward the deck above. Closing her eyes, Grace longed to dive back into the ignorance of slumber, but Spyglass resumed her kneading, pricking Grace with one of her claws.

"Ooh!" She grabbed the cat. "Very well, no need to stab me. I shall arise." Sitting up, Grace kissed the cat on the cheek, then set her down on the deck. She glanced over the cabin. Annette's blankets lay folded in the corner.

"Bonjour," a voice coming from the cot startled Grace. She rose and sat in the chair, studying the madame. Though it had been little more than a day, color had returned to Claire's cheeks and her eyes regained their luster. "Good morning, Claire. How do you feel?"

"Stronger." She looked at Grace as if she were an angel. "I owe you my life, mademoiselle."

"No. You owe God your life."

Claire drew in a deep breath and struggled to sit. She pushed a curl from her face. "I never believed God cared for me."

"He does." Grace retrieved the mug of lemon water from the table and handed it to Claire.

Taking it, Claire took a sip. "I am not so sure." She shook her head and dropped her gaze to the mug clasped between her hands.

Grace's vision blurred with tears for the sorrow this woman had endured.

Claire pressed her lips together. "Yet no one could have shown me the love you did after I treated you so horribly, unless God helped them." She chuckled and Grace smiled, unable to respond, her throat closed tight with emotion.

Claire's face reddened. "Forgive me for sharing such personal confidences with you during my illness."

" 'Tis quite all right. I had no idea your life had been so difficult."

"It is no excuse for my behavior." Claire sighed.

Grace clasped her hands together. Indeed, she used to believe there was no excuse for bad behavior. She had always looked down on those who could not control their passions and who chose evil over good. Then why did she find no disdain for this woman before her, only understanding and concern?

"I love him still," Claire said without looking up.

The words shot straight to Grace's heart as Rafe's name drifted through the air, unspoken. "I know."

"But it is too late for us. I see that now." The sorrow lining Claire's face made Grace's heart crumble even as a twinge of jealousy sprang from among the pieces. She shook it off as Claire continued, "And I am married to a monster." She trembled.

Grace took the cup from Claire's hands before she dropped it and placed it back atop the table. "You needn't remain so, madame."

Claire's eyes searched Grace's in confusion.

"Your husband has been unfaithful and continues to flaunt his philandering before you daily."

Claire shrugged. "What is to be done about it?"

"He has broken his covenant with you, Claire."

"Vraiment?" A spark of hope lit her eyes, but then her shoulders sank. "But where would I go?"

Grace leaned over and took her hand. "Perhaps 'tis time to start trusting God for your future and not man or money."

Claire swallowed and her hand trembled. "We shall see."

"Do you feel up to a stroll on the deck?" Happy that Claire seemed slightly open to the things of God, Grace would put off her talk with Rafe if she could continue the conversation. "The fresh air would do you good."

"Non. I am still too weak." She raised a hand to her forehead. "And tired. I believe I shall sleep some more."

"Very well." Grace assisted Claire back down onto the cot. "We will talk later." She brushed the hair from her face.

"Merci." Claire smiled then closed her eyes.

Rising, Grace splashed water on her face from the basin. She donned her petticoat, stays, and skirts and brushed and pinned her hair up as best as she could—no longer concerned with a proper, tight coiffure.

Out in the companionway, she headed for Rafe's cabin. Spyglass pranced beside her as if she knew exactly where Grace was going and thought it was about time.

Ignoring the fluttering in her stomach, Grace approached the captain's door. She must apologize for their kiss and inform Rafe it could never happen again. She did not want him to get the wrong idea about her affections for him. Whatever they may be.

She squared her shoulders and knocked.

"Entrez-vous," Rafe's resonant voice bade her entrance, and she opened the door and slipped inside, Spyglass on her heels.

Rafe's gaze swept over her, and his grin reached his eyes in a sparkle that sent a wave of warmth through Grace.

Spyglass leapt upon the captain's desk and began batting the feathers of a quill pen.

The door thudded shut, and suddenly Grace found herself alone with the captain. He leaned against his desk, arms folded across his waistcoat, but the grin that had taken residence on his lips, a grin that contained a mixture of admiration and hunger, caused her heart to flutter.

Grace clasped her hands together and she looked down. The hollow thud of his footfalls pounded over the deck. Black leather boots appeared in her vision. His body heat radiated over her, carrying with it his scent of tobacco and the sea. And her heart felt as though it would crash through her chest. Placing a finger beneath her chin, he tipped her head up until their eyes met. "You wish to speak to me, mademoiselle?" His tone was playful, inviting.

"Oui, I mean yes." Grace pressed her moist palms over her skirts. "But if you please, could you back away a bit? I cannot seem to breathe."

Chuckling, he took a step back. "Oui, bien sûr. Mais does my presence disturb you?"

Gathering her wits and her resolve, Grace stood and faced him. "Yes." She might as well be honest. "It does."

"C'est bon."

"There is nothing good about it."

"A matter of perspective."

Grace sashayed away from the door, putting some distance between them. What was wrong with her? She'd come here to tell Rafe she would not receive his affections again. But instead all she wanted to do was feel his arms around her and his lips upon hers. Her cheeks heated until she had to withdraw a handkerchief from her sleeve and wave it around her face. "It grows warm below deck."

"Feels quite cool to me." He raised his brows.

Grace swallowed and looked up at him. He wore his black hair tied behind him, revealing a jaw peppered with stubble that reminded her of crushed charcoal. The fading purple of a bruise circled one eye. He stretched his shoulders back, only a hint of their strength discernable beneath his gray coat. To the left of his long black breeches tucked into his cordovan boots, hung the rapier that rarely left his side. And suddenly as she gazed into his dark, penetrating eyes, all rational thought dashed away in fear, leaving her standing there speechless.

He stepped toward her. "Mademoiselle?"

Grace held up a hand and averted her eyes to the contents of his desk. A full bottle of brandy glittered amber in the morning sun. "I do not believe I've ever seen an untouched bottle in your cabin, Captain. Have you given up your drink?" She hoped her playful tone would douse the heat that rose between them.

"I have, but I will pour one for you if you wish." His gaze brushed over Grace, and she thought she detected a slight grin on his lips.

"I would never touch such a vile drink."

"Ah, mademoiselle, vile it is not. Mais that it offends you has become the bane of my existence."

"I am pleased to hear it, Captain."

He bowed. "I live for your approval, mademoiselle."

Spyglass jumped to the deck and began to circle her skirts.

"You mock me, Captain."

He cocked his head. "Never."

She turned her back to him. "Will you return me to my home?"

"As I have said."

Grace grabbed the chain around her neck and pulled out her cross, then moved toward the cannon in the corner. "What of your hospital?"

"I will find another way."

"What changed your mind?" The words were out before she realized the implication of what she asked. The only thing that mattered was that he *had* changed his mind. Then why did her heart cinch within her chest awaiting his answer? She must be truly daft. For if he spoke the words she yearned to hear, she feared it would be the end of her.

⤝⤞

Rafe rubbed his jaw and stomped back to his desk, the bottle of brandy luring him like glittering gold. Memories of their kiss last night warmed his body. Even though she'd fled with a look of horror on her face, Rafe had kissed enough women to know that Grace had enjoyed every moment of their embrace. And that thought alone had caused a spark to ignite in his heart—in a place long cold and dead.

Turning, he stared at the mademoiselle's back, green skirts flowing around her, trimmed in gold lace at the hem and waist. Coils of loose raven curls danced over her neck, taunting him like bait.

Why had he changed his mind? He shook his head, unable to deceive himself any longer. He knew why. He should tell her how he felt. Fear began a frantic pounding within him, erecting barricades, reminding him of the pain of rejection. It was bad enough he had allowed himself to fall in love again. But he would be a bigger fool to allow another woman to break his heart.

He straightened his shoulders. "I decided the don would most likely return you. Such a shrewish tongue would never survive a Spanish overlord."

She whirled around in a cloud of green silk, disappointment tugging down the corners of her mouth. "Shrewish?" Her face paled. "Of all the. . ."

Rafe's heart sank as the ardor, the affection, drained from her eyes, replaced by fury and pain.

"Very well. That makes what I have to say much easier." She lifted her chin, clutched her skirts, and headed toward the door, where she halted and drew a deep breath. "I came to inform you that I was remiss in accepting your. . .your"—she looked away—"kiss. And that it must never happen again." She gave him a venomous look, and he instantly longed to make things right.

Rafe moved toward her, his voice low. "I heard no objection while your lips were on mine."

She fanned her red face with her handkerchief. Tiny scratches lined one cheek and Rafe swallowed, longing to kiss them away.

"I am voicing them now." She took a step back. "Promise me you will not take advantage of me again, Captain."

"Take advantage, sacre mer." Rafe ran a hand through his hair, feeling his ire rising. "Mademoiselle, you have my word that I will take no further liberties with you."

Her lip trembled. "I shall hold you to that, Captain." She swerved about and opened the door. "Come, Spyglass," she called over her shoulder, and the cat promptly obeyed, stopping to hiss at Rafe on her way out.

He slammed the door shut after them and leaned back against it. The woman had not only stolen his heart but his cat as well.

CHAPTER 32

Grace leaned on the railing amidships and gazed as the setting sun spread a plethora of brilliant colors: persimmon, violet, saffron, and coral across the horizon. Yet the beauty was lost on her. For clearly she had gone mad. After her encounter with the captain, she had been unable to stop crying. For what reason her mind could not fathom. Finally this harrowing adventure would be over. She would be safe in her home in Charles Towne. She should be the happiest woman alive. Then why did tears continually spring from her eyes and her heart feel as though it had been mauled by a grappling hook?

A light breeze wafted over her, cooling the perspiration on her arms and fluttering her curls about her neck. Perhaps the fresh air was all she needed to clear her head and heal whatever ailed her heart. Soon the darkness would drive her back to her cabin. She drew a deep breath of the tropical air, allowing it to fill her lungs with its spicy aroma. She would miss it. The sea held a different scent than the harbor in Charles Towne.

Charles Towne. Where she would no longer have to deal with the French rogue Captain Dubois. The captain had not only called her a shrew, but he had claimed it was the reason he refused to sell her to the don. That she had been hoping for another reason, a more personal reason, brought her shame. That he seemed equally anxious to return her home and be rid of her himself caused her heart to shrivel.

Am I a shrew? Grace's eyes burned. What did she expect? Did she expect this Frenchman, this mercenary, this man who kidnapped her, to declare his love for her?

I am a silly woman, Lord. A silly woman who has been no good to anyone. Done nothing right except perhaps step out of the way so You could save Claire. At least I can go home with some dignity.

Footfalls sounded and Grace turned to see Annette inching across deck, a bundle in her hands. Behind the mulatto, the crew's eyes brushed over her, then swept away. In one corner, Monsieur Weylan, Mr. Fisk, Mr.

Holt—the three sailors who had assaulted Grace below—and one other man huddled together as they often did when on deck.

"Bonsoir, mademoiselle." Annette moved beside her. The setting sunlight cast a rainbow of colors over her tawny skin, making her look far more innocent than Grace knew her to be. Yet Grace no longer felt angry with the lady.

"Good evening, Annette. How is Madame Dubois?" Grace asked.

Annette flattened her lips. "Madame rests. She will recover." The sting of hatred so oft in her voice when she spoke of her mistress had lost its potency. "You did not tell her what I did?" She gazed down at the choppy waves pounding against the hull.

Grace shook her head. "No need, since you promised not to harm her again."

"You are very kind, mademoiselle." Annette unwrapped the bundle in her hands, revealing the stones, beads, rattle, and amulet she used in the rituals of her religion.

The hairs on Grace's arms bristled, but she resisted the urge to leave. She needn't be afraid of such things. She only hoped the girl didn't intend to use them again—especially right here in front of her.

With a flick of the cloth, Annette tossed them all into the sea. They splashed one by one into the dark waters and disappeared from sight. Then she uttered a sigh of resignation, folded the cloth, and slipped it into a pocket in her skirt.

Grace tipped her head curiously. "Why did you do that?"

"I have been thinking. Compared to your God, the religion of my ancestors is weak and harms others. I no longer wish to pray to my ancestors."

Grace nearly leapt out of her shoes. "I'm very happy to hear that, Annette." She stared out to sea again, where the sun sank further behind the horizon, and pondered what to say next, not wanting to fail again. "Perhaps you would like to pray to my God?"

"Non." Annette's reply disappointed Grace. "I do not, mademoiselle. If He is the one true God, then I want nothing to do with a God who enslaves my people."

"But you are mistaken, Annette." Grace laid a hand on hers. "He is—"

A deep, buoyant chuckle drew Annette's attention behind them to where Mr. Thorn had joined Weylan and his friends. The mulatto's dark eyes latched upon the first mate, and Grace nearly gasped at the ardor she saw within them. Turning, she studied the odd group curiously. They spoke in whispered tones and bore a camaraderie that could only be fostered by long acquaintance or a bond of common goals. Yet, how often had Mr. Thorn scorned these very men.

"Bonsoir, mademoiselle." Annette scurried away, dropping below deck before Grace could continue their conversation. Frustration joined her already troublesome thoughts and she turned back around.

The sun disappeared behind the sea, dragging with it the last traces of its brilliant glory and leaving the world in a shroud of gray that soon faded to black. Yet Grace could not pull herself from the railing. She did not want to face the captain. She did not want to spend hours in idle chatter with Madame Dubois. In truth, she wanted to be alone to sort out the chaotic emotions whirling within her.

An hour later, the tread of boots and bare feet sounded, followed by hushed voices. Familiar voices that caused her to slink further into the shadows beneath the railing. A group of sailors made their way to the capstan amidships, their dark gazes scouring the deck for any intruders. They didn't seem to see her.

Grace held her breath and craned her ear toward the group, trying to make out the words over the slap of waves against the hull.

"So, we are in agreement?" Weylan said.

"Aye."

"Oui, I have informed the others." A third voice.

"When?"

"The ship should arrive tomorrow at sunrise." Weylan again.

"The captain will not go down easily."

At the sound of Mr. Thorn's voice, Grace tossed her hand to cover her mouth.

"He will have no choice."

The men grunted their approval and then dispersed across the deck, some heading up to the quarterdeck, others to join sailors lumbering by the larboard railing. The rest dropped below hatches. Grace clutched her throat and released her breath. Her thoughts whirled with the content of the men's conversation. Though her mind refused to accept it, she knew what she had heard. Plans for a mutiny.

But Mr. Thorn, of all people?

Grace trembled.

She must warn Rafe. She dared not move for several more minutes, at least until her heart no longer pounded in her ears. Then slowly, she tiptoed out from her hiding spot and slipped down the companionway.

And barreled right into Mr. Thorn.

Wearing the grin of a panther who had just caught his prey. "What do we have here, a little ship mouse?"

Grace tossed a hand to her throat. "Mr. Thorn, you gave me such a fright. I was just going to my cabin." She heard the tremor in her voice and tried to skirt around him, but he blocked her way.

"Indeed? And where have you come from?"

"I was. . .I was up on deck getting some air." She tried to shove him aside. "Now if you please, sir."

He grabbed her arm. His tight grip pinched her skin and sent pain down to her fingers. "I cannot let you warn him, miss. You know that."

Grace lifted her gaze to his. Determined brown eyes with a hint of sorrow met hers. Her heart thrashed in her chest. She kicked him in the leg. He let out a moan and bent over to rub the wound. Grace gathered her strength to shoulder him aside when something hard hit her head with a *thunk*. A burning pain seared down her neck and back. The companionway spun in her vision and the last thing she remembered was Mr. Thorn's contorted expression before everything went black.

⟡

Rafe sat up in bed and rubbed his aching eyes. Sunlight poured in through the stern window setting everything aglow in its path. Rising, he tossed a shirt over his head, feeling more hopeful than he had in years, despite his lack of sleep. During the wee hours of the night Rafe had paced across his cabin—had suffered beneath the pain that, upon delivering Grace to Charles Towne, he would never see her again. And he had concluded that it would be worth the risk of confessing his love to her, if there was but the slightest chance she might love him in return.

Which was why Rafe must seek out Mademoiselle Grace straightaway. It was time to risk his heart again. He had been betrayed by everyone he'd loved, but maybe, just maybe, Grace would be different. Perhaps her God truly did exist and by following Him, she had become incapable of dishonesty and betrayal.

Donning his waistcoat, boots, and baldric, he strapped on his weapons and headed out the door when Monsieur Fletcher nearly barreled into him. "A ship, Capitaine!" the man said in an urgent tone. Setting aside his task for now, Rafe followed him above.

"Where away?" Rafe shouted as he burst forth upon the deck.

"Two points off the starboard stern!" brayed a sailor.

Plucking out his spyglass as he went, Rafe leapt upon the quarterdeck and drew it to his eye before reaching the helm. Only a hint of the cool night remained in the morning wind that whipped through his hair. He focused the glass on a trio of sails, their bellies gorged with wind, not more than a league off their stern.

Monsieur Thorn appeared beside him.

"What do you make of her?" Rafe handed him the glass and braced himself on the deck as the ship pitched over a swell. Still angry at his first mate for offering to help Grace escape at the deserted island, Rafe decided to let the matter go and relieve the man of his duties the next time they weighed anchor at some port. Sans doute the man suffered from a concern for Mademoiselle Grace's welfare. How could Rafe blame him for that?

Thorn pressed the spyglass to his eye and shrugged. "A merchant, perhaps? She flies the ensign of France." He lowered the glass and squinted into the rising sun. "Nothing to cause alarm, I am sure."

Rafe eyed him curiously. "Then why does she give chase?"

"Perhaps she needs our help."

"I see no *signal de détresse*." Rafe snatched the glass back, examining the narrow lines of the hull, the shape and position of her sails. At least she was not one of Woodes's two ships that had pursued them earlier. Sacre mer, was every ship in the Caribbean after him?

Lowering the glass, he turned to Thorn, surprised by the grin tugging at his first mate's lips. "All hands aloft. Loose topgallants. Clear away the jib."

"But our main-topmast, Captain." Thorn seemed in no hurry to obey.

"I am aware of the damage, Monsieur Thorn. Raise what sails we have left." Rafe ground his teeth together and gripped the hilt of his rapier. "And have Monsieur Porter clear the tackles and load the guns."

"Zooks, Captain, is that quite necessary?" Thorn chuckled and brushed specks of dried salt from his coat.

Scowling, Rafe turned a cold eye upon his first mate, a man who had never hesitated to obey him. "Do as I say, Thorn, or I'll find someone who will."

The first mate touched his hat, gave Rafe a grin laced with indignation and turned to bellow orders to the crew. Ignoring Thorn's impertinence, Rafe narrowed his eyes upon the ship that dared to intrude upon his waters.

Spyglass leapt into his arms and draped herself over his right shoulder. Purring filled his ears, and Rafe stroked her fur, releasing a familiar scent that delighted him. "So you have been with the mademoiselle." He grinned. "I do not blame you." His thoughts shot to the look of pain on Grace's face when he had called her a shrew. He had not meant to cause her any suffering, but only to cloak his true feelings. But he must not think of that now. For now he must shake this snake from his leg—this ship that dared to pursue him.

An hour crept by, and Rafe still was unable to determine either the ship's identity or her purpose.

The sun climbed midway between wave and topmast, and already the heat sent streams of sweat down his neck and back. The thunderous snap of sails glutting with wind sounded above. Shielding his eyes, he glanced at the line of men balancing across the foretop yard, as they adjusted sails to catch the shifting trade winds. At Rafe's direction, Monsieur Atton altered course repeatedly in an attempt shake off the nagging ship. But to no avail. "Zut alors, what does le irksome mongrel want?"

Rafe shrugged off his coat and tossed it to the deck by the railing, allowing the salty breeze to cool him. He stormed toward the taffrail and raised his spyglass again.

"She gains on us," Thorn shouted from behind him.

"Je sais!" Rafe wondered at the lack of concern in this first mate's voice.

Father Alers approached and squinted in the sunlight. The wrinkles around his eyes folded like the threads of an old rope.

Rafe adjusted the glass, bringing the ship into clearer view. A bark. Three-masted, fore- and aft-rigged. The French flag flapped lazily upon her bowsprit.

Shifting the telescope aft, Rafe focused on the ensign upon the mainmast. His heart leapt in his throat.

The figure of two black lions battling against the backdrop of a red coat of arms. The Dubois crest. Rafe lowered the glass and slammed it shut. "Sacre mer, my father's ship."

"Votre père?" Standing at the quarterdeck railing beside Rafe,

Father Alers flinched, his gray hair puffing around his head like a turkey displaying its feathers.

"Oui." Rafe's blood boiled.

Father Alers grabbed the glass and examined the ship himself. Lowering it, he scratched his gray beard. "I suppose he wants his wife back."

"He can have her," Rafe spat; then he marched to the quarterdeck railing.

"Egad, your father. How on earth did he find you?" Thorn appeared beside him.

"I wonder." Rafe shot an accusing glare at his first mate. In light of his impudent behavior toward Rafe, Thorn's recent deception regarding Grace began to reek of treachery rather than mere concern for the mademoiselle.

Rafe turned to the helmsman. "Hard to larboard, Monsieur Atton. Let's keep aweather of him. Perhaps he'll grow bored as he does with most of his intrigues."

"Hard to larboard, Capitaine," Monsieur Atton replied and adjusted the wheel.

Le Champion swept over the rolling waves under a full press of sails, at least the sails that remained. Rafe cursed. With his main-topmast damaged, he'd have trouble outrunning his father's ship.

"Perhaps you should see what he wants?" Monsieur Thorn lifted one brow.

"If he has come for his wife, I am happy to hand her over. Otherwise, I have nothing to say to him."

Rafe marched to the bulwarks, annoyed with his first mate's cavalier attitude. A gust of wind struck him, yanking strands of his hair from his tie. The ship bucked, and he gripped the railing until the wood bit into his fingers. Rafe had spent a childhood buried beneath his father's shadow, and the next several years of his life digging out from under it. Aside from his last unavoidable visit, he had vowed never to see the man again—the man who ruled the Dubois estate and most of Port-de-Paix with the iron scepter of cruelty.

But the sea was Rafe's territory. Was it not enough the man had stolen Rafe's childhood? Was it not enough he had stolen his fiancée? Did he want the sea as well?

Rafe grunted and gripped the pommel of his rapier. Whatever mischief his father was about, it would only end in disaster. Of that he was sure.

As the minutes passed, Rafe grew more agitated. His father's ship furled tops and mainsails, stripped to mizzen and sprit, and was now within one half mile of *Le Champion*, so close Rafe could make out her crew, as well as the yellow plume fluttering atop his father's cocked hat. Yet still Rafe waited. Waited for a signal to parley, a salute of the flag, anything to announce the man's intentions.

Finally, when the ship sailed just a quarter mile off their starboard stern, the flag atop her foremast dipped in a signal requesting a parley. Rafe narrowed his eyes, his gut churning with distrust. "Return the signal, but ensure our guns are loaded and ready. And man the swivels," Rafe ordered Mr. Thorn.

"But 'tis obvious he means us no harm," the first mate replied.

Rafe's jaw hardened, and blood surged to his fists. "Do as I say!"

"As you wish, Captain." Thorn's voice carried a sneering bite as he touched his hat and left.

Rafe shook his head. What was wrong with the man today?

Father Alers grunted and laid a hand on Rafe's arm. "Be patient, my boy."

"Never fear." Rafe sighed and crossed his arms over his chest. "Regardless that my father has never given me a reason to trust him, I will not fire upon him without cause. I shall wait to see what he wants."

His father's ship plunged through the turquoise sea, sending a foamy squall over her bow as she tacked alee then came even on *Le Champion*'s keel. Without warning, her larboard gun ports popped open one by one and the charred muzzles of ten guns spewed out from them like ravenous black tongues.

Father Alers gave a sordid chuckle. "Your wait is over, Capitaine."

"Zut alors." Rafe swerved on his heels. A string of rapid orders exploded from his lips, sending his men flying across the deck. "Helm's lee! *Adieu-va!*" he bellowed. Above him the sailors scrambled to let go the foresheets.

"Rise tacks and sheets!" Rafe braced himself on the deck as *Le Champion*, with straining cordage and creaking blocks, swung to larboard. She pitched over a swell, and foamy spray swept over the deck, slapping Rafe's boots. Lugsails flapped thunderously until the sails caught the wind in an ominous snap. *Le Champion* veered promptly about on an eastern tack, flashing the pursuing ship her rudder.

Boom! A volcano of hot metal fired from his father's ship, sending the air aquiver.

"All hands down!" Rafe dove to the deck. The crunch and snap of wood grated over his ears, and he looked up to see a gaping hole of jagged shards marring the taffrail. Rafe jumped to his feet. The other shots plunged harmlessly into the churning wake off their stern. He released a sigh and lifted a contemptuous gaze toward his father's ship.

Ten puffs of gray smoke curled upward from her hull like snakes beneath a charmer's flute. His father had fired upon him. After requesting a parley. Had the man no decency?

"Bring her about!" Rafe shouted to Monsieur Thorn, who was struggling to rise. "And ready the larboard guns."

The ship yawed widely to port as Rafe leapt down the quarterdeck ladder and marched across the main deck. Fury fanned his hatred into a roaring flame. His father may have oppressed him in his youth. He may have belittled him and defeated him, but Rafe was no longer a little boy, and he'd be keelhauled and strung from the yardarm before he'd allow his father to best him upon the seas.

Bracing his boots upon the slanted deck, Rafe glanced aloft as his crew worked furiously to complete another tack. Pride swelled within him at their skill and efficiency. He had taught them well. In a few minutes they'd be in position to deliver a well-deserved broadside to his father's ship.

A ship that now floundered in an effort to veer away from *Le Champion* as the crew no doubt sensed their imminent danger. Rafe grinned. He glanced over his shoulder. From the quarterdeck, Monsieur Thorn gazed at their enemy with the look of expectancy, rather than anger. Father Alers made his way over the teetering deck to Rafe.

Le Champion rose and swooped over the turquoise swells. The creak of her blocks and the rattle of flapping sails filled the air along with the silken rustle of the sea along the hull. The sting of gunpowder tainted the morning breeze. Rafe ordered top and studding sails reefed as they swung around and hove to, athwart the ship's bow.

His father's crew darted frantically across the deck and up into the ratlines, attempting to find the wind and turn their ship. Amidst the chaos, her larboard guns had not been reloaded and still hung from their ports in impotence.

Rafe had them. "Monsieur Thorn!" he bellowed.

"Yes, Captain."

"On my order."

"On your order, Captain." Thorn shifted his stance, not meeting Rafe's gaze.

Facing forward, Rafe studied his prey. Within seconds, they'd be in perfect position to loose a broadside. Within seconds, he would finally beat his father, sink his ship, and take the man prisoner. A tingle of elation ran through him at the prospect.

He opened his mouth to give the order.

"Wait, Captain. They raise a white flag," Monsieur Thorn said

Rafe glanced at the white cloth climbing toward the blue sky.

Father Alers turned to him with a look of censure. "They surrender, Rafe."

"He surrenders because he knows I have the advantage and could blast him from the water." Rafe grabbed his baldric. Yet a thread of relief wove through his knotted insides. No matter what his father had done to him, no matter the beatings, the humiliation, the belittling, the hatred, no matter the way he treated Rafe's mother, it was wrong to fire upon one's father.

Besides, Grace would not approve. Scanning the deck, he searched for a glimpse of her, but she was nowhere to be seen. She had admonished him to be a better man than he was. And right now, he wanted more than anything to prove to her that he could be. He turned around. Off their larboard side, his father's ship slipped through the sea, already positioned board by board. On her foredeck, the man who sired him stood awaiting his fate. If Rafe intended to loose a broadside, he must do so immediately or forfeit the chance to prove that his father had been wrong about him.

To prove that Rafe was not a failure.

Rafe clenched his fists until they hurt. "Stand down."

Mr. Thorn smiled. "Very well, Captain."

Shoving aside the angst churning in his gut, Rafe released a ragged sigh. "Arm the men and then signal my father to come aboard."

CHAPTER 33

Grace woke with a start. Pain burned through her head. Her lips ached. The taste of sweat-laden cloth filled her mouth. Why couldn't she move her hands and legs? She sprang up, and her head crashed into something hard. A crate? A barrel? Hard to tell in the darkness. Panic took over. She wrestled to free her hands, but the more she struggled the more her wrists stung until something warm seeped from them. Blood. She tried to scream, but her voice came out a muffled groan from behind the cloth stuffed in her mouth. *Lord?* As her mind cleared, she tried to recall how she ended up in this dark prison.

Mr. Thorn. The last thing she remembered was bouncing off his thick chest and the furtive look of treachery on his face.

The mutiny! They planned to mutiny!

Inching her backside over the rough planks of the deck, Grace used her bound hands to locate the door. She must be in some kind of storage room. She must get to Rafe. She must warn him. She had no idea how long she'd been in here. Lifting her legs, she kicked the door. *Pound. Pound. Pound.* She groaned a muted call for help. For several minutes, she repeated the process until her legs ached and her throat swelled.

Boom! Boom!

Cannon blasts fired in the distance. Grace's breathing took on a frenzied pace. Who was firing at them? Footsteps sounded on the deck above her like methodical drums. Muffled shouts and curses trickled down to taunt her ears. Grace screamed again and thumped her feet against the door. Nothing.

She would not give up. She must warn Rafe before it was too late.

⁓

Within minutes, Monsieur Dubois and several of his crew had boarded a cockboat and with oars to water, made quick work of the distance between the two ships. Rafe's father stood at the bow with arms at his hips and

910

yellow feather fluttering from his hat as if he were the conqueror of the world.

Familiar with his father's ostentatious display, Rafe ignored him, though he could not deny the fury that pulsed through every vein. "Steady, men." His piercing gaze scoured his crew as they stood armed with rapiers, pistols, and axes.

The cockboat thumped against the hull, and two of Monsieur Dubois's crew climbed over the bulwarks. Each gripped a pistol in one hand and drew their sword with the other. Three of Rafe's crew took a step forward, taunting the men with their blades and angry curses. Rafe stayed them with a lift of his hand.

Finally, his father clambered aboard, his face plump and red. "Infernal ladder," he grunted; then glancing at Rafe's crew, he lengthened his stance, adjusted his velvet waistcoat, and replaced his look of frustration with a veneer of confident insolence. He turned cold eyes toward his son. "No stomach for a fight, Rafe?" He waved a ruffled handkerchief in the breeze. "So much like your mother."

"If it's a fight you want, Père, it's a fight I'll give you. My men are well trained," Rafe replied, his statement confirmed by thunderous grunts behind him.

Monsieur Dubois shot his beady gaze across the deck as the remainder of his men jumped over the bulwarks and joined him. That made twelve men to Rafe's thirty.

"Have your men stand down, Father. I seek no battle between us." And that was no lie. He wanted his father to state his business, take his wife, and be gone. Rafe glanced across the deck, wondering why Grace had not come above but was thankful when he did not see her.

Monsieur Dubois tugged on the white swath of silk at his neck and directed his gaze to Mr. Thorn. The first mate shook his head and looked down.

"Very well, Rafe." Monsieur Dubois gestured for his men to lower their weapons.

Rafe glared at his father, questioning his decision to allow him aboard. "You should thank me for sparing your life, Father. For it was only our relation and our common bond to ma mère which stood between me and the cannons that would have sunk you to the depths."

"C'est vrai? I am more inclined to believe it was your cowardice that failed you." His father laid a hand on his hip and took a turn about the deck. "How you have succeeded as a mercenary I shall never know. Well, perhaps that is why you saw fit to steal my wife from me. Intending to sell her as well?"

Monsieur Thorn slipped from beside Rafe and disappeared behind him. Was the man so much a coward that he could not stand beside his captain in time of need?

"I did not kidnap Claire," Rafe shot back as he slid his fingers over the warm pommel of his rapier. One false move and he would silence his father's insolent tongue.

"Non? Is she not on your brig?" Monsieur Dubois's tone rose in sarcasm.

Rafe flexed his jaw. "Oui, but not by my doing."

"Then by whose? I suppose she stole away in the night and hired a boatman to bring her aboard?" He chuckled. "She has neither the brains nor the bravery for such an act."

A moan sounded from the companionway, and all eyes shot in the direction of the woman emerging from below.

"Ah there you are, ma chérie." Monsieur Dubois's features sharpened, but he made no move to aid his wife.

Claire walked across the deck, her blond hair shimmering in the noontime sun. The color had returned to her skin though her chest rose and fell from the exertion of climbing abovedecks.

Claire reached his side. "Henri. What are you doing here?" Disbelief and anger rang in her tone.

"I came to rescue you, ma chérie." His smile sent ice through Rafe.

Claire's face scrunched, and she eyed him with disbelief.

"What has Rafe done to you, ma chérie?" he went on. "Are you injured?"

"She has been ill," Rafe said. A gust of hot wind tainted with human sweat tore over the deck, tossing his hair.

Monsieur Dubois took Claire's arm and tried to draw the woman into an embrace. She stiffened, but he forced her against him. "Are you so inept, my son, that you cannot take care of one woman?"

Rafe snorted. "No more inept than a man who cannot hold on to his own wife."

Father Alers coughed.

Monsieur Dubois huffed and directed his gaze behind Rafe where Rafe heard the thudding of bare feet on the deck. He stole a quick glance over his shoulder but only Monsieur Thorn and a band of Rafe's men met his gaze. He faced forward. "How did you find me?"

"You are not the only one with skills upon the sea."

"Which is why your broadside splashed impotently into the water."

A vein pulsed on his father's sweaty neck. "Yet I believe it is I and my men who have boarded your ship."

"Only by my leave." Rafe groaned and stomped his boot on the deck. "Assez! If you have come for your wife, take her and go." He waved a hand in dismissal.

"No, please, Rafe," Claire cried. Fear and desperation scampered across her blue eyes.

"Silence, woman!" Rafe's father put his arm around Claire's shoulders, forcing her against him. Her face pinched. He glared at Rafe. "And leave her kidnapper unpunished?" Monsieur Dubois's eyes searched the deck. "And where is your other victim? I assume you stole Mademoiselle Grace as well?"

"Rafe did not kidnap me, Henri." Claire swallowed and stared at the deck. "I came of my own will."

Henri's face mottled in blotches of red and white. The veins in his neck pulsed. Rafe feared he would explode, but then a flash of anguish peeked out from behind the anger in his eyes. He shoved Claire to the side. "It matters not."

"Of course it matters, Father." Rafe shook his head. "We have no quarrel now." At least none Rafe cared to address. Then why did the hairs on the back of his neck suddenly stand on end?

Footfalls pounded on the deck behind him. Muffled voices bounced through the air.

The *ching* of sword against sheath. The cock of pistols. Rafe froze. The taste of metal filled his mouth.

Slowly he turned around. The tips of ten rapiers shot toward him. Sunlight glared from their blades and bounced over the deck like grape-shot. Toward the forefront of the mob of Rafe's own men stood Monsieur Thorn, wearing a look of haughty disdain. Beyond them, the remainder of Rafe's crew halted beneath the leveled aim of blades and pistols.

Rafe threw back his shoulders and lengthened his stance to cover up the fear tying his stomach into knots. He swung back to his father, whose blue eyes glowed with cruel deception. "What is this about?"

His father grinned. "This is what I believe you call a mutiny."

913

CHAPTER 34

Grace stopped pounding the door to catch her breath. Perspiration streamed down her face and neck. Her head ached. Blood dripped from her wrists, and her mouth was stuffed with cotton. But at least the cannons had ceased and the ship had slowed to a near halt. In light of what she'd overheard, however, that might not have been a good sign at all.

She continued battering the door with her feet and groaning through the saturated cloth in her mouth.

Finally, she heard shuffling in the hall. "Mademoiselle?" Annette's sheepish voice squeaked through the oak.

Grace groaned and kicked the door again. The latch clicked, and light spilled in around the mulatto's thin form.

"Mademoiselle!" Annette dropped to the deck and plucked the handkerchief from Grace's mouth. "Who did this to you?"

Grace coughed and tried to speak but her words emerged in a grating rasp.

Annette battled the ropes around Grace's wrists and feet. "When you not come back to the cabin last night, I worry, and come looking for you."

"Thank you, Annette," Grace managed to say. Tearing the loosened ropes from her ankles, she rose. A wave of dizziness swirled her vision, and she leaned on the bulkhead.

"Are you all right, mademoiselle?"

Grace gripped Annette's shoulders. "Where is Rafe?"

"Captain Dubois is on deck, mademoiselle." Annette's brows drew together.

"Come, we must hurry." Grace swept past her.

"It is not good." The *tap tap* of Annette's shoes behind Grace only added to her rising fear. "You should not go above, mademoiselle."

Ignoring the lady and the sinking feeling in her gut, Grace navigated

914

the narrow hallways and companionway. Then clutching her skirts, she climbed up the ladder and emerged into the sunlight, Annette fast on her heels.

A growling mob undulated over the main deck, and Grace ducked into the shadows beneath the quarterdeck. She strained to see through the horde of cursing sailors. Drawing Annette to her side, she circled around the mob until she spotted the yellow feather fluttering atop Monsieur Dubois's hat. Bright flashes caused her to squint and focus on their source.

Swords. Drawn swords. All pointed at Rafe. She was too late.

⮑

Rafe cursed himself as every muscle within him grew taut. How could he have been such a fool? He eyed his father, longing to draw his rapier and etch a permanent frown over his caustic grin. Stupide. Rafe shifted his gaze from his father to Monsieur Thorn. Despite the anger boiling in Rafe's gut, a sharp twang struck his heart. "So you joined mon père against me?" He formed the words his mind still refused to believe. That the man who had sailed with him for a year, the man he considered his friend, had committed the ultimate betrayal. But why not? Everyone betrayed Rafe in the end.

Thorn raised one shoulder. "So it would seem."

"And all of you!" Rafe yelled over their shoulders to those of his men who had joined the traitorous mob. "Have I not served you well?" He scanned their faces. Weylan, Holt, Fisk, Porter, Maddock, and a dozen other men who had been his companions. Some lowered their gazes, others gave him a sheepish look of apology, while others twitched their fingers over their weapons as if anxious to be done with him.

He turned back to Thorn. "Why involve my father in this?"

Thorn cocked a brow. "In the event there were not enough men willing to turn against you, Captain. And as it turned out, I needed his crew." He shook his head. "Even when I informed the men that you reneged on your promise to sell the mademoiselle and line their pockets, most still would not join us. A testament to you, I suppose. Though for the life of me, I find their loyalty confounding."

Movement on the fore- and quarterdecks drew Rafe's attention to groups of sailors who gathered at each railing, shock and fear tightening their features as some of their own companions held them at gunpoint.

Even Monsieur Atton, normally a solid rock of composure, stared at Rafe with a look of horror.

Weylan stepped forward, tugging upon the lace at his cuffs. "It's about her." He wagged a thumb toward his left, and Rafe glanced to see Mademoiselle Grace huddling in the corner beside Annette, her eyes wide, and her bottom lip quivering.

Zut alors, the woman always chose the most inopportune time to come on deck. His stomach tightened. What would happen to Grace now? "We heard you had grown soft on the woman," Weylan added with a sneer.

Rafe faced him. "What is that to you?" He gripped the hilt of his rapier, causing the swords pointed his way to jerk to attention. Grace gasped.

"Easy, messieurs." Rafe released the weapon and narrowed his eyes upon his father. "This has nothing to do with your wife." Rafe huffed as understanding dawned. "You planned this mutiny all along."

"Ah, gentlemen." His father glanced over the mob. "At last my son has regaled us with a smidgen of his acclaimed wisdom." His blue eyes flashed. "I had begun to doubt you possessed it."

Ignoring him, Rafe directed his attention to Thorn. "And you told him where to find us."

Thorn grinned.

Rafe nodded toward Claire who leaned against the foredeck, her eyes laced with horror. "Was she also a part of this?"

"My faithless wife?" Henri chuckled. "Non, she is merely a pawn. En fait, she believed she was running away to be with you. Had I known I was marrying a *souillon*, I would have allowed you to keep her."

Rafe gripped his baldric as a blast of wind tore over him. "But you did marry her. You won, Father. Why come after me?"

"Because I could not stand that she still wanted you, still loved you." Rafe's father shot a look toward Claire that burned more with pain than hatred, then he stomped toward Rafe, his eyes bulging. "Just like your mother. It was always about you. Smart, quick-witted, capable Rafe. Stronger, wiser, better." He spat to the side.

Rafe winced beneath the man's fury. He could find no cause for it. Nothing he had done in his childhood except succeed at all he did. Shouldn't a father be proud of such a son? "I was never in competition with you."

Henri snorted, his face reddening. "Oh, but you were. Every time you succeeded. Every time you won the affections of a lady I coveted, every time Claire's eyes lit up at the mention of your name. Every time I heard of your grand successes upon the sea and was bombarded by the people's praise for you in town." He snorted. "Assez!"

The loathing that twisted his father's features stunned Rafe. "So you devise a plan for me to appear to kidnap your wife so you can come after me and kill me?"

"How else to be rid of you within the bounds of the law? I am not a murderer." Henri lifted his shoulders as if shrugging off his anger, shrugging away his son.

"My crew will testify otherwise." Rafe said.

"Who would believe them over me?"

Rafe's heart collapsed into a ball of lead. His father was right. "I did not realize your hatred of me ran so deep."

Henri glared at Rafe for a moment. He licked his lips and looked away. "You are not my son."

A drop of sweat slid down Rafe's back. The sun fired hot arrows upon him. Waves slapped against the hull. Claire gasped.

Rafe's fingers went numb. "What did you say?"

Henri gazed over the sea, his stony face holding a trace of sorrow. "I said you are not my son."

"Then whose son am I?"

His father met his gaze. His eyes glinted like steel. "You are the son of the pirate Jean du Casse."

CHAPTER 35

Jean du Casse? Blood dashed from Rafe's head. Blinking, he caught himself before he stumbled backward. Jean du Casse, the admiral of the French navy? The man knighted by Louis XIV, the governor of Saint Dominique? The buccaneer who led the raid on Spanish forces at Cartagena? That Jean du Casse? The incredulous possibility swirled in Rafe's mind. Could it be true? Could he be the son of such a great man? Rafe raised a furrowed brow to Henri as his jumbled thoughts fled to his mother.

"I see where your mind takes you, Rafe." Monsieur Dubois stroked his pointed beard. "Straight to the source. En fait, I only discovered the truth after your mother died. Evidence of her duplicity in a letter I found stuffed in a drawer. I regret to dash your virginal memory of her, but she was nothing more than a souillon, a prostituée."

In a flash, Rafe drew his rapier and leveled its tip upon Henri's throat. "You will take that back, monsieur. If my mother found love in the arms of another it was because you drove her to it."

Blades flashed his way. A sharp tip pressed against his side. Rafe glanced in the direction to see Thorn's furious face at the end of the gleaming hilt.

"Stand down," Thorn ordered. "Or I'll run you through."

"Not before I slit his throat." Rafe pressed the point harder, and blood blossomed on Henri's white cravat as his eyes became transfixed in horror.

Thorn chuckled. "Go ahead. It matters not to me. "You may fall atop his dead body if that is what you wish."

Silence swallowed all sound aboard the ship except Henri's hurried breathing. Rafe's hand began to shake. Not from fear or even rage, but from the overwhelming desire to destroy this man who had destroyed Rafe's life.

"No, Rafe." Mademoiselle's quivering voice spilled over him from behind, followed by Claire's sobbing, "S'il vous plaît."

Lowering his blade, Rafe stepped back. Though he cared nothing for his own life, or for the life of Henri Dubois, he had Grace to consider. And as long as he lived, he would do his best to protect her. But he must live. He glanced her way. Green eyes, pooling with fear, met his. Claire, her face red and puffy, clung to Grace's left arm, while Annette stood as rigid as a mast off her right.

Father Alers's gray hair flared about him. He gripped the pommel of his blade and stepped forward from beside the three women. "Say the word, Capitaine, and I will fight by your side."

Henri chuckled. "How noble. Can you invoke no more loyalty than that of one old man?" He grinned, and the sailors joined his laughter.

"Non, mon ami," Rafe spoke to the former priest as he inclined his head toward Grace. "Stay with her. Keep her safe."

Father Alers nodded his understanding and took a step back.

Tears spilled from Grace's eyes.

Wrenching his gaze from her, Rafe thrust the tip of his rapier into the deck and leaned on the handle. "So, Henri, what will it be? Keelhaul? Hanging from the yardarm, or will you toss me to the sharks?"

"Such imagination!" Henri laid a finger on his chin. "Non, nothing so colorful. Monsieur Thorn has requested the honor of a duel to the death."

Rafe couldn't help the chuckle that escaped his lips. "To the death?" He directed a challenging gaze toward Thorn. "And what happens when I win?"

Henri smirked. "It depends on how long you can swim."

Rafe narrowed his eyes upon Henri, then plucked his sword from the deck and faced Thorn. "If you dare to challenge me, Thorn, you are a bigger fool than I thought."

But his words did not have the intended effect on Thorn. Instead, his first mate returned his gaze with hauteur. "You forget, Captain, I learned swordsmanship in His Majesty's Navy. And I have kept my skills sharp. Have you?"

Rafe grinned. "We shall see."

⤛

A duel to the death.

Grace's stomach lurched, and she realized if she'd had anything to eat in the past twelve hours, it would now be upon the rolling planks beneath her feet.

One hand on his hip, Thorn raised his blade and twirled it around Rafe's chest, taunting him. The captain stood his ground, a smug look on his face that was surprisingly devoid of fear.

Claire threw a hand to her chest and began wheezing then melted into Grace's arms. Father Alers helped lead Claire to a nearby barrel in the shade before he took a stance beside the women.

Rafe doffed his hat and flung it to the deck. "Are you going to fight or twirl your blade through the air like a woman?"

Thorn squinted, tightened his lips, then lunged toward Rafe. The captain leapt to the side and lifted his own blade to strike Thorn. Thorn recovered and met his thrust hilt to hilt. The *chink* of metal sliced over the ship.

Monsieur Dubois retreated to the railing as the crowd withdrew, allowing the combatants room. Shouts and jeers trumpeted through the air heavy with heat and sweat.

Grace's throat went dry. What if Rafe lost? What if he died? Horror stiffened her back. She could not imagine a world without Captain Rafe Dubois. She could not imagine this ship without him. And she could not imagine her life without him. The last realization stunned her the most. That, along with the awareness that her own welfare had not been foremost in her thoughts.

Rafe swung aside and drove his rapier in from the right. "We were friends once."

"We were never friends." Thorn dipped to the left and brought his blade up to strike the captain in the leg.

Rafe swerved about to avoid the thrust and circled his opponent. "Then you are a good liar."

Above them, loose sails flapped beneath a blast of wind as the brig rolled over a swell.

Thorn matched Rafe's stride until the two rotated over the deck like the spokes of a wheel. "Indeed I am a liar, but you are a murderer."

Rafe cocked his head, wiped the sleeve over his moist brow. "I am. But who do you say I murdered?"

Thorn charged him, his face a jumbled mass of red. "My sister."

Grace's breath halted in her throat.

Rafe met his attack and the clank of swords filled the air. "I have never killed a woman," he ground out with exertion.

The two men grunted, their swords slammed together. Rafe freed his blade and swept down on Thorn, nicking his right shoulder.

Thorn winced, a slice of purple forming on his blue waistcoat. He stared at it as if it were some strange occurrence, then his face grew hard and stiff.

"Who is your sister?" Rafe charged him again.

Thorn met his attack and gave Rafe a venomous look. "You do not remember her, then?" He pulled back. His lips curled in disgust and he charged Rafe like a mad bull, but his effort spent itself idly against the captain's skill. Rafe met each blow, each strike, with a calm defensive maneuver. Thorn stumbled, panting heavily, his mounting frustration evident on his face.

"You can take 'im, Thorn," one man yelled.

"Don't let that *cochon lâche* get the best of you!" another brayed.

"Finish 'im off, Capitaine!" Mr. Atton bellowed from the quarterdeck, echoed by several cheers, and Grace was thankful at least some of Rafe's men remained loyal.

Her eyes slipped to Monsieur Dubois. One of his hands clutched the larboard railing, the other was stuffed within his coat, as he watched the duel as if it were an afternoon's entertainment.

Even so, a measure of ease settled upon Grace's nerves. Rafe was indeed well skilled with the sword. Truth be told, in all her years of watching her father's swordplay with his friends in Portsmouth, she'd seen none to compare. But now her fear shifted to Mr. Thorn. For even though he had betrayed his captain—and her—she did not wish for him to die.

⤜⤏

Rafe eyed his opponent, noting that the look of insolence had spilled from his face along with the sweat that now ran like streams over his cheeks. "I know nothing of your sister."

Thorn stormed toward Rafe, brandishing his blade high.

Rafe met his thrust with a counter-parry, then he danced to the side and came in from the right. Their swords crashed, steel on steel, the sun glinting off their blades.

Pushing back, Thorn spit to the side and shook the sweat from his face. "Remember when you frequented Nassau upon your father's merchantman?"

Rafe kept his rapier aimed upon the rogue as his thoughts sped back in time. "Oui, I remember Nassau." A time long ago when his mother still lived. A time when Rafe believed that if he worked hard enough he might make his father proud.

"Elizabeth. Elizabeth Grayson," Thorn growled.

Rafe halted, his chest heaving. A vision of a young woman with eyes the color of lilacs rose from his memories. "Oui, Elizabeth." He furrowed his brow. "Your sister? Thorn is not your real name?"

"Does that surprise you?" Thorn lunged at Rafe, but Rafe batted his sword aside.

"I did not kill her." He'd had enough of this foolishness.

"Perhaps not her body." Thorn raged, his brown eyes flashing. "But her life, her future."

With a shake of his head, Rafe allowed his gaze to drop. All this had been caused by a woman's broken heart?

"Allow me to extend to you her compliments." Thorn swept down upon Rafe, and before Rafe could react, his arm exploded in searing pain.

At the sight of blood, the horde of sailors pressed in on them, assailing them with the stench of sweat and the clamor of shouts and curses.

Rafe pressed his hand over the wound and leveled his rapier at Thorn. "That is what this is about? Your sister?"

"You used her. You told her you loved her." He leapt toward Rafe and met his sword hilt to hilt. Pulling back he swung at him again. They inched over the deck, parrying back and forth. "Then you left her." Thorn heaved out in between breaths. "And destroyed her."

Suddenly the rapier felt as heavy as an anchor in Rafe's hand, as heavy as his heart. "I was but twenty. A foolish young man. I never meant any harm to her."

"Harm?" Thorn twisted, then came about and sliced his blade across Rafe's leg.

The sailors crowed in delight.

A thousand hot needles stabbed Rafe's thigh, and he stumbled back. Grace screamed.

Thorn grinned, wiped the sweat from his brow, and halted to catch his breath. "You ruined her so no one else would have her."

Tightening his grip on his rapier, Rafe shoved aside the pain in his leg, the pain in his heart. He could not allow his emotions to weaken him now. Not when Grace needed him the most. "Enough of your games, monsieur." Rafe clenched his jaw and set his mind on the task at hand. "Let us finish this."

Thorn rubbed a thumb down the red scar on his face and neck. "You don't remember me either?" He lunged toward Rafe.

Lifting his blade, Rafe met his parry with equal intensity. "Should I?"

"Do you remember the boy you fought after you left Elizabeth sobbing in the parlor? The boy who challenged you as you headed out to your ship to leave her forever?" In one swift move, Thorn dove at Rafe from the left. The chime of their blades rang over the deck.

Rafe halted. He swallowed. "Vous? That boy was but eleven or twelve. He drew a sword on me."

"I was thirteen."

Rafe shook his head, his frustration rising with the heat of the day. "I was defending myself."

"Now the boy has grown and you defend yourself again. Only this time you will not be so lucky."

Rafe fought off his advance. "I do not wish to fight you, Thorn. What I did to your sister was wrong. And for that, je suis désolé. Let us end this now."

"As you wish." Thorn charged him in a ball of red fury.

Rafe swept his blade up to receive him. Their swords clanked. Rafe slashed back and forth. Thorn stumbled, warding off each blow with difficulty. The sailors parted as Rafe forced Thorn backward through their ranks.

They shoved their fists in the air, cheering Thorn and cursing Rafe.

With one final blow, Rafe struck Thorn's blade, flinging it from his hand and sending it clanging to the deck. A look of horror branded the first mate's reddened face. He gasped for air.

Rafe leveled the tip of his rapier over Thorn's chest.

Monsieur Dubois appeared beside him, hands on his hips, and glared at Monsieur Thorn. "I thought you said you could beat him, monsieur." He huffed. Then turned to Rafe. "Well, be done with it. Kill him."

Thorn gulped. Rafe was baffled at the cruelty of the man he'd called Father.

The crowd parted, a flash of green crossed Rafe's vision, and Grace dashed to his side, Father Alers on her heels. She grabbed his arm and shook her head.

"Kill him. Kill him," the men began a new chant.

Thorn closed his eyes.

Henri adjusted his neckerchief and sighed in impatience. "Do you intend to kill him or not?"

Rafe eyed his trembling first mate. The man he'd considered his friend. The man who had betrayed him—like everyone else. For that, he deserved to die. Rafe blinked sweat from his eyes and gripped his hilt tighter as every ounce of him twitched to do the deed—to gain some recompense for the all the treachery Rafe had endured.

But then he glanced at Grace's pleading face. She did not approve. Her God would not approve. Perhaps there was a better way to live.

Rafe dropped the tip of his blade to the deck. "I do not."

Thorn's eyes popped open.

Henri snorted in disgust. "Très bien." He snapped his jeweled fingers. "Take le capitaine below."

Two sailors shoved Grace out of the way and grabbed Rafe's arms, twisting the rapier from his grasp.

Tossing one of the men off, Rafe drove his fist into the other's jaw and sent him reeling backward. But more hands latched onto him. He struggled, but to no avail.

Henri waved a hand. "Lock him in irons."

"No! Rafe!" Grace pushed her way back through the crowd. Her delicate hand stretched toward him from amidst the filthy mob.

But he could not reach out to touch her.

Would probably never touch her again.

He had finally seen a gleam of ardor in her eyes. But now they would be separated forever. He would lose Grace, lose his ship, and possibly his life. And his father—or rather this brute who had pretended to be his father—would once again win. Forcing his anger aside, he turned toward Henri. "Promise me you will take Mademoiselle Grace back to her home."

"I fear I cannot do that." His lips writhed in a crooked smile. "How do you think I arranged this mutiny?" He waved at the men in dismissal as he did all his slaves. "Non, I will sell her to the don and divide the money among the crew."

To which a cheer arose from the men.

He leaned toward Rafe, a maniacal spark in his eyes. "And then I will take you to Roger Woodes in Nassau. Where I am sure you will be tried and hanged, as the son of a pirate deserves."

"My father was no pirate." Rafe found a moment's joy in associating the word *father* with someone other than the man who stood before him now.

"Hmm. But you are kidnapper, non?"

"And you are a mutineer."

"Moi? Non." Henri laughed. "Monsieur Thorn and I have merely rescued these ladies from your brutal hands and relieved a criminal of his ship."

"Some of my crew know differently. You cannot kill them all."

Henri grinned. "A pocket full of gold does much to temper one's tongue. Non. They will not speak on your behalf. And those few who do will not be believed."

CHAPTER 36

Grace clung to the side of the cockboat and swallowed a knot of fear. A sliver of a moon frowned at her from above the gray horizon that wreathed a sea of ebony. The small boat crested a wave and water sloshed over the side. It soaked her slippers and sent a chill through her, despite the air thick with heat and moisture. The salt stung her raw ankle, and she tugged at the rope that bound her.

Monsieur Dubois perched at the bow, lantern in hand and face to the wind. His chest swelled as he peered through the darkness toward a shadowy mound up ahead. Behind him, two of his men grunted as they shoved oars through the churning water, sending the boat gliding toward its destination.

The coast of Colombia.

Where Grace would be sold to Don Miguel de Salazar.

She took a deep breath of the night air. The smell of earth and sea mingled in a fragrant symphony that would have otherwise soothed her nerves. But instead, her stomach coiled like a bundle of rope and her mind reeled with terror.

What would become of her? She could hardly consider it without breaking into a violent tremble.

For two days she'd been locked within her cabin. Twice a day, one of Monsieur Dubois's men had brought her food and changed her chamber pot, offering her only grunts and leers in response to her pleading questions. Then torn from her cabin in the middle of the night, she'd been lowered into this boat and shoved off without explanation.

But she knew where she was going.

Even in the gloom of the night, she could make out the pyramid of land looming ahead.

Oh Lord, how did it come to this? Please help me.

Amidst the fear, her thoughts veered to Rafe, as they often had during the past few days. The look on his face as he had been dragged away to

926

the hold would forever be carved in her memory. His dark eyes had locked upon hers, gulping her in as if she were a dying man's last drink. And though she tried to do the same, tears had filled her eyes and the vision of him had grown blurry. Just like her hope.

Would Henri turn over the man he'd raised as his own son to be hanged?

Grace drew out her cross and rubbed it as a blast of night wind tore over her. The splash of the oars and purling of water against the hull increased in both pace and ferocity. Moonlight glittered off the waves' rising crests as they crashed ashore in bands of light that marched ahead of her, leading her to her doom.

"Hold on, mademoiselle," Henri shot over his shoulder.

Grace lifted her slippers and placed them on the thwarts as they crested another swell. The wet rope chafed against the raw skin of her ankle, and she winced. The other end was tied to one of the oarlocks to prevent her escape over the side. Not that she would dare attempt it since she couldn't swim. Although drowning was beginning to seem preferable to the fate that awaited her at the hands of the Spanish.

How did I get here, Lord? She tightened her lips. *Whatever reason You had for sending me on this harrowing journey, I was open to Your will. I wanted to be used for Your glory.*

The croak of tree frogs and the call of the night heron met her ears. They were close now.

Grace's throat burned. She had done no good at all. She had not saved one soul, nor brought one person closer to God, save perhaps Father Alers. And even though Claire had been delivered of the curse Annette had cast upon her, she wavered in softening her heart toward God. Now Rafe would be hanged, Annette would remain a slave, Claire would go back to Monsieur Dubois, and Thorn would have his revenge.

The boat pitched over a wave then plunged down the other side. Seawater splashed over her, and she shook it off as tears filled her eyes. *I have done nothing good, Lord. Nothing. In fact, I have done worse.* She had stolen, lied, judged, broken a vow, faltered in her faith, and not only felt desire for Rafe but allowed him to kiss her. Some godly woman she was. How she had boasted back in Charles Towne of her righteous ways. How she had wagged her finger and flapped her tongue at others, so quick to point out their faults and failings and weaknesses.

Yet when faced with the same temptations, she had failed. She had sinned. She was no better than anyone else. She had judged people by their actions alone when she had no idea the path their lives had taken, the struggles and heartaches they'd suffered.

Nicole filled her thoughts. A trollop. A woman Grace would never have spoken to before. Yet she had been naught but kind to Grace. And Mr. Thorn, ever the presentation of propriety. Monsieur Henri, a godly man, a leader in his community—a man who spoke all the right words, who knew his scriptures. Both these men Grace would have gladly befriended a month ago. Yet inside, they were not godly men at all, but filled with hatred, jealousy, and revenge. And then there was Rafe. The ruffian, the rogue, but deep within, despite his cruel childhood, he possessed the heart of a saint.

How quick she was to judge others when it was her own heart that needed scrutiny.

Lowering her chin, she allowed her tears to fall. The boat canted over another wave, and she gripped the side, wishing they would capsize. She deserved nothing more than to drown beneath these foaming black waves.

The sailors adjusted their oars against the raging swells that came faster and more furious as they approached shore. Salty water crashed over her. She shivered as the boat struck land with a jolt. Splinters jammed in her fingers, and her knee struck a thwart. Pain etched up her thigh.

The sailors hopped out on either side. Waist deep in water, they dragged the bow of the boat onto the sand. Grace's breath heaved. Terror stiffened every nerve, every fiber.

Monsieur Dubois stepped onto the shore, fisted his hands at his waist and glanced about as if he were king. One of the crew untied the rope around Grace's ankle and offered her his hand.

Clutching her skirts, she splashed into the cool water. Her slippers sank into the sand as another wave crashed over the back of her legs, nearly toppling her. Grace froze as if the wave carried a serum of revelation. All through this harrowing journey, she had assumed that God had sent her to help someone else. She had assumed that once she had completed that task, she could go home. But now as she stood on the shores of Colombia, the jagged cliffs rising from the beach like ominous judges on a bench, the realization struck her just like the waves at her back. She hadn't been sent to help anyone else see the light. She'd been sent so that she would see the light. The light of her judgmental, prudish ways. The light that revealed deep down she was no better than anyone else.

"Come, come. *Dépêchez-vous.*" Henri held the lantern aloft and motioned for the men to bring her along.

Each sailor grabbed one of her arms. They dragged her out of the water and up the beach.

In the distance, beyond the rhythmic crash of waves, horses snorted and three men emerged from the dark forest.

"Captain Dubois." One of them approached Henri. The high-crested Spanish morion atop his head glimmered in the lantern light.

"Oui." Henri assumed Rafe's role with the ease of a man practiced at trickery.

"Is this Admiral Westcott's daughter?" the man said in a perfect Castilian accent.

"Oui, bien sûr." Henri laid a hand upon the hilt of his rapier. "As promised."

The other man approached Grace. He wore a suit of black taffeta with silver lace over which hung a corselet of black steel beautifully damascened with golden arabesques. A Spanish musket hung over his shoulder. He swept a contentious gaze over Grace and snorted before turning toward Monsieur Dubois.

"Then let us be about our business."

❧

Thorn leaned on the starboard railing and clasped his hands together. Beneath him, the sea lapped against the hull, pointing foam-laced fingers toward him—accusing fingers. In the past few days, instead of celebrating his victory with the crew, Thorn had sunk into a mire of despair, barely able to arise from his hammock each day. Wasn't this what he wanted? What he had worked for, for so long?

"Bonsoir," Annette said as she slipped beside him.

"Good evening." Thorn could not look at her—had been avoiding her for two days, too afraid to discover that she hated him for what he had done.

"Are you well?" She pointed toward the bloodstain on his right shoulder.

Her concern sparked hope within him. "Yes. It is not deep." Not as deep as Rafe could have made it if he had truly wanted to hurt Thorn. The thought chafed Thorn's conscience.

"Revenge is not so sweet, non?"

Thorn met her gaze, those dark, clear eyes that spoke more of understanding than condemnation. "No, it is not."

"Not for me either." She attempted a smile.

"I wanted to kill him for what he did to my sister. Can you understand?"

"Oui." She laid a hand on his. He squeezed it and held it tightly within his own.

"You do not fault me then?" he asked.

"How can I after what I did?" She gazed over the onyx sea then shrugged. "Perhaps it is not up to us to set things right in this world."

Thorn clenched his jaw. "My sister is still ruined."

"But the captain has changed, non?" Annette rubbed her thumb over his hand. "He is not the same man who did such atrocious things to your sister."

"People don't change."

"The captain did not kill you when he had a chance."

That fact had haunted him day and night for the past two days. Releasing her hand, Thorn gripped the railing until the wood bit into his fingers.

"Ever since Mademoiselle and her God have come on board." Annette shook her head and gave him a bewildered look. "I've seen many things I would not have believed before."

Thorn swallowed. "Indeed." He followed her gaze to the dark mound of Colombia in the distance.

"I miss her." Annette whispered then her voice grew hard. "You should not have let him take her."

Thorn shoved aside the agony he had endured since Monsieur Dubois had rowed away with Grace. "She was part of the bargain. I had no choice." He knew it was an excuse, but it was a good one.

But instead of agreeing with him, Annette gave him a look of censure that cut through his excuses straight into his heart.

"How am I to fight an entire crew?" he snapped.

She narrowed her eyes upon him, studied him for a moment, then shook her head and walked away.

Thorn leaned his elbows on the railing and dropped his head into his hands. Before the mutiny, he thought he knew exactly what he wanted—knew exactly what was the right thing to do. Now, nothing made any sense anymore.

~

Rafe yanked once again on the iron manacles clamped around his ankles. But he received the same result as he had the last time. And the time before that. Cramping pain searing over his feet and clawing up his legs. Blood dripped from his scraped ankles. The patter of tiny feet filled his ears, and he swatted away the rats.

He'd lost track of time. Two days? Four days? He had no idea how long he'd been chained in the hold. With nothing to gaze at but a darkness so thick it seeped into his soul, he'd begun to lose all hope.

That the ship had sailed for a few days, he could tell by the roar of the sea against the hull and the undulating roll that had tied his stomach in knots. But the thunderous sound had softened to the gentle slap of waves, and the grating of the anchor chain and ominous splash of iron had told him they had arrived at their destination.

Had his father truly sailed to Colombia to deliver Grace? Rafe ground his teeth together and grabbed the chain again. Groaning, he yanked upon it, straining the muscles in his arms. With nothing but putrid water, unfit to drink, for two days, Rafe could feel his body weakening. Soon, he would be unable to keep the rats at bay. He lay down on the damp planks of the hold, hoping for a moment's rest before the ravenous creatures crowded in on him, but the tap of a multitude of little feet drummed over his ears in warning. He sat back up and swatted them away.

Stripped down to his breeches, Rafe stood and fisted his hands, digging his nails into his palms. The stench of human waste and mold and decay clung to him like a garment. He tried to pace, but the chains forbade him. His swollen ankles cried out in pain. Bien. The pain kept him awake. He yanked his hands through his hair and thought of Grace. Sold to a Spanish don. A life unimaginable. Yet hadn't it been his fault, his doing, his idea?

What an imbécile Rafe had been. Fooled his entire life by a man claiming to be his father. Rafe didn't even look like Henri. Now this man, this imposter, who had ruined Rafe, and probably his mother. . .

Would finally win in the end.

Rafe shouted into the darkness, scattering the approaching rats and shaking the timbers of the hull.

When he had spent himself, he sank to the deck and lowered his head. Thoughts of the past month flooded his mind. Grace, sweet Grace. Even chained in the hold, he smiled at the thought of her. How she had changed him. How she had opened his heart again. Though her tongue was quick to judge, she'd had the best intentions—to love and care for others. If there was a heaven, Rafe suddenly wished to go there so he would see her again.

God, if You are there, save me.

Rafe surprised himself at his prayer. He heard the rats circling him. One of them chomped upon his toe. Pain spiked through his foot, but Rafe hadn't the energy to brush the rodent away. Then a hiss, scampering of paws, and the rats retreated. Something furry landed in his lap and began purring. Spyglass. Rafe drew the feline to his chest and scratched beneath her chin. "So you have come to my rescue, petit chat."

Or God had answered his prayer.

He set Spyglass down by his legs, and the cat stood guard, hissing and pouncing upon the rats who dared draw near.

A breeze blew over Rafe, and he rubbed the sweat from the back of his neck even as the hairs stood at attention. A breeze? In the hold? He peered into the darkness.

"I am here, son."

Rafe jumped at the silent voice. His heart hammered a frenzied beat. He shook his head. "I must be going mad."

He had wanted nothing to do with God. Not the God his father worshiped. Not the God whose rules his father had strapped to Rafe's back ever since he could walk. Not the God who blessed men like Henri with wealth and power and left good people poor, helpless, and starving.

Yet hadn't he seen Claire delivered from her illness? And what of Grace? She worshiped this same God. Through her eyes, this God was love and joy and light and goodness. Through her eyes, Rafe found himself yearning to know Him.

If only. . .

"God, are you there?" Rafe whispered then suddenly felt foolish.

Nothing.

Spyglass meowed.

Rafe caressed the cat's fur.

"I am here, son."

Rafe swallowed. Either God spoke to him, or he had become fou. Perhaps he was already dead. If so, Rafe had some questions for the Almighty. "Why has this happened?"

"I love you, son."

"Then why did You allow Henri to torture me all those years?"

"I love you, son."

"Why did You allow my mother to die?"

"I love you, son."

"Why did You allow Claire to betray me? And Thorn?"

"I love you."

Where frustration should have risen within Rafe at each repetitive answer, instead he found comfort in the words.

"Son."

Rafe scanned the darkness. *Son.* Did that mean God was his father? His real father? Hadn't Grace told him that God was the Father of all, especially those whose earthy fathers had failed them?

"Father?"

A presence descended on him. It swirled around him. It filled him. Joy and love as he'd never known. Rafe's throat burned. He rubbed his eyes. And in that moment, he knew that all his searching, all his yearning, had been in vain. This was what he wanted. No praise of man or praise of a father could surpass this feeling—this Presence. But then he saw himself as he was. Selfish and greedy and filthy. Even his charity toward the poor, if he admitted the truth, was done more to receive the praise of the people than for their ultimate good. To prove to everyone that his life had value, that he was not a failure.

"Leave me," Rafe cried out. "I have done so much wickedness."

"I love you, son."

A squeaking. A pinprick of light appeared above him. It blossomed, and footfalls sounded on the ladder. Spyglass nudged Rafe's side as if urging him to rise.

A circle of light advanced down the ladder, scattering rats in its path. Then a pair of brown boots followed. Not the boots of Weylan, who had been bringing Rafe his daily water.

Rafe stood.

And stared straight into the face of Monsieur Thorn.

Thorn approached him, holding a finger to his lips. His eyes landed on Spyglass, and he smiled then lifted his gaze to Rafe. An emotion flickered within his brown eyes that Rafe could not determine.

"Come to gloat?" Rafe hissed.

"No, Captain." He set down the lantern and clipped a set of keys from his belt; then he knelt and unlocked the irons around Rafe's bare feet.

CHAPTER 37

Rafe tossed the white buccaneer shirt over his head and thrust his arms into the sleeves, all the while keeping a wary eye on Thorn, who stood penitently beside Rafe's desk.

"Why are you helping me?"

Thorn released a heavy sigh and shrugged. "You did not kill me when you had the chance."

But Rafe had wanted to kill him. Even when Thorn had released him down in the hold, Rafe had wanted to throttle the man and lock him in the irons that had held Rafe captive.

But he didn't. Something had changed within him. He couldn't describe what it was. But he no longer harbored the same fury, the same hatred, toward those who had betrayed him. He donned the waistcoat, fastened the silver buttons, and shifted his shoulders. A weight had been lifted from them, a weight he'd been carrying around for years.

"Yet you betrayed me, lied to me all this time." Rafe strapped on his baldric and pistols while studying Thorn's expression.

Thorn scraped one boot across the deck planks and looked down. "I did."

Rafe buckled his belt about his waist. "I ruined your sister and scarred your face."

"You did."

"Then what has changed?"

Thorn fingered his chin and raised his gaze. "I have discovered revenge does not taste as sweet as I first assumed." He glanced out the stern windows into the darkness beyond. "You are a good man, Rafe. I saw true remorse in your eyes when you discovered what you had done."

Plucking his rapier off his desk, Rafe sheathed it with a metallic *ching*. Finally, he felt safe. If Thorn intended any *traîtrise*, he would not have allowed Rafe his weapons.

"Besides"—Thorn tugged at his once-white cuffs, now dirtied from their journey—"in the past few days, I have come to realize that what Miss Grace said was true. It is not for me to seek revenge. As with Annette's attempt to enact retribution upon her mistress, we only make things worse. I must trust in God's justice."

When Thorn faced Rafe, only sincerity burned in his eyes.

"Can you forgive me, Captain?"

Rafe stared at the bottle of brandy on his desk, his throat longing for a sip, yet his soul cringing at the thought. Forgive Thorn? For the lies, the betrayal, the intent to kill Rafe? Could he? Yet how couldn't he, after God had forgiven Rafe of things equally repugnant.

"I should ask your forgiveness for my beastly behavior toward your sister." Rafe sighed and ran a hand through his hair. "It was horrible of me." He gestured toward Thorn's face. "And to be so careless with a young boy."

Thorn rubbed his scar, and a spark of malice flashed in his eyes. But then it was gone. "I hope we can once again be friends."

Rafe cleared the emotion from his throat and spotted his boots perched in the corner. In one stride, he picked them up and took a seat. He did not have time to ponder Thorn's request. "I must rescue Grace. How long ago did Henri take her ashore?"

"Over an hour." Thorn's tone dove in despair, but Rafe would not allow his own hopes to follow. Cringing in pain, he tugged his boots over the raw scrapes on his ankles then stood. He glanced out the stern windows. Still black, but dawn would be here soon. It was a three-hour ride by horse to Don Miguel's mansion in Rio de la Hacha. But the horses would move slowly due to the darkness and the thick vegetation. Rafe would not. He pressed the wound on his thigh and winced. He must not let it hold him up. "You told Henri the signal?"

"Weylan did." Thorn pressed his lips together, his eyes heavy with guilt. "Don Miguel's men were waiting, just as you said."

A rap sounded on the door, and it creaked open to reveal Father Alers, tray of food and drink in hand. The old man gave Rafe a wide smile, revealing a full row of crooked teeth, and Rafe thought it the most pleasant sight he had seen in days. Father Alers set the tray down on the desk, and Rafe grabbed his arms and shook him. "It is good to see you unharmed, mon vieux. Monsieur Thorn informed me that my father. . .I mean Henri had chained you to one of the guns."

"It was nothing." He chuckled. "Besides, who would harm an

old priest like me?"

"And the rest of the crew?" Rafe asked Thorn.

"Those loyal to you were forced to swear allegiance to me and Monsieur Dubois or be tossed in the hold." He waved a hand through the air. "An act of preservation. They are still with you, I am sure."

"Bien." Grabbing one of the mugs from the tray, Rafe gulped down the rum-flavored water until it ran down his chin onto his shirt. The liquid, though warm and bitter, filled his mouth and trickled down his parched throat as if it were from a bubbling spring.

"Easy, my boy," Father Alers said. "You will make yourself ill."

Rafe smiled and wiped his sleeve over his mouth. "Merci." Then he chomped down on a hard biscuit. Normally he hated the crusty, bland flavor, but after not eating for days, it melted like butter in his mouth. "Are you sure my father will not return to the brig tonight?" Crumbs shot from his lips.

"Yes," Thorn replied. "As soon as he came back from shore, he gathered two of his men and rowed back to *Le Vainqueur*. To ready her for sailing at first light."

"What did he order you to do?"

"To sail with him back to Port-de-Paix." Thorn lifted his brow.

"He trusts you with *Le Champion*?"

"Why wouldn't he? I am his ally. Besides, he left five of his crew here, plus the men from your crew who joined him."

"Scalawags!" Father Alers spat then gave an apologetic look upward. "Forgive me, Lord."

Rafe drained the second mug of water and set it down with a *clank* on the tray. He flexed the muscles in his arms and back, allowing the nourishment to settle in and bring back his strength.

Swishing sounded and Claire flounced into the room, Annette following behind her. "You are well, Rafe. I was so worried. . . ." She grabbed his arm and squeezed him as if to make sure he was real.

Rafe stiffened as Claire's familiar scent of lavender filled his nose.

"I feared Henri would kill you." She lifted moist eyes to his.

"I believe that is still his intent, madame." Rafe pushed her back, noting that her close presence no longer affected him. Behind Claire, Annette and Thorn exchanged a glance of affection that startled Rafe.

He faced Claire. "Why did Henri not take you with him?"

"He is a proud man. Do you think he wants a wife who would betray him as I have?" She sighed. "No. Better for his reputation if he can say that he cast me aside."

Thorn stepped forward. "Monsieur Dubois will expect us to set sail with him. He has claimed this ship as his own."

Rafe studied his first mate, noting the gleam in his eye. "Mais, I suspect you have another plan?" He raised a brow.

Thorn exchanged a furtive glance with Father Alers. "Yes. Once out at sea, we fire upon your father's ship and take him by surprise."

Father Alers punched the air with his fist in excitement. "Then we board him and take both his ship and the doubloons he received for the mademoiselle."

Claire sank into a chair. "You will not harm my husband."

Thorn bowed toward her. "No, madame. Our only intent is to make him pay for what he has done."

Rafe eyed Thorn and Father Alers curiously. Perhaps he wasn't the only one who had gone mad. "The crew will never allow it."

"We have promised them double what Henri intended to pay them out of the money he received from the mademoiselle's sale." A pleased look overtook Thorn's features.

Grabbing a silk ribbon, Rafe tied his hair behind him and grinned. "I thought you were going to allow God's justice to prevail?"

Father Alers leaned toward him with a sly look. "Sometimes God uses men to enact His judgment."

Rafe chuckled. "And what will you do with all that wealth?"

Father Alers folded his aged hands over his belly. "I will give it to Abbé Villion in Port-de-Paix. I believe there's a hospital that needs building." His golden eyes sparkled with satisfaction. "En fait, I may join him in the effort. I feel God tugging me back into His service."

Rafe blinked. "When did this happen?"

"Mademoiselle Grace has opened my eyes. I no longer wish to run from God."

The ship creaked beneath a wave, and Rafe glanced out the window. A hint of gray spread across the horizon. He could afford no further delay.

Rafe started for the door and stopped to place a hand on Claire's shoulder. "When you reach Port-de-Paix, if Henri changes his mind and insists you come home, you do not have to obey him."

She nodded. "I do not intend to."

"A good decision." Rafe looked at Monsieur Thorn, hoping to elicit his help in settling Claire somewhere safe, but the man's eyes were riveted onto Annette.

Thorn cleared his throat. "Since you no longer need a maid—"

"She is free to go." Claire waved a hand toward Annette. "I cannot take care of her."

Annette's eyes widened, and she exchanged a glance with Thorn.

Rafe leaned toward Claire. "But who will take care of you, madame?"

She let out a tiny laugh. "Go save Mademoiselle Grace." Pain darkened her blue eyes. "We can talk about this when you return."

Rafe shifted his gaze over his friends, allowing the change in Claire, in Thorn, in everyone, to sink into him. What had happened during the two days he had been below? Had something been added to the water to make everyone so amiable? Or was it his sweet Grace and her God—his God now—who had changed them?

Thorn stepped forward, his brown eyes troubled. "Captain, we need you here. I need your expertise in sailing and in battle." His face grew tight. "This is your chance to beat your fa—Henri—to finally win."

Rafe hooked his fingers onto his baldric. *To finally win.* To finally best the man who had spent a lifetime battling Rafe—torturing Rafe, beating Rafe. The urge to stay and fight mounted within him, setting his senses aflame. A chance like this would never come again. And if things went wrong without him, Rafe could lose his brig, his livelihood, his means with which to provide for the poor. And with that, his purpose to live.

Mais non. What would any of that mean without Grace?

"I will not leave her." Rafe's tone conveyed the conviction of his heart.

"She is already in the hands of the Spanish, Rafe." The sorrow dragging upon Father Alers's face threatened to destroy Rafe's remaining hope.

"If you go ashore, we cannot wait." Thorn tightened his lips. "If we do not sail with your father, he will become suspicious."

Rafe gripped the hilt of his rapier. "Then go."

Father Alers gave him a sympathetic look. "Je suis désolé, Capitaine, but it is too late. If you attempt to rescue her, you will die."

CHAPTER 38

Grace shifted her legs over the leather saddle, trying to relieve the ache in her right thigh from sitting astride the horse for hours. In front of her, two Spaniards led their thickly muscled steeds down the narrow trail, chattering in Castilian as if they were on a Sunday outing. Behind her, the third rode quietly, save for the squeak of his armor and the clank of the metals adorning his horse.

With naught but a lantern to guide their way, they had forged through the thick undergrowth, following a path that wound deeper into the green mesh of vegetation. For hours, Grace had fought off vines and branches that struck her face as well as the insects that bit her tender skin. All around her, life teemed and buzzed. Frogs croaked and katydids droned. At one point during the night a deep, guttural roar sounded in the distance, raising the hair on her arms.

Quite possibly, she may not survive to meet her new Spanish lord.

The thought, though alarming, did not distress her overmuch.

Slowly, the hulking shadows around her—that she'd imagined to be monsters in the darkness—formed into trees, vines, and shrubs as dawn lifted its curtain over the Colombian forest.

Grace pressed her fingers over the scratches marring her face and ducked just in time to avoid another assault from a low-hanging vine. At least now she could see the attacking plants coming at her.

A myriad of birds took up a chorus of praise, ushering in the new day as if they didn't realize the horror that transpired beneath them. Grace glanced up to see patches of gray sky appear amidst the tangled mass of the canopy.

Her mouth went dry, and she gulped. She'd kept her fear at bay during the night by praying. Somehow it was easier to believe God was with her in the darkness, easier to imagine Him walking beside her, leading her horse, whispering comforting words into her ears.

But in the daylight, the reality of her situation struck her like the ray of sun gleaming off the morion of the Spaniard in front of her.

She drew a deep breath. Earth and life and air, perfumed with spice and flowers, filled her lungs, mocking the shroud of death that hung heavy over her heart. *Lord, where are You?*

One of the Spaniards cast a glance at her over his shoulder. His eyes were as hard as the steel breastplate he wore. He said something to his companion and they shared a chuckle. No doubt at her expense.

Something stung her neck, and Grace slapped the insect breakfasting on her flesh. Wiping away a trickle of sweat from her forehead, she tried to force her thoughts to good things. At least these men seemed disinterested in her. That was something to be thankful for. But then her thoughts sprang to Rafe, as they had often done during the night. And she took up her pleas to heaven for the French captain again.

Please, Lord, do not let him die. Help him to come to You. And forgive Thorn and Henri. Help Claire and Annette. And Lord, please save my sister Hope and bring her home. And help my sisters and my father to follow You always. Since Grace did not know how long she would live, she thought it best to cover all her loved ones with God's blessing before she passed from this world.

She also added a plea that her passing would occur soon. For the Spanish were notorious for their cruelty. Especially toward those they deemed infidels, heretics to Catholic Spain. Add to that whatever grudge this Don Miguel de Salazar had against her father, and her future appeared bleak.

Perspiration streamed down her back, and she gasped for air amidst the rising humidity. *Lord, forgive me for being such a Pharisee. Please grant me the strength to accept whatever consequence You send my way.* For she knew she deserved it. And much worse.

Thud.

A scream of pain.

The Spaniard who led the way toppled from his horse. With a snort, the steed bolted down the trail. The other horse reared and clawed at the air, screeching. The man on its back held on to the pommel of his saddle, trying to control the beast. He yanked on the reins and cursed. Finally calming the horse, he grabbed his musket and dismounted. A string of Castilian spewed from his mouth to the man behind Grace.

Grace's heart thundered. Her mind reeled. What was happening? Her horse started prancing about nervously.

The man behind her grabbed her reins. With one quick motion, he yanked her from the animal and tossed her to the ground. Pain shot up her back. She glanced at the Spaniard who had fallen from his horse. Blood oozed from an ugly wound on his head.

He wasn't moving.

More Castilian shot through the air. The man who'd knocked her down drew his pistol and sword, dragged Grace behind him, and crouched among the leaves. His comrade dove into a shrub on the other side of the trail.

The crack of a pistol sounded.

Two of the horses spooked and bolted down the trail.

Grace's heart bolted off with them. Her head spun. Who attacked them? Spain had many enemies. The French, the British, natives—a shiver ran through her at that final thought. Whoever they were, she wouldn't allow herself to hope that they were there to rescue her.

One of the men shouted something into the forest.

Grace scanned the mass of tangled green. No movement. Nothing.

"We travel on the order of Don Miguel de Salazar. Show yourself." The Spaniard attempted the command in English.

A flash of gray and black. Something pounced on the man across the path.

Grace shrieked and peered through the underbrush. *Rafe! It was Rafe!*

Grunts and curses flew through the air along with flailing limbs. The man beside Grace stood, pointed, and cocked his pistol upon the tumbling men.

Rafe clutched the man by the collar of his ruffled shirt. With his face red, his veins pulsing, his black hair flying about his face, the captain looked more like a wild animal than a man. He flatted his fist on the man's jaw then tossed him against a tree trunk. The Spaniard's eyes rolled up in his head, and he slid down the bark and landed on the damp ground with a *thump*.

The man beside Grace halted in fear at this unearthly apparition. Recovering himself, he pointed his quivering pistol at Rafe.

"Rafe!" Grace screamed and barreled into the man's legs. He stumbled to the side. The pistol fired. The blast echoed through the forest.

Wiping the sweat from his brow, Rafe met her gaze briefly and smiled.

The Spaniard tossed his smoking pistol to the ground, and drew his sword. But before he could point it at his assailant, Rafe had drawn his own rapier. With one swift strike, he sent the man's blade twirling through the air. The polished steel glittered in the rays of sunlight that had made their way to the forest floor before the tangled forest swallowed it up.

The Spaniard stood aghast as if he could not process how one man could have defeated three of Spain's finest soldiers. His chest began to heave beneath the decorated steel breastplate.

Rafe leveled the tip of his rapier at his neck. "Go tell Don Miguel de Salazar that I have changed my mind. Mademoiselle Grace Westcott is not for sale."

The man's dark eyes skittered about as if he were deciding whether it would be preferable to die at his attacker's sword or face the wrath of his master.

"Allez-vous-en!" Rafe barked.

At which the man turned and fled down the trail.

Grace tried to move but found her limbs had frozen. From fear, from shock, she didn't know. Perhaps she was afraid that if she moved, if she entered this vision, it would dissipate, and she would be back on her horse heading toward Rio de la Hacha.

Rafe sheathed his rapier. His dark eyes found hers.

"Are you real?" Grace asked.

"Come and see." He gave her a rakish grin.

Struggling to her feet, Grace rushed toward him. She fell against him and was comforted by firm, strong arms and his scent of tobacco and leather. She trembled.

"Shhh. . . You are safe now." He caressed her hair. Then holding her face between his hands, he brought her eyes to his.

The ardor, the affection, she saw within them both frightened and delighted her. "You came for me."

"Of course." He kissed her forehead.

"But you were locked in the hold."

"Oui, I seem to recall that."

A slight giggle escaped her lips, at odds with the tension of only a moment ago. Then as if a spigot had been opened, tears spilled down her cheeks.

Rafe wiped them away with a gentle thumb, and he gazed at her as if she were the most precious thing in the world.

Grace's belly fluttered. She knew she should back away from him. She knew she should resist the intense feelings bursting within her. For she had no idea where his intentions lay. Rafe was a man accustomed to the lavish affections of women. His charm, his virility, drew them to him like ships to a protective harbor. She would not become another one of his conquests. This ruffian, this French rogue. The man who had stolen her from her home.

But not until that moment did she realize he had also stolen her heart.

He ran his finger along her cheek and dropped his gaze to her lips. Yearning tingled across her own and she closed her eyes, wanting nothing more than for him to kiss her.

But no. Grace shot backward, tripping over a root. He grabbed her arm to steady her, and she lowered her chin, not wanting to be mesmerized by those dark eyes again.

She crossed her arms over her stomach and glanced down the trail. "You have no horse. How did you catch us?"

"I am a fast runner." He smiled. "Especially when there's something worth running to catch."

❧

Grace was alive. Rafe's heart soared. He silently thanked God for helping him deliver her from the Spanish soldiers. Now all he wanted to do was kiss her. He sensed her longing, but she had demanded he refrain from kissing her ever again. Though every fiber of him longed to do so, by the grace and strength of God, Rafe would honor her request.

He studied her, wondering whether the ardor brimming in those lustrous green eyes was because she was grateful for her rescue or because she loved him. He supposed it didn't matter. As long as she was safe.

He grabbed her shoulders, noting they still trembled slightly. "Did they hurt you?"

She shook her head. Rafe drew her close again. He must get her out of here as soon as possible. These were Spanish lands—enemy lands. He must get her back to shore where they had a better chance of escape. Perhaps Thorn would win his battle with Henri and come back for them. If not, Rafe would do what he could to keep them hidden and alive until he could figure out a way to get off the coast.

Or God would provide. Surely the Almighty hadn't gotten them this far to have them die. Rafe smiled. He could get used to depending on an all-powerful God. He had always believed such subservience would weaken a man. Now he discovered the opposite to be true.

After lifting Grace atop the remaining horse, Rafe leapt behind her and took the reins. She leaned back onto his chest. Her scent soothed his nerves. During the ride back to shore, Rafe regaled her with the tale of what had occurred in her absence: how Monsieur Thorn had delivered him from the hold, how he had changed his ways, how Madame Claire was finally free of Henri, how Father Alers planned on returning to God's service, and the strange love that had sprouted between Monsieur Thorn and Annette.

Grace smiled. "And I thought God had not used me at all."

"Mademoiselle, God has done more good through you than you know."

She sat up and stretched away from him, meeting his gaze. "Did you say God?"

Rafe smiled as he nudged the horse onward. "Hmm. Did I leave out the part about my conversation with God in the hold?"

"Why yes, monsieur, I believe you did." Delight sparkled in her green eyes. A lock of raven hair danced over her face, and Rafe brushed it aside.

"Let us just say, He and I have made our peace."

She nearly leapt from the saddle, and Rafe had to grab her waist to keep her from falling.

"I am most pleased." She kissed him on the cheek, sending a spark of warmth through him. He wrapped one arm around her, reveling in the feel of her in front of him.

Several minutes passed in silence, except for the thump of the horse's hooves and the buzz and chirp of insect and birds. Despite the sweltering heat, despite the danger, with Grace in his arms, Rafe wished this journey would never end.

⤚

Grace strolled along the beach. She dipped her bare feet into the cool waves, allowing the bubbles to wash over her legs. A gust of salty wind wafted over her from the sea, twirling her loose hair about her waist. Relishing the feel of it, she glanced over her shoulder at Rafe. He had spent the day building a makeshift shelter with banana leaves, and now he assembled logs for a fire to protect and warm them through the night. Beside him lay the cockboat he had dragged up on shore and the kegs of water he'd brought with him. Stripped down to his white shirt and breeches, his black hair grazing his shoulders, he looked every bit the dangerous mercenary he claimed to be, and Grace's heart swelled with love for him.

She shook her head, still having trouble believing all Rafe had given up for her. He had risked his life to rescue her, had forfeited an opportunity to beat Henri Dubois and retrieve the money for his hospital. He had abandoned himself on the shores of enemy territory, and quite possibly lost his ship, along with his livelihood. But was he prompted more out of guilt for his own duplicity in her situation or from his love for her? Rafe was a man of strong desires, to be sure. But Grace had no experience distinguishing fleshly longings from true love.

He raised a hand to shield the glare from his eyes and glanced at the sun sinking below the western horizon. His eyes met hers. He smiled, dropped the log he'd been using to prod the flames, and trudged through the sand in her direction.

Grace's breath caught in her throat, and she faced the sea again, dropping her skirts to cover her bare legs. She tried to focus on the ribbons of violet, gold, and crimson that spiraled over the horizon and not allow Rafe's presence to affect her. But to no avail. Her stomach tightened as he took a spot beside her and folded his arms over his chest.

"There is nothing like a Caribbean sunset." His nonchalant tone implied that her presence did not have the same effect on him.

Grace nodded. A wave caressed her feet, tickling her skin and loosening the sand beneath her toes. She dug them into the cool grains, seeking an anchor for her traitorous emotions. "How long do you think it will be before we are rescued?"

He turned to her, a wounded look in his eyes. "Do not fear, we shall not be here long."

"I would not mind if we were."

He cocked his head. "Vraiment? At one time you detested my company."

"Can you blame me?"

"Non." He chuckled and kicked the sand with his boot, staring at the turquoise waves. "What has changed?"

"*I* have changed."

945

He faced her. A warm breeze danced around them, fluttering Grace's hair, and Rafe ran his fingers through the strands. "En effet, you have changed. When I met you, you wore these curls so tight upon your head, I thought your skull would crack from the strain."

Grace laughed. "'Tis true." She studied him, wondering if she should abandon her safe shores and plunge into the deep. "That is not all that has changed."

"What else?" His tone was cavalier.

Grace bit her lip. "I have seen what a judgmental prude I have been."

"Oui."

"You do not have to be so agreeable." She mocked offense.

He grew sober. Lifting his hand, he slid a finger over her cheek. Grace's pulse raced. "What else has changed, mon petit chou pieuse?" He searched her eyes like a man digging for buried treasure.

"Can you not tell?" She gave him a coy look.

"Hmm, your face has tanned from the sun."

Grace ground her teeth together. "Not that." He taunted her. *The rogue!* Grace huffed. She turned to leave, frustration broiling in her stomach.

Rafe grabbed her arm. A mischievous grin lifted his lips. "Peut-être, have your affections changed for me?"

Grace narrowed her eyes at the man's presumptuous arrogance. "I suppose you are accustomed to women declaring their love for you."

"Oui, a common occurrence." He shrugged then grew serious. "Mais there is only one woman from whose lips I long to hear it declared."

Grace's body tingled with joy. She ran her fingers over the black stubble on his jaw. "Then you must know, Rafe Dubois, that I love you."

His dark eyes sparkled, and he knelt on one knee and took her hand in his. "My sweet prude pieuse, I have loved you since the moment I first saw you." He placed a kiss on her fingers and smiled. "Will you do me the greatest honor of becoming my wife?"

"Yes!" Grace could hardly contain her joy. She fell into his embrace before he could fully right himself. Stumbling backward, Rafe picked her up and swung her around as their laughter joined the crash of the sea.

When he placed her down on the sand, Grace puckered her lips and closed her eyes.

Nothing but a sharp wind scraped over her mouth. She pried open one eye and peered at Rafe.

He cocked a brow. "You ordered me never to kiss you again, mademoiselle."

"And of course that's the only one of my orders you obeyed." Grace huffed.

He licked his lips. "Do I have your permission?"

"You have it, monsieur. Now and forever."

He gave her that roguish grin that sent her heart aflutter and lowered his lips to hers.

EPILOGUE

Grace wiggled her toes into the sand and leaned back against Rafe's thick chest. He wrapped his arms around her waist, and his warm breath caressed her skin as he nibbled on her neck. She giggled and snuggled closer to him, amazed at the providence of God. A God who surely had a grand sense of humor. For who would have thought someone as pious and proper as her would be betrothed to a rogue like Rafe? Not only betrothed but enjoying every minute she had spent with him the past two days,

Boom! A cannon blast thundered.

Grace snapped her gaze to the sea where the puff of gray smoke clung to the red hull of a brig. The ball splashed harmlessly into the waves. A warning shot. Or. . .

Grace threw a hand to her throat. "I know that ship! That is my sister Faith's ship, the *Red Siren!*"

The cockboat crunched against the shore, and Grace could barely restrain herself from dashing into the waves to greet her sisters. Yes, *sisters*. Both Hope and Faith sat among the stern sheets of the tiny craft. Lucas and another sailor leapt over the side, but before they could hoist the boat farther upon the sand, Faith bounded into the water, followed by Captain Waite. Waves crashed over her as she waded toward shore, splashing her brown breeches and white shirt. When she reached dry sand, she rushed toward Grace with a beaming smile upon her face and her red hair flaming behind her. The scent of lemons rose to Grace's nose as she clung to her sister.

"I cannot believe we found you!" Faith stepped back and examined Grace, her nose wrinkling slightly. Behind her a man that looked oddly like Mr. Nathaniel Mason, the shipwright from Charles Towne, carried Hope from the boat and set her upon the sand. Lifting the skirts of her yellow gown, Hope rushed into Grace's arms, sobbing. "Oh, Grace. We were so worried. So very worried."

"Hope, Faith." Tears overran Grace's lashes and spilled down her face. "I thought I would never see you again. Oh, thank God for bringing us all together." Grace hugged her sisters and kissed them repeatedly on the cheeks as they laughed with delight.

Clank. Clink. The sound of steel on steel rose above the crashing waves.

Grace withdrew from her sisters and glanced up to see Mr. Waite holding his sword, hilt to hilt with Rafe, while Mr. Mason aimed a pistol to her beloved's head.

"No!" Grace dashed to Rafe's side.

"Relatives of yours, mademoiselle?" Rafe's insolent grin never faltered. "Is this how *les anglais* greet one another?"

Mr. Waite narrowed his eyes. "I saw this scoundrel accosting you on shore."

Grace cleared her throat. "This scoundrel is my betrothed, Mr. Waite, Captain Rafe Dubois."

Hope gasped and Faith flinched backward as if she'd been struck.

Mr. Waite's blue eyes shifted between Grace and Rafe. Finally he lowered his blade.

Nathaniel, however, kept his pistol aimed. "Then what, pray tell, was he doing?"

Rafe sheathed his sword and winked at Grace.

"Please lower your pistol, Mr. Mason," Grace said. "He was doing me no harm, I assure you." She couldn't help the flush that heated her face.

But Nathaniel would not be appeased. "Isn't this the Frenchman who kidnapped you?"

Grace gave Rafe an adoring look. "Yes."

Hope laid a hand on her hip. "You do have much to tell us, dear sister." Her gaze swept to Grace's loose hair. "I see this journey has done you some good."

Grace clutched her sister's hand. "More good than you know, Hope. I've been praying for you, dear sister. You left with Lord Falkland. We had no idea where to search for you."

"'Tis a long story," Hope said. "I have been praying for you as well."

"You, praying?" Grace blinked.

"Part of that long tale." Hope's eyes sparkled with more life than Grace remembered ever seeing within them.

"We all have stories to tell." Faith made her way to Mr. Waite. He put his arm around her.

With a huff of resignation, Mr. Mason stuffed his pistol into his belt and exchanged a loving look with Hope that sent the girl sashaying to his side. "It is fortunate we found you."

Rafe inched his way beside Grace. "How did you know where we were?"

Captain Waite folded his arms across his chest. "When we stopped in Charles Towne for supplies, we received your post, Miss Grace."

"And set sail straightaway for Port-de-Paix, but you had already left," Faith added.

"A local fisherman thought he saw a woman matching your description being brought aboard Captain Dubois's ship." Mr. Waite gestured toward Rafe. "Then of course we knew from your missive that you were headed to Rio de la Hacha."

Faith beamed "And here we are."

Grace shook her head at the providence of God. *Thank You, Lord.*

Lucas ambled forward, floppy hat in hand. "Good to see you, Miss Grace." He nodded her way, his dark hair coiling about his brown face.

"And you, Mr. Lucas," she replied.

"We have more good news." Hope almost leapt in the sand. "Along with yours, we also received a post from Father." She exchanged an excited glance with Faith before facing Grace again. "He is bringing Charity home and in fact, they may already be there now."

Grace blinked and glanced at Hope. "What of her husband?"

Lowering her gaze, Hope clung to Mr. Mason's arm.

"He is dead." Faith's tone held no emotion. "Killed in a duel over his entanglement with the wife of an earl."

"Oh my." Grace clasped her throat. How oft had she prayed for Charity to be delivered from the beast, but she certainly had not wished him dead. But Charity was coming home! And she would be finally free from the man's abuse. Grace could hardly contain her excitement. *Another praise to You, Lord.* "I shall be so glad to see her!"

Lucas glanced toward the west where the last traces of light fell below the horizon. "The sun sets, mistress."

"Aye, I don't feel safe this close to the main." Mr. Waite eyed the sea with caution. "There are Spanish *guardacostas* about."

But as quickly Grace's joy had risen, a sudden realization struck it down. She gazed up at Rafe. "Surely you wish to return to Port-de-Paix?"

It was his home, after all, and he had friends there. Would she have to be separated from him until they could be wed? She could not bear the thought.

As if sensing her fear, he brushed a curl from her cheek and caressed her skin with his thumb. "Oui. I need to get word to Monsieur Thorn that we are rescued. And to make sure his plan worked and that everyone is safe."

Faith turned to her husband. "I am sure Captain Waite would be willing to make a brief stop there to drop you off, Mr. Dubois, would you not, Captain?"

"Of course." Mr. Waite tipped his tricorne at Faith. "Anything for my first mate."

Grace gazed down at the mounds of crystalline sand at her feet and clasped the chain around her neck, seeking anything to cling to besides the sorrow overwhelming her. "How long will you stay there?"

Placing a finger beneath her chin, he lifted her to eyes to his. "You have attempted to escape me twice, mademoiselle, do you think I would allow it again? Non, you will not leave my sight." He smiled and raised his brows. "Ever."

Grace thought her heart would burst as Rafe took her hand and placed a gentle kiss upon it. She gazed up at him, tears of joy filling her eyes.

Mr. Waite cleared his throat. "Well, that being the case, I assume we will have no choice but to wait for you until you conclude your business at Port-de-Paix, sir."

Grace sent Mr. Waite a look of gratitude.

"I thank you, monsieur," Rafe nodded in his direction.

"Then it is settled," Faith said.

"And afterward we shall all go home." Mr. Mason held his arm out for Hope, and the couple turned and made their way to the boat. Mr. Waite and Faith followed.

Home. The word wrapped around Grace like a warm blanket. A gust of wind dashed over them, filling the air with the aroma of salt and brine and flowers—the scent of the Caribbean. Closing her eyes, Grace thanked God for seeing her through this harrowing journey step by step, for changing her judgmental heart into one of love, and for the incredible man standing before her.

She glanced up at Rafe, his black hair tossed by the breeze. He smiled at her, his sultry dark eyes burning with such love and admiration that her knees began to tremble. Then sweeping her up into his arms, he carried her to the cockboat to begin their new life together. Grace smiled. And what a life it would be, being married to Captain Rafe Dubois.

Sniffles (aka Spyglass) 1988–2009

DISCUSSION QUESTIONS

1. In today's Christian culture, there is prevalent belief that if you're a good Christian, love God with all your heart, and serve Him faithfully, God will bless you and nothing terrible will happen to you and your family. Many of those who preach this theology have scriptures to back up their beliefs. What is your opinion of this doctrine? Does the Bible contain verses that could be used to prove both sides of this doctrine? How do you rectify the seeming discrepancies in scripture and in people's lives?

2. Grace Westcott typifies many Christians in our western culture who were born and raised in a church environment and who know all the right scriptures and have never committed any obvious major sins. Would you describe yourself in those terms, or have you met other people like this? How do they come across to others, particularly to those who have led a more sinful life? What was Grace's major flaw? What does the Bible have to say about this particular sin?

3. What was the hero, Rafe's, main complaint against religion? Why did he turn his back on God? Do you know people like Rafe, who have turned away from God because of the example of certain people? Have you ever met someone whose hypocrisy could have done the same to you?

4. Have you ever met a man who grew up without receiving his father's approval, his father's praise and affirmation, or perhaps a man whose father emotionally and verbally abused him? If so, can you describe his emotional state, his goals, his temperament? What sorts of things did he aspire to? What things made him angry, sad? Can you see any of these qualities in Rafe Dubois?

5. Grace's heart was often in the right place. She loved God and didn't want anyone to end up in hell. Yet she rarely had any success in her evangelistic efforts. Why?

6. Why was Father Alers running away from God? Have you known people who have made the same excuse? What brought him back?

7. What was Justus Thorn's one goal in life, and how does it tie into his first name? Do you think he had a valid reason for his anger? What did he learn about revenge? And how did he learn this important lesson?

8. What was Claire Dubois's goal in life? What caused this desire within her? Can you understand this need? What decision in the past did this need drive her to make that she later regretted? Can you think of anything similar in your own life—some decision you made based on a human need that later caused you pain? What should Claire have done instead?

9. What two things did Annette and Mr. Thorn have in common? Did Annette's plan work out? Why? Why were they good for each other? What needs did they fill for the other one?

10. Do you believe there are demonic forces that can make a person sick? Can you find scriptures in the Bible that are similar to what Grace was able to do to deliver Claire?

11. Throughout the story, Grace believed that God had some important task for her to complete before He would bring her home safely. What did that task end up being? And can you name the things that happened to her along the way that brought about this change?

12. Did you enjoy Spyglass in the story? What role did she play? Can you think of a spiritual entity she may be an allegory for?

13. What ultimately changed Rafe's mind about selling Grace? Despite her shortcomings, what were the qualities he most admired in Grace? How did those compare with Claire? Have you ever been betrayed by someone? What was your first reaction? What caused Rafe to decide to trust Grace in the end?

ABOUT THE AUTHOR

M. L. TYNDALL

MaryLu Tyndall dreamed of pirates and seafaring adventures during her childhood days on Florida's coast. She holds a degree in math and worked as a software engineer for fifteen years before testing the waters as a writer. Her love of history and passion for story drew her to create the Legacy of the King's Pirates series. MaryLu now writes full-time and makes her home with her husband, six children, and four cats on California's coast, where her imagination still surges with the sea. Her passion is to write page-turning, romantic adventures that not only entertain but expose Christians to their full potential in Christ. For more information on MaryLu and her upcoming releases, please visit her Web site at www.mltyndall.com or her blog at crossandcutlass.blogspot.com.

OTHER BOOKS BY
MARYLU TYNDALL